P9-DUV-265

C = 33
LA = 8/92
12/93

92 H H

2 5

BEAUMAN, SALLY
DARK ANGEL

12/1

NOT RENEWABLE

DISCARDED

REDWOOD CITY, CALIF.

DEMCO

DARK ANGEL

DARK ANGEL

SALLY BEAUMAN

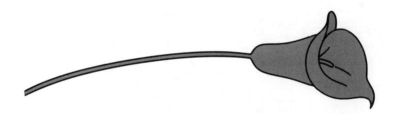

444

BANTAM BOOKS
NEW YORK · TORONTO · LONDON · SYDNEY · AUCKLAND

REDWOOD CITY PUBLIC LIBRARY
REDWOOD CITY, CALIF.
DISCARDED

DARK ANGEL
A Bantam Book / August 1990

All rights reserved.
Copyright © 1990 by Sally Beauman.
Book design by Barbara Cohen Aronica.
No part of this book may be reproduced or transmitted
in any form or by any means, electronic or mechanical,
including photocopying, recording, or by any information
storage and retrieval system, without permission in
writing from the publisher.
For information address: Bantam Books.

Library of Congress Cataloging-in-Publication Data

Beauman, Sally.
  Dark angel / Sally Beauman.
    p.   cm.
  ISBN 0-553-05762-6 / $19.95 ($24.95 Can.)
  I. Title.
PR6052.E223D3   1990
823'.914—dc20   90-111
                                                                CIP

Published simultaneously in the United States and Canada

Bantam Books are published by Bantam Books, a division of Bantam
Doubleday Dell Publishing Group, Inc. Its trademark, consisting of the
words "Bantam Books" and the portrayal of a rooster, is Registered in
U.S. Patent and Trademark Office and in other countries. Marca Registrada.
Bantam Books, 666 Fifth Avenue, New York, New York 10103.

PRINTED IN THE UNITED STATES OF AMERICA

RRH   0 9 8 7 6 5 4 3 2 1

For Ronald and Gabrielle Kinsey-Miles,
my father and mother,
with my love

The human heart is the starting point
in all matters pertaining to war. . . .
   —MAURICE, COMTE DE SAXE
      Reveries on the Art of War, 1732

ONE

From the journals

When men are gathered together alone, they discuss Sex. When women are similarly gathered, they discuss Love. What may we deduce from this paradox? Why, that women are hypocrites.

With Jarvis last evening, and two others at the club. With the second bottle of port, I posed them a question: Had any of them, ever, been so fortunate as to encounter a woman they could respect? (They might discount their mothers, I allowed. We could all grant mothers were a special case.)

No advocates for the female mind, I noted—though that scarcely surprised me. Jarvis became eloquent on the advantages of their apertures: for these, he claimed, he had the most profound respect. Hitchings, made bilious from the port, grew unduly passionate. Climbing upon a chair, he declared that—as God was his Judge—he respected all women. Were their instincts not more finely attuned than were ours? Did they not enjoy a delicacy of mind, a scrupulous sensitivity of heart denied our sterner sex? Women were undone (this was his thesis) by their dependency upon our favours—an unconvincing essay, this, in advocacy. Much fuddled Darwinism was to follow, in which men were brutes, first cousins to the Apes, while women (mysteriously exempt from the monkey chain) were their Guardian Angels. Since he fell off his chair at this point, it was agreed among us that his arguments might be discounted.

Returned home late. Had the child's nurse, against my desk, by gaslight. The light made her skin blue, like a cadaver.

At my crisis, the child cried out from the next room—her gull's cry, high and yelping.

She has contrived such ill-timing before, but when I investigated, she slept.

To Winterscombe for the comet (and other incendiary delights) at nine this morning.

I

THE
FORTUNETELLER
AND
MY GODMOTHER

I WENT TO A FORTUNETELLER ONCE. His name was Mr. Chatterjee; his premises were a small shop between a pastry maker and a silk dealer, in the middle of the bazaar in Delhi.

It was not my idea to consult Mr. Chatterjee; I did not believe in fortunetellers, horoscopes, Tarot cards, the *I Ching*—none of that tempting mumbo-jumbo. Neither, I think, did my friend Wexton, although it was he who made the suggestion to go.

Mr. Chatterjee had been recommended to Wexton. One of the Indians we had met on this visit gave him a glowing testimonial—it might have been Mr. Gopal from the university, or maybe the Maharani. The next day, on a visit to the bazaar, Wexton located his premises; the day after, he suggested I visit him.

Traveling with Wexton was always full of surprises. I thought, *Why not?*

"Won't you come too, Wexton?" I said. "He could read both our fortunes."

Wexton smiled his benevolent smile.

"At my age," he replied, "you don't need a fortuneteller to predict your future, Victoria."

A nod toward the graveyard. Wexton gave no sign of melancholy. I set off for my future the next afternoon.

On the way, pushing through the crowded alleyways of the bazaar, I considered the question of age. In a Victorian novel—the kind my father liked—a woman is old at twenty-five, over the hill by thirty. Now, in the 1980s, due partly to the influence of sudsy television, a woman is still judged young at fifty. But when I went to see Mr. Chatterjee it was 1968. People had begun to wear buttons that said DON'T TRUST ANYONE OVER THIRTY.

Wexton, well into his seventies, found that very amusing. I was not so sure I did.

When I went to visit my fortuneteller I was single, childless, a success—I suppose—at my chosen career. I was also almost thirty-eight years old.

The visit to India had been Wexton's idea. For the three months before we left I had been in England, at Winterscombe, helping my uncle Steenie to die—or at least trying to ensure that when he did, he did so easily, without physical pain.

Morphine cocktails work—indeed Steenie claimed they were nearly as good as champagne—but there were, inevitably, other pangs for which medicine was less effective. When Steenie finally died, I lost an uncle I loved, one of the last members of my family. Wexton lost his oldest friend, an iconoclast who had once, I suspected, been more than a friend—though neither Steenie nor Wexton ever spoke of this.

"Look at us," Wexton said, when we were alone at Winterscombe. "As gloomy as two bookends. We should go away, Victoria. How about India?"

It was a surprising suggestion. Claiming pressures of work (in fact fearing introspection), I had not taken a vacation in eight years. Wexton, whose poetry had made him internationally famous, never took holidays at all. American by birth, but an expatriate for some fifty years, Wexton had made his den in an untidy, book-filled house in Church Row, Hampstead; he disliked being coaxed out of it. It was entirely unlike him to accept an invitation to be lionized in Delhi, of all places. However, he did. He would go, he said; what was more, I would go with him. I was anxious to escape grief and the responsibility of Winterscombe (a great white elephant of a house—I would probably have to sell it), so I agreed. I rearranged my work schedule. Three days later we landed in Delhi.

Once there, Wexton gave his lecture at the university, read some of his famous poems to a distinguished audience of Indians, Europeans, and Americans, and then, gracefully but firmly, decamped.

Wexton has written lines that have stained my mind (as perhaps they have yours); as great poetry does, they have become an indissoluble part of my thinking. Many of his poems are about love, time, and change. As I listened to him read I thought of lost opportunities, a broken love affair eight years before, and my own age; I felt unspeakably sad.

Wexton, whose attitude to poetry was pragmatic, did not. He

gave his lecture; he hunched himself into a human question mark over the unreliable microphone. He pummeled, as was his habit, the great folds and crevasses of his face. He tugged at his hair, so it stood up in wild tufts. He looked like a huge and benevolent bear, bemused that these words of his should produce on his audience the effect they did.

Once the lecture was over, he strolled down from the platform, attended the formal reception in his honor, and annoyed his Embassy hosts by avoiding all the most celebrated guests. He talked for a great deal of time to Mr. Gopal, an earnest and excitable man whose position at the university was a minor one. He talked even longer to the Maharani, a woman of great good nature, mountainously fat, whose days of social eminence were over. The next day, to the consternation of his hosts, he left. Wexton loved trains; we went to the station and, for no very good or planned reason, took a steam train to Simla.

From Simla to Kashmir and a houseboat on the lakes, with curry-scented curtains and a wind-up gramophone. From Kashmir to the Taj Mahal, from the Taj Mahal to a baboon sanctuary where Wexton became beguiled by baboons, and Mr. Gopal, by then a disciple, caught up with us.

"Very brave man, your distinguished godfather," he remarked to me as Wexton fixed the baboons with a benign gaze. "These creatures give a very nasty bite." From the baboon sanctuary to the beaches of Goa, from Goa to Udaipur; from there, with numerous side visits to temples, fortresses, and railway stations, we returned to Delhi.

The pace was frenetic, which cheered Wexton enormously.

"Just what we need," he would say, settling back in another compartment in yet another train. "New places. New faces. Something's bound to happen eventually."

Something did, of course, once I'd been to see Mr. Chatterjee—but neither of us knew that then. I would embark on a very different kind of journey. I had been preparing for it, I think, for some time, without being aware of it. My uncle Steenie, and certain things he had said to me when he was dying—things that alarmed me—had pushed me closer to the journey. But it was Mr. Chatterjee who provided the final impetus.

Wexton, when he discovered my intentions, resisted. It was a mistake, he said, to explore the past—that was dangerous territory. He was being evasive, and we both knew why. My past involved Winterscombe (that was fine, Wexton said, though he was wrong). It also involved New York, where I grew up (that was all right, too, provided I did not dwell on the question of a certain man, still living there). Finally, it involved another godparent, in this case a woman. In this case, Constance.

Constance's name was one Wexton now refused to pronounce. She was his antithesis, of course, and I think he had never liked her. Wexton disliked very few people, and if he did dislike them, he preferred not to discuss them, since he was devoid of malice.

I had once heard him, in discussion with Steenie (who adored Constance) describe her as a she-devil. Such intemperate language from Wexton was exceptional—and it was never repeated. When I was to tell him of my visit to Mr. Chatterjee and the decision I had reached, Wexton never once used her name, although I knew she was uppermost in his thoughts. He became, for him, very gloomy.

"I wish I'd never listened to Gopal," he said. (Or was it the Maharani?) "I might have known it would be a mistake." He fixed me with a pleading gaze. "Think a little, Victoria. One hundred rupees on it, any bet you like: Chatterjee's a charlatan."

I knew then how keen Wexton was to convince me. He was not a betting man.

Mr. Chatterjee did not look like a charlatan. It had to be said, he did not look like a fortuneteller either. He was a small man of about forty, wearing a clean nylon shirt and freshly pressed tan pants. His shoes gleamed; his hair oil gleamed. He had confiding brown eyes of great gentleness; he spoke English with an accent inherited from the days of the Raj, the kind of accent that, in England itself, had been out-of-date in 1940.

His shop, compared to that of some of his rivals in the bazaar, was difficult to find and self-effacing. Over its entrance was a painting on cardboard of a crescent moon and seven stars. A small hand-lettered sign said: THE PAST AND THE FUTURE—RUPEES 12.50. This was followed by an exclamation mark, perhaps to emphasize Mr. Chatterjee's bargain rates; his rivals were charging upward of rupees 15.

Inside, Mr. Chatterjee's premises were austere. There was no attempt to evoke the mysterious Orient. There was one elderly desk, two clerk's chairs, a metal filing cabinet, and, on the wall, two poster portraits. One was of the present Queen of England, the other of Mahatma Gandhi; they were fixed to the wall with tacks.

The room smelled of the pastry shop next door and, slightly, of sandalwood. There was a multicolored plastic fly-curtain across a doorway, and from beyond that came the sound of sitar music played on a gramophone. The room resembled the bolt-hole of some minor civil servant, perhaps a railway official—and I had seen many of those the past weeks. Mr. Chatterjee sat down behind his desk and assembled charts. He gave me an encouraging nod and a smile. I was not encouraged. Mr. Chatterjee looked amiable, but as a fortune-teller he did not inspire confidence.

Not at first. Mr. Chatterjee took his task very seriously; it was lengthy, and at some point—I am still not quite sure when—he began to win me over. It was when he touched my hands, I think. Yes, probably then. Mr. Chatterjee's touch, cool, dispassionate, like that of a doctor, had an odd quality. It made me a little giddy—a tipsy feeling, the kind you get when you drink a glass of wine on an empty stomach and finish it too quickly.

I cannot now remember all the details of his routine, but it was both fluent and curiously moving. Herbs were involved—I remember that, for my palms were rubbed with a pungent substance, during which there was much discussion of birthplaces (Winterscombe) and birth dates (1930).

The stars were involved, too—that was where the charts came in. Mr. Chatterjee examined the charts closely; he put on a pair of spectacles. He drew linking patterns of lucid beauty, joining destinies and planets with a lead pencil that kept breaking. These patterns seemed to displease Mr. Chatterjee; more than that—they seemed to perturb him.

"I am seeing a date. It is 1910," he said, and shook his head. He prodded one particular area of that chart, an area that was beginning to resemble a freeway intersection.

As he prodded, Mr. Chatterjee paled. He seemed unwilling to proceed.

"What else do you see?" I prompted.

Mr. Chatterjee did not answer.

"Bad things?"

"Not too nice. Oh dear, no. Most definitely not." He resharpened his pencil. The sitar music stopped, then, after a pause, continued. Mr. Chatterjee seemed to have dozed off—his eyes were closed—or possibly he was transfixed by his 1910 intersection.

"Mr. Chatterjee," I said gently, "that's twenty years before I was born."

"A blink." Mr. Chatterjee opened his eyes. "Twenty years is a blink. A century is a second. However . . . I think we will be moving on. Try a new tack."

He bundled up the charts with an air of relief. He replaced them in the metal filing cabinet and locked it. Once the chart was out of sight he seemed cheered. For the second stage of his routine, gold dust would be employed—at least he said it was gold dust.

"If you would be so good. Please to close your eyes and consider most seriously those who are dear to you."

I closed my eyes and I tried. The sitar music scratched. A powdery substance was sprinkled against my eyelids and my cheeks. A lilting incantation began, in Hindi.

I felt hot. The dizziness increased. My mind began to track off in directions I would never have predicted. When the incantation came to an end and I opened my eyes, the gold dust was being carefully brushed back into its container, an ancient tin for Navy Cut tobacco. Mr. Chatterjee gave me a sad look.

"I am seeing two women," he said. "One is close, the other very far away. I am telling myself that you will have to choose between them."

He then told my fortune in some detail. His account of my past was unnervingly accurate. His account of my future was too roseate to be likely. He ended by telling me I was about to make a journey.

I was disappointed by that. I had begun to like Mr. Chatterjee. I had almost begun to believe in him. I became afraid he would move on to speak of tall dark strangers, voyages across water. I would have hated that; I did not want him to be tawdry.

A journey? I made journeys all the time. My work as an interior decorator meant I was always on the move, to the next house, the next commission, the next country. One week from now I would return to England. The next job was in France, the one after it in Italy. Was that the kind of journey Mr. Chatterjee meant? Then I hesitated. There were other kinds of journeys.

Mr. Chatterjee sensed that momentary skepticism, I think. He gave me an apologetic and gentle smile, as if my disbelief were his fault and not mine. He took my hands between his. He lifted them to my face.

"Sniff," he said, as if this would explain everything. "Smell."

I sniffed. The pungent substance rubbed on my palms was volatile. It contained oils, but also alcohol. The warmth of the room and of my skin released scents even more pungent than before. I sniffed, and I smelled India. I smelled crescent moons, honey and sandalwood, henna and sweat, affluence and poverty.

"Concentrate. To see, you must first close the eyes."

I inhaled again, eyes tight shut. I smelled . . . Winterscombe.

Damp and woodsmoke, leather chairs and long corridors, linen and lavender, happiness and cordite. I smelled childhood; my father and my mother.

"Concentrate. Again."

Mr. Chatterjee's grip on my palms tightened; a tremor passed through them. The scent in my nostrils was now unmistakable. I smelled the fresh greenness of ferns, then a ranker, more assertive undertone, musk and civet. Only one person I had ever known used that particular scent, and to me it was as individual as a fingerprint. I dropped my hands. I smelled Constance.

I think Mr. Chatterjee knew my distress, for he was then very kind to me. He talked me down. Then, with the air of a priest in the confessional—or, indeed, a railway official untangling a complex timetable—he gave me one final piece of advice. He told me to go back.

"Go back where? Go back when?" Wexton said mournfully over dinner that night.

"I'm not sure yet," I said. "But I know the route, and so do you."

The next day I wrote to her. When I received no reply—that did not surprise me; she had not replied when Steenie asked for her and I cabled—I changed my flight plan.

A week later Wexton flew back to England alone. I flew halfway around the globe to New York, and to that other godparent of mine, Constance.

Constance made me. I could say she brought me up, for that was true, since I went to her as a child and remained in her care for more than twenty years, but Constance's influence upon me was deeper than that. I regarded her as a mother, a mentor, an inspiration, a challenge, and a friend. A dangerous combination, perhaps—but then, Constance herself radiated danger, as the many men who suffered at her hands could have told you. Danger was the essence of her charm.

My uncle Steenie, who admired her and I think occasionally feared her, used to say she was like a matador. You watched her swirl the bright cape of her charm, he would say; the performance was so dazzling, so accomplished, you did not notice until too late how expertly she inserted the blade. But Steenie liked to exaggerate; the Constance I knew was forceful, but she was also vulnerable.

"Think of her dogs," I would say to Steenie, and Steenie would raise his blue eyes to the heavens.

"Her dogs. Indeed," Steenie once replied, in a dry way. "I'm never quite sure what to make of that one."

A puzzle. But then, Constance was full of puzzles. I grew up with her but I never felt I understood her. I admired her, loved her, was perplexed and sometimes shocked by her—but I never felt I knew her. Perhaps that, too, was part of her charm.

When I say "charm" I do not mean that slick and superficial ease of manner which passes for charm in society; I mean something more elusive than that. I mean the capacity to weave spells, to entrance. In this respect Constance was accomplished long before I met her. By the time I went to live with her in New York she was already secure in her reputation as a latter-day Circe. Because of the men, I suppose—although I, being innocent, did not understand about them, or even know of them.

"A trail of them, Vicky, my dear!" Uncle Steenie would later declaim, not without malice. "A trail of broken hearts. A trail of broken men. The debris, Vicky, of Constance's hectic career."

It was Steenie's view that if Constance damaged people, the damage was confined to the male sex. If women were damaged, he claimed, it was incidental and accidental; they were simply harmed in the fallout of Constance's main attack.

Steenie, I think, saw Constance not just as a sorceress but also as a warrior. She came at men, he claimed, her sexuality punching the air, using her beauty, her wit, her charm, and her willpower as weapons, hell-bent on some private war of attrition. Given his own proclivities, Steenie himself was exempt; this, he would explain, was how he could survive as her friend.

I believed none of that then. I thought my uncle liked to dramatize, and I loved Constance; after all, she had been unfailingly kind to me. When Steenie made his claims, I would say: but she is brave; she is resilient; she is gifted; she is generous. And so she was, all of those things, but in one respect my uncle was also right. Constance *was* dangerous. Chaos stuck to Constance the way iron filings cling to a magnet. Sooner or later (I suppose it was inevitable) Constance's zest for making trouble would affect my own life.

So it had, eight years before, when Constance succeeded in preventing my marriage. We had quarreled then, and for eight years the break had been complete. I had neither seen her nor spoken to her in that time, and until my uncle Steenie was dying, when she was invoked once more, I had tried very hard not to think of her. I had been succeeding. I was making a new life. Constance, a decorator herself, had trained me well; my career flourished. I grew accustomed to living alone, even grew to like it; I had learned the consolations of a crowded schedule and a full calendar. I had learned (I thought) to live with the fact that all adults coexist with regrets.

Yet now I was going back. I was on a plane flying east, a long journey with a great many stopovers. From Delhi to Singapore, from Singapore to Perth, from there to Sydney. On to Fiji, from there to Los Angeles, from L.A. to New York. So many time zones. By the time I landed at Kennedy, I was no longer certain whether it was yesterday or tomorrow—a state of mind that long outlasted the jet lag.

I was attuned to Constance. As soon as I stepped out of the airport terminal into the heat, I knew she was there, somewhere in the city, out of sight still, but very close. Bucketing toward Manhattan in a yellow cab, my ears buzzing from pressurization, my eyes scratchy from dry air at thirty thousand feet, my nerves twitchy from lack of sleep, filled with that false optimism which is a by-product of adrenaline, I was not only sure Constance was near, I felt she awaited me.

I think I envisaged some kind of final reckoning—not a reconciliation, but questions answered, the past explained, a neat line drawn under a neat balanced sum. This was the moment, I told myself, when Constance's and my arithmetic finally came out: Q.E.D. I understood myself; I understood my godmother; I was free, at last, to move on.

I was wrong, of course. I thought I was arriving, when in fact the journey was scarcely begun.

Constance never wrote letters, but she loved the telephone. She had several telephone numbers herself, and I called them all.

I called the house at East Hampton, on Long Island. I called all three numbers at the apartment on Fifth Avenue. The East Hampton house had been sold two years before; its new owners had not seen Constance since. None of the Fifth Avenue numbers answered—which was unusual, since even if Constance was away, there were servants who lived in.

Since it was a Friday, and past office hours, it was by then too late to call Constance's business headquarters on Fifty-seventh Street. I began calling Constance's friends.

It was late July; I was using addresses that might be eight years out-of-date. Not surprisingly, I drew a great many blanks. Friends had moved or were vacationing—but the reaction of those I did reach was very curious indeed. They were polite; they professed to be delighted to hear from me after all this time, but they did not know where Constance was, could not remember where, or when, they had last seen her. Not one of them expressed surprise that I was calling—and that was odd. After all, the breach between Constance and me was public knowledge, the source, I knew, of continued gossip and speculation. Constance and I had been business partners; we had been like mother and daughter, like the best of friends. I waited for someone to say, "How come the urgency? I thought you and Constance had a fight, way back." No one did. At first I thought this was tact. By the tenth call, I doubted it.

Around eight in the evening, fighting sleep, I took a cab uptown to Constance's apartment, the one where I had lived. A surly and unfamiliar doorman informed me Miss Shawcross was away, the apartment was closed up. There was no forwarding address.

I returned to my hotel. I tried to be practical and reasonable. After all, it was high summer and the humidity was way up— Constance was unlikely to be in New York at such a time. If she was not on Long Island, she would be in Newport. If she was not in Newport, she would be in Europe. Either way, there was a limited number of places where Constance would stay—and I knew all of them.

I telephoned them all, those hotels she had always favored, where she would always insist on the same suite. She was at none of them; not one had a booking in her name for the current year, let alone that summer. I was still unwilling to give up, even then. I could feel all the symptoms of jet lag, the false energy and the simultaneous exhaustion. I could also feel a more dangerous incentive— that tweaking of an invisible string felt by anyone who embarks upon a search, or a quest.

Constance was *there;* I could sense her. She was not in Europe, despite the season, but here in Manhattan, around the corner, just out of sight, amused and in hiding. One more phone call could locate her. I made two, in fact, before I admitted fatigue and went to bed.

The first (and I rang the number several times) was to Betty Marpruder, the nuts and bolts of Constance's workplace, the one person who always knew, without fail, where Constance was. I had never known Miss Marpruder to take a vacation; come to that, I had never known her to leave New York. Her number, the first I had called, had not answered when I dialed it at six; it still did not answer when I dialed again, at ten.

I went to bed. I sat up in bed, exhausted and alert, flicking through the pages of *The New York Times* supplied with the room. There, on the social pages, I found my perfect source. Conrad Vickers, the photographer, was passing through New York. He was preparing a fifty-year retrospective of his work at the Museum of Modern Art which would open that fall with a party for what the journalist described as *le tout New York*. Conrad Vickers had links with my own family that went back many years; he also had links with Constance. Apart from Steenie, Conrad Vickers was Constance's oldest friend.

I disliked Vickers, and the hour was late. Nevertheless, I called him.

Since Vickers also disliked me, I expected a brushoff. To my surprise, he was effusively welcoming. Questions about Constance were dodged, but not decisively blocked. He wasn't too sure where she was right then, but a few inquiries, he hinted, would locate her.

"Come for drinks. We'll discuss it then," he cried in fluting tones. "Tomorrow at six, dah-ling? Good. I'll see you then."

"Dah-ling," Conrad Vickers said.

He kissed the air at either side of my cheeks. He split the word, as he had always done, into two distinct syllables. It conveyed, in his case, neither affection nor intimacy, since *darling* was a term Vickers used both to close friends and to perfect strangers. He found it useful, I suppose, since it disguised the fact that he had often forgotten the name of the person he was greeting so warmly. Vickers did forget names—unless they were famous ones.

He made a few airy gestures of apparent delight. Conrad Vickers, in his customary plumage: an exquisite figure in an exquisite room in an exquisite brownstone on Sixty-second Street—a five-minute walk from Constance's apartment on Fifth Avenue. A blue silk handkerchief flopped from the pocket of a pale-gray Savile Row suit; it harmonized with the blue of the shirt; the blue of the shirt matched his eyes. A fuzz of soft white hair, now receding; the complexion of a girl. Conrad Vickers—once, like my uncle Steenie, a famously beautiful youth—had aged well. The vigor of his insincerity appeared undiminished.

"Such an age! I'm so glad you rang. Dah-ling, you look *radiant*. Sit down and let me look at you. Years and *years*. *Loved* what you did on the Antonelli house—and Molly Dorset's. *Terribly* clever, both of them. You *are* hitting your stride."

I sat down. I wondered why Vickers should bother to flatter me now, when he had never done so before . . . unless he had decided I was becoming fashionable.

"*Isn't* it hot?" Vickers was still in full flood. "Quite unbearable. What *did* we do before air conditioning? I'm a bird of passage, dah-ling, just *flitting* through. Trying to finalize these"—he waved a hand toward a pile of photographs. "Sheer hell. I mean, fifty years of work, dah-ling—where *does* one begin? Who to leave in? Who to leave out? Those museum people are *totally* ruthless, my dear. They want the Royals, of course. Margot and Rudy, Andy and Mick, Wallis and Lady Diana. Oh, and they want Constance, of course—well, they would. But anyone they haven't heard of is O-U-T out, dah-ling. I shall lose *half* my friends."

A small wail of distress. The next instant, distress forgotten, he was waving a hand at the arrangement of flowers on the table next to me.

"*Aren't* they divine? Don't you just *love* delphiniums? English garden flowers—I insist on them, wherever I am. And now I've found this *terribly* clever young man who does them just the way I want them. *Madly* original—I can't *bear* flowers that look *arranged*, can you? No, of course you can't—you're *far* too clever. Now, shall we have some champagne? Do say yes. I can't bear the martini habit—too noxious. One feels quite *blind* the next day. Yes, champagne. Let's be madly grand and open the Bollinger—"

Vickers came to an abrupt halt. He had just pronounced the name of my uncle Steenie's favorite champagne. Color seeped up his neck; his face reddened. He fidgeted with the cuffs of his shirt. He turned away to give instructions to the houseboy who had admitted me and who had been waiting by the door all this time.

He was Japanese, a pretty and delicate-looking young man kitted out in black jacket and striped trousers.

As the young man left the room and Vickers sat down, I understood at last why I had been invited. Vickers was more than embarrassed; he was guilty. This invitation of his owed nothing to Constance and everything to my uncle Steenie.

Since Conrad Vickers had been my uncle's friend for more than fifty years, and his lover—on and off—for at least half of that time, and since he had contrived to be conspicuously absent when Steenie lay dying, I could understand that guilt. I said nothing. I wanted to see, I suppose, how Vickers would wriggle out of it.

For a while he was silent, as if waiting for me to raise the subject of Steenie, and help him. I did not speak either. I looked around his drawing room, which—like all the rooms in all his many houses—was in perfect taste. Vickers's sense of loyalty might be weak and his friendships facile, but when it came to the inanimate, to fabrics, to furniture, his eye was as unerring as Constance's. This had seemed to me important once. I had believed there was virtue in taste. Now, I was less certain.

Vickers fingered the arm of his French chair. The silk that covered it, a clever pastiche of an eighteenth-century design, was one I recognized. It had come from the most recent Constance Shawcross collection. The chair was painted. It had been restored, I thought, and then cunningly distressed. A wash of color over gesso: Constance's workshops? I wondered. It was impossible to tell—almost impossible to tell—if the wash of pale slate-blue had been applied two hundred years before or the previous week.

"Last month," Vickers said, catching my eye. Vickers, for all his faults, had never been stupid.

"Last month." He sighed. "And yes—I know I can't fool you— that restorer Constance always uses. Oh, God." He leaned forward. He had apparently decided to take the leap.

"We'd better talk about Steenie. I know I should have been there. But I just couldn't . . . face it, I suppose. Steenie, dying. It seemed so out of character. I couldn't imagine it, and I certainly didn't want to witness it. Ah, the champagne." He rose. His hand trembled a little as he passed me the glass.

"Would you mind terribly if we drank to him? To Steenie? He would have liked that. After all, Steenie never had any illusions about me. I expect you think I'm a terrible coward, and of course I am. Sickrooms make me queasy. But you see, Steenie would have understood."

This was true. I raised my glass. Vickers gave me a rueful look.

"To Steenie, then? Old times?" He hesitated. "Old friends?"

"All right. To Steenie."

We both drank. Vickers set down his glass. He rested his hands on his knees; he gave me a long, appraising look. The blue eyes were alert. Vickers, for all his affectations, was a great photographer; he had a photographer's ability to read a face.

"You'd better tell me. I do want to know. When you called . . . I felt like a worm. Was it easy? For Steenie, I mean?"

I considered this. Was death ever easy? I had tried to make it easy for Steenie, as had Wexton. We had succeeded only to a limited extent. When he died, my uncle had been afraid; he had also been troubled.

He had tried to disguise this at first. Once he realized there was no hope, Steenie set about dying in style.

Uncle Steenie had always valued the stylish above everything. He intended, I think, to greet Hades as an old friend, remembered from past parties; to be rowed across the Styx as carelessly as if he took a gondola to the Giudecca. When he met his boatman Charon, I think Uncle Steenie meant to treat him like the doorman at the Ritz: Steenie might flounce past, but he would bestow a large tip.

This was achieved, in the end. Steenie went as he would have liked, propped up against silk pillows, amusing one moment, dead the next.

But that sudden departure came at the end of a long three months, months during which even Steenie's capacity to perform sometimes failed him. He was not in pain—we saw to that—but, as the doctors had warned, those morphine cocktails did have strange effects. They took Steenie back into the past, and what he saw there made him weep.

He would try to convey to me what he saw, talking and talking, often late into the night. His compulsion to make me see what he saw was very great. I sat with him; I held his hand; I listened. He was the last but one of my family left. I knew he wanted to give me the gift of the past, before it was too late.

It was often difficult, though, to understand what he said. The words were clear enough, but the events he described were scrambled. Morphine made Steenie a traveler through time; it gave him the facility to move forward and back, to pass from a recent conversation to another some twenty years before as if they happened the same day, in the same place.

He spoke of my parents and my grandparents, but only the names were familiar, for as Steenie spoke of them they were unrecognizable to me. This was not the father I remembered, nor the mother. The Constance he spoke of was a stranger.

One point: Some of Steenie's memories were benign; some, quite clearly, were not. Steenie saw, in these shadows, things that made him shake. He would grasp my hand, start up in the bed, peer about the room, address specters he saw and I did not.

This made me afraid. I was unsure if it was the morphine speaking. As you will see in due course, I had grown up with certain puzzles that had never been resolved, puzzles that dated from the time of my own birth and my christening. I had outgrown those puzzles, I thought. I had put them behind me. My uncle Steenie brought them rushing back.

Such a whirl of words and images: Uncle Steenie might speak of croquet one minute, comets the next. He spoke often of the Winterscombe woods—a subject to which he would return with increasing and incomprehensible emphasis. He also spoke—and then I was almost sure it was the morphine—of violent death.

I think Wexton, who witnessed some of this, understood it better than I did, but he explained nothing. He remained quiet, resilient, reticent—waiting for death.

There were two days of serenity and lucidity before it came, days in which Steenie gathered himself, I thought, for the final assault. Then he died, as I say, with a merciful speed. Wexton said Steenie willed himself away, and I thought: my uncle was indomitable, I loved him, and Wexton was right.

So—would you describe that as easy? I looked at Vickers, then avoided his eyes. I felt that Steenie, trying to stage-manage his farewell performance, would have wanted me to emphasize its bravura aspects.

Avoid those episodes in the wings. Be careful.

"He . . . kept up appearances," I said.

This seemed to please Vickers, or to relieve his guilt. He sighed.

"Oh, *good*."

"He was in bed, of course. In his room at Winterscombe. You remember that room. . . ."

"Dah-ling, who could forget it? Quite preposterous. His father would have had a fit."

"He wore his silk pajamas. Lavender ones, on the days the doctors came—you know how he liked to shock—"

Vickers smiled. "Makeup? Don't tell me he kept up with that . . ."

"Just a little. Quite discreet, for Steenie. He said . . . he said if he was going to shake hands with death, he intended to look his best—"

"Don't be upset. Steenie would have hated you to be upset." Vickers sounded almost kind. "Tell me—it does help to talk, you know. I've learned that. One of the penalties of age: All one's friends—at the party one minute, absent the next. Steenie and I were the same age, you know. Sixty-eight. Not that that's old exactly, these days. Still . . ." He paused. "Did he talk about me at all, at the end?"

"A bit," I replied, deciding to forgive him the egotism. In fact Steenie had scarcely spoken of Vickers. I hesitated. "He liked to talk. He drank the Bollinger—I'd saved some. He smoked those terrible black Russian cigarettes. He read poems—"

"Wexton's poems?" Vickers had regarded Wexton as a rival. He made a face.

"Mostly Wexton's. And his letters—old ones, the ones he wrote to Steenie in the first war. All the old photograph albums . . . It was odd. The recent past didn't interest him at all. He wanted to go further back. To his childhood, to Winterscombe the way it used to be. He talked a lot about my grandparents, and his brothers. My father, of course." I paused. "And Constance."

"Ah, Constance. I suppose he would. Steenie always adored her. The rest of your family"—Vickers gave a small, slightly malicious smile—"I should have said they weren't too frightfully keen. Your aunt Maud loathed her, of course, and your mother—well, I always heard she'd more or less banished her from Winterscombe. I never found out why. Quite a little mystery there, I always thought. Did Steenie mention that?"

"No," I replied, untruthfully, and if Vickers noticed the evasion he gave no sign. He poured more champagne. Something, the reference to Wexton perhaps, had ruffled him a little, I thought. Quite suddenly he seemed to tire of the subject of my uncle. He stood up and began to sift through the pile of photographs that lay on the table at his side.

"Speaking of Constance, look at this! I came across it just the other day. I'd quite forgotten I ever took it. My earliest work. The first photograph I ever did of her—terribly posed, too artificial, dated, I suppose, but all the same, I might use it in the retrospective. It has something, don't you think?" He held up a large black-and-white print. "Nineteen sixteen—which means I was sixteen, and so was Constance, though she subtracts the years now, of course. Look at this. Did you ever see this before? Doesn't she look extraordinary?"

I looked at the photograph. It was new to me, and Constance did indeed look extraordinary. It was, as Vickers said, highly artificial, very much in the fashion of its time and quite unlike his later work. The young Constance lay posed on what appeared to be a bier, draped in heavy white material, perhaps satin. Only her hands, which clasped a flower, and her head were visible; the rest of her body was wrapped and draped as if in a shroud. Her black hair, long then—I had never seen Constance with long hair—had been combed out and artfully arranged so that it fell in snaking tresses away from her face. Shocking in its luxuriance, as Vickers had no doubt intended, it brushed the floor. Constance lay in profile; a band of contrived light sharpened the strong planes of her face, so that her features, undeniably arresting even then, became a painterly composition, a pattern of light and dark. Black lashes made a crescent against a wide, high, almost Slavic cheekbone. Oddly, since her eyes (which were almost black) were Constance's most famous feature, Vickers had chosen to photograph her with them shut.

"*La Belle Dame sans Merci.*" Vickers, who was recovering, gave a high, whinnying laugh. "That was what I called it. Well, one did things like that then. Constance on a bier, the Sitwells on biers— nothing but biers for a whole *year*, which went down *terribly* badly, of course, because it was the middle of the first war, and people said it was decadent. Useful, though, all that outrage." He gave me a small glance. "It made me into an *enfant terrible*, always the best way to start. People forget I was ever that, now I'm a grand old man. So I thought I'd use this, in the exhibition, just to remind them. Oh, and her wedding photographs of course. They're too divine."

He riffled through the pile of photographs. "Oh, they're not here. They're down at the museum, I think. But look at this—now *this* will interest you."

The photograph he held out was an informal one, the kind of picture Vickers used to call a "family snap."

I recognized it at once. It had been taken in Venice in 1956. Constance and a group of her friends stood by the Grand Canal; behind them you could just discern the buttress of a church—it was Santa Maria della Salute. An elegant group in pale summery clothes; it included the legendary Van Dymen twins, both now dead. A moment before the picture was taken, I remembered, there had been some horseplay between the twins with a panama hat.

On the edge of the group, a little separated from them, were two younger figures. Caught in that golden Venetian light, with the shadows of the church just to their side: a tall, dark-haired man, his expression preoccupied, a man of striking appearance who might have been taken for an Italian but who was not, and a young woman at whom he was looking.

She, too, was tall. Her figure was slender. She wore a greenish dress above bare legs, flat sandals. Her most striking feature was her hair, which she wore long and loose. It waved about her face; the Venetian light intensified its color to red-gold, or auburn. A strand of hair, blown across her face, obscured her features. She looked away from the camera and away from the dark-suited man. She looked, I thought, poised for flight—this young woman, who had once been myself.

I had been twenty-five then, not quite twenty-six. I was not yet in love with the man standing next to me, but I had sensed, that day, a possibility of love. I did not want to look at this photograph, at the man, or at myself. I put it down without comment and turned back to Vickers.

"Conrad," I said. "Where is Constance?"

He prevaricated. He twisted and turned. Yes, he had made some calls, just as he had promised, but—to his great surprise—had drawn a blank. No one seemed to know where Constance was— which was unusual, but surely no cause for alarm. Constance, he suggested, would pop up suddenly, just as she always did; after all, hadn't she always been unpredictable?

"One of Constance's fugue states, isn't that the term? You know how she likes to take off. There's probably a man behind it somewhere."

He then showered me with suggestions. The apartment was closed up? How strange. Had I tried East Hampton? What, it was sold? He had had no idea. . . . He rushed away from that one very fast, leaving me quite sure he knew the house had been sold, for all the energy with which he denied it.

"She'll be in Europe," he cried, as if the idea had just come to him. "Have you tried the Danieli, the Crillon? What about Molly Dorset or the Connaught?"

When I explained that I had tried all these familiar ports of call, and others, Vickers gave a good impression of profound mystification.

"Then I'm afraid I can't help. You see, I haven't set eyes on her, not for almost a year." He paused, gave me an appraising look. "She's been getting very strange, you know—almost reclusive. She doesn't give parties anymore—hasn't for ages. And if you invite her, well, you can never be sure she'll turn up—"

"Reclusive? Constance?"

"Perhaps that's the wrong word. Not reclusive exactly. But odd—definitely odd. Plotting something, I'd have said, the last time I met her. She had that rather gleeful, secretive look—you remember? I said to her, 'Connie, I know that face. You're up to something. You're up to no good.' "

"And what did she reply?"

"She said I was wrong—for once. She laughed. Then she said she was taking a leaf from my book, embarking on her own retrospective. I didn't believe her, of course. And I said so. I knew a man must be involved, and I asked her who it was. She didn't tell me, naturally. She just sat there, smiling her Sphinx smile, while I played guessing games—"

"No hints? That's not like Constance."

"Not one. She said I'd find out in the end, and when I did, I'd be terribly surprised. That's all." Vickers hesitated. He looked at his watch. "Heavens! Is that the time? I'm afraid, in a minute, that I'll have to rush—"

"Conrad . . ."

"Yes, dah-ling?"

"Is Constance avoiding me? Is that it?"

"*Avoiding* you?" He gave me a look (an unconvincing look) of injured surprise. "Why should you say that? Obviously, you quarreled—well, we all know that. And I must say I *did* hear some rather titillating rumors: a certain man's name bandied about—you know how it is. . . ." He gave me an arch smile. "But Constance *never* discusses that. And she always speaks most warmly of you. She *loved* your recent work. That red drawing room you did for Molly Dorset—she *adored* that—"

In his efforts to convince me, he had made a lapse. I saw the realization in his eyes at once.

"The Dorsets' drawing room? That's odd. I finished that room four months ago. It was the last work I did before Steenie was ill. I thought you said you hadn't seen Constance for almost a year?"

Vickers clapped a hand to his brow; a stagy gesture.

"Heavens, what a muddler I am! It can't have been the Dorsets' then. It must have been some other room. Age, you know, dah-ling. Advancing senility. I do it all the time now: muddle names, dates, places—it's a positive *scourge*. Now, you mustn't be cross, but I'm going to have to *shoo* you away. I'm due down in the Village in half an hour—just a gathering of old friends, but you know how the traffic will be. The whole city quite clogged up with the most dreadful people—tourists, you know, car salesmen from Detroit, housewives from Idaho, grabbing *every* available cab. . . ."

He was steering me, a firm grip above the elbow, in the direction of the hall. There, the Japanese houseboy hovered. "*Love* you in that blue—too wonderful with the Titian hair," he chirruped, and, since Vickers often used flattery to secure a quick escape, it was no surprise to find myself, a moment later, out on the sidewalk.

I turned back, but Vickers, so famous for his charm in certain circles, had never been afraid to be rude.

A white hand waved. The Japanese houseboy giggled. The aubergine door of the smart little town house shut in my face.

I found that interesting: such a precipitate departure. I was then quite sure that Vickers, loyal to Constance if not to my uncle Steenie, had been lying.

Before going to Conrad Vickers's house, I had spent a disappointing and frustrating day, much of it on the telephone. The rest of the evening was similar. It had been a mistake to drink champagne, which left me with a thirst and renewed jet lag. It had been a mistake, also, to discuss with Vickers those three months I had spent with Steenie at Winterscombe. Above all, it had been a mistake to look at that Venetian photograph, to see myself as I used to be and was no longer.

There were people I might have called, had I wanted company, but I did not. I wanted to be alone. I wanted to decide, I suppose, whether to continue my search or abandon it and return to England.

I persuaded one of the windows in my hotel room to open. I stood there with the warm urban air on my face; I watched Manhattan. The transition hours, between day and night. I felt myself in transition, too, poised just this side of decisive change—and perhaps for that reason I became obstinate again. I would not be beaten this easily. I knew Constance was here; the sensation that she was close was more intense than it had been the day before. *Come on,* said her voice, *if you want to find me.*

Before I went to bed I telephoned Betty Marpruder again. I telephoned three times. I checked with Directory Assistance. I checked there was no fault on the line. I dialed a fourth time. Still no reply. I found that very curious.

Betty Marpruder—Miss Marpruder to everyone except Constance and me; we were allowed to call her Prudie—was quite unlike the other women Constance employed, since she was neither young nor decorative and no member of her family had ever adorned the Social Register.

Constance, like many decorators, was careful to employ women— and men—whose accents, clothes, and demeanor would impress her clients. She did so with a certain scornful pragmatism—window-dressing, she called it—but she did so nonetheless. Miss Marpruder, therefore, with her chain-store necklaces, her jaunty mannerisms, her brightly colored slacks, her aging invalid mother, her defiant yet sad air of spinsterhood, was always confined to a back room. There, she ruled the roost: She supervised the books, she tyrannized the workshops on Constance's behalf, she put the fear of God into manufacturers, and she never, under any circumstances, met the clients. Constance had always supplied the inspiration within the company, but it was Miss Marpruder, compensating for Constance's undeniable capriciousness, who did all the practical work.

In return for this, she had been granted certain favors; I was sure she would enjoy them still. Chief of these was that knowledge of hers of Constance's whereabouts. Miss Marpruder alone would be given the address of the villa or the number of the hotel suite; she would be entrusted with the details of the flights. She was given these privileged pieces of information because Constance knew how jealously she guarded them; Miss Marpruder, a worshipper at Constance's temple, was also Constance's high priestess.

In any decorating business there are constant crises; people relish them. In Constance's workplace they happened daily. Her clients were very rich; their riches made them whimsical. Costly material, a year on order, would arrive and fail to please. Rooms, hand-lacquered with sixteen coats of paint, would be completed and would disappoint. A drama would ensue. Assistants would scurry back and forth. Telephones would shrill. Clients would insist, *demand*, to speak with Constance, no one else.

In the midst of this melee, secure in her little back room, Miss Marpruder would wait. No, Miss Shawcross could not be contacted; no, she was *not* available; no, she would not telephone Venice or Paris or London or the airline—not just yet.

"Prudie has a perfect nose," Constance would crow. "When it comes to crises, she's a Supreme Court judge."

I listened to Miss Marpruder's telephone. I could see it quite clearly, this instrument, as I listened to it ring. I could see the lace mat on which it stood, the rickety table beneath, all the details of that sad room which Prudie, in her jaunty way, liked to refer to as her bachelor den.

I was parked with Prudie often as a child. She would take me down to Thirty-second Street, bring me through to say hello to her invalid mother, install me in her small sitting room, bring me little treats—homemade cookies, glasses of real lemonade. Prudie would have liked children of her own, I think.

Her sitting room was garish and brave. It had an air of scrimping, of insufficient money stretched to the limit by medical bills. There was a defiant couch, in an unhappy shade of red, draped with a shawl in a manner designed to imitate Constance's expensive, throwaway techniques. In Constance's rooms the shawl would have been a cashmere throw or an antique Paisley; in Miss Marpruder's it was Taiwanese silk.

She was exploited by Constance. When had I first understood that? To be loyal and indispensable, yet not to be well paid—or even adequately paid. How old was I when I first saw that as wrong? Whatever the age I was when liking fused with pity, it must have been in that small sitting room of Prudie's that my doubts about my godmother began.

There was the telephone, still ringing; there was its little lace doily, which Constance would have shuddered to see. It had been made for Miss Marpruder by her mother. Whenever she used the telephone she would smooth it into place.

"I love nice things," she said to me once, and I must have been in my teens, because her tone had made my heart ache. "Cushions, mats, doilies—it's the little touches that count, Victoria. Your godmother taught me that."

The memory made me angry. I went to sleep disliking Constance, rehearsing to myself the damage she did. But when I slept, I dreamed, and in my dreams my godmother came to me in a different guise. I woke to a sense of my own disloyalty. There had been reasons to love Constance, once.

A new direction to this search. I rose, showered, dressed. It was still very early. I telephoned Miss Marpruder one more time, and when there was no reply, impatient with the confinement of the room, I went outside to the heat of the streets. Brilliant light and clammy air. I hailed a cab. I think I decided where to go only when I climbed into it. I gave the driver the address.

"Queens?" Signs of reluctance, possibly resentment.

"Yes, Queens. Take the Triborough. Then I'll direct you."

"Green Lawns?"

"That's the place."

"Some kinda house?"

"No," I said. "It's a pet cemetery."

It was years since I had been there, and it took some time to find Bertie's grave. I walked past neat white tombstones, memorials to dogs, cats, and, in one case, a mouse.

ABSENT THEE FROM FELICITY A WHILE, it read. I turned, and almost fell over Bertie's iceberg.

There it was, just as I remembered: a grieving caprice on Constance's part, an attempt to re-create, at Bertie's final resting place, the landscape Constance saw as his ancestry. Bertie was a Newfoundland dog; Constance's knowledge of Newfoundland itself was poetic, also vague. Bertie dreamed of icebergs, she used to say; let an iceberg mark the place.

A stone had been designed. A stone had been carved. There had been arguments with the Green Lawns administrators, who liked neat tombstones and found icebergs unseemly. Constance, as usual, had triumphed, and there the iceberg was. From most angles the resemblance to ice of any kind was marginal; it helped if you knew what it was.

I had loved Bertie. I had grown up with Bertie. He was huge, black, as majestical as a bear. I read the inscription: TO BERTIE, THE LAST AND THE BEST OF MY DOGS. I looked at the dates of his birth and his death, faithfully recorded. Then I looked at something else.

Beneath the peaks of the iceberg, which was white, were runnels of green marble intended to represent a northern sea. These runnels extended from the base of the iceberg by at least one foot. Resting upon them, wrapped in a sheet of white paper, was a small bunch of flowers. Someone had chosen these flowers with care; this was no ordinary bouquet. It was as beautiful and as carefully arranged as the flowers I had seen the day before in Conrad Vickers's drawing room.

There were freesias, white roses, tiny side-sprigs of blue delphinium, pinks, pansies, lilies of the valley: flowers in season and flowers out of season, the kind of flowers it would be easy enough to pick in a garden like Winterscombe's, the kind of flowers that could be obtained, in New York, from very few florists.

I bent to smell the sweetness of their scent. I stepped back and considered them. It was, by then, midmorning. Bertie's grave was unshaded; the temperature in the sun was at least eighty degrees. The flowers were unwilted. They must have been placed there, at the very most, an hour before.

There was only one person in New York who would mourn Bertie, only one person who would bring flowers to the grave of a dog twenty-four years dead.

I scanned the lawns, the tombstones: no one in sight. I turned away, began to run.

Constance was in the city; compassion brought her close. All my love for my godmother came back, gripping my heart with an astonishing strength. Just like the old days, when Constance raced ahead and I panted to keep up. In pursuit, but—and I felt a moment's triumph—this time I was catching up.

*　　*　　*

I did something I had never done before in my life. I bribed a doorman. Not the doorman who had confronted me the day I arrived, and not the doorman I remembered—he would have retired. No, a new doorman, young, spruce, knowing, and amenable, who eyed me in a way his forebears would never have done.

"They're not answering." He replaced the telephone receiver. "I told you. Apartment's closed up."

I might have tried flirtation, I suppose; I preferred the twenty-dollar bill. I was expecting rebuff. To my astonishment, it slipped from my palm to his with the greatest of ease and disappeared into a pocket of his smart maroon uniform.

"Okay." He gave a shrug. "Go right on up. They won't answer. Fifth floor—"

"I know it's the fifth floor. I used to live here."

"If anyone asks"—he shrugged—"you sneaked past, okay? I didn't see you."

This was patently ridiculous. This was not the kind of apartment building in which people slipped past the doorman.

"Who else didn't you see today, apart from me?"

"What's that?"

"Miss Shawcross, for instance. Have you seen her?"

"No way. Not in weeks. I told you—"

I was making him nervous, I could see that. One more question and despite the twenty-dollar bill he might change his mind, refuse to admit me.

I took the elevator to the fifth floor. I walked along quiet red-carpeted corridors. Without a great deal of hope I pressed the bell for Constance's apartment. To my astonishment the door at once swung back.

I looked in, to my old home, to Constance's celebrated hall of mirrors. The glass on the right wall reflected the glass on the left; it created an illusory passage of space, reflections to infinitude.

"Count," Constance had said to me, that first day I came here. "Count. How many Victorias can you see? Seven? Eight? There are more than that—look more closely. You see? They go on forever."

"Constance," I said, thirty years later, and stepped forward. "Constance, it's me, Victoria—"

"No here. No here."

From behind the tall door a figure emerged. A Lilliputian maid, Filipino, dressed in a neat gray uniform. She stared in apparent astonishment, as if she had expected someone else. Then she barred my way with an anxious ferocity.

"No here," she said again, shaking her head from side to side. "Miss Shawcross—gone away—all closed up—no visitors." She gave me a tiny push.

"No, look, please—wait," I began. "I just want to ask, when did Constance leave? Where can I reach her?"

"No number. No address. No visitors—" Another tiny push. "All closed up now. Closed for the . . . for the summer."

"Then may I just leave a note? Please? It won't take a moment. Look, if you'd just let me in, Constance is my . . . godmother. It's urgent I see her—"

At the word *godmother*, clearly misunderstood, the maid's tiny features became very fierce.

"No children here—never any children here—"

"No, not now—but there used to be. I lived here as a child, with Constance. Look, surely you must have some number, some address—"

"Police." She gave me a more effective push. "You go right away now, or I call police, call them very quick—look, alarm button, right here—"

She leaned back a little as she spoke. She kept one hand on the doorjamb; the other reached for a small box on the wall.

"Panic button—you see?" The maid drew herself up to her full height, which was, at most, about four feet ten inches. She looked up at me—I am a great deal taller than that—and stamped one diminutive foot.

"Wait," I began, backing off a little, wondering when Constance (who never kept staff long) had hired this little spitfire. To have backed away was a mistake. A look of triumph came upon the maid's face. The door slammed shut. There was the sound of bolts, chains, locks being fastened.

I had come up to the fifth floor in one elevator; I went down in another. As soon as its doors closed upon me, I tensed. Those primitive, residual instincts we all still possess made the skin on the back of my neck prickle.

The elevator was not large, and the air inside it was close. There was a lingering humidity and also a lingering scent. I sniffed a familiar ambiguity: the fresh greenness of ferns with the earthier undertones of civet. Constance's scent, the one she invariably used, as memorable as her eyes or her voice. I felt a rush of the past to the head.

The descent seemed impossibly slow. I was convinced, even so, that she must have been just ahead of me, descending in the left elevator while I mounted in the right. It was for that reason the maid had answered the door with such alacrity. Constance must have just left, and the maid assumed she had reached the elevator, forgotten something, and returned. A matter of seconds: Constance might still be in the lobby, on the sidewalk outside.

The lobby was empty; the doorman's eyes were bent upon his desk. I ran out to the heat of the street. I scanned the faces of the passers-by. I looked uptown, toward the entrance to the park, the route Constance and I had taken almost daily, all those years before, with Bertie.

I think for one moment I almost expected to see not only Constance but also myself, a child, holding on to Constance's arm, the two of us laughing, chattering, and Bertie lifting his great head in anticipation as we approached the entrance to the park.

Time passes. The people on the sidewalk did not see our ghosts; I did not see Constance. No quick, small figure, no gesturing hands. I had sensed her in the air, and into the air she had evaporated.

The sense of loss was acute. I stood there, staring blindly across at the park. Then, because one sense of loss brought other losses close, I did something else for the first time—something much more foolish than bribing a doorman. I crossed the avenue and began to walk west, toward a street and an apartment block I had been careful to avoid for eight years.

Nothing had changed, which hurt. Seventy-sixth Street between Amsterdam and Columbus, the third building along on the left, heading west: a shabby red-brick, in a neighborhood Constance despised. I used to live there; the man in Conrad Vickers's photograph used to live there with me. Our apartment was on the top floor; on that fire escape, up there, we used to sit on summer evenings. Manhattan-watching, Manhattan-listening.

I looked up. The fire escape was empty. A dish towel fluttered on an improvised clothesline; someone else would live there now, some other couple.

I turned away. I was shaking. To believe you have cured yourself of the past and then to discover that its ill effects continue, that its pains recur like malaria—that, perhaps, is always a shock.

I went back to the hotel. I locked the door. I splashed water on my face. I watched the faucets weep.

Then I lay down on the bed, to will the past away. It refused to go, of course. It whispered with the air conditioning. It crept closer, then closer still, all the circuitous paths of my life, all of which led back to Constance.

The landscape of my past: It reminded me of home; it reminded me of England. All those paths through the woods. I dreamed of Winterscombe when I slept.

Imagine a valley, an English valley, and a clement one. The hills slope gently; the woods are of oak and beech and ash and birch. There is no indication, when you are in that valley, that—just a few miles to the south—the landscape changes abruptly to the chalk downs of Salisbury Plain.

This valley is not windswept; it is a sheltered place. Over the centuries its natural beauties have been refined by man. The course of its river, which abounds in fish, has been diverted, so its waters spill out into a lake, ornamental and felicitous.

On one side of the lake the woods begin. Drives have been cut through these woods, and paths through them are maintained; they lead to clearings or to eminences, some of which are left to nature, some of which are defined, in pleasing ways, with a statue, an obelisk, or a gazebo.

On the other side of the lake the hand of man is more obvious. There is a park and a small, somewhat ugly church, perched on a hill and endowed by my grandfather. There are lawns and grass tennis courts, herbaceous borders and a rose garden. There are, to one side, the walls of the vegetable garden and a glint of glass, which is the roofs of the hothouses where the gardeners, diminished now in numbers, still grow black grapes and melons and white peaches, which are rare and easily bruised and must never be picked by children.

You can see woodsmoke, which comes from the houses in the estate village, where some cottages are still occupied; you can see the gleam of the golden cockerel who rides the clock tower in the stables. Turn your eyes back to the lawns and you will come to a terrace; turn your eyes to the terrace and you will see my grandfather's house, which he built with my great-grandfather's money.

Everyone I know complains about that house: My mother says it is too large, that it was built for another world, and is now preposterous. My father says it eats money, because the rooms are so large and their ceilings so high, and the roof leaks and the windows rattle and the plumbing protests and wheezes and whistles. You can see the house eating money if you go down to the cellars and the boiler room and watch Jack Hennessy stoking the boiler with coke. The boiler is huge—it looks big enough to turn the turbines on an ocean liner—and Hennessy says that if he shoveled day and night he still couldn't satisfy its appetite. In go the shovels of coke—which I see as pound notes, for I've been taught to understand about economy—and out comes, upstairs, a wheezing and a rattling from miles of snaking pipes. The pipes are lukewarm; the radiators are lukewarm; the bathwater is lukewarm.

"This is not central heating—it's peripheral heating," my father says in a despairing voice; so the fires are lit as well and we all sit next to the fire, with hot fronts and cold backs.

This is how the house happened: My great-great-grandfather made a fortune, first from soap and then from patent bleaches. This fact is regarded as inconvenient by most of my family, especially my great-aunt Maud, who is grand and old and was once famous for her parties; only my father ever refers to bleaches or soaps, and then only when he wants to tease Aunt Maud or Uncle Steenie. My great-grandfather made even more money from his bleaches and his factories, which were situated in the Scottish lowlands. He didn't like to live too close to those factories, I think, and perhaps he, too, preferred not to be reminded of bleach, because he moved his family south, went into politics, purchased a barony, became the first Lord Callendar, and sent my grandfather, Denton Cavendish, to Eton.

My grandfather Denton was famous for his pheasants and his tempers and his American wife, my grandmother Gwen, who was beautiful but penniless. My grandfather built this house and created these gardens and enlarged these estates, and my father and his three brothers, like me, were born in it.

When my grandfather Denton built it, it was the acme of fashion. It was finished in the 1890s, when Queen Victoria was still on the throne, but in spirit and in design it was an Edwardian house. There it is, huge, crenellated, opulent, and absurd, made for the long summer days before the first war, made for a procession of house parties, made for billiards and bridge-playing, for croquet matches, for shooting weekends, and the discreet diversions of leisured adultery: Winterscombe, my home. I never cared if it ate money, and neither, I suspect, in their heart of hearts, did my father or my mother. They loved it; I loved it; I loved them. When I think of it now, it is always autumn; there is always a mist over the lake (which needs dredging); there is always woodsmoke; I am always happy. Naturally.

When I was older, and I went to live with Constance in New

York, I learned to love a faster life. I learned to value the charms of caprice and the pleasures of whim; I learned the luxury of carelessness.

At Winterscombe I never experienced such things, and I loved their opposites. Others might judge our family life dull; I liked the safeness of its rituals, and the sure knowledge when I went to bed that the next day would be almost precisely the same as the day before. Like my parents, I was, I suppose, very English.

In the mornings I woke at seven, when Jenna, who was my nurse, brought up the copper jug of hot water and a boiled wash-cloth. She scrubbed my face and my neck and the back of my ears until my skin glowed, and then she brushed my hair, which was red and curly—I hated it—for exactly fifty strokes. Then it was plaited into neat tight braids in an effort to subdue it, and fastened with elastic bands and ribbons, which were changed every day to match the blouse I was wearing. It was Jenna's religion to be orderly.

My clothes used to arrive twice a year, in white boxes from London; they were sensible and they never varied. In summer I wore sea island cotton undershirts and, in winter, woollen ones with sleeves. I wore long socks or woollen stockings in winter, and short cotton socks in summer. I had three kinds of shoes: stout brown lace-ups, stout brown sandals, and flat pumps, made of bronze kid, which were reserved for parties, although I went to very few parties. In summer I wore cotton frocks and cardigans Jenna knitted; in winter I wore gray flannel pleated skirts and gray flannel jackets. I had a succession of Harris tweed overcoats with velveteen collars, all of which were identical; a succession of identical pudding-basin hats that clipped under the chin with elastic. I hated the scratchy winter vests, but apart from that, I never thought about my clothes a great deal, except when I went to visit my great-aunt Maud in London.

Aunt Maud did not like my clothes and she said so, roundly. "The child looks *drab*," she would pronounce, fixing me with a stern eye. "I shall take her to Harrods. She has . . . possibilities."

I wasn't sure what those possibilities were. When I peered in my looking glass I could see that I was tall and skinny. I had big feet, which looked even larger in the brown lace-up shoes, which Jenna polished until they shone like chestnuts. I had freckles, of which I was very ashamed. I had eyes of an indeterminate green. I had that horrible curly red hair, which reached halfway down my back, when all I wanted was to have short straight black hair, and tempestuous blue eyes like the heroines in Aunt Maud's favorite novels.

No possibilities there that I could see, and the often-promised visits to Harrods never seemed to materialize. I think Aunt Maud, who was old by then and somewhat vague, may simply have forgotten; on the other hand, my mother, who found fashion frivolous, may have intervened. "I love Maud dearly," she used to say, "but she can go too far. One has to put one's foot down."

It is true that on one of my birthdays—my seventh—Aunt Maud did, as she would say, push the boat out. Aunt Maud's finances were a mystery, but as far as I could understand, she lived off paintings: a collection of paintings once given her by a very dear friend. Most of these paintings had been sold some years before, but a few had been kept in reserve—"For a rainy day," Maud said.

I think that, when my seventh birthday approached, a painting must have been sacrificed, for Maud acquired several new outfits herself and she also went to Harrods. From London, some weeks in advance, she sent me a party dress.

I can still see that dress, in all its magnificence, being unwrapped from its sheaves of tissue paper in the nursery. It was made of velvet the color of Chinese amber. It had a full skirt, with froths of petticoats; it had puff sleeves and a large lace collar.

"Oh dear, Brussels lace—Maud is so terribly extravagant." My mother looked at this dress in a sad way; and, over the top of her head, Jenna gave me a wink.

Later, when my mother had gone downstairs, Jenna drew the curtains and lit the lamps and set up the cheval glass in the middle of the nursery bedroom.

"Now," she said. "We'll try it on. And I'll do your hair for you. No looking till you're ready."

I was very excited, skipping about the room and fidgeting under Jenna's patient hands; it seemed to take so long. The cream silk party stockings, fastened with elastic garters, the bronze kid pumps, the petticoats. Even when the dress was on I was still not allowed to look. Jenna had first to brush my hair loose and tie it back from my face with a new black ribbon.

I think I knew there was a problem, even then, because it had been difficult to do up the dress; I had had to hold my breath, and I had seen Jenna frown. I forgot about that when I looked in the glass, because the dress was so beautiful and the girl who looked back at me was so transformed. I stood looking at this strange girl for some time; then Jenna sighed, and I began to see the things that were wrong. I was too tall and the skirt was too short; I was thin, but not thin enough for this dress, so the bodice strained across my ribs.

"I can let it out maybe—just a little." Jenna fingered the hem. "And look, Vicky, there's two inches here, maybe three. I'll let it down. Maybe your Aunt Maud wasn't too sure of the size. But don't you worry now, it'll be fine this winter. Charlotte's party—you always go to that. You'll be able to wear it to Charlotte's party."

Charlotte's party was the one dependable event in the winter calendar. Charlotte was a small thin blond girl several years my elder, a girl I did not greatly like. She lived in a large house some fifteen miles from Winterscombe. Charlotte had parties of unimaginable luxuriance, with magicians from London and, the previous year, an ice-cream cake. Her father bought a new Rolls-Royce every year and smoked cigars, and her mother wore diamonds in the daytime. Charlotte had once come to tea at Winterscombe and had pronounced it shabby. This had hurt. I quite looked forward to wearing this astonishing dress to Charlotte's party.

That year, Charlotte contracted measles and her party was canceled. The amber velvet dress hung in the closet, growing smaller and smaller as the weeks passed. I tried not to eat, but whether I ate or not, I seemed to grow taller and taller. When Christmas came Jenna let it out again, and we both began to hope: Surely I would be able to wear it at Christmas? Aunt Maud was coming for Christmas. I tried it on again, on Christmas Eve; the hooks and eyes would not fasten; I went down to Christmas luncheon as I always did, in sensible Viyella.

Aunt Maud had forgotten the dress by then, I think. On Boxing Day, I tackled her on another matter.

"Aunt Maud," I said, waylaying her in her room, "can you make freckles go away? Can you get rid of them?"

Aunt Maud raised her lorgnette and inspected my face closely. "Of course you can," she pronounced. "Fuller's earth. It whitens the skin. I've used it for years. It's unbeatable."

We tried. Aunt Maud took me into her bathroom and mixed up a grayish paste. She rubbed this paste over my nose and cheekbones, then sat me down in a chair and read to me from one of her novels while the paste dried. The novel was called *The Crossroads of the Heart*. It took place on an ocean liner. There were always what she called Good Bits in Aunt Maud's novels, and she read me one of the best of the Good Bits, toward the end; it was a tender scene, on the stern deck, by moonlight, and it ended with a most interesting description of an embrace. If my mother had heard it, I think she might have put her foot down, but it moved Aunt Maud a great deal, so much so that she started on one of her own stories about

Winterscombe and the parties there used to be there in the old days, when my American grandmother Gwen was alive.

"I remember once," she said, "there was a party for a comet. Halley's comet, you know. We were all to have supper and then gather outside, to watch the comet go over. . . ."

I sat very still. I liked these stories but my nose was beginning to itch; I wondered if it would be rude to interrupt and mention it.

"I wore my emeralds. Or was it my sapphires? No, the sapphires, I think, because I remember my dress was blue, and Monty—oh!" She gave a shriek. "The Fuller's earth, Vicky! Quickly!"

I was rushed back into the bathroom, and my face was scrubbed with Aunt Maud's special French soap.

"May I look now, Aunt Maud?"

Aunt Maud was staring at my face in a dubious way; with some reluctance, she handed me a mirror. I held it close to my nose and inspected. My nose was red; my whole face was a fiery red; the freckles winked. There seemed more of them than ever.

"I don't think it's quite worked, Aunt Maud," I began, and Aunt Maud snatched the mirror away.

"Well, of course it doesn't work in one go! Quick-smart, just like that! *Il faut souffrir pour être belle!* You must persevere, Vicky. Now, if I were to leave you a little packet, and you were to apply it every week . . ."

I took the packet of Fuller's earth. I tried it once a week for four weeks. When it was all used up and the freckles were still there, I acknowledged the truth. I loved Aunt Maud very much, but she had been wrong about three things: wrong about the dress size, wrong about the Fuller's earth, and wrong about my possibilities. I had no possibilities. My faith in Aunt Maud, though still strong, was dented.

Aunt Maud was one of the pillars of my life; she defined its boundaries. There were other pillars, too: There were my father and my mother; there was my godfather, Steenie's friend the poet Wexton; there was Jenna; there were my uncles; and finally there was William, who was called the butler but who did all sorts of things around the house that other people's butlers never seemed to do, including cleaning the boots and shoes—on which subject Charlotte (on that day she came to tea) was very scathing.

"The *butler* cleans your shoes?" she said.

It was winter, and we had just returned with muddy lace-ups from a walk in the grounds.

"Don't you have a bootboy?"

"Well, Jenna cleans mine. Usually."

"Jenna? But she's your nanny. She's not even a proper nanny—Mummy said so. My nanny wears a *brown* uniform."

This worried me more than I wanted to admit. When we had tea with my mother, I could see that Charlotte did not think much of her either. I could see her eying my mother's dress, which was the kind of plain dress she always wore on weekday afternoons, and over which she wore an elderly tweed jacket. I knew my mother's opinions about diamonds in the daytime, and—although I was sure she must be right—I began to wish she had worn something more dashing than a single string of pearls. She did have diamonds, after all; they were kept in the bank, and every six months there would be a debate about selling them.

I began to wish I could tell Charlotte about these diamonds and to plan how I might mention them, in a casual way, once my mother had left the room. On the other hand, I knew my mother would be ashamed of me if I did any such thing. I squirmed about in my chair and tried not to notice when Charlotte shivered and glanced toward the drafty windows.

My mother was telling her about her orphanage work, and Charlotte was listening with a small, tight, supercilious smile that made me more nervous still; she despised orphanages as much as she despised my mother, I could tell.

When my father joined us I relaxed a little. I was sure my father was beyond reproach: He was so tall and so handsome; he had fine hands and a quiet dry way of speaking; he was a good horseman, and when he wore his hunting clothes William said there wasn't a man to touch him in the county. I rather wished he were wearing his hunting clothes then, so Charlotte might see him at his finest; as it was, he was wearing one of his old tweed suits, but those suits were built for him, and William (who had the job of brushing them) used to finger their material and say, "That's quality."

I hoped Charlotte would see this. I hoped that when my father began to talk to her, that small supercilious smile would disappear from her face. My father stammered a little over certain words, which was a legacy from the Great War, but he was gentle and kind and he charmed everybody. It could only be a matter of time, I told myself, before Charlotte succumbed.

He asked her first about her lessons—which was perhaps a mistake, because Charlotte was now at boarding school and she had already, during our walk, given me her opinion of girls who stayed at home for their education.

"Your *mother* teaches you? I thought you at least had a governess."

"Well, I did. But she left." I hesitated, because that was difficult territory: None of the governesses had stayed long; we now no longer had a parlormaid and the cooks were always giving warning. This was because of wages, and the boiler in the basement, which ate money, and the orphanages, which ate up even more.

"She takes you for *everything*?"

"She's very clever. I do English and French and geography with her, and next year we shall begin on Latin. Mr. Birdsong comes over three times a week for mathematics."

"Mr. Birdsong? But he's the *curate*."

Definitive scorn. I was instantly ashamed of Mr. Birdsong, a mild and patient man whom I had always liked. Sitting in the drawing room, I now began to wish that my father would change the subject. Charlotte was lecturing him on Roedean, and the small supercilious smile was still on her face.

"And what about the summer holidays?" my father said, when that speech came to the end. He said it in his most polite and gentle way, but I could tell he didn't like Charlotte at all. In fact, I think he found her funny, but no one would have known, because his manners were perfect.

"Oh, Mummy says we shan't go to France next year. She says the Riviera is overrun. We may go to Italy. Or Germany. Daddy says Germany is on the up-and-up." She paused and swung her foot and gave me a sly glance.

"And what about you, Vicky? You didn't say."

"Oh, we have great plans," my father said in his easy way.

"Really?" Charlotte fixed upon him a small hard gaze.

"Yes. We shall stay here, you know. Just as we always do."

"All summer?"

"Definitely. All summer—shan't we, darling?"

He turned to my mother, and I saw an amused glance pass between them.

My mother smiled. "I think so," she said, in her quiet voice. "Winterscombe is so lovely in June and July, and besides, the boys come over—you know, from the orphanage. We have to be here for that, you see, Charlotte. Now, would you like a sandwich? Perhaps a piece of cake?"

When tea was over, my parents left us. Charlotte and I sat by the fire and played cards. We played gin rummy for a while and then, in a desultory way, took turns at patience. Charlotte told me about the new Rolls, which would be coming to collect her, and why it was so much better than the Rolls of the preceding year. She told me about Roedean, and how many name tags her brown-uniformed nanny had sewn on her new uniform, and she made it quite clear that playing patience was not her idea of after-tea entertainment.

I was very humiliated, and very afraid that Charlotte might return to the question of summer holidays, to the fact that we never took holidays abroad. When it was my turn to lay out the cards I did it very slowly, trying to pluck up the courage to mention my mother's diamonds. By that time I wanted to mention them very much indeed, because I could see that Charlotte thought my mother was plain and shabby, like the house. The thought of my mother's disapproval held me back, though, and so I continued to lay out the cards and scan my memory: There must be something I could mention that would wipe that supercilious smile off Charlotte's face—but it was hard to think of anything.

There were my two uncles, those other pillars of my life, and laying out the cards, I did consider them. Both my uncles were exotic in their ways: Uncle Freddie had had so many careers, including flying mail planes in South America, which must surely be glamorous. He had his enthusiasms, as my Aunt Maud called them, and the latest of these were two greyhounds, brought to Winterscombe the previous month and fed—to my mother's horror—on beefsteak. These dogs were "go-ers," Uncle Freddie said. They were going to win the Irish Greyhound Derby.

On the other hand, I was not too sure about these dogs, which spent most of the time, when not eating, asleep, and wouldn't listen to the special commands Uncle Freddie had been given by their Irish trainer. Uncle Freddie's enthusiasms had—as he would sadly put it—a way of "fizzling out." Better not to mention the dogs, perhaps, or South America, which Uncle Freddie had left in clouded circumstances. Uncle Steenie, then?

Uncle Steenie was definitely glamorous. He was an exquisite dresser and an exquisite speaker. He had the blondest hair I had ever seen, and the most beautiful pink-and-white complexion. Uncle Steenie knew everyone-but-everyone, and he called everyone-but-everyone "Darling" in a very warm tone of voice. He also said "too" a great deal: The journey was too impossible; the wine was too squalid; the last hotel was too quaint. Uncle Steenie had a great many friends all over the world, and, since he did not work, he was always visiting them. He was very good about sending postcards, and I usually received one every week. Their messages were brief: *Salut, Vicky! Here I am on Capri,* he might write, and then he would draw one of his little lightning pictures underneath, of himself or a tree or a shell. Uncle Steenie drew very cleverly and wrote in violet ink. I had a great collection of these postcards: That year alone he had been in Capri, Tangier, Marseilles, Berlin, and a villa in Fiesole which was too marvelous, and which was owned by his best friend, Conrad Vickers, the famous photographer. Uncle Steenie had a great many famous friends: He knew film stars and painters and singers and writers. My godfather Wexton, who used to be his best friend, had dedicated a whole book of poems to my uncle Steenie, poems he had written in the Great War which were called *Shells*.

Should I mention my uncle Steenie? He did not come to Winterscombe very often, it was true, and when he did, there were arguments about money: Uncle Steenie wanted to be the Best-Kept Boy in the World, and he used to remind people of this in a loud voice when he had finished all the wine at luncheon. I found this very odd, because although Uncle Steenie was undeniably well kept and had that beautiful complexion, he was not a boy and hadn't been a boy for quite a long time. When he talked about being one, he made my father furiously angry.

"For God's sake, Steenie," I heard my father say once, when I passed them in the library and the door was open. "For God's sake, you're almost forty years old. This can't go on. What happened to the last check I sent you?" Perhaps, on the whole, it was better not to mention my uncle Steenie, either. Charlotte would be sure to ask what he did—she always asked that; she even asked it about my father.

"But what does he *do*?" she said, after I had explained about the estate and my mother's orphanages and the lake, which needed dredging, and the boiler and its inexhaustible appetite for pound notes.

"I suppose he has a private income?" She made it sound like a dreadful disease. "Daddy said he thought he must. He said you couldn't possibly manage otherwise, not in this great barn of a place. Of course, there is the title. . . ." She wrinkled her nose. "But Daddy says titles don't count these days. Not unless they're very old—and yours isn't very old, is it? Daddy says they can be useful, of course. He wouldn't mind a title on his board, because there's still some people they impress. It's a pity he isn't in the City, like Daddy, don't you think? It must be horrid to be so poor."

"I don't think we're poor. Not exactly poor." I was red in the face. "Mummy says we're very lucky."

"Nonsense. You haven't two halfpennies to rub together—Daddy said so. He made a big killing last week and he told Mummy then. He made more money on that one deal than your father makes in five years. It's true! You ask him."

No, better not to mention my uncle Steenie, who did not work, or my uncle Freddie and his reluctant greyhounds; better not to mention my aunt Maud, who had been famous as a hostess once but who was now vague and old and wrong about my possibilities. Better, in fact, to stay off the subject of my family altogether.

I sneaked a look at the clock, hoping it would soon be time for Charlotte to go, and began to stack up my cards: black queen on red king; red knave on black queen: this patience (I could already tell) was not going to come out.

Charlotte sat opposite me, watching the pack as if she expected me to cheat. She tapped her fingers on the green baize cloth. Queen of spades on king of hearts. Suddenly it came to me: the perfect candidate, the trump card.

"Oh, by the way," I began—there was no time to be subtle— "I may go to America next year. Did I tell you?"

"*America?*"

"Yes. To stay in New York. My godmother lives there, and she wants me to stay with her."

"Your godmother? You never mentioned an American god-mother."

"Well, I call her 'aunt.' Aunt Constance. But she isn't really my aunt."

This was now more than a boast; it was a lie, since I called her no such thing, but I was launched, and scented victory. Charlotte's eyes had grown small and concentrated.

"Constance?"

"Constance Shawcross," I said.

I brought out the name with a flourish. I hoped, I suppose, that it would impress, for I knew, in a vague way, that my godmother was celebrated. She must, however, have been far more celebrated than I had ever imagined, for Charlotte's reaction exceeded my greatest hopes. She drew in her breath; her eyes rounded; her expression was of envy tinged with disbelief.

"No! *The* Constance Shawcross?"

"Of course," I said firmly, although I was at once afraid there might be two and my godmother the wrong one.

"Heavens!" Charlotte looked at me with new respect. "Wait till I tell Mummy."

Such triumph! I was a little afraid it would be difficult to

sustain, because I could tell that Charlotte was about to press me
with questions, to which my answers were sure to be wrong. But I
was saved. There was a scrunch of tires on gravel, the blaring of a
horn. Charlotte looked up. I took the opportunity to switch the order
of my cards.

"Your father's here," I said. "Oh—and look—this patience is
coming out, after all."

That was how the lie began; it was a lie that would have the
most terrible consequences.

When I mentioned Constance's name that afternoon at the card
table, all I really knew was that it was a name likely to impress. I
knew my godmother was famous, though for what I had no idea. I
knew that my uncle Steenie adored her and pronounced her incom-
parable; I knew that, when he came to Winterscombe, he would
sometimes produce magazines that charted my godmother's social
activities in breathless detail. I also knew that when he mentioned
her name he was met with silence and the subject was quickly
changed. The magazines, which Uncle Steenie would leave open
upon tables, would be removed the instant he left the room. I knew,
in short, that there was a mystery.

When I was born (Jenna had told me this) Constance had
attended my christening and, like a godmother in a fairy story, had
bent over my cradle to bestow a kiss. She had held me in her arms
outside the Winterscombe church and had given me as a christening
present a most extraordinary bracelet, in the shape of a coiling snake.
This bracelet, described by Jenna as unsuitable, I had never seen; it
lay lodged with my mother's diamonds in the bank.

After the christening Constance must have fallen from favor, for
she disappeared. More precisely, she was erased. There were numerous photographs of my christening, and Constance appeared in none
of them. She was never invited to stay at the house, although I knew
she came to England, for Uncle Steenie would say so. The only
reason I knew she was my godmother was that she told me so
herself; each year at Christmas, and each year on my birthday, she
would send a card, and inside them she would write: *From your
godmother, Constance.* The handwriting was small, the strokes of the
letters bold, and the ink black.

These cards of hers were arranged, with the others I received,
on the nursery mantelpiece. When the birthday was over I was
allowed to keep my cards, cutting them out and pasting them in

scrapbooks—all the cards, that is, except those from my godmother. Her cards were always removed.

This tactic was designed, I expect, to make me forget my godmother. Since I was a child, it had the opposite effect. The less I was told, the more I wanted to know, but to discover more was extremely difficult. My parents were obdurate: Nothing could persuade either of them to mention Constance by name, and a direct question was met with visible displeasure. They confirmed that she was my godmother—that was all.

Jenna had been provoked, once or twice, into discussion of my christening and the exotic bracelet, but after that I think she was warned off, for she too refused to discuss Constance again. Aunt Maud clearly hated her; on the one occasion when I risked an inquiry there, Aunt Maud drew herself up, gazed down her imperious nose, and sniffed.

"Your godmother is quite beyond the pale, Victoria. I prefer you do not mention her to me. I cannot imagine that she would interest you."

"I just wondered . . . if she had . . . tempestuous eyes," I persevered.

"Her eyes are like two small pieces of coal," Aunt Maud replied, and that was the end of the subject.

William the butler claimed not to remember her. Uncle Freddie shifted his eyes about whenever I mentioned her name; trapped, alone on a walk in the woods, he once went so far as to admit that he and his brothers had known Constance as a child. She had, he said, frowning at the trees, been jolly good fun—in her way.

"Did Daddy like her then, Uncle Freddie? I don't think he likes her now."

"Maybe, maybe." Uncle Freddie whistled. "I don't remember. Now, where are those wretched dogs? You shout, Victoria. Oh, well *done*. Here they come. That's the ticket."

That left Uncle Steenie. I had high hopes of Uncle Steenie, particularly if I could waylay him after luncheon, or when he was in his own room, where he kept a silver hip flask for restorative nips on cold afternoons. Uncle Steenie might not come to Winterscombe very often but when he did, he became expansive after a few nips. "Sit down, Victoria," he would say. "Sit down and let's have a *huge* gossip."

And so, on one of his visits, I evaded Jenna and the regulation afternoon walk and crept along to Uncle Steenie's room.

Uncle Steenie gave me a chocolate truffle from his secret

bedroom supply, sat me by the fire, and told me all about Capri. When he paused for breath I asked my question. Uncle Steenie gave me one of his roguish looks.

"Constance? Your godmother?" He clicked his tongue. "Vicky darling, she is an absolute *demon*."

"A demon? You mean she's bad? Is that why no one will talk about her?"

"Bad?" Uncle Steenie seemed to find that idea interesting. He had another nip and considered it. "Well," he said at last, in his most drawling voice, "I can never quite make up my mind. You know the little girl in the nursery rhyme, the one with the curl down the middle of her forehead? 'When she was good she was very very good, and when she was bad she was horrid.' Constance is like that, perhaps. Except, personally, I liked her best when she *was* bad. The great thing about your godmother, Vicky, is that she is never dull."

"Is she . . . pretty?"

"Darling, *no*. Nothing so bland. She's . . . startling." He took another nip. "She bowls people over. Men especially. Down they go, like skittles."

"Did she bowl you over, Uncle Steenie?"

"Well, not exactly, Vicky." He paused. "She was probably too busy to try. I expect she had other fish to fry. She and I are almost the same age, you know, so we were always friends. We met for the first time when we were—let me see—about six years old. Younger than you are now, anyway. We're both the same age as the century, more or less, so that must have been 1906. Lord, I'm ancient! 1906! It feels like eons ago."

"So she's thirty-seven now?" I was disappointed, I think, for thirty-seven seemed very old. Uncle Steenie waved his hands in the air.

"Thirty-seven? Vicky darling, in Constance's case, the years are immaterial. Age cannot wither her—though it does the rest of us, unfortunately. Do you know what I saw in the mirror this morning? A most terrible thing. A crow's footprint, Vicky. In the corner of my eyes."

"It's not a very big footprint."

"Darling, you reassure me." Uncle Steenie sighed. "And the reason it's small is my new cream. Have I shown you my new cream? It smells of violets, and it's too heavenly—"

"Would it get rid of freckles, do you think, Uncle Steenie?"

"Darling, in a flash. There's nothing it can't do. It's a perfect miracle, this cream, which is just as well because it costs a queen's ransom." He smiled mischievously. "Look, I'll give you some if you like. Pat it in, Vicky, every evening. . . ."

So my uncle Steenie changed the subject—more dexterously than the rest of my family, but he changed it nonetheless. That night there were storms and slammed doors downstairs, and Uncle Steenie became so upset he had to be helped up to bed by my father and William. The next morning he departed, early, so I never received my jar of violet cream, and I discovered no more on the subject of Constance.

For several months nothing happened: Charlotte contracted measles; her party was canceled; her mother took her to Switzerland for a period of convalescence. Christmas came and went, and it was not until January of the new year, 1938, that I saw Charlotte again.

I was invited to her house for tea, alone—an honor never accorded me before. To my surprise I was invited again the following week; the week after that there was a most pressing invitation to join Charlotte and her friends on an expedition to see a London pantomime.

My stock had risen, it seemed, not just with Charlotte but with her parents also. I was no longer just a dull child from an impoverished background; I was Constance Shawcross's godchild. I was about to visit her in New York. Quite suddenly I had acquired possibilities.

At first, I am afraid, I enjoyed this very much. I was given wings by Constance's surrogate glamour; I took those wings and I flew. Since I knew virtually nothing about my godmother, I was free to invent. I discovered the addictions of fiction.

In the beginning I gave Constance all those attributes I myself most secretly admired: I gave her black hair and dark-blue eyes and a fiery temperament. I gave her five gray Persian cats (I loved cats) and an Irish wolfhound. I made her a superlative horsewoman who rode sidesaddle to hounds. I let fall the fact that she ordered French scent in large flagons, lived at the top of one of the tallest towers in New York, overlooking the Statue of Liberty, ate roast beef three times a week, and insisted on Oxford marmalade for breakfast. All her clothes, right down to her underwear, came from Harrods.

"Harrods? Are you sure, Victoria?" Charlotte's mother had been eavesdropping on these boasts avidly, but now she looked doubtful.

"Well, perhaps not *all* of them," I said carefully, and cast about in my mind. I thought of my aunt Maud and her reminiscences. "I think sometimes . . . that she goes to Paris."

"Oh, I feel sure she must. Schiaparelli, perhaps Chanel. There's

a picture I saw somewhere—Charlotte, where did I put that book?"
Charlotte's mother always called magazines "books," and on that
occasion a much-thumbed copy of *Vogue* was produced. It was two
years old at least. There, in my trembling hands, was the first
photograph of my godmother I had ever seen. Sleek, insolently chic,
she was photographed at a London party in a group that included
wicked Wallis Simpson, Conrad Vickers, and the then Prince of
Wales. She was gesturing, so her hand obscured her face.

After that my lies became less pure. I had learned from that
error about Harrods, and I trimmed my image of my godmother to
suit the tastes of my audience. I gave Constance several motorcars (a
touch of malice there, for none was a Rolls-Royce); I gave her a
yacht, a permanent suite at the Ritz, a collection of yellow diamonds,
crocodile-skin luggage, silk underwear, and intimate friendship with
King Farouk.

I was learning fast, and most of these details I picked up either
from Charlotte and her parents or from the fat and glossy magazines
that lay scattered around their home—magazines that were never
permitted at Winterscombe. I think I liked this Constance less than I
did the Constance of her first incarnation, who lived in a tower and
rode to hounds at full tilt. But my preferences were unimportant;
I could see that these new details impressed my audience. When I
mentioned the crocodile luggage Charlotte's mother gave a sigh; she
herself, she said in a wistful way, had admired something very
similar, just the other day, at Asprey's.

There were dangers—I could see that. Both Charlotte and her
mother seemed alarmingly well informed about my godmother. They
consumed gossip columns; they tossed the names of people my
godmother seemed to know into their everyday conversation: "Lady
Diana's dress—what did you think, Mummy?" "Oh, a teensy bit
dull, not up to her usual standards." Did they *know* Lady Diana? I
was never quite sure, but I sensed I must be careful. Was my
godmother married, for instance? Could she conceivably have been
divorced? If she was divorced, that might explain her fall from favor,
for my mother was adamantly opposed to divorce. I had no way of
knowing, but I suspected that both Charlotte and her parents might
know. They also presumably knew—as I did not—why my godmother was rich, what she did, who her parents were, where she
came from.

So I spun the tales of my fabled godmother, but I spun them
more warily, avoiding all mention of husbands or antecedents. In
return for my inventions I gleaned certain facts, which I squirreled

away. I learned that my godmother had been born in England but was now a naturalized American citizen. I learned that she "did up" houses, although no one explained what this involved. I learned that she crossed the Atlantic as casually as the Channel, and adored Venice, which she visited every year. When there, she would stay nowhere but the Danieli.

"*Not* the Gritti. I told you, Harold." We were sitting in their drawing room, on a shiny brocade sofa. Charlotte's mother was drinking a martini in a frosted glass. She twirled the olive, set the glass down on a bright table of glass and chrome, and gave her husband a cold look. She turned back to me in her new apologetic way, as if I were an arbiter of taste, too, like my godmother. "We stayed at the Gritti last year, Victoria, because the Danieli was chockablock. Of course, if we had had a *choice* . . . but it was such a last-minute arrangement. . . ."

Holidays. I tensed at once, for there, of course, lay another danger: my own visit to New York. I had hoped Charlotte might have forgotten that part of my boast, but she had not. She also remembered I had given a date: this year.

But when, this year? As the weeks passed, the questions became more pressing. Charlotte returned to boarding school but as soon as the Easter holidays came around, the invitations to tea were renewed.

When, exactly, did I plan to leave? Had it been decided whether I should sail on the *Aquitania* or the *Ile de France*? Was I to travel alone, or was my godmother to visit England and collect me? Surely I could not be going to New York in the summer—*no one* went to New York then, and my godmother was usually in Europe.

There was a brief respite that spring, due to politics: Austria was annexed by Germany, and although I had no idea what that meant I could tell it was something serious, for my father and mother had long anxious conversations, which would break off when I came into earshot. Even Charlotte's father looked grave. Their own visit to Germany, planned for that summer, was canceled. They opted for Italy after all.

"Things seem so very uncertain," Charlotte's mother said with a sigh. "I wonder if your parents will let you travel, Victoria? It would be ever so disappointing if you had to cancel your trip, but I can see . . ."

"It might have to be . . . postponed," I said in a small voice.

"I can't see why." Charlotte, who was sitting next to me, gave me a hard look. "America is in the opposite direction. Nothing is happening *there*."

I mumbled something—something not too convincing, I think, for I saw Charlotte and her mother exchange a telling glance. Perhaps Charlotte was already beginning to believe that the visit to my godmother was a fiction; certainly she now looked at me in a measured way, with a hint of the old superciliousness. I might not have liked her, and I think I was already beginning to regret my lies. All the same I was desperate to regain her respect.

I knew what one did when one was desperate for something: One prayed. My mother had taught me that. For many years, after they were first married, my mother and father were childless; my mother had prayed for a child, and—eventually—her prayers had been answered.

"Did Daddy pray for one too?" I wanted to know, and my mother frowned.

"I expect so, Vicky. In his way. Always remember, it's important not just to pray for yourself. You mustn't treat God like Father Christmas and ask for too many things. But if you ask for good things, the right things, then God listens. He might not always grant your wish, or"—she paused—"He might grant it in an unexpected way, but He does listen, Vicky. I believe that."

Was my visit to my godmother a good thing, one it was permissible to pray for? I weighed the pros and cons for some time; eventually I decided it was quite a good thing. I had been taught to be methodical, and I was methodical about this. I prayed every night and every morning; I prayed on Sundays when I went to church. I bought penny candles once a week and lit them to give wings to the prayer, and I couched the appeal politely: Please-God-if-You-think-it-is-a-good-thing-may-I-go-to-New-York-to-stay-with-Constance-if-it-is-Your-will-thank-you-Amen.

Twice a day, every day for three months. At the end of that time, when it was high summer at Winterscombe, my wish was granted. I should have listened to my mother more carefully perhaps, because it was granted in a most unexpected way.

Until my wish was granted, I enjoyed that summer. I remember days of sunshine and of warmth, a sensation of lull, as if the world waited and held its breath. There was calm, but it was an expectant calm; somewhere, beyond the boundaries of that safe world, something was happening, and sometimes I would fancy that I could hear it, still distant, and soft, like a great, invisible machine in gear—events elsewhere, their momentum gathering.

For many years I had known, in a vague way, that the orphanages that took up so much of my mother's time and ate such a worrying amount of my father's money, had connections with their counterparts in Europe. So, that summer, when my mother took me aside and explained that plans had changed, that she and my father would be in Europe on orphanage work during July and August, I was surprised, but not greatly. Although we never went abroad for holidays, my mother had once or twice made such trips in the past, usually in the company of her closest friend, the formidable Winifred Hunter-Coote, whom she had known in the Great War. This time, she explained, my father had decided to go with them, because they were not just visiting European orphanages, as they usually did, but were seeing friends in Germany who would help them to bring certain children to England. Just for a while, she explained, it would be safer for those children to be here, rather than at home in their own country. They were not necessarily orphans, she said in her careful way; they were perhaps more like refugees. It was not always easy to persuade the authorities to let them leave, which was why my father was going with her and with Winifred, for his German was fluent. . . .

Here, in a way that was uncharacteristic of her, my mother paused, and I knew there was something she was leaving out, something she did not want me to know.

"Won't their parents miss them?" I asked, and my mother smiled.

"Of course, darling. But they know it is for the best. We shall be away quite a long time, and I shall miss you too. You'll write, won't you, Vicky?"

I did write, every day, joining the letters together so that they were like a diary, and sending them off once a week to a series of *poste restante* addresses. To begin with, it felt strange, a summer at Winterscombe without my parents, but after a while I became used to the new quietness in the house, and besides, there were diversions. My aunt Maud was brought down to stay, and arrived with packages of brightly bound novels. She was a little frail, for she had had a mild stroke the previous Easter, but her appetite for fiction was undiminished. Uncle Freddie arrived, complete with greyhounds; they had definitely "fizzled," I could tell, because Uncle Freddie no longer mentioned the Irish Derby. Jenna was there and William was there and Charlotte was safely distant, at the Danieli, so there was no need to worry about the lies for a while. There were strawberries to pick, and then raspberries and young peas and lettuces. High summer, and I was content, even though my parents were away. Best of all, I had made a new friend.

His name was Franz-Jacob, he was ten years old, he was German, and he was Jewish. He arrived with the first contingent of orphanage children, part of the small group of five or six German boys who stood a little apart from the English children who came to Winterscombe regularly every summer.

I think perhaps my parents had known his family, who were still in Germany, but whatever the reason—it could simply have been that he was known to be exceptionally clever—special arrangements had been made for Franz-Jacob which singled him out from the others. He lived with the other children in the dormitories, which had been built years before in the old dairy and laundry buildings. He was invited to join in their games of cricket and tennis, the swimming parties and nature rambles that were organized that year, as always. But he also came up to the house every morning to join me at my lessons.

Since my mother was away, those lessons were conducted entirely by Mr. Birdsong and concentrated on his own strong points: Latin, history, mathematics, robust and heroic English poetry. I was not very good at any of these subjects, and I think, looking back, that it must have been very tiresome for Mr. Birdsong to have to teach me, although, if so, he disguised his impatience well. From the first day that Franz-Jacob joined my classes, Mr. Birdsong blossomed.

I was still struggling then with long division and making little progress. Franz-Jacob, whose English was limited, provided Mr. Birdsong with a chance to try out his German—that was the first excitement. The second excitement was his ability at mathematics. They began, I remember, with equations: a textbook was produced and Franz-Jacob bent over his desk. The sun shone; the room was warm; his pen scratched. In the length of time it took me to complete two sums, Franz-Jacob had completed an entire exercise.

He took it up to Mr. Birdsong and presented the pages with a small bow; Mr. Birdsong checked them over. He nodded; he clicked his tongue in admiration; he appeared at first surprised and then became pink in the face, a sign of excitement.

"This is very good, Franz-Jacob. *Das ist werklich sehr gut.* My goodness me, yes. Shall we try our hand at some fractions?"

Franz-Jacob shrugged. The fractions exercise was completed equally quickly. From that moment on, Mr. Birdsong was like a man reborn: He entered the schoolroom with a new energy in his step. I saw, for the first time, a glimpse of the man he used to be: a gifted mathematician at Oxford who, at his father's behest, had abandoned an academic career to take up Holy Orders.

I was neglected after that, but I did not mind. Mr. Birdsong might set me poems to learn or might encourage me to write out the important dates of the Reformation, but although he remained kindly there was no fire in his eyes when he heard the poems or the lists of dates. The fire was reserved for Franz-Jacob. They had moved on to calculus, and Mr. Birdsong's hand shook a little when he opened the textbook.

I thought Mr. Birdsong's reaction was entirely proper. Franz-Jacob was exceptional—I, too, could see that. He was unlike anyone I had ever met.

To look at, he was small and slightly built, but with a wiry strength that made the bigger English boys wary of bullying him. He had a narrow, intense face, dark eyes, and thin black hair worn cropped short at the nape of the neck and long at the front, so it often fell across his eyes when he worked; he would push it back impatiently. He rarely smiled. There was in his eyes an expression I was unfamiliar with then, though I have seen it since many times, an expression peculiar to those Europeans whose families have been persecuted in the past and may yet be persecuted again: European eyes, which regard even happiness warily.

He was a solemn child, in many ways an old-fashioned one; he was lonely. I, too, was lonely, with my parents away; I think I was solemn, and I was certainly old-fashioned, for I had been brought up to believe in a way of life and a set of standards that were already dying. Perhaps it was not so surprising that we should become friends.

All summer Franz-Jacob and I were inseparable. At night, when he returned to his dormitory with the other boys, we would signal Morse code messages to each other from our windows, with flashlights. During the day, when lessons were over, he would remain with me at the house. He became a great favorite with my aunt Maud, whose German was idiosyncratic but effective. Aunt Maud bombarded him with stories about Kaiser Wilhelm, whom she had known but disliked. She took great pleasure in explaining Franz's dietary needs to the servants and the rest of the family.

"No roast pork for Franz-Jacob, William," she would pronounce in a ringing voice. "I believe I asked for salmon. Ah, yes, here it is!

Now, Franz-Jacob, you may eat that quite safely. I went down to the kitchens to supervise the cooking myself, and I know about such things! Have I mentioned my friend Montague to you? Yes, of course I have. Well, Montague was not entirely *strict*, you understand, but even so I made quite sure he was never offered bacon in my house. And as for sausages—I banished sausages from the breakfast table. And a very good thing too. I am suspicious of sausages. As I have always said, one never quite knows what goes into them. . . ."

My uncle Freddie took to him, too, especially when he discovered that Franz-Jacob liked dogs and was more than willing to exercise the greyhounds. Uncle Freddie had a new project, a new enthusiasm that required him to spend long hours in the library with notebooks—an enthusiasm whose precise nature he refused to explain. A stout man, reluctant to walk any distance, Uncle Freddie was delighted to be able to remain in the library, leaving the greyhounds to Franz-Jacob and to me.

All summer, it seemed, Franz-Jacob and I walked: We walked down to the lake and along the river; we explored the village and the decaying cottage, alone at the end of a lane, where Jack Hennessy lived. We walked up past the cornfields, which always produced such an unsatisfactory crop, and along the boundary walls of my father's estate.

We walked and we talked. I taught Franz-Jacob some English and he taught me some German. He told me about his father, who had been a university professor but who had, the previous year, been relieved of his post. He described his mother, his two older brothers, and his three younger sisters. None of these members of his family were to survive the coming war, and although he could not have known that, I used to wonder afterwards if Franz-Jacob had had some intuition of what was to come, for although he spoke of them with affection, his eyes were always sad. They were fixed on that European horizon, filled with a future, yet remembered, pain.

I had never had a confidant of my own age, and by nature I was not secretive. We explored Winterscombe and I told Franz-Jacob everything. I told him about the house and how it ate money; I told him about Uncle Freddie's enthusiasms and the way they fizzled; I told him my Uncle Steenie's mysterious ambition to be the Best-Kept Boy in the World; I told him about Aunt Maud, and the amber velvet dress that did not fit; I explained the terrible misfortune it was to be born with freckles and red curly hair.

Franz-Jacob, who knew better than I did what true misfortune was, was patient. Encouraged, I told him the more terrible things. I told him about Charlotte, my godmother Constance, and my terrible lie. I told him about the prayers I still said, every morning and every evening. I held my breath, for I was in awe of Franz-Jacob and I quite expected him to damn me.

As it was, he merely shrugged. "Why worry? This girl is a stupid girl, and your parents, they are good people. *Das ist alles selbstverständlich. . . .*"

No condemnation; he whistled to the dogs and we walked on. It was that day, I think, when we returned to the house, that Franz-Jacob—who had been talking about mathematics, which he said he liked because they were perfect and inevitable, like the best music— suddenly stopped on the steps that led up to the terrace.

He looked down into my face, his expression intent, as if he saw me for the first time. "You know how many freckles you have?" he said at last, stepping back.

"How many?" I remember thinking it cruel of him to count.

"Seventy-two. You know something else?"

"What?"

"I don't mind them. They're all right."

"You're sure?"

"Natürlich."

He gave me an impatient glance, as if I were being slow, the way he did sometimes when we took our lessons. Then he ran up the steps, the dogs at his heels, and left me at their foot, scarlet and rejoicing.

The special day came many weeks after this, toward the end of August. I didn't know it was going to be a special day until it was almost over, but it was an odd day from the very beginning.

That morning, for the first time in three months I left out the prayer about New York and my godmother Constance. I had begun to understand the folly of that particular fiction and the impossibility, once Charlotte returned from Italy, of sustaining it. Franz-Jacob's robust dismissal of Charlotte—*This girl is a stupid girl*—had given me strength. Why should I care what Charlotte thought? I neither liked her nor admired her. She might judge my family dull and shabby, but Franz-Jacob, who was a much better judge, said Winterscombe was a magical place—*ein Zauber Ort*—and he knew my parents were good people.

I felt clean for leaving out the prayer, and curiously freed. Even my lessons with Mr. Birdsong went better than they usually did; I could be promoted quite soon, he hinted, to algebra.

After lunch Franz-Jacob and I took the greyhounds for their walk. We took the path down by the lake, as we often did, and stopped to look at the black swans; then—and this was more unusual—we turned in the direction of the Winterscombe woods. For some reason Franz-Jacob disliked these woods, although I loved them at all seasons of the year, and particularly in the summer for the coolness of their shade.

That day it was very hot; Franz-Jacob gave one of his shrugs and agreed to go that way. We might, even so, have just skirted the edge of the trees and then branched off on the path to the village, but the two greyhounds caught a scent and raced off; we were forced to follow them, calling and whistling, deeper and deeper into the woods, where the paths became narrow and overgrown.

We passed the place where my grandfather had kept his pheasant pens, and then turned aside, down a path thick with brambles. I was a little ahead of Franz-Jacob; I could hear the dogs crashing in the undergrowth, and I could see in front of me the open sunlight of a clearing, where I had walked sometimes with Jenna.

"They're through here, Franz. Come on," I called back. I heard him hesitate, then the movement of the undergrowth and the snapping of sticks underfoot as he followed. It was only when he came out into the sunlight of the clearing, and I saw his face, that I realized something was wrong.

Franz-Jacob was always pale. Now his face was drained of all color; sweat stood out on his forehead; he shrank in the warmth of the sunlight, shivering.

"Come away. Come away." He pulled at my sleeve. "Come away from this place."

"Franz, what is it?"

"*Gespenster.*" He glanced over his shoulder toward the trees and the undergrowth. "Ghosts. *Ich spüre sie. Sie sind hier. Es ist übel hier. Komme, lass uns schnell gehen.*"

Fear communicates itself very quickly. I might not have understood that rush of German words, but I understood the expression in Franz-Jacob's eyes. A second later and I was frightened too. A familiar and pleasant place became lowering and full of shadows. Franz-Jacob seized my hand and we both began to run, faster and faster, slipping on moss, tripping over branches. We did not stop running until we were out of the woods and back on the lawns below Winterscombe.

"What happened there? Something happened there," Franz-Jacob said. He stood looking back across the grass toward the trees and the two greyhounds, who were just emerging from the under-growth.

"In those woods?" I hesitated. "Nothing. There was an accident there once, I think. But that was ages and ages ago. No one talks about it."

"It's there now." Franz-Jacob was still trembling. "I could feel it. *Ich konnte es riechen.*"

"What? What? I don't understand. What did you say?"

The dogs had reached us; Franz-Jacob bent over them. They must have caught a rabbit or a hare, for when he straightened up I saw they had blood on their muzzles and Franz-Jacob had blood on his hands.

"I said I could smell it." He looked at me with his wide, dark European eyes. "I could smell *this.*"

He held out his hand and I looked at it stupidly.

"Blood? You mean you could smell blood?"

"Nein. Nein. Du bist ein dummes englische Mädchen, und du verstehst nicht." He turned away. *"Ich konnte den Krieg riechen."*

I understood, that time. I understood that he thought me stupid and English. Tears came to my eyes. I was hurt, and because I was hurt, I lost my temper. I stamped my foot.

"I do understand. I do. And it's not me who's stupid. It's you. You're imagining things. You can't smell war. How can you smell war, in a wood?"

I shouted the question, then shouted it again. Franz-Jacob turned his back. He walked away, the dogs at his heels, and even when I ran after him, when I caught his sleeve and asked the question a third time, Franz-Jacob did not reply.

That night we had a party. It was an improvised party, suggested by Aunt Maud, who complained at being left alone all day. Aunt Maud, too, in her way saw ghosts—in her case, the ghosts of Winterscombe's glorious past, the sad specters of parties long gone.

"There were always people here," she said at dinner, in a mournful way, casting a reproachful glance down the long table. "Look at us now! Rattling around like four peas in a pod. Four people, and I remember when this table used to seat forty. There was dancing, and bridge—billiards for the men—music and champagne, Victoria! Footmen behind every chair . . . And what have we now? We have William—and his shoes squeak. Freddie, you must have a word with him."

William, who was standing three feet from Aunt Maud when she made this pronouncement, continued to stare straight ahead of him, since he was fond of Aunt Maud, used to her ways, and had been trained that the best servants should appear deaf.

Uncle Freddie blushed and ate a second helping of steak-and-kidney pudding. He cheered up later in the meal, when it came to gooseberry crumble. It was Uncle Freddie, I think, who suggested that after dinner we might try a little dancing. Aunt Maud, too, revived at this and became quite energetic. No, she pronounced, the drawing room with the carpet rolled back would not do; it would be the ballroom or nothing. As far as I knew, this ballroom was never used; it lay at the far end of the house, added on by my grandfather as if in afterthought, a cavernous place decorated in spun-sugar colors.

Uncle Freddie and Franz-Jacob busied themselves. William was called upon to fetch stepladders, light bulbs, and my mother's wind-up gramophone. Once the chandeliers were lit, the room revived and its gaiety looked less tawdry. Franz-Jacob and I explored the box that had been built for the orchestra. It overlooked the floor below like a box at a theater, with a curved front ornamented with gilded cherubs. It had pink silk curtains, now very tattered.

"Such a splendid evening!" Aunt Maud might have been referring to that evening or to others of the distant past; she unlocked the French windows and threw them back. Fresh warm air; a few moths, attracted by the blaze of lights. "Whenever was this place last used, Freddie?" Aunt Maud demanded, and from my perch in the orchestra box, I saw Uncle Freddie hesitate.

"I'm not quite sure . . ." he began, and Aunt Maud gave him a look of scorn.

"You remember perfectly well, Freddie, and so do I. Constance's dance. Her debut. She wore a most vulgar dress. Freddie, wind the gramophone!"

My mother's taste in music was not catholic: From a collection that mainly comprised Beethoven piano sonatas, with some Mozart and Haydn, Uncle Freddie had contrived to find two suitable records for dancing; both were Viennese waltzes.

To the strains of "The Blue Danube," Uncle Freddie and Aunt Maud took the floor, Aunt Maud erect and regal, Uncle Freddie quickly out of breath.

Then it was the turn of Aunt Maud and Franz-Jacob. Franz-Jacob danced, as he did everything, solemnly. Approaching my aunt he bowed, then put his arm around her waist. Aunt Maud was tall; Franz-Jacob was short for his age. The top of his head was on a line

with Aunt Maud's carefully corseted bosom. Franz-Jacob politely
averted his head and they began to circle the floor. Franz-Jacob was
wearing his best suit, which was brown, with trousers that ended at
the knee. On his feet he wore, as usual, stout and well-polished
boots, more suitable to a country lane than a ballroom. They made
an odd couple: Aunt Maud all Edwardian dips and sweeps, Franz-
Jacob neat and jerky as a marionette. Uncle Freddie and I watched
them for a while. I took a turn with Uncle Freddie, who confided he
had been a whiz at the Black Bottom and the Charleston, and that
this wasn't his line at all. Then it was the turn of Franz-Jacob and
me.

Aunt Maud seated herself on a small gilt chair and called out
encouragement: "*Bend*, Vicky—from the waist. Be supple! Goodness, how stiff the child is!" Uncle Freddie mused by the gramophone,
and Franz-Jacob and I plodded our way around the floor.

I had only the vaguest notion of the proper steps, though
Franz-Jacob's knowledge seemed sounder, but I did not mind that I
stumbled, that we were slow while the music sighed and sped. It was
bittersweet music, and a bittersweet dance. We turned, and I dreamed
of another world: of blue evenings and violet dawns, of melancholy
cities and young girls, of white shoulders and white gloves, the scent
of patchouli, the prospect of the distraction of romance. A Viennese
dream in an English house. I pretended to myself, I think, that I was
my godmother Constance. I could hear her whisper to me in this, her
ballroom, as we danced.

It was not until the gramophone was rewound, and Franz-Jacob
and I danced a second time, that I looked at him at all. When I did, I
saw that his face had a look of fixed concentration, as if he focused
upon the intricacies of the steps to avoid other, less pleasant thoughts.
I remembered his behavior that afternoon, his expression when we
looked back at the woods, and I wondered if he still saw his ghosts,
for his sad eyes looked haunted.

"You dance very well, Franz-Jacob. You know all the right
steps."

"My sister Hannah taught me," he replied, and stopped. "*Es ist
genug*. We will not go on."

He released me and stepped back. It was a moment before I
saw that he was listening. Then I heard it, too, cutting through the
dying fall of the waltz, muffled by the corridors but discernible: a
telephone ringing in another part of the house.

I am not sure now whether those things that happened next
happened slowly or swiftly; they seemed to do both. William sum-

moning my uncle Freddie; Aunt Maud chattering once he left the
room and then, when he returned, breaking off. Aunt Maud and
Uncle Freddie withdrawing together, and a silence in the ballroom
like the smashing of glass.

We were summoned back to the drawing room to find Aunt
Maud and Uncle Freddie standing before the fire, their manner
awkward, like that of two conspirators. I think they had meant to
speak to me alone but, faced with Franz-Jacob as well, could not
summon up the will to suggest he leave.

So it was that when Uncle Freddie told me there had been an
accident, and Aunt Maud told me things were not certain, but I must
be brave, their words seemed to come at me from a great distance.
To this day I cannot remember exactly what they said.

But I do remember Franz-Jacob: He stood listening by my side,
looking down at his brown laced boots. When Uncle Freddie and
Aunt Maud stopped, Franz-Jacob turned away.

He crossed to the windows, pushed back the old curtain, and
looked out.

A high full moon rode the sky; it silvered the cockerel who
crowed the dawn over the stables; it made the woods a mesh of
shadows, the lake gunmetal, light and dark. Franz-Jacob looked at
Winterscombe, then let the curtain fall.

He gave that shrug of his, that European shrug, one shoulder
lifted at the tricks of the world.

"*Es geht los,*" he murmured; then, seeing that I listened and that
I had not understood, he translated: "It is beginning," he said. "It is
beginning again. I knew it would. I heard it this afternoon in the
woods."

They finally told me that my mother and father were dead, but
it was not until a week had gone by. Then, I believed the talk of
confusion, of hospitals. I think, now, that Uncle Freddie certainly
knew they were dead when he received that first telephone call, and
decided it would be better, less hard, if I came upon the truth
gradually. He told me the truth, in the end, because he had a kind
heart and did not like to see me hope. Even when he told me, there
were confusions, and they remain to this day: No one could find out
for certain how my parents died and why, and neither Uncle Freddie
nor Aunt Maud seemed to mind that what information they could
obtain was conflicting.

Winifred Hunter-Coote, the person who had telephoned that
night in the ballroom, spoke of riots, street violence, and Nazi louts.

Aunt Maud, who knew Von Ribbentrop, the German Foreign Minister, once an adornment of London drawing rooms, wrote an imperious letter and was informed—in suave terms—that there had been a border incident, a case of mistaken identity which would, naturally, be investigated at the highest levels of the Reich.

Many years later, after the war, I tried to discover the truth and was thwarted. This was a minor incident in the months leading up to engagement; the records would have been kept in Berlin; those records had since been destroyed.

At the time, the newspapers took the matter up, briefly. I believe that one of my father's old friends asked a question in the House, but in the tension of that September such questions were quickly dropped. The death of my parents was no longer news once the British Navy was mobilized; by the time Chamberlain returned from Munich with the promise of peace in our time, the newspapers had lost interest. There were more vital matters to discuss.

Memory has its own way of applying salves, and there are many things about those subsequent weeks that I cannot remember. If I think back now, I see bright distinct images, a necklace of glass beads with gaps between them that I cannot fill. My parents' bodies were flown back to England, and the funeral was held at Winterscombe. The small church was very crowded and I remember being surprised at that, for my parents rarely entertained and I had supposed them to have few friends. My godfather Wexton came, for he had been close to my mother as well as my uncle Steenie; he stood in the pulpit and read a poem about time and change which I did not understand but which made Jenna, who sat with me, weep. There were one or two friends from my father's regiment in the Great War, and the parents of other friends who had fought in the trenches and never returned. There were people from children's homes and from the innumerable charitable organizations for which my mother had worked. There were the orphanage children, with black armbands on their brown suits, and my friend Franz-Jacob, who sat in the pew behind me.

When it was over, Winifred Hunter-Coote, who had sung the hymns very loudly, who was tall and magnificent in black bombazine, clutched me to her battleship bosom and gave me a mustachioed kiss. Then she fed me sweet tea and fish-paste sandwiches. She told me my mother was the finest woman she had ever known. "Ever!" she cried, with a glare around the room, as if expecting someone might deny her. "Ever. Bar none. She had the heart of a lion! I know!"

That night, when everyone else had gone and Aunt Maud had retired early to bed, looking ill and old, I went up to the schoolroom and fetched down my atlas and brought it to Uncle Freddie.

I had a fixed idea in my mind that I had not understood what had happened but that I might if I knew where the incident had taken place.

I explained this to Uncle Freddie, and opened the atlas to the double pages that showed the whole world.

There was that great expanse of red which was the British Empire, on which—Uncle Freddie had once explained—the sun never set. There was America, where my godmother Constance lived; there was Europe, where the boundaries changed so often and would shortly change again.

"Where did it happen, Uncle Freddie?" I asked, and Uncle Freddie looked at the map in a hopeless, confused kind of way.

I think, in truth, he was unsure, but he could see how eager I was, and so after a while he prodded Germany with his index finger in a firm way.

"There," he said. "It was just about there, Victoria."

I inspected the spot at which he pointed, somewhere to the left of Berlin. Then, to my great surprise, for Uncle Freddie was a grown man, he buried his face in his hands. When he surfaced, finally, and blew his nose, he looked at me with pleading in his eyes, as if he were the child and I the elder.

"It brings so much back, you see. Being here—when we were children. The war. Your father fought, you know, and I never did, Victoria. I could have done but I didn't. I was a coward, I expect."

"I'm sure you weren't a coward, Uncle Freddie. You drove an ambulance, you—"

"Yes, I was. I was a coward then. And I'm a coward still." He took a deep huffing breath and fixed me with sad brown eyes.

"This is terrible, you know. Absolutely terrible. I just can't think straight. Oh, Victoria, whatever are we going to do?"

"It will be all right. We'll manage. We have each other." I spoke very fast, in my mother's tone of voice, because I was very afraid Uncle Freddie might begin to cry.

"Uncle Steenie will be here soon," I said. "It will be better then. Uncle Steenie will know what to do."

This seemed to cheer Uncle Freddie, for he brightened perceptibly. "That's true. That's true. Nothing daunts Steenie. He'll find a way out. . . . Now, bedtime, I think, young lady."

I wanted to ask him why we needed to find a way out, but

Uncle Freddie gave me no chance; he bustled me upstairs, and when Jenna had settled me for sleep, he came up to the night nursery. He announced he would read me a book to help me nod off.

Uncle Freddie read with great vivacity, but his choice of reading matter was as unsuitable, in some ways, as that of my aunt Maud. That night, I remember, he read me a story that, in some ways, was similar to this one. Similar in certain respects, anyway, for it was a detective story and it contained a murder. That murder, as I remember, was done with a knitting needle.

Uncle Freddie, who relished gore, read it in a sepulchral voice with much rolling of the eyes.

"Over my dead body!"

Uncle Steenie had arrived, as promised in his cable, three days later, having been unable to obtain a berth on a ship from New York any earlier.

Uncle Steenie loved arrangements, the more complicated the better, and I could see the gleam of future arrangements in his eye when I followed him up to his room. He gave me a chocolate truffle, which was somewhat stale; he took several restorative nips from the silver hip flask.

"Now," he said, "I want you to know, Vicky darling, that everything is going to be all right. I've fixed things perfectly. First, though"—he gave me a hug—"first of all I have a minor battle to fight. Just a little skirmish. You wait upstairs—there's a good girl. I must talk to your great-aunt Maud."

I was alarmed by this reassurance. After all, I already knew that things were going to be all right—as all right as they could ever be, now. I would stay at Winterscombe with Jenna and William; Aunt Maud would be there some of the time, Uncle Freddie would be there some of the time; Uncle Steenie would make his usual flying visits. What could there have been for Uncle Steenie to fix?

I did stay upstairs for a while, as he told me. Then I crept out onto the landing; then—the skirmish seemed to be taking a long time—I crept down the stairs. The morning-room door was ajar and my uncle Steenie had a high, clear, carrying voice.

"Over my dead body!" Aunt Maud declared in furious tones, and Uncle Steenie interrupted her.

"Maud, darling—be sensible! There's going to be a war. If you believe the appeasers, I don't—and neither does Freddie. What else do you suggest? There's no money. Freddie can't look after her. I'm sure you wouldn't suggest I'd be suitable. The poor little thing looks quite crushed. What she needs is to go well away, to forget all this—"

"Never. Not that woman. I won't allow it, Steenie. There will be no more discussion, do you understand? This is one of your absolutely harebrained schemes, and it will go no further. There is no problem at all, except in your mind. Victoria will come to London. She will live with me."

"Harebrained?" Uncle Steenie began to sound peevish. "It's not harebrained in the least. It's thoroughly sensible. You happen to be prejudiced against Constance and always have been. She is the child's godmother—"

"Godmother! That was a mistake. As I said at the time."

"As soon as she heard, she offered to take Victoria in. Immediately. At once. No hesitation—"

"She will do nothing of the sort, and you may tell her, Steenie, that I should take it as a kindness if she would not interfere. Victoria will come to London with me."

"And when the war comes, what then? You'll stay in London, will you? That doesn't seem so sensible, I must say. Besides, you're not well. You're not as young as you were—"

"I am hardly in my dotage, Steenie, as you might have the goodness to remember."

"America is the obvious place—initially, anyway. Then, if there is a war, she will be perfectly safe. For God's sake, Maud, we're not talking about a permanent arrangement, just a temporary one. It would be good for the child. She would enjoy herself. She's always wanted to meet Constance—you know how she asks questions about her—"

"Have you been drinking, Steenie?"

"No. I have not."

"Yes, you have. Your eyes are distinctly pink. I can always tell. You are becoming quite wild, and I suggest you go and lie down. There is nothing more to discuss. You will forget this ridiculous scheme, and I will forget you ever raised it."

"I shall not forget it." Uncle Steenie now sounded truculent. "I might just point out, Maud, that Freddie and I are guardians, not you—so, technically, the decision is ours."

"Piffle. Freddie agrees with me—don't you, Freddie?"

"Well." I heard my Uncle Freddie sigh. He never liked to arbitrate. "Obviously, Maud has a point." He paused. "On the other hand, Steenie has a point too. I mean, if there was a war, America might be the best place. But I really don't think that Constance . . ."

And so it went on, for at least another half hour, wrangling and then more wrangling.

I felt quite sure, when I went to bed that night, that my Aunt Maud would win, for Aunt Maud, though aging and sometimes vague, had a formidable will when challenged. I prayed hard and long that Aunt Maud would win, that I would go to live with her in London.

If she lost, I could see a most horrible vision looming ahead of me. I would go to New York to stay with my godmother Constance, exactly as I had prayed to do, twice a day for so many months. The visit would have been made possible by my parents' death; their death would have been brought about by my wicked prayers. "Oh, please, God," I said that night, "I didn't mean it. Don't do this to me."

That night my Aunt Maud was vanquished, not by my Uncle Steenie's arguments but by the vagaries of her heart. At dinner she had complained of pins and needles in her arm; she had accused Steenie of upsetting her. That night in bed she had a second stroke, more serious than the first, which left her paralyzed on her right side, unable to speak or write or fend for herself for many months. She recovered eventually, but her progress was very slow, and in the meantime Uncle Steenie prevailed. I think Uncle Freddie put up spirited resistance to the idea, but he had never been a match for his younger brother. I tried telling both uncles that I wanted to stay in England, but Uncle Freddie was afraid to cross Uncle Steenie, and Uncle Steenie refused to listen; he was in full gallop, the bit between his teeth. Nothing I could say would rein him in.

"Nonsense, Victoria. It's the best possible thing. Lots of little girls would give their eyeteeth for such a chance. New York—you'll love New York! And Constance—you'll love her too, just as I do. She's such fun, Vicky. She goes everywhere; she knows everyone-but-everyone—you'll have the most wonderful time. She'll take you out of yourself, wait and see."

"I don't think Daddy would have wanted me to go. Or Mummy. They didn't like her, Uncle Steenie—you know they didn't."

"Ah, well, there were reasons for that." Uncle Steenie averted his eyes and waved his hands. "Forget all that, darling. None of it matters. All that is in the past." He took a small nip and gave me his most roguish glance. "Anyway, that's not strictly true. There was a time when your papa liked Constance very much indeed. . . ."

"Are you sure, Uncle Steenie?"

"Absolutely sure. And she *always* liked him. So that's all right, isn't it?"

He gave me his pink-and-white smile and, before I could argue any more, popped another stale chocolate truffle into my mouth. I left England on the *Queen Mary* on November 18, 1938, one month before my eighth birthday. We sailed from Southampton.

Aunt Maud was not well enough to accompany me to the docks, so I said my goodbyes to her in London, in her once-famous drawing room overlooking Hyde Park. I was escorted to Southampton by Jenna, who was to travel with me, by my two uncles, and—at my request—by my friend Franz-Jacob. They all gave me presents for the voyage. Uncle Freddie gave me a batch of detective stories. Uncle Steenie gave me an orchid, which had a carnivorous look. Franz-Jacob gave me a box of chocolates.

This present he produced at the last moment, on board ship, standing near the gangplank. Most of the other well-wishers had returned to the quay; my uncles were already ashore, and waving; the first confetti and streamers were being thrown.

"Here." Franz-Jacob pulled from his pocket a square gold cardboard box. It contained, I later discovered, eight exquisite hand-dipped chocolates, one for each year of my life. They were decorated with crystallized violets like amethysts, and with strips of angelica as green as emeralds. They lay couched in their smart box like so many jewels. Viennese chocolates: they must have been specially sent, I think, by his family. Franz-Jacob presented this present with a small stiff bow, so his lank hair fell across his pale forehead.

I was very touched that he should have gone to so much trouble but anxious not to embarrass him by appearing emotional. So I thanked him and clutched the box tight and hesitated. "I shall miss you, Franz-Jacob," I risked at last.

"You will not miss me. Distance is of no object between the hearts of friends."

He had prepared that small speech, I think, for he said it in a rehearsed and formal way. We looked at each other uncertainly; then, English fashion, we shook hands.

"I shall write every week, Franz-Jacob. You will write too? You'll let me know where they send you next?"

"But of course I will write." He gave me one of his impatient looks. He took from his coat pocket a pair of brown leather gloves, which he put on and carefully buttoned at the wrist.

"I will write each Saturday. I will enclose a mathematical sum in each letter." He came as close as he ever came to a smile. "I keep an eye on your progress—yes?"

"No algebra, Franz-Jacob. Promise me, no algebra."

"Certainly there will be algebra. Algebra is good for you. Please remember this."

I think he knew I might cry, and tears would certainly have embarrassed him. The ship's horns blew, which startled me. A woman next to me threw a bright-pink paper streamer into the air; I watched it coil out, flutter, then fall.

When I turned back, Franz-Jacob was walking stiffly down the gangplank, and out of my life. I did not know it then—which was fortunate—but Franz-Jacob, whom I would have trusted with my life, would not keep his promise. He never wrote to me.

The tugs were engaged, the hawsers freed; we began to edge away into the harbor. Jenna and I stayed by the rail for a long time, looking back through the drizzle of rain. On the quay a band played; my uncles waved; Franz-Jacob stood still. Their figures became smaller and smaller until, although we strained our eyes, we had to admit they were invisible.

That is what I remember of my leaving: Franz-Jacob, and the promise he never kept. I forget the voyage that came after it, and I never dream of it. The ocean liner, the view of the Atlantic from its decks—all that has gone. But I do dream sometimes, of the city that waited, the far side. I see Manhattan then as I saw it for the first time, a foreign place of startling loveliness. There is mist on the water; I can taste the morning on my mouth; winter sun glints upon a Babylon of pinnacles.

Constance stands waiting on the pier. She is dressed in black from head to foot, whereas I have only a mourning band sewn on the sleeve of my Harris tweed overcoat. In my dreams Constance greets me as she greeted me then. She advances. She clasps me in her arms. Her clothes are soft. I smell her scent, which is as green as ferns with a damper, hungrier smell under it, like earth.

She is wearing gloves. She touches my face with those gloves. Her hands are tiny, almost as small as my own. The gloves are of the finest kid, tight as a second skin. How Constance loves to touch! She touches my hair. She smiles at my hat. Her face becomes serious. She frames my face in her hands. She examines my features one by one. The pale skin, the freckles, the muddy and indeterminate eyes—and something she sees there seems to please her, for she smiles.

It is as if she recognizes me—although that is impossible. I stare at my godmother. She is radiant.

"Victoria," she says, clasping my hand in hers. "Victoria. It's you. Welcome home."

"It's you—"

Miss Marpruder was to say the very same thing to me, thirty years later, when she found me on her doorstep, unannounced.

"It's you—" she said again, and her face crumpled. She seemed unable to go on.

She did not add "welcome back." She simply stood there, blocking her doorway—Miss Marpruder, who had always been so hospitable. We stood there awkwardly, staring at each other, while an ugly blotch mounted her cheeks. Beyond her, I could see the familiar sitting room and that defiant red couch. One sagging chair had been drawn up, close to the TV set; the set was tuned to a hospital soap opera. Miss Marpruder's mother was dead now, I knew. She lived alone, and I could smell the loneliness; it seeped out into the hall.

"Prudie," I began, mystified by this reception. "I tried to call. I've been calling and calling, all weekend. In the end I thought—"

"I know you called. I guessed it was you. That's why I didn't answer."

I stared at her in consternation. There was no attempt to disguise the hostility now in her voice.

"Go away. I don't want to see you. I'm busy. I'm watching TV—"

"Prudie, please, wait a second. What's wrong?" She had been about to close the door in my face, then changed her mind. To my astonishment, her face contorted with anger.

"Wrong? You're wrong—that's what. I know why you're here— it's not to see me, that's for sure. You're looking for Miss Shawcross. Well, I can't help you—wouldn't, if I could. I don't *know* where she is. There. Is that plain enough for you?"

"Prudie, wait. I don't understand." I put out my hand to touch her arm. Miss Marpruder reacted as if I'd attempted to slap her.

"You don't understand? Oh, sure—believe that, you'll believe anything. Little Miss Successful—oh, we're doing real well now, I hear. All the big fancy clients. Kind of funny, isn't it—how many of them used to be your godmother's?" Her speech was rapid, as if

launched on a tide of pent-up resentment. Under its force I took a
step back, Miss Marpruder a step forward.

"You *used* Miss Shawcross—you think I don't know that? You
used her; now you're trying to use me. Eight years—I don't set eyes
on you in eight years."

"Prudie, I haven't *been* to New York in eight years. Only to
change planes. And anyway, I wrote to you—you know I've written.
I wrote when—"

"When my mother died—oh, sure." Miss Marpruder's eyes
filled with tears. "You wrote. So I'd owe you—that it?"

"Of course not. Prudie, how can you say such a thing?"

"Easy. Real easy—because I see now what you're like. I didn't
one time, maybe—but I do now, and it makes me pretty sick."

She advanced on me once more; she was trembling—with the
effort to convince me of what she said, I thought at first. Then I
changed my mind. It occurred to me that at least some of this anger
was self-directed; it was as if Miss Marpruder were also trying to
convince herself.

I held my ground. I said, as quietly as I could, "Prudie, all
right. I'll go. But before I do, I'd just like to make one thing clear. I
won't have you thinking I poached Constance's clients. It isn't true.
Constance and I work in totally different ways, you must know
that—"

"Is that so? How about the Dorset place? How about the
Antonellis?"

The names tripped off her tongue as if long rehearsed. I stared
at her in bewilderment. "Prudie, *listen*. They both asked Constance
to do the work first. When she refused, they came to me." I paused.
"Those are the only two clients of mine who ever had any connection with Constance. I have made my own way, Prudie. At least give
me the credit for that."

"She turned them down?" Miss Marpruder seemed to shrink
back into herself. She gave a puzzled look, a shake of the head.

"It's true, Prudie."

"I guess so. It could be. You may be right. Maybe I shouldn't
have said that. I was mad at you. . . . I'm tired. I guess I haven't
been sleeping too well. You'd better go now. I told you—I can't
help you."

"Prudie, is something wrong?"

"Wrong?" She said the word with great bitterness. "What could
be wrong? After all, I'm a lady of leisure now! No crises to deal with.
No rushing to get the subway every morning. Watch the TV twenty-

four hours a day if I feel like it. Oh, sure, I'm fine all right. I'm retired."

I stared at her. I could not imagine her retiring, and I could not imagine Constance's business functioning without her—unless there was some new and younger replacement, of course.

Pity twisted in my heart. Miss Marpruder, now the animus had left her, did look aged. There were runnels in the thick powder on her face. The tendons of her neck jutted. Her permed hair had thinned. I realized, guiltily, that I did not know her age.

"Sixty-five," she said, as if she read my mind. "And before you ask—no, it wasn't my idea. I never wanted to quit. Miss Shawcross . . . she retired me. Two months back. I argued, but she wouldn't listen. You know how she is, once she's made up her mind. . . ."

"Prudie, I'm terribly sorry—"

"I'll adjust. I'll get used to it. She's running it down, you know—the business. Like she's ready to quit, herself. That's why she let me go. I guess."

She must have read my expression, because she spoke again before I could frame the question.

"Oh, she's not ill—not her! Still beautiful. Still full of energy. But she's changed. Since you left—maybe it started back then. And it hit her hard, your uncle Steenie dying like he did. She's sick of it all, I reckon. She wants to travel—she told me that."

"Travel? Travel where? Prudie, I called all the hotels. She's made no reservations. Her friends aren't expecting her—at least, they tell me they're not—"

Prudie shrugged. Her face became closed.

"I wouldn't know. She had her route mapped out—she said that. I don't know where; I don't know when. And I didn't ask."

"Prudie, please. That can't be true. You must know where she is and where she's going. You always did. I must see her. I need to talk to her. Now Steenie's dead . . . she's my *past*, Prudie. There are things only she can explain. Surely you can understand that?"

She hesitated. She fiddled with the glass beads and for a moment I thought she would relent. Her expression became gentler. She nodded once or twice.

"Sure. I can understand. When my mother died, there were things, things I wished I'd asked her, things only she could've told me, but I hadn't asked, and then it was too late." She stopped in an abrupt way. Her face hardened. "So I understand. Makes no difference. I told you. I can't help."

She took a step back. Behind her the television blared a new tune.

"Can't, or won't, Prudie?"

"Take your pick." She shrugged. "That's my favorite program starting now. I don't want to miss it, okay?"

"Prudie—"

"Just leave me alone," she said, with another little spurt of anger. And, for the second time, a door was shut in my face.

I think, if that meeting with Prudie had not taken place, that I might have given up and gone home. The dream of Winterscombe had remained with me all evening, on the edge of my consciousness: I felt my home pulling me back.

I might have said then, the hell with Constance. But the meeting with Prudie changed that. Perhaps Prudie—once my friend—had turned against me of her own accord, but knowing Constance's ways, I doubted it. It would have been subtly done, I thought: no overt recriminations, just a matter of nuance, Constance's drip-technique of tiny asides, small but telling hints. Had Prudie understood, finally, that she herself had been used? Was that why she had been so quick to accuse me of using Constance? I considered that charge, which I knew to be untrue, and it made me angry. I suppose it also hurt; since I still loved Constance, she retained the power to wound me.

Two women. I remembered Mr. Chatterjee. I thought that by some fluke he had been correct, had pointed me, anyway, in the direction of resolution. Who was Constance? Was she the good godmother of my New York childhood, or the bad? Was it my mother, as Vickers had said, who had banished Constance from Winterscombe—and if so, why? What was it my mother had known about Constance that I still did not?

Your father liked her once, Victoria—liked her very much indeed. And she always liked him. . . .

A sly suggestion, made thirty years before, yet never forgotten. I wished that voice would go away; I wished they would all go away— but they would not.

It seemed to me, though, that I had reached an impasse. I believed Constance to be in New York, and I believed her to be avoiding me. If Miss Marpruder would not help me in this search, there was no one left who would—or so I thought. Then, gradually, an idea came to me. I was thinking of the flowers on Bertie's grave, their similarity to the flowers I had seen in Vickers's house the previous evening.

I thought of Constance and Vickers over the years, their shared worship at the altar of style. I thought of them forever swapping the names and telephone numbers of clever, talented young men: young men who could restore French chairs, drape curtains, paint *trompe l'oeil,* dye fabrics—or arrange flowers so they looked as if they had just been picked by the chatelaine of an English country garden.

I telephoned Conrad Vickers at once. He sounded wary at first, as if expecting more questions on the subject of Constance. When he discovered all I needed was the name of his marvelous florist, he relaxed at once.

"Dahling, of *course*! They're for a client—a potential client? My dear, say no more. His name's Dominic. He'll do them *perfectly*. One millisecond—I have the number here. . . . Oh, and when you call, do mention my name. He can be the *teensiest* bit difficult. Last year he couldn't be helpful enough, but this year—well, you know how it is! A touch of the temperaments. *Folie de grandeur.* He's beginning to drop names to *me* now—which, when you think about it, is really rather silly. Oh, and by the way, *don't* be fobbed off with his frightful assistants. Speak to Dominic himself—he'll melt before your charms. Yet another feather in his cap. Byeee . . ."

"Ye-es?"

Dominic spread the one word over several syllables. With those syllables, he contrived to convey languor, grandeur, and incipient obsequiousness. Cooperation *might* ensue, said that voice, in certain circumstances: if a duchess were on the other end of the line, for instance, or should it turn out that the First Lady happened to be calling Dominic, in person, at seven o'clock on a Monday morning.

I considered. In my work I had to deal with many Dominics. It seemed to me I had a straight choice: Be assertive or be flustered. Fluster might create an ally; it seemed worth a try. I used my English accent, not my American one; I gave a Knightsbridge wail.

"Dominic? Is that Dominic himself? Thank heavens I've reached you! There's been such a *flap* . . ."

"Calmez-*vous*," said Dominic in a very bad French accent.

I gave him a false and resounding double-barreled name.

"*Love* it," he caroled. "*All* of it. *And* the accent."

"Dominic—I do hope you can help. You see, I'm the new assistant—and you know how Miss Shawcross is. One mistake and

I'll be the *ex*-assistant. She's in a terrible state about the order. You *are* working on the order?"

"Dah-ling!" It was a near-perfect imitation of Conrad Vickers. "Of course! I'm working on it now."

"You are sending delphiniums?"

"Sweetheart, of *course*." He was now, definitely, an ally. "Delphiniums, the most *gorgeous* roses, some *cheeky* little pansies—"

"No lilies? You're sure, no lilies?"

"*Lilies?* For Miss Shawcross?" He sounded rattled. "*Would* I? My dear, she *loathes* them—more than my life's worth."

"Oh, thank goodness. There must have been a mistake. Miss Shawcross thought someone mentioned lilies. . . ." I paused. "Last problem then. Dominic. Which address are you sending them?"

"Which address?"

A note of wariness had crept into his voice. My heart was beating very fast.

"Are you sending them to the Fifth Avenue apartment?"

It worked. It was Dominic's turn to wail.

"Fifth, dah-ling? No. *Park*. The same as last week. And the week before. Look, it's here, right in front of me: Seven Fifty-six Park Avenue, apartment Five-oh-one. *Don't* tell me it's Fifth, because if it is I shall *crucify* that assistant of mine—"

"No, no, it's not. Park is correct," I said hastily, writing down the address. "Oh, what a relief! And they'll be there . . . when?"

"At ten, sweetie. You have my *word*."

"Dominic, you've been marvelous. Thank you so much."

"*Rien*, dear, absolutely *rien*. Oh, by the way . . ."

"Yes?"

"Did Miss Shawcross like that special bouquet I did for her? She needed it Sunday—to take out to her little girl's grave, you know? She rang me *personally*. I could hear the tears. It really got to me—*un frisson*, dear. I mean I guess I never thought of her in that way. As a mother. I never even knew she'd *had* children. . . ."

There was a silence.

"No," I said. "No, Dominic. Neither did I."

Constance had never given birth to a little girl—or a little boy, come to that. Constance—and she had once explained this to me, at length—had been unable to have children of her own. I was her daughter, she would say. She had always insisted on that.

Had she been embarrassed to explain that the flowers were for a dog she once loved very much? If so, why elaborate? Why make up a story like that when no explanation was necessary? I thought I knew the answer to that one: Lies were part of Constance's nature. She once told me a very terrible lie, and I had realized then that Constance lied for one very simple reason: Lies delighted her; she reveled in their ramifications. "What is a lie?" It was one of her favorite maxims. "A lie is nothing. It is a mirror image of a truth."

I was standing outside her apartment building on Park as I thought this. It was nine-thirty, and under my arm was a huge box of flowers purchased earlier, in my American accent, from Dominic's. A flamboyant box, it bore his name in large green letters. It seemed appropriate, I thought, that I should find Constance at last through duplicity.

I had tracked her down at last. This, then, was where she was hiding. I looked up at the building. Presumably the apartment must be borrowed from a friend; even so, it seemed, for Constance, a curious choice.

Constance was full of irrational strictures—one could stay here but not, for some reason, there—and on the subject of Park Avenue she had always been cutting. It was a dull, safe, predictable, bourgeois place. "Park," she would say, "is unimaginative."

It was not particularly imaginative to live on Fifth, of course, but I knew what Constance meant. Furthermore, if Park was respectable and dull, this building she had selected was the dullest, the most irreproachable for blocks. Twelve stories of red sandstone; a grandiloquent doorway reminiscent of the Knickerbocker Club. It seemed an odd place for Constance to hole up. Still, it was a temporary arrangement, I told myself as I entered an august lobby. I was nervous. Another few minutes and I would be speaking to Constance herself. Would she welcome me? Reject me? I advanced on the front desk.

"I'm from Dominic's—with the flowers for Miss Shawcross. I'm a little early, I guess. Can you check if it's okay to go up?"

I was inept when it came to falsehoods. I blushed as I spoke. I waited to be denounced as an imposter. I was astonished when the man replaced the phone and said, "Five-oh-one. Go right on up."

I counted to fifty outside the apartment door. My hands had begun to shake.

It was not Constance herself who opened the door; it was a maid. Worse than that, it was the same maid, the Lilliputian termagant of the day before. I should have foreseen that possibility, I suppose, but I had not. In despair, I waited for her to recognize me.

I am five feet ten inches tall; her gaze began somewhere mid-chest. It mounted slowly. I waited for more miniaturized rage, for a door shut in my face. To have come so far and then to fail was more than I could bear. I put my foot in the door. I looked down to do this. When I looked up I saw something astonishing.

No sign of hostility. The maid was smiling.

"Victoria—yes?" She gave a tiny giggle. "On time—very good. You come in. Through here—quick."

She took the box of flowers, disappeared behind them momentarily, set the box down, and set off at a smart pace down a narrow corridor. She opened a door with a flourish, then stood back to let me pass.

The room beyond, overlooking the avenue, was empty. No Constance stood there. I turned back to the maid in bewilderment. A telephone in the hall began to shrill.

"You wait. One minute. Please excuse."

The maid disappeared. She closed the door behind her. From the hallway beyond I heard long silences, mouselike maid squeaks.

Confused, I walked across to the room beyond: a bedroom. No one lurked; no Constance waited just behind the door. Both rooms astonished me. I could not imagine Constance, even *in extremis,* living here.

You should understand: Constance was a decorator, an obsessive arranger of rooms. Everything in her rooms, even her hotel rooms, had to conform to her taste. Constance would no more sit in a room she found unsympathetic than a concert pianist would listen to an amateur mangle Mozart.

Could Constance, in any circumstances, live here?

Constance liked flamboyant rooms; she liked strong, vivid, daring colors: budgerigar yellow, finch green, Prussian blue, or—her favorite, this—a garnet that gave a womblike effect and that she called, inaccurately, Etruscan.

She liked these vivid rooms to be enclosed, sumptuous spaces, crammed with rare and surprising things. Out of colors that in less sure hands would have clashed, out of furniture whose derivation and date were discordant, Constance made harmony.

Japanese screens—she had always loved them, indeed loved screens of any kind. An abundance of flowers, always. Chinese porcelain. Some charming curiosity—a birdcage, say, shaped to resemble a pagoda, a bowl filled with shells, an antique wooden toy. Painted furniture, always; and mirrors everywhere, old ones, their mercury stained and foxed. Could Constance live here? No, she could not.

This room was painted off-white. It was a symphony of Syrie Maugham creams and beiges. It sang the song of the cocktail age, 1925 to 1930 at the latest, a period Constance had always detested. It was rectilinear, chaste, with a nod toward Bauhaus brutalism. Constance could not be here, I decided. I had come to the wrong place. As I turned to the door, the maid reentered and I discovered my mistake.

Constance *was* here in this room with me. This was, I suppose, where I found her, and—as I might have foreseen—she was waiting to play another trick.

"Present." The maid gestured across the room toward a table of bleached wood. She gave another little giggle. "Miss Shawcross—on phone. Flight being called. Big hurry. Left present for you. You take it with you, yes?" She gestured again at the table. She gestured toward something on the table.

I walked the length of the room. I looked at it. It seemed a curious kind of present. There on the table was a stack of notebooks— about twenty or twenty-five of them, I estimated. Each was about twelve inches by fourteen; all had identical black covers. They resembled an old-fashioned school exercise book. The top book in the pile bore no label or identifying mark of any kind; the rest, I was later to discover, were similarly anonymous. They had been carefully and neatly stacked, the pile tied with well-knotted string.

In case there should be any doubt that this was a present, and intended for me, a note had been attached with my name on it. Heavy white paper; familiar handwriting: the strokes of the letters were bold, the ink black, the message brief.

Whistle and I'll come to you, Constance had written. *You've been looking for me, dearest Victoria. Well, here I am.*

I went back to England. Back to Winterscombe. I took Constance's present with me, the notebooks still unopened, still tied together with string. I suppose I knew there was no point in pursuing Constance herself any further, no point in calling friends or hotels or airlines. I had the notebooks instead: *Here I am.*

Even so, I was reluctant to undo that parcel. I was made uneasy by the manner and the circumstances in which it had been given. I was also irritated by the note Constance had attached: *Whistle and I'll come to you.* It was a quotation, I thought, and a familiar one, but I could not place it. A line from a poem? I was not sure.

When I arrived at the house I put the parcel of notebooks away in the library. I avoided the room; I avoided them. This was easy enough at first; Winterscombe distracted me.

In order to come here I had had to postpone some commissions, delegate work to others. Better not to delay, I told myself as I locked up my town flat; several weeks had already passed while I extricated myself from London. It was, by then, September. Winterscombe was in a poor state of repair. It would not do to leave it closed up, empty, another winter—that was the argument I used to myself. It was not the whole truth. The truth was that after years of avoiding it, my home pulled me back.

Memories should not be monkeyed with—I had felt that. I had wanted Winterscombe to remain the house of my childhood, the house I had loved between the wars. Even when Steenie lived there I had been reluctant to visit it. During the years I lived in America, avoiding Winterscombe was easy. I had avoided it still, even after I returned. It was simple enough; I purchased the London apartment, though I spent less time in it than I did in hotel rooms. If Steenie pressed invitations upon me (and he did, at first) I could always plead pressures of work. Until the months of his final illness, I had revisited the house no more than three or four times. I had never spent a night under its roof. I had dreaded the house, dreaded to see its proof of change, of time passing. Yet now—and I felt this very strongly—it called to me.

A matter of practicality, I told myself. Winterscombe would have to be sold. But before it could be sold, before I telephoned Sotheby's or Christie's about auctioning its contents, I would have to go through the house. I did not want the dispassionate hands of an auctioneer or an appraiser sorting through the trunks and boxes, examining old clothes, old toys, papers, photographs, letters. That sad task—one with which anyone middle-aged will be familiar—was mine. This was my past, and my family's. Only I could decide what to discard and what to keep.

I had allowed myself one month. Almost as soon as I arrived I realized that a month would not be enough; Steenie had left Winterscombe in chaos. During the years when, down on his luck, he had lived there, many rooms had been closed. In the months of his last illness I had had no heart to explore them. Now, when the caretakers came up from the lodge, when rooms were unlocked, windows opened, cupboards exposed, I saw to the full the havoc that Steenie had wrought.

At first I thought it carelessness; Steenie never minded disorder. Then, as the days passed, I changed my mind. What Steenie had been doing, I realized, was searching for something, searching with increasing desperation, going from room to room, opening a desk here, a trunk there, spilling the contents out, then passing on. Steenie had left a trail of some kind—a trail it was impossible to follow.

In that old disused ballroom where Franz-Jacob and I once danced, I found a box of my grandmother's dresses. Another lay, half-unpacked, in the room always known as the King's bedroom; a third, spilling whalebone corsets, turned up in the stables.

There was a croquet set in a bathroom, a collection of moth-eaten teddy bears on a back landing. Parts of a once-opulent dinner service lay in the china pantries; the rest were stacked under the billiard table. And the papers—there were papers everywhere, glimpses of a family past I never knew existed. Love letters from my grandfather to my grandmother, letters home from the trenches from her sons. Ancient bills, theater programs, children's drawings, photograph albums, envelopes containing clippings of babies' hair, ledgers recording fishing catches or numbers of pheasants shot, designs for orphanages never built, drafts for speeches in the Lords, newspaper cuttings, pictures of long-dead dogs, of favorite ponies, of unidentified women in huge Edwardian hats, of unidentified mustachioed young men playing tennis or posed on the portico steps wearing World War One uniforms.

There were treasures here for me in this welter of papers: I found journals kept by my mother which I had never known existed. I found letters my father sent her long before I was born. I looked at these things with pleasure and with unease, wanting to read them, uncertain if I had a right to do so. I felt like a trespasser, and (this increased my unease) I was clearly not the first person to trespass here. Where I searched now, Steenie had searched before me—that much was clear. Letters had been tossed to one side, envelopes torn, diaries opened, then thrown down. It was as if Steenie had been looking for something, failed to find it, and become increasingly frantic. A nasty suspicion came to me: Could my uncle have been looking for those notebooks which now lay downstairs, neatly parceled, in the library?

During the day, when the caretakers were with me, when the sun shone and there was work to do, it was easy to push such suspicions to one side. It was less easy after nightfall. Then, when I was alone in the house, the presence of the notebooks pressed upon me. I would go into the library. I would look at them. I would go out.

On the third night, still tempted, still drawing back, I telephoned Wexton in London.

"Wexton," I said, when we had finished with the usual updates and pleasantries, "Wexton, may I try a quotation on you? It's been bothering me for weeks. I've heard it before but I can't place it—"

"Sure." Wexton sounded amused. "I'm a pretty good dictionary. Try me."

"*Whistle and I'll come to you.* Is it a poem, Wexton?"

Wexton chuckled. "No. It's not a poem, and it's not complete. 'Oh, Whistle and I'll Come to You, My Lad.' It's the title of a story. M. R. James—nothing to do with Henry, by the way. Linguist, medievalist, biblical scholar. Heard of him?"

"Vaguely. I've never read him."

"Well, he's dead now, of course. Besides the scholarly works, he also wrote stories—not bad stories, in their way. That's the title of one of the nastiest."

"Nastiest?"

"They're ghost stories. That's what he wrote. Extremely chilling ones too. If you're embarking on him, don't do it at Winterscombe. Not if you're alone at night."

"I see." I paused. "And this particular story, Wexton—can you remember what it's about?"

"Sure." Wexton sounded amused. "It's probably the most famous one he wrote. But I don't want to tell you the plot—not if you intend reading it. I don't want to spoil it—"

"Just the gist, Wexton. That would do."

"Well," Wexton replied, "it's about . . . a haunting. As you might expect."

That decided me. Constance was not a great reader—indeed I could not remember her ever finishing a book; it was one of the great differences between us. But Constance *was* a great borrower of other people's books, a great dipper-in to them. If she had chosen that quotation (perhaps expecting me to recognize it at once) she would have done so deliberately—yet another little trick in the game of hide-and-seek she played with me. Or was it cat and mouse?

I had had enough of Constance's games by then. Since she had given me the present, I would look at her notebooks, have done with them, and then forget them, but I would do so on my own terms and in my own way. If Constance intended to haunt me (and she would have liked that idea) she would not succeed. I would exorcise her first.

I began the preparations the next day. The weather had changed, and it was a cold one. Winterscombe felt chill, with that damp and clinging cold peculiar to houses after long disuse.

I persuaded the caretaker to tackle the old boiler in the basement, the one I used to see as burning crisp pound notes. After much coaxing, and protesting, it caught. I returned upstairs. Pipes wheezed and rattled. I could sense the old beat of my house's heart, coming back to life.

That night, when I was alone, I took Constance's parcel of books to the drawing room. I lit the fire. I closed the old and tattered curtains. I moved furniture from place to place. Some pieces were still missing, lost in the intervening years, but there were enough left to re-create, by lamplight, the illusion of the past. The sagging sofa, the worn rugs, my mother's chair, the writing desk between the windows, the chaise longue where Aunt Maud held court, the stool where my friend Franz-Jacob always sat—when all these pieces were in their accustomed places, my house began to speak again. I was almost ready. There was just one component left.

I found it at last, stored away in a closet: the folding table at which, in another life, a girl called Charlotte had once sat with me, playing cards.

I set the table up. I placed a chair for myself, and another chair for a girl I had not seen in thirty years. Then—I suppose I had known I would do this—I put Constance's black notebooks down on the green baize. This was where Constance had entered my life; this was where she would depart from it. *Here I am*.

The room was still. I closed my eyes. I let Winterscombe seep through my skin and inhabit my mind: damp and woodsmoke, leather chairs and long corridors, linen and lavender, happiness and cordite. When I opened my eyes, the room was peopled.

My uncle Steenie yawned and stretched; he flipped the pages of a magazine. My aunt Maud read a romance called *The Crossroads of the Heart*. My uncle Freddie snoozed, his two greyhounds at his feet. My mother left her account books, unbalanced, on her writing desk; at her piano she played Chopin, a few desultory bars. My father watched her, then bent toward the fire. He stirred a log with his foot. The wood crackled and the sparks flew upward.

Beyond them, quiet but substantial, waiting as if to be greeted, there were other figures: my third uncle, the one I never knew, who died in World War One; my grandfather Denton, dead before I was born; my American grandmother, Gwen, who died so soon after him. They were waiting, with the humility of supplicants; because they were there, and I trusted them, I cut my parcel's string.

They were journals or diaries of some kind; I think I had expected that. I opened the first of them, to see a date, 1910, and a location, Winterscombe. Lines of neat copperplate marched across the page; this handwriting was one I did not recognize.

I stared at the page in confusion. There was something familiar on this page, but I could not place it. It was there, out of reach, nagging away on the edge of memory. Whose writing was this? Why should Constance send me journals this old? I opened the next notebook; the same unfamiliar writing. I opened the third—a different hand, this, and one I did recognize. A letter fell out, tucked between cover and first page.

That letter was the first and the last letter I ever received from Constance. I was to reread it, many times. I have it beside me still, quintessential Constance.

My dearest Victoria [she wrote],

> *Are you sitting comfortably? Good. Then I shall tell you a story—a story you think you already know. It is about Winterscombe, your family, your parents and me. It is also about a murder—is it a murder?—so pay attention as you read. I should hate you to miss the vital clues.*
>
> *Well now, where shall we begin? With your christening, and my banishment? You might like that, I think—a chance to resolve all those mysteries! But I prefer that you wait. We shall come to your part in this story eventually; to begin with, I am center stage.*
>
> *I may surprise you, I think! You may find you do not know this Constance. You may also find you do not know this mother and this father—we may even shock you a little. Never mind that—it is good to be shocked occasionally, don't you think? Take my hand and come back with me: Look, I am a child, and the year is 1910.*
>
> *Tonight your grandmother Gwen, who is still young and still beautiful (the age you are now, my dear Victoria), is giving a great party. Tonight, a comet—Halley's comet—will pass. We shall all watch its progress—that is one purpose of the party. A comet is not, perhaps, the best omen for an occasion like this, but your grandmother*

forgets that; she has other things on her mind. What's that? You've heard about that night, and that party? I'm sure you have. Well, listen again: I shall give you the uncensored account.

Read my father's version of events (yes, the first two notebooks are his). Then read mine. But don't stop there—not if you want to catch up with me. For that, you must read on to the end. There is a great space of time in these little journals of mine!

Then, when you have finished reading, shall we talk? I should like that, for I miss you, you know, my little godchild with the moral eyes! Yes, let's talk. Give me your solution. I should like to hear that. You tell me who the murderer was and who the victim. You explain to me the nature of the crime.

Meanwhile, it is 1910. Does that sound very distant to you? It isn't, you know: blink, and it's yesterday. Look, here is the house. Here are the gardens. There are the woods where your clever little friend Franz-Jacob once smelled blood. . . .

The past. That is a good present to give someone, don't you think? And the moment seems right—for you, and for me. Listen, here is the past; here is a present only I can give you. Do you know what it looks like? Like my hall of mirrors in New York, the hall you used to love so much. Back and back; one reflection, then another behind that, on and on, all the way to infinity.

When you've finished reading, you tell me: How many fathers can you see? And how many Constances?

She had meant to intrigue, and she succeeded. I began to read. I let Constance and her father be my guides—to begin with, anyway.

I had remembered, by then, where I was the last time the year 1910 was mentioned. I heard sitar music, faced a portrait of a latter-day saint, smelled India, smelled Winterscombe. Magic, perhaps, of a kind. When I turned to copperplate handwriting, and a date in April 1910, I felt as if Mr. Chatterjee joined the other watchers at my side.

> *To the Stone House in the gardens,* [I read]. *This morning, with Gwen. The new black ribbons in my pocket, safely concealed. Once there, alas, that great bore Boy required us to pose for a photograph. What a simpleton he is! Infernal delays, a long exposure; an imprint of adultery: which sweet fact Boy, a fool indeed, never suspects . . .*

I read on: what follows is what I was shown not just by Constance and her father, but also by those other witnesses then summoned to my house. I will show it to you as I saw it then: as a story, but also as a puzzle. It was a puzzle whose pieces did not always fit, a puzzle (I sometimes feared) with key pieces left out.

Perhaps you will be quicker than I was in seeing how the pieces joined. Perhaps you will be quicker and more ingenious than I was in solving what might, or might not, have been a crime.

One word of warning, though, before we begin: Who was telling this story, in the main? Why, Constance. And what is Constance? A decorator.

Take care with decorators! It is not always wise to trust them. Like those other compulsive rearrangers of reality, like con men, photographers, or writers, they marshal deception among their tools.

Consider: what is the first rule in the decorators' manual? What is the first technique they must learn?

To trick the eye. Or so Constance used to say, in the days when I was her pupil.

TWO

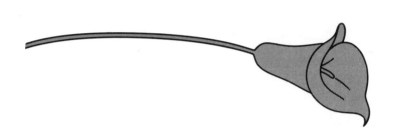

I
A COMET
AND A
COPULATION

The year is 1910; the month is April, the day a Friday, the weather fine. My family relish spring at Winterscombe. They cannot know they approach the end of an era, that they are poised, even now, on the cusp of two worlds.

One month from now the King will be dead—Edward VII, who has stayed, on one occasion, at Winterscombe. His funeral, which my grandfather will attend, will be a glorious affair: Nine kings will ride in the procession, and Edward's nephew, Kaiser Wilhelm of Germany, will have the position of honor, directly behind his uncle's hearse. Those kings, the Kaiser, the numerous archdukes, princes, and queens, divide Europe among them; many, by birth or intermarriage, belong to the same family, the progeny of Queen Victoria— dominant from Britain to the Urals. Four years after this funeral, that family will be at war.

My own family, who have their own smaller conflicts to come, cannot know this, naturally. It has not yet occurred to them, or to anyone else, that the sightings of Halley's comet this spring could be ill-omened. That suggestion will be made, at Winterscombe and elsewhere, but only with hindsight.

Not now. Now, Halley's comet is a cause for celebration. To my grandmother Gwen, it is the excuse for a party. That party will commence in a few hours' time; meanwhile, it is morning. The air is sweet, the lake serene; visibility is good, the light excellent for the taking of photographs.

My grandmother Gwen prepares to pose for the camera of her eldest son, Boy.

Turning her head, she rests her lovely but astigmatic eyes on the figure of her lover, Edward Shawcross. He is eight feet away from her, his outline slightly blurred. She holds out her hand to draw him closer; she smiles.

"Eddie," she says, "Eddie, won't you stand by me?"

Gwen knows nothing of comets or stars, could not identify with any certainty even such constellations as the Plough, or Orion. Halley's comet has captured her imagination all the same. She feels she knows how it will look: a great bolt of light, blazing across the sky. The comet's tail could be two hundred million miles long, Eddie has told her (consulting newspapers who have been consulting astronomers). Two hundred million; Gwen glances at Eddie with pride. He is a writer; he understands, Gwen feels, the poetry of facts.

Tonight, she will watch the comet with him. There will also be some forty other guests, of course, and the servants will watch from the kitchen garden side of the house, but for Gwen the other comet-gazers are an irrelevance. This momentous evening will belong, she feels, to her and to her lover. They will watch together; under cover of darkness, she may hold Eddie's hand; then, later . . .

But that is later. Now it is morning, and (the servants are well-trained; all arrangements were completed weeks before) Gwen has nothing to do. She may give herself up to the spring air, to the delights of the oyster faille of her new dress (already admired by Eddie). She may enjoy Eddie's proximity and her husband Denton's absence. She can relish the fact that she has escaped the house, and is now settled at her favorite place at Winterscombe, a small rustic building fronted by a loggia, tucked away in the gardens, a place Gwen has made her own. The Stone House it is called.

She can relax here in her Petit Trianon, as Eddie calls it, which she has furnished simply and charmingly to her own taste. Winterscombe is Denton's house; years ago she made a few desultory attempts to set her mark upon it, and—in the face of Denton's irritable intransigence—soon gave up. Easier to retreat here, where she keeps her watercolors and her easel, her wildflower press, her embroidery silks and frames, the American books she loved as a child, and one or two pieces of furniture, simple but good, which she had shipped from Washington, D.C., when her mother died.

Here she can enjoy the light on the lake in the distance, the pale green of the woods beyond just coming into leaf. Earlier, in the distance, she glimpsed Denton, together with his head keeper, Cattermole, disappearing into those woods, probably to check on the pheasants, possibly to shoot rabbits or pigeons, possibly because Cattermole has been complaining about poachers yet again.

That momentarily spoiled the view, but now Denton and his keeper are out of sight and unlikely to return again for at least an hour, so Gwen feels at peace again. She sighs. The air at Winterscombe, Gwen likes to maintain, is not merely fresh; it is *benign*.

Her youngest son, Steenie, aged ten, pulls at her skirts, and Gwen bends to lift him up onto her lap with a fond smile. Eddie Shawcross, as bidden, has moved forward; he has taken up his place behind her. She can smell the smoke of his cheroot. Feeling they make a charming group, almost a family group—herself, Steenie, her lover—Gwen lifts her face so its most flattering angle is turned to the lens of her eldest son's camera.

This camera is the latest thing, an expensive Adams Videx, mounted on a tripod. Her son Francis—always known as Boy—is bending over it, fiddling and adjusting. Boy is eighteen; he has left school; he is about to embark on military training at Sandhurst and a career as a soldier. Gwen cannot think of Boy as grown up; to her, he remains her child.

The Videx was a present from Gwen for Boy's last birthday; Boy is in love with it. In the last few months photography has become his obsession—which does not please his father, Denton, at all. Denton's present to Boy on that eighteenth birthday was a matched pair of Purdey shotguns. These guns (a status symbol, we might call them—Denton likes status symbols) are the finest of their kind. They took two years to make. Denton himself supervised every detail of their design. He escorted Boy to the Purdey fittings, and— although he knows the guns are a piece of ostentation, particularly for an eighteen-year-old boy who is a poor shot—Denton remains proud of them. Her husband (and this pleases Gwen, though she would not admit it) is jealous of the Videx.

Boy takes photographs all the time now, of the family, of the servants, of the house. He took them last fall at the Winterscombe shoot, when he should have been shooting guns, not film; this made his father furious. Boy, usually frightened of Denton and his rages, has in this respect shown a new and unexpected obstinacy. He continues to take his pictures; he will not give up.

Now, draping the black camera cape over his head and shoulders, Boy squints through the viewfinder. Like his mother, he is pleased with the composition, the family group—and Eddie Shawcross is such an established friend that, as far as Boy is concerned, he almost counts as one of the family. Boy's eyes rest on the inverted image of his mother: She is thirty-eight and a remarkably handsome woman, although our tastes in beauty may have changed. She has given birth to seven children and lost three of them, but she has retained her figure. It conforms to the Edwardian ideal of an hourglass shape. Her features are strong, her hair dark and loosely gathered up, her expression placid. There is in her pale eyes a dreaminess suggestive of lassitude, which many men find sensual and which her husband, Denton, when angry, attributes first to stupidity and second to laziness.

Gwen sees Boy is ready to take his photograph. It will involve a one-minute exposure, during which everyone must remain absolutely still. One quick glance down at Steenie, who is looking up at her with gratifying adoration; one quick glance back at Eddie; yes, all is well.

No, all is not well. From the corner of her eye Gwen catches a blur of movement, a dart of black. It is Eddie's daughter, Constance.

Until this moment Gwen has succeeded in forgetting Constance is present—an easy thing to do; the child is forever skulking in corners. Now, in the nick of time, Constance has insinuated herself into the picture. She darts forward, kneels at her father's feet, to the side of Gwen's chair, and turns her small unattractive face obstinately toward the Videx. Forgetting herself, Gwen frowns.

Boy, under his camera cape, looks through the viewfinder, hand poised to press the bulb. A moment ago the composition was excellent. Now Constance has unbalanced it; it is spoiled. Boy is too polite to say so; he ignores the expression on Constance's face, which is characteristic, if hostile. He checks the others: Steenie—pretty, charming, delicate. Shawcross—well-groomed, handsome, negligent, every inch the writer. His mother . . . Boy ducks out from the camera cape.

"Mama," he says urgently, "Mama. You must smile."

Gwen casts Constance a small look; she turns back to Boy. Eddie Shawcross, sensing her irritation, presses his gloved hand against her shoulder. One thumb (invisible to Boy) massages the nape of her neck. Gwen, mollified, decides to forget Constance. She tilts her chin back to the flattering angle. Leather against bare skin; suede against bare skin. It is delicious. Gwen smiles.

Beneath the camera hood the bulb is pressed. For a minute the camera whirs; for a minute no one moves.

In the distance, from the direction of the woods, a shot rings out. (Denton, or Cattermole, and another rabbit dead, Gwen thinks.) No one reacts to the shot—which was quite far off—and so, luckily, Boy's exposure is not spoiled.

One minute later, Boy emerges, flushed.

"There," he says triumphantly. "It's done."

Another shot rings out, farther away this time. Steenie yawns and climbs down from his mother's lap. Boy is busy dismantling his tripod. Gwen, sure neither son is watching her, arches her back a little. For a second she feels against the nape of her neck the press of her lover's thighs. She stands, stretches, meets his eyes, reads the message in them, falters, and looks away.

She turns, feeling guilty now, and happy enough to be generous, feeling she should make amends to Constance. She ought to make more of an effort to befriend the child, to include her. Gwen looks in every direction. But no; Constance has gone.

Later the same morning: Boy has set up his tripod in another part of the garden, by the croquet lawn. Two players: his other brothers, Acland and Frederic. Acland is winning; one can tell this not so much from the position of the croquet balls and hoops as by the expression on the brothers' faces.

Acland is a year younger than Boy, and is now some four months away from his eighteenth birthday. Frederic is not yet fifteen; sometimes he resents this.

Freddie is in a temper; his face is dark with it. His mouth scowls; his brows are drawn together. The resemblance to his father, Denton, is marked. Father and son—both powerfully built, wide-shouldered, square-hipped, something about their stance suggesting the boxer, squaring up to the world, picking where and when to land the punch. Both expression and stance are misleading; unlike his father, whose famous rages may rumble for weeks, even months before they erupt, Freddie's temper blazes quietly, then dies away and is forgotten. Fifteen minutes after this photograph is taken, Freddie's anger will have passed.

For the most part, Freddie enjoys life; his demands are few and simple. He likes good food (he is already a little stout); he is developing a taste for wine; he likes to flirt with pretty girls, though he chafes at his lack of opportunity.

A sunny nature, Gwen will say of Frederic, the least troublesome of her sons. Freddie has none of Boy's agonizing shyness—indeed, he will chat as openly and happily to a complete stranger in a railway carriage as he will to his family. He is not highly strung, as Steenie is. Freddie seems to have been born without nerves. Freddie's great quality (Gwen maintains) is his *simplicity*; he may talk too much, but to be with him is to bathe in the easy warmth of a June day. So peaceful, Gwen will think, so cheering, so jolly, so . . . *unlike Acland*. And here she will pull herself up guiltily, then sigh and acknowledge the truth: Acland is the most difficult of her sons; she loves him, but she does not understand him.

Acland, in Boy's photograph, stands a little to the side of the frame, and (unlike Freddie, who stares straight at the lens) Acland's head is slightly turned, as if he distrusted or disliked this fixing of his image in a picture. A tall young man, thin compared to his brother. His clothes are elegant and his stance (croquet mallet in hand) is a studied one, carefully negligent. But Boy is a subtle photographer, and he has caught something in Acland's attitude—a hint of arrogance, a suggestion of triumph. Not only has Acland won this game, he is pleased to have won, and cannot disguise his pleasure in his victory.

In the photograph the light glances across Acland's face, and the wind has lifted his hair from his forehead. The picture (sepia) cannot show this, but Acland had fair hair lit with red; his eyes (the most remarkable feature in an arresting face) were perceptibly different in color, the left eye hazel, the right clearest green.

When he was a small child, Gwen—delighting in this son who resembled no one in the family—gave him fanciful nicknames. She called him her changeling child, her Ariel—until Denton, enraged by this sentimentality, put a stop to it. Then Gwen desisted (she was usually obedient to Denton); but in the privacy of her own room or the nursery, she would use the nicknames again.

Acland was so quick, so bright, so strange and unpredictable, so fierce and sudden in his passions. He was made of fire and air, Gwen would think—there was nothing of earth in him.

In those early years Acland was Gwen's delight. She was proud of his quick intelligence, she delighted in his company; she discovered—and this touched her to the heart—that Acland was vulnerable. He raced after things, must always acquire more information, must always *understand*—and this pursuit of his, as if he always chased something just out of reach, made him hectic.

This driven quality in him, marked even when he was very young, made him always restless: Gwen discovered that when he was so, she could calm him—not with words, not with arguments (they were always useless) but simply with her presence.

"Ah, Acland," she would say, "you can't fight the world," and she would take him in her arms, watch him become peaceful.

When he was a boy. Later this changed. Perhaps when Acland first was sent away to school, perhaps when her last child, Steenie, was born—Gwen sometimes cites these events by way of excuse, but she knows that, truthfully, neither episode explains what happened. Suddenly, apparently without cause, Acland grew away from her. If he needed solace he no longer turned to his mother, and by the time he was twelve the break was complete.

He no longer confided in her as once he did; he seemed to fear betraying his emotions, and he judged people, Gwen thought, judged them in a way she grew to hate—and fear. He showed little sympathy and made no allowances; mention the frailty of human nature, and Acland would exhibit scorn. No, he looked, estimated, judged, and then, too often, he dismissed.

To be dismissed by Acland, aged fifteen or sixteen, was not a pleasant experience. It was withering. Gwen told herself that it was youthful arrogance, a by-product of Acland's intellect, that it would pass—but by that time Eddie Shawcross had come into her life, and Acland's implacable refusal to accept Shawcross cut Gwen to the heart.

She could hardly plead on her lover's behalf, although she tried from time to time to emphasize his strengths. She gave Acland copies of Shawcross's books—and then suffered in silence when Acland remorselessly explained why he thought them bad. She tried—in the first year or so—to throw them together; and then she gave up. It occurred to her that Acland *knew*, that he was not deceived, as the rest of the family were, about the true nature of her relationship. Then Gwen became truly afraid. Acland did not just judge the world in general, she saw; he judged her, his mother, judged her and—presumably—found her wanting.

I have lost a son, Gwen would think sometimes, close to tears, and she would yearn to throw her arms around Acland, to tell him everything, to *explain*. Fearing him, she never did so. Acland, she knew, might be brought back to her, but there would be a price, and that price would be Shawcross. To regain her son's confidence and respect, her lover would have to be sacrificed—and this Gwen, for all her occasional unhappiness over Acland, cannot bring herself to do. She loves Shawcross; she cannot give him up, and this her son would never understand. Acland, Gwen tells herself, is too contained; passion does not exist in Acland's universe.

In this judgment Gwen is quite wrong, for Acland himself is in love. In the past year a universe has been unlocked by this love, yet he does not speak of it to his mother or to anyone. Acland protects the love from the gaze of others behind a barrier of sarcasm and nonchalance.

Meanwhile, all that hidden away, Acland poses for Boy's photograph. He swings the mallet, rests it, holds still (although he hates to be still, and Boy's endless photographs make him impatient). A glowering Freddie, an inattentive Acland.

"Keep *still*," Boy commands, and the camera whirs.

"Such a day! Such a day! Such a day!" Acland shouts when at last the exposure is over, and he throws himself down full-length upon the grass.

Freddie and Boy regard him, face lifted to the sky, arms outstretched, expression rapturous.

Freddie grins. Boy, dismantling his tripod, gives Acland a prim glance. Acland's moods are too precipitate, in Boy's opinion. They veer from heaven to hell, from the black to the sublime, too easily. Boy finds these moods pretentious.

"Oh, for God's sake, Acland," he says, and tucks his tripod under his arm. "Do you have to be so extravagant?"

"Wrong," Acland replies, and does not even glance in Boy's direction. "Wrong, wrong, wrong! I am not extravagant. I am . . . *steadfast*."

He proclaims the word, perhaps to his brothers, perhaps to the sky, perhaps to himself.

Freddie's response is an amiable kick; Boy's response is to leave. He proceeds across the lawn and, at the edge, looks back. Acland still has not moved. He lies on his back and stares up at the sun, but his expression has changed, and his face—as pale and precise as a marble monument—is serious.

Shall we move on? Boy took a great many other photographs that day—that key day—and some of them are helpful.

Here is one of the houseguests, Mrs. Heyward-West, formerly the King's mistress. She is descending from a motorcar, wearing furs, a huge hat, and a motoring veil, which she has just lifted. Nearby, another houseguest, Jane Conyngham—plain Jane Conyngham as she was unkindly known, and one of the great heiresses of her day. Jane, whose long-widowed father owns adjoining estates in Wiltshire, has known the Cavendish family from earliest childhood. She has been invited this weekend for a special reason: Lord Callendar plans to marry her off to his eldest son, Boy; a proposal is imminent.

We shall come to Jane in due course. Meanwhile, dressed in an unflattering walking suit, she stands next to Acland, and her gaze is fixed upon him. Jane has an intelligent face. We would not call her plain now, perhaps, for our standards in beauty have changed. She stands next to Acland, absorbed, and Acland—predictably—is looking the other way.

Next, a group of servants, lined up outside the servants' hall in serried ranks, as if for a school photograph. How patient Boy must have been! Toward the back, at the end of a line, is a girl called Jenna Curtis.

She is then aged sixteen and has been in service at Winterscombe for two years; both her parents, now dead, worked there before her. Jenna has been steadily promoted over the past two years and is by this time a between-stairs maid. For this party of Gwen's, however, she has a new role: Jane Conyngham's personal maid has fallen ill; Jenna has been pressed into service. Today, it is she who will unpack Jane's dresses and iron them and lay them out. It is she who will help Jane Conyngham dress her hair for the great dinner, and she will do so with such tact, skill, and patience that Jane (shy herself, and easily intimidated by smarter maids) will actually remember her and will—a few years later—promote her marriage. A mistake.

The sixteen-year-old Jenna is pretty. By modern standards she is plump. She looks rounded, soft as a dove; her eyes are wide and dark and calm. A lovely girl, even though her uniform is drab and her cap is unbecoming.

My Jenna, I thought, when I first found this photograph. She was unrecognizable as the Jenna I remembered. But then, the Jenna I found in the notebooks was different too. Words and pictures: I placed them side by side, and I considered.

One last photograph. Come with me; we are indoors now. Boy has abandoned people for interiors; he has had trouble lighting this.

Boy, it seems, has a project of his own, not yet revealed to anyone. It involves photographing each of the rooms at Winterscombe, mounting the pictures in an album, and then presenting it to his father, Denton. The gift may bring his father 'round, Boy thinks; Denton may see that there is a use to the Videx after all, for Denton is immensely proud of his house.

Above all, he is proud of this room in which Boy now stands. Unblushingly, Denton refers to this room as "the King's bedroom." All the other bedrooms have names too: There is the Blue room, the Red room, the Chinese room, the Honeysuckle room . . . but those names are rarely conjured by his father. The King's bedroom, however, he mentions at every opportunity, especially to guests new to Winterscombe.

It is one way of reminding them (should they not know) that Denton's house has received royal visitors. It provides Denton, a patriot, a monarchist, and a snob, with the lead-in he seeks. He can then launch himself on the anecdotes his family have come to dread: how King Edward graciously complimented him on the excellence of his shoot, his claret, his view, his architect, his plumbing, above all his perspicacity in marrying such a beauty as Gwen.

Denton will mention the King's remarkable good humor while at Winterscombe (the King's temper being notoriously unreliable); he will attribute it to the excellence of the Winterscombe air, unequaled (Denton believes) in any other part of England. Denton will mention the King's cordial invitation to shoot with him at Sandringham; he will neglect to mention that this visit never materialized.

Then, ignoring Gwen's frowns (Gwen, being American, finds all this glorification of the monarch tedious), Denton will occasionally take his guests upstairs so that they can view for themselves the room where the King slept.

He will pace about a room which is swaddled and stuffed. He will punch the ballooning pregnancies of the red velvet chairs, smooth the bulges of the crimson curtains, caress the curvatures of the four-poster bed. The whole room was redecorated for the King's impending visit, and in the bathroom beyond, the wonders of German plumbing were installed at vast expense, but it is the bed, which Denton himself designed, which remains his pride and his delight.

It is so large it had to be erected by the estate carpenters in the room itself. Steps are required to mount it. At its head is a canopy embroidered with the royal arms; at its foot, two cherubs disport themselves suggestively. The mattress, hand-stuffed with horsehair and finest wool, is eighteen inches thick; Denton, to demonstrate its luxury and resilience, will—occasionally—bounce on it. However, he does so with a certain reverence, for to Denton this bedroom is a shrine, a hallowed place. Sometimes Denton allows himself to speculate on the mysteries this bedroom may have seen. (When the King visited, the Queen was indisposed, but his current mistress was of the house party.) He speculates, but he maintains respect. And for this reason, the King's bedroom has not been used in five years. Until this weekend.

This weekend its sanctity will be broken—Gwen has insisted upon it. With so many guests for her comet party, and only eighteen bedrooms at her disposal, Gwen finds herself short of accommodation. For once, and with a hostess's authority, she has insisted, and

Denton—furious—has been overruled. The King's bedroom shall be occupied. Gwen has decreed that Eddie Shawcross shall sleep in it.

Her lover has in fact been nagging her for months to let him use this room. Shawcross has a lively sexual imagination, and Gwen knows that he must have particular plans for this room—though he will not tell her what they are, for he is secretive. The unspecified plans have inflamed her own imagination; for months, temptation and timidity fought a fierce battle. Finally she took the risk and, to her own astonishment, found Denton could be vanquished.

After her victory, it is true, Gwen felt some anxiety. She would look at her husband, wonder if he suspected, ask herself if she had gone too far. But in the past few days these anxieties have receded. Denton's temper is bad, but there is nothing unusual in that, and (Gwen thinks, is almost sure) her husband still does not suspect. This is partly because she and Shawcross have been commendably discreet; partly because Denton is unimaginative; mainly (she tells herself) because Denton is not interested.

Since the birth of Steenie, Denton has stayed away from her; the punctual weekly peremptory visits to her room have ceased. Instead, Denton makes punctual weekly visits up to London, where— Gwen assumes—he keeps some woman. True, he does not like Shawcross and does not bother to disguise his dislike, but this is just snobbishness on his part, Gwen thinks. Denton dislikes Shawcross because of his class, because of the school he went to, because he is a writer—a profession for which Denton has the most profound contempt. But this snobbishness is, in a way, helpful; it would not occur to Denton that a man such as Shawcross could be his rival.

So, on the whole, Gwen feels safe. Because she feels safe she is gradually becoming less cautious. She has begun to chafe at her marriage to Denton; she has begun to resent his churlishness. She is thirty-eight; Denton is sixty-five. When she finally nerved herself to make the announcement that Eddie would sleep in the King's bedroom this weekend, when her husband's face purpled with rage, she found herself asking a new question: Must she remain tied to Denton for the rest of her life?

This question she keeps to herself. She does not dare to hint of it to her lover. For what is the alternative? Divorce? That would be out of the question. She would lose her children, lose her place in society; she would be without money and she would be ostracized. Such a route to freedom is unthinkable, and, Gwen suspects, Eddie Shawcross would not welcome it. His only source of income is his writing; he finds it hard even to support Constance and often complains of that. And besides, he is not a man renowned for his fidelity. When Gwen first met Shawcross he already had a considerable reputation as a ladies' man, with a particular penchant for women of the aristocracy; Shawcross, it was said, did not like to bed lower than the wife of an earl, and his men friends made unsavory jokes about his methods of rising in society.

In the circumstances it is a continuing source of wonder to Gwen that she attracted Shawcross at all, and that, having attracted him, she has held on to him. Their affair has endured four years; Gwen does not like to ask but she thinks that, for Shawcross, this is a record. However, he has never in all that time admitted to loving her, and with him Gwen never feels secure. Divorce? Separation? No, she would not dare to mention such ideas to Eddie; the least suggestion of pressure, and he might leave her.

Instead, just of late another idea has come to her; it came to her, in fact, for the first time when she insisted Eddie should sleep in this room, when Denton's face purpled, when he shouted and slammed out of the room. There it was, curling into her mind like smoke: *What if her husband were to die?*

Gwen is ashamed of this thought, but once admitted, it will not go away. If her husband were to die she would be rich—very rich indeed—and that fact might alter Eddie's attitude considerably. Gwen, shying away from this speculation, tells herself that she is only being sensible. After all, Denton is much older than she. He eats too much. He drinks too much. He is overweight; he has gout; he has that choleric temper about which his doctors often warn him. He *could* die; he *might* die . . . He could have a seizure, an apoplexy. . . .

Gwen does not want Denton to die. Indeed, the very thought of his death causes her distress, for despite his irascibility Denton is in many ways a good husband and Gwen is protective toward him. Providing he is humored, Denton is easy enough to live with. He loves his sons and is fiercely proud of them; he can be gallant to Gwen, even considerate. She and her husband are, for the most part, comfortable together; Gwen is wise enough to know that this easy marital steadiness suits her and should not lightly be thrown away.

On the other hand, there is Eddie. On the other hand, she would like to be free. . . . Except what does it mean exactly, that word *free*? Free to be with her lover, free to give herself up to him? This freedom she enjoys already. But free to be with Eddie permanently? Free to marry him? No. Gwen shies away from that thought.

Eddie is a lover; she is not always sure she would like him as a husband.

Meanwhile, she has the best of both worlds. Denton does not know; Shawcross does not complain, and the demands he makes on her (such demands! Gwen glories in them), though intense, are limited. *Don't rock the boat, Gwen,* he said to her once, and though she was hurt by the remark and found it somewhat coarse, she later accepted that what he said was sensible. The great thing is, they are safe.

Was Gwen right about this? We shall see. Certainly she was right as far as her eldest son was concerned. Boy—honorable, devoted to his mother, in awe of his father—could not conceive of either parent as an adulterer. As far as Boy is concerned, his parents must love each other, for they are man and wife. As for Shawcross, he is a good, loyal, trusted friend. Boy cannot understand either his books or his jokes—and this makes Boy feel humble.

Now, setting up his tripod, screwing the last nuts into place, Boy sees only a room, a room whose photograph may please his father; he has sensed no undercurrents before and he senses none now. It is simply . . . a bedroom. He regards the undulations of the bed, the billowing curtains that divide the sleeping quarters from the dressing room; he frowns at the heavy draperies across the windows and, fussily, adjusts them to let in more light. Why, someone could hide in this room and never be discovered, Boy thinks, and then forgets the notion at once, to concentrate on technical matters.

Indoors, with less natural light, the exposure must be longer. Two minutes, Boy decides, hoping no one will come in to spoil the shot. Two minutes . . .

Remember this bedroom, please. It is important.

"Why are you called Boy?"

Boy looks up from his camera, startled. The girl has come into the room silently, has perhaps been there for some while, watching him. Luckily, his photographs are complete, and Boy—busy dismantling his Adams Videx—had thought himself alone. The girl is standing just inside the door and seems uninterested in the answer to her question, for she is already looking away from him, a small frown on her face. Her gaze circles the room; it takes in the royal arms, the fat bed, the undistinguished oils of Denton's Scottish estate, and the curtains. Boy hesitates and she looks back at him.

"You're not a boy. You're a man. You look like a man. So why do they call you Boy?"

Her tone is irritable, almost accusing. Boy, easily embarrassed, finds himself beginning to blush. He bends his head to hide it, hoping the child will go away.

To be truthful, Boy does not like Constance, and this makes him ashamed, for he is generous-hearted and he knows it is uncharitable. After all, Constance is motherless, does not even remember her mother, Jessica, who died of tuberculosis in a Swiss sanitorium when Constance was just two years old.

Yes, Constance is motherless, and her father treats her coldly, almost cruelly. Boy, observing this, seeing how Shawcross mocks his daughter in front of friends, has told himself that Constance must bring back painful memories, must remind her father of the loss of his wife. But even if there are reasons for this behavior, it is not kind, and Boy feels sure Constance must be very lonely. He should not dislike her; Constance should be an object of pity. After all, it is not as if she stays at Winterscombe all the time. Surely, on those brief occasions of her visits he can afford to be friendly?

On the other hand, to be friendly to Constance is not easy. Constance obstinately repels pity; whenever Boy feels it welling up in him, the child seems to sense it and deflects it at once. Her manner is abrupt, prickly, rude. She seems to have an unerring instinct for the weaknesses of others; she homes in on those weaknesses at once, and Boy can never make up his mind whether this is policy on her part or accident. He tells himself it is accident. After all, Constance cannot help her manners; it is just that she has never had the right guidance. She must have a nurse or governess to help her, but such a figure is never in evidence at Winterscombe, and perhaps Eddie Shawcross cannot afford to employ a lady of the right type.

If there were such a person, Boy thinks, looking at the small figure in front of him, she would insist that something be done about Constance's appearance. Her hair is always unkempt; her face, hands, and fingernails are often grubby; she wears cheap, ugly, unflattering clothes. No, Constance deserves kindness; her rudeness must be caused by lack of training, not ill-nature. After all, Constance is only ten years old.

Now, Constance is waiting for an answer (yet again, she has homed in on a weakness), and Boy does not know what to say. He loathes the nickname Boy, wishes his mother and family would drop it now and forever. He fears (correctly as it happens) that this will not occur. Now, trapped, he has to say something. He shrugs.

"It doesn't mean anything. Mama called me that when I was

little, and it stuck, I suppose. Lots of people have nicknames, family names. It isn't important."

"I don't like it at all. It's foolish." The child pauses. "I shall call you Francis."

To Boy's surprise, Constance then smiles at him. The smile lightens her normally tight, sullen little face, and Boy's guilt and shame at once deepen. For Constance, too, has nicknames, though she may not be aware of them. Her father refers to her simply as "the albatross." "Where is the albatross now, I wonder?" Eddie will remark archly to his audience, and will sometimes even mimic the weight of that ill-omened bird around his neck.

Boy and his brothers use a different name: Constance Cross, they call her. It was Acland's idea. ("Well, she is always cross," he explained. "She is also a cross we have to bear. Several weeks a year.")

Constance Cross, the albatross. It is very unkind. Boy decides, there and then, that he must make amends.

He smiles at Constance shyly and indicates his Videx.

"I'll take your photograph if you'd like. It won't take long."

"You took it this morning, earlier."

A flat answer. His overture is rejected as usual. Boy perseveres.

"Yes, but that was with the others. This will be just you. On your own . . ."

"In here?" The child's face shows a sudden glimmer of animation.

"Well, if you liked—I suppose I could. But the light's difficult. I really meant outside—"

"Not outside. Here."

Her tone is now definite, even demanding. Boy caves in. He begins to remount tripod and camera, bends over to screw the tripod legs into place.

When he looks up again, he is startled, almost shocked. The child has struck a pose for him. She has clambered up onto the King's bed and is now sitting on it, legs swinging, her skirts slightly hitched up. Boy stares at her in dismay, glances toward the door.

It is not just that the child is sitting on the sacred bed and probably creasing the counterpane, which would make Denton Cavendish roar with rage; it is the *way* she is sitting.

Boy stares fearfully at a pair of dusty buttoned boots that end at the ankle. Above the boots he can glimpse wrinkled white cotton stockings and a layer of none-too-clean petticoats.

Constance has tossed back her long, untidy black hair, so that it snakes over her thin shoulders. Her face is pale and concentrated, its expression taunting. As Boy looks at her, she first bites her lower lip with her small white teeth and then licks her lips so that they appear very red against the pallor of her skin. Boy stares, wrenches his gaze away, and concentrates on his camera. A few adjustments; he pulls the black hood over his head and adjusts the viewfinder.

An image of Constance Shawcross is in his gaze, upside down but perfectly in focus. He blinks at it. It seems to him that there is now an even greater amount of stocking visible, less drab skirt, more grubby petticoats. He clears his throat, tries to sound magisterial.

"You must keep absolutely still, Constance. The light is poor, so I need a long exposure. Turn your face a little to the left. . . ."

The child turns her head, tilts her small pointed chin. Boy sees that she is posing stiffly and self-consciously, as if anxious the photograph should be a flattering one. She is a plain child, and Boy is touched.

Under the hood he reaches for the shutter bulb, adjusts the aperture. A half-second before the bulb is pressed, too late for Boy to stop, the child alters her position. Two minutes; silence and whirring.

Boy emerges from the hood, scarlet. He stares at Constance accusingly and she stares back at him. In that half-second she parted her thighs and altered the position of her hand. She has posed with her left hand lying across her thigh, her fingers outstretched, point-ing downward into her lap. A garter, a patch of bare skin, a knicker-leg are visible. It is a gesture capable of innocent interpretation . . . just. It is also (coupled with the brazenness of her stare) the lewdest, the most lascivious gesture Boy has ever seen in his life.

To his horror, to his shame, his body has stirred. He remains behind his camera, grateful for its protection, telling himself that he is foul, evil. Constance is a ten-year-old child; she is motherless, innocent. . . .

Constance bounces down from the bed. She seems now in an excellent humor.

"Thank you, Francis," she says. "You will give me a print of the photograph, won't you?"

"Oh, yes—that is, certainly. If it comes out . . . I'm not sure about the exposure I used, and—"

Boy lies badly. He has already decided to destroy the plate, although later, when he sees it, he will change his mind.

"Oh, *please,* Francis—"

To Boy's utter consternation, Constance reaches up (Boy is over six feet tall) and, as he bends awkwardly, plants a childish kiss on his cheek. Boy drops, and loses, one of the wing nuts from his tripod, although in his confusion he does not realize this. It rolls across the carpet to rest under a desk—from where Boy will have to retrieve it, somehow, later. Constance, kiss over, skips to the door.

"I shall give it to my father," she says, with one backward glance over her shoulder. "Papa will like that, don't you think?"

"Fetch out the traps." Denton takes a large swallow of claret. "The hell with the law. This is my land. Fetch them out—see how the beggars like that! Traps rusting away in barns—what's the sense in that? Set them. I shall tell Cattermole. Patrol the woods. Get four men in there, six if necessary. I won't stand for it. I must have lost fifty birds this past month. Fifty! Three last night alone. How they get in I don't know, but I intend to find out, and when I do, they'll damn well regret it. Blast of shot up the backside—only thing they understand, these fellas. Blast of shot, then up before the magistrates. Old Dickie Peel—been on the Bench since the year dot. He knows how to deal with them. Maximum sentences, the full weight of the law. Mind you"—another hefty swig—"prison's too good for them. Poachers? You know what I'd do if I had my way? Ship 'em out, that's what. Ship 'em off to the colonies—America, Australia. Get rid of 'em for good. No respect for a man's property. It makes my blood boil."

Denton does indeed look as if his blood could have reached one hundred degrees centigrade: His face is livid as an overripe plum; one large index finger is raised in admonition at the entire table; he waggles it, glares from face to face, as if his luncheon guests might be guilty of poaching his pheasants, given half a chance.

He fixes each of his three elder sons with his gaze, glowers at Mrs. Heyward-West's mild-mannered little husband, scowls at Jarvis (a friend of Eddie Shawcross, invited at his request—something to do with Art; no one is sure exactly what).

Jarvis is wearing a cravat that is perhaps a trifle bright; in St. James's London this cravat pleased Jarvis; now, as Denton's ripe gaze fixes on it, Jarvis feels less certain of its shade. He winces, and Denton's gaze roves on. It fixes finally on the trim person of Eddie Shawcross, seated on Gwen's left at the far end of the table. Staring at Shawcross, Denton's features become, if possible, even more empurpled.

"Poachers. Trespassers. *Interlopers*," Denton pronounces with special savagery, and Shawcross, more used to these outbursts than some of the other guests present, amused enough by them to recount them in malicious detail in his journals, returns him a polite even smile. Denton makes a gurgling noise in his throat, indicative to his family of extreme fury, and Gwen's treacherous heart gives a tiny leap. Seizure? Apoplexy? Now, at her luncheon table, in front of her guests? But no, it is merely the residue of rage, the result of Denton's inspection of his woods with Cattermole that morning, the honest indignation of a man whose most passionate belief is the sanctity of property. It is not directed particularly at Eddie Shawcross, and it is even now subsiding.

Gwen's instincts as a hostess rise to the surface. There are ladies present, which Denton seems to have forgotten. They have already endured "backside" and the clumsy emendation of "buggers" to "beggars"; it is more than possible that, even with his rage spent, Denton might actually swear or blaspheme.

Gwen leans forward to intervene, but Acland is quicker.

"One small point, sir," he says into the silence that has fallen. "Just that the Declaration of Independence was signed in 1776 . . . which means America hasn't been a colony for quite a long time."

"So? So?" Denton looks up with new belligerence.

"Well, it might be difficult to dump our felons there. Even the poachers. The Americans might object, don't you think?"

Acland's voice is exceedingly polite; his father, head lowered like a bull about to charge, is regarding him with suspicion, sniffing for heresy, but he is deceived by Acland's tone.

"Inconvenient, I grant you. But a bit of a poser nonetheless."

There is another silence, during which Shawcross smirks behind his napkin. Mrs. Heyward-West (charming and tactful Mrs. West, Gwen thinks) comes to the rescue. She is seated on Denton's right, and she leans forward, her hand brushing his arm. She is still a well-preserved, a handsome woman.

"America!" she says in her deep voice. "How I love that country. And the Americans themselves—so welcoming, so very very kind. Did I tell you, Denton my dear, about our last visit there? We were staying in Virginia, with some friends who breed quite magnificent horses. Now I know, Denton, what you are going to say. You're going to say I'm no judge of a horse at all, and I'm sure you're right. But—now this will interest you—"

The miracle has been achieved; Mrs. Heyward-West has his full attention; Denton's somewhat bulging blue eyes revolve, then fix on her. Everyone relaxes (even Jarvis of the lavender cravat), and at the far end of the table Gwen and Shawcross exchange glances.

The moment of drama is past, and from then onward the luncheon passes very pleasantly. Gwen employs a good cook, and the meal—by Edwardian standards—is light, in view of the feasting to come at the comet party that evening. On Gwen's left, Eddie Shawcross is being most charming to an elderly deaf neighbor, last spinster member of a once-prominent Wiltshire family. He is discussing the work of George Bernard Shaw. (Eddie never lowers his metropolitan standards, even in the country.) The neighbor has never heard of Shaw, that much is obvious, but no matter—Eddie is being witty. On Gwen's right, George Heyward-West, a dignified little man who has always seemed quite unaffected by the past scandals concerning his wife and the King, is explaining the intricacies of the stock market to Denton's sister, the famously beautiful Maud, a spectacular girl, who married so high that Eddie claims she gives him vertigo. Maud (now, Gwen notes with satisfaction, becoming a little *too* plump) hitched her star to that of an Italian princeling. The Italian princeling is never much in evidence, and is not present now; Maud claims he is in Monte Carlo, gambling.

Maud has, in fact, considerable knowledge of the stock market herself, but she is woman enough not to betray this to George Heyward-West, who is patiently explaining the difference between bonds and equities. Money, as a subject of conversation over luncheon, is not strictly speaking *de rigueur,* but both are clearly enjoying themselves, so Gwen does not intervene.

Instead, pleasurably, she allows herself to dream. The room is warm, the wine has made Gwen feel gently soporific, and all her guests seem animated—she may indulge herself a little.

Fourteen at table now, all her sons present except Steenie, who is upstairs in the nursery wing with, thank goodness, Constance Albatross, firm instructions to Nanny that both children should remain there all afternoon. (Steenie is delicate and needs to rest; Constance will have to put up with the confinement. One of the things Gwen most dislikes about Constance is the way she is always creeping about, as if she were spying on her father, from whom, once found, she refuses to be parted. Like a limpet, that child.)

Fourteen at luncheon, forty at dinner. Gwen is pleased by her dinner menu: mock turtle soup, oyster patties, and—always a triumph this—a ragout of lobster. Then the plainer fare, which will ensure Denton's good temper: roast goslings, roast saddle of mutton, a boiled capon. Guinea fowl—did she remember to ask for guinea fowl, which Eddie so likes? Yes, she did. And then the puddings, of course, which always look so pretty: little champagne jellies in crystal glasses, and maids-of-honor, cabinet puddings, and the tiny lemon water-ices served in baskets of mint leaves—Steenie loves those, and she must remember to have some sent up for him in the nursery. Finally, the dessert. Gwen, who has a sweet tooth, loves this part of a meal, when the cloth is drawn and her table sparkles with silver dishes: tidbits and sweetmeats, purple Carlsbad plums sticky with sugar, tiny pyramids of preserved cherries and frosted grapes, filberts, figs from the hothouses, pale glasses of ice-cold Sauternes—oh, it will be glorious.

They will eat inside; then she and her guests will assemble outside, on the terrace, and the comet will pass across the sky in a blaze of glory.

Gwen will don her furs at this point. Denton has not yet seen the new sealskin with the ermine collar, nor the bill for it (when he does, it will not please him, for Denton is tightfisted). However, by the time Gwen puts it on, she will be safe. Denton will be far too drunk to notice.

Then they will return to the house. A little music perhaps: Jane Conyngham, a gifted pianist, has promised to play for them; Gwen herself may sing one or two of the sentimental ballads she loves. And after that, no haste, let it all remain very easy, very dégagé (as Eddie would say), people may follow their own inclinations.

Denton will disappear, that is a certainty. He will go off with his cronies, smoke his cigars, and down plenty of port (despite the gout) and then he will heave himself up to bed, late, late—it does not matter how late; Gwen will not have to listen to his snoring. Yes, Denton will disappear drunk, as he always does; the snooping Constance will be safely asleep; her guests will divert one another, and then—at last—Gwen and Eddie will be free to be alone. Somewhere.

Gwen is in a reverie, but as her thoughts crystallize and focus on that sweet moment which still lies ahead, she is seized with an acute impatience. She wants Eddie; she needs Eddie; the desire for him is so intense that she feels hot, breathless, as if she might faint.

This morning at the Stone House, after the children had left them, Eddie took her hand and slipped it into the pocket of his jacket. It closed on something soft; she drew out several lengths of black silk ribbon. She looked at these ribbons in silence, a familiar lassitude building in her body. She did not need to question him about these ribbons; already her mind raced ahead—to the King's bedroom, perhaps, or to the clearing in the woods where she and Eddie sometimes met. The places danced in her mind; so did those ribbons, and the use Eddie might make of them.

Gwen looks at Shawcross now. He does not appear to be thinking of her as she is thinking of him. On the contrary, his manner is urbane, amused, detached. He is talking across the table to his friend Jarvis about some painter. Jarvis, as far as Gwen can understand it, is a middleman. He hopes Denton may commission some pictures from a painter of his acquaintance; the painter is good, Jarvis says, with the only subjects Denton considers fit ones for art—to wit, horses, dogs, stags, and foxes.

Now Eddie is discussing some art gallery of which Gwen has never heard. The black ribbons may be in his pocket even now as he speaks with such assurance, dark-gray eyes glinting, reddish beard shining with pomade, his small ladylike white hands gesturing, gesturing. . . . "My dear fellow," he says, "please. I'm not interested in your daubers. Words. Sentences. The sting of the novelist's perceptions—*that's* the thing. All art aspires to the condition of literature—not music, and certainly not your humdrum painting and sculpture. Why, if I had my way, we should all live like monks: books aplenty, and *bare walls*. . . ."

Shawcross, as he pronounces the words *bare walls*, casts an insolent glance at the walls of the Cavendish dining room. They are crammed with large Victorian oils: two stags *montant;* one hare being torn in two by greyhounds, and several murky sea battles purchased by Denton's father.

Gwen, forgetting silk ribbons in an instant, snaps back to attention, ceases to be Eddie's mistress and remembers she is hostess. Her eyes scan the guests anxiously. What has happened? *Something* has happened. Denton looks purple and thunderous once more. Acland is watching him, detached as always. Freddie is trying not to laugh, Boy is scarlet with embarrassment, Jane Conyngham is staring studiously at her plate, and Mrs. Heyward-West, the most equable of women, is frowning in annoyance.

Could it have been Eddie's last remark? But no—whatever was said or done, it occurred earlier. Gwen, flustered, hesitates, and to her horror, her husband leans across the table—silver tinkles against glass—lifts again that waggling accusatory finger, and points it straight in the direction of a now-silent Shawcross.

"You, sir," Denton roars. "Yes, you, sir. You would do well to mind your manners. You will remember, if you please, your position here. You will remember you are a guest in my house. *My* house, sir . . ." And—more horror; really, this time Denton has gone too far—Denton rises. No waiting for the ladies to withdraw, not the slightest pretense of civility; Denton rises, turns his back, and stumps out of the room. The door slams. Gwen is so vexed she feels she could weep, or faint. This behavior cannot be excused or passed off.

Suddenly she sees the evening ahead of her, her beautiful party, quite ruined.

It is Acland who saves her. He looks along the table at the embarrassed faces; as Eddie Shawcross starts to apologize, Acland cuts him off with a contemptuous glance.

"Don't worry, Shawcross. It was nothing you said. The loss of his pheasants always makes my father quite savage. I imagine he has gone to strangle some poachers. Probably with his bare hands. Mama?"

There is a nervous rustle of laughter. Acland turns to her, and Gwen seizes her opportunity. She rises; the other women rise. Gwen manages their exit with some dignity.

And later—half an hour later, when they are outside again on the terrace and the guests are making their various plans for the afternoon—Gwen feels consoled. The situation has been retrieved. Most of these people are family friends; they understand Denton's moods and eccentricities. Indeed, now he has disappeared, the mood lightens; nervousness transmutes into gaiety.

"My dear, my brother Denton is a beast. I shall tell him so later," Maud says kindly.

"Dear Gwen, you must not worry," says the elderly, deaf Wiltshire neighbor as she takes up her crocheting. She herself spent sixty years deferring to a tyrannical father; now she pats Gwen's hand. "Men will have these little moods. We women become used to them. . . ."

The Heyward-Wests decide to stroll down to the lake; Maud announces her intention of retiring to write letters to Monte Carlo; Boy agrees to play tennis with Jarvis, Acland, and Jane. Freddie drifts away; the other guests drift away. Soon, Gwen and Eddie Shawcross are alone on the terrace with the elderly neighbor, who nods off to sleep over her crocheting.

Gwen raises her parasol and feels her fears and embarrassment fade. She looks out across the gardens, feels the soft breeze against her skin. It is three o'clock. (We must remember the time; it is important.) Eddie rests his hand on her arm, removes it, and allows the back of his fingers to brush against her breast.

Gwen looks up at him. The silence is now loud. Their eyes meet, and Gwen sees in Eddie's face a fixity that can mean only one thing.

"What time do your other houseguests arrive?" he asks.

"Not before five . . ."

"And tea?"

"At four-thirty. For those who want it. But I must be there."

Gwen's voice is faint. Eddie consults his pocket watch with a maddening slowness. He puts his hand into his pocket (the pocket) and removes it again.

"What a temper your husband has," he remarks levelly, and Gwen understands at once: The husband's rudeness adds piquancy to the lover's plans.

"You must tell me more about Denton's rages," Eddie says, and rises and offers his hostess his arm. They turn back to the house at a leisured pace. By the French windows they pause.

"My room, I think," Eddie says, his eyes scanning the garden.

"Now? Eddie . . ." Gwen hesitates, furls her parasol, steps into the shadows of the house.

"My dear Gwen"—Eddie turns away—"do you intend to waste one and a half hours?"

"Galoshes!"

Boy stops in his tracks, just outside the house, and looks down at Jane's feet with a mournful expression.

"I really think . . . the grass is so damp, and if we are to go down through the garden . . . yes, galoshes would be the thing."

"I don't need galoshes, Boy," Jane replies with some asperity, for Boy's irrepressible gallantry irritates her.

Beside them, Acland surveys them lazily, his face expressionless. He swings his tennis racquet, looks up at the sky, looks away.

"It rained last night. The grass still hasn't dried out. You could take a chill. It's a long way to the court. Really—galoshes! I insist on it!"

Boy's voice has taken on that stubborn note it always does when his protectiveness is challenged. Jane can hear that faint hesitation before certain consonants, a residue of the bad stammer Boy had as a child. It returns whenever he is nervous—in conversation with his father, for instance, or on those occasions (frequent) when Acland teases him. It returns when he is with Jane because he is ill at ease with her. There is that general understanding, thick in the air as a conspiracy, that sooner or later Boy will propose; it is what his father wishes. Jane knows this, and also knows that Boy does not wish to propose, for he does not love her. For that reason Boy is solicitous to a fault. Poor Boy: he does not find it easy to be a hypocrite. Jane, pitying yet still irritated, gives a sigh.

"I didn't *bring* my galoshes, Boy. Please, don't fuss."

She stops, aware that Acland, turning back, is inspecting her. His gaze travels from head to foot: the crisp tennis blouse with its sailor collar; the wide black belt with its silver clasp; the long, pleated white skirt, which reaches to her ankles; the trim shoes, which the maid Jenna has whitened and powdered.

This outfit is new; Jane ordered it, with a light heart, for this visit, just as she ordered the green silk dress she will wear this evening. Hours looking at pattern books, hours posing in front of a mirror while her aunt's dressmaker knelt, pins in mouth, and tucked and adjusted.

Of the green dress Jane is still a little uncertain: not the color she would have chosen. But her aunt, who brought her up and whom she dearly loves, had bought the material, bringing it back in triumph from an expedition to London. So proud, so pleased, so anxious, that Jane had not had the heart to demur.

"Bourne and Hollingsworth," her aunt said fondly, stroking the silk. "A most obliging girl there, and she assured me it was the latest thing. A very special dress for a very special evening."

A little pause then; a meaningful glance exchanged with the elderly dressmaker, and there the word lay among the three of them, unspoken but understood: a proposal. At last.

"My agate necklace, dearest Jane," her aunt had said, bringing forth a polished leather box just as Jane was leaving. "My agate necklace—an engagement present from William when I was eighteen. Dearest Jane, it will look lovely with your dress."

Her aunt had been widowed fifteen years; her uncle was, for Jane, no more than a whiskery memory, but Jane was touched. She kissed her aunt; she will wear the necklace, as promised, this evening. Not for Boy, as her aunt expects, but for the benefit of someone else, someone who is looking at her and at her crisp new tennis clothes, and smiling.

Under that gaze, quizzical, possibly amused by Boy's fussing, Jane grows self-conscious. She smooths her skirt, blushes, averts her gaze. Minutes before, looking at herself in her glass, telling herself that yes, she looked well, that simple clothes suited her best, Jane had felt confident—confident of the clothes, confident of herself, confident (in some odd and irrational way) of the immediate future. There was the afternoon; it hovered brightly before her. There were the stairs down to the afternoon, and there, at the foot of those stairs, waiting, was Acland.

How long has she loved Acland? Jane hardly bothers any longer to ask herself this question, which, in any case, she has never succeeded in answering. All she knows is that she loves Acland now and has loved him for as long as she can remember.

When they were both children and their two families constantly met, she loved him as a brother, perhaps. Her own brother, Roland, whom she idolized and who was much older, could be censorious on the subject of Acland. Acland needed discipline, Roland claimed; Acland was wild, but the right school eventually would tame him.

The right school did no such thing, but Roland did not live to see that, because he went away to Africa to fight in the Boer War and never returned. After Roland died . . . Was it then? But no, Jane was only eleven then and still too young, so it must have been later, perhaps when she was fifteen or sixteen, that she finally realized the feelings she had for Acland were not sisterly.

One occasion she remembers vividly. She and Fanny Arlington, who was her best friend, whose father's land bordered her father's land—Fanny, with whom she shared a governess; Fanny, who was sweet-tempered and featherbrained, who had curly blond hair and eyes blue as hyacinths—they were both at Winterscombe, with Hector (Fanny's brother) and Boy and Freddie and Acland. It was spring. The boys climbed one of the oak trees; she and Fanny stood and watched them.

Higher and higher, and which of them—of course—had to go highest of all? Why, Acland. Twenty feet up, thirty. Hector and Acland's brothers gave up; Acland continued climbing. Jane stood in silence and watched. Beside her, Fanny fluttered her hands and clasped them; she sighed and gasped and called out admonitions in a voice Jane had never heard her use before, until quite suddenly a bitter thought sprang into Jane's mind and lodged there. Fanny was *encouraging* Acland: "Oh, no further!" she would cry, and "Please don't, Acland—you'll fall. I cannot bear it." And Acland would mount a foot or two more, and the oddest, most complacent smile came upon her friend's face as he did so.

Was this performance of Acland's, then, for Fanny's benefit? Jane became convinced that it was. For the first time in her life she experienced jealousy. It sliced into her mind; for a moment she hated her friend, hated her for her curly hair and her hyacinth eyes, and hated Acland, who must be doing this for Fanny's benefit. Acland, who presumably did not care—why should he?—that Fanny was stupid.

Jane, then, would have liked to shout aloud: Look at me, she wanted to cry; look at *me*, Acland. I can speak French and construe Latin. I have a quick mind for mathematics. I am interested in politics. I read poetry and philosophy, which makes Fanny yawn and turn up her eyes. All those things, and more, she would have liked to cry. And yet what was the point, for what were such accomplishments, and what man or boy would care for them? You could *talk* to me, Acland, she wanted to cry . . . and she turned away from the tree, knowing it was hopeless, for why should Acland want to talk when he could gaze at delicate pink cheeks and hyacinth eyes?

I am plain, Jane thought, realizing her plight fully for the first time, and just at that moment, when she felt the most bitter regret, Acland climbed down. He jumped the last twelve feet, rolled over on the grass, and sprang up unhurt.

Fanny rushed to him. She must brush his jacket and cling to his arm and assure herself he was safe. Acland unexpectedly—and, to Jane, triumphantly—pushed her aside.

"Don't hang on me, Fanny. It bores me," he said.

No attempt to disguise the rebuke. Fanny's eyes rounded in dismay. Acland walked away.

Well, that was a long time ago. Fanny married at eighteen and lives in Northumberland now and has two children, and Jane, still her best friend, is godmother to the first. Jane visits her twice a year, and sometimes, when they talk about the old days, Jane suspects that Fanny *knows* of her feelings toward Acland. Nothing precise is ever said, but somehow the hints are there, and this throws Jane into a panic. *No one* must know her feelings for Acland. She never speaks of them, never admits them, not even to her closest confidante, her Aunt Clara. They are her secret, lodged in her heart, and she hugs that secret to her. It is a quick, bright, painful thing, her love for Acland; Jane protects it fiercely.

If Acland guessed at her feelings, Jane knows he would bring their friendship to an end. Meanwhile—because Acland does not know, does not suspect—they can be friends. They can meet constantly, play tennis, dance one regulation dance together at their friends' balls, ride occasionally, walk. . . . Walk, and talk—above all, talk—and those conversations, which Acland probably forgets the instant they are over, are precious to Jane. For years she has recorded them in her journals, noting Acland's most casual remarks in painstaking detail. Sometimes, although she knows them by heart, she will read them over, trying to see in them a pattern, and in that pattern the lineaments, the sense, of the man she loves.

Such a nihilist! Jane will think sometimes as she reads. Acland seems to believe in nothing: He decries the religion he is made to practice; he denies the existence of a god. He takes a perverse delight in denying all the other beliefs sacred to his family and his class. Patriotism; the benign and civilizing influence of an aristocracy? Acland will have none of it. The sanctity of womanhood? Marriage? On these subjects, too, he can be scathing—although Jane has noticed that his sarcasm is directed at these targets less of late.

Acland, Jane tells herself, is a radical, a freethinker—and that is part of his attraction for her, of course. He is, to an extent, her surrogate, exploring heresies Jane knows to exist but from which she herself shrinks.

And then, for all his nihilism, there is much to admire in Acland. He is fierce in his loyalties, obdurate in his rejection of hypocrisy, considerate to those he loves or respects. Acland is noble, Jane tells herself; his faults are large, not petty. He is impatient, impetuous, arrogant, certainly—but then he is very clever, so Jane would expect a certain arrogance of mind. There is nothing wrong with Acland that could not be cured; sometimes Jane catches herself thinking this, and she knows the corollary: Acland could be cured . . . *by the love of a good woman.*

This thought checks Jane. She sees Acland as he could be in the future: quieter, more stable, kindlier; Acland, a contented man. *I could save Acland from himself;* that idea, too, will steal into her mind. She is always careful to dismiss it. As far as Acland is concerned, she is a friend. Beyond that, he is blind to her. It is not a situation likely to change.

Yes, Acland likes her; he seems to respect her mind. Just occasionally, Jane finds this unbearable.

Now, standing in the damp grass, while Boy still fulminates on the question of damp grass, chilled feet, and the fragility of womankind, Jane turns away. She sets her face in its usual mask of casual indifference.

Acland is showing signs of impatience. Boy is being adamant. There is a cloakroom, he points out (an untidy cloakroom, nicknamed the hellhole); in that cloakroom are innumerable pairs of galoshes. One pair must surely fit Jane.

"Oh, for God's sake, Boy," Acland says with sudden irritation, and looks at his watch. "Are we going to play tennis or not? We've wasted half the afternoon already."

"I merely thought," Boy begins in a ponderous way, and Acland throws his racquet down on the grass.

"I'll get them then, if you insist. But you're being ridiculous. Jane doesn't want the damn things anyway."

With which Acland disappears into the house. Boy starts to

apologize, thinks better of it, sinks down onto a garden bench, then rises again until Jane is seated.

They wait five minutes. Jane tells herself (as she has done before) that Boy is kind, that when he is being most annoying—as he is now—it is because he so lacks confidence and therefore must be assertive in trivial matters. She begins to add up his good qualities: He is honest; he is honorable. She reminds herself of her age—twenty-two and humiliatingly old, given her fortune, to be still unmarried.

Ten minutes have gone by. Boy has remarked on the weather twice. Now he looks at his watch and rises to his feet.

"What on earth can Acland be doing?" he remarks to the sky. "All he had to do was find a pair of galoshes— Oh." He breaks off. From the darkness of the doorway Acland emerges. The light catches his hair, his face is lifted to the sun, and he is laughing, as if at a remark just made and broken off. Behind him, clutching a pair of black galoshes, is the maid Jenna.

"At last," Boy says with reproach in his voice, but Acland ignores that.

"Do you *know* how many pairs of galoshes there are in there? Thirty at least. And all mismatched, and half of them with holes, and then I had to guess the size—for Jane's feet are very small—and then, luckily, Jenna was passing, and so . . ."

"Thank you, Jenna," Jane says, and takes the galoshes from the maid. Cursing Boy and mustering what dignity she can, she puts on the galoshes. She stands, takes a step or two. The galoshes make a squelching, rubbery noise. Jane stops, blushes with humiliation, sees the amusement in Acland's face.

"Can we go now, Boy?" she asks sharply, and Boy takes her arm. They have progressed a short way along the grassy path before they notice that Acland is not following. He has thrown down his racquet, stretched out on the garden bench.

"Acland," Boy calls. "Aren't you coming? That fellow Jarvis will be waiting. I said we'd make a four."

"Changed my mind. Don't feel like it. It's too hot for tennis," Acland calls in a careless way. Boy pauses, as if he might argue, and then changes his mind. He walks on at a faster pace.

"Just as well, really. Acland has such a devil of a serve," he says more cheerfully. Jane nods agreement, scarcely listening. All color has gone from the afternoon; it is now without Acland and without expectation. Already she has begun to erase the next few hours from her mind and to think ahead. Tea—she will see Acland at tea. And then this evening, and she will wear the green dress and the agate necklace.

"Hates losing though. And shows it," Boy adds. "Not that he does very often." Arm in arm, they round a large and gloomy yew hedge, turn a corner, walk between the herbaceous borders in the direction of the tennis court.

"Very fine, these," Boy says, when they are halfway down, gesturing to right and left. "In the right season, of course."

Jane glances up at him in surprise. Boy always makes this remark but usually waits until they have reached the end of the border. "When the roses are out," Jane answers, as she always does. One last time, she glances back.

Trees and shrubs, the great bulge of black yew. Only the roof of Winterscombe can now be seen, and Acland is invisible.

"Now," Acland says, the second Jane and his brother have rounded the yew hedge. "Now, Jenna."

He takes her hand. He draws her back from the doorway and out into the sun.

He lifts her hands, both of them, presses his own palms flat against them, and stands still, looking down into her face. They remain in this way, neither moving, neither speaking, for some while. Jenna is the first to step away.

"It can't be now. There's things I'm to do. Ironing. Miss Conyngham's dress—I've to iron that, for this evening."

"How long to iron a dress?"

"Ten minutes. Fifteen maybe. Unless it's too crushed from the packing."

"And then?"

"Very little. Lay out her things. That's all. I unpacked her cases this morning."

"We have an hour then. Nearly an hour."

"No, we don't. I'll have to be back for four. She'll change for tea. She may ring for me."

"My love."

Acland, who has been still all this while, suddenly moves. With a new agitation he presses Jenna's palm against his lips. Jenna can sense both his urgency and his anger—in Acland the two are always closely allied. She stands quietly, looking up into his eyes; a grave look, a still look. It is the tranquility of Jenna that he loves, Acland thinks, a gift she possesses and he does not.

"Snatches," he bursts out at last, knowing it would be better not to speak but unable to stop himself. "That is all we ever have. Snatches of time. An hour here, a few minutes there. I don't want that. I hate that. Everything and nothing. Lies and subterfuge. I despise it. I loathe it. I want . . ."

"Say it. Say what it is you want."

"Time. Our time. All the time in the world. An eternity of time. It still wouldn't be enough. I'd *die* wanting more time."

"Everyone dies that way," Jenna says drily. "I reckon."

She tightens her arms around his neck. She knows these storms that spring up in Acland; she also knows that she can cure them—with her body. Glancing over her shoulder first, she draws Acland closer. She presses his hand against her breast. They kiss. Jenna intends that they should kiss, then part—but this does not happen. It never happens. Once they touch, the need is intense. Acland pulls her back into the doorway, out of sight, then into the cloakroom beyond. It is shadowy there, pressed up against coats; they are both breathing fast. Acland kicks the door shut, opens her mouth under his.

"Quickly. Here. We can do it here. No one will come in." Acland has undone her dress. Still he has to fight his way through under-bodice and petticoats to touch her skin.

"This stuff—damn this stuff. Why must you wear so much of it?"

"Keeps me decent." Jenna has begun to laugh. "I'm a decent girl. Don't fight it so. Look, it's easy."

And she parts her bodice, so her breasts spill out.

"Decent? Decent?" Acland, too, has begun to laugh. He whispers the words against her hair. Her breasts feel heavy in his hands, full and slightly damp. In the cleft between her breasts there is a runnel of sweat. He licks it. Her skin tastes of salt and smells of soap. "*Decent* is a horrible word. An obscene word. I should hate you to be decent—"

"It's Jack's word. That's what he says—"

"Damn Jack. Jack is an alibi, that's all. Forget about him. Come here—"

"Come and get me—"

Jenna darts away, laughing again. Acland makes a grab for her. His arm comes around her waist. He swings her up and off her feet. The next moment they are tumbling back against the coats, onto the floor. They roll across the floor, panting, struggling, laughing. They kiss again. Acland is the first to draw back.

"I can't make love to you on a pile of old galoshes. Well, I could . . ."

"I can tell that," Jenna says.

"But I won't. Come outside, to the birch grove."

"What about the dress? I must iron that dress."

"Damn and blast that dress—"

"Oh, I'll say that, shall I, to Miss Conyngham?"

Jenna kneels; she presses her mouth against his. Acland feels her tongue flicker across his lips; her breasts brush against his palms. Her eyes, which slant upward in her face and are full of light, tease him.

"I'll come. But I'll do that dress first. Skip the petticoats—she'll not notice. Ten minutes—you can wait that long."

"I can't."

"If I can, you can. You'll have to."

Jenna can be firm; she is always practical. Now, she buttons up her dress with quick deft fingers. The beautiful breasts are hidden away, the starched bib of her apron pinned back in place, her hair—in considerable disarray—twisted expertly back and pinned in a loop at her neck.

Acland watches with fascination. He watches her hold the hair-pins between her teeth, watches her bend her neck, gather the hair, twist it, pin it; it is done in a matter of seconds. Acland loves this matter-of-factness in Jenna; he loves to watch her dress or undress; he loves the absence of coyness.

The first time—and Acland will never forget the first time— they went to the boathouse, down by the lake. Acland was in a torment of physical desire and mental anguish. His heart raced; his body pulsed; his mind popped with questions, arguments, justifications, explanations. He was then sixteen, a virgin, as was Jenna. It seemed to Acland that to explain to Jenna that he loved her was a matter of terrible magnitude. He could not lay one hand on her until he was quite sure she understood that. On the other hand it was becoming pressingly urgent to touch her, and not to speak at all. Acland stood in the boathouse, scarlet with emotion, torn by instinct, a highly developed intelligence, and an education—an expensive education—that had always emphasized the primacy of words.

Jenna, standing a few feet away, frowned at the water. Its reflection made patterns of light and shade on her face; her mouth, then her eyes, seemed to dissolve in its brightness. She turned, gave the still-silent Acland a long and considering look. Then, without a word, she began to undress. She took off all her clothes, as neatly and practically as she now, in the cloakroom, refastened them. She folded them in a small pile. She unpinned her hair. She stood in front of Acland, the first woman he had seen naked. Her skin was roseate. Her body's curves astonished him. Light moved against her thighs and her breasts. He stared at the unexpected darkness of her nipples, at the secret lineaments of legs, arms, waist, throat, hair.

"Let's," Jenna said.

Jenna, Jenna, Jenna, Acland thinks now, leaving the house, taking the path that leads to the birch grove. He does not say her name aloud, but the words are like a great shout of triumph in his mind. In the distance, over the woods, the black rooks rise from the branches, as if they, too, heard that silent shout and were disturbed by it.

They circle, cry their raucous cries, then settle. *I have found my religion,* Acland the unbeliever thinks to himself—and, because his mind still delights in ideas, paradoxes, ironies, he smiles to himself, develops the notion in his mind, toys with it.

By two-thirty Steenie is asleep. Constance, who has been waiting for this moment, creeps into his room and looks down at him. His cheeks are faintly flushed; he breathes evenly.

On two occasions in the past—once as a baby, with croup, once when he was eight years old and contracted the deadly scarlet fever—Steenie almost died. Constance wonders if it is the fact that he was twice so close to death that makes his mother love him. But it cannot just be that. Gwen also loves Boy and Acland and Freddie, and they are all strong and healthy; they never had to rest every afternoon, as Steenie does.

Constance frowns. Perhaps if she herself were close to death—would that make her father care? Would he sit by her bedside right through the night, the way Gwen told her she did when Steenie was ill? *He might,* Constance thinks. He might, even though he is a man and always so busy. Busy, busy, busy—that is the problem: busy writing and must not be disturbed, busy changing to go to a party or to make a speech at some literary gathering, busy even when just sitting in a chair, because when he is sitting (he once told her impatiently) he is occupied; he is thinking.

Hate him being busy, Constance thinks; hate him being here, at Winterscombe, where he is busier than ever, busy with Gwen, always with Gwen. . . . Constance clasps her hands, twists around in an odd tight little pirouette of rage. She would like to stamp her foot or cry or tear something or smash something. But she must not do that—she must not wake Steenie. If Steenie wakes, she will never get away.

She tiptoes to the door and peeps through into the day nursery, and yes, it is safe. No sign of Steenie's governess, and old Nanny Temple, who must be a hundred (she was Denton's nurse, which is unimaginable), is fast asleep by the fire. Easy! Constance creeps past her, out into the corridor, and along to the back stairs. One floor down and she is at the far end of the East Wing. Here there is a maids' service room, where the hatboxes and trunks are unpacked and the dresses of the women guests can be hung up, sponged, and pressed.

She peeps into the room. There is a maid there, ironing one of the frocks. Constance can feel the heat of the stove used to warm the irons; she can smell the hot scent of drying cotton and linen. She edges around the door, and the maid starts, then smiles at her.

Constance knows this maid. Her name is Jenna; she lives in the village with the Hennessy family, for she is an orphan, and she is walking out with the head carpenter's son, Jack Hennessy. Constance has seen them together in the village; she has watched their sedate walks with interest. She has also watched other assignations of Jenna's which were much less sedate. Jenna, she hopes, does not know this.

Jenna changes irons; Constance sidles into the room.

"Miss Conyngham's dress," Jenna says, indicating the flounces of silk. She holds the new iron close to her face to test its warmth and then eases it, with an expert hand, along a length of frilling. "I'm dressing her tonight. Doing her hair for her. Everything."

Constance looks at Jenna with scorn. Jenna, it is true, has a lovely face. She has long, heavy hair, and that hair shines, is the color of chestnuts. Her complexion is clear, and—Constance resents this—she has particularly beautiful eyes, of a dark hazel color; their gaze, which is steady, is also perceptive. Not a fool, Jenna. However, her hands, damaged by housework, are square and reddened, and she has a marked country accent. Constance prefers to think of her as stupid. Jenna looks content to be doing this task, even proud, and Constance finds that pathetic. Why be proud to iron another woman's dress? Proud to wear it, perhaps—but to press it?

"It's an ugly color," Constance says. "Green. Nasty dark-green. Green isn't fashionable, not in London."

The maid looks up and stares at her. Then she says quietly, "Ah, well. It looks pretty enough to me. I dare say it will do—in the country."

There is possibly a mild reproach in that remark. Constance looks at Jenna more carefully, and the maid, who cannot be stern for long, as Constance knows, gives a sudden smile; her cheeks dimple.

"See." She puts her reddened hand into the pocket of her apron. "I kept you something. Don't say where it came from, mind now. And don't let no one catch you. You're supposed to be resting." She holds out to Constance a little sweetmeat, one of the *petits fours* Gwen serves with coffee. It is a tiny marzipan fruit bedded in a wisp of chocolate, an apple tinted green and pink, with a clove for a stem and strips of angelica for leaves.

"Don't you go swallowing the clove now. Leave that bit. I don't want you choking."

Constance takes the sweet. She knows she should thank Jenna, but somehow the words will not be spoken; they stick in her throat, as thanks always do. Constance knows this is one of the reasons everyone hates her.

The maid seems not to mind, though; she just nods at Constance and goes back to her ironing. She seems anxious to finish it and her hands move deftly. Constance edges back to the door. She studies Jenna a moment—Jenna, who is only a few years older than she is; Jenna, who is sixteen and content with her lot; Jenna, who will always be a servant—and then, with a jerky little movement she runs out, down the back stairs, and out into the gardens.

There, hidden by a bush, she pauses. Some guests are outside; she can hear the murmur of their voices in the distance. But not her father's. Where will her father have gone after luncheon? Constance's head lifts, like an animal's. She waits for a moment, listening, calculating, and then—keeping out of sight of the house—runs in the direction of the woods.

When she reaches the woods she is more careful. She pauses to catch her breath, chooses judiciously the path she will take. Not the main paths, of which there are two: one leading in the direction of the village and one to a small Gothic folly, which Gwen, stupid Gwen, calls a gazebo. No, neither of those paths; Constance ducks aside, and takes a small track. This track, narrow and overgrown, winds its way around to the far side of the wood, on the other side of the coverts. Only the keepers are supposed to use it, but they do so infrequently, preferring the more direct route from the village.

Here it is quiet, still, a little frightening; here you are unlikely to meet anyone else. Constance, however, knows that other people use this path besides herself, for that reason. Her father uses this path; Gwen Cavendish uses this path. Constance has spied on them—oh, yes, Constance has seen them.

It is muddy here, and brambles catch at her skirt; young nettles brush her ankles and sting her, but Constance does not pause. She does not take any of the other little tracks. She presses on, deeper into the woods, toward the clearing.

Still, she must be watchful; Constance knows this. She scans the undergrowth ahead, for there are traps in these woods, and not just for animals. Cattermole uses man-traps, Freddie told her, to catch the poachers. Freddie described them. There are steel traps with jagged jaws that close on a man's leg. There are pit traps, with sharpened staves, for the unwary. Constance was not sure she believed Freddie when he told her this with such relish. Man-traps, she knows, have been illegal for some years. Even so, she intends to be careful.

Every few yards she stops, listens, pokes at the undergrowth ahead of her, but there is nothing there—just celandine, the scent of wild garlic, and silence. All the same, Constance is a little frightened; when she reaches the clearing she is out of breath. Here the grass is short and safe. She sits down, panting. Will Gwen come this afternoon? Will her father? It must be past three o'clock by now. If they do come, it will be soon.

Then, just as she is lying back on the grass, feeling its coolness and dampness seep through her dress, she hears the noise. A rustling, then silence; then a rustling again.

She sits up, startled, ready to run away. She hears the sound again, just behind her, in a mound of brambles. She sits as still as a stone, listening to her heart hammering; then she realizes how foolish she is being. No person could make such a little noise. It must be an animal, a small animal.

And when she goes to investigate, parts the thorns and foliage, bends down, she sees a rabbit. At first she cannot understand why it does not run away, why it is twitching and jerking like that, and then she sees the snare around its neck, the thin twist of wire. With every jerk the wire noose is tightening.

Constance gives a little cry of dismay. She bends to the rabbit; the rabbit, terrified, jerks more vigorously.

"Oh, keep still, keep still," Constance cries aloud.

No way of releasing the noose from the neck—it is too tight and the rabbit is bleeding. She must first unwind it from the sticks it is fixed to—and that is hard. The job has been done well, cunningly. She twists and pushes, tugs at the sticks. The rabbit is still now, just a tremor of movement, and Constance feels a surge of hope and happiness. The rabbit *knows;* it *knows* she is rescuing it.

There! The snare is released from the sticks. She can lift the rabbit clear of the undergrowth, which she does.

Very gently, cradling the rabbit in her arms—it is only a small rabbit, almost a baby—she brings it back to the grass of the clearing and lays it in the sun.

She kneels down, strokes the gray fur, wipes at the runnels of blood with her petticoat. The rabbit lies on its side; one eye, almond-shaped, looks up at her. She must disentangle the noose now, Constance thinks, untwist it. . . . She reaches forward, and the rabbit convulses.

Constance draws back in terror. The rabbit's head lifts, jerks, falls. Its paws scrabble at the earth. It urinates. A tiny drop of blood drips from one nostril. Then it lies still. Constance knows at once that it is dead. She has never seen a dead animal before, let alone a dying one, but she knows for certain. Something is happening to the rabbit's eye. As she looks at it she can see it is clouding.

Constance kneels back on her heels; she is trembling. There is a tight pain in her chest. She cannot swallow. She knows she would like to scream; she knows she would like to kill the person who did this.

Suddenly, wildly, she jumps up. She picks up a stick; she whirls around the circle of the clearing, smashing at the undergrowth, at the nettles, the brambles, the places where more snares might be hidden. And then she sees it. Just to the right of the track she came by, disguised by branches she has now knocked aside. She stops, lets the stick fall, stares down in disbelief.

There is the man-trap, just the way Freddie described it. A metal mouth, two jaws of steel edged with rusty teeth, a springing device; in the sunshine the jaws grin at her.

Constance stands very still for a moment. Does the trap still work? It must be an old one, a broken one. . . . Constance looks more closely. It does not look broken. The undergrowth around it is trampled, as if it were newly placed. The branches that were over it, the ones she moved, are freshly cut; their leaves are only just wilting.

She stares at the trap for a long time, fascinated and repelled, tempted to poke at it with a stick, frightened to do so but wanting to know for certain if it works. The jaws grin; the branches of the trees lift in the breeze and fall. Quite suddenly Constance loses interest in the trap. She has remembered the time; it must be three-thirty by now. The wood is silent; her father must not be coming. She will go and look for him.

But first she must bury the rabbit. She cannot just leave him.

She goes back to the rabbit, touches its fur, which is still warm. The blood on the fur is drying. Poor rabbit. Sweet rabbit. She will make a fine grave for him.

She picks up her stick again, selects a place, scratches at the earth under a small birch tree. The ground is soft after weeks of spring rain, but even so the job is difficult. Discarding the stick, she digs with her bare hands. It hurts her hands and tears the nails, but she manages it. After some fifteen minutes she has made a shallow indentation in the earth. Into this, absorbed, concentrated, Constance lays a bed of pebbles, then covers the pebbles with grass. The grave looks inviting now, a nest, a bed for her rabbit. She picks some of the wildflowers from the edge of the clearing: yellow celandine, a violet, two early half-opened primroses.

These she lays around the edge of the grave, kneeling back on her heels to admire her handiwork. Then, gently, she picks up the rabbit. She lays it in the grave, on its side, and puts a celandine between its front paws to take with it on its journey. Then she covers the body of the rabbit with tufts of sweet grass. At first she lays the grass so the rabbit's head is still uncovered, so it looks as if it has a green quilt. Then—she does not want the earth to go in the rabbit's eye—she covers its face. A sprinkling of earth; more earth; she tamps it down firmly and rearranges grass and leaves on top of the mound.

Her rabbit. Her secret rabbit. Constance kneels beside the mound, head bent. It is only when she pushes a strand of hair back from her face that she realizes there are tears on her cheeks. Sweet rabbit. Secret rabbit. Is it for the rabbit that Constance—who never weeps—has been crying?

From his perch in the branches of the oak tree, Freddie has a commanding view. In one direction he can look down the path from the woods to the estate village; in the other he can look back across the lawns to the house. He himself cannot be seen, which is precisely why he has come here.

Freddie leans back, settles himself as comfortably as he can, with his back against the trunk of the tree, his bottom well supported by a smooth branch. Then, smiling to himself, he extracts from his pockets the cigarette he purloined that morning from Acland's bedroom. He unwraps the paper he has secreted it in, lights it, and inhales. He coughs a little, but not very much, and he is pleased with himself: He is making progress.

The first cigarette (cadged from Cattermole, hand-rolled) made him violently sick, which caused Cattermole great amusement. Since then, Freddie has been practicing: one a day, occasionally two—no more, or Acland might notice his supply was depleted. Acland's cigarettes, the best Virginian tobacco, supplied by a firm in London, are a great improvement on Cattermole's. They are mild yet pungent; they produce in Freddie an agreeable light-headedness. He now has it down to a fine art: the whole business of lighting the cigarette, wafting it around in a devilish sophisticated manner, and finally extinguishing it. He has modeled his performance on that of the actor Gerald du Maurier, whom he saw playing the gentleman burglar Raffles a few years previously. Du Maurier, the man Freddie most admires in the whole world, had a certain way of holding his cigarette which Freddie is hell-bent on copying. Now, he feels he has succeeded; slightly narrowed eyes—that was it—the tube of tobacco held at a negligent and rakish angle . . .

He makes the cigarette last and extinguishes it with reluctance. He consults his pocket watch—almost three—considers what he might do now the high point of the afternoon is over.

In the distance, from the village, a thin column of woodsmoke rises into the clear spring sky. From his vantage point Freddie can see two men standing on the path from the woods, talking. The one leaning against the gate is Cattermole; the other—Freddie squints—the other is Jack Hennessy, son to his father's head carpenter. Hennessy has a clutch of sons, all of whom work on the estate, and this son, Jack, is walking out with one of the Winterscombe maids, the plump pretty one called Jenna. Freddie has gleaned this information from his valet, Arthur Tubbs, a thin, acned Cockney boy brought down from the London house and not greatly liked by the other servants, most of whom are local. Freddie does not much like Arthur either, but he is a source of information, particularly on the subject of girls.

Arthur's information in this department is a great deal more vivid than the often-conflicting information Freddie has received from boys at his school. The remarks concerning Jenna and Jack Hennessy were rather less welcome. A few years before, when he was thirteen, Freddie conceived an unspoken and unrequited passion for Jenna, so that when Arthur said she and Jack were courting, Freddie experienced a brief bout of jealousy. Now, however, that has worn off, and Freddie realizes it was foolish. No point in mooning about a maid, even a pretty one. Another year or so and Freddie will enjoy much more satisfactory conquests.

He turns his head. Cattermole and Jack Hennessy have broken apart; Cattermole has turned back to the village; Hennessy is striding in the direction of the woods. Freddie looks toward the house and gardens, where Boy and that pansy art fellow from London, Jarvis, have been playing tennis; Boy is handing his racquet to Jane Conyngham, and Jane, standing on the base line, has just served underarm straight into the net.

Boy does not stay to watch her play, Freddie observes, and grins to himself. They all know why Jane Conyngham is here today: She is here because Denton and Gwen have plans for her. They intend her to marry their eldest son, thus securing for Boy an estate of twelve thousand acres and an income conservatively estimated at fifty thousand pounds a year. Jane Conyngham does not interest Boy in the least, of course. For which Freddie does not blame him.

Freddie looks scornfully at Jane's distant figure. Tall, thin, gawky. She has straight sandy hair and a narrow, freckled, sandy little face. She wears spectacles for reading (and she is always reading). What is more, the stupid woman cannot hit a tennis ball. Even Jarvis looks as if he is losing patience.

Freddie is growing bored; he feels the need for company. Perhaps he should wander back to the house? His eyes scan the terrace. But no, there is no sign of diversion there—just old Mrs. Fitch-Tench, who is fast asleep over her crocheting. Freddie's mother is just going back into the house—Freddie sees her close her parasol and disappear from view—and Eddie Shawcross, whom Freddie does not much like, is wandering around the side of the house in a distracted way, glancing once or twice over his shoulder.

Freddie watches until Shawcross also disappears into the house, probably making for the library. Freddie begins to climb down from his perch. He will go and seek out Acland, he decides. Acland may prefer to be on his own—he usually does—but that is just too bad. Freddie, a gregarious boy, feels in need of conversation. Also, he is considering whether he might admit to Acland the truth about the cigarettes, whereupon Acland might—might—give him another.

And he knows exactly where Acland will be. By the birch grove, in the gazebo. He goes there now almost every afternoon.

When Freddie finds Acland, he is indeed in the gazebo, sitting on one of the seats with a book in front of him. Freddie, catching sight of him from a distance, assumes Acland has been there some while. When he enters the gazebo, however, he wonders. First, Acland does not seem pleased to see him. Second, Acland is out of breath, as if he has been running, and third, the book in Acland's hand—a novel by Sir Walter Scott—is upside down.

Freddie wonders whether to comment on this and decides it would not be politic. Acland has a secretive side; he does not like to be spied on. "The trouble with this damned house," Acland will frequently remark, "is that it's impossible to be alone in it."

Instead, Freddie flops down on the stone seat and mops his brow. He is feeling the weight he has put on this past winter, and the waistband of his new plus-four trousers is definitely too tight. Stupid tailors. He should not have eaten two helpings of pudding at luncheon. Thinking of the luncheon brings back the scene with his father, and Freddie lets out a sigh.

"God, what a day. First I lose to you at croquet. Then that fellow Shawcross bored me to death. Then Father made that terrible scene. I didn't know what to do! My face was like a beetroot, and I haven't blushed for a year and a half. I thought I'd stopped. Did you notice?"

"Not particularly." Acland now has his book the right way up. His face is bent to its pages.

"Damned embarrassing." Freddie has been practicing swearing as well as cigarette smoking. "Why are we saddled with a father like that? I ask you—no one else we know has to put up with a lunatic for the head of the family."

"Lunatic?" Acland looks up. "Would you say so?"

"Yes, I would," Freddie says in robust tones. "I think he's crackers. Mad as a March hare. Always in a foul temper. Flies off the handle for no reason whatsoever. Mutters to himself. He drank his shaving water the other morning. Arthur told me."

"Arthur is hardly a reliable source of information."

"It's true. In fact, if you want to know, I think Father's going senile. I mean, he could be, couldn't he? He's as old as Methusaleh, and he dribbles—have you noticed? When he drinks his wine. And he farts. He let off the most enormous one the other night. I was playing billiards with him, and he leant over the table and—woof! —out it came. Sounded like a gun going off. Then he glared at the dog, as if he did it, and kicked it out the room. As if that would fool anybody. . . . And he's foul to Mama. He's foul to Boy. He's foul to everybody. Getting Boy those embarrassing guns, when he *knows* Boy hates shooting and isn't any good at it anyway. And his own shooting—well, you've seen. Even Cattermole was worried, he told me. He can't control the gun at all anymore. It wiggles around all over the place. He nearly winged Shawcross last November. I mean, I know Shawcross was wearing that frightful hat, but that's hardly an excuse, is it? You can't shoot a man because he doesn't know how to dress properly. I tell you, he's mad. Look at that scene at luncheon. I thought he was going to explode. All right, so it was rude of Shawcross, all that stuff about the pictures—did you see how he looked at them? Personally I can't see what's wrong with them. The greyhound one's damned good, if you ask me, jolly lifelike, but—"

"It was nothing to do with the pictures. Or Shawcross's remark." Acland closes the book. He looks at Freddie with an expression of mingled exasperation and amusement. He feels in his pocket, checks his watch, then produces his gold cigarette case. "You'd like one, I take it, Freddie?"

Freddie, to his consternation, blushes again. He hesitates.

"Well, it appears to be one a day now, occasionally two. You pinched one this morning, so I thought you might like another."

"Acland . . . I . . ."

"For God's sake. If you want one, take one. It might make you stop talking. With luck, it might make you go away."

There is a pause. Freddie lights up, hoping Acland will notice the Du Maurier proficiency; perhaps Acland does, for he smiles narrowly but makes no comment. He, too, lights a cigarette, inhales, exhales, leans back against the walls of the gazebo thoughtfully.

"What provoked the outburst," Acland continues after a while, "what occasioned it, was Boy's remark. Didn't you notice?"

"Boy? No. I was listening to that pansy fellow Jarvis. Boy was talking to plain Jane. I think he was talking to plain Jane."

"Indeed he was. Boy is nothing if not obedient." Acland stands up, wanders to the doorway, looks out. "Boy was talking to Jane, and Jane—who has a kind heart—was asking him about his photography. I must warn her not to do that, by the way. Once Boy is launched on that subject, he's unstoppable. So, we had a detailed list of all the photographs Boy had taken between breakfast and luncheon. The last one was of the King's bedroom. He was unwise enough to say so, and our father heard him. That's all."

Acland pronounces the phrase *King's bedroom* with distaste. Freddie goggles at him.

"That caused it? But why should it?"

"Because, Freddie, because that room is to be occupied for the first time in five years, this evening. By Shawcross, no less. Papa would prefer not to be reminded of that fact. He's sensitive about that room, as you know."

"And he doesn't like Shawcross."

"True. True."

"In fact, he can't stand him. Arthur told me. Arthur says it's because Shawcross isn't a gentleman—"

"And what do you think, Freddie?" Acland turns as he asks this question.

Freddie, surprised by a new note that has entered his brother's voice, frowns. "Well, *I* don't know. Maybe that. Shawcross *is* a cad. He's supercilious and vain, and he has horrible little white hands—have you noticed? Also, he wears those frightful suits." Freddie laughs. "You remember the ghastly blue one he wore with the brown shoes? And the hats . . ."

Acland begins to smile. He turns away, though, and Freddie has the feeling that Acland is concealing something from him.

"Of course," Acland says in his most flippant voice. "Of course, Freddie. How clever of you. I'm sure you're right. The suits, absolutely. And the hats . . ." He pauses. "Now push off, Freddie. I'm going for a walk. *On my own.*"

Freddie knows when his brother is mocking him; he gives Acland a grumpy look, a suspicious look, then sets off back toward the house.

Once he is out of sight, Acland throws down his book, glances to his right and left, turns toward the birch grove, and begins—after a few yards—to run.

Jenna is there before him. As soon as she sees him, she knows there is something wrong. Acland's face does not disguise emotion well; the effort to conceal his feelings from Freddie has left his face white with anger, his green eyes glittering.

Jenna knows that expression. She also knows who provokes it. This they have discussed, many times.

"Oh, Acland, Acland." She puts her arms around him. "Don't. Let it be. Don't think of him—"

"Don't think?" Acland jerks away. "How can I? He's here. I have to look at him. Sit at the same table with him. Pretend he's just a guest like all the other guests. Pretend I don't see the little smiles, the touches when they think no one's looking. It makes me want to—"

"Acland—"

"Have you noticed his hands? He has horrible small white hands—soft hands. He's vain of them. I think he puts something on them, some lotion—they stink of carnation. I look at his hands—they're never still, always gesturing, gesturing—and I think, she must like them. My mother must like those hands. How can she be so blind? How can they all be so blind? Shawcross. The family friend. The *writer.* I read his books—she made me read his books. Little thin cheap snide things—they made me want to vomit—"

"Acland don't, not now—"

"I could kill him, do you know that? I could actually kill him. Put him down, like a sick dog."

"You don't mean that—"

"Don't I? You're wrong. It would be easy enough. One shot. Or maybe my father will do it for me—I'm not sure he didn't try, last autumn. Except he missed. Unfortunately."

"That was an accident, Acland—"

"Was it? Or was it a warning? In which case he's been warned—six months ago—and he's still here. Insulting us. Smirking. Reeking of cheap scent. Rolling his tongue around titles. Using us and despising us. He despises my mother too. He doesn't love her—he doesn't even like her. He's always talking down to her. This painter, that writer—'Oh, but my dear Lady Callendar, haven't you read . . . ?' I'd like to get hold of his throat and shake and shake, so I never had to hear it again—that horrible mincing affected voice. How can she bear to listen to it—"

Jenna steps back. Acland is trembling with anger. The imitation of Shawcross (Acland is a good mimic) was exact.

"You shouldn't talk like that." She hesitates. "I don't know you, not when you talk that way."

Acland does not answer her. He stands still, in the center of the circle of birch, their shadows blueing his face. It is as if he does not see her at all.

"Shall I go?" Jenna says. "Maybe I'd better go. . . ." She starts to turn. This, at last, seems to reach Acland.

"No, don't. Jenna—" He catches hold of her, pulls her toward him roughly, looks at her face, touches her face, then angrily buries his head against her hair.

"Oh, God, oh, God, oh, God. Don't go. Let me touch you. Hold me, Jenna. Jenna—make it go away. Make it all go away."

"My goodness me. Where has everyone gone?"

Ancient Mrs. Fitch-Tench has roused herself from her slumbers. She has straightened her bent back as far as she can, mopped at her rheumy eyes with a handkerchief abstracted from the leathery object she still calls a reticule, and is now scanning the gardens. Mrs. Fitch-Tench may be deaf but she has excellent eyesight, particularly for distance. The gardens are empty.

"I don't know, Mrs. Fitch-Tench," Freddie says grumpily.

"What was that, my dear boy?"

"I said I don't know, Mrs. Fitch-Tench," Freddie shouts. "I expect people have gone to change. It will be time for tea presently."

"Tea? Tea? Surely not. We have only just had luncheon."

"It's almost four o'clock, Mrs. Fitch-Tench," Freddie yells. "Tea is at four-thirty. Luncheon was over hours ago. You've been asleep."

Mrs. Fitch-Tench looks offended.

"Nonsense, my dear Freddie. I never sleep. I was merely resting. I was quite alert—quite alert. Oh, dear me, yes . . . However, if we are to have tea soon, I shall perhaps go inside, as you say. . . ."

Freddie stands. He assists Mrs. Fitch-Tench to her feet, assists her with her reticule, parasol, crochet-bag, lorgnette case, slim volume of poems, and shawl. When Mrs. Fitch-Tench is safely stowed inside, Freddie returns to the terrace.

He feels grumpier than ever. He is guiltily aware, despite earlier resolutions, that he is hungry again. He is also bored, which does not improve his mood. He feels left out of things. There is no sign of his mother, or any of her guests. Boy is nowhere to be seen. Acland, Freddie has just glimpsed returning to the house via the side entrance, as if hoping no one will see him.

His father has also returned. Freddie glimpsed him pounding out of the woods like a bull elephant, puce in the face again, waving his arms and shouting at poor old Cattermole. Then he stumped across the terrace, his bitch Daisy at his heels, and disappeared into the house. He passed within inches of Freddie without appearing to notice his son's presence at all.

Lunatic! Freddie scowls at the harmonious view before him, checks his watch—ten minutes past four; tea in twenty minutes—and decides to return to his room to wash his hands. He will use extra tooth powder on his teeth—yes, better remove all scent of tobacco from his breath before he next encounters his mother.

Activity and the proximity of tea restore his good temper. Freddie goes into the house whistling. He pats the head of the stag shot on Denton's Scottish estates by Denton ten years ago. His humor improving by the minute, he bounds up the main stairs two at a time, turns down the corridor to the West Wing.

Segregation of the sexes is the practice at his mother's house parties. The West Wing is where the bachelor guest rooms are located, although (as Freddie well knows) no one seriously expects the bachelors to remain in them. Their ability to find the room of whichever women they seek is facilitated by Gwen's practice of placing name cards in slots on the outside of bedroom doors. In this way the proprieties are simultaneously observed and circumvented.

Passing doors, Freddie notes names. He glances toward the end of the corridor where, separated from the rest of the house by a small lobby, the King's bedroom is located. The best room in the house, with its own stairs down to the service quarters below. Freddie grins; tonight Edward Shawcross should be in clover.

Freddie's own room is on the second floor, almost directly above the King's bedroom. These are his and his elder brothers' quarters. Still whistling, he bangs on Acland's door, throws it open, and finds the room empty. He bangs on Boy's door, receives no response, and gives it an amiable kick.

It swings back to reveal Boy sitting on his bed. His head is clasped in his hands; he appears to be staring at the floor. On the bed next to him are his camera and his tripod.

"Tea!" Freddie shouts. "Come on, Boy, tea in fifteen minutes. Shake a leg! I say—" Freddie stops, stares at his brother. "Is something wrong? You look awfully greenish."

"I don't feel like tea." Boy looks up at Freddie. His face is pale. It has a greasy, streaked look to it, so that for a moment Freddie has the appalling suspicion that his eldest brother has been crying.

"Gosh, Boy. You do look queer. Are you all right?"

"Perfectly all right." Boy stands. He turns so that his back is toward his brother. He begins to fiddle, in a fussy way, with his tripod. "It's just hot up here. Airless. Damn this bloody thing."

This astonishes Freddie, for Boy never swears. He looks to see what could have caused the outburst.

"There's a nut missing," Freddie says in a helpful manner. "One of the wing nuts, from the legs. It won't stand up properly, not without that—"

"I know that, Freddie."

"I expect you've dropped it somewhere. Do you want me to look?"

"No. I don't. For God's sake, push off, will you, Freddie?"

To Freddie's astonishment, Boy rounds on him quite savagely.

"I can find it on my own. I don't need help. And I don't need you to explain the workings of a tripod—"

"All right, all right—only trying to help. There's no need to bite my head off. What's the matter with you anyway?"

"I told you. It's hot. I have a headache. Look, just leave me alone, will you?"

Making a face at Boy's back, Freddie does so.

Once in his own room, whistling again—first Acland in a bad mood, then Boy; well, the hell with both of them and their moods—

Freddie advances on his washstand. He is just about to embark on the teeth brushing when he pauses, turns. Did he see this as he came into the room? Yes, he did. There, on his bed, laid out for him by Arthur, are his evening clothes. Trousers, tail coat, white boiled shirt, and . . . Freddie stares. There, in the middle of the snowy shirt, there is . . . a sweet: one of the marzipan *petits fours* his mother serves with coffee. It lies inside a frilled paper case and so, fortunately, has not marked the shirt, despite the fact that it is melting.

Freddie is not amused. Is this Arthur's idea of a joke?

He jangles the service bell, then marches to the head of the back stairs.

"Arthur!" he bellows. "What the hell is the meaning of this?"

There is no answer, no sound of running feet. Freddie is about to slam back into his room when he hears—quite distinctly—a scream.

He stands still, considerably startled, thinking for a moment that he must have been mistaken.

But no, he hears it again, a second time. A woman's scream, or possibly a child's. Freddie listens, head on one side. The second scream is followed by complete silence. Whoever it was (Steenie, Constance, playing games?) and whatever happened, no one screams again.

"Get ready," Shawcross says as Gwen comes into his bedroom, the King's bedroom. He locks the door that leads out onto the West Wing corridor and gives the instruction over his shoulder, not looking at Gwen at all.

Gwen hesitates and, as Shawcross turns, reaches out her hand, as if to delay him or caress him. Shawcross brushes her hand aside; Gwen, whose lack of control Shawcross despises, gives a small moan. "And hurry up," Shawcross adds, for good measure. He has one reason for haste, one only, and a simple one: They have just over an hour at their disposal, and Shawcross wishes to make full use of it. Gwen, however, will waste half the time if he lets her. Without the assistance of her maid she is slow at undressing, just as she is slow at everything else: slow in her movements, slow in her responses, slow—come to that—in her thinking. Big, stately, clumsy, stupid Gwen. Shawcross wonders sometimes whether Gwen realizes that it is her stupidity, above all, that attracts her to him. Now, predictably, she has been hurt by his tone.

"Oh, Eddie," she says, and Shawcross, anxious not to waste further time on idiotic questions and reassurances, turns back to her with reluctance. He knows the quickest way to ensure Gwen's cooperation. He has used it before, and she has yet to see through it. Without preliminaries, staring down into her eyes, he rubs the palm of his hand against her breast.

Gwen changes her clothes at least four times a day, and so the oyster faille of the morning has been replaced by a luncheon gown of pale-blue crêpe de Chine. The material is thin; through its pleats and pin-tucks he feels the largeness of her breasts, the predictable hardening of her nipples. Gwen sighs, moves closer to him. Her eyes widen; the pupils dilate; her lips part.

When she looks thus, both loving and aroused, Shawcross despises her most. That expression on her face, which makes her look both beautiful and soulful, infuriates him. It makes him want to punish her.

Now, bending his head, he pushes his tongue between her lips. Gwen shudders, reaches for him, and Shawcross at once draws back.

"You wanted me, during luncheon. You were thinking about it. You were sitting opposite your husband, and you wanted it. Did you think I didn't know? What does that make you, Gwen?"

Gwen does not answer. To Shawcross's irritation she hangs her head, even though she knows what the answer should be; they have rehearsed it often enough.

Shawcross grips her chin in his hand; his fingers close on her mouth, distort its shape, squeeze it painfully.

"Come on. Answer me. What does that make you, Gwen?"

He relaxes his grip on her mouth; Gwen lifts her eyes to his.

"Wanton, Eddie," she says in a low voice. "It makes me wanton, wicked, like . . . like a whore."

Shawcross gives her a small tight smile by way of reward. It took three months of coaching to get this word past Gwen's lips; she still has relapses of infuriating modesty, when for several weeks the word will be withdrawn from the repertoire. Now it is back; that is something.

"And what effect did that have on me, Gwen?" He bends closer to her. "Come on. You know. Say it."

"It . . . it made you want me, Eddie."

"Precisely. It made me impatient. So. Hurry up. Get ready."

To his relief Gwen reaches for the small pearl buttons at the throat of her dress and begins to undo them one by one. Shawcross at once turns away. He knows full well that only two tactics can persuade Gwen to be hasty in her preparations for sex: One is impassioned declarations on his part; the other is insistence on the urgency of his male need. Of the two, insistence on the urgency of his own desire is preferable. It is quicker, less boring, and marginally more truthful, although truth is of little concern to Shawcross with Gwen, or any other woman.

Now, however, he has won. Gwen is actually undressing. With a sense of relief Shawcross pushes aside the curtains at the alcove, passes through the dressing room and into the bathroom. There, he takes out the black silk ribbons shown to Gwen that morning and runs them between his fingers. They are wide petersham ribbons, of the kind used to trim hats, and they are strong. Shawcross considers them, then replaces them in his pocket. He decides he will remain fully dressed, a variation employed once or twice before (though not, so far, with Gwen).

The decision at once arouses him; his penis, well attuned to the devices of his imagination, stirs, and hardens. Casting a cold look at the opulence of the bathroom fittings, Shawcross turns to the basin and washes his hands.

This hand-washing is important to him; he does it like a surgeon preparing to operate. Three times the hands are lathered with French soap that smells of carnations; three times they are rinsed. The nails are scrubbed. Shawcross will, on occasion, make love to a woman with hands that have not just been washed (in the woods, for instance, what is the alternative?) but he prefers it this way. All sex, to Shawcross, is dirty; its allure lies in his sense of degradation. In his fastidious mind he associates women with dirt; even when he touches them, even when he pushes his own flesh into their orifices, they disgust him. He loathes them, these soft, giving receptacles, with their seaweed odors, their wet and sticky effusions. Do they know, Shawcross wonders sometimes, how obscene they look, these women, with their fat milky breasts, their pale fleshy buttocks, their ugly wet purses of flesh?

They seem not to know. For this stupidity, not just because they are dirty, not just because they disgust him, Shawcross likes to punish them. And the ways of punishment are infinite: He can punish them by making them wait, until they are sweating for it, begging for it; he can punish them with his words. (When he makes love Shawcross is rarely silent, and no words of endearment ever pass his lips.) Above all, he can punish them with all the convenient weapons his body affords, with hands that can squeeze, pinch, slap, scratch; with teeth that can bite; with his weight; and with his sex, which Shawcross likes to watch as it plunges back and forth—like a sword, Shawcross thinks (with no great originality).

The more outwardly respectable the woman, the more exalted

her social position, the more Shawcross relishes this punishing. Bought women hold no interest for him; they have been humiliated too often by other men. But a married woman, a renowned woman, a virgin, or a wife who has never taken a lover—such women are a prize. To teach such virtuous women exactly what they are, to force them to acknowledge their need for him, that, for Shawcross, provides an excitement that transcends mere sex. Seduction, he might say if questioned by a man, is a kind of moral crusade.

Gwen of course thinks that she loves him. She probably even believes that he loves her, and so, in the name of love, all excesses can be justified. Well, Shawcross will disillusion her on that point in due course. To demonstrate his absolute contempt, to end an affair by expressing fully the distaste he has always felt and the disloyalty he has always practiced—that, for Shawcross, provides the final, most excruciating thrill.

With Gwen, that moment has not yet been reached. It lies (Shawcross considers as he dries his hands) perhaps five or six months further off. He does not find it quite as easy as he once did to replace his mistresses, and as a result of past indulgences a number of great houses (good hunting grounds) are now closed to him. Meanwhile, Gwen suffices; he enjoys her subjugation still, and besides, through Gwen he humiliates her husband.

Gwen, with her lazy, foolish mind *and* her lout of a husband: a double prize. Fingering the silk ribbons, Shawcross turns toward the bedroom, checks himself, remembers. There is another door to this suite of rooms: the door from the dressing room, which leads to the service stairs. It will be as well to lock it.

Shawcross pads through to the dressing room. He opens the service door, closes it again. There is no key in the lock, no bolt he can fasten. He pauses, considers: It is unlikely that anyone will disturb them at this hour; if the manservant assigned him for the evening were to come, he would certainly knock. Shawcross turns away, crosses to the bedroom, pauses in the doorway alcove, and (just to make doubly sure) draws the heavy velvet curtains across.

Gwen is waiting. She is sitting on a fat ottoman at the foot of the King's bed, leaning back against the pair of gilded cherubim. By now she has wit enough (Shawcross has taught her) not to undress fully. She sits there in her tight-waisted corset, quiet and patient, her hands clasped in her lap like a well-bred schoolgirl; her dress is neatly folded on a chair.

As Shawcross enters, her face lifts and her eyes light. Then, seeing he is still fully dressed, an expression of bewilderment crosses her features.

Shawcross moves to stand directly in front of her; he puts his hands in his pockets, rocks back and forth on his heels.

"You want it?" he begins.

"Eddie, I—"

"You want it, then say that you want it."

"I want you, Eddie. I love you."

"If you want it, then get it out."

Gwen colors. Her fingers (clumsy, clumsy Gwen) fumble against his crotch, but Shawcross will not help her. He waits, looking down at her, looking at the unnaturally tiny waist, the swell of her breasts above her stays. Below the waist she is naked (as instructed, many times). Shawcross can see the blue veins in her thighs, can glimpse the dark triangle of pubic hair. Her stomach, hidden from view by wisps and frills of organdy silk, is stretch-marked from childbirth, as are her upper thighs. Shawcross sometimes pinches these marks and comments on them, because he knows they make Gwen ashamed.

"In your mouth," Shawcross says as she parts his trousers and draws him out. "Tilt your head back," he adds, and Gwen, well-trained Gwen, who hates this, who was introduced to the practice by Shawcross, obliges.

She is not proficient at it, even now after months of tuition. Shawcross, hands in pockets, hands playing with the black silk ribbons, grows impatient and bored.

He dwindles in her mouth, pulls back. Gwen looks up, eyes wide with anxiety. Shawcross would like to hit her; nothing would give him greater satisfaction than to wipe that stupid fearful expression from her face with one blow. However, he restrains himself; the perfect use for the black ribbons has just occurred to him. Until now he had allowed himself only to imagine their possibilities in the most general terms. Now a specific scenario forms in his mind. He at once hardens again. Gwen gives a small triumphant moan of pleasure; she reaches for him.

Shawcross knocks her hand aside, lifts her, pushes her.

"Turn around," he says. "Kneel down."

Obedient Gwen turns her back; she straddles the ottoman. Shawcross loops the ribbons around her wrists, tightens them, fastens them to the wooden pillars at either side of the bed. Gwen's face is now hidden from him, pressed against the wings of the cherubim. This, Shawcross thinks, is an advantage; when he touches her he prefers not to see the expression in her eyes.

Standing between her thighs, Shawcross surveys the scene; since Gwen cannot see him, he fondles himself; his clean, carnation-scented white hands move gently at first, then more rapidly; his mind fires. He leans forward, rubs himself against the cleft between Gwen's buttocks, notes (pleasurably) that she is now quite helpless and he may do as he wishes. This sense of power and ascendancy excites him further; he considers the idea (a new one this, as far as Gwen is concerned) of rubbing against her and spilling his semen onto her back; then he decides differently. The desire for outrage is intensifying, and also the desire to inflict pain; he slips his hand between Gwen's thighs, feels the wetness there, and (face taut with distaste) rubs.

Women are slimy creatures, he thinks in passing (like snails, like slugs, both of which he loathes). He inserts one thumb into Gwen's soft orifice and rotates it. Predictably, Gwen shivers against him; predictably, Gwen moans.

Time to begin the litany: Shawcross speaks in a mechanical voice, hardly conscious of the familiar words; the more he touches Gwen, the less he sees her. She has become, for him, a nothing; as his desire sharpens and becomes compelling, it is images of her husband, Denton, that fill his mind.

"How big am I, Gwen?"

"Big. Very big."

"Bigger than your husband?"

"Much bigger, yes."

"What would he do if he could see us now, Gwen?"

"He'd be angry. He'd be hurt. He'd want to kill you."

"Did he ever do this? Or this?"

"Never. Never."

"Did he get hard?"

"Not as hard as you. You're so big. So hard. It frightens me. You—you fill me up. I want you to fill me up. . . ." Gwen hesitates, but Shawcross is too far gone by this point to notice. His body trembles; he reaches forward and clutches at Gwen's breasts, squeezes her nipples between finger and thumb. At that point, when Gwen foolishly departs from the script and murmurs again how much she loves him, Shawcross decides.

He releases his grip on her breasts, draws back, stands, holding himself in readiness and looking down at her; anger flares in his mind. He sees the black ribbons, Gwen's spread white flesh; he smells her terrible wet pungent female smell. He looks at the folds and purses of flesh, two orifices; the desire to violate, to punish, grows stronger. Stupid, stupid Gwen.

Finally, aided by a little saliva, quietly applied, he plunges.

Half in. He has never done this before; Gwen never knew such a thing was possible, and the pain is intense. Half in. Gwen screams. All the way in. Gwen screams a second time. Shawcross, gratified, clamps his hand across her mouth. Gwen writhes. It is over.

When he withdraws, finally (disgusted with Gwen, disgusted with himself), Shawcross knows he has made a mistake. It is twenty minutes past four; he has just ten minutes in which to calm Gwen down, help her dress—and he senses it is not going to be enough.

Face set, he unties the ribbons. There is nothing for it—he will have to act the lover. He does this, but it has little effect. Gwen is shaking; her face is blotched with tears; she will not look at him.

She seems not to hear the comforting lies; she seems not to understand when he speaks of the need for urgency.

"My dear, let me help you. Quickly. We must be quick. Your hair—and your face. You must wash your face. Gwen, think. It's late. Your guests will be waiting."

Slowly, Gwen lifts her head.

"You shouldn't have done that," she says in a dead voice. "You shouldn't have done that, Eddie. You hurt me."

"Dearest, I know. I didn't mean . . . it happened . . . on the spur of the moment. I wanted you so much—Gwen, it's something people do—men and women—they can do that. You remember, I explained. There are many things, other things, that you hadn't done before. This is just the same. It's no different. I know it hurt you—but you have to understand, Gwen, *nothing* is forbidden. Not even pain sometimes. Men's needs are different from women's—you know that. Now listen, just stand up. Walk around a little, Gwen, try—"

"It was *wrong*, Eddie. Wicked."

Gwen turns her face again and covers it with her hands. To the despair and irritation of Shawcross, she again begins to weep. In such a situation, given more time, Shawcross would usually risk coldness; he knows from experience that nothing brings Gwen to heel as quickly as the threat of offending him. His ultimate weapon is always her fear of losing him, but now Shawcross hesitates to deploy it. Now all that matters is getting Gwen back on her feet, into her clothes, and out of his room.

Shawcross sighs; he takes her hand. It will have to be said, there is no other way out. He looks at Gwen, a burning glance. In an injured voice, a passionate voice, he says, "Gwen, I love you. And because I love you, nothing we do can be wrong."

This, to his relief, reaches her. The sobs cease; Gwen is very still. She lowers her hands and looks at him. Shawcross has never said this before (thank God, he thinks, that he kept something in reserve for emergencies). He waits for Gwen to melt, to fling herself into his arms; after that, it will all be easy. But Gwen does not melt; she does not fling herself into his arms. She looks at him, looks for a long time, and then, in a flat voice, a voice Shawcross does not like at all, she says:

"Do you, Eddie? I wonder."

Then, to his immense surprise, she rises. Turning away from him she dresses, quietly and—for Gwen—efficiently. A sequence of seed-pearl buttons, thirty of them, each slipped into place, until bodice and jabot are fastened.

"I shall go back to my room now, Eddie. I will see you downstairs."

Shawcross does not like this voice at all. It alarms him. Gwen sounds like a sleepwalker, looks like a sleepwalker, as she moves to the door.

Shawcross stands; it is he who hastens to her and reaches for her hand. Now, he is fearful; this new Gwen, this transformed Gwen, looks as if she might be capable of anything. She might be deciding the affair is over; she might be contemplating a confession. Shawcross, a physical coward, intends above all else to avert *that* possibility. Images of Denton Cavendish, horsewhip in hand, lurch through his mind. He embraces Gwen with passion.

"My dearest. Say you are not angry with me. Say you haven't changed towards me. Gwen, please, you must let me explain—"

"I have to go downstairs."

"Now you have, yes—but later. Gwen, this evening. We can talk then. We can meet then. Promise me, my darling. Swear you will. After dinner, after the comet—we can be alone then. You know we can—you said so. I'll come to your room—"

"No, Eddie."

"Then here. No, not here—" Seeing her expression, Eddie changes tack quickly. "In the woods then. Our place. Our special place. We can slip away separately and meet there. We could meet at midnight, under the stars—think, Gwen, just think of it. My dearest, say you will. I want to hold you in my arms. I want to look at you. I want to worship you. Gwen, please. Say you will."

There is a silence; Gwen opens the door, looks out, checks that the corridor is empty, then turns back.

"Very well. I promise," she says, and slips out through the door.

Left alone, Shawcross gives a sigh of relief, checks his pocket watch once more. He must go downstairs soon (it would hardly do to arrive at the same moment as Gwen, even from different directions). First, however, he must wash.

He moves quickly in the direction of the dressing room. As he approaches the curtained alcove he stops for a moment, thinking he heard something—some movement. He pulls the curtains aside; the room beyond is empty; the bathroom is empty. Yet something is wrong: The service door is unlatched. He closed it—surely he closed it? Now it is open a crack; even as he looks at it, it moves a fraction on its hinges and then subsides, as if some distant draft had caught it.

He must not have closed it—which was careless. Shawcross feels a spurt of alarm. He crosses to the door, flings it back, and looks out.

At once he feels foolish. There is no one there. Of course there is no one there. The landing is empty; the service stairs are empty. No cause for alarm.

Shawcross returns to the bathroom, runs clear water, reaches for the carnation soap; a little pomade to his beard (Shawcross is proud of that neat beard), a comb through the hair, a fresh collar. Within minutes he feels confident once more; within minutes he is ready.

Downstairs on the terrace it is becoming chilly. A breeze has blown up and Mrs. Fitch-Tench takes her tea in a mittened hand; two shawls around her shoulders, her knees well swaddled with rugs. Eddie Shawcross strolls across the terrace to join the group, a book under his arm. They are all assembled: Denton, Maud (who is pouring the tea; Gwen is still not in evidence), the Heyward-Wests, Jarvis (now wearing a more somber cravat), Jane Conyngham, the three older sons, and Steenie.

As Shawcross approaches—*So sorry, quite forgot the time, I was buried in my book*—a shadow detaches itself from a corner and Constance falls into step behind her father. Shawcross looks down at her with irritation.

"Oh, there you are, little albatross," he says in a light voice, settling himself in a vacant chair. "Fly away now, there's a good child. Don't hang about me."

Constance retires several feet; a few smiles greet this remark, but not many. Shawcross accepts a cup of tea; a maid hands him a tiny napkin trimmed with lace, a tiny plate and silver knife, and offers sandwiches. Shawcross balances these (he has no appetite in any case) and allows the conversation to flow over him. When at last there is a pause, he interjects—in an admirably casual tone, he feels—"And where is Lady Callendar? Has our hostess deserted us?"

"Resting, I expect."

It is Acland who answers him, Maud who backs him up with some remark, and Constance who—startling everyone—contradicts them.

"No, she isn't," she says distinctly. "I saw her just now on the stairs."

"Mama came up to see me," Steenie interjects. "She said she'd fallen asleep and forgotten the time. Now she's changing."

And indeed, Steenie seems to be correct, for even at that moment Gwen appears, looking composed, rested, lovelier than usual. Her hair is freshly brushed and fastened with tortoise-shell and silver combs in a heavy chignon; she wears a new dress, Brussels lace over café-au-lait silk, which rustles as she moves.

The men rise; Gwen smiles and begs them to be seated. She takes her place beside Maud and accepts a cup of China tea.

"You must forgive me," she says to the circle around her. "I've been asleep for such an age. Now, you must all tell me, how have you spent the afternoon? Maud, did you write your letters? Ross will frank them for you and send them down to the village to post if they're ready. Mrs. Heyward-West, did you find the path by the lake? Did you see the swans? Isn't it delightful? Denton my dear, have you recovered from your ill-humor?"

This last is said with particular charm; as she makes the inquiry, Gwen takes her husband's hand in hers. She smiles at him like a coquettish young girl.

Denton pats her hand, presses it, then says in a gruff voice, "Quite recovered, my dear. Quite myself again. But I owe you an apology. Owe everyone an apology, for that matter. Hope you'll all forgive me. In a state—you know how it is. Got myself worked up because of those d— those pheasants. . . ."

There is a murmur of general forgiveness; Maud laughs at her brother; Boy blushes crimson, and Eddie Shawcross looks away. It has not occurred to him until this moment that Gwen (stupid Gwen) is such an accomplished actress. The realization does not please him; Gwen's behavior to her husband does not please him.

Shawcross thinks of the scene just half an hour ago: Could he have underestimated Gwen? Could she have tricked him into those hideous, those demeaning and unnecessary avowals? Shawcross's mood is often one of ill-temper when he has just been with a woman; the sexual act leaves him, he finds, with a sourness, a spiritual residue of bile. Now his mood is not improved, either by Gwen's assurance or by the fact (the undeniable fact) that—as often happens at Winterscombe—he is being ignored.

The circle of guests is chatting with some animation. As usual they are discussing the activities of friends they have in common. Even Jarvis seems included (Jarvis, invited at Shawcross's behest, so that Shawcross should not be the only outsider). Shawcross looks from face to face. How he detests these people! How he despises them, all of them, with their mindless chatter, their inexhaustible fortunes, their calm assumption that they should never have to do a day's work.

They have money; Shawcross does not. They are the patrons, and it is he who must accept their patronage. He knows himself to be their superior in every way, yet they look down on him—he senses it. Out of politeness they smile at his witticisms (pearls before swine). They even listen attentively to his stories about London literary life, but Shawcross knows he does not really engage them. They do not know what it is to be insolvent, to have to scrape a living by reviewing books, by contributing essays. They do not have to grovel to literary editors (editors Shawcross despises, for he knows he could do the job far better if only someone would push the job his way). They do not have to fight for a reputation in a world where genuine talent and ability constantly lose out to the fashionable. Shawcross knows the merit of his own writing; he knows the sweat that has gone into his three novels (well, novellas really). For Shawcross these words, tenacious, dangerous, challenging, are electric with life. The critics, so far, have taken a different view—but then, Shawcross despises most critics also; to a man they are venal.

But what do these people here understand of all that, of the struggles of an artist? Nothing. They are not even interested. If he were perhaps more celebrated . . . But no, even then there would still be barriers. Bitterly, and for the hundredth time, Shawcross reminds himself of the truth. He was born the wrong side of a social and financial divide, and it will remain a divide impossible to cross— except in bed. Except there, where he enjoys a brief dominion between the sheets.

Shawcross feels a familiar acid flow through his veins; he looks from face to face. He feels he would like to stand up and denounce them all, these friends of Gwen's. To their faces he would like to tell them what they are: degenerates, philistines, parasites.

His gaze revolves around the pathetic circle: Denton, the cuck-old; fat, fatuous Freddie; Boy—well named—an immature, gauche, and boring fool; sister Maud, with her playboy prince and her diamonds; Jane Conyngham, a spinster in the making if ever he saw one. Acland Cavendish, the son Shawcross most detests—Acland, who is clever, cold, and condescending; Acland, the only one among them who never bothers to disguise contempt.

Yes, he would like to denounce them, and yet it remains prudent not to do so. Their time will come, Shawcross reminds himself; their class will not endure much longer. Their days of supremacy are numbered, and meanwhile, with their country houses, their careless luxury, their parties, introductions, and their patronage, they have their uses. Oh, yes.

Shawcross eyes them, vindictiveness now in full flow. He takes a savage bite from a cucumber sandwich, looks away, and catches his daughter Constance's eye. As usual, she is watching him. She sits a few feet away, squats on the grass munching a piece of seedcake, alongside Steenie. Steenie is immaculate in velveteen breeches; Constance, Shawcross realizes, is filthy. Her hair is tangled and uncombed; her dress, torn at the hem, is muddied; she has not washed her hands, and her nails, Shawcross observes, are black.

His temper snaps. If he cannot denounce the Cavendishes and their guests, he can turn on Constance, the child he never wanted, the child who cramps his style, the child who is an interminable expense. Constance has certain advantages, the chief one being that she cannot answer back.

"Constance, my dear." Shawcross leans forward, his voice pleasant and mild. Constance (who knows that tone, and dreads it) blinks.

"Constance, I know you like to be a little gypsy, my dear, but really, don't you consider you are taking things too far? We are not among tinkers here. We are at Winterscombe, and I rather think, Constance, that it might have been a good idea had you washed and changed before honoring us with your presence at tea. . . ."

Shawcross has begun this speech amid chatter; by its end, there is silence, a lovely still pool of silence into which his words fall with maximum effect.

There is a small rustle of embarrassment from the circle. (Several of those present, if you remember, both dislike Shawcross and resent his bullying of his daughter.) Shawcross, sensing the disapproval and finding it, in his present mood, an added sting, continues:

"Have you heard of soap and water, Constance? Can you recognize a hairbrush? What can you have been doing, child, this afternoon? Climbing? Tunneling?" Shawcross laughs. "Yes, tunneling, I think, to judge from the state of your fingernails."

"Nothing," Constance says. She stands and looks at her father. "I was doing nothing. I was in the nursery. With Steenie."

She looks at Steenie as she says this, and Steenie (who knows it is not true; he woke up and Constance was not there) nods agreement. Steenie, alone of Gwen's sons, actually likes Constance. He does not like Shawcross, who takes up too much of his mother's time. Steenie decided long ago—he is Constance's ally. His support irritates Shawcross further; he sets down his plate with a sharp clatter.

"Constance, please do not lie," he says. "Lying merely exacerbates the matter. I will not tolerate untruths. You will go to your room. And while you are there, you will be good enough to apply a little water, a little soap, to your person."

"I will take her up."

To everyone's surprise it is Jane Conyngham who speaks. She stands and holds out a hand to Constance, which Constance ignores.

"I'm going in, in any case," she says. "The wind is getting up. Gwen, if you will forgive me. I feel a little chilly."

It is a snub. Shawcross knows this at once. A snub from a plain, stupid heiress, and to make matters worse, his anger is dulling his brain. No suitable rejoinder springs to his lips, and before he can make even a lame remark, Jane has left them. She puts her arm around Constance's shoulders and half leads, half propels her into the house.

Another silence. Mrs. Heyward-West remarks upon the volatility of spring weather; Freddie coughs; Boy stares in a fixed way in the direction of the woods; Daisy, the Labrador bitch, rolls over on her back and offers her master, Denton, her belly.

"Tea, Eddie?"

Gwen is holding out her hand for his cup. She has now taken over the teapot from Maud and is enthroned behind the tea table. A silver tray, a silver teapot, silver sugar bowl and tongs, silver milk jug . . . Shawcross regards the glittering array, considers that these few objects, if sold, would provide enough capital to support him for a year—two years. In style. No more seedy compromising of his artistic intentions; his genius would have the freedom to flourish. . . .

"Thank you."

He extends his hand with his cup. He glances at Denton, sitting beside Gwen, nodding off in his chair, his large, liver-spotted hands slack in his lap. It occurs to Shawcross (for the first time, oddly enough) that if Denton were to die, Gwen would be a very rich woman.

"No. No sugar. Thank you."

A very rich *widow*. Who might, in due course, marry again. Who might marry *him* (it would hardly be difficult to persuade her). Always supposing, of course, that he could face the idea of a second marriage, considering the boredom, the suffocating confinement of the first.

If Denton Cavendish were to die . . . Shawcross lets the possibility eddy through his mind; he accepts his cup of tea from Gwen. Their fingers do not touch, but (is it possible Gwen has read his mind, or is she just remembering the events of the afternoon?) Gwen's hand shakes. It is a tiny movement, a brief weakness; cup tinkles against silver spoon. Shawcross notes it, however; so, he observes, does Acland.

Shawcross sips his tea, which is too hot, and burns his lips. Acland's gaze, cold, hostile, knowing, meets his. An uncomfortable moment; Shawcross maneuvers in his seat.

"Shawcross . . ." Acland leans forward, speaks in a polite voice. He asks a question, and Shawcross has the unpleasant feeling that the answer is known. "You never told us. Did you spend a pleasant afternoon? How did you divert yourself? Tennis? Croquet? A walk in the woods perhaps? Did you visit the swans on the lake? Enlighten us, Shawcross. Surely you cannot have been reading all afternoon?"

II
AN ASSIGNATION AND AN ACCIDENT

From the journals

A memory of my mother: *The gentility was thin but hard—you could see through it, as you can the best bone china. After I'd kissed her she would blot her lips with a white handkerchief. When I was very small I prayed that one day she would let me kiss her without wiping the kiss off after. I asked her if she would, but she said kisses carried germs.*

A memory of my father: *When he belched, his stomach moved. You could see it, pumping the wind out. A man full of gas: gaseous matter, noxious matter. A man festering inside. You could smell the putrefaction when he died.*

Loose lips and large hands. I can see his hands, paddling inside her dress. I was three years old the first time I caught them at it; my mother panted.

A memory of my daughter: *Twelve months old; Jessica already starting to die in the next room, coughing day and night to stop me working. The child learned to walk in the middle of a chapter, and the bitch of a nurse brought her in to show me, of course. Five tottering paces, then she clasped me by the knee. An ugly thing, this Constance that I fucked into the world: yellow skin, Asiatic hair, a Semitic hook to the nose, malevolent eyes. I wanted to kick her.*

Write about hate—and its purity.

Tonight, the comet. Conceived by an accident of elements—like my daughter. Hot and gaseous—like my father.

Odd, the associations of the mind. I miss my mother. Dead these twelve years, well-rotted by now. I think of her every day still. Blotting her lips after every kiss. She was clean and cold and distant. Like the moon.

"Tinkers. Romanies. Gypsies. Vermin. Mark my words. They'll be at the back of it."

Denton takes a hefty swallow of port, swills, gulps, and glowers. Dinner is over; the women have withdrawn. To his left and his right Denton has his cronies; certain of their sympathy (they are land-owners, too), he has reverted to his current *idée fixe*.

"Thought they'd been moved on," remarks Sir Richard Peel, chief among the cronies (old Dickie Peel, chief magistrate, fearless huntsman), and he frowns. His estate adjoins Denton's; if Denton Cavendish loses pheasants this month, he is likely to lose them next.

"Moved on? Moved on?" Denton almost chokes. "Of course they were moved on. But they're back. Down by the railway bridge. Filthy ramshackle lot. Thieving. Spreading dirt and disease. Hennessy's boy Jack saw them up near my woods last week, told Cattermole. You want to see to it, Peel."

"Common land, down by the bridge. A bit difficult . . ." Sir Richard says musingly, and Denton's nose purples and quivers.

"Common land? What's that supposed to mean? Means they can do what they like, does it? Means they can sneak into my woods at night and pick my birds off as they please? Means they can come into my village with their filthy flea-bitten lurchers—disgusting brutes; poisoning's too good for them. One of them got at Cattermole's best bitch last year. Mounted her, right outside the church—nothing Cattermole could do. Drowned the puppies, of course. Sunk them in a sack in the river—but that bitch of his hasn't been the same since. Not the dog she was. Got into her system, you know, tainted her. Spoiled her. And she was a good bitch once. One of the best. Fine nose, nice soft mouth. And now . . ."

For some reason the sad fate of Cattermole's bitch seems to affect Denton deeply. His chin sinks against his chest; his eyes glaze. As his cronies leap in with other similar stories of Romany outrage, Denton seems not to hear them. He shakes his head, mumbles to himself, grasps the neck of the port decanter, and slops more port into his glass.

His third glass, Shawcross notes from the far end of the table. Drunkard. Sot. Philistine. Denton the cuckold was already drunk by the time they sat down to table; now he is well and truly soused.

Shawcross takes a small and ladylike sip of the port, which happens to be excellent, and then pats at his small neat mouth, his beautifully pomaded beard, with a snowy napkin. The sight of the cleanly napkin, his own small cleanly hands with their carefully buffed and manicured nails, pleases him. His nostrils quiver; the smell of carnation soap, of his own fine cologne, generously applied, reassures him. With a tight supercilious smile he averts his eyes from Denton's end of the table and surveys the guests closer to him. To his left, receding into the distance, are a senile earl, a prim bishop, his acquaintance Jarvis (who has cornered some Cavendish neighbor with a fine collection of Landseers). Nothing very promising there.

To his right sits the prominent financier Sir Montague Stern, in conversation with George Heyward-West (percentage points again, no doubt of it). Beyond them, a group of younger male guests, including Hector Arlington, whose father's land adjoins that of the Conyngham family. Arlington, an earnest and studious young man, is rumored to be an amateur botanist of some distinction. Shawcross permits himself a small sneer—a botanist! Nothing there.

Beyond Arlington, a group of elegant young Etonians with braying accents and, beyond them, interspersed with a number of unnervingly prominent men, sit Gwen's trio of elder sons: Boy, who is looking flushed and anxious; Frederic, who has contrived to become slightly drunk; and Acland, who has been silent and preoccupied for most of the evening.

Shawcross sees Acland stifle a yawn, and notes that Acland seems to be drinking only water. He notes, too, that Acland appears to be listening to the man next to him, but in fact is not; he sees that Acland's gaze moves from face to face, and he has the impression that that gaze misses very little.

Acland's regard is always unsettling to Shawcross, and he turns away now lest he should be forced to meet Acland's eyes. Shawcross has the feeling—it has intensified these last months—that Acland does not merely dislike him, Acland *knows*. He knows of the affair with Gwen; he knows, or senses, the contempt Shawcross feels for Gwen—a contempt Shawcross had always believed well hidden. That question, earlier, tossed by Acland across the tea table: *Shawcross, you never told us. How did you divert yourself this afternoon?* No accident, that question, Shawcross feels, and carefully calculated to cause him unease. God, how he loathes that boy. . . . Shawcross makes a small ceremony of lighting a cheroot, conscious that Acland's eyes are upon him now. He shifts in his seat. Apart from anything else, he hates that Acland should see him as he is now, socially disadvantaged, speaking to no one, yet again left out. Clearing his throat, Shawcross leans forward and interrupts the monetary murmurs to his immediate right.

George Heyward-West breaks off with a look of surprise. The financier, Sir Montague Stern, is more urbane. He takes Shawcross's interjection in his stride, admits him to their conversation, turns it to include him. Within seconds they have passed from equities to opera; Shawcross is mollified.

Montague Stern is known as a prominent patron of Covent Garden; Shawcross, who is unmusical, knows nothing of opera and cares less, but at least it counts as one of the arts; at least it is a subject of some sophistication, preferable to belchings and grumblings about gypsies and hounds.

He manages a quite passable witticism (he feels) on the subject of Wagner, and eyes Sir Montague's waistcoat, an unconventional affair of embroidered crimson silk. Shawcross relaxes, and Sir Montague, a generous man, does not correct him when he confuses Rossini and Donizetti.

Shawcross sips his port more heartily, aware that he is becoming slightly, pleasurably, indulgently drunk. A couple of swallows and he feels ready to dazzle. Opera into theater, theater into books . . .

Conscious, at the back of his mind, that Acland's eyes are still watching him, Shawcross grows more expansive still. Let Acland watch; let him try to find fault if he can! Shawcross is not the outsider now; he is in full metropolitan flood, and the names of fashionable deities (all friends, all such close close friends, Wells, Shaw, Barrie—such a charming little man, Barrie) pour from his lips like rosewater, nectar, balm.

Sir Montague listens quietly. Occasionally he nods; once or twice (Shawcross does not notice) he shakes his head. Shawcross feels elation take its hold, even risks a small triumphant glance in Acland's direction. Safe, safe on his gracious and bountiful home territory, literature in general, in particular those works of literature penned by himself. Here, on these heights, no one can snub him and no one can sneer—no one present at this table anyway. Sir Montague? A cultured man, certainly; an intelligent and sophisticated man, yes, but Sir Montague's attention only adds to the sense of security Shawcross now feels.

For Sir Montague, alone of the men present, is in no position to patronize and look down. He cannot despise Shawcross for his breeding, his schooling, his manners, his way of dress. And why not? Why, on the contrary, can Shawcross feel that sweetest sensation of all: that it is he who can condescend, he who can patronize?

Simple: Sir Montague is a Jew. He came—or so rumor says—from the very humblest origins, and though he may have risen high, very high, he cannot leave those origins, racial and social, behind. They are marked in his features, recognizable in his waistcoat, traceable, just occasionally, in his voice, which has a richness, a cadence that sings of Central Europe, not the English shires.

Splendid, as far as Shawcross is concerned, for of course he despises Jews, just as he despises women or the working classes, the Irish, any person with a dark skin. . . . To ally himself with Sir Montague against the philistines, yet to be sure at the same time that he, Shawcross, is innately superior—oh, the pleasure is exquisite. His witticisms spiral to new heights. He feels acute disappointment when the port drinking ends and his performance is curtailed.

"My dear fellow," he says, and rests his hand on Sir Montague's arm. "You haven't read it? But you must. You would appreciate my finer points, I feel sure. Once I return to London—no, please, I insist! I shall send 'round a copy—signed, naturally. Just let me have your address. It shall be with you first thing." Sir Montague inclines his head; he gives a small (foreign) half-bow.

"My dear fellow," he says—his tone is gracious; Shawcross sniffs no irony at all—"My dear fellow. Please do."

Later the same evening. The party now is in full swing, and Gwen's drawing room glitters with laughter, warms with conversation. Later the same evening, as spirits mount and the advent of the comet draws near, Boy Cavendish takes Jane Conyngham to the gun room.

The visit is prompted by Jane, and it springs from desperation. Hours before, over dinner, when they were paired yet again, Boy exhausted the only subject—photography—that ever animates him. Valiantly, as course succeeded course, he and Jane tacked back and forth on the choppy seas of polite conversation. Boy's replies were distracted, often monosyllabic. By the time Jane was toying with cabinet pudding, they had finally foundered on the sandbanks of travel. There they discovered that while Jane (who loves museums, who never moves a step without her Baedeker guide) has been to Florence, Rome, Venice, and Paris, Boy's expeditions abroad have been more limited. He spends his summers at Winterscombe, his autumns at Denton's Scottish estates, his winters in London. Prompted by Jane, Boy recalls that he did, once, make an expedition to

Normandy with his aunt Maud, but that was when he was very young, and the food made him sick.

"Papa," Boy says, blushing painfully, "Papa doesn't really approve of 'abroad.' "

Once the men join the women in the drawing room after dinner, things improve, for Acland draws Boy to one side and Jane is left—to her relief—with Freddie. Freddie is less pleased by this situation; he does not wish to be trapped with Jane. He frowns in the direction of his elder brothers, who both look pale and appear to be arguing. He turns back to Jane and, mustering his training, compliments her on her dress.

In fact, Freddie does not like this dress—a particularly gloomy green—but he manages to inject some sincerity into his remark, for Jane does look well. Her thin face is flushed with faint color; her hair is attractively arranged in soft waves, which emphasize the height of her forehead and her wide-spaced hazel eyes. Acland has contended in the past that Jane is not plain, that her intelligence shines through her face, lending her a kind of beauty. Freddie would not agree with this (Acland being perverse) but he does manage the remark about the frock. Jane frowns.

"Freddie, please don't be polite. The dress is . . . a mistake."

"I'm sorry?"

"It had good intentions, this dress. . . ." Jane pauses. "They have not been fulfilled."

Jane glances toward the figure of Acland as she says this. Freddie finds the remark incomprehensible, possibly a joke—and he never understands Jane's jokes.

An awkward silence falls. Freddie scans the drawing room for assistance and finds none. He manages to catch the eye of Hector Arlington, but Arlington, seeing Jane, moves rapidly away.

Freddie knows why this is: Arlington was once expected to marry Jane—expected to do so by her family, anyway. The match was promoted with great energy by her aunt. Arlington—a confirmed bachelor, according to Acland—managed to extricate himself before gossip compromised him. Freddie doubts Boy will have such an easy escape. Not if his father has anything to do with it.

What a fate, to end up with a bluestocking! Freddie gives Jane a sideways glance. According to Acland (again) Jane was offered a place to study literature at Cambridge and refused it when her elderly father fell ill. Freddie squirms in his chair and wonders how he may decently leave. He cannot decide whether the idea of university women is appalling or funny.

"Is Boy unwell?" Jane asks, with a suddenness that startles Freddie.

"Unwell?"

"He looks so pale. I thought at dinner he seemed a little distracted. . . ."

Probably worrying about the proposal, Freddie thinks to himself, and hides a smile.

"It's the weather, I think. He said earlier that he had a headache. Oh—and he'd lost one of the bits of his camera tripod. You know how he fusses about that camera! It won't stand up without it. I expect he's fretting about that."

"I don't think so. He must have found it. He was taking photographs earlier, by the lake. The swans, you know. I was with him. It was just before dinner."

Again Freddie suppresses a smile. So: clearly Boy has had an opportunity to propose and has funked it.

"Yes, well, I can't think of a reason then," he says politely. "Anyway, he's coming back now," Freddie adds with relief as Boy leaves Acland's side. "Perhaps you'll excuse me?"

He makes a speedy exit. Boy sits by Jane, and—to her increasing despair—the appalling stilted conversation begins again. Nothing, it seems, can animate Boy, not music, books, the other guests, the advent of the comet—nothing. Somehow the conversation comes around to shoots, from there to guns, from guns to the famous Purdeys. Jane remarks that they must be very fine. She remembers her brother, Roland, settling for Holland guns, which he said were good, but not quite as—

"I'll show you them, if you like. I'll show you them now." To Jane's astonishment, Boy interrupts her. He rises to his feet. He holds out his arm. He sets off at a fast pace, Jane in tow. He appears not to notice the knowing smiles and indulgent glances as they leave the room, but Jane sees them. So, people think the proposal is imminent—and they are wrong.

Hastening along corridors and down stairs, Jane believes she knows the reason for Boy's alacrity. There are many places in which a conventional man may be expected to propose: by a lake, for instance, overlooking some charming vista; on a terrace by moonlight; perhaps in a conservatory—yes, that would suit Boy. Any of those places, but a gun room? Never. In the gun room, safe from proposals, they discover something astonishing: The matched pair of Purdeys is missing.

This discovery—which takes some time to confirm, for Denton's gun room is a veritable arsenal of weapons—seems to make Boy very nervous indeed. In a testy and abstracted way, he explains: His father has organized this gun room with fetishistic care. There are only four keys to the room: His father has a key, he has a key, Acland has recently been granted one, and the last is in Cattermole's safekeeping. Other keepers are occasionally admitted to the room to clean guns, but only when his father or Cattermole is there to supervise them.

Despite the fact that the glass-fronted case containing the Purdeys is unlocked, and the guns clearly not there, Boy refuses to accept that they are missing. He hunts high and low, in corners, behind cupboards, his manner becoming more and more agitated.

"Papa will be furious, absolutely furious! Please"—he takes Jane's arm in a pleading way—"please don't mention this, will you, to anyone?"

"Of course not, Boy," Jane replies, and she keeps her word. The incident will be recorded in her journals, but it will never be discussed, just as Boy's announcement that the guns have been found after all (two days later) will never be discussed. Boy will never mention the matter again—not even when he is called upon to give evidence to an inquest intended to examine all the events of this night in fine detail.

In the gun room Jane sees on Boy's face a look of childish dismay. *Poor Boy,* she thinks. Boy, who is unmanned by his father, is not really worrying about his father and the Purdeys; he is worrying about his father and a proposal.

She feels a spurt of pity for Boy, trapped in this farce every bit as much as she is. She will tell him, she thinks, and tell him now: she does not want him to propose, and if he does, she will certainly refuse him. All the sentences are there, stacked waiting in her mind. They are there, but they are never spoken.

At that moment a gong is struck. It echoes, reverberates, through halls and passageways: a ghostly sound. Boy jumps. But that gong is only a signal: a signal for the comet, a signal for the guests that it is time to gather outside.

Boy seems to greet it as another reprieve.

"Better hurry," he says, and Jane, knowing her moment of honesty has been lost, looks around at weapons, then follows him.

So many people, outside on the terrace at Winterscombe, gazing up at the night sky. A breeze blowing; a calm night; expectation.

"Over there!"

It is Acland who glimpses it first, and points. All around him people mill and push, crane their necks, fill in the waiting minutes by trying to identify the constellations.

The polestar, Orion, Cassiopeia, the twins Castor and Pollux, the Great Bear, the Little Bear. Tonight the sky is clear of cloud; the stars are glorious. They look (Acland thinks) like bright seeds scattered across the heavens by the hand of a generous, a profligate God; their profusion dazzles his mind. He moves away from the others so that the buzz of their conversation will not intrude on him, so that he can be—as he prefers it—alone.

He looks up at the sky and feels exultant. On such a night all things are possible; all the shabby things of life, all nuance and subterfuge and compromise and untruth are banished. For a moment, just before he sees the comet, he experiences a great soaring of the spirit, as if he left the dull gravitational pull of the earth far behind him and was swept up among the stars.

The sensation does not last. It is already fading when he glimpses the comet first, and the comet sobers him. He had expected it to be a disappointment, this comet, this much-heralded phenomenon. Random particles, gases, and dust. He had been sure it would be less than spectacular.

As soon as he sees it, he knows he was wrong. The comet awes him; it awes his companions. As he shouts, and points, the conversation dies away; the people on the terrace are silent.

One long curvature of light. The comet arcs; the stars pale; the darkness flares; the great trajectory is silent.

It is this, Acland thinks, that makes the apparition so unearthly and so fearsome. Volition, blaze, and silence. With such speed and conflagration, he expects noise, the crackle of flame, the burst of an explosion, even the roar of an engine (like a motorcar or a steam train, like an aeroplane—Acland has seen an aeroplane, once).

But the comet is as silent as a star, and it is this (Acland decides) that is so awesome. This, and—just for an instant—a perception of the future. For this comet will return, of course, some seventy-six years from now; that much is certain.

Acland looks and calculates (as perhaps, just then, each person looks and calculates). The comet will next be seen in the year 1986. The digits sound foreign, unimaginable, bizarre. By then, he will be . . . ninety-three.

He will not live that long—of that fact Acland is at once sure. It is too ancient, too unlikely, too far beyond the allotted span of three-score years and ten. He keeps his eyes on the comet, watches light curl. He knows: once only in a lifetime; he will never see it again.

Acland watches and (briefly) understands his own mortality. It saddens and angers him. So few years, Acland thinks; before it is over, he would like to do one thing daring, one thing extreme, one thing glorious.

He turns impatiently, furiously, away. He must be with Jenna; he must be with her *now*—and he does not care who sees him leaving. *Life is so short*, Acland thinks, and turns in the direction of the stables; there, Jenna has promised to meet him. He quickens his pace. No one sees him leave except Jane Conyngham (who always watches him).

The air is sweet in Acland's lungs. The exultancy has returned. *Tonight, I could do anything*, Acland says to himself, begins to run, and glances back, once, over his shoulder.

But no. No one calls after him, no one shouts his name, and, much later, no one will ask where he has gone.

And the other watchers? Some of them, too, are frightened. Even Denton feels melancholy steal upon him; he thinks of his stiff joints, his shortness of breath, the closeness of the graveyard. Gwen, wearing her sealskin trimmed with ermine, standing next to Shawcross just as she planned, understands how expectation can be shriveled by reality.

She had envisaged an unclouded happiness. Now her mind is troubled, rent in two by hope and panic. For the first time, today, she has questioned her own adultery. She no longer dismisses all the doubts at the back of her mind. She has admitted them; they throng. She loves Eddie; she does not love him. He loves her; he does not love her. She is a mistress; she is a mother. And now, for the first time, those two roles collide, and she fears, obscurely, some punishment.

She has sinned. She looks at the comet and she knows it. Not erred, sinned. Eddie would laugh at the word, but for once she will not be influenced by Eddie. Nothing, she decides, can excuse what she has done. The shame of it sickens her. Again she sees herself, a child, sitting in the parlor listening to her father read from the Bible, and she knows now as surely as she ever knew then: Sin invites retribution.

Eddie has taken her hand but she tugs it away. She will make amends, break off this affair, and she will never be tempted again.

Eddie glances at her, but Gwen does not even notice. She is trying to calculate her punishment and, with a swoop of irrational terror, understands whence it will come.

She will not be hurt—of course not. That would be too easy. No, someone she loves will be hurt. The loss will be her punishment. Frantic now, she searches the faces of the crowd for her children, her husband. Then, turning away, she stumbles back across the terrace toward the house.

"Gwen, where are you going?" Shawcross calls. Gwen does not look back.

"To see Steenie," she says. "I have to see Steenie."

Steenie and Constance have been allowed to stay up. They are kneeling side by side at the window of the nursery. The window is wide open and they lean out over its ledge dangerously. Steenie's face is flushed, excited; Constance's face is pale and closed. They both stare at the sky, watch the light fade on the horizon.

Nanny Temple, her gray hair in a pigtail down her back, well wrapped up in a red flannel dressing gown, fusses behind them. When Gwen rushes into the room and sweeps Steenie into her arms, Nanny Temple is aggrieved. The nursery is her domain.

Gwen covers Steenie's face with kisses. She insists that she must take him back to bed, give him his glass of milk, settle his pillows, feel his forehead, tuck the sheets and blankets up to his chin. Even then, she is inclined to linger. She remembers the nights she sat here when Steenie was ill, certain that if she left him her protection would cease and he would die. The fear of those nights is with her again; only when she is sure that Steenie is asleep, his breathing regular, will she consent to leave.

Then, abstracted, she scarcely notices that Constance has been forgotten, and that only now is Nanny Temple insisting the child come away from the open window.

The window is shut; the curtains are closed.

"Time for the sandman," Nanny says briskly.

"Goodnight, Constance," Gwen calls, leaving. Constance, who knows she will not sleep, allows herself to be led to her bedroom.

"I buried a rabbit today," she tells Nanny as she is tucked into bed.

"Of course you did, dear," Nanny says, extinguishing the night light. Nanny Temple (who does not like her) is well used to Constance's lies; her policy is to ignore them.

"It was a baby rabbit. A gray one," Constance adds.

"Off to dreamland," Nanny says, and shuts the door.

In the darkness Constance lies rigid and still. She flexes her fingers. She thinks. She hums, flatly, a metallic little tune. She waits, and after a while the albatross comes, as he comes each evening.

Constance watches as he circles the ceiling; she listens to the slow beat of his huge white wings. This albatross is no bird of ill omen—how stupid people are. This albatross is her counselor, her friend, her guardian among the angels.

And he is beautiful. Each day he flies to the ends of the earth and back again; each day he traverses the oceans of the world. One day he will take Constance with him—he has promised her that. She will sit on his back, and rest between his wings, as secure as a nut in a shell—and then she, too, will see the world. Constance looks forward to that. Meanwhile, she watches and she waits. Patiently.

Downstairs, it is eleven o'clock; the chandeliers are illumined, the Cavendish drawing room glitters; Jane Conyngham is playing the piano.

To begin with she has played the expected pieces: a tinkly waltz or two, a gentle mazurka, the kind of music a gentlewoman should play, the kind of music Jane detests and despises.

To begin with, people were listening to her; they gathered in a circle, perhaps expecting that their hostess would join Jane at the piano, as she often does. Gwen has a sweet voice and her repertoire is designed to pluck at the heartstrings. But tonight, re-joining her guests with an easy apology, Gwen has declined to sing.

Jane, lifting her eyes from the piano keys (she knows the wretched mazurka by heart), sees Gwen begin to circulate. Gwen begins with her most distinguished guests, the elderly earl and his wife, who rarely appear in society. She moves on to Denton's sister Maud, and to Sir Montague Stern, the financier. She greets colonels and captains, statesmen and politicians, City men and stockbrokers. She encourages Boy and Freddie to circulate among the young women present. With a laugh and a smile she shepherds her husband and his sporting cronies in the direction of the smoking room, or billiards. A word here, a touch on the arm there. Gwen is good at this, Jane observes.

The mazurka comes to an end. The circle around the piano disperses. Her playing will be background noise from now on. Jane rests her fingers against the keys. She does not mind; to be on the periphery is to be private.

For a while, resting between pieces, she watches the other guests, remembers the comet. She did not look at it at first, not for some while, for her eye was held by the figure of Acland, separate as always, outlined against the light of the sky, arm outstretched, finger pointing.

Jane bends her head to the keys. She is aware that Acland is not in the room and that he did not return from the gardens—although no one else seems to have noticed. No matter; she is being ignored, and so she can allow her mind to dwell on Acland. She thinks of his reddish hair, and how with that unearthly light from the sky, it flared like a halo around his head. She itemizes his features, which, for Jane, possess an endless fascination. Acland has pale skin of great translucence; it betrays his emotions as litmus does chemicals. When Acland is angry (and she has often seen him angry), he pales; when he is happy or excited or amused, color washes thinly over bone. When she thinks of Acland it is always in terms of speed. He has a quick mind, a quick tongue, a precipitate judgment. He must always move on—to the next place, the next idea, the next person, the next project, and in his company Jane often feels fearful. Acland, she senses, can be destructive; he is splendid, but careless.

When she watched him earlier, outside in the garden, Jane felt as if a struggle took place inside her own skin. It was as if something inside her, something wild and rebellious, an incubus, were fighting to get out. Now that incubus is back; Jane can sense it. This incubus—which is no such thing, of course, but merely temptation—makes devilish suggestions. It sings a song of a wild world, a world outside the careful boundaries in which Jane lives. There, a different Jane could forget about such tiresome concepts as duty, discretion, and obedience. She could forget about her ailing father and the hopes of her widowed aunt, and she could be . . . free.

Jane hesitates, then closes the music in front of her. She lifts her hands to the keyboard and begins to play from memory. This time, a piece of music she loves, one she respects, for this music has no pat answers and its cadence does not reassure. Chopin's "Revolutionary Etude," *not* a piece for a drawing-room gathering.

Free, free, free. It is a difficult piece. As she approaches its close, she becomes aware that someone is standing behind her. A man. While the music lasts, she is convinced that it is Acland.

But it is not Acland. It is Boy. He waits until she has finished; he claps politely.

"I wonder," he says as Jane closes the piano, "would you like some fresh air? I thought we might go into the conservatory."

*   *   *

Jane rises and goes with him. She knows what will happen in the conservatory; she knows she does not want to think of it. Instead, she keeps the music in her mind, and the comet, and an image of Acland pointing, not to the comet now but to a path, a route, a different course she might take.

Camellias brush her arm; Boy kneels (he actually kneels); he places one hand in a tentative gesture in the region of his heart.

"Miss Conyngham ·. . . Jane . . ." he begins.

Jane fixes on the comet, on a halo of hair, on an absolute silence that, for her, echoed and reechoed, like guns.

". . . your hand in marriage."

Boy stops. Jane waits. There is a long silence. Then the daring of a few minutes ago deserts her, as she feared it would. Long lean years of spinsterhood—is that what she wants? And that is what lies in wait for her, after all. More christenings to attend—and all for other women's children. What of the future when her father dies and her aunt dies and she is left all alone with her fortune?

Spinsterhood. Or Boy, who is almost certainly her last chance. Turning toward Boy, she accepts (though she insists, in the next breath, that there must be a long engagement). She is prepared to wait, she would prefer to wait, until he is twenty-one.

Boy's face falls. Then his eyes brighten. He stands up. His knees make a cracking sound. Jane would like to laugh, it is all so absurd, but instead (pitying them both), she holds out her hand to him, and smiles.

It is a night for proposals, possibly a night for love. While Boy and Jane become engaged, other promises and assignations are taking place.

In the drawing room Freddie flirts with a young girl called Antoinette, vaguely connected to his aunt Maud by marriage, and even more vaguely chaperoned. Antoinette (fourteen but precocious) flirts back. Freddie swaggers.

On the far side of the crowded room, his aunt Maud (wearing her famous sapphires) discovers she has much in common with the financier Sir Montague Stern. As they discuss opera, Maud eyes his waistcoat (loud and luxurious; it fascinates her). She tries to remember what she knows of this man whose name is a byword in London circles. A man who has risen fast, and a man of great influence certainly, rumored to have the Prime Minister's ear; Jewish, of course, though that fact is discussed only behind his back, usually by those who owe him money. What is his real name?

Not Stern, she is sure of that, and there are stories she has heard about him which she recalls vaguely as sinister, though the details escape her. A man some few years her junior, she estimates; around forty, though it is difficult to be certain, and he could be younger. A powerful man; a saturnine man; both amusing and unshakably urbane. It occurs to Maud that she has never been to bed with a Jew, and just as she is thinking this, she finds she has accepted an invitation to the Stern box at Covent Garden.

"Delightful," Maud murmurs, and casts her eyes around the room. "And your wife? Shall she join us? Is she here tonight?"

"I have no wife," Sir Montague replies, and something in the measured way in which he says this causes Maud's heart to quicken.

He waits a beat, exactly the correct beat, then inclines his head. "And your husband, the Prince?"

"In Monte," Maud says, her manner firm. They smile at each other. It is at once clear to them both that the Prince is disposed of; he need never be mentioned again.

Sir Montague takes her arm; he steers her through the press of people toward a servant with a silver tray and champagne. They pass the elderly earl, who acknowledges Sir Montague in a formal way; a politician, who greets him with more warmth; Eddie Shawcross, who is perhaps slightly drunk, weaving his way toward Gwen.

"Such a very unpleasant man," Stern says; he glances in Shawcross's direction and gently steers Maud to one side. The comment, coming in mid-anecdote, surprises Maud, for she had not expected Sir Montague to be frank.

"Gwen likes him," she answers, and at once regrets both the remark and the manner in which she made it—certainly indiscreet. Maud, who likes Gwen, who has no illusions as to how unpleasant it would be to be married to Denton, who finds it touching that Gwen should bother to be so private about her affair, now hesitates.

"That is," she adds awkwardly, "Gwen is interested in art, you understand. In books. And my brother Denton—"

"But of course," Sir Montague says in even tones, and at once changes the subject.

Maud is reassured—as perhaps she was intended to be. All her instincts tell her this man will not gossip; her indiscretion is safe with him. Yet she also has the impression that this piece of information, inadvertently given, will not be forgotten. Just for a second, as her eyes meet his, she senses a man whose mind is banked with secrets, with snatches of information—possibly useless, possibly useful—all of which are stored away against some future contingency.

A banker; a bank; stored power—is it this that gives Sir Montague that air of containment? Maud is not sure, but some power she can sense, and it is erotic; her pulse quickens again.

A small silence between them; Maud looks into Sir Montague's eyes, which are dark, heavy-lidded. She looks away.

"In which room do you sleep tonight?" Sir Montague asks, and because he asks in this way, without preamble, without subterfuge, when only a few hours have passed since they were first introduced, Maud answers him at once.

No coyness; no pretense at shock. Sir Montague likes her for that.

"The first door on the left," Maud says crisply. "At the head of the stairs to the East Wing."

"Twelve?" says Sir Montague, with a glance at his watch.

"How impatient you are!" Maud replies, and lays her hand on his arm. "Twelve-thirty."

"In half an hour," Eddie is saying. His voice is a little slurred. He grasps Gwen's hand.

"Impossible. It's too soon."

"At midnight then. I'll slip away just before, and I'll wait for you there. You'll come then? You won't be frightened?"

Gwen releases her hand, glances to right and left. Of course she will not be frightened; she is never frightened. She has met Eddie before in the woods, in the dark, and if she was afraid picking her way along the path in the dark, then the fear enhanced the excitement when she was embraced in Eddie's arms.

"Is it safe?"

Gwen stares at Eddie, not understanding him for a second.

"Is it safe?" he repeats, more urgently. "What about the keepers? You remember—at luncheon—your husband said the grounds would be patrolled."

This concern irritates Gwen; it smacks of timidity, and timidity is not a quality she expects from a lover.

"Not tonight," she says. "The whole village had the evening off. They've been watching the comet. There was a dinner for them too. They're probably all drunk by now. Far too drunk to be worrying about poachers."

Eddie presses her arm. "At twelve then," he says, and moves away.

Gwen turns to another guest. Later, fifteen minutes before the appointed time, she sees Eddie slip out onto the terrace; five minutes after that and she, too, has left the room.

The party is in full swing; no one notices her leave. She hurries up the main staircase to her bedroom. One hour, she tells herself. For one hour she will not be missed. She pauses on the landing and listens.

From the billiard room comes the sound of male laughter; she listens. She can (she is sure) detect her husband's voice. It is drunken; it is baying.

In the stable yard Acland waits and listens. He lifts his face to the night sky and hears from the distance, beyond the kitchen gardens, the murmur of voices. The estate workers, the villagers, some of the indoor servants—they, too, watch the comet. In a moment Jenna will slip away to be with him. Five minutes, ten—every minute is one too many. *Hurry, hurry*, Acland thinks, and glances back at the grayness of the house.

There, on an upper floor, one light shines out. Silhouetted against the light he can just make out two small figures: Steenie and Constance. Even as he looks, Steenie disappears, retreats out of sight to the sound of distant protests; Constance remains at the window alone. For a second Acland has the sensation that she is staring at him; he draws back into the shadows. Constance Cross, the albatross. Acland dislikes her.

A second later and he knows that *dislike* is not the correct term; he is *wary* of Constance, and this angers him, for Acland is wary of very few people, and why be wary of a ten-year-old child?

She snoops, of course; that is one reason. Constance is a great listener at doors; she snoops and she pries—and when caught in the act (and Acland has caught her on several occasions) she exhibits a brazen-faced calm that astonishes him. "Do you make it a practice, Constance," he said to her once, "to read other people's private letters?" And Constance, then nine, caught red-handed going through Gwen's desk, with a letter from her father in her hand, merely shrugged.

"Sometimes. Why not? I wanted to know what my father had to say. Neither he nor your mother is likely to tell me."

This silenced Acland, the more so because he, too, might have liked to have read that letter. Furthermore, there was in Constance's tone an inflection, a knowingness that shocked Acland deeply. For him to have had suspicions about his mother and Shawcross was one thing. To hear them suggested, almost confirmed, by a nine-year-old girl was another. Constance had this knack—he had marked it before—of involving others in her guilt. As she stared at him with that habitual stonelike expression on her face, derision flickering in her eyes, Acland felt tainted and involved—and then very angry.

"Put that back." He stepped forward and grasped her hand, shaking the letter out of it. Possibly he hurt Constance, for she drew back with a small grimace, but no cry.

"Why, you're angry, Acland. You're white. You always go white when you're angry." The black eyes glittered, as if it pleased Constance to have provoked this response. "And you hurt my hand. Don't do that."

With which, she reached up and, before Acland could move, scratched his face. One quick bunched movement of the hand, her nails against his cheek. She drew blood, and the two of them stood looking at each other, neither moving, neither speaking, until—a second later—Constance laughed and left the room.

An incident never spoken of again, by either of them, but it has remained with Acland, puzzling him and occasionally perturbing him, for he experienced emotions then that he did not understand and is still at a loss to explain. In a peculiar way Acland respects Constance. She is the antithesis of all he admires, with her deceits and her flagrant lies and her tight, barbed little remarks—and yet, in her way, she is honest.

Constance sees too much: This thought speeds into Acland's mind. It makes him uneasy. There are certain things he prefers Constance not to see, his hatred for her father being one of them. He glances once more at the house, but now the figure of Constance is gone; the light from the window is obscured; the curtains are drawn. Acland feels freed. He opens the door that leads to the loft stairs, and mounts them.

A sweet smell of hay; from below the rustle of straw as the horses shift in their stalls. Acland moves to the dormer window to the west. The night is still, the gardens dark; the comet's light declines. Some exultancy lingers in his mind: *Oh, let Jenna come soon.*

He fixes his mind on her: Jenna, who drives out the dark. When he is with her he can forget . . . everything—even his mother and Shawcross.

He throws himself down on the hay, smells its sweet dustiness, closes his eyes, summons the parts of her body, as another man might count the beads of a rosary: her hair, her eyes, her mouth, her throat. When he hears her footfall on the stair, he springs to his feet, then clasps her in his arms.

It is very quick. Jenna can feel his anger beating down on her. Knowing the source of that anger, she waits. Then, when Acland is calmer, she takes his hand.

"Still him?"

"Him. My mother. Everything. The comet maybe."

Jenna kneels. Acland will not look at her. He fixes his eyes on the window to the west, his body taut, his face scowling.

"Why the comet?"

"No reason. Every reason. Urgency, perhaps. I could see time . . . slipping past me. And nothing changing. This place, this house, that man—it made me . . . violent. I wanted to do something extreme. Kill someone. Put a bullet through my brain. Set fire to the house—stand there and watch it go up, every picture, every stick of furniture, every evasion, every lie—one great, glorious conflagration." He stops. "Is that mad?"

"Yes."

"Well, maybe it is. But it's what I felt. It's gone now—nearly gone. Did I hurt you? I'm sorry if I hurt you."

"Shall I make you forget all that?"

"Can you?"

"If you'll be slow, I can. But you're to do as I say, mind."

Acland turns. He looks at her hair, her eyes, her throat, her breasts. Jenna, peering through the dusk of the loft, watches his face. A new concentration comes to it. She rests her hand on his thigh; she moves her hand a little higher; Acland sighs, leans back.

"I believe you. I almost believe you. Show me."

Upstairs, her hands shaking, Gwen changes satin slippers for leather shoes. She retrieves her sealskin coat—if she is to meet Eddie, return, and not be missed, she must be swift—and then, the coat still in her arms, pauses, stares at her own reflection in the cheval glass.

Such a flurry of indecision: What will she say to Eddie? What will she do? Shall she break it off, this liaison of hers, or shall she wait until the morning, when she is calmer, and decide then?

Who is this woman? she thinks as she looks at her strained white face in the glass. Despite her thirty-eight years, Gwen feels a girl still—but it is not the face of a girl who looks back at her.

Oh, let me be wise, Gwen thinks, and turns away from the glass with a little moan. As she does so, she hears a sound.

A light tapping at her door. Gwen stands still. It must be her maid, she decides—and what will her maid think when she sees the sealskin coat? Frantically she tries to push it back onto its hanger, but the fur catches on the embroidery of her dress. She has just freed it when the door opens; Constance comes into the room.

"It's Steenie," she says without preamble. Gwen pales, feels a cold and shivering sense of premonition.

"He has been having a nightmare, I think." Constance's eyes never leave Gwen's face. "He was calling your name and crying. He feels very hot. I went in to him, and touched him. He didn't wake up. I think he has . . . a fever."

Constance speaks clearly and precisely; her eyes waver, turn from Gwen's white face to the sealskin coat, now tossed across the bed. "Oh. You were just going out," she continues flatly, as if this is not surprising at all. "I'm sorry. Shall I go and wake Nanny?"

Gwen does not pause to answer this question. She does not pause to observe the oddness of the situation, for Constance has never come to her room before. She does not even notice that Constance has just apologized (and Constance *never* apologizes). By the time Constance has finished speaking, Gwen has almost forgotten her. She is already running to the door.

She runs along the corridor, runs to the stairs of the nursery wing, runs to Steenie, her last child, her baby, the son she loves best. And as she runs, her mind streams with prayers: *God forgive me, God forgive me, let Steenie be safe.*

She flings back the door of the night nursery and rushes to the bed. Steenie sleeps. As she kneels beside him he flexes, murmurs, rubs at his nose; he turns from his right side to his left. Gwen bends over him.

Constance comes into the room after her, but Gwen sends her away. "Just go back to your room, Constance," she says, averting her face. "Go back to sleep. I'll stay with Steenie. He'll be all right if I'm here."

Constance slips away; the door closes. Gwen remains on her knees by her son's bed. She rests her hand on his forehead; she feels for his pulse. All the old terrors flare up in her mind: Haviland, the local doctor, saying he must be honest and there was very little hope. One of the dead babies . . . which dead baby? The little girl, that was it, lying in her arms, a yellowish tiny waxwork with blue lips. The rattle of croup, the terror of the scarlet fever, when Steenie's throat swelled so badly he could not swallow saliva, let alone water. A week to the crisis; she had sponged his body hourly with vinegar and cool water to try to lower the temperature. At the height of the fever Steenie did not recognize her, could not speak. . . . *Please, God.*

Gwen rests her head against the rise and fall of her boy's chest. His forehead is cool; his breathing is regular; the pulse does not flutter. Gwen counts heartbeats, and slowly, slowly, she grows calmer.

There is no sign of fever. Constance must have been mistaken; it was simply a nightmare, that is all. Steenie is safe and God is merciful.

But (it is 1910, remember; penicillin will not even be discovered for another eighteen years) Gwen is a mother, and as a mother she knows the fragility of the division between life and death. It is a hairsbreadth; easily severed; the commonest childish illnesses are something to be feared. Measles, mumps, influenza, bronchitis, even a minor cut, infected—all these can be killers. Gwen knows this; she knows she has been warned.

This time, she thinks, burying her face in her hands, this time she has been spared. God has not punished her, but He has reminded her of His might. Silently she repents her affair with Shawcross; she will break it off, never see him again. From this night forward she will conform to an ideal laid before her since earliest childhood: She will be a loyal wife, a virtuous mother.

To her surprise the decision is neither painful nor difficult; it brings her an instant respite. This morning she would have believed the bonds that bound her to Shawcross could never be severed; tonight, the bonds are gone.

Head bent, Gwen tells herself that she is making a moral choice—between right and wrong, between holy matrimony and fornication. But in her heart it does not feel like that. It feels like a choice between lover and son—and in that, of course, there is no contest.

Gwen stays in Steenie's room that night, letting its peacefulness work on her; then she descends to her guests.

The fires in the drawing room are still well banked, her servants are still circulating, but the evening's party has reached its climax of energy and is beginning to run down. The elderly earl and his wife (who have been anxious to leave for some time) take their departure.

This is the cue for other guests to leave—guests who are not staying at Winterscombe. There is a flurry of thanks, of congratulations, of farewell; people's spirits are high. Servants hurry to fetch hats and coats and walking sticks; motorcars (and some carriages) are brought around to the front of the house. The houseguests linger for the departures, and then they, too, one by one, come to Gwen to wish her goodnight.

For correctness' sake Denton should be at Gwen's side for these thanks and farewells, but he is not, and Gwen (used to this) is not greatly worried. By now, Denton will have consumed the best part of a bottle of port, possibly some brandy. He is probably still in the smoking room or the billiard room.

When she discovers this is not so, Gwen is still not concerned. Boy comes to her, his manner agitated. He announces he has been looking for his father for the past hour and cannot find him. He is not in the smoking room. There is no one playing billiards. . . .

"Boy, leave it until the morning," Gwen says fondly, kissing him. "Your father will have gone to bed, that is all. You know how these evenings tire him."

Boy does not question the euphemism. Politely he escorts Jane Conyngham to the door of her room; politely he wishes her good-night and, once her door is closed, flees to the sanctuary of his own room. There he surveys his collection of lead soldiers, his collection of birds' eggs, his rows of adventure stories—all the familiar and much-loved totems of his boyhood. He sits on his bed, chin in hand, and stares into the coals of his fire. He will not sleep, he knows that. He also knows his boyhood is finally over.

In her room Jane Conyngham rings for the little maid Jenna Curtis, who dressed her hair so flatteringly this evening, and thinks—as the girl unfastens her dress, unlaces her stays, loosens her hair, and then, once Jane is in her cambric nightgown, brushes it for her—how pretty the girl is.

Her fingers are deft; her cheeks are flushed; her eyes sparkle. *I am engaged. I should look like that,* Jane thinks, looking at her own reflection; *I should, and I do not.* She sighs. Fifty brushstrokes—but nothing will make her fine hair look the way this girl's does, shining, heavy, profuse, a glorious weight of chestnut hair, escaping even now from the confines of her neat maid's cap, and that cap slightly askew, as if it has been pinned in place hastily.

"Did you see the comet, Jenna?" Jane says as the girl lays down the heavy silver brush, picks up Jane's green dress, and bobs a curtsey.

"I did, Miss Conyngham. We—all the servants—watched it."

"It was beautiful, didn't you think?"

"Very beautiful."

"But frightening, I thought. A little frightening." Jane looks at the girl's reflection in the glass; Jenna does not answer.

"I felt as if . . . oh, I don't know quite. As if the world were changing. Something was altering. I—"

Jane breaks off. That was not what she felt, and she knows it. She also knows her feelings cannot be discussed with a maid—or, indeed, with anyone. She speaks more briskly: "Imagination, I suppose. Very foolish. Still, it was a remarkable night. One we shall never forget. Goodnight, Jenna."

Below, in the drawing room, the last guests wish their hostess goodnight. Gwen, alone, turns to a mirror, smooths her dark hair, sees that the decision she has made can be read in her face: It is serene now.

She touches the emeralds that lie about her throat like a necklace of water: an engagement present from Denton, given when she was eighteen years of age, newly arrived in England with her widowed mother, part of that fishing fleet of American girls who came to England in search of an aristocratic suitor. So long ago. She had believed Denton an aristocrat then; now, she is less certain.

Some fresh air, she decides, before she retires for the night. One last look at the stars.

There is the figure of a man in evening dress leaning against the balustrade, looking out over the gardens. From a distance Gwen thinks it is Shawcross. She is about to withdraw—she does not want to meet her lover now; their interview must wait for the morning— when the figure turns, looks up. She sees it is Acland.

She smiles with relief and crosses to him. Of course it was not Eddie, she thinks; Eddie will long ago have given her up and returned to his bed in a bad temper.

She puts her arm around her son's shoulders and reaches up to kiss him goodnight.

"Why, Acland," she says, "your coat is quite damp. Where have you been? You should go in, my dear, before you take cold."

"I'll go in, in a minute, Mama."

Acland does not return her kiss; in a cold manner he disengages her arm.

Gwen turns back to the house. In the doorway she looks back. Acland is still in the same place, still leaning against the balustrade.

"Acland, you should go in," she repeats, more sharply. "It's past one o'clock. Everyone's left. What are you doing anyway?"

Acland turns away again. "Nothing, Mama," he says. And then: "Thinking."

*   *   *

It is Cattermole who discovers that there has been an accident, Cattermole who wakes at five-thirty the next morning with a thirst and a hangover.

He heaves himself out of bed, leaving his wife fast asleep, and goes downstairs to the kitchen of his cottage. There, he stokes the stove and gets a blaze going. Then he fills a pitcher with ice-cold water from the pump, stands at the sink in his shirt-sleeves, tips half of the water over his head, and lets out a growl when it hits him.

The kitchen is small and warms up quickly. Cattermole puts the kettle on to boil, lays newspaper on the kitchen table, sets a knife, a fork, a plate, and a big tin mug in readiness. He is already beginning to feel better; he whistles to himself as he cuts a thick rasher from a side of bacon and puts it in the pan to sizzle. Two eggs, a large hunk of bread, four spoonfuls of strong India tea in the big brown pot—let it sit to keep warm; Cattermole likes his tea well mashed—and then he is ready for his breakfast. Cattermole is an early riser; he is used to getting breakfast for himself. He is thoroughly domesticated. Arms on the table, rump to the fire, Cattermole munches his way through his meal.

When he has finished he uses the last of the hot water in the kettle for his shave at the sink, using a cutthroat razor, stropping it first on its leather. That done, he creaks up the stairs again to put on the rest of his clothes. Two pairs of thick woolen shooting stockings, stout brown boots that once belonged to his father and still have a good few years left in them, Harris tweed breeches, woolen shirt, moleskin waistcoat, Harris tweed jacket—nothing to beat that for keeping a man warm.

Downstairs once more, he pours a cup of tea, which he takes up for his wife, Rose, and leaves by her bedside. Downstairs again: cartridge case, cartridge belt, walking stick, shotgun. He checks his gun (also once his father's), squints down the barrels, breaks it, rests it in the crook of his arm. Outside now, and the mist is lifting, the air cool and fresh, the ground still damp with dew, pungent with spring.

The dogs are ready as usual. He goes to their kennel and lets two of them out, his two black flat-coat retrievers, Dancer and Lightning, father and daughter, better dogs by far than any of those spoiled brutes up at the Hall.

Dancer and Lightning greet him and go at once to heel; each gets one pat, one touch on their damp muzzles. They look at him expectantly. Cattermole knows that they look forward, as he does, to these morning expeditions through the woods.

Six-thirty now, which is late by Cattermole's standards. One thin high whistle and they are off, dogs and man, to the woods.

Cattermole skirts the village, looks toward the Hennessy cottage. He wonders if the Hennessy family will be late rising this morning, as he was. Jack Hennessy drank too much the previous night, no doubt of that; he missed most of the celebrations, disappeared halfway through dinner. To meet that girl Jenna—that was his wife Rose's opinion, but Cattermole is unsure if he agrees. Last night Jack Hennessy was drunk before they sat down to eat, too drunk for dalliance, in Cattermole's opinion, and downing the drink in that odd way he had sometimes, as if he wanted to be in a stupor.

A junction of two paths; Cattermole turns left, heads deeper into the woods, silently now, no whistling. There is a ritual to these walks from which Cattermole rarely departs. He quarters the woods, then makes for the clearing on the far side from the village, where he has a quiet five-minute smoke. Then he makes his way back, checks (at this time of the year) the pheasant pens, unlocks the bins, and gives the birds their allowance of corn.

Today, by the time he reaches the clearing, the sun is well up. Cattermole settles himself with his back against an oak, takes out his tobacco tin, takes out his papers, rolls a fat and aromatic cigarette.

Dancer and Lightning know they have five minutes of freedom now; they may weave back and forth in the clearing, sniffing and marking their territory. They may engage in mock fights and roll in the damp grass; they are off duty.

Cattermole watches them for a while, feet spread, bottom protected from the dew by Harris tweed, cigarette pungent. He removes his cap and lifts his face to the sun; he thinks of the comet the night before. His father saw that comet, the very same one, when he was a boy, back in 1835—saw it from much the same place, most likely.

He puffs the cigarette down to a small stub, then buries it. He stands up, notices for the first time that there is an odd little mound in the grass, just over to his right, a mound that was not there the previous morning. He is inspecting the mound—children's work, by the look of it, and children shouldn't be in this part of the wood, not by rights, they shouldn't—when the dogs begin barking.

Cattermole straightens up. Neither dog is in view but they are close by and they are yelping. Cattermole knows that bark, a high repetitive yipping sound, the sound they make when they've put up a fox or a rabbit.

He waits, but neither dog emerges and the barking continues.

Puzzled, Cattermole crosses the clearing, starts to turn down the path that traverses the woods, and then stops dead.

Cattermole has seen death before. He has even seen what a man looks like who has taken the blast of a shotgun full in the face—and although that was thirty years ago Cattermole has not forgotten it. But he is not prepared for what he sees now. He stares in horror, and in terror, for he at once fears that he will be blamed for this. He stares; his gorge rises; he turns away to the bushes to vomit. Sweat breaks out on his brow; he is shaking. It is when he straightens up that he hears the groan. He swings around.

Dear God, he thinks, *so much blood and still alive. It isn't possible.*

"There's bin a haccident. An 'orrible haccident."

It is Arthur who brings Freddie the news, bursting into Freddie's room, wrenching back the curtains and filling the room with light and agitation.

Freddie surfaces from deep sleep and stares at Arthur in confusion. Arthur is normally more painstaking with the disposition of his aitches, but in his excitement Cockney returns.

"In the woods. Last night. Mr. Cattermole just found 'im. Sent Jack Hennessy up to the 'ouse. The doctor's telephoned for, and they're fetchin' 'im up on a stretcher. Blood everywhere, Jack said. Blood like you wouldn't believe. You'd better get up, Master Frederic—"

Who, who? Frederic wants to know, but Arthur cannot tell him. Jack Hennessy didn't know, or didn't say, and for the moment Arthur is too drunk on disaster to care. Sufficient that there has been an appalling occurrence, that cook is in hysterics, the house in an uproar. "Blood, blood," he keeps repeating in gurgling tones, eyes rolling with the drama of it all, as Freddie bundles back the bedclothes and struggles to get dressed.

To Freddie's fury, Arthur departs for the kitchens and fresh information, leaving Freddie to find his own shirt and tie.

Freddie wastes precious minutes, during which he hears running footsteps, distant shouts, the hooting of car horns, and the crunch of tires on gravel. His fingers fumble; Arthur does not return. Peering from his high window, Freddie sees a group of people gathering on the drive outside. He sees Boy, Acland, his mother, his aunt Maud; he sees the butler, Ross, and—this is when he realizes there is indeed something terrible afoot—he sees Ross, staid, irreproachable, unflappable Ross, actually break into a run.

Ross waves his hands in the air like an agitated goose flapping its wings. He seems to be trying to shoo the maids back into the house, but he is having no success. Still they come out at a run, the streamers of their caps blowing in the wind; they gather, flutter, regroup. One of them—Jenna Curtis—is crying.

With a growl of anger, Freddie leaves his collar agape, his tie askew, his shoes half-laced, and runs for the stairs.

Down past the stag's head, across the hall, onto the portico steps. The scene in front of him is now one of pandemonium.

Jack Hennessy has disappeared—gone back to help the stretcher party, someone says. No one is certain exactly what has happened, or to whom it has happened. On all sides Freddie hears little snatches, gasps, rumors and counterrumors. He stares from face to face. Boy, looking bewildered, hurrying to their mother's side; Acland, white-faced, standing apart and staring in the direction of the woods. The head parlormaid weeping; Ross demanding sal volatile, and quickly; Nanny Temple trying to catch hold of Steenie and chivy him inside; and Steenie, running wild, leaping across the gravel from group to group, evading Nanny Temple's clutch, and yelling.

His mother, too, has dressed in haste, Freddie sees. Her hair is not properly fastened and is already escaping from the pins at her neck; she has rushed outside without her coat.

"But what can have happened? What can have happened?" she says, over and over again. She turns; Freddie sees her eyes scan the terrace. She registers his own presence, the fact that Boy is there, Acland is there, Steenie is there. For a moment her face quietens, and then she cries out:

"Denton? Where is Denton?"

Heads turn; a group of maids eddies apart; Ross speaks in an urgent voice to one of the manservants; the man departs inside at a run. No sign of Lord Callendar, and now, alerted by the noise, other guests are appearing on the steps: Montague Stern, majestic in a padded dressing gown of crimson silk, apparently unconcerned at this departure from convention, stands for a moment at the head of the steps, surveying the scene. He turns to Acland.

"What has happened?"

"An accident of some kind."

Acland's voice is terse, his manner distracted.

"Is the doctor sent for?"

"The doctor, I think, is here."

As Acland says this, and runs forward, the noise of a car is heard. It bucks up the driveway at some speed; it crunches to a halt in front of Freddie, gravel spluttering. From it emerges Dr. Haviland, red in the face, unshaven, whiskery, hat jammed low on his brows. He clutches his alligator medical bag, and at his appearance—the appearance of authority amidst chaos—a sigh goes up from the cluster of maids.

The doctor's arrival is a diversion. As he goes to Gwen's side and her family groups around her, only Acland stands apart, just as he did the night before for the arrival of the comet. Acland stands apart, and Jane Conyngham, coming out onto the steps with Mrs. Heyward-West, sees Acland's head lift, sees him raise his arm to point, just as he did the night before.

Jane turns, screws up her shortsighted eyes. At first she can see nothing; then, gradually, she discerns the group to which Acland is gesturing.

There is a thin mauve mist in the valley below, as there often is on spring mornings. It shrouds the edge of the lake and the woods, and it is from this thin mist that the group of men gradually emerges. There are nine, perhaps ten of them, headed by Cattermole, by Jack Hennessy, and by Hennessy's other brawny sons. They progress slowly, awkwardly, in fits and starts, with many muffled shouts and cautions to watch their step, to go easy now.

They are carrying something. Jane narrows her eyes. They are closer now; she can see that four of the men support an improvised stretcher. On the stretcher is a pile of rugs, the familiar tartan rugs that at Winterscombe are always brought out for shooting luncheons or for picnics.

"Oh, my dear," Mrs. Heyward-West says in a low voice, and reaches for Jane's hand. The groups on the terrace fall silent. Jane knows they are all looking for the same thing—a face, and whether that face is covered.

The group of men is coming closer now. Jane can see that their faces are blanched with shock, that Cattermole, the most stalwart of men, is greenish and shaking. He has removed his tweed cap, and as he advances he turns the cap around and around in his hands, like a nervous child up before a teacher. Fifty feet away, the group pauses, as if reluctant to advance. By the house, no one moves and everyone is silent.

Twenty feet, fifteen; the men stop. They are sweating in the chill air; their breath comes in clouds. A word from Cattermole, and gently, reluctantly, averting their faces, they lay their burden down.

A little flutter from the group of maids; Montague Stern draws in his breath; Acland tenses. Jane stares; Freddie stares. They can see the bundled form now, under the tartan rugs; they can see the remnants of a white shirtfront; they can see blood, and a head lolling.

It is Gwen who goes forward first, and Jane has never admired her more than she does at this moment—Gwen, who, brushing aside Boy's restraining arm, steps forward. She walks toward the bundle of rugs, bends, kneels in her silk dress on the gravel. Cattermole lifts a hand, as if in warning, then lets it fall. Gwen lifts the tartan rugs to one side.

She had assumed—everyone had assumed—a shooting accident, but no gun would have produced these kinds of injuries. Gwen stares, bewildered, shock slowing the processes of her mind. The body in front of her is so badged with blood that at first she cannot locate the source of the injuries, cannot recognize the man before her. His hands, arms, face, are lacerated; gobbets of blood spew from his mouth; his lips are retracted so that he appears to snarl.

The nails on his hands are ripped, and the stumps of his fingers are black with congealed blood; the hands are clenched like claws, clutching at the shreds of his clothing. The hands are not moving, and the smell—for a second Gwen averts her face—the smell is terrible.

Gwen lifts her face to Cattermole in bewilderment. Cattermole hesitates, and it is Dr. Haviland who, reaching her side, setting down his bag, twitches the rugs back a little further.

Gwen stiffens. From behind her there is a groan, a sigh, a scream from one of the maids. The man's right leg is fragmented. Below the knee it is twisted and foreshortened. One foot, shoeless, is bent up under his body; the shinbone, snapped in two places, protrudes through the flesh; a sliver of bone glistens.

"Dear God," Dr. Haviland says, very quietly. He lifts his face to Cattermole. "Dear God, man, what happened?"

"A trap, sir," Cattermole says in a low voice. "He must have been in it for hours before I found him." He hesitates. "He'd have gone wild, sir, trying to get out of it, just like an animal would. That's why his hands . . . and his tongue, sir . . ." He bends toward Dr. Haviland's ear, lowers his voice even further so that Gwen will not hear him. "He's bit it, sir, bit it bad. . . . But he's alive, sir, that's the thing of it. At least, he was alive—when we got him out. . . ."

Dr. Haviland turns away, his face grim. Beside him, Gwen has not moved; she remains kneeling on the gravel, her head bowed. The doctor bends toward her. He is a kind man, a conventional Edwardian; his first thought is that this is no sight for ladies.

"Lady Callendar . . ." He reaches for her arm to help her to her feet; he glances back toward the butler and motions him forward with the sal volatile.

"Lady Callendar, please . . ."

Still Gwen does not move; the doctor looks around at the silent group helplessly. There is a moment's silence. Boy, the eldest son, who should be the one to help, seems transfixed. It is Acland who finally steps forward. He, too, bends, takes his mother's arm, presses it.

"Come away," he says in a low voice. "Come away, Mama. Let Haviland see if—"

Acland never completes the sentence. Suddenly he is aware, from the corner of his eye, of a rush of movement, a dart of black. He looks up, and it is Constance—Constance Cross the albatross— and she is running. Down the steps and onto the gravel; past Jane; past Nanny Temple, who tries to grasp her and misses; past the maids, and Montague Stern, and Maud, who has begun to weep; past Boy, past Freddie.

She swoops down upon the group by the stretcher, darts between the men, black hair flying, black skirts billowing, and—before Acland can stop her, before anyone can stop her—she hurls herself with appalling force onto the rugs, onto the stretcher, onto the body it is supporting. As she does so, she screams. It is a sound Acland will never forget, which no one who hears it that day will forget, a sound both terrifying and primitive. It is not a child's cry; it is a scream of anger and grief, as raucous as the cry of a gull. The pure high note echoes in the air; then Constance buries her face against a twisted throat, a once-neat and pomaded beard.

"Father," she cries, and then again, shaking him, "Papa . . ." There is absolute silence; Shawcross's body twitches; his head rolls.

Constance looks up. She lifts her pinched white face and she stares in accusation at the silent group around her: at Gwen, at Acland, at Boy, at Freddie, at the doctor, at Cattermole. "You killed him," she cries at the circle of faces. "You killed my father."

Acland has never heard such hate in any voice; the venom is chilling.

He stares at Constance, and, her gaze growing still, Constance fixes her eyes upon him. Her blanched face is expressionless; her black eyes seem blank and unseeing. A stone face, a Medusa face, Acland thinks, and then—just for an instant—the quality of Constance's stare alters. Something flickers in her eyes as she looks at Acland, and he knows she sees him. A tiny moment, but in that moment Acland feels something pass between them, a pulse of recognition, like signaling to like.

Acland would prefer to turn aside but finds he cannot do so. The idea that this child and he are in any way akin is repellent to him, yet he finds he cannot break the compulsion of her eyes. He remains still, transfixed; behind him, no one moves, and it is Constance—finally—who snaps the moment's thread. She rises; she sways on her feet. (For a moment, Acland thinks she is going to faint.) Then she recovers herself. She stands absolutely still, a thin, erect child, an ugly child, in a shabby black frock. Her eyes are chips of flint. She lifts her clenched hands over her head; then, on a rising note, she repeats the same phrase, over and over again.

She says: "I loved him. I loved him. I *loved* him."

And it is melodramatic, of course, Acland tells himself. Melodramatic, self-indulgent, and disgracefully ill-bred—yet he cannot tear his eyes away, because he knows that this display is beyond manners, beyond convention, and that, for all its theatricality, it is truthful.

Constance ends on a high keening note, one last yelping cry of grief. Then she is silent. In the slow motion of shock, three things happen.

First, the body of Eddie Shawcross emits a bubbling groan.

Second, Jane Conyngham steps forward. It is she who takes Constance by the arm and, with quiet determination, leads her away. At the top of the steps, Constance pauses, confronted by Sir Montague Stern and that blood-red dressing gown. They look at each other: a small child in a black dress, a tall man dressed in red. Then Stern moves to one side. The third thing occurs: One final person makes his appearance on the steps.

It is Denton Cavendish, fully dressed, moving stiffly, blinking in the daylight, everything about his appearance and demeanor that of a man awakened with a hangover.

Acland sees his father lift his hand to his forehead, look about him with apparent bewilderment, with bloodshot eyes. He looks, in a blank way, at the doctor's car, at the group below him, at the stretcher. The old Labrador bitch Daisy appears at his side, waddles up to him, rubs against his legs.

"Good dog, good dog," Denton says in an absent voice as his eyes rove over the group. They light upon the figure of Sir Montague Stern, always the observer, Stern in his barbaric red dressing gown. Denton's eyes pass on; they return; his expression of confusion changes to an outraged glare.

"Has something happened? Has something *occurred?*" Denton booms in the direction of the dressing gown. His tone implies that nothing short of Armageddon could excuse this garment in this place.

The absurd words echo in the morning air. Before anyone can reply, Denton's bitch Daisy lifts her head.

Like that patient observer Stern, Daisy senses that something here is wrong. Perhaps it is just that she scents blood; on the other hand, like Stern, perhaps she can smell guilt, and fear (someone in this group is both guilty and afraid). Whatever the reason, Daisy's hackles rise. Her throat pumps.

Denton clasps his head; he thwacks the dog's rump. His bitch ignores her master, and his hangover. She continues to howl.

It was clear that Shawcross would die. It is possible that even now, with modern medical practice, he might have died. He had been long hours in the trap, and the loss of blood was severe. Then, there was no hope for him; it was simply (Haviland explained to Gwen) a matter of time.

But how much time? An hour? A week? A day? Gwen pressed the doctor for an answer. The doctor replied, "Not as long as a week, I fear."

The nearest hospital was some thirty miles away. Dr. Haviland pronounced that the journey there would kill Shawcross. Gwen scarcely listened to this. She would not consider a hospital in any case; Eddie must stay at Winterscombe.

And so Shawcross must be returned to the King's bedroom, and the King's bed with the cupids cavorting at its foot. He must lie there beneath the royal arms, with Gwen and Maud in constant attendance; private nurses in starched uniforms must be hired. Shawcross must be cared for twenty-four hours a day.

Dr. Haviland did not expect his patient to survive the first of these twenty-four hours, but he did what had to be done. The wounds were washed with antiseptic; the fractured leg was straightened and splinted; Shawcross regained consciousness, screamed in agony, fainted again. This done, there were problems, and Dr. Haviland hinted at them gravely: The leg should have been set in plaster, but Haviland feared gangrene.

How long had Shawcross lain in the trap? No one could give him a certain answer, but it was obviously a matter of hours. Once the blood supply to a limb was cut off, gangrene could commence in thirty minutes. Haviland touched Shawcross's blackened foot, sniffed, and decided: No plaster; it was not worth the agony it would cause—not for a man he expected to die within hours.

Apart from this question, other problems. They fenced him in on all sides. Shawcross must be suffering starvation of blood to the brain; it therefore might be efficacious (he had seen it practiced) to lay the patient at an angle, head lowered, feet raised.

On the other hand, the supply of blood to the injured leg and foot must be maintained, so perhaps the head should be raised and the feet lowered? Haviland frowned and pondered, while Maud, fluttering in the doorway, reminded everyone of the excellence of good beef broth, and Gwen, fluttering beside the bed, begged the newly arrived nurse to bring her a little eau de cologne.

The women seemed to feel that dignity was paramount: They were all for arranging Shawcross decorously, his shoulders propped against monogrammed linen pillows, his smashed leg protected by a cage under smooth sheets. Haviland, seeing this and knowing their efforts were hopeless, gave up. Let the man lie as they wanted him; let him have the beef broth by all means, if he could take any; yes, yes, cologne dabbed on the forehead did have very often a most soothing effect.

Haviland's bedside manner came to the fore: Gravely he listened to the beat of his patient's heart, and forebore to say how it raced and fluttered. Impressively, magisterially, he examined the patient's eyes with a small torch, and the bitten tongue with a small spatula; he recommended quiet, he administered morphine, and—while giving no false hopes—he remained silent on such questions as fever and delirium. Septicemia, a matter at the forefront of his own mind, was never mentioned; ladies unacquainted with this term had, he found, a tendency to ask its meaning in plain English, and *poisoning of the blood*—the alternative term, and a death sentence—was one that could reduce the calmest woman to hysterics.

Haviland was certain that Shawcross would not survive the first day, let alone the first night; he was astonished to be proved wrong. Shawcross made it through the first day and the first night; he made it through the second; he was still alive on the morning of the third. Both Maud and Gwen were triumphant at this. Both were in that state of optimism and false elation which ensues from shock and lack of sleep; both were beginning to believe, Haviland saw, that Shawcross could recover from this ordeal.

"Oh, Dr. Haviland, he took a little water from a glass this morning," Gwen cried as she came to greet him on the third morning.

"And a spoon of broth last night," Maud added eagerly. "We wondered—perhaps something very light? A little dry toast? Do you think a coddled egg?"

They looked at him with expectant faces. Haviland said nothing. He looked down at his patient, opened his medical bag, caught—across the King's bed—the practiced eye of the senior nurse, and saw her mouth turn down at the corners. He looked at Shawcross and marveled—as he had marveled many times in the past—at people's capacity to deceive themselves.

Shawcross had a mounting fever; that much was obvious even before the doctor laid his hand on the hot dry skin. In two days he had wasted, so the skin of his face now seemed stretched tight across his bones. His lips were dry and cracked with dehydration; his eyes, open and unfocused, darted from side to side. Even as Haviland bent over him Shawcross began to shiver, and beads of sweat broke out on his brow.

"Lady Callendar, if you would perhaps leave us a moment, while we change the dressing?"

He saw Maud and Gwen exchange looks—frightened looks. Both left the room without speaking. Haviland twitched the bedclothes aside, lifted the cage that supported them.

The sickly smell told him immediately, even before he looked down at the dressing.

"When was this last changed?"

"An hour ago, Dr. Haviland." The nurse paused. "His temperature is a hundred and three. It's risen two points since six this morning."

"Delirium?"

"There was some distress in the night. Nothing intelligible. He hasn't regained consciousness this morning."

Haviland sighed. With the nurse's assistance the dressing was changed once again, and further morphine was administered.

Then, his face grave, he went downstairs once more, where he requested an interview with Lady Callendar and her husband.

In the morning room the doctor looked from husband to wife. Lady Callendar's face was puffy from lack of sleep and weeping; her husband, moving slowly and stiffly, seemed to have aged years in the past days. Composing himself, Haviland made the small speech he had been rehearsing in his mind for two days; it was sad and regrettable, but he had to inform them that it was now a matter of hours. Once death had ensued—really he understood how painful it must be to them to consider such a matter at a time like this—the police would have to be informed. An inquest would be necessary, a formality, of course.

The doctor, having pronounced these difficult words, fell silent. Lady Callendar, he noted, made no reply. Her husband, hunched before the fire, fumbled at the rugs wrapped around his knees like an old and infirm man. He would not meet the doctor's eyes.

"I won't have Cattermole blamed" was all he said. "Won't have it, d'you hear? It was an accident—an accident."

Was it an accident? Constance does not think so, for one. Constance is not allowed into her father's room, has not seen him since he was brought into the house. She is confined to the nursery, watched over by Nanny Temple. She is a prisoner, she feels.

Constance cannot sleep. She lies awake night after night, staring at the ceiling of her room, listening for the beat of her albatross's wings. Constance waits for the albatross, who flies everywhere and sees everything, and the albatross tells her it was no accident—someone wanted her father to die.

But who? On this question the albatross is silent, so Constance is left to the speculations of her own mind. Denton Cavendish? Gwen? Boy? Acland? Freddie? Any one of them could have slipped away from the party, as her father must have done, and then . . . What? Followed him? Pushed him? Called to him? Lured him? Threatened him—with a gun, perhaps, so he backed away from them, off the path, into the undergrowth, into that horrible, horrible thing, with its jaws grinning?

Constance holds her breath and listens to the beat of the great bird's wings, white and slow and sure as it circles her room. Not an accident, not a mistake: Constance saw the rabbit and she knows. Someone meant to hurt her father; someone meant to snare him.

She would like to cry; her eyes scratch, but tears will not come. In a minute it will be morning. She can see light edging the curtains now; in the gardens outside, birds are singing. It will be morning, and then the albatross will leave her. She will be alone again.

When the room is gray with light she pushes aside the bed-clothes and steals quietly to the door. It is very early, and if she is very very quiet, now, when her jailor Nanny Temple must surely be sleeping . . . She tiptoes in bare feet out of her room, across Steenie's room, through the day nursery, and out onto the landing. No sound, no stir; her courage rises. They will not keep her away, they will not, these Cavendishes who pretend not to despise her.

But not the back stairs—there a maid might catch her, for the maids at Winterscombe also rise early. The main stairs: there she is safer, and then, once she is in the hall—cold feet on a cold stone floor—into the side hall, and then a passageway and another passageway. Past the silver room and the china pantry, past the housekeeper's room and the stillroom: such a warren of rooms and corridors, and Constance knows all of them intimately. One danger point as she nears the kitchens and the sculleries—she can hear voices there—but then, around a corner and she is safe.

She pushes through a green baize door, and stands, heart beating hard, on the other side of it. Here, on her right, there is a small bare room with an iron bedstead and a washstand. This room, once used by the King's manservant, is never used now. Immediately opposite it, on her left, are the stairs that lead up to the King's dressing room. Does she dare to go up? Constance knows this is forbidden but she does not care. She will not care! They have no right, *no right*, to bar her from her father.

Silently she steals up the stairs. The door at the top is closed, and Constance listens. She can hear footsteps, the rustle of skirts—the nurse perhaps, in her starched uniform. A clink of glass against metal, a murmur of voices, and then silence.

But her father is near. Constance knows this, and although she dares go no farther, the knowledge brings her peace. She sinks down to the floor; she curls up there, like an animal. She thinks herself into her father's mind, so that he will know she is there, his little albatross, his daughter, who loves him. She closes her eyes. After a while, Constance sleeps.

Inside the King's bedroom, beside the bed, Gwen does not sleep. She has been awake all night, she has seen the deterioration in Eddie's condition, she has seen the expression on the face of the nurse, and she no longer deludes herself. She knows the crisis is near.

The nurse has withdrawn. Gwen is alone with Eddie, the silence of the room broken only by the shifting of coals in the fire and the ticking of the clock. Gwen looks at the clock—it is nearing six—and wonders how many more minutes Eddie Shawcross has left. She is ashamed of herself, but she has reached that stage of exhaustion in which she hopes it will be soon. Once she had accepted the idea that Eddie must die, she began to be impatient for the end and to chafe against death's protraction. She knows this is wicked, and hardhearted; still the involuntary prayer springs into her mind: *Let it be soon. Let it be soon, let it be quick—for his sake.*

Her hands twist against the silk of her dress; she turns to look at her lover's face and finds it difficult to believe that this is the man she loved.

His lips are cracked; his once beautifully manicured hands fumble and pull at the sheets; Gwen averts her eyes from the broken nails and the bandages. She looks away, and into her mind—there before she can push it away—comes an image of herself and Eddie, here in this room, just a few days before. She sees herself, wrists bound with black ribbons, and although she is alone her face crimsons with shame. She rubs at her wrist, thinks of bondage and pain, the scent of carnation soap, the allure of the forbidden. As she tries to force the image out of her mind, Shawcross stirs. Gwen turns back to him.

Sweat has broken out again on his brow (the fever goes in cycles). His eyes are open and fixed; his lips slacken, shape dry and incomprehensible noises, and then slacken again.

Gwen reaches for the bell for the nurse. In truth, Shawcross's appearance now frightens her, and she does not like to touch him. Before she can ring, however, Shawcross begins to talk—a rush of words and phrases, some of which are comprehensible.

Rats. Shawcross begins to talk of rats: large ones, black ones, rats who squirm, rats whose eyes bulge, rats who nibble, rats in pantries, rats in haylofts, rats in sewers, rats in—yes—traps, and the half-rhyme seems to please him, for he gurgles and quivers and repeats the word, and then, rising up in the bed with a strength Gwen did not suspect he possessed, he moves on, from rats to ribbons.

"Black ribbons," Shawcross screams, and though his voice is slurred the word is quite distinct. "Black ribbons. Stamp on their heads. That's it. Stamp on 'em. . . .."

Gwen is transfixed with horror and disgust. Ribbons, ribbons—oh, why should he talk of ribbons? She tugs hard on the bellpull and forces herself to bend over him, to make her voice soothing.

"Eddie," she says softly. "Eddie, my dear. You must rest. You must not talk, please, Eddie. . . ."

Eddie's voice has subsided; he slumps back against the pillows. From his throat comes a series of bubbling guttural noises; spittle froths at his lips. Gwen stares down at him fearfully. Can this be a death rattle? She yanks at the bellpull again, and as she does so, Eddie's eyes stop their darting and flickering; they seem to focus on her face. He looks directly at her and says, with perfect lucidity:

"You called to me. In the woods. I heard you call to me."

"No, Eddie," Gwen begins, terrified that the nurse will come in and hear this conversation. "No, Eddie, you're mistaken. You're feverish. Please lie still. . . ."

But something has happened, even as she speaks: a small paroxysm. Less than a shudder, not violent in any way, no more, really, than a slight clenching of the facial muscles, followed by a relaxation. In that fraction of a second the greatest of boundaries is crossed, and Gwen knows it instantly, even before the nurse—now at her side—reaches across, touches Eddie's throat, sighs, checks her watch, and says, "He's gone."

It is a quarter past six, the beginning of a new day. Dr. Haviland is summoned at once, and there is one final nastiness—though, fortunately, Gwen does not witness it.

Before rigor mortis sets in, Shawcross must be washed and laid out. At seven-thirty, just when this process is almost complete and Haviland is preparing to depart, there comes from the bed a most horrible noise, a gurgling, an eructation. The doctor and two nurses swing around; one of the nurses (the less experienced, and an Irish Catholic) touches her crucifix and crosses herself. The sight that greets their eyes is not a pleasant one, nor a common one, though Dr. Haviland, in cases of severe blood poisoning, has seen it before. From all the orifices of his body Shawcross weeps. A sticky yellowish substance, like honey but not so sweet-smelling, issues forth from his ears, from his nostrils, from his mouth. . . .

The washing must be done again. The laying-out must be done again; the nightshirt must be changed, the pillowcases, the sheets. The more experienced of the two nurses, tight-faced, sends a message down via the kitchens, for flowers from the hothouses—if possible, lilies.

They are sent, and finally, at around nine, the other formalities take place. The blinds have already been lowered throughout the house, and in this dim light the members of the Cavendish family come to pay their final respects. Boy, Acland, Freddie. Steenie is spared the ordeal, since his nerves are delicate, but Constance is not. She comes in last, standing rigidly between Denton and Gwen Cavendish at the foot of the King's bed.

She looks at the cherubim, at the embroidered royal arms, at the bed on which—just a few days ago—she posed for Boy's photograph. She looks at her father—eyes closed, linen sheets up to his chin. When led forward by Gwen, she bends over his body and places a dry kiss in the air beside his cheek.

The room reeks of lilies, a flower Constance will loathe forever afterward. She does not cry; she does not speak. She listens for the sound of a bird's wings, for, even though it is daylight, she knows her protector is here with her in this room. She listens and it comes, a sussuration of the air; for the first time she bends her head.

Constance's silence, her lack of tears, alarm Gwen. She takes the child back to her room, sits her down, and talks to her quietly and as gently as she can for some while. Gwen knows that the things she says to Constance are banal; she says them nonetheless. She wonders if she should mention Constance's presence on the dressing-room stairs (where she was discovered by the nurse) but decides against it. The child is capable of deeper feelings than anyone guessed, Gwen tells herself. Let the matter rest.

"Constance, I want you to know," she says at last, "that we feel responsible for you, my dear, and we care for you. The matter will need thought, but remember, Constance, you will always have a home here with us, at Winterscombe."

Constance has been expecting this. She understands that although Gwen's eyes are tearful, the invitation springs from guilt and not affection.

"I understand," she replies in her stiff way. She pauses. She fixes Gwen with her eyes. "When will they take my father away?"

Gwen is flurried by the question.

"Later today, Constance. This afternoon. But it is better not to dwell on it, my dear—"

"When he has gone . . ." Constance lays one small grubby hand on Gwen's sleeve. "Then. May I sit in his room on my own? Just for a little while. So I may say goodbye to him?"

"Of course, Constance. I understand," Gwen replies, touched by the request.

And, later the same day, when Gwen is sure that the undertakers have departed, she herself leads Constance back to the King's bedroom. She opens the door and switches on the lamps. (She does not want Constance to be frightened.) She checks that the bed has been remade and the lilies removed. She settles Constance in a chair.

"You're sure you want to stay here alone, Constance? Would you like me to sit with you?"

"No. I should prefer to be alone," the child replies in her odd formal way. "Just for a little while. For half an hour. I want to think of him."

"I'll come back at four," Gwen replies, and leaves her.

*　　*　　*

When Constance is alone in the room, she looks over her shoulder, toward the bed. Its curtains have a frightening look; they billow at her.

She stands and, in a cautious way, approaches the bed. She darts out a hand and pulls the coverlet back. The pillows reassure her. They are clean and smooth. They bear no imprint of a head.

Constance smooths the coverlet into place. She backs away from the bed. She walks about the room slowly, touching the furniture as she passes. The back of a chair: its horsehair-cover bristles. The back of another chair: velvet this time. She smooths out a crease in the antimacassar. She goes into the dressing room, then the bathroom beyond, switching on the lights as she passes. She looks at the great copper shower, at its levers and spouts, at the wonders of German plumbing. From the basin she purloins a small tablet of carnation soap, which she pockets.

She returns to the bedroom. She becomes more purposeful. There, laid out upon his dresser, are her father's personal possessions, removed from his evening clothes when he was brought up here. A few coins, the case containing his cheroots, a box of matches, his pocket watch and chain, a clean and unused linen handkerchief.

Constance picks up this handkerchief, but it is freshly laundered; it does not smell of her father. She sniffs it. She presses it against her face. She replaces it upon the dresser. She picks up the silver watch chain.

She opens the case of the watch, which is dented. She examines its face. The watch, not wound for several days, has stopped. Its two small black hands point off in opposite directions. Constance closes the case. She holds the watch tight in her hand. She glances once more, over her shoulder, toward the bed. The bed is still empty.

In a crablike, sideways manner, Constance inches her way from the dressing chest to the writing desk, which stands between the windows.

The desk is not locked. In its bottom right-hand drawer, however, underneath some sheaves of papers and printer's proofs, there is a wooden traveling writing case. This is locked, as always. The key to this writing case is small and silver. It hangs upon her father's watch chain.

Constance bites her tongue between her small teeth. She bends forward. She concentrates. She fits the key into the lock and turns it.

Inside the writing case there are a number of letters and bills, which she does not pause to examine. Beneath these, there is an exercise book with a black cover. It is the kind of book a pupil might use in school. It bears no identifying label.

Constance's hands are a little afraid to touch this book. They advance toward it and then they draw back. Finally they delve into the box. They remove the notebook. Its cover is not stiff. It may be rolled up, this notebook, like a newspaper.

Constance rolls it as tight as it will go. She thrusts it down into the deepest pocket of her full black skirt. She examines the skirt. Does the bulge show? No, it does not.

After this, she is quick. She relocks the writing case and closes the drawer. She replaces the watch chain upon the dressing chest. She does not look in the mirror on the chest, because she fears it. If she looked there, she might see her father's pale face, his neat beard. He might do something very terrible: He might beckon to her.

She returns to the chair where Gwen stationed her. She sits down quietly, in an obedient way. She thinks about her father. She tries not to think where they may have taken him. Wherever it is, she is sure it will be cold, and lonely.

Shall she say goodbye, now? Shall she say it out loud? Constance hesitates. She can feel that her father is very close. It seems foolish to say goodbye.

"Goodnight, Papa," she says at last, in a small voice.

The following week there was, as Dr. Haviland had foreseen, an inquiry of sorts. You would not expect it to be too thorough, that inquiry, and you would be right.

Desultory might describe it; *tactful* might describe it. The local police, overawed, had no intention of offending such a prominent local landowner as Lord Callendar, whose cousin was Chief Constable of the County and whose closest friends were so prominent on the local judiciary.

There was an inquest. Not one member of the Cavendish family appeared; they all gave written evidence. That evidence established with some accuracy the time Shawcross was thought to have left the party. It emphasized that Shawcross—a writer, after all—often took walks alone. Beyond that, it told the jury nothing.

Cattermole, who did appear and who rather enjoyed the experience, was more forthcoming. Having explained that, for many years, the traps once used to deter poachers had been stored in a disused barn, where they rusted away, no one giving them a second thought, he moved on. Before the coroner could stop him, he reminded the jury that there had been Gypsies in the area for weeks. These

Gypsies, he continued, had been found to have decamped on the very day the accident was discovered. Since neither he nor any of his men (he could vouch for them) would have positioned traps known to be illegal, he drew his own conclusions. The jury might do the same, he continued, as the coroner leaned forward to interrupt. In his view, it was the Gypsies who had placed the trap, intending mischief to his keepers or to him.

The jury was composed of local men, including several tenant farmers from the Cavendish estates. Their verdict? Death by Misadventure. The matter was closed.

Was this verdict accepted in the privacy of Winterscombe? Perhaps by some—though I think there were other members of the family who had their doubts. The only person to express those doubts out loud was Sir Montague Stern. He voiced them the day after the inquest, in his chambers in Albany in London; there Maud was visiting him, for the first time.

"Death by Misadventure," Stern said in his even way. "That is convenient. And neat."

Maud, who was distracted both by the attraction she felt toward Stern and by the details of his drawing room—such a restrained, perfect room, and full of perfect things, a great contrast to the man himself—did not take this in at once. When she did, she gave a small shriek.

"Montague! Whatever can you mean? Obviously that was the only verdict. We all know it was an accident."

"Do we?" Stern stood by the windows. He looked into the street.

"But of course. The Gypsies—"

"I am not convinced by the talk of Gypsies."

Something in the way he said this drew Maud closer. She advanced a few steps. She looked at Stern, who was tall, whose complexion was pale, whose features bore the marks of his race, and whose eyes were heavily lidded. Those eyes told her nothing. He looked toward her, his expression appraising yet cool. They might have been discussing a dinner party, not a death. Again she had that sensation, experienced at Winterscombe, of a contained man, of contained power. She was shocked by what he said; also excited.

"You cannot mean . . . If it was not an accident, then it would be a question of—"

"Murder?" Stern gave a slight shrug, as if he found the word distasteful. Maud was tempted, but sensible. She stepped forward another pace, then stopped.

"That is ridiculous. Unthinkable. Why, for a murder, you would need a murderer—"

"Indeed. I would have said there might be candidates."

"Preposterous. I shall not listen to this. I believe you are trying to frighten me." She hesitated. "Who?"

Stern smiled. He extended a hand to her. Maud stared with some fascination at his hands, which were fine-boned, and at his cuffs, which were exceptionally white. A glint of gold at the wrist.

"It is pointless to speculate." Stern sounded more brisk. "The matter is resolved. It is unlikely to be investigated further. I like puzzles—that is all. I like to try to solve them. Purely for my own entertainment, of course."

Maud decided to change the subject; she debated whether to take his hand. She felt flurried.

"This is a very beautiful room," she began in a rushed way—a gauche way, and Maud was rarely gauche.

"I am glad you approve." He gave that odd, foreign half-bow. He gestured in a slightly dismissive way toward certain paintings on the walls and certain austere porcelain vases upon the shelves. "I like these things. I am a collector, of sorts."

Something in the steady way in which he said this, and something in his eyes as he did so, decided Maud. An acute memory came to her, of this man in her room at Winterscombe.

Forgetting talk of inquests and more sinister matters, she took another step forward, grasped his hand.

Stern also seemed to have forgotten their earlier conversation. Moving away from the window, his manner deliberate yet circumspect, he took Maud in his arms.

The inquest over—the matter resolved—and it was time for the funeral. But where should it take place? Not at Winterscombe. That suggestion, made tentatively by Gwen, was scotched by Denton at once. In London, then, where Shawcross had rented rooms in Bloomsbury.

Gwen took on the arrangements, for Shawcross seemed to have virtually no family. She worked hard, her mind busy sanitizing the past: an obligation, to an old family friend. By the time the ceremony actually took place, Gwen almost believed this herself.

The funeral was not well attended. Gwen opened up her Mayfair house for the occasion. She did her best to ensure a large and distinguished congregation. On the day, she was mortified by the thinness of the turnout.

Her family were there in force—naturally. But where were the many literary friends of whom Eddie had spoken with such warm familiarity? She had written to them all, these famous men. Now, where were they, the illustrious novelists, the poets of advanced views, the influential editors, the titans Eddie claimed to dine with so often?

None in evidence. The arts were represented by Jarvis of the lavender cravat—who left the ceremony hurriedly, refusing an invitation to return to Park Street—and by a young American, introduced as Hitchings. He claimed to represent a New York journal. His breath smelled of whisky.

Gwen, returning to her Mayfair drawing room, eyed the awkward gathering. She could have cried from pity and humiliation. A thin, chilly little group. Her own family; Boy's fiancée, Jane Conyngham; Maud; Sir Montague Stern (invited at Maud's suggestion, he sent an outsize wreath). There was Constance, who had a cold and whose nose was running. There was a sad-eyed student who rented rooms in the same Bloomsbury house as Shawcross. There was an aging widow whose name Gwen did not catch, who claimed once to have introduced Shawcross to some literary editor.

Apart from these, there was only one other mourner: a reedy young man, a solicitors' clerk in a rusty black suit, who had never met Shawcross himself but was there to represent the firm's partners.

Jane Conyngham talked kindly to the student. Gwen's family massed, to present a united front. Montague Stern, in a patient fashion, engaged the uncommunicative Constance. Gwen, feeling she could bear this no longer, motioned the solicitors' clerk to one side.

She drew him into the library. There, the young man enumerated some gloomy facts: Shawcross had been prevailed upon to make a will, it seemed, after the death of his wife; its beneficiary was Constance. Shawcross had, however, left his daughter very little. His banking accounts were overdrawn; his landlord and his tailors were clamoring for payment. All Constance would inherit, the young man said in a prim and reprimanding way, were her father's books, his personal effects, and a batch of debts.

There was a further problem: Inquiries had naturally been made of the most thorough kind; Shawcross, it seemed, possessed no near relatives. His parents were dead; he had no brothers or sisters; the nearest family still alive were his mother's sister and her husband, who had a small business in Solihull.

"In Solihull?" Gwen was not quite sure where this was, but whatever its location, she did not like the sound of it.

These relatives had been contacted, went on the reedy young man, fingering an ill-fitting and yellowing collar. They had expressed their grief and wished their condolences to be conveyed to the child. However, they had made one thing clear: Their means were slender; they regretted, but they could not be made responsible for a child they had never met. Circumstanced as they were, it was out of the question—*out of the question,* the young man repeated impressively—for them to take Constance in.

Gwen was offended by this. She was offended by the young man, by his collar, which had a tide-mark, and by his Adam's apple, which jiggled as he spoke. She did not like the way he pronounced her name, rolling her title on his lips. She did not like the way his eyes added up her library and its contents.

Gwen had learned hauteur. She gave the young man a diminishing glance. She dismissed these uncharitable relatives and the unpleasant place in which they lived; she dismissed the question of these footling debts, which she would ensure were settled. She dismissed, finally, the question of Constance.

Constance would be taken in, she said, by her own family. This had been their intention from the first. Mr. Shawcross had been an old and valued family friend. Anything else—and she turned upon the young man a cold eye—would indeed have been out of the question.

The young man possibly resented this remark and the way in which it was said. His sallow skin colored. He remarked that his firm would be much relieved, and matters would be facilitated.

"Of course, there is the matter of the Bloomsbury accommodation. The rented accommodation." He paused at the door. "That will have to be cleared. The landlord requires the rooms. We have already had Communications."

This he said in a nasty way, with a supercilious glance at a tiger-skin rug. Having thus disposed of Shawcross, who might have rich and titled friends but who was nonetheless insolvent, he took his leave.

Two days later—her last task, she told herself, and felt relief—Gwen set off for Bloomsbury with Constance in tow. Constance insisted on accompanying her. She needed, she said, to pack her own things. It would not take long. One suitcase would be ample.

The house was tall and gloomy. The communal hall smelled of

wax polish and, more faintly, of boiled cabbage. Gwen leaned against the wall; she began to feel faint.

It was Constance who insisted they must press on, Constance who led her up the wide stairs to the first landing and then on, upward, a steep climb, to the second floor.

Gwen had been supplied with a key; the door to the Shawcross apartment was unlocked. She entered, for the first time, the place where her lover had lived.

They had never met here, and these rooms were not as she had imagined them. Although she had known Shawcross was not rich, Gwen had a benign imagination, and in her mind's eye she had seen these rooms as a pleasant and bookish place, a writer's domain. She had envisaged bookcases, the glow of leather bindings in firelight; a desk, perhaps with a green-shaded lamp; neat piles of papers; an easy chair; some spaciousness. It had given her pleasure, often, when they were forced to be apart, to think of Shawcross here, sitting at this imagined desk, working, then breaking off to think of her.

She had imagined him, perhaps, taking a meal, brought to him on a tray by some servant. She had imagined him, from time to time, inviting to this room some of the celebrated men whom he counted as his friends. She had seen them sitting either side of a bright fire, discussing life, art, religion, philosophy.

This room resisted all such images. It was, in the first place, cramped, having been at some time subdivided. There were bookshelves, but they were gimcrack affairs; the books they contained, though numerous, were dusty. There was a desk, set in front of a grimy unwashed window overlooking a noisy street, but the desk, too, was cheap. There was an ugly lamp upon it. It was scattered with a confusion of letters, papers, proofs, bills. Gwen found this disturbing. Shawcross had taken such care over his appearance. He had always seemed to her so tidy.

"There are three rooms altogether."

Constance had set down her small black case. She stood in the middle of the room. Her face looked pinched.

"There's my father's bedroom—that is through there." She pointed toward a door. "My room is next to it, across the corridor. It has two beds. My nurse slept in the same room."

She said this with an air of some importance, as if the fact that she shared with her nurse gave status.

"Of course, she left some years ago. Papa did not replace her. I was older then. We managed very well without." She paused, lifting her sharp small face to the window.

"Do you like it here? I like it here. If you lean out of the window, you can see the square. And there is a church at the end of the street. I could hear its bells on Sunday mornings. St. Michael and All Angels. I always liked that name. All Angels—it sounds powerful, don't you think?"

Gwen made no answer. She sank down into an uncomfortable chair before an empty grate. On the shelves opposite were several empty bottles, a number of dirty wineglasses. She pressed her gloved hand to her brow.

"Constance, perhaps . . . It is a little soon, I think, to do this. I am not sure I am quite able. It must be upsetting for you. Perhaps we need not stay. I could just arrange . . . well, for everything to be removed to Winterscombe. Then we could go through it later. That might be the best thing."

"I need my clothes." Constance sounded obstinate. "I have some books. Some things of my mother's—her hairbrushes. I left them here. I want them."

"Of course, of course." Gwen attempted to rouse herself. She half rose, then sank back in her chair. She began to wish she had never set foot in these horrible rooms. She could so easily have sent someone else. She sighed. Curiosity, she told herself, curiosity of the worst kind had brought her here. Just once, before she relinquished him, she had wanted to see Eddie's home. Well, now she saw it.

"You stay there." Constance was looking at her in a concerned way. "You look tired. I can do it—I know where everything is. It will not take long."

She rummaged around among the papers on top of the desk, bringing to their surface a letter on mauve paper. She picked up a bundle of proofs and pressed these into Gwen's hand.

"Look. These are the proofs for Papa's new novel. You might like to look at those while you wait. I know how much you liked his work. He would have wanted you . . . to read this."

Gwen was touched. She took the proofs. Constance gave her an approving nod. She picked up her case, then turned toward the bedrooms.

Once the door was closed upon Gwen, Constance was swift.

She went first into her father's bedroom. She fetched a chair and, standing upon it, scrabbled around on the dusty top of his wardrobe. She found the key she sought, and with this key she unlocked the small cabinet beside his bed. This cabinet had two shelves. On the top was a collection of medicines, ointments, lotions, and pillboxes, for her father had suffered mild hypochondria. On the shelf below, neatly stacked, was a pile of black notebooks.

Constance knelt. She leaned back upon her heels. What she was about to do frightened her a little, because these notebooks were secret—she knew that. Her father wrote in them every night. If she came in while he was writing in them, he covered them up or closed them. He always locked them away. He kept the key in his pocket, except when he went to Winterscombe, and then he put it in the dust on the wardrobe, out of sight.

Would he want her to have them? Constance thought that he would. They were his special books, and now that he was dead they belonged to his daughter. *I shall look after them for Papa*, Constance said to herself. She pulled the notebooks out and arranged them in the bottom of her case. Her hands felt itchy. She wiped them on her skirt. Standing, she carried the case across the corridor and into her own room.

She did not want to stay here a moment longer than necessary. From her closet she took two dresses—that did not take long. She pushed them into the case in a tangle. Some blouses, some crumpled petticoats, a nightgown, one pair of buttoned boots, which needed mending, and one pair of slippers.

She had to sit on the case to shut it. When it was closed she realized she had forgotten the hairbrushes. She looked at these brushes, which belonged to someone she had never known: a stranger. She decided to leave them behind.

When she returned to the sitting room she was out of breath. Her sallow cheeks were flushed. Her hands shook with her own daring.

Gwen must have tired of the proofs, Constance saw, for they had been replaced on the desk. Gwen was standing now, next to that desk. She had seen the mauve letter then. . . . Well, Constance had half intended that she should. Why hide it, after all? The letter had lain there, in the rest of that muddle, for weeks. Her father had not bothered to reply. Gwen might not have written to her father; other women, less discreet, had no such scruples.

The letter—only one page—lay open. The paper on which it was written smelled of scent. The writing on it—a large, impulsive female hand—could be read at arm's length. Gwen, who—unlike Constance—did not stoop to read private letters, had, it seemed, been unable to avoid the contents of this one.

For a moment Gwen seemed quite unaware that Constance had

returned. She stood by the desk, frozen in the act of turning away. The blood had rushed into her neck; as Constance stood looking at her, it suffused Gwen's face. Gwen made a small sound. She blinked. With some dignity she turned to the door and, at the door, lowered her veil.

Big, slow, stately Gwen. She gave orders to the carriers, when they finally cleared these rooms, that all letters and private correspondence should be boxed and brought down with the other effects to Winterscombe. At Winterscombe, when they arrived, she gave explicit directions. These boxes should be left sealed. They should then be burned at the earliest opportunity.

Gwen returned with Constance to her Mayfair house. Constance walked stiffly into the house in her black coat and hat, with her small black suitcase in her hand. The rest of the family were having tea by the fire in the library.

To Gwen's surprise, Constance marched into this room, still in coat and hat, still carrying her pathetic little suitcase, and took up a position center stage, before the fire. Denton sat opposite her, clearly stupefied by this interruption, a rug over his knees, the hand holding his cup half raised between lap and lips. His four sons, quicker to take in the situation than their father, were in the act of rising to their feet.

Constance looked from one to the other with apparent equanimity. "I have my things now." She indicated the case. "I want you to know. I shall be very glad to live with you. It is very kind of you to take me in."

Gwen, in the doorway, looked at Constance with an impotent distress. Her plans for Constance, discussed with the child, and with Denton, who had given them his resigned and bewildered consent, had not been discussed with her sons.

They took the news—that Constance Cross the Albatross would now be with them all the time, not just for a few weeks a year—in a predictable way. Steenie clapped his hands with genuine delight; his three elder brothers could not disguise their dismay.

Boy blushed crimson; he fixed his eyes on the carpet at his feet. Freddie gave an audible groan, which he attempted to disguise as a cough. Acland, who found it difficult to conceal dislike, and usually did not bother to try, gave Constance a cold and suspicious look. He glanced up toward his mother. Across the room his oddly beautiful eyes met hers; he was perhaps angry, perhaps—and this was odd—amused. Gwen, disconcerted, found it impossible to tell.

Constance regarded her new family with apparent poise. Her small sharp chin tilted. The very model of a dutiful and loving child, she advanced upon Denton. She reached up on tiptoe. Denton, outflanked and outfaced, had to bend to receive the kiss.

She turned next to Steenie, whom she hugged. She paused, then solemnly advanced upon each of his brothers in turn. Boy, Freddie, Acland: each must have his kiss.

All three older boys were well schooled in manners. Being much taller than Constance, each was forced to bend to receive the proffered peck on the cheek.

Only Acland, the last to be kissed, spoke. He did so quietly, into Constance's ear, as her face was lifted to his. One word only, which Constance alone heard.

"*Hypocrite*," he said. That was all.

Yet Constance was delighted. She stepped back from Acland, and a sudden and genuine animation could be read in her face. Her eyes lit; her lips curved. She considered the word, she later wrote, a declaration of war.

THREE

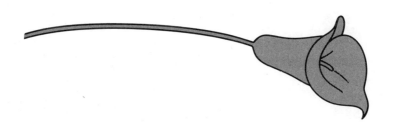

I
A DECLARATION
OF WAR

"SO, HOW'S IT GOING?" Wexton called through the open door of his kitchenette. "Are you advancing or are you stalled?"

I could hear the sounds of cans being opened; an electric toaster popped. Wexton was preparing supper for me from his much-loved hoard of convenience foods. Wexton's kitchen gods were Heinz and Campbell; he never ceased to be delighted and surprised by the glories that came in cans. What would it be tonight? Oxtail soup, with a dash of sherry, or corned-beef hash with Worcestershire sauce, or would it be that favorite of his, a concoction dating back to the days of rationing, involving ketchup and toasted cheese and known as a Blushing Bunny? Whatever it would be, Wexton had one inviolable rule: No one was allowed to watch when he was cooking.

"I'm not sure," I called back through the door. "Running very fast on the spot, I think. The appraiser from Sotheby's came yesterday. I saw the estate agents today. So I suppose I'm making progress. But, Wexton, there's so much *stuff*—"

"Damnation." Wexton gave an anguished cry. A smell of burning toast filled the air. There was the sound of a toaster being punched. I knew better than to interfere in Wexton's love-hate relationship with his toaster. I moved away to the window, maneuvering through piles of newspaper clippings and books.

Wexton, the least violent of men, seemed to have his mind on violence: All these clippings concerned the violent events of the past violent year. The war in Vietnam, the civil war in Nigeria, assassinations in America, potbellied Biafran children in an advanced state of starvation. Wexton's quiet and donnish room was stacked with the evidence of man's current inhumanity to man.

Leaning against the window, I looked out. The view was tranquil; it gave the illusion time could stop. Apart from the presence of motorcars, it was a view that had changed little in two hundred years. The old streetlamps had been retained; the Queen Anne and Georgian houses, much prized, were carefully restored. This street (the reason it was prized, I suppose) resisted the twentieth century.

I could just see the church at the end of the street, and the trees that flanked the south side of the old Hampstead cemetery. Wexton liked to live near graveyards, or so he said. He liked to read old tombstones. This graveyard was his favorite in London; he visited it every day when he took what he would describe as his morning constitutional.

Out of his house, along Church Row, up past the graveyard with its urns and graceful sepulchers, through the warren of small lanes and passageways to the top of Holly Hill, from where he would descend to the village shops, to stare lovingly at the soup cans in the grocer's.

This daily progress of his, reported once in a Sunday newspaper, was now celebrated. It attracted fans. They would lurk in Church Row, waiting for the famous poet to emerge, adjust his battered hat, lift his great lined face to the sky, and sniff the morning air.

Wexton-spotters. The previous day, apparently, one had asked for his autograph. It was the first time this had ever happened.

"Did you give it to him, Wexton?"

"It was a her. She was wearing a long velvet dress, Indian beads, and a peace badge. Sure, I gave her an autograph. I wrote, 'All the best, Tom Eliot.' She was delighted."

I picked up a book from the top of the pile next to me. Perhaps Wexton's mind ran on Eliot as well as violence, for it was a dog-eared copy of *The Waste Land*. I read the lines about Madame Sosostris, famous clairvoyant, with her wicked pack of cards. *I will show you fear in a handful of dust.* I put the book down. I had not yet told Wexton how I had spent the past week at Winterscombe. Or about Constance's journals.

"Deviled sardines. On toast. Unburnt toast." Wexton advanced, with a tray.

Between us we managed to clear enough space among books and clippings to put the tray down. We balanced our plates on our knees, sat in front of Wexton's fire—he liked coal fires—and munched. The room was peaceful and companionable; the sardines were peppery and excellent. Wexton, who surely knew I was keeping something back—he always did—steered the conversation within careful boundaries.

"So. Tell me about the appraiser," he said, still munching.

"He likes the Victorian furniture. The Pugin chairs, and that Philip Webb painted cabinet. When he saw the William Morris hangings he went into a rapture. His name's Tristram."

"Wow," said Wexton.

"That's nothing. The real-estate agent is called Gervase. Gervase Garstang-Nott."

"Does he have raptures too?"

"Not noticeably. Think laid-back. In fact, think horizontal. Think if-it-was-Blenheim-I-might-just-get-interested."

"As bad as that?"

"Worse, really. Nothing but negatives. Wrong date—everyone wants Queen Anne. Too far from London. Too far from the station. Too big—only institutions want houses with twenty-five bedrooms, apparently, and institutions won't spend money. A nibble when I mentioned the woods—because the timber might be worth something. A flicker when we got around to the acreage—*if* planning permission could be obtained to build. He's coming down next week. He made it sound as if that were a great favor."

Wexton gave me a keen glance.

"Depressing?"

"Yes. I suppose it was. I don't want the woods cut down. They're beautiful. I don't want to see houses on all the fields. Maybe that's selfish, but I don't. And I'd have liked someone to want the house. Barring an eccentric millionaire, apparently that's not very likely. I know it's large, Wexton. I know it's Edwardian. I know it's dilapidated. But I love it. I think of all the care that went into it, all the things that happened there—" I stopped. "Anyway. What I feel is irrelevant. Other people don't feel that way, it seems. Either I'm blindly biased or there's something wrong with me."

"Have some ice cream." Wexton rose. "It's a new brand I discovered. American. We can have it with cherries. Tinned cherries. They're really pretty good."

"I don't think I could eat anything else, Wexton. This was lovely. Sorry."

"Okay." Wexton sat down again. He hunched over in his chair. "Look," he said at last. "Why don't you tell me what's really wrong?"

I told him. At least, I told him some of it. I explained about the chaos Steenie had left behind, the boxes and trunks, the family papers, the bundles of letters, journals, photograph albums—all that fallout from the past. I did not tell him about Constance's journals. I almost did but, in the end, held back.

Wexton would not have approved of those journals. He might have told me to get rid of them, burn them—and it might have been sound advice. There were things in those journals, especially those written by Constance's father, that sickened me, and to which I had no wish to return. There were other things that, placed side by side with other evidence still in the house, both alarmed and intrigued me. It was like an addiction, this investigation of the past—I could already see that. The past gave me a fix.

Perhaps that was why I was secretive—and with Wexton, of all people. Wexton, with whom I was always frank. As an alcoholic might hide bottles, I hid the fact of those journals. That way it was easier: I could pretend I did not need them, that I wouldn't take another drink. I'm quite sure Wexton knew I was being evasive; always careful of others' reticence, he did not prompt. I felt ashamed. I loved Wexton, and with those you love, evasion is as bad as a lie.

"It . . . muddles me, I suppose, Wexton," I finished. "There the past is. I thought I knew it, and I find I don't. I recognize the places, but I don't recognize the events. They sound so different now, not the way I remember people telling them at all. And I don't recognize the people, either—that's the worst part. Aunt Maud, Uncle Freddie . . . well, maybe I recognize them. But Jenna. My father and mother. . . . They're different, Wexton. And it hurts."

"That's predictable, you know," he said quietly.

"I know it is. It's predictable, and stupid—I know that. Obviously they're different. Obviously they had lives before I ever knew them, and they grew up and changed. . . ." I hesitated. "But now I feel as if I never knew them at all, as if all my own memories were false. I suppose that's it. I want them back."

"Then stop. You don't have to read all that stuff. All right, you don't want to junk it. Okay. But you can just pack it away. Look at it some other time. When you're older, maybe—"

"Oh, come on, Wexton. I'm almost thirty-eight. If I can't cope with it now, when can I? Besides . . . I can't explain. The moment feels right."

"I guess it is right then. Trust your instincts." Wexton looked at his hands. "You're following some chronology? How far have you got?"

"Oh, 'round about the first war. No. Not as far as the war. Just before: 1910, 1912. I'm not being too meticulous—just trying to put things in some kind of order. When Constance first went to live at Winterscombe, her father's death—there's a lot about that."

"Before my time. I was still in America then."

"But you heard about it, Wexton? I mean, Steenie must have talked about it, or my parents. About Constance and her father and the . . . accident he had. They must have talked about that?"

"Maybe. I don't remember too well. Why not ask Freddie? After all, he was there."

"I can't. He's away. His annual expedition. He was thinking about Peru, but in the end they settled for Tibet."

Wexton smiled. My uncle Freddie's annual excursions to the more remote parts of the globe delighted Wexton; he found them, as I did, impressive. Also comical.

"May I make a suggestion?" Wexton, still hunched in his chair, gave me a considering look.

"Of course, Wexton. I know I'm floundering about. Maybe you're right and I ought to stop."

"I didn't say you should stop. I said you *could* stop. Why not take a look at the war years?"

"The First World War, you mean?"

"It might be an idea." He shrugged. He made a church steeple of his fingers. "Maybe the problems you're having—not recognizing people you thought you knew—well, why not think of it as a generation gap? You see, you weren't yet nine when the last war began. You spent the war years in America. But if you'd been, say, five years older, if you'd been in London at the time of the Blitz, it would have left its mark on you. Take anyone who fought in that war—it doesn't matter what nationality; they could be Russian, American, British, Australian, German, Polish—they still have a common ground, a common experience. They can be difficult to understand, if you don't share that."

"And the first war was the same, you mean?"

"Of course. That war above all. It marked all of us. Your grandparents, your uncles, your father and your mother—especially them, I think. Even . . . even Constance."

I turned back to the window. I was surprised Wexton should mention that name. I also knew he might be right. I could already see it was to war that these journals were leading. *War* was one of Constance's favorite words, although when she used it, it often had no connection with politics or with military matters. I turned back to Wexton uncertainly.

"How do I look at the war, Wexton? The letters from the front line—is that what you mean?"

"No. Not exactly." Wexton answered me quietly. He looked abstracted, distant, as if his mind were far away from this room, from me. There was a long silence; then he seemed to rouse himself. He stood and put an arm around my shoulders.

"You're tired. I can see all this has upset you. Don't listen to me. I'm getting old—and I'm probably barking up the wrong tree. I've got war on my mind at the moment—that's probably it." He waved his hand at the piles of newspaper clippings.

"The thing is, I've never been to these places. Africa. Southeast Asia. But that's not the point. It's not the terrain that interests me, or the politics or the weaponry. I'm not writing about napalm. The journalists do that better than I ever could, and when they've finished, the historians can take over. No, it's not that. I wanted to write about—"

He stopped, in the middle of his sitting room. Wexton rarely discussed his own poetry; when he did so, it always made him first agitated, then self-deprecating, then gloomy. His manner was never that of the sage. He resembled someone trying to explain a particularly abstruse knitting pattern.

"I wanted to write . . . about war as a state of mind. Yes, I think that's it. It does exist. I've seen it. Soldiers—they have to be trained to attain it. But other people reach it as well. Some are born with it, perhaps. People who've never carried a gun. People who've never been near a front line. It's inside us all, waiting. Bayonets in the brain. That's what I wanted to write about . . . I think."

His face fell. The creases and crevasses rearranged themselves into mournful folds.

"I even finished it. Yesterday. The first part of it. Of course it was no good at all. When I looked at it this morning, I could see—it was embarrassing. Dishwater verse."

"What did you do with it, Wexton?" I asked him gently.

"Tore it up," he said. "What else?"

I knew Wexton, I knew his hints, and I respected them. Wexton rarely gave advice. If he did so, it was usually astute. The more casual and dismissive his manner when he made a suggestion, the better it was likely to be.

When I returned to Winterscombe, and returned to the past, I opened Constance's journals at my uncle Freddie's nineteenth birthday, the day war was declared.

I was camped in a corner of the drawing room. In the rooms beyond, Tristram Knollys and his team of assistants were embarking on an inventory. They were making lists: every painting, every rug, every piece of furniture. Constance, too, made lists that day, but her lists were very different.

This is what she wrote:

August 4, 1914

How good to begin a new book, on a new clean page. Do you see, Papa—I have found some journals exactly like yours! The same size, the same paper, the same covers. I was so happy to find them! I wanted them to match.

It is so very hot again today. Francis measures the temperature every morning. I am helping him to keep a chart. At eight o'clock it was seventy-five degrees Fahrenheit, imagine that! I put the mark in, and joined up the graph. It looks like mountains. It looks like the Himalayas. Up and up and up. So hot. And the house is full of that hot word 'war', so I ran away here, to the birch-grove to write. It is cool under the trees. Floss is licking my leg. Acland used to meet Jenna here, but now he is changed, and they do not meet, not here, not anywhere. I am interested—a little interested—in that.

Now, shall I make my list, Papa—the one I promised you? Here it is. The ones on the left had a motive, and the ones on the right had the means.

Denton	*(jealousy)*	*Denton*
Gwen	*(guilt)*	*Cattermole*
Francis	*(if he knew)*	*Hennessy*
Acland	*(he did—hate)*	*Acland*
Jack Hennessy	*(jealousy—not of you)*	*Francis*
Gipsies	*(a mistake)*	*Gipsies*

There. Does that help? Please tell me, Papa, what you think.

Today, on the way here, Floss and I found a hedge-sparrow nest. There were seven eggs, of the most beautiful hue. They were as blue as your eyes, Papa, and no bird to sit on them. Floss said the nest was abandoned.

Abandoned is a good word. It has two meanings. You would like that. Some words have three, and a very few have four. Maybe I will make lists of them too. Would you like that?

It is very quiet here. The bushes are stealthy. Oh, Floss is beginning to growl. He says, Be careful, Constance. Stop now. Someone is watching.

Acland paused, just beyond the gazebo. Through the trees he could see a patch of blue. He hesitated, then walked a few paces farther forward. There, in the center of the birch grove, her back against a silver tree trunk, sat Constance. Floss was with her, stretched out at her feet. Constance's attitude was one of concentration, her dark head bent toward her lap.

Acland took another step forward, a quiet one. She was writing, he saw, writing in a slow and painstaking way, as if completing a lesson. Every so often she would break off, stroke Floss in an absent-minded way, then continue. She wrote in a notebook, he saw—a notebook with a black cover.

She seemed absorbed. Even when his foot cracked a small dry branch, and the dog's ears pricked, Constance did not look up.

Acland was fascinated by Constance. Sometimes he resented this. He liked to watch her (especially if she did not know she was being observed); he liked watching her as a child likes to look down the tube of a kaleidoscope. He liked to see her patterns shift, re-form, and scintillate; he liked the patterns for their brilliant hues and their complexity. They tricked his eye with their iridescence, so that each pattern seemed new and never repeated. There must be a finite number of these patterns, but the speed and the dazzle with which they altered and re-formed pleased him; he preferred to believe they were infinite, and infinitely arbitrary.

Acland knew about kaleidoscopes; he had been given one as a child. Once, in an effort to resolve its mysteries, he had taken it apart. He had been left with a cardboard tube and a handful of glittering particles, mixed together in his palm, the colors muddied. All the variety and contradiction were gone. He had learned his lesson. Constance fascinated, he told himself, precisely because he watched, and from a safe distance at that; he did not intend to investigate further.

In four years Constance was greatly changed. The fact that Gwen now chose her clothes, and Jenna—now Constance's maid—tended both her clothes and her unruly hair, had made a difference, of course. But the chief change was one Constance had wrought: She was then, as Acland watched her, in the process of inventing herself.

Later, when she had herself down to a fine art, Acland would still admire her, for the defiance and the energy of her artistry. But in some ways he admired her more when she was younger, still rough around the edges, as she was then, in 1914. Constance's energy, always formidable, was then as tangible as a force field. She bristled with it—so much so that Acland sometimes felt that if he put out his hand and held it above her hair, his hand would tingle with static electricity.

She was small, fierce, unpredictable, and quick. Her face had the natural plasticity of the actress: She could look as sad as a clown one second, as imperious as a dowager the next. Everything about her seemed to fly off from some center of energy; her hair, which Jenna brushed religiously and tried to tame, had a will of its own. Constance was still too young to wear it up, and so it tumbled and snaked across her shoulders and her thin back—black, thick, resilient hair, as coarse and abundant as a horse's mane. Gwen despaired of this hair, which she felt in a vague way was impolite. It made Constance, even when on her best drawing-room behavior, look like a Gypsy.

Constance never learned to be sedate and ladylike: If she could cross her legs, she would; if she could squat on the floor, she would; if she could run, she would. All the time—running, sitting, standing, talking—her hands moved. Constance had small hands; they gestured and spoke, and—since Constance had a magpie fondness for small bright pieces of jewelry—they glittered, for she wore too many rings, jamming them on her fingers with a carelessness Gwen found vexing. Gwen once examined these rings and found a valuable ring, of chaste design, given by herself, on the very next finger to a trumpery affair that had come from a Christmas cracker.

Constance could not resist such things; she could not resist bright colors. It occurred to Acland, as he watched her through the trees, that he had never seen Constance wear muted shades or pastels. Her dresses were as bright, and often as clashing, as the feathers of a hummingbird's wings: scarlet, fuchsia pink, an electric shade of violet, marigold yellow, an iridescent blue so bright it bruised the eyes—these were the colors Constance loved, and the dresses she cajoled from Gwen. When she had them, she would preen in them; then, surreptitiously, day by day, she would trick them out until they were more garish still. A fragment of lace, sequins, a bright square of embroidery, a diamanté buckle on an otherwise irreproachable shoe; Gwen would sigh, and give in. She could see that, however much she disapproved, these things suited Constance. She took oddities and scraps and excesses, and out of them fashioned herself: a quick, bright thing of contradictions. Look at me, said this creature: I divert! You cannot tame me! Watch me—look how I sparkle when I dance!

That day, in the birch grove, Constance wore a dress of blue material, acid as prussic crystals. It had begun life plain but was now adorned by a zigzag line of scarlet picot trimming, which marched around her tiny waist and navigated the now-discernible peaks of her breasts. Acland, looking at this trimming, wondered if its disposition—and the attention it drew to Constance's figure—was accidental. He decided it was not. Constance might be many things; she was not an innocent. She was, that day, tranquil—and that was unusual. She wrote, paused, wrote again. Occasionally she would break off from her writing to stroke Floss.

Floss, given her by Boy, was the first of Constance's dogs: a pretty thing, a small tricolored King Charles spaniel with an impudent air and a tail as smart as a feather. He had an inexhaustible appetite for affection; he encouraged Constance's strokes and pats unashamedly. After a while, he rolled over on his back and offered her his stomach, but he did so in a lazy way, as if he were a potentate and Constance was just another useful hand from the harem.

To his own surprise, Acland was touched by this vision. Those who do not know they are watched are always, in some way, defenseless. Constance's defenses were usually thick and impenetrable —she had discovered, Acland suspected, that charm was a better barrier than the sullenness she had displayed as a child. Now, because she did not see him and therefore made no attempt to tease, provoke, challenge, or please, as she usually did, Acland felt drawn to her.

She looked like a child, although she was close to fifteen, almost a woman. She looked sad and studious and lonely, this girl with her dog and her notebook and her pencil. What did she write?

Acland was about to step forward when Constance, closing the notebook, looked up.

"Oh, Acland," she said. "You startled me."

"You looked busy." Acland approached, then stretched out full-length on the grass, as he liked to do. He felt the sun on his face; he levered himself up onto one elbow and looked at her.

Constance had curious eyes: They were large, a little slanted toward the corners, and their color was indeterminate; sometimes Acland thought they were navy-blue, sometimes a very dark green, sometimes black. He could see himself in them now: a tiny reflection. These eyes resisted interpretation; they rested upon him, yet they seemed, in their darkness, blank.

There was always the temptation, with Constance's eyes, to look closer, to look deeper, to surprise a truth they cloaked. Acland felt from time to time that he would like to touch Constance's eyes, and to trace their shape with his fingers. Also her lips, which he suspected she brightened with some salve; the upper lip was sharply defined; the lower, softer and more sensual. Between her lips, which were slightly parted, were small, even white teeth. Acland drew back.

"Aren't you coming to Freddie's picnic?"

"Is it time yet?"

"Nearly." Acland lay down again on the grass. "I was just going back to the house."

"I'm avoiding the house." Constance made a face. "War, war, war. That's all anyone talks about. Sir Montague says it's inevitable, then Aunt Maud argues, and your mother weeps, and your father brings out his maps again, and Francis talks about his regiment. . . . I decided to escape."

"What were you writing? You looked very absorbed."

"Just my journal." Constance pushed the notebook beneath the folds of her bright skirt. Acland smiled.

"*You* keep a diary? I can't imagine that. And what do you write in it?"

"Oh, my girlish thoughts, of course." Constance gave him a sideways glance. "I write about serious matters. My latest dress. My new shoes. Whether my waist is now sixteen inches or sixteen and a half. My dreams—I never leave out my dreams! My future husband—I spend a great many paragraphs on him, as girls do. . . ."

"Do you indeed?" Acland, who believed little of this, continued to regard her, slightly lazily. "And what else?"

"Oh, the family. I write about them. What Steenie said. What Freddie wants from me for this birthday of his. About Francis and his photographs. His wedding to Jane, and how it has been postponed yet again . . ." She paused and gave him a sly look. "Sometimes— not often—I write about you."

"I see. And what do you write then?"

"Well now, let me see. I write about your progress in the world. The books you read and the things you say about them. I write about those you admire and those you don't. I describe you, of course. I say you remind me of Shelley—you do look like him, Acland, you know—"

"What nonsense." Acland, who knew it was nonsense, was still flattered. "You've never even read Shelley, I'll bet."

"Very well then, perhaps I don't write that. Perhaps I write . . . that you are changed."

Constance's voice altered as she said this. The teasing note left it. She gave him another sideways glance. Acland began to pull up tufts of grass. He said in a light voice: "Oh—and am I changed?"

"But of course. You have left Oxford now. You are quite the coming man—or so everyone says."

"You believe it, do you—what everyone says?"

"Naturally. I trust gossip implicitly. I would lay down my life for a rumor. Acland the party-giver. Acland the golden boy of Balliol. Also . . ."

"Also what?"

"I make observations of my own. I record my data. No scientist could be more industrious. Of course, sometimes my findings do not tally with your reputation—"

"In what ways?"

"Ah, you are listening now, quite intent! What egoists you men are—you always want to know what we women think of you. Very well, I shall tell you. I write that you are older, less impetuous, that you have acquired a measure of caution, and that you fight life less—"

"A dull dog. I sound like a banker."

"Perhaps I mean fight *me* less—for you have certainly called a truce there."

"A truce? Is that what you call it? A tactical withdrawal, that's all. Fighting is exhausting. Besides, you've changed. You're a little less obnoxious than you used to be."

"Thank you, Acland dear."

"You have improved. You'd admit there was room for improvement?"

"Oh, yes. And I shall improve myself even more. Wait and see. I'm an anchorite when it comes to self-knowledge and self-improvement. Why, I've hardly begun! I shall work on myself, Acland, you'll see—polish and hone away until I make myself quite dazzlingly perfect." She paused. "However. I am beside the point. Don't turn the subject. We were discussing you. How you have changed. I left out the most important thing of all."

"Oh, and what was that?"

Constance gave a small smile. "Why, *Jenna*," she said.

Acland stood up. He walked away. He was angry with Constance. He would have liked to slap her for her spying ways and her deviousness. He would have liked to slap her for her precocity, for the way in which—as and when it suited her—she made a provocative transition from young woman to young girl. Her words stung him, as she had known they would do—stung more, since he knew they were right. If he was changed, it was because of Jenna, and the ending of their affair.

Looking back over his shoulder at Constance, who had returned to her notebook without sign of concern, Acland thought (as he had thought before): *Constance sees too much.*

It was not simply that Constance should know of an affair he believed secret, or even know that it was over—it had been over for almost two years. But Constance had seen more than that: She had seen that he had changed. For the worse, he assumed, since the end of the affair had been shabby.

He had gone up to Oxford hot with love and promises: eternal fidelity, unaltered love. That state of mind had not lasted three months. Jenna was, quite simply, eclipsed. He lost sight of her behind new friends, new intellectual challenges, new horizons, new books. When he had next returned to Winterscombe, already wary, already experiencing guilt, he found a Jenna unaltered, yet unrecognizable.

He could see that she was pretty, where he had believed her beautiful. The redness of her hands, the calluses on her fingers— these offended him. Her accent, the slow manner of her Wiltshire speech, these which he had loved before, now irritated him. Acland had a head full of new friends, new ideas, new books, none of which he could discuss with Jenna.

This disloyalty made him ashamed. Shame bred guilt; guilt eroded desire. Acland discovered a bitter fact: Love was not immortal, as he had believed, and neither was physical want; both were capable of vanishing overnight.

Jenna, who had probably seen the change in him before he did, said not one word of reproach. With an air of quiet resignation, explaining their plight in truisms that made Acland wince, she said she understood it was over, that it might be for the best, that she would settle to it, given time, that, no, he was not to blame; no one was.

There was a look in Jenna's eye, when she said these things, that made Acland deeply ashamed. He saw himself as shallow, profligate, irresponsible, snobbish—yet, even then, at the very same moment that he despised himself, he was heaving a silent sigh of relief.

His friend Ego Farrell (and Farrell, to the mystification of many, for they appeared so unalike, was Acland's closest friend) said Acland had been a boy, confusing love and sex—in love with his idea of a woman, not with Jenna herself. He implied, in his dry way, that Acland might profit from the experience, that self-flagellation was unnecessary, since the affair had been the means to grow up.

Acland could accept that this was sensible; however, a residue of guilt and self-dislike remained. It had occurred to Acland while at Oxford, and it occurred to him again, standing on the edge of the birch grove, that to grow up in such a manner might also be to diminish. Was he less now than he once was—or more?

Acland was unsure. He had excelled at Oxford; he had also learned to distrust that excellence. At the very moment when the quickness of his mind, his grasp of the abstract, had earned him plaudits, at the very moment when (as Constance said) that golden future was forecast, Acland doubted. He saw himself as tainted, flawed, and self-deceiving. *I lack will,* he would say to himself, and he would see himself as confined by his class, a prisoner of the ease of his upbringing.

Jenna might have freed me from that, he would think, and the doubts would intensify. Yes, he was a fine sprinter (his First from Oxford told him that), but in the long term, did sprinters stay the course?

"Why did you say that?"

He had returned to Constance. He glowered down at her.

Constance closed her notebook and gave a shrug.

"About Jenna? Because it is true. You loved her once. You used to meet her here. I saw you kiss her once—oh, years ago, now. Then I saw her weep, one Michaelmas term. Now I hear she is to marry that horrible Jack Hennessy. . . . I told you: I collect my data. I make my observations."

"You're a little spy. You always were."

"That's true. Another thing to cure. I shall make a note of it. Thank you, Acland. And don't scowl so. Are you afraid I'll gossip? I shan't, you know. I am very discreet—"

"Go to hell, Constance."

Acland began to turn away. Constance caught hold of his hand.

"Don't be angry. Here, pull me up. Now, look me in the eyes. You see? I meant no harm. You asked if you had changed. I answered you. You have, and for the better."

Acland hesitated. Constance was now on her feet; she stood very close; her hair brushed his shoulder; her face was lifted to his.

"For the better?"

"But of course. You are harder now. Steelier. I like that. In fact, I sometimes think I like you best of all, even better than your brothers. Still, it's useless to tell you that. You won't believe me. You think me a hypocrite—or so you once said." She paused. "Do you still think that, Acland?"

Acland looked down at her. Her face, serious now, was still lifted to his. There was a small bead of sweat on her temple, like a tear. Her nose intrigued him. Her wide flat cheekbones intrigued him. He was intrigued by the abundance of her hair. Looking down into her face, Acland was possessed by an extraordinary, an irrational thought: If he could only bend just a few inches, if he were to touch that springy hair, if he were to kiss those parted lips, he would have the answer to her question once and for all. Was she a hypocrite? The taste of her mouth would tell.

He turned away abruptly, releasing her hand. He said stiffly, "I'm going back to the house."

"Oh, wait for me. I'll walk with you." She put her arm through his. Floss cavorted at her heels. Ignoring Acland's silence, she chattered about Freddie, his birthday, the picnic, the present she had bought, what they might eat, whether Francis would take a photograph. . . .

"Why do you call Boy that?" Acland said, out of a lingering irritation, a sense that he had been outsmarted and outplayed. "Why Francis, for God's sake? No one else ever calls him that."

"It's his name. Why not?" Constance gave a skip and a jump.

"You do it so deliberately. You make such a point of it—"

"But of course." She gave another skip. "Francis likes it. You must have noticed that." She released his arm, then ran ahead of him, Floss barking at her feet. The distance between them widened. Acland, suspecting she meant him to chase her, slowed his pace.

They were out of the woods now, on the edge of the lawns. Acland stopped. Constance ran on, not once looking back. From a distance she was very much a child still, a tiny swift figure, a flirt of blue skirts.

On the terrace beyond, his family were gathering. Straight as an arrow to its target, Constance ran across the terrace to Boy.

Boy was given to sudden outbursts of coltish exuberance; Constance, Acland believed, liked to play on that. She did so then. As Constance launched herself at him, Boy gave a whoop of delight. He caught Constance up, swung her around in a blue circle, set her down on her feet again. It was the kind of horseplay an uncle might indulge in for the sake of a small child. Except that Boy was not

Constance's uncle, and Constance—in Acland's view—was not a child.

From the edge of the lawns he glared at the spectacle: Boy making a fool of himself; Constance teasing Boy as successfully as she teased him.

Hypocrite, he said to himself.

They began the picnic with a photograph.

This is how Boy arranged them: in the center, Denton and Gwen, with Freddie, the guest of honor, enthroned between them. Acland and Steenie were to flank their parents, balanced on one side by Maud and on the other by Jane Conyngham. There were two other male guests to be accommodated: Ego Farrell and James Dunbar, Boy's friend from Sandhurst and now his fellow officer.

Dunbar, a young man who wore a monocle and had no apparent sense of humor, was the heir to one of the largest estates in Scotland. Farrell was stationed by Jane, Dunbar by Maud; the two men knelt, to improve the composition. Maud promptly obscured Dunbar's face with her parasol.

Since Montague Stern had remained at the house, awaiting news, the picture was then almost complete. Only one last component was missing: Constance.

Boy fussed; Maud complained that the sun was in her eyes. Freddie, who was eager to open his presents, had begun protesting volubly. In the end Constance appeared; she darted forward and seated herself right in the center of the group, in front of Freddie.

Since Freddie was tall and Constance tiny, this seemed to settle the matter. Boy disappeared beneath his camera hood.

"Smile!" he commanded, one hand snaking out, ready to press the bulb.

Everyone smiled; Freddie, leaning forward, put his hands on Constance's shoulders; Constance, arching back a little, whispered something. Freddie laughed. Boy emerged from under the hood.

"I can't take it if you talk."

"I'm sorry, Francis."

Boy retreated beneath the hood. The bulb was pressed; the Videx whirred; the picture was taken. It is in one of the old albums still, sepia, distinct, the corners dog-eared, the only photograph I have ever seen of Constance, with my family, at Winterscombe.

Constance holds her little dog Floss in her arms; she gazes directly at the lens; her hair flies out; her fingers are crammed with rings. Constance loved to be photographed; when you looked at a photograph, she used to say, you knew who you were.

Freddie liked to receive presents. It was pleasant, for once, to be the center of attention, pleasant not to compete with Steenie's dramatics or Acland's wit. By the time Boy began to unpack the picnic food, Freddie had a pile of the most satisfying gifts beside him. Constance's present, the last to be given, lay on his lap: a flamboyant cravat made of Paisley silk, the kind of cravat Sir Montague might have envied. Freddie looked at it uncertainly.

"Don't worry," Constance said in a whisper. "That's your public present. I shall give you your proper one later." These words scratched away in Freddie's mind, as Constance had probably intended. "Proper present." "Later." Freddie began to fidget.

"Constance," Boy said in a stern voice, "would you prefer the chicken or the salmon?"

He looked up from the picnic basket in the manner of a man requesting that Constance make a serious and moral choice—between good and evil, salvation and damnation, perhaps.

"Oh, salmon, I think, Francis," Constance replied in a careless way, and withdrew to the shade of a small clump of birch.

It was very hot. The air felt moist and steamy; the surface of the lake was without ripples. Freddie munched his way contentedly through the staple fare of Winterscombe picnics: gulls' eggs, poached salmon, chicken in an aspic (which was beginning to melt).

He shared a cold steak sandwich with his father; he ate raspberries, then a slice of apple pie. His birthday was toasted in pink champagne. Freddie tilted his Panama hat over his eyes and leaned back against the bank. A pleasant somnolence began to steal over him.

Before this picnic, Acland had taken each person to one side; he had banned the topic of war, which so upset his mother. War might be uppermost in everyone's mind, but consideration ruled. It was not mentioned. As Freddie lay back and began half to listen, half to dream, fragments of conversation drifted into his mind and out again. His father spoke of Scotland and salmon; Gwen and Maud discussed dresses; Acland and Jane talked about a book they had both read; Steenie gave a running commentary on the sketch he was making of the family group. Freddie half-closed his eyes. Steenie's charcoal scratched on the drawing paper; Constance's words scratched away in Freddie's mind, like mice behind a wainscot. Constance, he saw (watching her beneath his eyelids), was laying siege to James Dunbar.

Boy's friend was not promising material, but Constance was not deterred. She liked to practice her charms on the intractable, Freddie sometimes thought; she did so with an air of sweet perseverance, like a would-be pianist practicing scales.

After some while, Boy, who had also watched this display, began on a game. He picked up small twigs and pieces of branch and whittled at them. He began to toss them for Constance's dog, and Floss chased after them. Floss was not an obedient dog; he had none of the instincts of a retriever. Once he had caught the sticks, he refused to return them to Boy. He pounced on them, toyed with them, flopped full-length, then gnawed at them.

Constance leaned across; she smacked Boy's hand.

"Francis," she said, "don't do that. I've told you a thousand times. He will chew the bark. It makes him sick."

"Sorry."

Boy seemed to ignore the sharpness of the reprimand.

Constance turned back to Dunbar and continued her attack, which was taking the form of an inquisition.

"Tell me," she said, laying one small ringed hand on Dunbar's sleeve, "are you a good soldier? Is Boy? What makes a man a good soldier?"

Dunbar screwed at his monocle. He looked perplexed—such a question seemed not to have occurred to him before. He glanced across toward Gwen and then, judging she was out of earshot, decided to risk a reply.

"Well now." He cleared his throat. "Courage—of course."

"Oh, I thought you might say that." Constance gave a small pout. "But you must be more specific. I'm a woman, and women don't understand male courage. Our own kind is so very different, you see. What makes a man courageous? Is it daring? Is it stupidity?"

Dunbar looked nonplussed. Acland, who had caught the remark, glanced up and smiled. Boy, seeing that Constance once more had her back to him, threw another, larger stick to her dog.

"No, not stupidity," Constance ran on. She smiled at Dunbar winningly. "That is *quite* the wrong word. I can't imagine why I said it. Lack of imagination—that is what I meant. I've always thought the greatest heroes must lack imagination. They must refuse to imagine all the terrible things—pain and disaster and death. That is why they are strong—don't you think?"

As Constance said "strong," Freddie noticed her place her small hand once again on Dunbar's sleeve. Dunbar looked confused. He fiddled with his monocle cord; he let out a stertorous sigh. The argument might not have convinced him (it was, in any case, truly aimed at Acland, Freddie thought), but the eyes did. Dunbar made protective noises; he capitulated.

Freddie smiled to himself. He knew quite well that Constance had considerable scorn for Dunbar, whom she called "the tin soldier." He watched Boy throw one more stick, and Floss caper after it. Then he closed his eyes. He began to drift toward sleep.

Words eddied toward him. "The thing *is*," his father was saying in an aggrieved tone of voice, "they're so damnably fussy about where they spawn. You give it the optimum conditions, and what does your salmon do? It goes up Dunbar's river, that's what it does. . . ."

"I almost think, Gwen, that I prefer Mr. Worth. I saw the most charming ensemble there last week. Montague would have adored it."

"It is a perfect book."

"Can anything be perfect?"

"Books can. While one reads them."

"Women *are* the weaker sex—I've never doubted it," said Constance, who believed no such thing. "A woman looks up to a man as she would to a father. He must be her protector, after all. . . ."

"Because the thing is—your salmon is a contrary creature. Concentrate on the trout, I sometimes think, and forget the damned salmon altogether. . . ."

"Little pin-tucks. Then, on the skirt, the most cunning embroidery . . ."

Freddie heaved a comfortable sigh; a muddled vision swam through his consciousness: salmon in ball gowns, rivers flowing with books. He saw himself assembling a new fly and heard himself pronounce, with great authority, that with this fly he would catch them—by the volume. There he was, in his waders, up to his thighs in rushing water, playing the book on his line, and it was a book he had seen Constance reading the previous day (a book borrowed from Acland), a devious brute, a fifteen-pounder at the least, which he reeled in just so far when it started fighting. . . .

"*Floss!*"

A sudden high cry of distress, so sharp it wakened Freddie at once. He sat up, blinking.

His aunt Maud had jumped to her feet and was flapping her hands in a distressed way; Acland was rising; Constance was running toward the reeds in a blur of blue skirts.

"Boy, that was your fault." Jane stood. "Constance told you not to do it."

"It was only a game." Boy stammered a little on the *g*.

"It was a stupid game. Constance, is he all right? What has happened?"

Freddie stood up. Constance had reached the reed bed. He saw her bend and pick up her dog. She cradled Floss in her arms. Floss wriggled; he squirmed. It was some while before Freddie realized that he was choking.

"He can't breathe. He can't breathe." Constance's face was white and waxy; her voice rose in distress. "Francis, I *told* you—you see! There's something stuck in his throat. Oh, help me someone, help me—quickly. . . ."

Floss was making a kind of dry retching noise. A shudder passed through the length of his body from nose to tail. He squirmed, opened his mouth as if to yawn; his small tongue threshed; his paws scrabbled. Then he fell still. Constance gave a moan. She crouched down, head bent, clasping her dog more tightly, as if she wanted to hide his struggles from view.

"Hold him still."

Acland pushed past Freddie. He knelt down beside Constance and grasped the dog's throat. Floss jerked his head; he struggled so violently that Constance almost dropped him.

"Hold him *still*."

"I can't. He's frightened. Stay, Floss—stay. . . ."

"Damn it, Constance, hold his head. That's it."

Acland forced the dog's throat back; he prised the clenched teeth apart; he hooked his finger into the dog's mouth. Blood and saliva flecked his hand. A quick movement, then his hand was withdrawn. Acland closed his palm, then opened it. In it lay a fragment of stick, no more than an inch long. As they all looked at it Floss gave another tremor. He shook himself. He seemed to decide he could breathe. He snapped at the air, then licked at his muzzle. He made a heroic leap, and bit Acland.

That done, he recovered rapidly. Hearing the sighs of relief and the endearments, knowing he was the center of attention once more, he vibrated with new energy. He batted Constance with his front paws and nuzzled her hand with his nose; he pranced about the group and raised his smart feather of a tail. It was at this point, when it was clear that the accident had been averted and Floss was saved, that Sir Montague Stern joined the group unseen, from the path behind them.

It took a moment, amid the celebrations, for Stern's presence to be registered. It took a moment more to understand the expression on his face. Once it was understood, the group wheeled and turned. They pressed upon Stern, pelted him with questions: It was certain, then? How did he know?

War, war, war. The banned word was released, in spite of Gwen. Having been imprisoned and suppressed for so long, it seemed to leap from person to person with new vigor, like a tongue of flame.

All eyes turned upon Stern, except those of Freddie. Freddie remained looking at Constance, and so it was Freddie alone who witnessed the strange thing that happened next.

Despite the appearance of Stern, despite his news, neither Constance nor Acland had moved. They remained kneeling, facing each other, Floss sniffing and panting just to their left. They did not look at Floss but at each other.

Acland said something that Freddie could not catch. Constance replied—again, he could not hear her words. Then Constance reached forward and took Acland's hand. It was the hand Floss had bitten, and although the bite was neither serious nor deep, it was visible: a red half-moon of teeth marks. It had not broken the skin.

Constance raised Acland's hand to her face; she bent over it and pressed her mouth against the sickle of the bite; her hair fell forward, obscuring Freddie's view.

For a moment Acland did not move; then, in a slow way, as if he might at any second draw back, Acland lifted his hand too. He held it a few inches above Constance's head; he lowered it, and let it rest upon her hair.

They stayed thus, poised as two figures in a *pietà*, apparently deaf, blind, and indifferent to the lake, the sun, the family group, the cries and exclamations. This stillness, in two people Freddie associated with speed and constant movement, astonished Freddie and silenced him. He had been about to interrupt—perhaps to intervene. He did not.

Walking back to the house a few minutes later, Freddie felt confused, a little truculent. There was something sour at the edge of his mind, a malaise as diffused but definite as a hangover. Acland walked ahead, his arm around his mother, who had begun to weep. Freddie brought up the rear of the procession. He glared at the sky.

Constance came skipping after him, Floss bounding at her heels. She caught his arm; she registered the glare.

"We knew it would happen, Freddie," she said, in a kind voice. "It's been inevitable for weeks."

"What has?"

"War, of course." She quickened her pace; the news seemed, if anything, to raise her spirits. "There are things to look forward to, even so." She squeezed Freddie's arm. "Don't be a grump, Freddie. There's your present, remember. I shall give it to you later."

"When?" Freddie asked, with some urgency.

"Oh, after dinner." Constance released his arm. "I shall give it to you then."

She tossed back her hair; she quickened her pace to a run. Freddie followed more slowly. His mind felt like a logjam. War and a present; war and Constance.

Then, and later (this confused him), he found it impossible to dissociate the two.

"Look here, Acland, Farrell—what will you do? Wait for conscription, or volunteer?" Dunbar, at dinner the same night, cut into a slice of beef; he surveyed the table with a manly monocled eye. It was clearly a relief to him that after the constraints of the afternoon, he could now speak of war.

"I haven't decided yet." Ego Farrell looked away.

"You should volunteer—both of you. Shouldn't they, Boy? After all, the whole shooting match could be over by Christmas. It may never come to conscription at all."

"I would counsel patience," Sir Montague Stern put in. "You might be being a little optimistic, Dunbar. Things might drag on longer, you know."

"Really, sir? Is that the verdict in the City?"

Dunbar's voice was one degree short of the overtly rude. By "City," he clearly meant moneylenders; by moneylenders he implied Jews. The remark was designed, in short, to remind Montague Stern of his place, which—in Dunbar's opinion—was not at a table such as this. True, certain prominent Jews, Stern among them, moved in London society, occasionally joined house parties such as this. That would not be the case, Dunbar seemed to imply, in Scotland, on his home ground.

"The City?" Stern, who was used to this kind of jibe, appeared unperturbed. "No. Downing Street, actually. Last week."

It was rare for Stern to allude to his influence or his contacts. It was rarer still for him to put those who were offensive in their place. Silence followed his remark. Steenie, who disliked Dunbar, giggled. Constance, who admired Stern for his composure, gave him an approving glance. Dunbar blushed scarlet. Maud was quick to intervene. She was always sensitive to all slights to her lover. She had also noticed, as Dunbar had not, that his remarks were causing Gwen dismay.

"Monty, my dear," she said lightly, "you are usually right, but you are a terrible pessimist. Personally, I have immense faith in our Foreign Service, especially now Acland is to join it. In my opinion, the whole matter will be resolved by diplomats. Why, it may never come to battles at all! The Kaiser, I'm sure, is at least a reasonable man. Once he understands what he is taking on—the British Navy; think of the British Navy!—he will back down. These gallant Belgians are all very well—one cannot stand by and see them overrun, I suppose—but really, when you examine it, what is this silly war all about? A great many peculiar countries in the Balkans, which I for one couldn't *begin* to name—why, I couldn't even place them on a globe with any degree of certitude. Besides which, I had it on *immensely* good authority—only last week, at dear Lady Cunard's— that . . . ."

At the far end of the table Gwen scanned the faces of her sons. All but Steenie were of an age to fight. Even Freddie, whom she thought of as a boy still; Freddie, who had only just left school.

Gwen pushed aside her food, untouched. The worst thing was that her present fears must remain unspoken. To voice them would be both cowardly and unpatriotic. She had already disgraced herself by weeping; any further exhibition of her true feelings would make Denton angry and her sons ashamed.

My hostages to fortune, Gwen said to herself; as the conversation continued she began to make silent and panicky plans. Denton would not help—that much was certain. Denton was in favor of war, would be proud for his sons to fight. In any case, Denton was almost seventy and showing his age. Gwen looked down the table, watched her husband's hands tremble as they conveyed food to his lips. Poor Denton—the fire had gone out of him. His great rages were rarer now, and for the past year, two years, Gwen had found herself again growing fond of him.

In some way she could not understand, the death of Shawcross, that terrible accident, marked a dividing point in her husband's life. Before then he was, if irascible, still vigorous: after it he became an old man.

The advent of war might have revived him a little, but Gwen knew that would not last. No, Denton would revert in a few days to the quieter way of life he had adopted. Days would be dozed through; Denton would begin again to speak, as he now loved to do, of the distant past. For that period, his childhood, his memory was vivid—yet, increasingly, he forgot events from the previous day. Names escaped him, also dates, and these sudden and unpredictable gaps in his memory, far from enraging him as they might once have done, now made him oddly humble.

More and more, Denton turned for comfort to Gwen.

"Talk to me, Gwennie," he would say sometimes of an evening, when they were alone. Or: "Sing to me, Gwennie. One of your old songs. You have such a sweet voice."

Gwen took a sip of her wine. The conversation had now, with Maud's assistance, been turned to other things. She began to feel a little more courageous. She began to make plans. *Friends*, she said to herself—friends in politics, friends in the armed forces, friends—that was what she needed. Friends who, at her behest, could pull strings.

Boy must have a staff position—an adjutant, perhaps, well behind any front line. Acland—well, Acland had that First from Balliol; he had passed the highly competitive Civil Service examination; he was due to take up his work at the Foreign Office shortly. An illustrious future was foretold for Acland. Gwen saw him as an ambassador very soon. The Foreign Office: surely, on the strength of such vital work, Acland would—if it ever came to conscription—be classified exempt? Not so very difficult to achieve, Gwen thought. Which left Freddie. Freddie, she decided, must have some health defect. She began to think about weak hearts, flat feet, and obliging doctors.

With these plans, her spirits rose. She would begin this campaign, she told herself, immediately after dinner. No delay. She would begin with Maud, and Montague Stern.

Looking across at Stern (wearing tonight one of those flamboyant waistcoats of his, jade-green with, yes, *gold* embroidery—Constance had given it a covetous look), Gwen felt a passing envy of Maud, a jealousy, there, then gone. With the advent of Sir Montague, it had to be admitted, Maud's life had been transformed.

With notable lack of scandal, Maud had allowed her Italian princeling to drift out of her life. Maud no longer had to endure debts, constant traveling, perpetual uncertainty, and a succession of younger mistresses. Now Maud was the owner of a splendid London establishment, bought for her by Stern. It overlooked Hyde Park. Maud now dressed in Paris, with the best *couturiers*. Maud was, month by month, establishing herself as a prominent hostess. At her London parties, where Gwen often felt like a country bumpkin, Maud assembled a heady cast: royalty, both British and European; maharajahs; rich Americans (with whom Stern had many business contacts); celebrated names from the worlds of music, literature, opera, painting, and the dance.

Maud gave parties for the Ballets Russes. She invited Diaghilev to tea. She patronized Covent Garden, where Stern explained to her the plots. Augustus John had just completed her portrait. Maud was triumphing; she was becoming a close rival, even, to that doyenne of hostesses, Lady Cunard.

Gwen found these triumphs dazzling. She did not envy Maud her worldly success. No, she loved Maud, who had a kind heart and a shrewd mind, belied by her manner of speech. But, just occasionally, Gwen would look at Maud and feel a little wistful. Maud, after all, was older than she; her age might be a closely guarded secret, but she approached her late forties, Denton said. At—what?—forty-seven, forty-eight, Maud had a man by her side who was wise, reliable, considerate, discreet. A man who was younger, who was energetic, active, vigorous. Maud had, in short, a lover and a friend. Gwen spent her days with an old man whom she protected like a son.

Gwen sometimes felt it would be pleasant to have a man she could lean on, a man she might be kissed by, a man she could embrace. However, she did not. Nor would she have, she reminded herself, for Shawcross had cured her of that. Such days were over. Now, at forty-two, Gwen felt she had crossed the summit of the hill; she rested on the gentle incline downward. In her heart she neither resented that fact nor chafed at it. It was restful on that slope. When she considered it, she was content. After all, Maud had no children. She herself was a mother; that was her fulfillment.

My dearest sons, Gwen thought, half including Denton in that group. *My dearest family*.

"Nursing." Jane Conyngham's clear voice cut across her thoughts.

"Nursing," Jane repeated. "I shall begin to train at once. I made inquiries a month ago. Guy's Hospital will take me, I think."

"Oh, I shall *knit*," Constance interjected, with a demure glance toward Montague Stern. "That is, I cannot knit yet—I never mastered it—but I shall. I shall knit *constantly*. Balaclavas and woolen vests, little useful pouches and belts. Don't you think that would be fitting, Sir Montague? For a woman, that is?"

Seated beside her, Stern smiled. He had detected the ridicule in her voice—as, perhaps, had Jane, at whom it was directed.

"Most fitting," he replied. "Though difficult to envisage in your case, Constance."

"Well, we must do *something*." Jane blushed. "I did not mean
. . . It is just that nursing . . ."

Nurses? Gwen frowned at Jane, whom she liked but found
untactful. Her sons would not need nurses. Of that she was
determined.

She leaned across, touched Stern's arm.

"Monty, my dear," she said, "after dinner, might I have a
word?"

"How much longer?" Freddie demanded with mild irritation as,
from behind a screen in Constance's sitting room, the shrieks and
giggles continued.

"Not long. *Wait*, Freddie. Steenie, keep still. Stop wriggling, I
can't do it up . . ."

Freddie shrugged; he began to pace about the room. It annoyed
him that Constance should have insisted on Steenie's joining them
here; that she insisted on performing this charade. Dinner was over
now. Constance's present, yet again, was being delayed.

It would not do to betray his irritation, however; Freddie knew
he must be careful. Too much protest on his part and Constance
would be angry. No present then; its offer would be withdrawn, with
a toss of the head, a stamp of the foot.

Best not to complain. In any case, being made to wait even
longer had its consolations. Anticipation was sharpened, for one
thing—as Constance, of course, would know. Constance's favorite
word (one she constantly used to him) was: *wait*. So, resigned,
Freddie hummed to himself and continued to pace up and down. He
lit a cigarette and looked around him with curiosity.

Some years earlier Constance had been moved from the nursery
to this small set of rooms. She at once made them her own in a way
that fascinated Freddie. This sitting room had become, for himself,
Constance, and Steenie, a kind of headquarters. It was where they
all three retired when the activities of the older members of the
household threatened to become boring. For Freddie this room was
part of a puzzle, a clue to the mysteries of Constance herself.

When Constance was moved in here, the room was redecorated
on the instructions of Gwen. Gwen, not greatly interested in matters
of interior decoration, had suggested in a vague way that the room
should look fresh and feminine.

Accordingly, its colors were pale, and there was a certain amount of
frippery: lace curtains, small ornaments, decorative little cushions. All

this had been overlaid by a different and stronger hand: Constance had claimed the room and set her mark upon it.

Now, it resembled some Gypsy caravan, or the tent of a desert nomad. Gwen's chairs were covered with rugs and throws of brilliant material, which Constance had rescued from the attics. The lamps were dimmed by pieces of bright silk; there were always candles burning. On the old screen (behind which Constance and Steenie were still conspiring and giggling) Constance had glued a mass of vivid images, cut from periodicals and cards or painted for her by Steenie. By the window was a large brass cage containing a fuchsia-pink parakeet. Under its cage were the homes of Steenie's and Constance's other pets—their menagerie: one white rat, called Ozymandias (Steenie's contribution); one bowl of goldfish; one grass snake, given to Constance by Cattermole. This snake, a harmless and somnolent creature, Constance loved. She would hide him in her pocket, let him coil about her arm, tease Maud with him. She seemed almost as devoted to the snake as she was to Floss, but Freddie accepted this. Constance, he thought sometimes, preferred pets to people.

Freddie yawned, puffed at his cigarette, settled himself in one of Constance's chairs. Yes, he liked this room. Constance always derided it, of course. Constance maintained that, if she had her way, she would inhabit a room that was black and silver and red. Freddie did not take this seriously. It was just another example of Constance's need for drama, Freddie told himself, then shifted somewhat uneasily in his seat. Some of Constance's little dramas (to which Freddie was addicted) made him afraid. With Constance there was always danger: Would she go too far, or (on the other hand, in some ways worse) would she not go far enough?

"Ready!" Constance cried from behind the screen.

A small scuffling, more laughter; then Constance and Steenie emerged. Freddie stiffened, blinked, stared. Constance surveyed their audience of one with steely concentration.

Constance and Steenie had exchanged clothes. Constance stood before Freddie dressed as a young man. Steenie, though taller than Constance, was very slender. His stiff shirt and black evening trousers fitted her well. Freddie had never before seen a woman in trousers. He gazed, fascinated, at Constance's slim legs, her narrow hips, and—as she pirouetted for him—her pert and erotic bottom.

Beside her, Steenie gave a languorous sigh and fluttered his eyelashes. He looked, Freddie thought, quite horrible. He was wearing Constance's dark-green dress, under which, in the area of the bosom, there was some lumpy padding. He had rings on his fingers, rouge on his lips and cheeks; his longish hair was scraped back in a bun at the nape of his neck; on his nose was a pair of small round reading spectacles. As Freddie stared, Steenie leered at him. He wiggled his hips in a lascivious manner. Constance cast him a look of disapproval.

"Steenie's overdone it. As usual. I told him he didn't need padding. Jane's bosom is like an ironing board. And as for all that face paint, have you ever seen Jane wear the merest *smudge* of it? Really, Steenie, you are the most terrible little queen."

"You've cheated as well." Steenie seemed unmoved by this criticism. "You don't look anything like Boy. Boy's heavy. Well, stout—let's be kind. Sort of square-shaped, anyway. I told you, you should have stuck a cushion up—much more convincing."

"Be quiet, Steenie. Wait. Now . . ." Constance turned back to Freddie with an imperious gesture. "Now. Tonight, before your very eyes, and for one performance only, we bring you a most solemn and historic moment. We bring you, just as it occurred, the betrothal—the famous proposal of the Honorable Boy Cavendish to Miss Jane Conyngham, Spinster and Heiress of our neighboring Parish. Now, for your delectation: The Night of the Great Comet. We are in—I'm sorry about this, but Boy isn't imaginative—we are in: the conservatory. At Winterscombe."

Constance turned to Steenie; Steenie clasped his hands to his bosom and smirked; Constance struck an attitude, and—yes—Constance was a very clever mimic, and there, before Freddie's startled gaze, she was translated. Of course she was not tall enough, of course she was far too thin, of course she still looked like a girl—yet also, by some magic of observation, she was Boy. She had Boy's odd stiff stance, with his feet slightly apart; she had Boy's puffed-out chest and nervously squared shoulders; she had—to the last detail—the inconclusive gestures of Boy's hands. Before him Freddie saw his brother, and pitied him—for his awkwardness, his good intentions, his good heart, and his stupidity.

Constance sank to her knees at Steenie's feet and placed one hand in the region of her heart. It lay on the starched shirtfront, inert, like a dead fish on a platter.

"Miss Conyngham . . . Jane . . ." Constance began, and although she could not match the depth of Boy's voice, she had the manner of his speaking. She had caught the ponderous solemnity, the underlying insecurity—even the way Boy hesitated over certain consonants, that legacy from his childhood, when Boy stammered.

"... I shall, of course, speak to your father. That is, if you want ... if you would like. But meanwhile, I have the honor, I should like to ask if you would do me the inestimable honor, of accepting ... that is, I should like to ask for your hand in marriage. ..."

Freddie listened, heard his brother drowning, heard him tussle with the words, and finally end with his head, just, above the water. It was, as Constance played it, amusing. She carried on, with calm conviction, despite the fact that Steenie was overplaying his part grotesquely. Constance, ignoring this, swept on like the professional she was, and by the end both Steenie and Freddie were reduced to helpless laughter.

"Oh, *God*. He can't have ... he didn't. Oh, Boy is such a fool. Constance, are you *sure*?" Steenie was clutching his sides, doubled up with malicious amusement.

"His very words. To the letter." Constance gave a toss of the head and, the performance over, pulled off the band holding her hair; she shook it loose over her shoulders.

"Poor Boy." Freddie, still chuckling, reached for another cigarette. "No wonder he made such a mess of it. He doesn't love her, you know. Boy can never hide what he feels. I can just see his face, lighting up, the sigh of relief when she insisted on a long engagement. ..."

"Oh, she was relieved too." Constance threw herself into a chair and grinned at them both. "Very relieved. She doesn't love Boy any more than he loves her. I should think they'll be engaged for the next thirty years. And Jane will nurse a broken heart all that time. ..."

"A broken heart? Jane? Whyever should she?" Freddie looked up in surprise; Constance and Steenie glanced at each other.

"Oh, come on, Freddie, don't be slow." Steenie winked. "You must have noticed. Jane is not as prim as she looks. Years—ages— she's always carried a torch for ..." And Steenie paused maddeningly.

"Who for? Who?"

"Acland, of course," said Steenie and Constance in unison, and began laughing once more.

Their laughter and their conspiratorial air sobered Freddie. He stopped smiling and looked at them. What they were suggesting seemed to him unlikely and absurd, but their certainty was impressive. As sometimes happened on such occasions, Freddie felt left out.

This, obviously, was something Steenie and Constance had already discussed, one of their many secrets. And Freddie resented those secrets, resented the fact that Steenie and Constance had this effortless bond.

"Rubbish," he said after a brief pause. "You're making it up. Jane carrying a torch for Acland? I never heard anything so stupid. I don't believe it. In fact, I don't believe any of it. It's typical of you two. You just made the whole thing up, invented it. How could you know, anyway?"

"Oh, Constance knows," Steenie said, with a little smile.

"Oh, Constance was there, I suppose," Freddie began, with weighty sarcasm. "Constance just happened to be sitting in the conservatory when Boy and Jane came in, and Constance said, 'Don't mind me, just go ahead and propose in front of me.' Rubbish. You were both in bed. Up in the nursery. Where you belonged."

"It wasn't *quite* like that. . . ." Steenie giggled. "Was it, Constance?"

"Not quite." Constance's face took on a closed expression.

"In other words, you made it up. Just as I said."

"Oh, no. It's true. Word for word. And Constance wasn't in bed, were you, Constance?" Steenie gave Constance a sly little smile.

"Not then." Constance looked away. Her expression was now one of boredom, yet Freddie had the impression she disliked this interrogation and wished Steenie would stop.

"The truth of the matter is . . ." Steenie continued, delving a hand into the bosom of his dress and pulling out yards of stuffing, "the truth of the matter is, Constance used to be a terrible snoop, didn't you, Constance? Winterscombe's very own little spy. Once upon a time. When she was younger. Not anymore, naturally."

"Oh, I wouldn't say that." Constance roused herself. She stood and met Steenie's eyes. "I see all sorts of things, Steenie. Even now. I can't help it—it just seems to happen that way. I see things people would much prefer I didn't see, and I hear things they'd prefer I didn't hear. But then, it doesn't matter, because I never talk about them, do I, Steenie?"

Constance reached across as she spoke. She lifted her hand and, in a deliberate way, rubbed her finger across Steenie's rouged lips. The rouge smeared across his cheek, and there was a small and dangerous silence. Steenie's eyes were the first to fall.

"No," he said in a flat voice. "No. You're very discreet, Constance. It's what we all love about you. Heigh-ho!" He gave an exaggerated yawn. "How late it is! I think I'll go to bed now."

He retired behind the screen, and in the room beyond, Freddie and Constance looked at each other. Freddie shifted from foot to foot, aware that the atmosphere in the room had changed in a way he did not understand. He could sense both hostility and threat—which were inexplicable.

And yet Constance, now, seemed quite unmoved. As Freddie looked at her uncertainly, Constance blew him the smallest of kisses. She nodded in the direction of the door.

She mouthed some words at him—*"Your present"*—and at once Freddie's heart began to beat very fast. It pounded a tattoo in his mind, and he felt it again, that familiar ache of expectation, that lassitude and alerting.

Constance now produced this effect upon him very easily. She had done so for some time. *How long,* he asked himself as he moved to the door. *Why?*

The door closed. Freddie waited, well schooled, on the landing. *How long? Why?* Familiar questions now, and yet Freddie could never quite answer them.

How long? It began, he supposed, quite soon after the death of Constance's father, which meant it had been going on for more than four years. Yet it began in such small ways, and it crept upon him with such stealth that Freddie was not even sure of that fact.

Step by step, inch by inch, meeting by meeting: Constance, Freddie felt sometimes, laid siege to him.

"Did you find the present I left for you, Freddie? The little marzipan apple? I left it on your shirtfront. In your bedroom. It was my present, especially for you, Freddie. . . ."

"Did you find the book in your room, Freddie? The one I left? Did you see what I wrote in it? Mind you don't show it to anyone else. . . ."

"Oh, Freddie, did you know what I was thinking at dinner? Could you tell, when you looked at me? I saw you blushing. . . ."

"See, Freddie, I've brought you another present. It smells of me. Do you recognize that smell, Freddie? Is it nice?"

Wicked magic. In his mind all these separate occasions blurred and commingled, the innocent and the less innocent, and Freddie was now uncertain in which order they had happened, or when. Did Constance say these things (and do these things) when she was eleven, or twelve—surely that wasn't possible? Or was it later? Did it, in fact, begin in a more gradual way than he now remembered?

Freddie never felt sure. All he knew was that (when she wanted) Constance had him in thrall. She could summon him with a click of the fingers, a glance of the eyes, an inclination of the head. And Freddie would go, wherever Constance's whim commanded—sometimes the woods, sometimes to the cellars, once the gamekeeper's hut, ripe with the smell of hanging pheasants, and dark. . . . Where else? Oh, an infinite number of places. In London once, in his mother's bedroom, with the door half open for added danger, the two of them in front of his mother's mirror. Once here at Winterscombe in the King's bedroom. Once in the attics (no, twice in the attics). Once in the library, under Denton's desk.

And what did they do in those places—in a dark hut, in front of a mirror, on rugs up in the attics? Never enough, as far as Freddie was concerned, but just enough to make him ache for more.

A cockteaser. Freddie knew the term, naturally, and once or twice, when angry, had been tempted to apply it to Constance. He rarely did so for long, for he knew it was inaccurate. Too ribald, too cold, too obvious, too slight. Constance teased, yes, but not just his body, or parts of his body. Constance teased his mind, and his imagination, which was why she was so powerful.

Constance teased, and when she did (what would his present be?) it was magic. Wicked magic.

"Acland's room," Constance said when she joined him on the landing, in her green dress, with her hair in black snakes over her half-bared shoulders. "Acland's room. Quickly."

Acland's room? For once, Freddie hesitated, and consulted his watch. He was afraid of Acland—his sarcasm, his anger, his cutting tongue. It was now almost midnight. What if Acland should come up? What if he should find them?

"He's downstairs, playing billiards. Arguing about the war. Who cares? Hurry up, Freddie. You want your present, don't you?"

By then Freddie did want his present very much; his mind was exploding with the possibilities of that present. Who cared about Acland, indeed? He quickened his pace, hurried along the corridors. From the East Wing to the West Wing; as they passed above the hall Freddie heard music and voices, hesitated once more, and then again quickened his pace. Up to the second floor; Constance flitted through the shadows ahead of him. They were now above the King's bedroom, in that corridor where (so many years before) Freddie had heard the two mysterious screams. (He had long ago forgotten them.)

His room, Boy's room, Acland's room; outside the three doors, Constance paused.

"Maybe I'll show you something first," she said. "Maybe I will. Just quickly."

And, to Freddie's surprise, she opened the door to Boy's room. She switched on the light, smiled over her shoulder at Freddie, who faltered in the doorway. Constance crossed to the corner. There, next to a large roll-top desk, under the shelves that still contained all Boy's childhood trophies, the birds' eggs, the lead soldiers he painted, the books, the school photographs—there, in the corner, was a large wooden cabinet ranked with shallow drawers. In this cabinet, Freddie knew, Boy kept his photographs.

"You thought I was being unkind to Boy earlier on, didn't you?" Constance looked back at him.

"No. Well, not exactly. You hit him off very well—but, all right, you did go a bit too far. Boy may be awkward and slow, but he's kind. He's a good sort; he means well. He's never done anything to hurt you."

"Hasn't he? He nearly killed my dog today—or didn't you notice? It's you who can be stupid, Freddie. You take people at face value. Just because Boy's your brother, you look up to him, pretend he's all sorts of things he isn't."

"Look, let's leave it, shall we? Yes, Boy's my brother. Obviously I care for him. I respect him. So what? What are we doing in here anyway? Why are we wasting time?"

"We're not wasting time, Freddie. And I don't want you to think I'm unjust. Not to Boy, not to anyone. Boy is not so slow. He's an artist. Watch. Wait . . ."

As Freddie stared at her in puzzlement, Constance produced a small key from her pocket and held it up.

"Where did you get that?"

"Don't ask. I have it. Maybe Boy gave it to me. Now. Look . . ." Constance bent, unlocked and then opened the last of the cabinet drawers. It was a deep drawer; at the front of it was a neat pile of envelopes and leather-bound albums. These, with an air of contempt, Constance pushed to one side. She reached her hand into the back of the drawer, scrabbled around a little, and eventually withdrew a thick bundle wrapped in what appeared to be white cotton.

"What's that?"

"That? An old petticoat of mine. And inside it, some prints of his photographs. Not the plates—he hides those somewhere else."

"Your petticoat?"

"My petticoat. My photographs as well. At least, Boy took them, but they are all of me. *Not* the kind of pictures Boy would leave around in an album in the drawing room. Look."

Constance unwrapped the petticoat. She laid the bundle on the bed, and Freddie took a hesitant step forward. One by one, as he bent his head to look, Constance held up the pictures.

As she said, all the photographs were of Constance, exposure after exposure, and all of them had clearly been taken when Constance was younger. In them Constance stood, sat, lay, in a variety of curious costumes. Sometimes she wore a thin and bedraggled shift; more often she appeared to be wearing little more than rags. Her hair was tousled and her feet always bare. She seemed to be wearing an odd kind of makeup: In some she looked as if her face were streaked with mud; in others her lips were grotesquely smeared with rouge, so that she looked sometimes like an urchin, sometimes like a prostitute.

This impression was deepened by the poses Constance had struck. Somehow she contrived to look both deprived and depraved. Sometimes the rags or shift clung to her thin limbs, as if the material had been wetted; sometimes a sly hand would draw attention to a forbidden part of her anatomy. There, the point of a nipple, the small bud of a just-developing breast; there (Freddie drew in his breath sharply, for he had never seen this much) Constance parted her legs; between them was a cleft in plump flesh, a hint of pubic hair.

Freddie stared at the photographs, and sickness crawled in his stomach. They disgusted him and they appalled him; they also (and this was shaming to him) aroused him.

"It started when I was ten, and it stopped when I was nearly thirteen." Constance's voice was matter-of-fact. "My breasts grew too much then. I started to look like a woman, and Boy didn't want that. He likes little girls. Poor little girls. I expect what he would most like to do is visit the slums of London and photograph girls there. Maybe he does—I don't know. As it was, I had to pretend to look poor and dirty. Boy helped. He used to make me up, rub the mud on my face, that sort of thing. It started before my father died. Boy took my picture the day of the comet party—in the King's bedroom. And then, a few months later, he asked if I would pose for him again. It developed from there. Curious, isn't it? I think it made Boy feel guilty. I had to promise never to breathe a word to a soul. And I haven't—until now. But I thought you ought to see, Freddie. So you'd know—he isn't quite what he seems, your brother."

"Oh, my God." Freddie turned away. There was no doubt in his mind that these pictures were pornographic, but there was also a curious tenderness and restraint to them, which confused him. He swung around to Constance. "But *why*, Connie? Why did you agree? Why did you do it?"

"Why not?" Constance looked at him calmly. "I was very young and there seemed to be nothing wrong. Not at first. I liked Boy. I wanted to please him. And by the time I was old enough to realize that it wasn't normal, it wasn't right—well, we stopped then. I was too old anyway." She gave Freddie an intent glance and then, with an unusual gentleness, covered his hand with hers.

"It's all right, Freddie, really it is. I wasn't hurt. Boy never touched me, never did . . . anything. I wouldn't have let him touch me anyway. I would have known that was wrong. I don't let anyone touch me—except you sometimes."

Freddie hesitated. Constance was looking him full in the face, and her expression was one of limpid honesty. What she said flattered him, excited him, touched him—and yet he was not quite sure if he believed her. He had learned from experience that Constance could lie.

"Freddie, I've upset you. I'm sorry." Constance rose. She wrapped the photographs back in the petticoat and locked them in the drawer, took Freddie's hand, and switching out the light, closing the door behind her, drew him out onto the landing.

There it was dark, and Freddie's eyes adjusted slowly to the sudden absence of light. Constance was only a dim shape, close to him, as she pressed his hand, released it, edged away.

"I shouldn't have done that. I wanted you to know, I suppose." Constance's voice was now sorrowful. "You won't want your present now, I expect. Never mind. I can give it to you another time. Tomorrow. Or the day after."

Freddie felt dazed; his heart was thumping fast yet again; he had that familiar breathless tightness in his chest. Flaring in the recesses of his mind were images and memories: the small curve of Constance's childish breast, peeping out beneath a damp petticoat; shadows between thighs; the touch of a hand, the brush of a damp palm, the smell of Constance's skin and hair. He tried to fight against these memories and images, but it was useless.

"No. No. I want my present now," he heard himself say, in a low voice, and beyond him, somewhere in the shadows, Constance sighed.

"Very well, Freddie," she said, and she opened Acland's door.

* * *

"Watch," Constance had said, and *"Wait . . ."*

And Freddie had obeyed her. Only a candle lit, the candle Acland kept by his bedside. (Constance loved the ambiguity of candlelight.) Acland's room was bare and monastic. Constance lay on his bare and monastic bed; the candle flickered; Freddie stood at the foot of the bed. On the floor by the bed was a curl of petticoat, a rustle of green silk, the green dress discarded, sloughed off like a skin.

In the candlelight Constance's complexion was creamy, and her sharp little body appeared languorous. Very slowly, Constance stretched. In her hand she held her pet snake, which had been curled up in the pocket of her dress; its appearance startled Freddie. Now Constance held her pet aloft; the snake's head moved from side to side and its tongue flickered. Slowly Constance lowered the snake and rested it between her small uplifted breasts; she stroked its spine, and it lay still, a necklace of *S*'s against the pallor of her skin.

Where should Freddie look first? At Constance's black hair, which coiled across her shoulders? At her red lips, which were parted very slightly, so that Freddie could see her small white teeth and the pink tip of her tongue? At her breasts, which he had never seen, although he had been allowed to touch once or twice? At the angles of her waist, at her flat and boyish stomach, at that mysterious, alluring, terrifying triangle of hair, which looked so soft but which, once, he touched (one touch only, fumbling under skirts and petticoats) and found to be crisp and resilient?

Freddie looked at all these things, all these components of Constance's wicked magic, and his vision swam. Looking was not enough (was looking to be his present?); looking only increased the agony. Freddie reached out a hand.

"Wait," Constance said more sharply. *"Wait. Watch."* Then she parted her legs, and her snake began to move. Usually this snake was lazy; not now. Now it began a complex journeying: It coiled and uncoiled between her breasts, slithered up to the curve of her throat, nestled in the hollows beneath her collarbones, darted out its tongue, and began a descent. Across Constance's rib cage, slithering across her thighs, through the pubic hair, down to her ankle, around which it coiled like a slave anklet. There was now an expression of concentration on Constance's face. She frowned, passed her tongue across her lips, bit the tip of her tongue between her sharp white teeth. Then, just as the snake seemed to decide on a final resting place (curling on the cream of her stomach, a pattern of jet and diamonds), Constance began to touch herself.

First her breasts, which she cupped in her hands and stroked, then pinched. Her nipples stiffened, and Freddie—who had heard of this happening but had never witnessed it—felt his body give a demanding, mutinous lurch.

After that, Constance's movements became more businesslike, less desultory. Constance had small square hands (they were not her most beautiful feature); her fingernails were bitten. One of these hands she now insinuated between her thighs; the other remained at her breast, flicking at the tip of one nipple in an idle way, as if she were bored. The right hand, the hand between her thighs, moved deftly, and the fact that it was so small, crammed with cheap rings, that the fingernails were bitten, added to the eroticism for Freddie.

Freddie could not quite see what this hand was doing, and he leaned forward against the footboard of the bed, which creaked. This alarmed Freddie—one infringement of the rules, he knew, and Constance would curtail the entertainment.

Now, however, she was merciful; her eyelids flickered open, and her dark blank eyes fixed on Freddie as if she did not see him at all. Or perhaps Constance liked the fact that he watched with such concentration; perhaps—for she smiled.

"Open the door, Freddie," she said in a dreamy voice.

"What?"

"Open the door. . . ."

Freddie did so. From below he could hear voices still, and now they were more distinct; actual words could be discerned. *War,* Freddie heard, then murmurs, then again *war:* a tocsin of a word, and Freddie hesitated. Supposing Acland came up? Supposing his valet, Arthur, should put in an appearance? Supposing Constance's current governess, the bristling Fräulein Erlichman, should arrive on the scene?

But these were (apart from Acland) unlikely appearances: Arthur, who grew insolent and lazy, would come only if rung for; Fräulein Erlichman retired early. Besides, as Freddie had learned, fear of discovery had its uses—it could sharpen desire. Freddie hesitated a second only, no more; then he was back at the foot of the bed. Constance's eyes were still open and they remained upon him while, with delicacy and precision, she parted the lips of her sex.

No details; Freddie's mind could not deal with details now. What he saw was a blur to him, and later, when he tried to conjure the details, they continued to escape him. A pursed softness, mauve flesh; a dampness. Freddie groaned.

"Let me touch—oh, Connie, please. Let me touch you. Quickly, quickly—someone may come up."

Constance pushed his hand aside. "Watch. Wait," she said (as she always said), and Freddie, terrified to disobey, withdrew his hand. He clenched it, thrust it into his pocket, touched himself. Below him, on Acland's bed, Constance's face became blank and concentrated.

Her little hand moved faster; one finger rubbed and glistened. Freddie—who by then could not understand what she was doing at all, but who was beyond caring—rubbed himself against the warmth of his own palm. Yet, something was happening to Constance; even the pet snake seemed to sense some danger. Constance's body lifted; the snake slithered toward her head, and rested coiled on the pillow by her hair.

Constance bent her knees; she raised her haunches from the bed; her throat arched back as if in spasm, and her eyes closed. She shuddered, jerked, and then was still. It was like a minor convulsion, even a little like death. Freddie was, for a moment, terrified; urgent though it was to touch himself, his hand fell still.

A brief pause, then Constance opened her eyes.

She wiped her damp hand on Acland's bedcover. She made a deep and purring sound of contentment; she stroked the back of her snake, outlined the dark diamonds of its spine with one finger. Then, composed once more, she lifted her arms, folded them behind her head, looked up at Freddie.

"You can do it now, Freddie," she said, in the sweetest voice Freddie had ever heard her use. "I know you do it, in your room with the door locked. You were half doing it then. Go on—do it properly. I want to see it. I want to look at it. I want to see you. You can do it on me if you like; then we won't make a mess in Acland's bedroom. Please, Freddie, dear Freddie. I want to watch. Do it. Do it now. . . ."

Was that her birthday present? Was that Constance's gift, first to let him watch her and then to watch her watching him? To be at once both surreptitious and free, to obtain a glorious release, in a way he had never imagined possible with a woman, in a way that he later decided was dirty, depraved, and probably taboo (and therefore all the more glorious). That, Freddie told himself, that had indeed been his birthday present.

The next day he was less sure. He remembered the events of the previous night more coolly then, against the background of impending war. He watched his mother, weeping, as Boy and Dunbar departed, recalled to their regiment. He watched the other guests depart. He watched all these things, and by the end of that long, hot, oppressive day, when Sir Montague had gone and even Acland had left for London, he found himself alone, the last young man of their party still at Winterscombe. By nightfall a nasty and sick certainty took hold of him: Constance's present had been given before they even entered Acland's bedroom. Constance's present had been the bundle of Boy's photographs; Constance's present had been the destruction of his image of his brother.

That day, Freddie had found it very difficult to meet his brother's eyes. He had been distant when Boy took his departure, even though he knew it was possible that something terrible might happen and he might never see Boy again.

Guilt came to Freddie once his brother had left; guilt, and gloom, and disgust at his own behavior. He was very cool to Constance that day, indeed avoided her. He was cool the next day as well, and the day after that. Then it occurred to him that if Constance had noticed this coolness, she seemed unaffected by it. She behaved as if nothing had happened at all.

Freddie found this maddening. A curious, unaccountable jealousy seized him. From worrying about his brother and his own behavior, he turned to worrying about Constance. Did she hate him? Was she disappointed in him? Would she ever be with him, look at him, touch him, again?

A week. Constance waited a week, and then (perhaps when she judged that Freddie had argued himself back where she wanted him) she made another assignation. After that, more waiting, more agony and indecision and longing on Freddie's part. Then the crumb of another little meeting was tossed his way.

Meeting after meeting, hiding place after hiding place, summer into autumn, autumn into winter. It was a strange time.

Looking back later, Freddie would know that it was not a happy time; as the months passed he felt no contentment. All around him his life was changing, and the pillars that had held up the structure of his world were falling. Boy had sent for his manservant; he was overjoyed to be posted to northern France. Acland was away in London, at the Foreign Office, doing work that—Gwen stressed—was of national importance. One by one, as the weeks passed, the servants were caught up in the war fever: Denton encouraged the men to join up (even threatened with dismissal those who were tardy in doing so); Arthur Tubbs left, surprising Freddie; Jack Hennessy enlisted, and his three brothers followed him; all the younger footmen left, and the drivers and the gardeners and the keepers and the estate workers. Freddie himself helped to bring in the last of the harvest that year; he worked in the fields bitterly, surrounded by old men.

War, war, war: no one talked of anything else; it was the only subject in the newspapers, and the expectation of an early victory was still strong. At the breakfast table, letters from the front were read: Boy sounded elated and cheerful; waiting for a posting to the front line, he had passed an afternoon near Chartres, bird watching.

Little to fear from this war. Freddie associated it with the packing of food parcels, the rousing tunes of the bands that accompanied the recruiting officers through the villages. He associated it with excitement, with a new sense of national purpose, and—in his own case—with frustration and shame.

For what had happened, within weeks of the declaration of war? Why, he had been escorted by Gwen to a famous Harley Street specialist recommended by Montague Stern. This specialist examined Freddie at length. His blood pressure was taken, before and after exercise. Feeling a great fool, Freddie ran up and down on a small moving platform, dressed only in undershirt and underpants. His pulse was taken. Blood samples were taken. An X ray was taken. A most thorough and exhaustive physical inspection was made. At the end of this, Gwen was readmitted. The specialist looked grave.

It was, he said, quite out of the question for Frederic to join up, and if conscription ever came, Frederic would be exempt. Frederic, he explained, had a slight irregularity in the heart valves. Had he perhaps experienced palpitations, episodes of dizziness? Freddie had, of course, and very recently, too—but those were not occasions he could mention then. He denied any malaise. The doctor remained adamant. Frederic had a weak heart; he should lose weight, exercise gently, avoid excitement, and forget the army. Freddie was shocked by this; his mother seemed shocked too. She left the consulting rooms with a white face and returned home weeping.

In the privacy of his own bedroom that night, Freddie swung his arms, ran up and down on the spot, and waited to drop dead. Nothing happened. The man had seemed very certain, but Freddie was not convinced. However distinguished the physician was, he could have made a mistake.

He pleaded with his mother for a second opinion. He tried to explain how dreadful he felt, the only man among his contemporaries at Eton who was still languishing at home. Gwen fell into such a paroxysm of weeping, such a violent clutching and clinging, that Freddie gave way. He remained at Winterscombe. He preferred to stay within the grounds. Visits to London made him very nervous. Freddie was tall, heavily built; he looked much older than nineteen. Every time he set foot in the street he expected to be accosted, to be given the white feather symbolizing cowardice.

Freddie's obsession with Constance grew stronger. Constance was his confidante and his consoler. When Freddie felt less than manly, Constance could prove to him just how manly he was, in the only way (she said) that really mattered. Constance kissed the war away. In her arms, drugged with the scents of her body, Freddie forgot about patriotism and cowardice. Weeks went by in a priapic daze. Freddie learned the delights of enslavement, an enslavement in which nothing was more urgent than their next meeting, nothing more intoxicating than their last. Constance's hair, skin, eyes, the whisper of her voice, the suggestions and ambiguities of her touch; hot days, hot thoughts; sweet delays and shocking promises—such a summer that was!

Constance, experimenting with techniques that she was later to use to even greater effect, was an artist in sex. She understood that hints, promises and caprice, delays and deviations were a more effective drug than fulfillment. Step by step, kiss by kiss, she took Freddie down into the maelstrom. His body sweated for her; his mind itched for her. At night he invented; then he dreamed of her. Sometimes she would give more, then—for weeks—less. Freddie's days passed like a dream; the second he left her, he would be imagining some new excess.

One thing: she would not let him fuck her. This word—one Constance used casually and frequently, a little time device triggered to great effect in mid-embrace—would reverberate in Freddie's mind like gunshots. He could not understand why Constance, who appeared without shame, who dismissed all sexual taboos, who introduced Freddie to practices he had neither heard of nor suspected, should impose this arbitrary, this incomprehensible stricture. Yet, on this point she was immovable: any variation—but no fucking. And then she might smile: *Not yet.*

Constance's favorite variation, Freddie discovered, was to risk danger when one of his family was nearby. The threat of discovery from a servant, a gardener, a farm worker—that worked to a more limited extent. Freddie was beginning to recognize when Constance was most excited: It was when his mother, his father, or one of his brothers was at hand.

The most outrageous example of this occurred in London, at the Cavendish house in Mayfair, in January of 1915. With his parents and Steenie, he and Constance had been visiting friends with an estate on the South Coast. From there, Freddie heard for the first time the famous and fearsome sound of the gun batteries across the Channel. Gwen heard them, too, and they sent her into one of her flurries of fear and protectiveness: They must stop off in London, she decreed. She could not return to Winterscombe without seeing Acland. Acland was duly telephoned at the Foreign Office, and agreed to meet his mother at home at five o'clock.

The Cavendish house in Park Street had a tall and spiraling main staircase, which led upward around a vertical shaft from the hall on the ground floor to the attics four stories above. There, it was possible to lean over the banisters and look down a vertiginous well to the marble floor of the hall below. Freddie—warned against the dangers of that staircase as a child—still retained an odd, almost atavistic fear of it.

Just before five, at Constance's insistence, Freddie joined her on the shadowy, ill-lit third landing. By five, Constance was leaning forward against the banister, and Freddie was behind her, pressing against her sharp and agile little bottom. He was in a state of violent tumescence. (Indeed, just the thought of Constance these days provoked an erection.) He had one hand inside her dress (bright scarlet that day, and unfastened down the back). His other hand— weeks since he had been allowed to do this—his other hand was under Constance's skirt. Constance was not wearing any knickers.

Freddie's left hand squeezed and caressed Constance's breasts; his right hand groped and explored a soft damp place. So excited was Freddie that he hardly heard the slam of the front door or the footsteps across the hall. He became aware of Acland only when Constance called out to him.

Acland came to a halt at the foot of the stairwell. He looked up and greeted Constance; Freddie he did not greet, for Freddie— whose hands stopped their explorations and became rigid—was invisible from below. Constance then proceeded to have a conversation with Acland. Indeed, she protracted the conversation most amusingly. At the same time she made it quite clear to Freddie (who had been about to withdraw his hands) that she did not want him to stop.

She wriggled and rubbed against him; she pressed down hard against his right hand, so hard that—for the first time—Freddie found the miraculous aperture he had long been seeking. Two of his fingers slipped inside her; Constance gave a small tremor. While continuing to converse cordially with Acland, she rotated her hips, as if screwing herself down on Freddie's fingertips.

By then Freddie was too excited to stop. The fact that he was hidden from view, the fact that he was continuing to do this indelicate thing while Constance continued to speak, her voice quite as usual— all this combined to make Freddie both angry, aroused, and afraid. Fear, anger, and desire—oh, Constance understood the cocktail of sex. Freddie pinched and stroked at her nipples; from beneath Constance's skirts he was aware of small sucking noises—she was very wet.

"We could hear the guns, Acland; the wind must have been in the right direction, for we could hear them quite clearly. . . ."

Constance's voice paused only a fraction; a hiatus before the ending of the adverb, and in that tiny space Constance had her orgasm. Freddie felt her body grow rigid for a second; then his dipping fingers felt the pulse from inside. Constance came; he had brought her to climax, something he had never done before, for usually Constance liked to do this herself, sometimes (she said this amused her) with Freddie timing her. Her record was thirty seconds.

Freddie knew she would reward him, and—when Acland, suspecting nothing, finally left the hall—Constance did; she was scrupulous about such things. She knelt, unbuttoned his trousers. She took his penis in her hand. With a fixed, set face, she said, "I want you to say something, Freddie. Just three words."

"Anything," Freddie muttered, frantic now and reaching for her.

"Say, 'In your mouth.' Just that. Nothing else. All right, Freddie?"

In your mouth: Freddie's mind spun away into some vortex. This, Constance had never done, and the brutish simplicity of the words slipped the last of his controls. Heady; like diving into black water from a great height. Freddie said the words, and Constance obliged him.

That evening, Acland stayed for dinner. Throughout, Constance was unusually quiet—so much so that Gwen asked her if she felt ill, and Constance, replying that she was tired, retired early.

Freddie sat on for another hour, while his father slumbered before the fire; he tried to read a detective story but found himself unable to concentrate on the plot. Fragments of conversation between his mother and Acland drifted toward him.

"Ego has joined up—Ego Farrell," Acland remarked once, in a casual voice. "Gloucestershire Rifles. I saw him today, before he left."

"He might have had more sense," Gwen said in a high strained voice. "I cannot imagine Ego's fighting—and it cannot be necessary. He's such a *quiet* man. Surely they have men enough out there?"

Acland changed the subject. Later, Gwen took out her most recent letter from Boy, and read sections to Acland. Freddie, who had already heard the substance of this letter at least four times, used the moment to say goodnight. All he could think of was seeing Constance. He crept up the stairs and along the landing to Constance's room. The London house was smaller than Winterscombe; here they had to be very careful. Constance was waiting for him.

She was sitting at a table, a pile of black notebooks in front of her. As Freddie entered and closed the door, he saw that Constance was sitting in a stiff position; on her face was that dark, closed expression she had always had as a child. Without acknowledging him, she opened one of the black notebooks, flicked a page or two.

"My father's journals." She picked up the book and held it out to him.

Freddie looked down at the book; he glimpsed a date, lines of neat copperplate handwriting. These journals, which Freddie had never seen before, had not known existed, did not interest him in the least: Freddie, just then, had a mind that blazed with other matters.

However, Constance mentioned her father rarely; if she chose to do so now, he could not brush it aside—perhaps, after all, in her own secretive way, Constance still mourned for him.

"You shouldn't look at them, Constance," Freddie began. "It's bound to bring things back. Much better to try and forget. Here." He put his arm around her. Constance pushed it aside.

"They are about his women," she announced in a flat voice. "For the most part. Sometimes other things, but usually women."

This provoked Freddie's curiosity; he at once felt more inclined to look at the journals. He glanced down at the page before him again, and there made out a word—several words—that startled him. Good God! And he had always thought Shawcross such a cold fish!

"Have you read them, Connie?"

"Of course. I read them constantly. Read and reread them. It is like a penance with me. I don't know why I do it, quite. Perhaps I would like to . . . understand."

This statement seemed to agitate Constance a little, for the dead note in her voice changed.

"Let's look at them later, Connie."

Freddie had just managed to insinuate his hand beneath Constance's skirt. He could feel the top of a stocking, a strip of silk garter, a taut thigh. His priorities at once adjusted themselves: No words, however shocking, could compare with the suppleness of Constance's skin, with the agility and aggression of her body, with the way in which, teasingly, she would sometimes part her legs wide and then scissor them shut.

"Later, Connie, please."

"Not later. *Now.*"

Freddie at once withdrew his hand.

"I want you to read this, Freddie. It concerns you too. Look, here, on this page. This is where it all begins."

"Where what begins?" Freddie drew back a few steps. Although he still did not understand, there was something in Constance's expression that alarmed him. She had looked like this, he remembered, in Boy's room, the night she showed him the photographs. He could feel the doubts begin; he felt uneasiness seep and creep into his mind.

Constance sighed. She said in a weary voice, "Just *read*, Freddie."

Freddie hesitated once more; then curiosity had the better of him. He bent his head and began to read from the top of the page:

. . . had not done it since her husband died—or so she said; I went on with my own calculations. Twenty minutes at the most, preferably fifteen: I liked her mouth—a liverish colour, with slack lips—but I had that train to catch.

I had her up against the bedroom wall before the door closed, but her cunt was not to my taste: too vast, too loose, and I prefer them small. So I shoved her down on her knees, and went for the mouth after all. What should I discover then? Why, that the husband must have been a man of liberal tastes, for she was an old hand at this. She went at me like a sow for ripe potatoes, snuffling and guzzling; it put another inch on me at least. She pleasured my balls, gave a grunt and a heave, and there I was inside, the whole length of me, with those rubbery lips clamped round the stem of my cock, and her tongue lathering me.

The best suck in years. The old bitch swallowed the lot when I spent, and licked her lips, and unbuttoned her blouse and thrust her great drooping breasts at me. Her turn now, she had the gall to imply, so I let her beg for a while, and made her say the words—all of them. If her friends could have seen her then, all those friends who would not give her the time of day were it not for her money!

I left her then, unsatisfied, with some speed, not pausing even to wash, and caught my train with only minutes to spare. I felt soiled, had the notion I could smell her mouth and cunt on me, but on the train I became calmer. Variation! The very fact that I was unwashed . . .

Freddie had come to the end of the page; he looked up at Constance. Constance said, in a flat voice: "Turn over."

Freddie did so; he began on the next page.

. . . began to suggest some interesting possibilities. Circumstances were with me; my conveyance was on time, and my other albatross was waiting, alone, in her boudoir.

I waited until the maid was out of the room; then I went for her. I had her down on all fours, with her great arse up in the air—she was slavering for it, as she always is, and came almost at once, in her usual fashion, noisily. I rammed on, like a madman, for a good five minutes, keeping the image of the other bitch in my mind all the while. My cock was burning like a poker thrust into coals, but I had a fear I might not be able to bring matters to their natural conclusion. I managed it however, and came. Just a few squirts, then I made her smell me.

An attempt at the appropriate rapture—though I knew in truth she was embarrassed—and her embarrassment gave me one last happy notion. I washed as usual—that excellent carnation soap—but I would not let her wash. I wanted her there, downstairs, sitting in her blue chair, with that lout of a husband of hers spread out, the way he always is, on the red sofa. There, with her other guests, with her tea table at her side, and her fine china cups and her silver teakettle, her cunt oozing my sperm and her juices.

Which she did: I begin to have her well trained, I think. Could the husband smell sex? I wondered—and almost hoped he did, which was certainly imprudent.

I was charming, even loquacious—always guaranteed to put him in the foulest of tempers. At six I retired, to bathe and change for dinner.

Twice within a matter of hours was a reasonable performance, I thought, although when younger I could have exceeded that tally easily. A well-banked fire in my room; a whisky in my hand; some proofs to correct before dinner; a good cigar to be savoured. Ah, Shawcross, I say to myself as I write this, the rewards of adultery are sweet—as sweet as those of retribution.

Freddie had come to the end of the entry, and the end of the page. He stared at it, the words shifting before his eyes: a blue chair, a red sofa. He would never look at this foul thing again, he told himself (although in the coming weeks he would in fact read this notebook, and several of the others, again and again).

"A blue chair?"

"A blue chair."

" 'My other albatross'? What does it mean?"

"You know what it means. Just as I do."

"I don't. I don't." Freddie grasped Constance by the wrist and shook her. "You tell me. He's your father."

Constance jerked her wrist free. Saying nothing, her face tight and pale, she picked up the notebook again, turned back a page or two, indicated the heading.

Winterscombe, Freddie read. *October 3, 1906.*

"Nineteen-six?"

"It began that year. In the summer. It went on a long time. Four years. It's all in there. He often calls your mother that—'the other albatross.' You can see if you want to."

"Four *years?*"

"Oh, yes. Four years. Until the day he died, actually."

Quite suddenly, Constance's face altered: Her features seemed to crumple. She closed her eyes; she shivered; she clasped her arms tight around her chest; she began to rock back and forth, as if in some terrible ecstasy of grief.

Freddie, who had been about to burst forth in denunciations of Shawcross, was frightened by this. He stared at Constance, whose mouth moved in wordless cries. Then, in a hesitant way, reluctant to touch her, he stepped forward.

"Connie, don't—don't. Please don't. You scare me. Wait. Think. Perhaps it's all lies—it could be. Perhaps he made this up, like one of his novels. It can't be true. My mother . . . It cannot be. Connie, please, be quieter. Look at me—"

"No!" Constance cried out. She jerked away and hit out at him.

"It's true. All of it. I know—I've worked it out. I've looked at the dates. And anyway, I know. I saw them together—"

"You saw them? You can't have."

"I did. By accident. Once or twice—in the woods. They used to meet in the woods. I saw them there, and I ran away. And once on the stairs—they were coming down the stairs. Yes, that's it. I remember it. . . ."

Freddie began to cry. The tears spouted suddenly from his eyes, although it was years since he had cried. He saw his mother in the garden, calling to him; saw her come into his bedroom and kiss him goodnight; saw his mother in a thousand guises, yet always the same: gentle, kind, devout, growing a little shortsighted now, so he teased her. His mother, and—blotting out the sense of her touch, the tranquility of her skin, the sureness of her care—another image, gross and grotesque.

"Connie, please . . ." He groped for her hand. "Look, I'm crying too. It's—"

"Don't touch me, Freddie." Constance backed away from him. She backed up against the wall, backed farther, into the corner of the room. She huddled there, and then, as Freddie stepped forward, she sank to her knees.

"I want to die." She said it in a small flat voice. "Yes. That's it. That's it. I want to die."

II
A DECLARATION
OF LOVE

From the journals

A memory of my father: *When he wrote it was on quires of white paper,*
which he cut himself with a silver knife. He wrote in ink; his inkwell was
glass, with a brass lid. The pens he used scratched. The script was copper-
plate, all the hooks and loops perfectly formed, the lines marching straight
across the page like soldiers going into battle.

It was easy to read his writing, but not so easy to read my father.
The pomade he used on his beard smelled of lemons.
The soap he liked best was carnation.
Sometimes he chewed cachous, so his breath smelled of cloves.
His cheroots came from Cuba.
He changed his shirt twice a day, like a gentleman.
He polished his own shoes, then spat on the toecaps to make them shine.
I liked his blue suit the best—it made his eyes blue.
Once he let me help him steam the jacket, to bring the pile up. There was
an accident. The steam scalded my hand.

His voice was melodious. At Winterscombe he was careful with his
accent; at home, less so. At Winterscombe he could sound affected. Acland
thought he was affected. And common. I heard him mimic him once.
He was short. His books were short.
If he hadn't died, he would have loved me.
Constance can hear his pen scratch. She can hear him rustle with her
nurse.

She can smell the carnations and the lemons and the cloves.

She can see the blue suit and the gold pin in his tie and the brown shoes; she can see his hands, which are as white as lilies. A lily-white man. One is one and all alone and ever more shall be so.

Constance can see her father. She can. She can. He is very close. He is at his black desk on his black chair with his white paper.

No, he isn't. He is closer than that. He is as close as close can be. He does love her. He says he loves her. But he only says it when they are all alone.

Then.

How my mind cracks. I don't understand. I ask and ask. I say—who put the trap there. I say—who pushed you, Papa. He never answers. I don't understand why he never answers.

Where is he?

When I came to this entry of Constance's (it was about a week after I had supper with Wexton in London) I could see that she was ill.

It was not simply *what* she wrote; it was the handwriting itself. It was becoming smaller and smaller and increasingly difficult to decipher. The slope of the letters, always consistent before, was now wildly uneven, slanting first to the right, then to the left. I turned the page, then the page after that. What followed was a series of lists.

Constance had used lists before, as you have seen; now lists seemed to have taken her over. There were more and more of them, crammed upon the page: lists of random things—colors, shapes, words, names, birds, countries, rivers, mountains, cities, battles. It was as if Constance, sensing mental breakdown, had been frantic to impose an order, or a geography.

I pitied her deeply. It was impossible not to pity her, no matter what she might have done to Freddie. She had witnessed the appalling injuries to her father; she had made the terrible mistake of reading his journals. To see her, five years after his death, trying to ward off the delayed effects of trauma with a series of schoolroom lists, with those sad small details of her father, was like watching a small child armed with a stick warding off attack from a flame thrower.

I was puzzled, though, that the breakdown had been delayed so long; I was also puzzled because, in all the years I lived with her,

Constance had never once referred to this illness of hers. Had she been ashamed? That seemed likely, for Constance hated to admit weakness. She had never, for instance, given any indication to me that her childhood had been anything but happy. She had loved her father; she had loved my family. Of the accident that separated those two periods of her life she rarely spoke. I wondered now: Had she been shielding me from something?

That thought made me uneasy. If Constance had protected me in the past, and had now decided to impart some hidden truth, then that truth hinged on her father's death, on the possibility of murder. To that theme Constance returned, again and again. She juggled the names of possible culprits; she put forward, at different times, different theories as to method and motive; she reexamined the events of the day on which Shawcross died, who had been where, and when. Her final short list of suspects was brief and homogenous: everyone on it was a member of my family.

If it had been Constance alone who expressed these suspicions, they might have been easier to dismiss, particularly in view of the mental stress I saw in the pages of these diaries. But it was not just Constance. There were other hints, from other, much cooler witnesses. If Constance had shielded me from the truth about Shawcross's death, so, it seemed, had others equally close to me.

There were cryptic remarks in a letter from my aunt Maud to my grandfather Denton; Boy wrote to Acland from the front, referring to his missing Purdey shotguns in a way I found incomprehensible. Finally (and this perturbed me most of all) I found, among a mass of Steenie's drawings and papers, a letter begun to Wexton and never sent. It was dated the year of my own christening. *I know what you said*, Steenie wrote, *but the more I think about it, Wexton dear, the more convinced I am that we were wrong. Too Grand Guignol for words! Sorry, Wexton, but we're no good at playing Holmes and Watson. It may be dull, but I think the inquest was right: an accident.*

I thought so too. I wanted to think that. I might want to know what Wexton's theory had been (why had he never mentioned it?) and I intended to find out—but whatever his solution was, he had been mistaken. Doubt is like a disease, I told myself, and Constance's doubts had infected other people. If shock and memory contributed to Constance's illness, so did an overactive imagination. Once Constance recovered from this breakdown, the references to murder would surely cease.

How and when had she been cured? I wondered when I went to bed that night. I would find out the next day, if not in Constance's journals, then elsewhere. I fell asleep, half-aware of some incident nudging at my memory. Constance might never have spoken of this illness of hers, but someone else had, though I could not remember who it was, or the circumstances.

The next morning there was no opportunity to return to the past; the present intruded. It intruded in the form of a Prince of Wales check suit, a Turnbull and Asser shirt, tasseled Gucci loafers, all transported from London in a low-slung, dramatic sports car: Mr. Garstang-Nott, the real-estate agent.

It was his fourth visit in eight days. Garstang-Nott, aged about forty, possessed of excessive good looks, retained his alarming sang-froid but was beginning to exhibit the occasional flicker of interest (in the house, I hoped, though it was difficult to be certain).

On his first visit of inspection, his attitude had been one of guarded pessimism. On his second (longer) he grew more expansive: He told me that his father had been at Eton with my father, and with my uncle Freddie, to whom he sent his regards. On the third (longer still) he told me that my client Molly Dorset was his aunt; he admired the work I had done on her house, in particular her red drawing room.

The flattering photographs of Winterscombe had now been taken; the measurements and details of rooms were complete; every out-building had been itemized; plans of the garden, grounds, and farmland (now rented) had been finalized. All that remained, on this fourth visit, was to go over the draft of the sales particulars. I had expected it to take, at most, an hour. Two hours and one glass of sherry later, Garstang-Nott still lingered.

He told me that he might (he stressed the *might*) have located a potential buyer.

A millionaire, it seemed—in this case not an eccentric one. The man concerned (Garstang-Nott was not yet at liberty to divulge the name) was in the market, specifically, for a property in Wiltshire. A *large* property, with a certain status attached to it, since the man in question was newly rich, having made a fortune in those sixties' careers, development and corporate raiding. There had to be room to entertain clients; there had to be stables and land; a suitable site for a helipad would be advantageous.

This seemed too good to be true.

"You mean, if he was interested, he wouldn't want to pull it down, or build?"

"Absolutely not. He has a place in Spain and another in Switzerland. But this is his first English country house. He wants *gravitas*."

"Not Queen Anne?"

"Frankly, I don't think he'd know the difference."

We were, by this time, out of the house, approaching Garstang-Nott's dramatic Aston-Martin. He patted the bulge on its hood.

"Hit a hundred and ten on the way down. Just outside Reading. I don't suppose you're free for dinner tonight? We could discuss it then."

"The Aston?"

He smiled narrowly. "No. The house. Obviously."

"I'm afraid I'm not free."

"Oh, well. Some other time perhaps." He paused. "Well, I'll be in touch."

"This potential buyer—you'll be sending him the details?"

"Oh, Lord, we'll *send* them. We'll see if he bites. I'm afraid I don't hold out a lot of hope."

I felt he might have held out more hope had I agreed to have dinner with him. He climbed into the car, sped off down the drive with a spurt of gravel. I returned to my house, which no one but me seemed to care for, and to Constance's journals.

Sad pages of lists, followed by several pages left blank, followed by a page with only one word: *Floss*.

Then it came back to me—where I had been, when and with whom, the first and only time this illness of Constance's had ever been mentioned.

Thirty years before. My parents were recently dead. I was waiting to be shipped off to America. One day, about a week before I sailed, I went to tea in London with my uncle Freddie. He must have been summoning his nerve, I think, for on that occasion he did raise the forbidden topic of my godmother. Then, I had been disappointed by his revelations. Now, with thirty years' hindsight, I could see I had been wrong. What Freddie had told me that day (and what he had *not* told me) was interesting.

"I expect," he had begun, "I expect you'll be wanting to know about Constance."

We were having tea in Uncle Freddie's rented house, a large house with crumbling white stucco, which overlooked the canal basin in that district of London known, because of the waterways, as Little Venice. It is a smart district now, but it was not then. I had never been there before. The first thing Uncle Freddie did when I arrived was apologize for the disorder of his sitting room.

I could not see why: I liked the room. It was stuffed with the spoils of Uncle Freddie's past. Uncle Freddie often described himself as a rolling stone; the term suited him—he was by then very stout. This rolling stone, it seemed, had gathered plenty of moss: There was a brass table, brought back from India, supported by a rearing brass cobra base. There were many rickety tables and lacquer screens acquired in Japan; a stuffed otter in a case—that came from Winterscombe. There were masks from Peru, puppets from Bali, a Tiffany lamp, and many bright posters from German cabarets in which angular women wore top hats and smoked cigarettes in long holders.

Before he raised the topic of Constance, Freddie—to my great relief—talked nonstop. I can see now that he was perhaps nervous. He put off the topic of my godmother and, prompted by the objects in the room, launched himself on long reminiscences. He told me all about flying mail planes in South America. He told me about his spell in Chicago, selling encyclopedias. We had the tale of the Berlin zoo, where Uncle Freddie had been in charge of the bears, and the period—more recent this—when he had had a half share in a nightclub, now defunct, called the Pink Flamingo.

En passant, we also had Uncle Freddie's numerous past enthusiasms: We had the stamp-collecting period, the crossword period, the Irish greyhound period. These, like their predecessors, had now decisively *fizzled*—I could tell that. They had been returned to Ireland. Uncle Freddie had a new enthusiasm. It was this which had been occupying him in the library all that summer at Winterscombe, while Franz-Jacob and I walked the dogs.

It was, Uncle Freddie said with a flourish, *detective novels*. Freddie, always a fan of that particular genre, had now decided: if he could read them, why not write them? With this enthusiasm Uncle Freddie was, in fact, to find his métier: Later, after the war, he was to enjoy considerable success with his detective fiction. Then, however, he was still refining his methods, which he explained at length.

"Three murders, Victoria," he said in a confiding way. "There must be at least three—that's what I've decided. I tried one. I tried two. But I'm settling for three. Yes, three—that's the ticket!"

He was standing at his desk, shuffling his manuscript as he said this. Then, without a pause, as if the one topic led naturally to the other, he embarked on the subject of Constance.

I can see now that Uncle Freddie must have found that subject difficult, full of pitfalls. I think, in retrospect, that he must have doubted the wisdom of Steenie's plan far more than he indicated. He had been steamrollered. I think he must have felt guilty and concerned, possibly even worried. But he had trained his memory to be comfortable even then: The picture of Constance he painted was a plaintive one.

"The thing *is*," he said, "I often think your godmother must be lonely."

"Lonely, Uncle Freddie?"

"Yes, well, you see—in some ways she's had a sad life. Her marriage, you know. I don't think that exactly worked out. . . ."

I sat very still. A marriage?

Uncle Freddie seemed lost in thought. After a long pause I finally dared the great question: Was my godmother divorced?

"Oh, no, no. Goodness me, no." Freddie, knowing my mother's opinions on that subject, shook his head violently.

"But—there were difficulties. That can happen, Vicky. Your godmother lives alone now—"

"Is her husband dead?"

"Well now, I'm not sure. He might be. He was very very rich, and the thing is . . . the thing is . . . your godmother never had children of her own. That is, she did have a baby once, a long time ago now, the year before you were born, I think. But she lost it. That made her very sad, of course—"

"Did she pray for another one, Uncle Freddie? That's what Mummy did."

"Well now. I can't quite . . . Constance isn't very religious, you see. Still." He brightened. "Perhaps she did. You never know. And now she'll have you to look after, so—"

He stopped. I considered that while I was praying, Constance might have been praying too. Both our prayers were being answered, if that were the case. This frightened me, and perhaps Uncle Freddie saw that, because he changed tack quickly.

"She loves animals!" he said, with the air of a conjuror producing a prize from a hat. "Goodness—now I look back, she and Steenie had a whole menagerie. There was a cockatoo, and some goldfish, a tortoise. Why, there was even a grass snake once—"

He stopped. He shifted in his chair. He switched on the Tiffany lamp. Its stained glass made the walls jeweled.

"Does she like cats, Uncle Freddie?" I prompted at last, when Freddie had been silent some while.

"Cats?" He roused himself. "No, never cats, not that I remember. But she loves dogs. She's had a whole succession of dogs. The first one was a King Charles spaniel—she adored him. His name was Floss—"

He stopped again. I waited. When he did not go on, I prompted again. I asked what had happened to Floss.

"Well, Floss came to rather a sad end. And your godmother was very upset. She loved him, you see, and afterwards—well, she grieved so much it made her ill. Seriously ill."

"Like measles? Like scarlet fever? Uncle Steenie had that once, he told me."

"Not exactly like that, no. Some people said . . . it wasn't just Floss. The doctors, you know. And your aunt Maud. But now I look back, I can see . . . Yes, Floss—he was her best friend, you see. It all began one day in the park. . . ."

Uncle Freddie then told me the story of what happened to Floss. It was indeed a sad story. It showed my godmother in a very sympathetic light.

"How did she get better then, in the end?" I asked. "Did someone buy her another dog?"

"No, no. It was Acland. He . . . had a long talk with her. Sorted it out. She was as right as rain, then. In fact, it was then that she really came into her own—"

He stopped. He looked as if he regretted what he had just said. At that moment, his "help," a Mrs. O'Brien, who had already served us the tea, appeared in the doorway. Mrs. O'Brien was quite unlike the servants at Winterscombe, in that she wore carpet slippers and a flowered apron. She shuffled in now. Uncle Freddie rose. He seemed glad of the interruption.

"Jesus, Mary, and Joseph—just look at the two of you now, sitting there in the dark," Mrs. O'Brien pronounced. The Tiffany lamp did not count, it seemed, for she switched on the overhead light.

In its glare all the magic colors vanished—and my godmother Constance vanished with them. Uncle Freddie did not mention her again.

Thirty years later, however, others did. Once I began to look, there was a great deal of evidence concerning Constance's illness, and not everyone agreed that it had been caused by Floss. Jane Conyngham, for instance, who had been summoned (as a nurse as well as friend) to attend a family conference on the matter in the spring of 1915, was cautious. *Constance's symptoms*, she wrote. *They are: refusal to eat, rapid physical decline, severely troubled sleep, cessation of menstruation. Could this be caused simply by the loss of a dog? I believe Constance's troubles lie deeper than that. But the last of her symptoms could not, in mixed company, be discussed, its nature being delicate. And I was overruled by Maud, whose diagnosis was vigorous: anxiety at the war, exacerbated by the incident in the park. . . .*

"The incident in the park!" Maud cried to the assembled company: Gwen's Park Street drawing room, that emergency conference. "Forgive me, Jane. I bow to your medical knowledge, obviously. But I feel you complicate the matter. Let us consider this reasonably. It is perfectly straightforward—"

"It isn't. Jane's right." Steenie, who had been sitting in the window seat, sprang to his feet. "It isn't just Floss. It's something more. In any case, it doesn't matter what caused it. The point is, she's getting worse. She won't even speak to me now. She just turns her head to the wall. And she looks so horrible—I can't bear it. All her bones stick out. She has these dreadful sores on her skin—"

"Steenie, that is enough. You are upsetting your mother. We all know this. She doesn't eat enough to keep a sparrow alive. Broth, a little dry toast . . . Gwen, we have to find a way to stimulate her appetite."

"We have *tried*, Maud. Steenie has tried very hard. He spent three hours with her yesterday. She never said one word. A swallow of barley-water . . . I'm at my wit's end—"

"I blame the doctors. That last man was a perfect idiot—talking about a 'decline'! That term went out with my grandmother. In my opinion we should blame the war! The incident in the park, too—but mainly the war. We worry—all of us worry—about our friends, about Boy in particular. And Constance worries, too—she was always most attached to Boy, if you remember. Why, she used to write him the longest letters. I posted one for her myself, once—before her illness, of course. Now—"

"Constance writes to Boy?" Acland, speaking for the first time, looked up.

"Of course. Whyever shouldn't she?"

"I've never known her to write more than a postcard, ever."

"Then that proves my point! She wrote to Boy *because* she worried on his behalf. In fact, it seems to me I may have hit the nail on the head. Anxiety about Boy—now that would explain every-thing. Am I not right? Acland? Freddie?"

Acland gave a gesture of annoyance but said nothing. Freddie stared at the wall. Mention of Boy reminded him of Boy's photographs. He was feeling sick.

Maud, whose questions were often rhetorical, rushed on. "Gwennie, dear, don't look so distressed. Now, listen to me. I think we need another opinion. I disliked that new man—such a graveyard face! What we need is a homeopath. Maud Cunard recommends the most *excellent* man—a Pole, I think, or was it a Hungarian? Anyway, he cured her sciatica, quick-smart, just like that. I think you should call him in. Jane, Montague—don't you agree with me?"

Montague Stern was sitting on one side of the room, reading a newspaper. Now he looked up patiently.

"Possibly, my dear. It would do no harm to try, I imagine." He folded his newspaper in half. " 'Canst thou not minister to a mind diseas'd,' " he murmured.

"A mind diseased?" Maud gave one of her shrieks.

"It's only a quotation." Stern returned to his newspaper.

"Well, it is hardly an apposite one," Maud rejoined smartly. "There is nothing whatsoever wrong with Constance's mind. And I may say . . ." She drew herself up, cast a firm look around the room. "I may say that I very much distrust that kind of new-fangled notion. Viennese doctors? I believe they require you to write down your dreams. Such nonsense! In my opinion they are quacks, every last one of them. A friend of Gertrude Arlington, I hear, had the greatest faith in one of these men. She visited him three times a week—at twelve guineas a time, mark you—lay down upon a couch, and talked! I told Gertrude, I never heard anything more silly. If that is what one needs, one can do it for nothing. One simply invites a friend to tea, and—"

Acland rose. "Shall we try and stick to the point?"

"I am upon the point, Acland. I never *depart* from a point—"

"I should like to know what the new doctor said." Acland turned to Gwen. "Mama?"

"The new doctor?" Gwen stared fixedly at her hands. "It was rather horrible. He was so stern. He said . . . well, he said that if there was no improvement by the end of this week, we should have to consider more aggressive measures. He said, if she cannot be persuaded to eat—eat properly; the barley water and the broth will not do—then they would have to *make* her eat. He would bring in a new nurse and they would . . . feed her by force."

There was a silence. Then Steenie stamped his foot.

"Force-feed her? That's disgusting. They wouldn't do that."

"Of course they will not do it." Maud rose. "Gwen will never allow it. What can this man be thinking of? Does he imagine this house is a prison, that Constance is some species of suffragette?"

"Maud, he said we might have to. He said, if she refuses to eat, it's the only way. She could die otherwise. He said so—"

"You can't. You can't, Mama—please." Steenie's voice had risen. He was almost in tears. "You can't let them do that—not to Constance. It's horrible. I know what they do. I read about it. They strap them down. They put this tube down their throat. Then they take a funnel and—"

"Steenie, please! That is more than enough." Maud glared at him. "None of us requires details. Gwen, let us be calm about this. You are distressed. You're not thinking clearly. Monty, would you fetch my smelling salts? Thank you. Now. Let us try to consider this thing in a sensible way. I shall telephone that homeopath—yes, that's the first thing to do. And then, tonight, if we were to arrange a special dish, her favorite food, Steenie could take it up to her. Then perhaps Freddie could go in, and Acland. Acland, you should—you hardly ever sit with her. They could talk about pleasant things, ordinary things. Then, I feel sure— Why, Freddie, where are you going?"

Freddie, who could bear this no longer, had risen to his feet.

"I think I'll go out," he said. "Just for a bit of a walk. Then I can think. I need some fresh air . . ."

Acland stood.

"I'll come with you," he said.

"Walk—or drive?" Acland said when they were on the stairs.

"Oh—drive."

"Your motorcar or mine?"

"Yours." Freddie shrugged. "It goes faster."

" 'Round London, or out of London?"

"Oh, God. Out of London."

"I agree," Acland said. "Out of this house and out of this city. Come on, Freddie. Hurry."

In the mews behind Park Street, where Denton had once kept his carriage horses, there were now garages. In the first was Denton's Rolls; in the second was Freddie's nineteenth-birthday-present runabout; in the third, huge, magnificent, a beast of a car, was Acland's new acquisition: a red Hispano-Suiza Alfonso. Freddie stroked its long hood with love and with respect.

"What will she do?"

"Flat out? On the straight, sixty—maybe seventy. Shall we find out?"

"Let's."

Acland cranked the engine: a full-throated roar.

They climbed in; Freddie glanced at his brother, whose face was tight and abstracted. Acland looked miserable. He eased the car out of the mews, paused at the junction with Park Lane.

"Where are we going, Acland?"

"Out of London by the fastest route." Acland opened the throttle. "Anywhere. Somewhere. It doesn't matter, does it?"

He accelerated down Park Lane, heading south. Somewhere the other side of the river—Freddie had no idea where, for his knowledge of London was mostly confined to Mayfair and the streets around Hyde Park—Acland slowed.

"Ego's dead," he said. "His mother had the telegram last week."

"Oh. I see." Freddie hesitated. "I'm sorry, Acland."

"It happens."

"Is that what's wrong, Acland? I knew something was wrong. I could tell it by your face."

"Yes. That." Acland accelerated once more: they were reaching the suburbs now; Freddie could see open country ahead.

"That. And other things. Constance, I suppose. The war. Everything. I just can't stand the house, that's all. It's as if there's a blight on it." He changed gear, the noise of the engine mounted, and the wind began to whistle in Freddie's ears.

"Never mind all that, anyway. Let's not talk. Let's just drive—fast."

They drove fast—into Kent, Freddie thought, seeing houses give way to fields, and fields to orchards. They drove, and they thought.

Freddie thought for a while about Ego Farrell, whom he had liked but had met infrequently—Farrell, who had seemed such a quiet man, and such an unlikely friend for Acland. He wondered how Farrell had died, whether he was shot or bayonetted or blown up by a mine or a shell.

He tried to imagine what the war must be like, and how it would be if a doctor had not lied (Freddie was almost sure the doctor had lied) and you had to go to the front line and the trenches and the mud. Freddie had heard some stories about conditions in France, though Boy, when home on leave, had said very little, and most of the other officers Freddie had encountered in London had been similarly reticent. He read the newspapers, he read the statistics, but the newspapers then seemed to concentrate on victories; even retreats were made to sound ordered and tactical.

They used gas now—the Germans used gas, and Freddie had heard accounts of the terrible injuries the mustard gas caused. But even so, he found that his idea of the war was an insubstantial one, unfixed and imprecise, cloudy and shifting—a gaseous thing indeed. Freddie told himself there was a reason for this: It was because he was a coward.

A double coward. He was a coward not to defy his mother and fight; he was a coward about Constance. He was the one person who knew what was wrong with her, after all; he knew it was not simply the incident in the park, as the rest of his family claimed. Constance's illness, her visible wasting away—these things were caused by her father. It was her father, and in particular her father's journals. Constance was dying of the past, Freddie believed, and he was too much of a coward to say so.

Such thoughts were familiar to Freddie now; indeed, they went around and around in his head every day, a nasty tangled web of thoughts, which made his head ache and his stomach feel queasy. The journals, and Constance, and the things they had done, which were like the things Shawcross wrote about—Freddie could see that now. And his mother. That, too, for Freddie now found he could not bear to touch his mother, avoided even speaking to her, and shied away from her most casual embrace.

These were the things that made him ill; these were the things that made Constance ill. Not just the war, not just the incident in the park, although they, perhaps, contributed. No. The past, he told himself again as the motorcar reached the brow of a hill and swooped downward. The past had poisoned them, and Constance—he was sure of this—had come to a decision. Since she could not force the past out of her system, since there was no emetic for a poison of this kind, Constance was willing herself to die.

She would persevere, and within a few weeks she would succeed. After all, he had never doubted her willpower.

"Was it Floss? Was it the incident in the park?"

Acland had stopped the car, somewhere, anywhere, by the side of the road. He and Freddie were now walking. Along a farm track, along the side of a shallow valley. Freddie looked out upon the beauty of England in late spring: green fields, sheep with newborn lambs in the distance, a farm couched in the hills, with woodsmoke rising, the pale thread of a river below. He hesitated.

"It *seemed* to begin then," Freddie replied cautiously.

"Possibly, but I'd have said earlier. Several months earlier. It grew worse then, that's all."

"She did weep, Acland. Maud was right about that. I never saw her weep before."

"Yes. She wept," Acland said, and came to a halt. He leaned against a stile, his eyes fixed on the river and the fields below. Freddie, kicking at some nettles first, then leaning also against the stile, saw not the fields but the open expanse of Hyde Park, some two months before.

Tea: they had been to Maud's for tea, in the smart house Stern had bought her, which overlooked Hyde Park and the Serpentine. His mother had been there, and Jane Conyngham, Steenie, Acland, and Constance herself.

Constance had brought Floss with her. It had been a fine day, one of the first fine days of the year, and everyone had seemed in good spirits. Gwen read aloud her recent letter from Boy; Maud regaled them with the latest scandals. Floss begged for tidbits in such a pretty and charming way that no one could refuse him.

Freddie, feeding the little dog with morsels of cake, felt for the first time in weeks an extraordinary well-being, a new, bounding optimism. When Maud proposed they should stroll in the park, Freddie took his mother's arm.

The first time he had done so for several weeks. His mother glanced up at him, saying nothing, but she smiled, and Freddie, who knew he made her happy, that it was simple to make her happy, felt happy too. He loved his mother; no matter what had happened in the past, he loved her. He was out of the labyrinth.

They made a circuit in the park; they stopped to admire a group of riders who cantered along the sand track close to the Serpentine; they watched the rowboats, and the children playing.

"How far away the war seems on such a day!" Maud said, and Constance, who was playing some foolish game with Steenie, let Floss off the lead.

They paused then, near the water, to watch Floss race back and forth. He dug a hole; he rolled in the grass. Steenie climbed a tree and tore his jacket. Then they decided to turn back, and it was then, just as they had almost reached the park gates, that the accident happened.

The horses and riders they had watched earlier were making a second circuit of the park, still only at a canter, but it was enough.

Floss had trailed behind, sniffing at trees. As the horses drew level he looked up, saw Constance on the far side of the sand track, and with a bark and a whisk of the tail, ran to join her.

Freddie doubted that the riders even saw him. One second he was still running toward Constance; the next, he was tangled in the horses' hooves. They tossed him up into the air, a small bundle of fur. Black, white, tan—it was as if he performed with delight a clever somersault, of his own volition. His new trick, and Floss had had many tricks. He was dead, his neck broken (Acland later said) before he hit the ground.

"She carried him all the way home," Freddie said now, leaning against the gate. "She wouldn't let him go. Do you remember? And she did cry. She made those awful choking noises. She sat with him on her knees, and she stroked him."

He looked away. He could see the moment quite clearly: Constance, in a scarlet frock, clutching Floss tight, and the consternation because no one could persuade her to relinquish him.

"Constance, come with me," Acland had said finally, as evening approached and the light began to fade. "We'll go out into the garden and we'll bury him there."

Constance had seemed to accept this. Freddie and Steenie went with them, and at the end of the garden, beneath a lilac just coming into bud, Acland and Freddie dug a grave.

"I don't want him to lie on the bare earth," Constance said when they had finished. "I don't want the earth to go in his eyes."

She looked, and sounded, like a sleepwalker. She laid Floss down very gently; she stroked him. She began to pull up tufts of grass. Freddie, finding this unbearable, would have stopped her, but Acland took his arm.

"Leave her," he said.

Constance filled the grave with grass. She picked Floss up and laid him upon the grass. Then, to Freddie's horror, she slumped down full-length. She lifted Floss's head; she stroked his muzzle; she began to make the most terrible high, keening noise in her throat.

"Please, Floss. Don't die. Don't die. Please breathe. I know you can breathe. Lick my hand—oh, Floss, please lick my hand. I love you so much. *Please,* Floss—"

"Constance. Come with me. I'm going to take you inside."

Acland knelt down. He put his arm around Constance's waist. He tried to lift her, but Constance fought him off.

"No. No. Don't move me. I won't go. I have to hold him—"

Acland lifted her bodily in his arms. For a moment Constance fought him. She struggled, eel-like, her hair flying out, her face streaked with tears and mud. Acland tightened his grip. His gentleness astonished Freddie. Then, quite suddenly, Constance became still. She went rigid in Acland's arms; he carried her into the house.

There, she was put to bed by Gwen. She remained in bed the next day, and the day after that. She had remained in that bed ever since, taking some water but eating almost nothing. First she set about starving herself, and then—as if intent on punishing herself more—she ceased speaking.

The last time Freddie had heard her voice had been a week before. Then, clasping her thin wrist, Freddie had become very agitated; it was the first occasion on which he had realized that Constance actually might not get better.

"Constance, I'm going to burn those journals," he burst out. "I'm going to burn them. They did this. It wasn't just Floss, was it? It's them. I hate them. Oh, please, Connie—stop this. Was it my fault? Was it what we did? Please, Connie—I want you to be better."

"I should like that too," Constance had said. She almost smiled—a ghost of a smile, a ghost of a joke. Then she turned her face away, and the next time Freddie came to see her, she said nothing.

By then he had discovered that Constance's desk was locked, and he did not have the nerve or the resolve to force the lock or touch the notebooks.

"Does she talk to you?" he said now, turning back to Acland. "Does she? She never says a word to me. I think she maybe can't talk anymore. I'm not even sure she can see. Acland—she's dying."

"I know that."

Acland turned to look down at Freddie. Freddie looked at his brother's hair, that helmet of bright gold; he looked at his brother's eyes, the right greener than the left. It was not easy to lie to Acland.

The compulsion to speak was strong, but even so he hesitated. Acland reached across and touched his arm.

"Tell me," he said.

"I don't know where to begin."

"Begin at the beginning," Acland said, and turned away once more. The perfect confessor, he looked out across the fields.

"Well," Freddie said, "it began—it really began—a long time ago. I went upstairs to my room . . ."

"At Winterscombe?"

"Yes. At Winterscombe. And Arthur had laid my evening shirt out on my bed. There was a sweet on it. No, not a sweet—one of those *petits fours* things Mama orders. It was a little apple made of marzipan, and—"

"When was this?"

"It was the night of the comet. It was the night Shawcross died."

"Ah, *then*. The night of the accident."

Something in the way Acland said this brought Freddie up short.

"Why do you say it like that? You mean you think it wasn't an accident?"

"Never mind that. It doesn't matter. Here, have a cigarette." He lit one for them both, cupping his hand to protect the flame. Then, seeing that Freddie, once begun, wished to continue, he turned away once more.

"A marzipan apple," he said. "Go on."

"On and on and on."

"Until she was ill?"

"No. It stopped before that. After she showed me the journals the first time. It stopped then. It was the journals that did it. I'm sure of that. They got into her system—like germs. Then they got into mine. Do you understand?"

"Yes. I understand."

Freddie had talked for a long time. The sky grew first mauve, then gray; the fields beyond were now indistinct, the sheep scarcely visible. Dusk hid the expression on Acland's features. He stood still, quiet, although Freddie could sense a gathering tension in his brother's body. Freddie watched the end of Acland's cigarette glow; then, with an impatient gesture, Acland tossed it down. A red glow of a stub in the damp grass. Acland ground it underfoot.

"Let's go back." He took Freddie's arm.

"Now? I don't want to go back. I can't bear it there. Acland, couldn't we stay down here—till later? We could find a place to have a drink. Something."

"No. We're going back. Come on. Hurry."

Acland led the way back down the path. Freddie stumbled to keep up with him. His leather-soled shoes slid on damp grass; mud squelched.

"Stay away from her."

They had reached the car. Acland stopped, one hand on the door. He turned back to his brother.

"Freddie, stay away from her. I won't tell you to forget this—obviously you can't forget something like this. But—try to move away from it. Try not to let it touch you."

"It's not just Constance. It's not just that horrible father of hers—and the foul things he wrote. It's everything." Freddie slumped against the car. "The war. Mama. That doctor she made me see—I think he lied, Acland."

"Why should he do that?"

"I think Mama persuaded him. She's terrified I'll join up."

"I'm sure you're wrong."

"Maybe. Maybe. But I feel so useless. So utterly useless. Boy's fighting. You have important work—"

"Important work? You couldn't be more wrong."

"It is. It is. Why sound so bitter? Even Stern said it was vital—I heard him. And what do I do? Nothing. I stay at home. I go out with Steenie's friends—and they're all younger than me. Even they do things. They paint. They write. They take photographs. That's better than nothing. It's better than being like me. Useless. Of no use—to anybody."

Freddie's voice cracked. He blew his nose loudly and made a great business of refolding his handkerchief. Acland put his arm around his shoulders. He bent his face closer. Freddie looked at his brother's pale skin, at his green eyes. They did not appear stern, though he thought Acland was angry.

"Find something. There must be something you could find to do—something that would make you feel useful. Freddie, you don't have to fight. Not everyone has to fight." He paused, then opened the door. "I'll talk to Jane Conyngham. Go and see her at Guy's. She'll be able to help. They need people at the hospital—porters, auxiliaries, drivers—"

"Drivers?"

"Ambulance drivers. Now, get in."

Freddie climbed into the car. Acland cranked the engine, then sat beside him. He opened the throttle. The car trembled, then roared. Acland swung it in a tight circle. When they were facing toward London once more, he accelerated. The body of the car shuddered; it gathered pace.

Freddie had thought they drove fast on the way out; on the way back they drove faster still. A corner swerved toward them, and then another one. The camber tilted; the car ate the road. Freddie peered ahead through the gathering darkness; hedges pressed closer. He suggested Acland might slow down, but the slipstream caught his words and rushed them over his shoulder.

He gripped his seat with his hands and braced his feet on the floor. The tires whined. A bend rose up to block them. Freddie closed his eyes. He had a clear sensation: He was going to die. If not at this bend, then the next, or the one after that. Sudden impact.

He did not open his eyes again until they reached the suburbs and Acland slowed. Up Park Lane; the tires screamed as they turned into the mews. Acland was already out of the car and making for the house before Freddie decided it was safe to let go of the seat.

"You're angry," he said, running after Acland and catching him by the sleeve.

"Yes. I'm angry." Acland stopped. He looked up at the sky. He took in a deep breath.

"With me?"

"No. Not with you. With her. For what she did to you—and what she's trying to do to herself. I'm going up there now. So she can see just how angry I am."

"Now? Acland, you can't do that. Don't do that."

"Yes, I can. Everyone's out. They've gone to the opera with Stern. There will be no one there—just Jenna and the nurse."

"Acland, please don't—she's ill."

"Do you think I don't know that?" Acland pushed Freddie aside. "You've just been telling me how ill she is."

Perhaps Constance had been asleep, or in that daze she often experienced then, when time passed without her being aware of it. Either way, she did not hear Acland come into the room or sit down on the upright chair by the bed. When she opened her eyes, it was some while before she noticed him.

She was looking toward the windows. She liked to watch the sky beyond, the light altering, the clouds moving; she liked to listen to the sounds from the street, but in the last few days she had noticed something curious. The sounds were becoming more distant and more muted, and the light—that was changing too. It was no longer bright, even at noon; the window seemed farther away than it used to be; even the curtains framing it were less distinct. In fact, she had to concentrate very hard in order to see the outline of the windows at all, or the furniture in the room.

It had occurred to her—yesterday? the day before?—that she was going blind, and she had tried to concentrate on this thought, too, for that was an important development, surely, to become blind?

But the thought would not fix, or stay still long enough for her to assess it. It eddied forward, then billowed, then drifted away. *Perhaps I am dying,* she thought, an hour later, or a day later, and for a moment that idea was huge and bright in her mind, as if she were staring at the sun; then it, too, went away, and the darkness returned. She preferred the darkness. It was peaceful.

That night, that significant night, she opened her eyes; she turned them toward the place where the window ought to be, and she saw . . . violets. Not the shape of the flowers, but their color and their scent. She could see the color scudding—every conceivable hue, from the palest, most opalescent gray, through lavender to a dark grape-purple. The sight, and the scent—of dampness and earth— were so delightful to her that Constance cried out, and the sound curled away from her, gunmetal and smoke.

"Touch them."

When Acland spoke—and she knew at once that it was Acland— his voice seemed very loud to her, so loud she was sure she dreamed. But then he said the words again, so perhaps it was not a dream after all. Then—how long it took, like watching the world spin—she turned her head on the pillow and she could see him, there, then receding, then coming closer, his thin face intent. He was frowning. He held something in his hands; he held something out to her; he put his arm under her shoulders and lifted her. He held something close to her face.

It was violets, a small bunch of them. Acland had just plucked them from a vase on the dressing table, but Constance was not to know that. She was astonished they were there, that she was not blind. She wanted to touch them, but her hand was too heavy to lift.

"Smell them. Look."

Acland held the flowers close to her face, so that the petals brushed her skin. She could see that each flower had an eye, and these eyes looked at her. The leaves were veined. The scent of earth was overpowering. Drowning in violets. Acland grasped her wrist.

"It's time for your veronal. I'm not going to give it to you. Drink this. It's just water. Slowly."

He held the glass to her lips, and because her mouth was

becoming stupid, her throat obstinate, some of the water spilled. Acland did not mop it up, as the nurse did or Jenna did. He put the glass down and he looked at her.

Perhaps it was the effect of the water, perhaps the shock of its coldness on her skin; Constance found that she could see him. She could see the way in which his hair curled against his brow, so that it appeared sculpted; she could see the thin high bridge of his nose, the pallor and concentration of his features. She saw that his eyes were examining her, their expression severe.

"Can you see me?"

Constance nodded.

"What color is my jacket?"

"Black."

It took a long time for this word to surface; by the time she thought she said it, Constance was no longer sure it was the right one. Presumably it was, however, for Acland nodded. He stood up, crossed into the swirl of colors; then he came back. In his hand he held a mirror.

"Sit up."

Again he lifted her, propping her against the pillows. Then he did an astonishing thing. He held the glass up to her face, although mirrors were forbidden, and had been for weeks. Jenna had covered the large one on the dressing table with a shawl.

"Look. Can you see? Look at yourself, Constance."

Constance looked. At first the surface of the mirror was misted and gray and pearled, like the inside of a shell, but she wanted to obey Acland, so she peered, then peered again. She blinked her eyes. After a while she found she could see a face.

The face shocked her. It was the face of no one she knew. It was ashen; the bones stood out sharply; there were sores around the mouth; the eyes were sunken, ringed with shadows. She looked at this face in an uncertain way, and her hands began to move in the way they did now, of their own accord, back and forth, small plucking movements against the cool of the sheets.

Acland put down the mirror; he grasped one of these hands. He held it up before her face, circling the wrist with his fingers.

"Do you see how thin you are? Your wrists are matchsticks. I could snap them—just like that."

This seemed to make Acland angry, so Constance inspected her wrists. She supposed they were shocking, so ugly and bony. Surely they had not been like that yesterday? She frowned at her wrists and, as she did so, found she could see not just her wrists but also her hands, and Acland's hands, and the crisp white linen of the sheets, and the coverlet, which was red, and the chair Acland sat upon, which was made of some black wood, carved and fretted.

"I want you out of that bed."

Acland pulled back the covers.

"It's all right. I know you can't walk. You don't need to walk. I shall lift you."

He picked her up. The sudden movement was dizzying. The room tilted and lurched, and Constance felt her hands scrabble, in their silly useless way, at the lapels of his jacket.

He took her to the window. When they reached it, Constance gave a small cry, for it was open. He took her out onto the small iron balcony. Such air! Constance could feel its lightness, filling her lungs and clearing her mind. She gazed around her: the shapes of houses and clouds; the hiss of traffic. The sky swooped. She cried aloud again.

"It's raining."

"Yes. It's raining. It's raining quite hard, and there will be a storm. You can feel it in the air. Can you feel the rain? Can you feel it on your face?"

"Yes," Constance replied.

She let her head fall back against Acland's shoulder. She let the rain wash her skin. It whispered to her. She closed her eyes and felt the pinpricks of rain against her eyelids, her cheeks, her mouth. It was pleasant at first; she luxuriated in it. Then the rain began to penetrate her nightdress; it grew clammy and chill against her skin.

"Take me back inside," she heard herself say. Her voice surprised her, for it was like her old voice, only more cracked than before. Acland did not move, so she said the words again.

"Take me back inside, Acland."

"No," Acland said. It was then that Constance understood that he was angry—more angry than she had ever seen him.

"Can you hear what I'm saying, Constance? Can you understand?"

"Yes," Constance began, but before she could say anything else, Acland gave her a cruel shake that jarred every bone in her body.

"Then listen to me, and remember what I say. You're killing yourself. You seem to expect that everyone will stand by and let you do it. I won't do that—do you hear me? So, you shall choose, and choose now. Either you go back inside and begin living, or I'll simply let go of you. I'll stand here, on the edge, up against the balustrade, and I'll let you go. It will be a great deal quicker, and less painful, than starving yourself to death. This way, it will be over in an instant. Forty feet down. You'll feel nothing. You decide. Which is it to be?"

As he spoke, Acland moved forward. Constance felt the iron of the balustrade brush her feet. She looked down; she could see the street below, heaving, then distinct. Forty feet at least.

"You wouldn't do that."

"Maybe no. Maybe I'm not quite callous enough—though I'd like to be. Very well. I'll let you choose yourself. I'll set you down. Look, the balustrade is quite low—you would only have to lean over the smallest amount, and you'd be over. There."

Acland lowered her. The paving was cold against her feet. Her knees buckled.

"Hold on to the balcony rail. Like that. You can do it. You'll have to do it. Let go of me."

Acland pulled her hands away from his jacket.

Constance swayed against the balcony rail, reached for it, missed, and then managed to grasp it. Acland was behind her. Was he still close—or had he moved farther away? She thought she could sense him, just behind her, but when he next spoke, his voice was receding. Constance looked over the rail; the street beckoned.

"Decide."

Certainly farther away now. Constance could scarcely hear his voice; it was being swallowed by rain and wind and sky. She could jump, she thought, and perhaps Acland was right: That was what she wanted. She would not even need to jump, as he said; all she had to do was lean, a very little. Then it would be done with: the black notebooks, and the black dreams, and the black worms that nibbled away at her heart in those dreams. Easy!

Constance bent her head. She looked down at the street below with great concentration. It still beckoned, but with less vigor than before. Constance considered how it would feel, and how it would look, to be smashed on that pavement, to be easily crushed like the shell of an egg. Everything over; all done. It might be easy to drift toward death; to leap to it was another matter.

She lifted her face to the rain and sniffed the damp urban air. She sniffed a future—there was a possible future there, after all. If she could will herself to die, she could also will herself to live: years and years of a future. She frowned at that future, and saw that it could beckon, too, for it was secret, and unknown, and therefore seamed with the loveliness of possibilities. Let go, or go on.

Gamble, and go on: She could hear these words said to her

distinctly, in a small clear voice. At precisely the moment she decided this voice gave good advice, which she wanted to take, her hands began to slip on the balcony rail. The street rushed up toward her with a speed that made her head buzz. She thought she cried out. Acland's arms came about her. He had been much nearer than she thought.

They stood still. The rain fell; in the distance lightning wavered; the sky growled.

A summer storm. Acland, turning her toward him, looked down into her face. He looked puzzled, Constance thought, as if something was happening to him that he neither welcomed nor understood. A dazed look in his eyes, as if he had been struck an invisible blow.

An expression of distaste came upon his face, a tightening of annoyance to his lips. In a quiet and weary voice he said, "Constance. Come inside."

"I cannot change," Constance said to him, and it was much later the same night. She had taken some food. She felt new. She felt stronger. "I cannot change altogether. You do know that, Acland?"

Acland had been holding her hand or, if not holding it exactly, had laid his own hand very close to it, on the bedcover, so their fingers touched.

"I never asked you to change. You are what you are." He paused. "Was it Floss? Was it the accident?"

"Not just that. No."

"Freddie then? Your father's journals?"

"You've talked to Freddie?"

"Yes. Tonight."

"Did he tell you what I did? What we did?"

"Some of the things. I imagine he left out others."

"I shall not apologize. I shall not beg forgiveness." Constance began to speak rapidly, her hands twisting back and forth. "Now you know me for what I am. You know me at my worst. I expect it was no surprise—I expect it just confirmed everything you ever thought. You never liked me, Acland."

"I disliked you, once upon a time, very much."

"Very well then—so you were right. I will not argue with that. I often dislike myself. I often hate myself."

"Is that why you punished yourself?"

"Punished myself?" Constance was stung by his tone, as he perhaps meant her to be. She turned away.

"You set out to die. You were fixed on it. That seems a punishment, of a kind."

"Maybe it was that. Perhaps." Constance began again, more slowly. "I did not like myself. I thought I damaged people. I can't explain it, Acland, and I'm not always like that. Sometimes I almost feel I might be good—or better, anyway. But then—something happens. I change, and I have to do harm. My father used to say . . ."

"What did your father say?"

"Nothing. It doesn't matter."

"You should forget your father. You should . . . cut him out of your mind."

"I am my father's daughter," Constance replied, and her hands again began to twist back and forth upon the sheets.

She seemed feverish, Acland thought; he rested his hand against her forehead, which indeed felt hot. At the touch of his hand, Constance's eyes closed. She moved a little, in a restless way, and then lay still. She should rest, Acland told himself; she should sleep. He moved away from the bed, sat down, then stood up and began to pace the room. After a while Constance's breathing became regular. Acland crossed to the window, reluctant to leave her, and looked out.

Freddie's account had shocked Acland, although he had tried to hide that fact from his brother. He had been shocked by what Freddie told him, and shocked by what he was sure Freddie left out. Freddie censored his story. There were gaps, and Acland found it was these gaps that obsessed him. He tried to concentrate his mind on the facts Freddie had imparted: the fact that Shawcross had kept journals; the fact that both Constance and Freddie had read them; the fact that Freddie now knew of their mother's affair; the fact that, in some physical way, Constance had seduced his brother.

"She liked to go to places where we might be caught," Freddie said. "I don't know why. Father's study, or the back stairs. We went to your room once."

"*My* room?"

"We went to everyone's room, except hers or mine. Then . . . she'd touch me. Or I'd touch her. You know, Acland . . ."

Acland, standing at the window, watching the storm recede, turned back to the bed. *My room,* he thought.

Constance still slept; her cheeks were flushed, her hair disordered, spread out upon the pillows. She was a child still, Acland said to himself. He knew at once it was untrue. Constance had never been like a child, even in the days when he first met her. Even then her gaze—defiant, watchful, as if expecting hurt—had been that of someone much older.

Someone had robbed her of her childhood. Acland took a step toward the bed. Constance cried out. She had begun to dream; he saw her eyelids pulse. She began to struggle, wrestling with the sheets. She pulled at the ribbons that fastened her nightgown. She cried out again. Then, eyes still tight shut, breath coming quickly, she lay still.

Acland moved to the bed. The sheets had been kicked to one side; they were tangled with her legs. Her nightgown was disordered. Constance now lay as if a man had just made love to her: her arms flung out, her hair tumbled about her throat and face. One leg was still covered, the other bare. He could see her thigh, the darkness of sexual hair through the thin material of the nightgown. Her right breast was covered, the left exposed. That this child possessed breasts, that they remained full, the aureole wide and dark, despite her thinness, checked Acland.

He reached across to draw the nightgown across her breast. His fingers touched its ribbons. Constance stirred. Her hand closed over his.

"Touch me," she said, eyes still tight shut. "Oh, yes. Touch me like that."

He felt the curve of her breast against his palm, the point of her nipple. Constance shuddered. Her eyelids flickered.

Acland snatched his hand back. Constance opened her eyes. She pushed back the tumble of hair. She stared at him, her eyes wide, dark, and blank. Then comprehension flickered.

"Oh, Acland. It's you. I had a bad dream. A horrible dream. Take my hand. Please hold it. There. I'm better now. No—don't go. Acland. Stay with me. Talk to me a little."

"What shall I talk about?"

Acland felt wary; he hesitated, then sat down by the bed.

"Anything. It doesn't matter. I just want to hear your voice. Tell me, where is everyone else?"

"At the opera, with Stern. They'll be back soon. The nurse is here, and Jenna, too, if you want them."

"No, I don't want them. That nurse is so grim. And Jenna fusses so. What a time I've slept. Has she married Hennessy yet?"

"Not yet. Rest, Constance. Hennessy is in France. He joined up, don't you remember? They'll marry after the war, presumably."

"Don't let's talk about them. I don't want to hear of them." She moved her head on the pillows. "I hate Hennessy. I always did. He killed beetles. He would pull off their legs, shut them up in a box—he showed me once, when I was little—"

"Constance. Rest. Forget Hennessy."

"He's simple, just a little. That's what Cattermole says. But I don't believe it. I never did. I think he's clever. Clever and grim. So huge. Does Jenna think he's handsome, do you think? I suppose he is. Like a great oak. But he killed beetles. And moths. And spiders. He killed my father, I used to think—"

"Constance, stop this. You shouldn't talk. You're feverish. Lie still."

"Am I? Am I feverish? Is my forehead hot?"

She struggled against the pillows. Acland, growing alarmed, wondering if he should ring for the nurse, laid his hand against her forehead. It still felt dry, a little hot.

"You see? No fever. No fever at all."

She lay back on the pillows. She fixed her eyes on his face.

"I don't think that now. I was younger then. Now I think—who took those Purdey guns?"

"What?"

"Francis's guns. Someone took them. They were missing—Francis told me. He might have lied, of course. He might have taken them himself—"

"Constance. I'm fetching the nurse."

"Don't you know about the guns then, Acland? I thought you might. Or your father might. Don't fetch the nurse. Wait. I'll tell you a terrible thing—"

"Constance—"

"My father and your mother were lovers. They were. On and on. For years. Even Francis found out in the end. He saw them, that very day. Your mother, going into my father's room. He'd lost something—Francis had. What was it? Something he needed . . . for his camera—that was it! Yes, he'd left it, and he went back and there she was, just closing the door of the King's bedroom. Francis wept."

"Lie still."

"And Freddie. Both of them. Such tears. Did you weep, Acland? Oh, no—you knew. You already knew. Of course. I'd forgotten that. Acland, my head aches so. Hold my hand. No, tighter. There, you see? I'm calmer now."

"Constance. You must forget all this. It was a long time ago, five whole years—"

"Acland, will you tell me one thing? Just one? That night—the night he died—where were you, Acland?"

"I was at the party, obviously—"

"Yes, but later. Acland, Francis says he looked for you, when the party was over. He couldn't sleep; he wanted to talk. And he couldn't find you. You weren't in your room, you weren't downstairs—"

"Boy says that?"

"He said it once."

"Well, he wouldn't have found me. I wasn't there. I was with . . . someone else."

"With Jenna?"

"Yes. Now, can we leave this?"

"All night?"

"Yes. All night. It was dawn when I left. I never went to bed—"

"All night. With Jenna."

Constance gave a deep sigh. All the strain and anxiety left her face. She lay back against the pillows.

"There. You see? You have put my mind at rest. I knew you could. You see, I was so afraid—"

"Constance—"

"No, truly. I feel as if there had been this terrible weight on my back, pressing me down. And now it's gone. You've cured me, Acland. Cured me twice. Once on the balcony, and once in here. I'll never forget that—not as long as I live."

She stopped. She took his hand once more.

"Stay a little longer. Talk to me. Tell me quiet things. Ordinary things. Then I'll sleep. Tell me about your work. Where you go. What you do. Who your friends are. Please, Acland, don't go."

Acland hesitated. For a moment his instinct was still to fetch the nurse, to leave the room—but Constance drew him to her. He wanted to leave; he was reluctant to leave.

He looked around the room and found it lulled him. The stillness of a sickroom, the warmth of the firelight, the red of the coverlet. Constance's eyes rested quietly upon his face. A strange evening, he thought, an evening out of time, set aside from the rest of life.

"Very well," he began. "My work. My work is very dull. Pieces of paper: I read reports and I write reports. I draft memoranda. I attend committee meetings. I am assigned to the Serbian desk, and the more I learn about events there, the less I understand. I have two wooden trays, Constance, one on the right side of my desk and one on the left, and by the end of the day I have to transfer all the pieces of paper from the left to the right, and that is what I do. Every day."

"Do you come to decisions?"

"Decisions? No, not for at least the next ten years. No, I make recommendations—and then watch them being ignored."

"So it doesn't suit you?"

"No. It doesn't suit me."

"What would you rather do?"

"I wish I knew. I'm not trained to do anything. I'm trained to read Greek and Latin and philosophy. I'm being trained—now—to take up some sort of position in the world, a powerful position, I suppose. It's the expected thing. It doesn't greatly interest me."

"Why not?"

"Because it is so very predictable, I suppose. Look at us: Boy will return from the war. One day he will inherit Winterscombe. They'll find some suitable profession for Freddie, just as they found one for me. Steenie may escape—but the rest of us?" Acland paused.

It surprised him that he should say these things, since he had never voiced them to anyone else, not even to his friend Ego Farrell. Acland looked down at his own hands. They were narrow and pale; the skin was soft: the hands of a gentleman.

"I lack will," he said, and surprised himself again, for it was not his habit to admit weakness. He looked away. "We were all given too much—perhaps that's it. Too much, too soon, too easily. So we never learned to fight."

"You could fight." Constance struggled to lift herself against her pillows. She reached across and grasped his hands. "You could—you could, Acland. You could go anywhere, be anything, if you chose. Look at me. There! I can see it in your eyes. I recognize it. I always could. . . ."

"Constance, you're tired—"

"Don't patronize me. It's there in you, just as it is in me. We're alike. You're not meek and weak, any more than I am. You're not one of nature's Christians, Acland." She smiled. "You're like me. A pagan."

"Nonsense." Acland returned her smile. He lifted his hand and began to count off upon his fingers. "Christened, Church of England. Confirmed, Church of England. Eton and Balliol. Son of a High Tory squire. Grandson of a High Tory squire. The imagination in my family died out years ago. It died out as soon as they acquired money. In a few years' time, Constance—maybe not quite yet, but it will come—you'll look in my eyes, and you know what you will see? Complacency. The sang-froid of the Englishman. I shall have it to perfection by then, because it takes at least three generations to acquire—ten, probably, if you want the truly finished article."

"You're lying." Constance's eyes had remained fixed on his face. "You're lying, Acland—and you're also leaving something out. What is it? There's something else, isn't there? Something you haven't told me?"

"I've joined up." He extricated his hands from Constance's grasp. There was a silence.

"I see," Constance said at last. "When?"

"Three days ago."

"Which regiment?"

"The Gloucestershire Rifles."

"Ego Farrell's regiment?"

"Yes. Ego is dead."

"Ah—" Constance drew in her breath. "You mean to replace him then?"

"In a sense. I felt I owed him something—that I owed him that. No one knows yet. I shall tell them tonight. Tomorrow perhaps. I have to train first, in any case. I'll have to learn to kill. They'll send me to officer training camp."

"Draw back the curtains, Acland."

"You should rest now—"

"In a minute I will. But not yet. Stay five minutes more. It's raining again, I think. I can hear the rain. Draw back the curtains. Just for a moment. I want to look."

Acland hesitated; then, as much to placate her as anything, he did as she asked. He returned to the side of the bed.

"Switch off the lamp for a moment. Look . . ." Constance's thin face strained toward the window. "Look, there is a moon."

Acland turned. He looked through the shadows of the room, at a moon almost full and at clouds scudding. They obscured the light one moment; the next it shone forth. Acland looked and, as he gazed, found he saw not just the moon and the clouds, but thoughts, possibilities, and imaginings. They sped formless through his mind, opening up a bright space and then clouding it. A moon, glimpsed; a sick girl, who had been intent on dying.

He remained still, with his face turned to the window, yet the proximity of Constance beat in upon him. He could feel her hand, a few inches from his own, as surely as if he touched it; her hand, her skin, her hair, her eyes. At the same moment they turned to look at each other.

"Acland. Will you hold me? Just for a moment? Will you?"

Constance lifted her arms; Acland bent. It happened, a curious embrace, although he was not conscious of moving, or of taking the decision to move. One moment he still stood by the bed; the next he felt Constance's thinness strain against him.

He could feel each bone in her rib cage; he could have counted the hard knot of each vertebra. He could feel the heat of her face, which she pressed against his neck. Her hair, made lank by her illness, felt damp, a little greasy against his skin. He lifted a lock of this hair between his fingers, as he had done once before; this time, he pressed it against his lips. Constance was the first to draw back.

Her hands gripped him, so she forced him to look down into her face. When she began to speak, she did so with great intensity.

"No explanations," she said. "No repercussions or promises. Just this. Just this one time and this one incident. I always knew it was there. You knew it was there, too—the day by the lake, you knew then. Did you know then? No. Don't answer me." She pressed one hot thin hand across his lips. "Don't answer me. I don't want answers any more than questions. Just this. I need it—to give me strength."

She broke off. She lifted her hand and touched his hair, then his face, then his eyes. She covered his eyes with her hand. When she removed it, Acland saw she was smiling.

"Later, you'll tell yourself this was my illness peaking. That's all right—later. But don't believe it now. I won't let you believe it now. I'm not feverish. I was never more calm. You can go in a minute—but not yet. Before you go, you have to promise me something."

"Promise you what?"

"Promise me not to die."

"It's a little difficult—to promise someone that."

"Don't smile. I mean this. I want you to swear. Lift your hand—press it against mine. Like that. Promise me."

"Why?"

"Because I want to know you will live. That you are there. Even if we never meet. However much time passes and we change, I want to know you are there, somewhere. It's important. Promise."

"Very well. I promise."

*   *   *

He moved toward the door. A curious promise; a curious bond. Again, as he had earlier, Acland sensed he crossed some invisible divide: a time out of time; a step through the looking-glass.

He opened the door. Constance's eyes were now shut, her breathing regular. He wished her goodnight but she did not answer him. He lingered at the door, unsure. A clock ticked.

On the landing outside, he passed the room where the nurse sat, door ajar, asleep in a chair. He walked farther along the landing, reached the stairwell, and looked down. At the bottom of those stairs waited the ordinary world, a family returning from an opera, the explanation that he was going to the war.

He ought to go down and wait for them, but he was reluctant to leave the shadows of the landing. He was not ready yet. He was not yet . . . depressurized—yes, that was it, like a diver who had been down to the depths of the ocean and had to wait to breathe ordinary air. Full fathom five. He rested his hand on the banister; there remained, in his mind and in his body, something insubstantial and unresolved, a vestigial need. After some while he understood that the need was for a woman.

He turned back. He walked quietly along the corridor. The door of Jenna's room was also ajar; he looked in. She was seated with her back to him, at a table, writing. Acland leaned against the wall. He closed his eyes. The corridor was full of whispers.

Did you sleep with her, Freddie?

No. She wouldn't. Everything else, but not that.

Everything?

She liked to touch. And watch. Sometimes—

Sometimes what?

She likes the dark. She likes mirrors. She says words—

What kind of words?

Those words. The words women don't use. She learned them from the journals—

I don't understand. Are you making this up?

No. She'll do anything. And she frightens me.

Acland opened his eyes. He looked through into the lighted room. A pen scratched. The air was full of Constance. She pursued him from the bedroom into the passageway; she led him on, beckoning. A chair, a table, a bed, a woman—Constance was in there waiting; he could sense her detonations. He could smell her hair and her skin. He could put his hand between her thighs. He could stroke her breasts. Her hair brushed his eyes. She took her small jeweled hand, crammed with cheap rings, her child's hand, and she touched him as a woman would touch. She ran her hand up his thigh; she made his cock rigid. This was what Constance did—to someone else.

He pushed back the door, entered. Jenna started. She turned, gave a low cry, scraped back her chair.

"What's wrong? Is it the fever again? I'll come—"

Acland closed the door.

"Constance is asleep. I came to see you."

Jenna stopped. Her face became rigid.

"I was writing—writing to Jack. I just began. I owe him a letter. Acland, what's wrong?"

"Wrong? Nothing is wrong."

"You're white. You look so white—"

"I've been with Constance. Also, I've joined up. I wanted to tell you. I think I wanted to tell you—"

"Shhh." Jenna took a step forward. "Keep your voice low. The nurse will hear us."

She came closer. Her lips moved. She was speaking again, and Acland could hear some of her words, but the closer she came the farther away she seemed. She looked small, distant, a figure gesturing on a platform while he rushed away on a steam train, a troop train. Going to the war. The room was small, too—he could see that now; all its details were precise, meaningful and meaningless, as if he viewed them from the wrong end of a telescope. A chair, a table, a bed, and a woman. The woman had begun to touch him. She touched well enough, and he wanted sex; sex was the way through, his depressurization chamber. Constance, sex, war: that was the progression.

"Look at me. Acland, look at me." She had taken his hand. "I know why you came. We can. If you want, we can."

She was whispering now, drawing him toward the bed. But something was wrong; there was something lacking. *She liked to go to places where we might be caught. Your room, Acland . . .*

Acland turned. He opened the door. He left it three inches ajar. Jenna's eyes widened. When she began on another whispered protest, Acland rested his fingers on her mouth. The room sighed its assent; it settled.

As he moved toward the bed, and a woman (who might have been crying), Acland thought: *Your turn to watch, Constance. I'll show you—about fucking.*

The next day, or perhaps the next week—the entry was undated—Constance wrote this in her journal:

Three facts:

1) The night Acland came to my room, he told me one lie. A serious lie. Interesting.

2) He went from me to Jenna. That is all right. I like Jenna. She may be my understudy.

3) He is going to the war. When he told Gwen this, she fainted.

Gwen also wept, cajoled, insisted, pleaded. When Acland proved obdurate, his decision irreversible, Gwen gave in; she had never had the stamina for prolonged opposition.

Once he had left for his training camp, Gwen set her mind to ensuring his survival. There were techniques she had already learned from Boy's absence at this war; now she redoubled them. Gwen believed that the fate of her sons depended upon herself; she could protect them now from wounds as she had once protected them, when children, from illness. It required concentration of mind: If she could remain busy enough, brave enough, if she thought constantly of her sons and willed their safety hourly, then her love would have the power of an amulet. No bullets, mines, or shells could pierce this invisible shield.

She became—more than ever before—superstitious. She banned the color green from her house and her wardrobe. She felt a horror of the number thirteen, even on a passing omnibus. She skirted all ladders. She kept, about her room and her person, many small charms and relics of her boys. Every day she would invoke the powers of these articles; she would pray over them. Scraps of her sons' hair, cut when they were babies; drawings they had made for her as children; a Saint Christopher medal; a pair of blue satin baby shoes; the letters her sons now sent from the front: Gwen believed in the powers of these inanimate things. She felt it pulse when she touched them.

She was furtive about these prayers and invocations—Denton would have dismissed them angrily. She was also sentimental. She was also lonely.

To be afraid, yet unable to speak of the fear, intensified it. Gwen knew this, but there was, at first, no one to whom she could turn. Maud, whose interest in the war was intermittent, was caught up in a round of parties. Denton slumbered whole days away by the fire. Both Freddie—who had been found a job by Jane Conyngham, driving an ambulance in Hampstead—and Steenie were occupied with their own lives. Steenie would bring his new friends back to the house: Conrad Vickers, a would-be photographer; one Basil Hallam, well connected but an actor; an odd shambling bear of a man, American, always known as Wexton. Gwen did not know what to make of these friends. They seemed worryingly Bohemian. With the possible exception of Wexton they seemed unaware there was a war on. So, Gwen was lonely, but this loneliness did not last. She was to find a new companion, a new confidante—and that was Constance.

At first the process was gradual. Constance was recovering from her mysterious illness, which had ended as abruptly as it began. Gwen took pleasure in her convalescence. The empty weeks were punctuated with small victories: Constance came downstairs for the first time; she took her first walk in the park; she ate dinner with the rest of the family.

This process cemented a new friendship between them. As the weeks passed, Gwen discovered something else: Constance could be excellent company.

There seemed no scars; there was no sign that the illness had left any legacy of lassitude or depression. On the contrary, Constance had a new and avid zest for life. She talked—how she talked! Gwen discovered that Constance had healing powers: Whenever she felt sad or afraid, Constance could console her.

She was amusing, of course—that was part of it. She had zip and drive. She loved to gossip; she listened attentively to all the stories of London society that Gwen received at second hand from Maud. She loved to discuss feminine things: hats, gloves, dresses, the count-less fine shadings of fashion. She liked to make shopping expeditions with Gwen—brief ones at first, then more lengthy and adventurous ones. Returning from these expeditions, small parcels dangling from their wrists, pausing in a smart tea shop to take tea, they would discuss these spoils enjoyably.

Gwen had never had a daughter; these harmless delights were new to her. For the first time in her life, she accepted Constance. A residual wariness, always there before, passed away. "Constance," Gwen would say, "what would I do without you?"

And then, Constance was adaptable. She was not always a fount of gaiety. Her instincts were subtle—she knew when Gwen wanted diverting; she also knew when Gwen needed to be quieter.

Constance, sensing this need, would draw her out. She would encourage Gwen down the gentler pathways of nostalgia. Sitting by the fireside on these restful afternoons as autumn turned to winter, Gwen opened her heart to Constance. She described her own child-hood in Washington, D.C.; she described her parents, her sisters and brothers. All kinds of details would come back to Gwen as she spoke—details that, until then, she had forgotten. The brougham her father kept up; the rides they used to take, across the river to visit cousins in Virginia; the dresses her mother had worn; the readings her father gave each Sunday morning, from the Bible.

None of Gwen's family had ever shown great interest in these stories, but Constance did. She would sit, concentrated and still, apparently rapt. "Oh, America," she said on one occasion. "America. I should love to go there. A new world. How lucky you are, Gwen, to have traveled."

Encouraged by this, Gwen moved on. She told the story of her meeting with Denton, and their engagement. Winterscombe, and the birth of her children. Gwen passed over the Shawcross years— and on that period, Constance never prompted her.

From the immediate family to Denton's. Gwen filled in some of Maud's background. She described the Italian princeling, Maud's Monte Carlo life. She approached the advent of Sir Montague Stern, said perhaps too much, and halted. This was not, she realized, a topic to discuss with a girl. Constance smiled.

"Oh, you need not be delicate. I am not a child now. I know Stern is Aunt Maud's lover. Why shouldn't he be? He is younger than Maud, of course, but such a clever and generous man. . . ."

Gwen was shocked at first. The word *lover* was unexpected. She might have preferred some more decorous term—*protector*, perhaps. But Gwen was not staid; she had a sense of humor, and Constance was now looking at her in such a way, amused, slightly conspiratorial. . . . Times were changing. Gwen was tempted to go on.

"Well, of course, he is a Jew. I am not too prejudiced, I think, on that score. But some people are. Most people are. It makes it hard for Maud, I often think. Even Denton, you know . . ."

"Denton? But he invites him so often!"

"I know. I sometimes find it curious. But there you are—one cannot always account for Denton's actions. And of course, Stern does have the most powerful connections. . . ."

The moment of resistance was over; Gwen was launched. She and Constance had a most interesting talk on the subject of Maud, Stern, the rumors about Stern, the lack of positive information, his discretion, his generosity, and his riches. It was at the end of this conversation, which both enjoyed very much, that Constance sighed. She reached across and pressed Gwen's hand.

"You know," she said, "you should go out more. It makes me feel guilty—I shouldn't like to think you stayed here on account of me. I am quite strong again now. *We* could go out more, you know. We could go together. . . ."

Gwen was touched by this.

"I suppose that we could now . . ." she began, somewhat wistfully.

"But of course we could! It would do us both good!" Constance sprang to her feet. "Let's! We could begin tomorrow."

In this way, Constance's entry into society began. It began at a tea party of Maud's, the next day.

There followed a most hectic and enjoyable period, which was to last some nine months. It began in the autumn of 1915, when Acland was still at his officer training camp; it continued even after Acland left for France.

Gwen had made brief forays before into the glittering world in which Maud held court, but she had always held back, fearing she was not brilliant enough to be accepted by such a world. Now, encouraged by Constance, Gwen ventured. She discovered acceptance was much easier than she had imagined.

Many of the other women who sat on the pinnacles of this society were American, too, among them Maud's great crony and sometime rival, Lady Cunard. These women took to Gwen, and to Constance, whom Gwen or Maud would chaperone. They were blessed with a powerful energy; Gwen and Constance were quickly swept up in an unceasing whirl of activity. There were the luncheon parties, the tea parties, the soirées, the "crushes," the suppers, the balls; there were the committees—an endless number of them, raising money for soldiers' wives, raising money for the select private nursing units, which sent titled women, women of good family, to nurse in France. Gwen's presence on these committees was sought after, she found, and so were the checks she persuaded a reluctant Denton to write on the charities' behalf.

Where her diary had been relatively empty, it was now full: not an hour free—and if there was, it could be pleasurably spent, for attendance at all these functions required a radical revision of her wardrobe.

"No, Gwen, you *can't* wear that dress again," Maud would proclaim, delighted to have found a new ally and recruit. "What's more, Constance hasn't a *thing* that's suitable. We need a shopping expedition. Immediately."

So, as the months passed, the shopping expeditions increased too. Under Maud's expert tutelage Gwen rediscovered the seduction of luxury.

"Silk, Gwen, next to the skin! It's the only thing!" Maud would cry, and Gwen, who had some years before taken up cotton in response to Denton's demands for economy, experienced a rapid conversion.

It was heady—and it was expensive. Occasionally, waiting in a scented salon for a model to parade irresistible dresses, Gwen would become anxious. Maud would brush these scruples aside.

"Rubbish, Gwen," she would cry. "Denton is such an old miser. He doesn't understand money at all—all he understands is saving. Besides, don't worry—they're terribly good here. They don't send the bills for months. . . ."

Credit! It was hardly difficult to obtain; these places that parted Gwen from her husband's money were discreet. The actual cost of a dress or a hat or a pair of French-made shoes or a hand-embroidered petticoat of shantung silk—such a vulgar matter as price was not mentioned. It seemed to Gwen crude to inquire. After all, had she not always assumed, in her vague way, that the Cavendish fortunes were inexhaustible? They could hardly be dented too badly by expenditure such as this. Dresses, one or two pieces of jewelry. Why, as Maud said, it was a nothing!

There was another dimension, too, to all this activity, to the succession of parties and the succession of shopping expeditions, and that was the transformation they produced in Constance.

Constance, Maud said, in her tart but affectionate way, had the instinct for luxury. She reveled in the intricacies of excellence; she was a quick and a clever pupil.

"No, Constance, dear. I know you like colorful things, and they suit you—but that green is *too* bright. Now *this*"—and here Maud held up a length of silk that was twice as expensive—"this is the real thing. Feel it, Constance. You see?"

Constance did see. She began to understand subtlety, although her taste remained dramatic. She began to understand about line. She saw that fashion was akin to disguise.

Yes, Constance learned fast. Maud discovered—as Gwen had done before her—that it was pleasant to teach; it was pleasant to see how quickly her pupil advanced. One day, early in January 1916, Maud took Gwen to one side. It was at one of her tea parties, and Constance, at the far end of Maud's drawing room, was much in demand. The two older women looked back; they regarded her with pride.

"You know, Gwen," Maud began in a thoughtful way, "Constance has possibilities. I know there are problems—lack of family, lack of money—but those things do not matter quite as much as they once did. They are certainly not insurmountable! You see how amusing she is? Always so quick and so animated. She has *charm*, Gwen. She may not be beautiful, exactly, but she is striking, don't you think?" Maud gave Gwen a sidelong glance. "People like her, Gwen. Even difficult people. Maud Cunard was stiff with her at first—you know how she can be—but now she's *quite* won over. She can see Constance as an *asset*—and she is an asset, Gwen. She has such energy! She makes a party go! Women like her. More important, *men* like her. They are intrigued by her. I think, Gwen, if we set our minds to it, that Constance could make a really very good marriage."

"Marriage?" Gwen started. Maud gave her a dry look.

"Darling Gwen, you can be slow. Constance will be seventeen next May. You were eighteen when you married, and so was I. We should look ahead, Gwen, and start to plan. In fact, I mentioned it to Monty just the other evening. There are simply masses of candidates—I wouldn't rule out a title, not if we played our cards the right way. After all, she's practically your adopted daughter; she has your name behind her now. And if not a title, certainly *money*."

"Money?"

"Oh, Gwen, *think*. Why shouldn't she marry money? There's enough of it about. Monty has heaps of friends in the City, men who've worked their way up, who are now looking around for the right wife. They're a good deal older than Constance, of course, but when did disparity of age matter in love? Look at Denton and you, after all. So—there is the City contingent, several candidates there. Or what about an American? Monty has innumerable American business contacts: There's that man Gus Alexander, for instance—you know, Gwen, the construction king! He's still a little rough at the edges, so Constance would be just what he needs. On the other hand, what about a Russian? I *love* Russians—such romantic manners. Flamboyant—Constance would love that. Maud Cunard has a *very* diverting one in tow at present, trots him out at every opportunity. Prince-Something-unpronounceable. Dark, with flashing eyes and rather bad breath—but I'm sure that could be dealt with. Now, how about him, or—"

"Maud, stop. I can't keep pace with you." Gwen had begun to laugh.

"You *shall* keep pace with me." Maud was suddenly firm. "It's always important to plan. I shan't let you drag your heels on this, Gwen, I warn you. Strike while the iron is hot! Women's looks don't last forever, and just now Constance is a novelty. Capitalize upon that, Gwen! You know what you should do? You should *launch* Constance. Tell Denton so. A ball—that would be the thing. This summer, at Winterscombe . . ."

"I don't know. Denton might object. A ball would be such a huge expense. . . ."

"Nonsense. My brother isn't a complete fool. And he certainly won't want to support Constance for the rest of her life. Make him see it as an *investment*, Gwen—one that could pay very high dividends! And if you won't persuade him, I will. I'll make Monty talk to him. Monty can always make Denton see sense. . . ."

And so it was decided: the launching of Constance; a summer ball.

Montague Stern took luncheon with Denton at Denton's club, the Corinthian, which would shortly afterward admit Stern as a member. Not long after this luncheon, Denton himself broached the idea; before Gwen knew what was happening, the arrangements had begun.

They would open up the ballroom—how many years since that had last been used? There should be a marquee upon the lawn. There were a thousand decisions to be made, and they were not easy decisions, as Gwen, at first, naïvely believed.

Maud began to take charge, seeing Gwen falter, and once Maud took charge, everything became much more elaborate. The orchestra Gwen had envisaged hiring—they certainly would not do! That was last year's orchestra, not this year's. The same was true, Gwen discovered, of the caterers, the wine merchants, the florists.

To compose the guest list was worst of all: Who should be on? Who should be off? Gwen was under siege. Steenie could not bear for any of his group to be left out; Freddie had further suggestions; Maud's mind changed from day to day, according to whom she had met the previous evening.

Only Constance was quiet, and modest, making few suggestions, apparently content to let Gwen and Maud make all the decisions. There was about her a quiet air of contained expectation, Gwen thought, in the months that led up to this dance. It was as if Constance were waiting for something, planning something, serenely confident that it would fall into her lap.

Only natural, Gwen told herself, though she found this new

concentration in Constance somewhat odd. Constance was looking forward to the ball, Gwen told herself. She was nervous at the grandeur of the plans—yes, that must be it! Gwen was touched by this evidence of insecurity in Constance; she found she liked her the more.

The ball was to take place in June; the invitations were sent out in March. Gwen's absorption in her new task, and her happiness in it, faltered only once—in April 1916, when Acland returned from France on a four-day leave.

Gwen, overjoyed to have him home again for those four days in London, anticipated no difficulties. After all, Boy had returned, over the past eighteen months, on two occasions, and although he refused to discuss the war, Gwen had been encouraged by his demeanor. He had seemed so very cheerful—far more so than she ever remembered. None of his odd morose moods; no sign of agitation; she had not heard him stammer once. It had almost been exhausting, Boy's insistence on joining in every social activity, when—for once—Gwen might have preferred to sit quietly at home with him and talk.

Boy had not wanted to talk. He had wanted to go out. He spoke in new, ringing, confident tones, in a hearty, jocular way. Once or twice Gwen had found that heartiness strained, and Boy had developed a new habit—of shaking his head, as if he had water trapped in his ears—which she found worrying. But Boy dismissed her fears; it was just that London seemed so quiet, he said, compared to the front and the constant boom of the guns.

That was the only occasion on which he mentioned the war. He at once changed the subject. By the time he returned to France, Gwen was reassured: Boy was well and strong and in good spirits. Her prayers were being answered.

She assumed, therefore, when Acland returned for the first time from France, that his visit would be similar. Acland would want to go out—as Boy had expressed it, "to make up for lost time."

This proved not to be the case. Acland returned from France a very different man. He was leaner than Gwen remembered, and he had always been thin. He was quieter, too, and abstracted. He had no intention, he informed Gwen somewhat curtly, of going anywhere or meeting anyone. He had only four days. He preferred to stay at home.

Stay at home he did, and Gwen stayed with him. But she found Acland very difficult to talk to now. Perhaps he regretted the terseness he had shown when he first arrived, for he did seem to make an effort. He asked all the right questions. One by one he went through the litany of the family: How was his father? how was Steenie? Freddie? Boy? . . . He paused. How was Constance?

The trouble was, it *was* like a litany. There was none of his usual animation. Acland listened in a polite way to her answers, then put another question, as if going through some list in his mind. Gwen felt he did not listen to her replies at all.

This change in her son made Gwen very nervous. She felt she was not simply boring him but also failing him in some way. The war—she ought to ask about the war. But she could not think of the right way to frame the questions, and Acland's dismissive replies, when his father began on that inquisition, were no encouragement.

Instead—and she was aware of this—she began, whenever they were alone together, to babble in the most stupid and trivial way, especially about the arrangements for Constance's ball. Once she began on these babbles they grew worse and worse; she found she could not stop.

"I thought—I have almost decided, Acland, this brocade. Do you agree?"

It was the last night of Acland's leave. Denton slumbered by the fireside; Steenie, Freddie, and Constance were at the opera with Maud and Montague Stern. The scrap of brocade Gwen held up was the material she had chosen for her ball dress. Now that she looked at it again, she found it drab.

"And the style, Acland," she went on. "Now that is very difficult. I don't want to look passé. Maud cut out this drawing for me, Acland, from one of her periodicals. The new narrower look. I was not quite certain. . . ."

Gwen stopped. Acland had turned, first to the scrap of material, then—in his polite way—to the sketch she held out. Gwen felt he saw neither. She lifted her eyes to his face, and there—before he had time to compose his features—she saw an expression that cut her to the heart.

She could not have described it: desolation, perhaps, mixed with anger. Acland looked at a fashion sketch as if into a pit in which unimaginable horror crawled.

"Acland, I am sorry. Forgive me." Gwen dropped the piece of brocade.

"Don't apologize. Please, don't do that. I understand." For the first time since he had returned, Acland looked at his mother as if he saw her. He took her hand and held it for a time, while Gwen bent her head and fought back sudden tears.

"Tell me about your dress," he said. He stood up and moved away to the window, his back to her. "I mean it," he said after a pause. "I prefer it. Truly. Tell me about your dress and Maud's dress and Constance's dress. How the ballroom will be decorated. Who is coming and who is not . . . all those things."

"They're trivial, Acland. I know that."

"Are they? Well, perhaps they are, and perhaps that is why I like them. Tell me."

So Gwen began to speak, slowly at first, then more rapidly, for she saw Acland did listen, and her words seemed to calm him.

After a while he moved back to her and sat down next to her. He leaned back against the sofa cushions and closed his eyes.

Gwen looked at his pale features. She reached out, greatly daring, and stroked his hair.

Acland did not push her hand aside. Feeling that she could, after all, soothe him, Gwen began to speak again: first the coming parties, then past parties, then—such an easy loop!—other reminiscences from the past, long days at Winterscombe, the summers when Acland was a child.

The span of the years shrank. She was back in the nursery with this boy, her Ariel, her changeling, for Steenie was not yet born and she had never met a man called Edward Shawcross.

"I called you that, Acland," she said in a low voice, with a cautious glance toward Denton, who still slept by the fire. "It was because of your eyes. And then you were so very different from Boy or Freddie. Do you remember that, Acland? You were so very young."

"Remember what?"

"The names I called you then. Silly names. They made your father furious. But I didn't care. You liked them. We were very close."

"I think I remember. I think so."

"You were always so restless, Acland! It was as if there were some place you were always trying to reach, and failing—and when you failed you used to become angry, you know! Angry with yourself. When that happened, I'd sit you on my knee. I'd talk to you, just as I do now. It was so calm and peaceful, by the fire there. I remember once . . ."

Gwen talked on in a low voice. Acland kept his eyes closed; he listened to her words and tried to concentrate his mind on that nursery, those vanished summers.

If he could concentrate well enough, he felt, the image would go away. He tried, but perhaps his concentration was poor, because the image remained there fixed in his mind, as it had been for some weeks.

Not such a terrible image, really. There were others, he supposed, that were worse—yet they did not intrude, as this one did. There it was again: a part of a man. Not a foot this time, or a hand; not even the hands which, stiffened by rigor mortis, thrust up through the waves of mud, and which—the first time he had seen them, at a distance—he had taken for branches of trees.

No, not a hand: a jawbone—eaten clean by rats. The teeth were still intact; it was possible to count the blackened fillings.

"Give us a kiss, love." One of the men with him had picked it up; he articulated the jaw so that it seemed to be the broken mouth that spoke. *"Just one kiss, love."* The man laughed, then tossed the jawbone aside; he said it stank.

Acland opened his eyes and sat up.

"Where's Constance?"

"Constance?" Gwen, her reminiscences interrupted, looked at him with surprise. "You remember—I told you, Acland. She's gone to the opera with Steenie and Freddie. In Monty's box—"

"Which opera was it?"

"Verdi, I think. Now, was it *Rigoletto?*"

"Would you mind if I went out?" Acland leaned across and kissed his mother. "I'd like to walk for a while. . . ."

"Walk, Acland? In London?"

"Just for a while. I might go to the club." Acland was already moving to the door. At the mention of his club, Gwen's face brightened.

"Ah, so you do feel like seeing people, after all! I'm so glad, darling." She rose and crossed to him and took his hand. "Did it help, darling—just to sit quietly and talk? I think it must have. There—you look better already." She reached up to kiss him, then drew back, holding his face and looking into his eyes.

"Acland, you do know that I love you, darling? You do know how much I care for you?"

"I love you too. Very much," Acland replied, in a stiff way. It was many years since he had said this to her, and at that, Gwen's worries vanished.

As he left the room, Acland had a distinct picture in his mind. It was a picture of a small and anonymous hotel, next to Charing Cross station, which had been mentioned to him several times by fellow officers.

He had never visited the place, but in his mind's eye he saw it clearly, down to the last details of the room he could hire there—by the hour, his friends said; no questions asked if a man were in uniform.

Acland was not in uniform, but even so, few questions were asked. He signed false names for himself and Jenna, they were given a key, and they went up to the room. It was as he had expected.

It had all been so easy, and so quick: a word with Jenna on the back stairs; a touch, a glance; a meeting in a mews a few streets away; a taxicab; signing a form, being given a key. So quick, so easy.

When he did all these things—which took so little time—Acland had felt quite certain on one point: His mother could not drive the image of the man and the jawbone from his mind, but a woman could. Constance would have banished it in a moment, he felt, if he could have been with her alone, but he had been alone with Constance only once since his leave began. Possibly she was avoiding him.

"You are keeping your promise?" She had said that to him, in a fierce way, catching him by the hand as they delayed, the last two people to leave breakfast.

"As well as I can," he had replied. "I thought you might have forgotten it."

"Don't be a fool." She had seemed angry; she dug her nails into his palm. "I shall never forget it. No matter what I do, or you do. Ever."

Then she had gone. Tonight she was at the opera in Stern's box, and Stern had, over the past four days, performed one discreet service for Acland. At Acland's request he had introduced him to a solicitor, whose name was Solomons and who operated from dingy premises on the edge of the City.

The best there is, despite appearances, Stern had said, and Acland assumed Stern to be a good judge. He could hardly consult his father's solicitors in a matter such as this.

Acland had made a will; it was signed and witnessed. Not a very impressive will, he had thought, reading it over, but the best he could do, since his family money was tied up in trust until he was twenty-five—if he were ever to be twenty-five. His motorcar to Freddie; his clothes and other personal belongings to his brothers; his books to Constance, for she sometimes borrowed them, though he doubted she read them. All the money not in trust, some two thousand pounds, to Jenna, who might—one day—need it.

It would bring in an income, Solomons had said, of some one hundred and fifty pounds a year—hardly munificent, but adequate. In the pocket of his jacket, Acland now had a card with Solomons' address; before they left this room—and they would not stay long—he must give it to Jenna, and explain.

The necessity of doing this vexed him; the room vexed him. Now that he was here Acland wondered how he could have imagined that it would do any good. He was using Jenna as he had used her three or four times before, visiting London from his training camp. He knew this to be a betrayal—of Jenna, and of himself. Her acceptance of the fact that he came to her for one purpose, and one only, made no difference.

I should leave here. I should go now, Acland said to himself wearily. But his capacity for disgust—even self-disgust—was exhausted. Without speaking to Jenna, he began to undress.

He lay back on the sagging bed, on the cheap blankets, and pillowed his head on his arms. Jenna undressed more slowly, thinking perhaps that he watched her; but although Acland's face was turned in her direction, he scarcely saw her. He was a prisoner of the war, he thought to himself. If the experience of the war could have been communicated to anyone, to Jenna now, he had a vague sense that he might begin to be free. It could not be communicated; he refused to communicate it. It would be like passing on to someone else—knowingly, and with intent—a disease.

"They're sending me to the Amiens area next," he said. "At least that's the rumor."

"Amiens?" Jenna lifted off her petticoat. "Where's that?"

"Farther north than I was before. Just a place. It's near the river Somme."

Jenna did not reply. She removed the rest of her underclothing. Then, when she was naked, she sat beside him on the bed. She began to touch him. She did this now: She made love to him in a new bold way Acland rather disliked, although it was effective.

He averted his eyes. He thought of the brothels in France, the queues of men—officers in one queue, men in another. Inside, flimsy partitions, usually no more than curtains; the sighs and grunts of soldiers. The women had a sullen yet avid air; they wasted no time on preliminaries. They earned more money that way.

"No kissing," one of the girls had said to him. She had unruly black hair, worn loose; a trick of the light made her resemble Constance. "No fucking," she said. They seemed to be the only two English phrases she knew.

She had made a fist about his penis and jerked at it in the dark; she was efficient enough. It was over very quickly. It worked—as this was working now.

Jenna lowered her body onto his; she moved above him, rising, then sinking, her eyes closed, her expression rapt. Pleasure of a kind: Acland felt it narrow to the sharpest point of light. When it was over, Jenna lifted herself free; no words. There was a washstand in the room; she moved across to wash herself there. The water ran; Jenna soaped her thighs, then toweled them.

From some very distant place, the place from which he watched her, Acland said, "Will it be all right?"

"Of course it will be all right. I'm careful. I count the days."

"I'd rather it wasn't like this." Acland sat up. "I'm sorry, Jenna."

"Don't be. We're not children now. We take what we can, and we give what we can."

She hesitated then, and Acland saw her face change. For a moment he feared she would take him in her arms—but perhaps she saw the instinctive recoil, for she drew back.

"I do still love you, you see," she said in a careful voice. "I wish it would go away, but it won't. I know you don't love me. I know you won't ever come back. And so—I'd rather this. It's this—or nothing."

She reached for her petticoat, then looked back. "It won't go on much longer anyway, will it?"

"Perhaps not. Perhaps better not."

"Was this the last time, then?" She put the question like a child, standing there, still naked, clutching her petticoat in front of her.

"I think so. Yes."

"Ah, well. Here—let me help you with your shirt."

No pleas and no recriminations. Acland felt diminished, but also relieved.

When they were both dressed, Jenna turned and looked back at the ugly room. Beyond the window a train whistled. Acland reached into his pocket and took out Solomons' card; he gave it to her. He explained: If anything happened to him, she must go to Solomons at once; the solicitor would take care of everything.

"I never wanted money from you." Jenna stared down at the piece of pasteboard.

"I know that, Jenna. Even so." He made an awkward gesture of the hands. "I have nothing else to give."

"I don't believe that." For the first time there was passion in her voice. "Not to me—but there are other people. I remember you, Acland. The way you used to be. When we were happy—"

"It was simpler then. I seem to have lost the gift."

He smiled then. Jenna, who had grown used to his indifference, found she could not bear to see that smile.

"Take care." She opened the door. "I'll go now. It's better if we leave separately."

Separately indeed. Acland stayed a while, alone, in the shabby room, listening to the trains shunt back and forth. He was not cured, but then he had not really expected to be cured; the relief of sex was always temporary. He smoked a cigarette, then left.

He walked back through quiet streets, avoiding main roads, reaching Park Street just after eleven, the time the opera party should have returned.

They had not returned. They had telephoned, his mother said, and they were going on for supper at Maud's.

Climbing into the first of the taxicabs Stern had summoned, Steenie—who had never seen *Rigoletto* before, but knew its more famous arias—hummed to himself. *"La donna è mobile"*—that melodious celebration of infidelity. Steenie liked this refrain. He sat on the jump seat; he began to whistle it.

On the backseat, somewhat crushed by the large figure of Freddie, sat Jane and Constance. Next to Steenie, on the other jump seat, sat his new friend Wexton. Wexton, a large and ungainly man of great benevolence, sat hunched up; his elbows protruded. He apologized for his knees, which he tried to telescope beneath the seat. They protruded too.

Wexton was wearing a borrowed opera cloak and a borrowed collapsible top hat. Its mechanism seemed to fascinate him. He flipped the hat up and down. He twirled it in his hands. Steenie watched him happily. He was in love with Wexton; he began to suspect Wexton might love him.

Opposite him, Freddie and Jane discussed the opera. Jane ventured an opinion on the tenor who had sung the part of the Duke, and the baritone who had sung the part of the hunchback father, the jester Rigoletto. Freddie, who usually avoided the opera, said even he had enjoyed it; he especially liked the last act, which was bloodthirsty.

"That bit when Rigoletto thinks it's the Duke dead in the sack, and then discovers it's his daughter. That was jolly good. Oh—and the curse—"

"*La maledizione?*"

"That's it. It sounds better in Italian. That was terrific. It made my hair stand up on the back of my neck."

"Oh, yes—and just after that, when the assassin comes to Rigoletto to offer his services. The scoring is for muted solo cello—and double bass, I think. There are these *pizzicato* strings. It's—"

Jane stopped. Freddie was looking at her blankly. She smiled, then hid her smile with an odd defensive gesture of the hands.

"What is it?" Wexton leaned forward.

"Oh, it's . . . effective. That's all. Very effective."

Wexton leaned back. He made no comment. He flipped his opera hat up and down. Steenie continued to whistle. Constance, who had stared out the window all this time, and who had not spoken since they left their box, straightened up.

"Do stop whistling, Steenie. It's beginning to mangle my nerves. Anyway, we're here. Maud's taxi is just behind us. Come on."

Maud's post-opera suppers were always informal affairs. She and Stern led the way to her dining room; the younger guests followed. Servants were dispensed with. Maud waved her hand in a vague way toward a sideboard on which chafing dishes were laid out. Wexton, who was always hungry, eyed these. To Steenie's amused delight, he refused caviar, which he said he never ate, then consumed three helpings of scrambled eggs.

Maud, who knew that at these gatherings it was usually Jane who was left out, concentrated her attentions there. She asked Jane about her work at Guy's Hospital, not that it greatly interested her—Maud found hospitals depressing—but because she knew it was the best way to break down Jane's barriers of shyness. Like the accomplished hostess she was, she contrived to listen to Jane with animation and encouragement while never losing sight of her other guests.

She noticed, therefore, the way in which Steenie was looking at this young American, Wexton, and decided it would be better not to mention it to Gwen. She watched Freddie bumble about from group to group in a lost way. She watched her lover, Stern, who in his urbane manner was making an attempt to converse with an unresponsive Constance.

Stern stood before the fire, leaning against the chimneypiece. He was wearing evening dress; Maud, gazing at him fondly, thought how handsome, how distinguished he looked. His stillness, his capacity for concentration—these things she loved. Now, although Maud knew Constance's conversation was unlikely to be of great interest to him, he listened with every appearance of close attention, his sleek and tawny head bent toward the tiny figure at his side. Constance toyed with scrambled eggs. Stern put a series of polite questions to which Constance replied in a sullen way, without animation. Then something Stern said seemed to catch her attention. She put down her plate and began to speak more rapidly. Maud, curious, left Jane to Freddie and approached.

Maud did not catch the beginning of Constance's remarks, only the tail end.

" . . . I was afraid," she heard. "The storm was terrible. And then, at the very end, when he finds his daughter in that black sack, I wanted to know what he would do. I could have cried when the curtain came down. He did love her so much! I think he killed himself. I think he threw himself into the river with his sack. Yes, that's what he did, after the curtain came down."

She gave herself a little shake. She looked up at Stern in a childlike way.

"I am glad I came. Would you say it was Verdi's best opera?"

The naïveté of this seemed to amuse Stern. He greeted Maud and drew her toward them.

"Well, now. Is it his best opera? What would you say, Maud?"

"I like it. But I prefer *Trovatore*." Maud smiled. "Monty, of course, prefers Wagner to Verdi. We must take you, Constance. You have stamina. *Tannhäuser*, perhaps. You would like that. Or *The Ring*."

Not long after this, to Maud's relief, for she grew tired, her guests left. Stern remained, standing in a thoughtful way by the fire, and Maud—who loved the ends of evenings, when she and Stern were alone—sat down and stared into the coals for a while. The quiet was companionable. Maud fetched them both a glass of wine. Stern lit one of his cigars.

"Isn't Constance odd?" Maud began, for she liked postmortems and meant to steer the conversation to the interesting subject of Steenie. "So quaint! That question about Verdi. She can be such a child sometimes—and at others . . ." She sighed. "Well, she is grown-up now. It will be her ball soon. I think that will be a success. We must find her a husband, Monty."

"At once? Quick-smart?" Stern smiled.

"Well, as soon as possible. You promised to think. What about that Russian—"

"Lady Cunard's? No. I think not. He has debts. A sponger, or so I hear."

"Really?" Maud looked up. "Then what about the American—

Gus Alexander? You like him—you said so yourself. And he's awfully rich. He sent Constance two hundred red roses."

"Did he indeed?"

"You don't think he'd suit?" Maud frowned. "I don't see why not. I think he's fun. Not pretentious in the least. Who then?"

"My dear"—Stern leaned forward; he kissed her brow—"I cannot think of a single suitable candidate. There is a limit to the number of men who want a child-wife. The responsibility is too great. Particularly one of that type. Constance will be a heartbreaker. I wouldn't wish that on my friends—no, not even at your request. And now—I know you like to matchmake, but you do it better on your own—I must leave you, I fear. It's late. I have work to do."

"Oh, Monty, you won't stay?"

"My dear, nothing would give me greater pleasure, as you know. But I must be at the War Office tomorrow morning, and I have a board meeting after that. Tomorrow?"

"Very well. Tomorrow." Maud, who knew better than to argue, kissed him goodnight.

When he had left the house, she could not resist running to the window, so she might watch him walk along the street. He turned in the direction of the chambers he still kept up in Albany, near the Burlington Arcade.

Maud watched him lovingly. He walked at a slow pace, she saw, hatless, stopping once or twice to look up at the night sky. This was unusual. Stern's habitual gait, neither fast nor slow but measured, conveyed a sense of purpose. He walked in the manner of a man whose days were strung with appointments, appointments that caused him no anxiety. Stern, though punctual, was rarely seen to consult a watch and never gave an impression of haste. The appointments would wait, his gait seemed to suggest; they would wait because their outcome rested with him.

That was how he usually walked; not that night. That night he looked like a man preoccupied, even uncertain of his route. Maud, struck by this, watched him attentively. She craned her neck. She saw him reach the corner, where it was his custom to pick up a cab. He stood there some while, a tall and solitary black-coated figure, the light from a gas lamp striking his bared head. He stared out fixedly across the street. Several taxicabs passed him, their FOR HIRE signs illumined, but Stern hailed none of them. Once, in an angry way he turned about, and Maud, heart lifting, thought he must have changed his mind and was returning to her.

But no. Stern walked a few paces, stopped beneath a second

lamp, looked up again toward the sky. For an instant she could see the pale oval of his face; then he bent his head, turned back. Without hesitation now, as if he had come to a decision, he set off on foot in the direction of Albany. Maud watched him until he was out of sight.

Maud was puzzled. Seeing her lover thus, at a distance, from a window, as she might have seen a stranger, she had been struck by how vulnerable he looked. A man in love, Maud might have said, but it had been a stranger she watched, a man perplexed by some word, gesture, or glance from the beloved. This thought (my aunt Maud was a romantic even then) gave her a *frisson* of pleasure. The next moment, recollecting herself, she turned away with a smile at such foolishness.

Stern, though accomplished at lovemaking, was not a man to allow sentiment to ruffle his composure; he did not betray his feelings in the bedroom, let alone standing in the street by Hyde Park corner. Maud knew she might like to imagine that Stern, standing there, thought of her. She also knew it was unlikely. His mind would not have dwelt on her—or indeed on any other woman—and if she were to admit to Stern that momentary suspicion of hers, he would dismiss it with impatience. When he was apart from her, he claimed, his thoughts were always occupied with his business.

Maud, reminding herself that she was not a mooning girl, was disposed to believe this. What then could account for this oddness in Stern's behavior? Some problems with his munitions works? Some crease in the well-ironed affairs of his bank? Or could it be—and here Maud began to feel anxious—could it be that Stern was considering some of his loans, and one loan in particular?

That loan, to a member of her own family, made Maud increasingly uneasy. She began to see a day when that debt must be written off or called in—and when that happened, what would be her lover's reaction?

Stern always said that the lending of money was a straightforward business matter; the identity of the debtor was irrelevant. Explaining this creed, Stern could be cold. On such occasions Maud found him both alarming and exciting. On such occasions she sensed power, even a certain rapacity; she could not approve this, but she found it erotic.

This confused her. Two creeds of her own collided. Brought up to believe that all debts should be honored eventually, she also believed that a lender should show mercy. To pursue a debt to the point of ruination, Maud judged vulgar. It smacked of commerce; it was tradesman's behavior, not the attitude of a gentleman.

As far as this particular debt was concerned, Maud had always assumed in a vague way that it would be repaid—in due course. Should the debtor experience serious difficulties—which seemed unlikely—then she herself would intervene. She would plead on the debtor's behalf, whereupon Montague would waive the debt. Of course he would; any other course of action was unthinkable!

Certain, now, that she had hit upon the reason for Stern's odd, preoccupied air, Maud was anxious to question him. If Stern was worried, then the matter must be pressing. It had better be discussed—and at once.

Maud (always precipitate) telephoned Stern's chambers in Albany. There was no reply. She waited fifteen minutes, then telephoned again. Still no reply. It was incomprehensible!

Maud was fond, her imagination vigorous. She saw a street accident; she saw her lover set upon by thugs. She called again, and again. At two in the morning, Stern answered.

He sounded curt. He sounded displeased to be telephoned, even more displeased when Maud embarked on a rush of worries. The matter of the loan to her brother was not pressing, he said. There were other things on his mind.

"But where have you *been*, Monty?" Maud began.

"Walking the streets."

"At *this* hour? Monty, why?"

"I wanted to think. There was a matter I needed to resolve."

"*What* matter? Monty—are you anxious?"

"Not in the least. That matter is resolved."

"You've come to a decision?"

"Yes. I've come to a decision."

"Monty—"

"It's late. Goodnight, Maud."

That same morning, Acland was returning to France. He saw his family only briefly.

Both Freddie and Steenie had overslept. His mother had risen early to bid him goodbye; so had his father. These farewells took some time; the others were more perfunctory.

Freddie emerged, looking guilty, rubbing his eyes, with half an hour to spare. Steenie arrived some five minutes later, in a distinctly foppish suit. He ate his breakfast standing up, humming *"La donna è mobile."* Constance did not appear until they were all gathered in the hall.

She came running down the stairs, her hair loose and unbrushed, her cuffs unfastened, complaining that Jenna grew forgetful. She had failed to sew on missing buttons. It was time for Acland to depart. He stood in an irresolute way by the door, dressed in uniform, his bags at his feet, his cap under his arm. Outside, his father's Rolls waited.

A gruff handshake from his father; a less gruff handshake from Freddie. A hug from Steenie; a long and tearful embrace from his mother. Constance hung back. Only at the last moment did she kiss him goodbye: two quick and distracted kisses, one for each cheek.

She did not remind him of his promise again. This first hurt Acland, then made him resentful.

Constance followed him out onto the steps.

"I'm sorry you shall miss my ball," she called out to him as he climbed into the back of the car.

She waved her hand, one quick careless gesture.

"Oh, I hate goodbyes," she said with sudden intensity, and ran indoors.

The Rolls drew away from the curb. Its great engine whispered. Its silvery and ghostly hood pointed the way to the station, to the troop ship, to the trenches.

Acland leaned back in the seat; he watched the streets pass.

It was in this way, angry with Constance—and suspecting she had meant him to be angered—that Acland returned to France.

III
ENGAGEMENTS

From the journals

Winterscombe,
June 12, 1916

There was a war in me—not a great war, like the war in Europe, just a small one—and it is over now. I am better. This is because of:
my rabbit
my dog
my Acland
myself
Because I am better, I shall write down the secret thing. I shall do it now, before I go downstairs to my ball. I want the paper to have it. I don't want it in my mind anymore. Listen, paper: you can remember. I can forget.

Once upon a time, when I was five years old, I made my father very angry. It was nighttime, and he came to my room. The nurse had left. No more wages, he said—but he missed her, I think.

He had wine with him, and while he drank the wine, he told me the story of his new book. He had never done that before! I listened very carefully. I felt so proud, and grown-up. The hero was very fine—he was Papa, I could tell that! I thought he would be pleased I had seen this—but when I told him, he became very angry. He picked up his wineglass and threw it at the wall. There was wine, glass, everywhere. All the room was red with it.

He said I was stupid, and he meant to chastise me. He said I was wicked, and he would beat all the wickedness out of me.

He put me across his lap. He pulled my nightgown up. He bared me, and then he hit me.

I'm not sure how many times. It might have been five. It might have been twenty. Something happened, then, when he was hitting me. He stopped. He stroked me.

Then he did a wicked thing. I knew it was a wicked thing. The nurse told me. You shouldn't touch down there, or look down there—but

Papa did. He said, Look, I can open you up, like a little purse. You see how small you are? There is a little place there, such a tiny place; he held up one of his white fingers, and he said—Watch. This will go in.

It hurt. I cried. Papa held me very close. He said we were close, and he loved me so very much, and because he loved me, he would show me a secret.

He unbuttoned himself. He said, Look. There, coiled up between his thighs, was this strange thing, like a sweaty white snake. I was afraid to touch it, but Papa laughed. He said he would show me some magic. He put my hand on it, and it pulsed. It was alive. Stroke it—Papa said. Stroke it, and you'll see, Constance, you can make it grow.

Pretend it's a kitten, he said. Smooth the fur very gently. So I did—and it grew bigger, just as he said. It uncoiled. It sprang up at me. I said—Look, Papa, you have grown a new bone—and when I said that, he laughed again and then he kissed me.

Usually, Papa did not like mouth kisses, because of germs, but that night was different. He kissed me, then he told me there was something he wanted very much. I could give it to him. He held his new bone in his hand. He spat on it. He said he could—

Stuff it up me. Push it up me. That big thing. I knew it would never fit—and it wouldn't. It made me bleed—but Papa was not angry. He washed me. He washed me clean. Then he sat me on his lap. He gave me a glass with some wine in it. The glass was like a thimble. The wine was like my blood.

Don't cry, Papa said. Don't worry. This is our secret. We can try again.

The first time he did it, it was a Sunday. I knew it was a Sunday—I could hear the church bells ring. There was a church at the end of our street, Saint Michael and All Angels. If you leaned out the window a long way you could almost see it. All those angels.

He used an ointment that time. I had to rub it on till he was slippery. Then it went in all the way and Papa gave a great shout. It hurt me, and I thought it hurt him too, because he shook and I could see his eyes hated me. He closed his eyes and when it was over he wouldn't look at me.

Always on a Sunday after that. Sometimes he said—Touch my snake. Sometimes he said—Stroke the kitten, Constance. Sometimes he said the bad words, all the short ones. Once he sat me on his lap and put it in that way. Once he said I was his own little girl. Once he did another thing—I don't want to write down the other thing. It made me sick. When I was sick, his eyes hated me. He always said he loved me, but his eyes always hated me.

After he met Gwen, which was the next year, this stopped. I was glad and I was sad. After it stopped, he never said he loved me. After it stopped, he called me the albatross, which he never did before, and then he'd laugh at me. I said—Please, Papa, don't call me that, not when other people can hear. And he promised me to stop—but he didn't. He said it again, the very next day.

Little albatross. It made me very lonely.

There. That is how it was. There it is, the most secret thing of all. I have given it to the paper, and the paper can decide if he loved me, or if he lied.

I shall close that book now, and begin a new one.

I shall close that Constance.

I shall close that life.

I shall go and dance. I am ready to dance now. I am wearing my new white dress. I am going to choose a husband. From now on, I'll be very very careful. I wouldn't want to be an albatross again—not to anyone.

So Constance went down the staircase at Winterscombe to dance. There she is, at the top of these stairs; the music begins; it drifts upward on the air. She is wearing her ball gown, which is white, decorated with sequins.

Little rings are crammed on her small fingers. Her hair is up for the first time. Her eyes slant upward at the corners. There are pearls around her throat, pearls that Maud has given her. *Full fathom five thy father lies* (Constance thinks); *Those are pearls that were his eyes.*

She stands very still. The words perfume her mind. The music drifts. Her mouth turns down at the corners, her waif face, her sad little clown face. She gathers her will. There is an ink stain on one finger. Constance waits to feel cured. She waits to feel free.

Full fathom five is a long way down, yes—but in Constance's case, would it have been deep enough?

Actually, a fathom isn't so very much: it's six feet. So, full fathom five, which sounds such a long way down, is only thirty feet. I think Constance could have consigned her father much, much deeper than that—thirty fathoms, forty, it would have made no difference: Shawcross couldn't be drowned, or not in his daughter's subconscious anyway. Sooner or later, and probably sooner, he'd rise up.

Constance, who had never heard of the subconscious mind, thought she could contain her father in a book. She thought she could net him with words, drown him in paragraphs, hammer down the hatches, close that book and close that life. She couldn't, of course; memory does not work like that. None of us controls memory—it controls us.

We cannot forget. We are the stuff of memory: all those images, all those details, sequences, episodes, which we all carry around with us in our heads and which we call the past—that is what we are. We may try to control it—as Constance did, and I had done too—selecting an image here, an event there, turning our own pasts into ordered, linear, comprehensible narratives. We are all novelists, I think, when it comes to our own lives—but the past resists this kind of tweaking. I'm sure it does. It has a life all its own, sometimes benign, sometimes virulent. It is as tough as a microbe, as adaptive as a virus, and just when we think we've composed it in a pattern that suits us just fine, it re-forms; it transmutes; it assumes a very different shape. And if we ignore this, turn a blind eye—or, if you like, suppress—what does it do? It sends up a subversive little message: Up comes an image, an event, we thought had been safely forgotten. Hey, says the memory (which refuses to lie down), what about this? Don't you remember that?

This had happened to me. I had spent eight years trying to forget happiness. That had been hard enough, and one of the things I'd discovered at Winterscombe was that I had not succeeded. How much harder for Constance then, who was trying to forget abuse.

When I'd read that particular entry in her journal, I did not want to go on. Like her, I closed the book. I walked around Winterscombe, from room to room. I went into the ballroom, where Constance began the next stage of her life. I went to the foot of the stairs and looked up.

It was just a ballroom. They were just stairs. There was no twang from the past. That seemed wrong. I felt that the vitality and the violence of past events ought to have left some discernible imprint; the quality of the air here ought to have been different, so that even someone who knew nothing of the house or its history could have stood here and sensed . . . what? A chill in the air, a concentration of molecules—all those sensations that people describe when they try to define a haunting? Even I, knowing what I knew, could sense nothing. The ballroom remained a room; the stairs remained stairs. They were stubbornly inanimate.

I went back to the journals, which were not. I went back to the photographs of Constance, taken that night. I thought of her standing at the top of those stairs. I pitied her, and I also feared for her—because, to some extent, I knew what happened next.

I knew that Constance did choose a husband, the night of her coming-out ball; I knew who that husband was, and I knew something of subsequent events. In fact, many of the things I thought I knew at that point were wrong; Constance's marriage, like her childhood, was full of secrets. Then, I looked at Constance at the top of those stairs, and I thought: *She is about to make her worst mistake.*

I thought Constance had tried, pathetically hard, to free herself of her father—and I was certain she had failed. Shawcross the escapologist was out of that notebook, off its pages, before Constance even left her room. Shawcross was not even dead. In Constance's memory he lived on. He stood there with her at the top of the stairs; he went down with her to the ballroom, and out with her into her future life.

Constance might have been certain that she selected her husband of her own volition, her own free will, but I didn't agree. I didn't believe that at all. Constance's choice of a husband caused mayhem. It was a choice that had her father's fingerprints all over it.

A husband it had to be. After all, what were the alternatives? Constance was—she saw this—a prisoner of her time and her society. Women of her adopted class did not work; women of her own class did—and depressing work it was, too. Constance had no intention of dwindling away her days as a governess or a companion. To become a secretary, some menial species of clerk? Never. Nursing? Constance rejected that at once. It was the war alone that made nursing a socially acceptable profession, and even this war could not last.

No, marriage it must be—marriage, which would release her from the confines of the Cavendish family and their charity. Marriage, which Constance, who was still very young, associated with freedom. Marriage—but to whom?

As she went down the stairs, Constance had in her mind a clear but abstract idea of the man she needed. She had made one of her lists. He must be rich, obviously; well connected, preferably; titled, possibly; single—for simplicity.

The right man, she had decided, must be already established. Constance was too impatient for life to make do with a man still climbing the ladder. He need not be handsome—Constance had

observed that handsome men were often vain; she found that tedious. She thought she might prefer him to be clever; whether his
nature was kindly was immaterial. Of course, if she could select a
man who had looks *and* wit, fortune *and* position, the marriage might
be more agreeable. Constance might be decided upon a husband,
but she did not relish being bored.

When she drew up this list for herself, Constance thought of
Acland. He fitted each category, after all, as snugly as a well-made
glove shaped itself to fingers.

This idea she rejected almost at once. Constance had Acland
locked away in a separate compartment of her mind. She respected
him too much to classify him as husband material. A husband was a
means to an end; Acland was . . . himself. She preferred to think of
Acland as a temptation that must always be out of reach. In that way,
his uniqueness was preserved.

So Constance put Acland, with his bright hair, in a little lacquered mind-box. She locked the box. She threw away the key (until
some years later, when she decided to retrieve it again). Inside that
box, with him, was impossibility, excess, music, and gunshots—the
chaos of life. Inside the box, Acland was safe. He could never be
ordinary. So, Acland was ruled out. Constance had to select another
candidate.

She told herself, when she reached the foot of the stairs, that
her mind was open, that in no way did she lean more toward one
man than another.

In her heart, I suspect, she knew that was not entirely true.
There was already a bias there, but Constance would not acknowledge it. It might be anyone, she said to herself. The possibilities
made her giddy.

She was arrogant, of course. I don't think that it occurred to her
for one moment that the man, once selected, might fail to respond.
But then, beauty gives confidence, and Constance was very beautiful
that night.

Anyway, there she is, at the foot of the stairs, with the music
drifting. Lifting the hem of her white dress in her white-gloved
hand, she walks toward the ballroom where, some twenty years later,
I will dance with Franz-Jacob, in his brown boots, and not understand that when he stops dancing, it is because he fears for a
sister in Germany, for a telephone ringing in another part of the
house.

She approaches the ballroom. Its pink curtains are not tattered, the orchestra plays in its box, the chandeliers are lit, and the air is brilliant.

She is wearing new dancing slippers; the heels are a little too thin, so she finds balancing difficult. She looks like a woman, but she walks like a child.

She is greeted by Gwen, who kisses her. By Sir Montague Stern, who bows over her hand in his odd foreign way. By Maud, who tells her how lovely she looks, and who draws her forward with pride in her protégée. As convention demands, she dances the first dance with a slow and gouty Denton. She dances the next, in an inattentive way, with Freddie.

By the end of this dance, her spirits are soaring. As he leads her from the floor, she stops, turns to him, clasps his arms.

"Oh, Freddie," she says, "the future. I want it so much. And I can hear it now. I can. It's there—listen . . ." She breaks off, tilts her head. Freddie finds himself blinded by the loveliness of her face. He stammers some reply, but Constance interrupts.

"Oh, Freddie, will you forgive me for all I did, all I was? I know I hurt you—and I swear to you, I shall never hurt anyone, ever again. I feel so very happy tonight. I can't bear for you to look sad. You and Francis and Acland and Steenie—you're the best brothers in the world. I love you all so much. I love you to death. I shall *make* you be happy. Look, I'm going to put some luck in your hand, now, quickly, in your palm. Close your fingers over it and hold it tight. There! All the past has gone away and we need never think of it again. You see what I've given you? Tomorrow. Just like that, in the palm of your hand. Now, go and dance, Freddie." She smiled. "With *someone else.*"

Freddie did as she asked. He danced a polka, then a foxtrot, then a waltz. He enjoyed these dances, up to a point. He was curing himself of Constance, he told himself, though he knew he was not cured quite yet.

In a way, he thought (returning to one of the small gilt chairs at the side of the floor, sitting down beside Jane Conyngham), he was glad to relinquish Constance. She went too fast. She muddled things; she muddied things, and Freddie preferred these things, whatever they were—life, he supposed—to be slower, more cautious, above all *simpler.*

Freddie sat down in a puffing way, out of breath from the spins of the waltz. He mopped at his forehead and greeted Jane. He looked around the floor in a hopeful way, at the passing dancers, at the women in particular. Freddie was not anxious to fall in love—too much of an upheaval, just then—but he would have been quite glad to find some ordinary girl whom he could see from time to time. Someone to take to the theater, so he did not have to tag along behind Steenie all the time.

None of the passing women held his eye, and he found his gaze strayed back, in the most irritating way, to the small and animated figure of Constance. She had not sat out one dance. Freddie, knowing it to be foolish, resented this. He resented the men who were her partners.

Wrenching his gaze away, he turned to Jane with some relief. He had grown to like Jane after all. She was kind. She was sensible. She was easy to talk to; she was both resilient and astute. Freddie, who had been exposed through his ambulance work to aspects of life from which he had previously been shielded, began to understand a little the rigors of her work. Because of this, he respected her. He was not pleased, therefore, when Jane turned his attention back to the dance floor and, even worse, back to Constance.

"Who's that dancing with Constance now, Freddie?" she asked.

Freddie averted his gaze with a jerk. "Oh, God, I don't know," he said irritably. "One of the devoted swains."

"Is it that American, the one Maud mentioned? What was his name? Gus Something. Gus Alexander, that's it."

"I can't see," said Freddie, refusing to look. "If he's wearing diamond shirt studs the size of pigeon's eggs, then it probably is."

"His studs are quite large. And they do glitter." Jane's voice was dry.

"Then it's him. Can he dance?"

"Not terribly well. He looks as if he's wearing boots."

"Then it's definitely him. I can't stand him. He talks about money all the time. How much he's made—down to the last cent. Also, he thinks he's in love with Constance. Do you know how many roses he sent her the other day? Two hundred. Red ones. In a horrible gold basket thing. The kind of thing Stern would have chosen."

"And was she pleased?"

"Of course she was. Constance loves extravagant gestures. She says people ought to be more vulgar."

"Does she indeed? Well, you know, Freddie, I sometimes think Constance might be right about that."

"Right? How can she be right?"

"Oh, I don't know." Jane frowned. "We make all these rules and regulations, and most of them are arbitrary and silly. We decide you must hold a knife a certain way. Or we decide it's not done to talk of certain things—like money. Why not? Why not just be like Mr. Alexander and say what you think?"

"And eat your peas off your knife while you're doing it?"

"There are worse crimes, Freddie." Jane paused. "When I am at the hospital . . ."

Jane never completed this sentence. She stopped, and Freddie did not prompt her. She looked out across the ballroom, at the tiers of hothouse flowers, at the chandeliers, which made the air as lucid as glass. She saw the ballroom; she also saw the hospital.

The transition from one world to another was abrupt; Jane found it difficult. She felt she ought to be able to separate the two worlds and see them as distinct, but increasingly she found this impossible. This inability to separate the parts of her life frightened her. She believed it was caused by overwork; sometimes she found it a little mad.

That morning at Guy's, she had been treating the wound of a small boy. His name was Tom. Tom slept in a crib in the women's ward because the hospital suffered from chronic overcrowding. Tom had (among other things) rickets; like most of the children, and many of the women, he came from the East End and he suffered from malnutrition. He also had a diseased kidney; the previous day it had been cut out, leaving a neat round hole, like a bullet wound.

Jane wanted this boy Tom to live. She always wanted the children on the ward to live, with a passion she feared, for it made it harder when—as did happen—the children died.

Tom would survive; Jane was determined of that. Sitting on her small and absurd gilt chair, Jane wished that she was with him, and that she had not left the hospital. On the other hand she was glad to escape the hospital, too, for at the hospital, she lied.

She had been taught to lie; it was necessary. Above the bed of each woman on the ward there was a number. (The women were known by numbers, not names.) Next to the number was a fatal diagnosis: carcinoma. Sometimes of the stomach, or the lungs, or the skin, or the brain; always carcinoma—it was, after all, the cancer ward.

The women were not told that. Most of them were illiterate; they could not read their own placard, and if they could, they were deceived by the Latin term.

"It isn't cancer, is it, dearie?" they always asked, sooner or later.

"Of course not," Jane would say in her new, bright, well-trained voice. "Let's shake up the pillow and make you comfortable, shall we?"

The ward sister said that was the only thing to do. Once, Jane had believed the ward sister. Now she was no longer sure she did. She would have liked to ask Freddie's opinion. She would have liked to tell Freddie how the hospital would not go away but pursued her everywhere.

But it would have been ill-considered, ill-mannered to have done so. Etiquette again. Also unfair to Freddie, who was young and (Jane thought) unhappy. This was her burden; she must carry it.

So, Jane began on the sentence about the hospital but left it incomplete. She leaned forward, resting her chin on her hands. I should like you to see her as she was then. Like Constance, she was changing.

She was thin; she sat, in a nervous way, on the edge of her gilt chair. Her hands were reddened and coarsened by the work at the hospital, which involved (she was a voluntary nurse, and therefore given menial tasks) much scrubbing with carbolic.

It was characteristic of her to hold these hands in front of her face, as if she wished to hide it, particularly when she spoke. She still lacked confidence, and so, when she did speak, it was often in a disconcerting way: She would begin briskly enough, but halfway through a sentence her poise would desert her; she would finish the rest of the words in a rush. She would take refuge in safe phrases, clichés, little earnest rushes of dull and incontrovertible obviousness, and then—because she was intelligent, and despised this timid and evasive language—she would break off. Jane's sentences tended either to blur or to hit an invisible cul-de-sac; men found this tiresome.

She had a narrow, fine-boned face, the high forehead of a child, and—at her best—eyes that were unwavering. She no longer considered these eyes—hazel, flecked with brown—her best feature; she no longer considered her face at all.

One other thing: she had cut her hair. This, in 1916, was daring.

Jane did not care. She cut it herself, for practicality at work, and she liked it cut. It suited her. Her face was often anxious and striving, but her hair had a new character of its own. It framed her face and exposed the delicacy of her neck; it was obedient to the comb and lay straight and smooth against her scalp, clipped like a helmet, the color of newly cleaned copper. It was assertive, that hair; Jane herself was only just beginning to assert, and when she did so, she sometimes had a curious sensation: It was her hair that showed her the way. Cut, it had a new authority.

She might have authority too, one day, Jane felt. Meanwhile, she was still tentative, even with Freddie. So she began on the sentence about the hospital, then hid her mouth with her hands and left the sentence unfinished.

Instead, after a pause, she directed Freddie's attention back to the less difficult (she thought) topic of Constance, and the beauty of Constance's dress.

Freddie looked: Constance was in the act of selecting her next dance partner from a crowd of eager young men. Her quick small hands gestured in the air; her hair, pinned up and fastened with glittering combs, looked lovely and yet precarious, as if it might tumble about her shoulders at any moment. She turned from man to man; a white glove against a black shoulder—Constance, who made a ballet of flirtation.

Freddie rose. It was not a ballet he wished to watch any longer. He left Jane to the ministrations of the approaching Hector Arlington (on leave; in uniform), and went in search of champagne. Since the war continued as it did, there was a shortage of manservants; the champagne was brought him, in the end, by Jenna.

She looked pale, ill, and exhausted—so much so that it was a moment before Freddie recognized her. When he did, it depressed him further. She had once been so pretty, and now she was aged. Age, time, change. Freddie felt thoroughly gloomy. So much for Constance's luck.

He stood underneath the orchestra box and drank his champagne very fast.

"Who's that?" Denton said in querulous tones. He screwed up his eyes and peered at the dance floor.

"Where, dearest?"

"There, Gwennie, there! Dancing with Hector Arlington. Who's that?"

"It's Jane, dearest. Boy's fiancée. Jane Conyngham," Gwen replied, with increasing emphasis as Denton's face took on an obtuse expression, as if he had never heard of Jane, let alone met her.

"Ghastly get-up." Denton scowled. "What the hell's she done to her hair? Looks as if she's been scalped."

"She's cut it, dearest. It's the new thing, I believe. I think it rather suits her. So much less severe. She looks years younger. Almost pretty."

"Hideous frock." Denton was not listening. "Perfectly ghastly. Yellow, is it? Looks like sick. You should have a word with her, Gwennie."

"Jane isn't very interested in clothes, dearest. She never has been, if you remember. Besides, I like that dress. It suits her coloring. Of course, she is so very thin . . . but she has a kind heart, Denton, a kind heart."

"A kind heart, and a *fortune*," Denton remarked, and chuckled.

Gwen cast him a suspicious glance. Denton now seemed to recall Jane perfectly; for an instant Gwen suspected he had done so all along.

Gwen now found her husband's memory—or lack of it—an increasing puzzle. For small things—dates, names, certain words, in particular adjectives—Denton's memory seemed to her indubitably bad. Denton, describing someone or something, had grown alarming in his incapacity to grasp the opposite word:

"He's . . ." he would begin, and his eyes would revolve like Catherine wheels; his hands would gesture convulsively.

"Tall?" Gwen would prompt in a patient voice. "Big? Well-built? Stocky? Stout?"

Really, she would think, she needed a thesaurus.

"Broad-shouldered? Of a military build? Very large? Gigantic?" This, in response to Denton, who had grown purple in the face and whose right hand, by then, would be indicating some vast stature.

"Tall," she would conclude. "I feel sure you just mean tall, dearest. More than six foot—like you and Boy and Acland. Very tall—is that it, Denton?"

"*Hairy*," Denton might then pronounce, with a wild and wicked gleam in his eyes. Hairy, or bald, dwarfish or sly; whatever the word Denton finally produced, it had little to do with the charade he had just been enacting.

On such occasions Gwen felt sure she was being teased, and could become irritable. Could her husband's lapses of memory be a

matter of perversity? It did seem odd to fail to recognize Jane
Conyngham one moment, yet recall her fortune the next. Gwen
sighed; she reassured herself. Of course the problem was genuine.
Denton's mind had become an imperfect conductor, that was all.

"Are you tired, Denton?" she asked, leaning forward to him in
the motherly way that had now become second nature. "It is growing
late. No one will mind if you retire early."

"Not tired. Not tired at all. Enjoyin' myself," Denton replied in
a firm voice. He looked down at his brandy glass, which was empty,
and which Gwen did not intend should be refilled.

"Not sure about some of these people, though." He surveyed
the room. "Woman over there—the one with all that paint on her
face. Looks like a . . ."

"Denton!"

"Hussy. Looks like a hussy. What did you think I was going to
say? And that fellow with her, damned dago. Who invited him? And
what about that one? Prancin' over there in the corner. A bugger by
the look of him. Long hair. Wearin' disgustin' red stuff all over his
cheeks. Ought to be out at the front. That'd knock some sense into
him."

Gwen raised her new lorgnette and gazed at the young man
Denton had just indicated. He had his back to her and was talking
with some animation to Freddie and a group of other younger men.
They included Conrad Vickers, the would-be photographer; that tall
shambling bear of a boy everyone called Wexton; and, to the edge of
the group, Basil Hallam, the actor.

Gwen still disapproved of these friends in a vague way: Vickers,
in particular, seemed to her excessively animated. The young man
accused of prancing by Denton still had his back to her, but Freddie,
she noticed, was deep in conversation with Wexton. He (or so Jane
said) was about to join an ambulance unit in France. Just as Gwen
was thinking how wary she must be—the last thing she wanted was
for Freddie to emulate him; ambulance driving in Hampstead was all
very well, but ambulance driving at the front was another matter—
the prancing young man turned round. Gwen saw that it was Steenie.

"See what I mean?" Denton waved a liver-spotted hand in his
direction. "Paint. Plastered all over him. Vomit-making."

"Denton dearest. Please do not be foolish." Gwen gave Denton
a repressive glance. "That is Steenie, as you could see if you would
wear your spectacles. And he is simply a little flushed, that is all. It
is hot in here, and he has been dancing—"

"What's more"—Denton's gaze roved on and lit upon the figure of his sister—"what's more, take a look at Maud. Mutton dressed as lamb, hanging on his arm—that fellow, what's his name? The Israelite."

"Denton, *please*. Maud may hear you—"

"Damn good thing if she did. Might bring her to her senses. What in God's name does she think she's doing, eh? She's *English*—dammit, she's *my* sister. First she marries a wop, and now this. A . . . moneylender. I ask you, how does a man like that come by a title?"

"Rather in the same way your father came by his, I imagine," said Gwen, with asperity. "He purchased it, I should think."

"Preposterous! If I had my way—"

"Hush now, Denton my dear. You know what the doctor said. And anyway, you quite like Monty, you know you do." Gwen motioned one of the elderly footmen forward and watched while Denton's brandy glass was refilled. The measure was small, for the servants had their orders, but it sufficed. Denton subsided.

"Leech," he muttered. But his anger was spent. A moment later and he appeared to have forgotten both Maud and Sir Montague. Gwen felt relief.

These outbursts on the subject of Stern had grown more frequent of late, and—coupled with certain little hints and evasions from Maud—Gwen sometimes found them troubling. It had occurred to her once or twice that Denton might have borrowed from Stern, as, she knew, many of their friends had done. Stern was known to have a sympathetic ear for those with expensive habits, whether it was something foolish, such as gambling or speculation, or something sounder, such as outlay on estates.

The Arlingtons, for instance: according to Maud, in the strictest confidence, Hector Arlington, advised by his mother, the formidable Gertrude, had turned to Stern and had been assisted. A temporary embarrassment, of course, something to do with death duties. Even Sir Richard Peel, Denton's old crony and the most conservative of men, had, it was rumored, turned his portfolio over to Stern and been delighted with the results. Peel was of the old guard, and unashamed of that fact.

"Can't have the fellow in my house," he had once remarked to Gwen. "Know he comes here, know he goes about, but I can't do it. Habits of a lifetime—you know how it is. And the great thing is, he understands. Never pushes. Tactful chap, for a Jew."

Had Stern been useful, in a similar way, to Denton? In the past few weeks Gwen had begun to consider this possibility; she considered it now, gazing across the ballroom to where Stern stood, Maud on his arm, talking quietly.

Until recently, it had never occurred to Gwen that Denton could need either financial advice or assistance. After all, they lived very simply: only three houses—Winterscombe, London, and the hunting lodge in the Highlands which Denton liked to visit in August and September, for the deerstalking and the fishing. Their entertaining was not lavish; the number of their servants was much reduced by the war. No, it was incomprehensible that Denton should need to borrow. If he did have connections with Stern, it must be for advice on investments, that was all.

Yet, there were oddities: Denton was so close with money, and always had been, so she feared to show him the recent bills for her dresses. On other occasions he would be—without explanation—lavish, casting caution to the winds. His presents to his sons were always more than generous; he had even encouraged the arrangements for this ball. On the other hand, there was that inexplicable insistence, going back years, that Boy should marry an heiress, an insistence that offended Gwen, for it smacked of the mercenary. Why should Boy need a rich wife?

"Bed," Denton suddenly remarked. He rose. "Bed now, I think. I'm becoming too old for this kind of thing, Gwennie."

"Nonsense, Denton darling." Maud had joined them, Montague Stern at her side. She leaned across to give her brother a kiss.

"You can't retire now—you've danced only once. Make a little circuit with me, just a small one. . . ."

"Far too old. Far too stiff," Denton growled. He reached for the walking stick, which (Gwen considered) he did not need but which he enjoyed flourishing; Denton liked to play the valetudinarian.

He straightened up. At that moment Constance appeared at his side, her silvery dress shimmering.

"Nonsense, Papa," she said, with a winning smile, and leaned upon Denton's arm. "Please, it's been such a lovely evening. Won't you give me one last dance before you retire?"

Denton, who never seemed to mind when Constance called him "Papa," returned her smile in what seemed to Gwen his most foolish manner. He doddered a little and shifted his cane and rolled his eyes—how Gwen wished he would not roll his eyes!

"Can't be done," he said. "Can't be done, I'm afraid. Not even for you, my dear. Like to dance with the belle of the ball again— would have done once, but not now. Too old. Gammy foot. Look here—maybe Stern will stand in for me."

With which remark he took a firm grasp on Sir Montague's arm, just above the elbow. He propelled him forwards with surprising strength.

Constance seemed amused by this; Stern seemed disconcerted. Possibly he resented this abrupt manhandling; possibly he had no inclination to dance with Constance. Either way, he recovered quickly.

"Constance," he said, his manner urbane once more, "I am sure I am an imperfect substitute, but I am delighted if I will serve."

"Oh, you will serve," Constance replied in her light way. She permitted herself to be led onto the floor. They glided away, Constance looking very small and frail in Stern's arms. Maud watched them with a benign, an approving smile. Both were accomplished dancers.

It was a Viennese waltz.

"How do you prefer to dance, Constance?" Stern remarked when they had made just one circuit, their pace graceful but somewhat slow. "We are decorous, but a fraction behind the rhythm, I think."

"Oh, I like to dance *fast*," Constance replied. "I like to be . . . danced off my feet."

Stern smiled at this. His left hand gripped hers more tightly; there was a slight but perceptible increase in the pressure of his right hand against her spine. Their pace quickened. As it did so, a most curious thing began to happen. For the first of their new, faster circuits, Constance concentrated on the steps of the dance, on the guidance of Stern's hands. With the second circuit, she began to concentrate upon him.

She had promised herself to select a husband, yet the ball was almost over and still the choice was not made. When they began on the third circuit, it occurred to her that perhaps it had been made after all—decided by a certain bias in her mind, before this evening began.

Constance liked to speculate. It was true that she had—just once or twice in the past—speculated on the question of Stern. A time, long before, when she had looked around the dining table at Winterscombe and understood that Denton had been usurped, that it was Stern who had become the unofficial patriarch of this family; that it was to Stern that Gwen turned when she needed advice or help; that it was Stern, the outsider, as she was, who had come to dominate this family.

Constance did not know that Denton had also turned to Stern

for advice—although she discovered that later. She was never to
know that both Acland and, later, Jane had consulted him. Such facts
were immaterial. Constance's instincts were acute; she recognized the
smell of power.

They reached a corner of the ballroom; they spun, once, twice,
three times. Constance gave Stern a considering glance.

She recalled her discussions with Gwen on the subject of this
man. She recalled an episode from several months before when, at
the end of one of the shopping expeditions with Maud, she was
taken to meet Stern, who awaited them at a West End gallery.

He was in the act of purchasing a painting. Constance had no
eye for art, no ear for music, a resistance to literature. Even so, as
Maud said, she learned fast. She looked at the paintings on the
gallery walls. They all looked much the same to her; she even found
them dull. Constance liked paintings to be large and to contain
people. Stern's taste, clearly, was different. These paintings were of
modest size, and all were landscapes. However, she could scent
reverence and deference as acutely as she scented power. The man
who guided Stern from painting to painting was deferential—she
knew that at once. Yet he was not obsequious; it was to Stern's
judgment he deferred, not his bank balance.

Stern passed along the line of paintings slowly. Beiges, browns,
duns, terra-cottas. Constance had never been to France; she had
never heard of Cézanne. She looked at these images; she tried to
puzzle them out. She wanted to yawn.

Stern stopped, finally, at one painting.

"Ah," he said. "Now *that*—"

"Oh, yes." The gallery assistant had also stopped. Like Stern,
he sighed.

Reverence! Constance stared at the painting in question. She
stared very hard. It might have been a mountain, she thought, and
there were certain shapes that could possibly be trees, but on the
whole it was an abstract and inconclusive affair. She could not like it.
She suspected Maud did not like it either.

Stern bought the painting. The salesman congratulated him.
Constance, looking quickly down at the price list she had been given
when they entered, saw that none of these pictures were expensive,
but the one Stern had selected had the highest price. Good things
were always costly—Maud had taught her that. Constance at once
revised her opinion of the painting. She also revised her opinion of
Stern. He had not even consulted a price list: he had selected the

best (it must be the best) on instinct. He saw something here, and she, Constance, was blind.

A mystery—and Constance was always attracted to mysteries. There were new areas of excellence here which Stern understood and she did not. She glimpsed them again, once or twice, on other occasions, when he selected wine, when he discussed books with Acland or Jane, when he took her with the rest of the family to the opera.

Occasionally, sitting to one side of Stern's box, she had stolen a glance at him, this composed and influential man. His concentration upon the music was absolute. He leaned forward, his elbow on the edge of the box, his chin upon his hand. He heard something in these sequences of notes that Constance did not. Constance found that unbearable. She wanted to be admitted to the temple and its secrets, at once. And, on one occasion, she had waited for the intermission, then tapped him on the arm. She had asked some question—the wrong question, to judge from his expression.

With a patient air (the opera was *The Magic Flute*) he had explained the plot. It seemed to Constance quite ridiculous, a fantastical thing. She had had the wit to keep this to herself; even so, she could see that Stern was irritated.

She had tried harder after that. She had tried particularly hard on the occasion their party went to *Rigoletto*. She had asked Stern about Verdi; she had wanted him to see that she could be his pupil, that he might enjoy being her tutor.

Her tutor? The waltz was coming to an end. As the last notes faded, Constance decided. Not just a tutor—Stern could be far more than that. He could be a husband.

The obviousness of this choice—did he not fulfill every single one of her requirements?—dazed her a little. She found it difficult to believe she could have been so slow. He was single (Constance did not give Maud a second thought). He had authority, wealth, position, even wit. His appearance was striking; his discretion—his legendary discretion—was intriguing. He was old enough to be her father, of course, but age was immaterial, and—above all, best of all—she did not know him. He had been part of the family circle for six years of her life, yet she had not plumbed his depths. She had no idea why he was, who he was. He was still, after all that time, the considerate, the urbane, the polite, and the elusive stranger.

Constance hesitated no more—but then, she was always precipitate.

"No. One more dance. You dance so well," she said when the waltz ended and Stern began to steer her from the floor.

Stern seemed surprised by this.

"Please. You cannot refuse me. No one can refuse me to-night." Stern looked as if he doubted this. He looked as if he could refuse her easily, as if he had half a mind to do so, there and then.

Then his practiced manners reasserted themselves. He gave an inclination of the head.

Taking her arm in his, he led her back to the center of the floor.

In his arms, Constance concentrated. She believed implicitly in the transference of thoughts. She would imagine, and after a while Stern would imagine too.

She waited a short while; then, in a most convincing way, she missed a step. She stumbled, pressed a little closer to him, allowed her gloved hand to brush his throat.

She relied upon silence. Then—when she judged the moment was correct—she made some small remark, turning upon Stern as she did so her most deadly glance. A slow turn of the head, which might give him time to take in the polish of her features, to notice the provocation of her lips, before he registered the more subtle provocation of her eyes.

This sounds vain—and perhaps it was—but Constance's own attitude toward her appearance was practical. To her, her features were weapons that she happened to have in her armory. Her skin was still unlined; her complexion had a porcelain finish. Her hair was abundant, wiry with life. Her nose had a useful symmetry. Her lips were naturally red. God—if there were a God, which she doubted—had given her expressive eyes, of ambiguous coloration. These gifts were not of her making; had they not been supplied she would have managed without. As it was, they produced a discernible effect upon men. She fully intended that they should do so then.

One thing she had perfected herself: the speaking glance. In this glance, Constance had confidence. So she rested her eyes upon Stern, summoned her will, and waited for the thoughts in her mind to pass into his.

She thought of touches and whispers; she considered sexual matters. She let herself imagine how Stern, the man of power, might behave when he was Stern the lover. She fixed Stern with these imaginings; she saw them as arrows piercing his skin. As many arrows as a Saint Sebastian! Stern, to her delight, met her eyes. To her consternation, he then looked away.

Constance was severely shaken. The look she had surprised in his eyes, before he could disguise it with his habitual charm, was an expression of tedium no woman could misconstrue.

He performed this task—dancing with a family friend, dancing with a child—from tact, from politeness. That was all. Her imaginings meant nothing. Constance was erased.

She said nothing. She completed the dance with an air of patient concentration, her face absorbed. That expression of hers always meant trouble.

The dance over, Stern escorted Constance to her next partner. He returned to Maud's side. They conversed with evident affection; shortly afterward, they left.

Constance watched this quietly and patiently, as a cat watches a mouse or a bird. Stern was not easy prey, of course, and Constance knew this; the knowledge drew her on.

Constance was her father's child. As with Shawcross, the easily accessible was never to attract her. Of course, her father had left her another legacy, too, one that would remain with her, influencing her, for the rest of her life.

The one thing Constance could not stomach from a man was indifference, even when veiled.

"Do you ever think about love?"

Steenie put this question to Wexton a few days after Constance's ball. They had been visiting a small gallery in Chelsea where Steenie hoped to have an exhibition of his paintings. They were now having tea at the kind of café—steamy, busy, unsmart, with pert waitresses in neat black-and-white uniforms—that Wexton most liked. Steenie, who was nervous, refused anything to eat. Wexton, after great deliberation, had ordered a cream bun.

Wexton did not answer Steenie's question. He gave him a cautious glance, then poked at the cream bun with the small fork provided.

"Are you meant to use this?" He held up the fork.

"You don't have to." Steenie's voice came out in a squeak. He cleared his throat. Then, in a high voice, he asked the question again. "Do you ever think about love?"

It sounded ridiculous. Steenie colored. Wexton appeared to consider.

"Sometimes." Wexton sounded doubtful. "There are so many different kinds."

"Are there?" squeaked Steenie, who thought there was only one.

"Well. Children love their parents. Parents love their children. Then—you can love a friend. A man might love one woman, or several women. He might love them one after another, or he might love, say, two at the same time. He might be *in* love, or he might love. There're lots of possibilities."

Steenie was not interested in these possibilities, and the reference to men loving women made him feel slightly sick. A horrible possibility occurred to him: Could he have been wrong about Wexton?

He took a large gulp of tea. It scalded his mouth. He put the cup back in its saucer. He fixed his eyes on Wexton's face, which was an extraordinary face, a lived-in face, its habitual expression one of sweet and slightly bewildered melancholy. Wexton, who looked much older, was in his early twenties. Steenie thought he was the wisest, as well as the kindest, man he had ever met.

Steenie felt that if he was going to say what he was going to say—and he would; they had reached the Rubicon—he could not do it and look at Wexton at the same time. He was too afraid. So he turned his gaze to a woman in a preposterous hat who sat at a table behind Wexton. He stared fixedly at her hat, from which protruded a pheasant's tail feather.

"Also," he began, his voice hitting high C. He cleared his throat again. "Also. I suppose, a man could . . . love another man."

"Oh, yes." Wexton took a bite of cream bun. He chewed it with apparent contentment.

"This is very good," he remarked.

Steenie knew he was about to die. Any second. He had at most one more minute to live. His heart had stopped beating, for one thing. His head was churning concrete. His lungs had collapsed. His ears were stopped up. There was definitely something wrong with his eyes. Even the pheasant feather was now invisible. Thirty seconds. Twenty. Ten.

"For instance," Wexton went on, in a reasonable tone of voice. "I love you."

"Oh, my God."

"I hadn't planned to mention it. Then I changed my mind."

"I'm having a heart attack. Yes. That's definitely it. Look, Wexton—my hands are shaking."

"Is that a symptom of a heart attack?"

"I don't know."

"Neither do I. I don't think it is."

"Maybe it's happiness." Steenie's voice was returning to normal. He risked a look into Wexton's eyes. "I think it is. Extreme, sudden—happiness." He paused. "Also a heart attack of a kind. Because of course I love you. I love you madly, Wexton. Totally. Irresistibly." He leaned across the table and took Wexton's hands in his. He looked into Wexton's kind and melancholy eyes.

"I know what you must think." Steenie began to speak very fast. "You must think I'm very affected. And frivolous. Feather-brained. Idiotic. Superficial. I expect you do think that, don't you?"

"No."

"I'm not like that really. I know I sound like it, but that's mostly camouflage. Well, not entirely. I exaggerate—I know I do. But words are so approximate anyway that one might just as well, don't you think? What did you just say?"

"I said 'no.' "

"Oh, God. Would you mind saying it again?"

"No," Wexton repeated in an obliging manner. He had finished the cream bun. He drank his tea, then poured more, a cup for Steenie, one for himself. Steenie watched him do this with delight.

"Wexton. That tea is far too strong. I'm sure they don't drink tea like that in Virginia. You could stand up a spoon in it. It's perfectly disgusting."

"I like it."

"I shall always love you, you know." Steenie's grip on Wexton's hands—already attracting some attention from neighboring tables—tightened.

"I shall love you, Wexton, forever and ever, world without end. Anything else is unthinkable. Oh. You don't believe me. I can tell."

"Let's wait and see."

"No. Absolutely not. You must believe me *now*."

"Right now?" Wexton gave him a sad and yet benevolent smile.

"*Right* now."

"Okay. I believe you now. Shall we get the check?"

"The check?"

"The bill."

"Can I come back to your flat?"

"Sure."

"Will you read me some more of your poems?"

"Uh-huh."

"Will you tell me you love me again?"

"No."

"Why not?"

"I've said it once. Once is enough."

"I might need reassuring."

"Too bad."

When they reached the street outside, Steenie capered. The sun shone. The streets were crowded. Steenie would not have cared had it poured with rain, but the fine weather pleased him nonetheless. The elements were on his side. They knew he was in love.

"Do you think," he began, stopping dancing, taking Wexton's arm, and falling into step beside him as they turned into the King's Road. "Do you think other people are in love like us, Wexton? I'm sure they're not. No one else could possibly be this happy—don't you think?"

"I wouldn't say that," Wexton began cautiously. "We haven't cornered the world's supply. I guess there's some left over."

"Nonsense. Who?"

"Well." Wexton considered. "Lots of people. Your mother and father, for instance. They love each other in their way. Your aunt Maud and that man Stern—she's crazy about him—"

"Aunt Maud? She's as tough as old boots. She couldn't be crazy about anyone—"

"Then there's Jane—"

"Jane? You're mad."

"She's engaged, isn't she?"

"Oh, God, yes. But she doesn't love Boy. You'd know if you saw them together. She *likes* him, yes. And she used to be mad about Acland."

"Acland?" Wexton appeared interested.

"Oh, that was ages ago. It's probably worn off. All she thinks about now is hospitals." Steenie gave a few more capers and prances. He shot Wexton a look of triumph.

"You see? You're failing miserably. Not one single candidate. No one to touch us. Who else had you in mind? Freddie? Poor old Freddie—he always seems at such a loss."

"No. Not Freddie."

"Who then? Admit it. You've failed."

"Any of the people here." Wexton waved a hand in a vague manner at the people who passed. "Any one of them. At any time. That's the way it is."

"Them?" Steenie dismissed the passers-by with one lordly wave of the hand. "They don't count. We don't know them."

"Okay. I give up."

"Just us?"

"If you like."

"I *knew* it." Steenie gave a happy sigh.

They walked on a little way in silence. They turned into Wexton's street. At the corner Steenie gave Wexton a sideways glance.

"Of course, there is someone we left out. Neither of us mentioned Constance."

"That's true."

"After all, everyone's waiting for Constance to fall in love. Or to be married, anyway. That's what the ball was all about. So maybe we should have considered Constance. How odd that we didn't."

"It's not odd at all. It's because neither of us can imagine . . ."

"Constance loving someone?"

"Yes. She might *think* she did. She might talk herself into it."

"She could *hate*, I think." Steenie paused. "Yes, I can see Constance doing that. It's quite a frightening thought."

"She's frightening altogether."

"Do you think so?" Steenie stopped. "I suppose she is, in a way. All that energy. Except—I do like her, Wexton. I always have. She had a vile childhood, you know. Her father was perfectly ghastly. Horrible to her. Well, horrible to everyone, really. And then he died—in a particularly gory way. Have I ever told you about that?"

"No."

"Well, I might. One day when I'm feeling strong. It was at Winterscombe. Everyone said it was an accident, but . . ."

"You didn't think so?"

"I don't know. I was very young. But there was . . . something odd. It never felt quite right. The edges didn't stick down. Anyway"—he shook himself—"I don't want to think about that. Not today of all days. Whyever did we start on all that?"

"Because of Constance."

"Oh, yes, Constance. And love. I think she'd *like* to love, Wexton—I think she *wants* to, very much. I *think* she loved her father, for instance—she always seemed to. You know what he used to call her? 'My little albatross.' Can you imagine? He really was the vilest man. He was a writer too."

"Thanks."

Wexton had reached the door of the house where he lived. He was fumbling from pocket to pocket, looking for his keys. Steenie, having checked that the street was empty, gave him a hug.

"Oh, God—I didn't mean *that*. He wasn't a proper writer, anyway. And he didn't write poems. Just horrible affected little novels. You'd hate them. Even Constance hated them. She knew they were no good, I think, and she couldn't bear it. Do you know what I caught her doing once?"

"No. What?"

"Cutting them up. One of the novels. The last one, I think. She was sitting there on the floor of her room, cutting it up. Page by page, with a pair of nail scissors. She cut up the whole thing, until there was just the covers left. It took ages. When she'd finished she put all the bits in a bag and put the bag in her desk. It was quite spooky. Then she cried. It wasn't long after he died, you see. And she was grieving. She was very peculiar then. She got over it a year or two later."

"Aha! Found it." Wexton produced his key. He frowned at it in a reproachful way, as if it had been hiding from him. He inserted it into the lock.

Steenie felt a certain excitement, and a certain apprehension, since this would be the first time he had ever visited Wexton's flat. He hoped he would not fail it. He mounted the steps cautiously. He was ushered through a small hallway into a pleasant room. It was full of books.

"It's rather a mess, I'm afraid."

Wexton looked about him in a fond yet apologetic way. There were books on shelves, books on tables, books on chairs, books on the floor.

Steenie advanced into the room. Wexton approached a gas ring, lifted the kettle.

"We could have some coffee. Or some more tea. I could fix us something to drink."

"That would be lovely."

"All of them?"

"Any of them."

"All right." Wexton still appeared to hesitate. He turned back to Steenie, the kettle still in his hands.

"One thing. I mean, I don't want to keep harking back to her. In fact, I'd be glad to forget about her. But before we do. At Winterscombe—at that ball . . ."

"Yes?" Steenie, who had begun to smoke, using a holder, was about to light a cigarette. He paused. He eyed Wexton, who seemed unwilling to go on. Steenie sighed.

"Oh, Wexton. I'm not blind, any more than you are. I knew you'd noticed. And I know exactly what you're going to say."

"Constance and Stern." Wexton frowned. "When they were dancing together. Right toward the end. Didn't you think—"

"Wexton. I most *certainly* did. My eyes were on stalks. Absolutely no one noticed, except you and me. And it was *so* obvious."

There was a silence. "Her, did you think?" Steenie said at last. "Or him?"

"Definitely her. Him—I'm less sure. Probably not. He looked kind of impatient."

"Precisely what was interesting." Steenie put out the cigarette. He stood up. "Stern never is—impatient, I mean. Absolutely nothing ruffles him. You could introduce him to death, and he wouldn't turn a hair. But that night, he was ruffled. Peddling backwards *quite* fast, I'd have said. I saw him when he left. I bumped into him in the cloakroom. I don't think he even saw me. He looked like thunder—no, like ice! Terrifying! Then, the next moment, he was back with Aunt Maud, and he was perfectly charming. He's usually perfectly charming. And just the tiniest bit coldblooded. So maybe I imagined the whole thing."

"Maybe." Wexton shook the kettle. "It's interesting anyway."

"It's interesting—*up to a point,*" Steenie replied in a new firm voice. He hesitated, then took a step forward. He became rather pink.

"Up to a point?" Wexton put the kettle down.

"Wexton—do you think you could put your arms around me?" Steenie became pinker still. His voice rose, then sank. He advanced another pace. Wexton held his ground.

"Just one arm, Wexton. To begin with. One arm would do."

"What about the coffee?"

"The hell with the coffee."

"You're very young. Steenie, I—"

"Oh, for God's sake, Wexton. I have to begin somewhere. I want to begin now. With you. I love you, Wexton. If you don't put your arms around me, right now, I shall do something terrible. I shall probably cry. I might have another heart attack."

"Well, I guess we wouldn't want that," Wexton said. He shuffled about from foot to foot. He gave Steenie his benign smile. He pulled at the tuft of his hair.

Then, looking sad, as he always did when happy, he held out both arms.

Steenie rushed into them.

"And so, Gwen, they will have to sell up. Lock, stock, and barrel. The house. The estate. Everything. Isn't it sad? *Tragic,* when you think: there have been Arlingtons there for three hundred years."

The end of June, some two weeks after Constance's ball: Maud was enthroned behind the teacups and the spirit kettle, in her London drawing room. One of her more elaborate tea parties. Other guests were expected, but she and Gwen (as was their practice) could have a few moments of enjoyable intimacy first. Also gossip, of which Maud always had such a fine store.

At the far end of the large room there was a cluster of younger guests: Constance, Steenie, Freddie, and Conrad Vickers, the young photographer. Wexton, who had gone to train for his ambulance driving, was absent.

Next to the flamboyant figure of Vickers, who wore his hair several inches longer even than Steenie, sat a stiff row of young officers on leave. Several of these men seemed inclined to take exception to Vickers—which was predictable. A number of the others stared at Constance with bemused rapture. That group, as far as Maud was concerned, could take care of itself. She and Gwen had more important matters to discuss.

"I can't believe it," Gwen said in a gratifying tone of shock. "The Arlingtons? There must be some mistake. It's unthinkable. Who told you, Maud?"

"Heavens, I can't remember! Was it Jane? Their land borders hers, as you know, so . . . But no, of course it wasn't Jane—she's always the last to hear anything. Now, who could it have been? Someone at Maud Cunard's last night . . . but goodness, there was such a crush, I can't remember who . . . Anyway, it doesn't matter, because it's definitely true. Monty said so, this morning. You see, Gwennie, the thing *is*"—Maud leaned forward confidingly—"Gertrude Arlington was forced to borrow—only in a modest way, of course. I believe Monty helped her to arrange some of the loans. But he warned her, years ago, and now the price of land has fallen in this shocking way, so she daren't borrow more, and anyway she hasn't the security. And then—" Maud rattled to an abrupt halt. Gwen stared at her. It was not like Maud to break off in the middle of a story.

"And then what? Go on, Maudie, go on."

"Well, the thing is . . ." Maud hesitated, but could not resist the plunge. "The thing is, if you remember, it's only two years since poor Gertrude lost her husband. The death duties were crippling then, but she and Hector managed somehow. Then Hector joined up—well, I always said he would never make a soldier, but apparently nothing would keep him away. He was adamant, just like Acland, and now—"

"He's dead? Hector Arlington is dead?" Gwen interrupted, her voice sharp. "That's not possible. He was on leave. He came to the ball. I saw him just the other week. He danced with Jane, I remember, because Denton was remarking on her hair, and her dress."

"He went back two days later, Gwennie. I thought you must have heard." Maud hesitated. She leaned across and pressed Gwen's hand. She should not have embarked upon this story. It was now imperative to keep details to the minimum; better not to mention that Hector, in the same regiment as Boy, had (like Boy and Acland) been posted to the Somme, that it was there the sniper's bullet had hit him. "They say it was very quick, Gwennie. No pain. But for Gertrude . . . well, it had to be the final blow. To lose her only . . . She was devoted to Hector, as you know. And then, death duties again. Within two years. I blame the government, and I told Monty so. Death duties, and such punitive ones, such socialistic ones—it cannot be right, Gwennie. So inhumane, so insensitive. Three hundred years, a whole way of life. If this continues, we shall all be wiped out. Even Monty agrees with me there."

"Hector." Gwen set down her teacup. Her eyes had a vacant look. "I can't believe it."

"Now, Gwen . . ." Maud's voice took on a warning note. "Now, Gwen, you promised me. I shouldn't have told you. I wouldn't have told you. I thought you must certainly know."

"He stammered."

"Who, Hector? No, he didn't."

"Yes, he did. Very slightly, when he was a child. Like Boy. He was such an earnest child. The others used to make fun of him—"

"Gwen . . ."

"I'm sorry, Maud." Gwen's eyes had filled with tears. She leaned forward and attempted to pick up her cup, but her hand was shaking and she let it rest.

Maud leaned forward again. She took Gwen's hand once more and pressed it. "Dearest Gwennie, I know it's sad, and I'm sad too. Now listen, that wasn't the only thing I had to tell you. I had good news, too, and I saved that for last because I knew it would cheer you. Don't cry. You don't want Freddie and Steenie to see you. Take a deep breath—that's it. *Now:* Monty says, and he has it on the very best authority, you understand, that this is almost over. The war! The whole wretched thing! Truly, Gwennie—another few months at most, Monty says. The generals are convinced, even those dreadful pessimists at the War Office. By Christmas, Gwennie—think—it could all be over." She had invented this rigmarole on the spur of the moment, for Stern had given her no such assurance, and the last time the matter was discussed, his predictions had been gloomy. Maud, in that moment, cared for none of that; the words tumbled out. She had her reward when she saw hope flicker in Gwen's eyes.

"Oh, Maud, are you sure? Is Monty sure?"

"Darling, I promise you. He's at the War Office now, and he said he'd look in on the way back. Ask him yourself then. Since he went into munitions he hears everything—and anyway, he and that horrid Lloyd George are like *that*." Maud held up two fingers, crossed. "Think, Gwen! By Christmas, Boy and Acland could be home. We could all go down to Winterscombe. We could have a family party, just as we always used to do. We can see in the New Year together. We can be reunited; we can drink to 1917, and peace at last . . ."

"Death to the Kaiser?" Gwen put in, and managed a wan smile, for this currently was Maud's favorite toast.

"Death to the Kaiser, absolutely," Maud replied with spirit.

"I always thought him the most vulgar little man."

Death to the Kaiser, Constance heard from across Maud's splendid drawing room, above the languid monotone of Conrad Vickers, who had taken up a position of worship at her side.

She glanced across and saw Maud lift her teacup, her expression so fierce it seemed she might dash it to the ground, Russian fashion. Stupid woman, Constance thought to herself, watching Maud rise to her feet to greet a group of new guests; she gazed at Maud jealously. Maud was, in fact, not stupid at all, but shrewd, and her manner of speech was misleading. Constance knew this, but that afternoon she did not feel kindly toward Maud, or indeed anyone else; she felt tense and on edge.

In part this was because two separate matters pressed in upon her and divided her energies. Constance never liked that. She was always happiest when her mind could focus with perfect clarity on one course, when all her willpower could be directed to one end. Today, she had come here with just such a purpose in view: She would see Montague Stern, and she would behave in such a way that the indifference in his gaze when he looked at her would vanish forever.

That had been her purpose when she entered this drawing room, but more than half an hour had passed—time in which she had been forced to listen to Conrad Vickers's inanities. Constance was beginning to believe that she would be thwarted yet again, that Sir Montague might not even appear.

Whereupon her mind, with a facility that infuriated her, began to dart off at a tangent. It began to dwell instead upon the quite separate matter of her maid, Jenna.

Jenna was not well: Constance had been aware of that fact for weeks, but the excitement of the ball and its aftermath, her plans for Montague Stern, had diverted her. Today, when Jenna came to help her dress for this tea party, she had looked so ill that Constance could no longer ignore it. Jenna's normally contented expression had gone; her eyes were puffy, as if from lack of sleep, or weeping; her manner was silent and distracted.

Constance, alerted by this change, watched her. She already knew a great deal more about Jenna's affairs than her maid ever suspected. It was torture to Constance to think there might be other secrets to which she did not have access. Jenna still wrote to Acland, for instance, and must receive some replies; Constance knew that. At least she deduced that, for on three occasions, following at a discreet distance, she had observed Jenna make a pilgrimage: out of Park Street, down to the post office at Charing Cross Station. There she would post a letter and collect one from one of the numbered boxes. Such letters, Constance concluded, could come from only one person; anyone writing openly to Jenna would have written to the house.

Discovering this, Constance had been impatient to know more: Why did Jenna write, and why did Acland reply? Was their affair over, as she had believed and Acland had confirmed? If it was over, why continue to write? At times, speculating upon this, Constance ached with a most painful curiosity.

Once or twice the temptation was so strong that she almost gave in. Jenna must hide these letters somewhere, and there was at least the possibility that Constance could find them. Yet something held her back. She could imagine Acland's disdain, his contempt—to creep into a servant's room . . . No, tempted though she was, for once Constance could not do it. *How moral I have become!* she thought to herself, and she glanced toward the door to see if Stern had yet made an appearance.

He had not. Conrad Vickers continued to discuss his tiresome photographs, and how daring they were.

"So, I posed Constance on a bier," he was saying. He gave an adoring glance in her direction, which Constance knew meant nothing at all; Vickers was immune to the attractions of women.

"Then—and this was the *pièce de résistance*—I put one white rose in her hands. Well, I wanted to use a lily, but Constance hates lilies.

Anyway, the rose looked very well. She looked like Juliet on her tomb. No—rather more dangerous than Juliet. That divine hawklike profile of yours, Connie dear! It was positively *perturbing*."

"I can't see why you should want Constance to look like a corpse," remarked one of the young officers with a chilly glance in Vickers's direction.

Vickers raised his eyes to the ceiling.

"Hardly," he squeaked. "Connie looked magnificently alive— just as she always does. I'm not taking family snaps to stand on the piano, you know. The whole point is to make a *statement*. The *essence* of Connie—that was what I was after. Not a *likeness*—any fool could do that."

"Yes, but why make her look dead?" The young officer, perhaps more experienced than Vickers in matters of mortality, was not to be repressed.

"Not dead—dead*ly*. A *femme fatale*," Vickers replied on a note of triumph, for he loved nothing so much as explaining the obvious to the philistines.

"*La Belle Dame Sans Merci*—that's how I see Constance. Perhaps . . ." He paused magnificently. "Perhaps you are not acquainted with the poem?"

"I've read the poem. Everyone's read the poem. Perhaps you ought to print it next to the picture—just in case anyone misses the point."

"My dears!" Vickers sighed a deep sigh. "I couldn't. I wouldn't. I simple *loathe* the obvious, don't you?"

Constance turned away from this bickering. She glanced down at the small jeweled watch she wore pinned to the breast of her jacket—almost four; would Montague Stern never come?—and forced herself to look around her, to examine the drawing room in which she sat.

This drawing room, she felt, could assist her. Maud might lay claim to it, but Constance doubted that. Stern had certainly paid for these things. Perhaps chosen them. In this room, and in these objects, there could be a key to the man she sought.

The drawing room was already, in its way, famous. Its modernity, its eclecticism, had already been celebrated at length in numerous periodicals, all of which Constance had read. It was not, perhaps, to Constance's own taste, for it was an understated room—arresting, in the first instance, because of its absence of clutter.

It was a room some of Gwen's friends might have judged vulgar, for—with a peculiarly English snobbishness—they held that a room should look a little shabby, that anything too perfect or too obviously expensive declared itself as nouveau riche.

Perhaps this room was a little too careful, a little too rich, but Constance did not mind. She looked at it, she listened to its stream of coded messages, and she understood: The person who created this room was a paradox, an ascetic who could not resist beautiful things.

For beautiful things—and rare things—lay all around her, displayed with a museum's care: *sang de boeuf* porcelain, ranked upon a French commode; a rug beneath her feet which was as complex and delightful as a flower garden. And then the pictures! These paintings, which Constance had previously never liked, now sang to her.

Looking at them, and at their jeweled colors, she knew beyond a doubt that it was not Maud who had selected the objects here. Maud might boast of these paintings—and indeed did—but she would never understand them.

No, this room was Stern's. He paid for it; he chose it; he assembled it. Stern, the collector of rare things.

And I chose him, Constance said to herself. In that moment, when she felt she might understand him, that she might dwell in his mind, that she might work on him—just then, Stern came into the room.

One of his fleeting visits, although Stern gave no indication of this. He gave the impression, as he always did, that he had all the time in the world. He greeted Maud. He greeted the twenty or so assembled guests. He appeared delighted to see them. As soon as he judged they were engaged once more, he extricated himself from the conversation. He withdrew, as was often his custom, to the other end of the room.

Constance bided her time. This meeting, every detail of which she had carefully planned in her mind, must not be rushed.

She waited, therefore, while Maud addressed the company at large. She saw Stern wince when Maud explained he had been that afternoon at the War Office and could not now stay long, for he was going on to Downing Street that evening. Stern, who was almost always negligent and modest about his access and his powers, disliked these fond boasts, Constance thought.

She watched the skill with which he extricated himself. She noted the slight sigh of relief he gave as he withdrew. She watched him choose a seat with its back to the rest of the room. She watched him pick up a newspaper.

None of the other guests seemed to find this withdrawal odd. They had been well trained by Maud. Stern was an important man;

they accepted that he had weightier matters on his mind. Besides, his withdrawal left them free to gossip. When it came to scandal and innuendo and revelation, Stern's excellent manners sometimes failed. He was known to be a source of information, naturally; that information, however, was filtered through Maud.

This assisted Stern's useful reputation for discretion. That reputation Maud guarded fiercely. She might be a great gossip, but she gossiped with care. No gaffes; and—since Maud revealed so much—people were inclined to make revelations in their turn. These, Constance had no doubt, were then repeated to Stern when Maud was alone with him.

She looked at Stern appraisingly. She considered whether he might actually love Maud, or whether Maud was merely useful to him. She was not sure, and because she was uncertain, she was all the more determined to proceed with care.

Constance could spot tedium in the eyes at twenty paces—and what did Stern find most tedious? Why, the blandishments of women—that she had begun to observe.

For Stern, she had decided, most women were mere gadflies. It was power that interested him, and most women had no power. So, charmingly, politely, he brushed them aside. She had learned her lesson the night of the ball: With Stern it would be useless to employ the flirtatious tactics usual to young girls.

Other strategies were required. Since these were already decided upon—it was too late to go back—Constance felt herself grow calm. Time for first strike. She allowed a few more seconds to pass; then, detaching herself from the group of young men, she stood up.

Her most beautiful dress, selected for this occasion: silk the color of Parma violets, a plain black ribbon wound tight about her throat. On her fingers, just one ring: a black opal, given by Maud, which superstitious Gwen had tried to persuade her not to wear.

Constance looked down at this ring: lightning imprisoned in jet. She liked the unpredictability of opals. She was not superstitious and never would be.

She half believed in luck, from time to time; she had greater faith in willpower. Determination: that was the thing. When she was determined enough, she felt she could do anything. She advanced across the room. She looked at Stern's back. As she did so, the most unlikely memory came into her mind. The day they brought her father back to Winterscombe on the stretcher. A black black day; everything about it was black. She could not see into the detail of the memory. Then someone took her arm; someone led her up the portico steps—and her way was blocked, by this man, by some garment. She could not remember the garment at all—only its color. It had been red. Her father's blood had been red too. A red and black day, which made her mind twang and ache.

She stopped halfway across the room. Maud, looking up, made some passing remark to her. Constance answered it in an absent voice. Then, despising her own hesitation, she took up her position, her planned position, just behind Stern's chair.

"How old are you?" Constance said. She said it without preamble, just as she had planned. All that had happened was that Stern had turned, risen, greeted her—"Ah, Constance my dear"—and drawn out a chair for her. He had then seated himself again with his back to the room, put down his newspaper with a certain reluctance, and smiled. He had not been paying attention. He was paying attention now.

"How old?" He hesitated, as if puzzled, then gave a small wave of the hand. "Constance, I am ancient beyond belief. I am thirty-nine years old."

Constance, who had consulted Gwen and who knew he was forty-three, was encouraged by this. She lowered her eyes, then looked up at him boldly.

"Oh, you are too young," she said in a charming manner. "I feared you would be."

"Too young? Constance, you flatter me. I think of myself as a graybeard, my dear, particularly when I am in the company of such a delightful young woman as yourself. Too young for what?"

"Do not tease me," said Constance. "I am not fishing for compliments. I ask for good reason. I wondered, you see, if you might have known my mother. Her name was Jessica Mendl before her marriage. She was a Jew."

This was one of her trumps, and the second it was played, Constance knew the trick of gaining attention had been won. In the first place, as she knew it would be, this information was unexpected. In the second, it raised a topic usually barred.

Stern might not practice his religion; on the other hand, he made no attempt to disguise he was a Jew. His race, however, was never discussed to his face. To Constance's delight, Stern frowned.

"I am sorry, Constance. I do not understand."

"It is very simple." Constance leaned forward. "My mother was Austrian. Her family lived in Vienna, I believe. She came to London to study art at the Slade, and while she was there she met my father.

They married. Of course her family were appalled. She had been living with cousins in London. They closed their doors to her. She never saw her parents again." Constance paused. "I was born a year after the marriage. Not long after that, my mother died, as you probably know. It is foolish, perhaps, but I often feel I should like to know more of her."

A reminder, just the most delicate hint, of her sad status as an orphan. Constance was careful not to overdo it, since Stern was not a sentimental man.

"Are you certain of this, Constance?" He was looking at her now with an expression of disbelief. "I always assumed . . . I certainly never heard—"

"Oh, no one knows," Constance replied quickly. "Not even Gwen. My mother died long before my father ever went to Winterscombe, and I doubt he would have spoken of her there. He could have been ashamed—anyway, he was a secretive man." Constance, now sure of Stern's attention, lowered her eyes. "I was told by the woman who nursed me when I was a child. She had looked after my mother before she went to the sanitorium. She hated me, and I hated her. She said it to wound me, I think. She probably thought she could make me ashamed. But she didn't. I was glad. I was proud."

"Proud?" Stern gave her a sharp glance, as if he suspected insincerity.

"Yes, proud." Constance looked up at him. "I should hate just to be English. The English are so smug, so pleased to be parochial. Parochialism is their chief religion, I think. I have always felt like an outsider—and glad of it. Do you ever feel like that? But no, of course you do not. Forgive me. That was both stupid and rude."

There was a brief pause. Stern looked down at his hands. When he looked up at Constance once more, the expression in his eyes disconcerted her. For a moment she had the feeling that Stern knew what she was about, that her little tricks and ploys made him angry. He appeared to hesitate. Constance waited for some cutting reprimand. Yet it did not come. When he spoke, his manner was calm.

"My dear, you are intelligent. Do not pretend to a stupidity you do not possess. Look at these people." He gestured behind him. "Look at me. I am everything these people loathe and distrust—can you doubt that? I am tolerated, occasionally even sought after, because I can be of use and I am not poor. My abilities are at these people's disposal because I choose to make them so. If they wish to believe I act from the profit motive solely, why should I care? Their opinions are a matter of indifference to me. I *pass*, my dear Constance, no more than that—as you must certainly know. And no, Constance, I am not acquainted with any Mendls of Vienna. Perhaps I am too young, as you say. More likely, they and their London cousins moved in more exalted circles. The people I grew up with did not send daughters to study art at the Slade. I am a Whitechapel Jew, Constance. My father was a tailor. I cannot help you."

Constance was silent. Stern's words made her feel small; perhaps he had intended them to do just that. She hesitated. She decided it would be better not to pursue the matter of her mother. Her mother, in any case, did not greatly concern her—had she not always thought of herself as her father's child? Constance swiftly decided to alter her line of attack.

"These people?" She turned to look back across the drawing room. She made the question sharp. "These people? Not all of them, surely? You can hardly mean to include Maud."

She stood up as she spoke. As she well knew, the reference to Maud was daring on the lips of a girl. It was rude, in that it implied reproof. And, most perfect of all, it brought out into the open that other aspect of Stern's life which was never discussed to his face: his sexual relationship with a woman Constance addressed as Aunt Maud.

Constance now contrived to speak to Stern not just as a family friend, or a Jew, but as a man. Lest he should be in any doubt of that fact, she fixed her eyes upon his. She passed her tongue across her lips. She bit them so that they reddened.

An old trick. Stern had possibly been about to take offense. Slowly, his expression altered. He looked at Constance intently. He seemed amused, yet a certain speculation could be detected in his eyes.

Constance, feeling stronger now, met his gaze. She examined him: the beautifully shaped skull, the clean-shaven olive skin, the foxy tone of his hair, the narrow-set and watchful eyes, the mouth, which she judged sensual, and the strong nose. She liked that nose, she decided, and she approved that face. She liked the luxury and flamboyance of Stern's clothes—so much more fun than the drab conventional suits of the Englishmen present. She liked the fact that he was born a tailor's son in the East End and had made his own way in the world—for was not that just what she intended to do?

She liked, she found, everything about Sir Montague Stern: his sharp intelligence, his foreignness, his exoticism, the lingering scent of cigar smoke on his jacket, the whiteness of the exquisite handkerchief that protruded from his breast pocket, the flash of gold at his cuff.

She liked the richness of his voice and the anger she had glimpsed earlier in his eyes; she liked the fact that he did not belong, any more than she did, to this hidebound, narrow-spirited world in which they were both forced to operate.

Above all—no dupe, this man—she liked the fact that he was now making no attempt to disguise the quality of his interest in her. His gaze had become one of overt sexual appraisal—and that appraisal seemed to amuse him, for he began to smile.

That was good: The best flirtations, the best affairs, were tempered with humor, surely? Constance returned his stare and felt her mind skip. This course she had embarked upon—it was no longer just a challenge, a means to an end. It was amusing.

"I like you," she announced suddenly, and was sincere. "I like you, and I think you are . . . splendid. This room is splendid too. And the paintings—especially the paintings. You chose them, didn't you? I never saw paintings like these before." She paused. "Won't you show me them? Won't you give me a guided tour?"

"The postimpressionists?" A lazy smile. "The ones in here, or the others? There are some on the stairs, and others in the main hall. The best ones are in the library upstairs."

"Oh, the best ones first, obviously," Constance replied.

"You like the best? That is your preference?"

"I am learning to make it so," Constance said, and took his arm in hers.

"My dear," Stern said in passing to Maud, who had looked up as they moved to the door, "Constance requires educating in matters of art. May I take her to inspect the Cézannes?"

"Of course, Monty," Maud replied, and returned to her enjoyable conversation with Gwen. All the women present were by then deep in the byzantine love affairs of Lady Cunard.

In the library, with the door closed, Sir Montague looked at Constance closely.

"Do you want to see the Cézannes?"

"No."

"I thought not." He paused. "I am beginning to understand, Constance, that I have underestimated you."

"Not underestimated. You simply did not look at me. Now you do."

"Is that why you told me about your mother? To make me look at you?"

"Yes."

"And why should you want me to look at you?"

"Because I intend to marry you. Mainly."

At this, Stern smiled.

"Do you now? Have you not heard, Constance, how confirmed a bachelor I am?"

"I heard. And I did not believe it. That was before you met me."

"Well, well, well." Stern took a step forward. He looked down into Constance's up-tilted face.

"You're very direct, which is unusual in a woman. And very precise. 'Mainly,' you said. Was there an additional reason to make me look at you?"

"But of course. I should like you to make love to me."

"Now?"

"We could make a beginning now."

"And my position in this house? Your position? The people downstairs?"

"I do not give a fig for them—any more than you do."

"And your reputation, Constance? You really should consider that."

"My reputation is safe with you. You are a gentleman."

"A gentleman would most certainly refuse you. He would send you packing with—at the least—a tactful reprimand; at worst, a smacked bottom."

"You are an unusual kind of gentleman. Had I thought you likely to treat me as a child I should not have come up here."

There was silence, during which they regarded each other somewhat warily. There was a brief knocking to be heard in the distance, the sound of servants and of conversations in low voices. Neither Stern nor Constance noticed this; they continued to look at each other, though there was a curious blindness in that stare.

After a while Stern stepped forward another pace. He lifted Constance's chin in his hand. He turned her face, first this way, then that, as if he were a portraitist and she his model. At his touch, and for the first time, Constance displayed an agitation. She grasped his hand.

"Tell me," she said with sudden vehemence. "Tell me what you see."

"I see," Stern answered slowly, "a woman. Not a beautiful woman, in the conventional sense. You have an interesting face, Constance—the face of someone who likes to rewrite the rules. I see . . . a very young woman, which deters me somewhat, for I distrust

young women and I am not a seducer of little girls. A clever woman,
though, and perhaps a predatory one—"

"Am I ugly?"

"No, Constance, you are not ugly."

"My father always said I was ugly."

"Your father was wrong. You are . . . striking. Probably unprin-
cipled, and certainly tempting. Provocative, too, as I am sure you are
aware. And so I think that—on consideration—yes."

With which, Stern bent his head and kissed her on the lips.
Possibly this kiss was intended to be a brief one, a seemly one. If so,
the intentions were not fulfilled. It became protracted. It became an
embrace; it became an intimate embrace, and the quality of that
embrace startled both of them.

They broke apart, looked at each other, then reached out again.
Constance's arms locked around Stern's neck; his arms tightened
around her waist. Constance, who seemed greatly aroused, opened
her lips; she gave a small moan, which might have been of pleasure
or distress. She reached for his hand and pressed it against her
breasts. Then, in a kind of angry ecstasy, she pressed herself close
against him; feeling him harden, she gave a cry of triumph.

When, finally, they parted, neither was composed. They looked
at each other with a cautious respect, like two combatants. Constance's eyes glittered; her cheeks were flushed. She smiled, then
began to laugh. Stepping forward, she took Stern's hand.

"Tell me you did not expect this."

"I did not expect it." Amusement deepened in his eyes. "Why?
Did you, Constance?"

"No. How could I have? I suspected . . . but I might have been
wrong. It might have been . . . forgettable."

"And it wasn't?"

"Not in the least. It was . . . addictive."

"Dangerously addictive, I should say. I must have lost my
reason. However . . ."

He reached for her again, but before he could take her in his
arms, there came the sound of footsteps on the landing outside, a
discreet cough. Then the door opened upon the figure of Maud's
butler, an elderly man.

It was an intrusion of farce, Constance thought. She moved back
and, with commendable presence of mind, began to speak. She was
just praising the Cézannes, and requesting she now be shown the
further paintings in the hall, when she registered the expression on
the servant's face. He appeared neither suspicious nor shocked. At

first Constance took this for good training on his part; then she observed something else: The man's face had an ashen look. In his hand, which was shaking, he held a silver salver. Upon the salver lay a telegram.

"It is for Lady Callendar, sir." The man looked up at Stern and then away. "The boy took it to Park Street, and they sent him straight here. I was not sure, sir, if I should take it up directly. I thought it best to inquire of you. In the circumstances you might feel it more appropriate, I thought, to speak to Lady Callendar first."

The man's voice faded. Both Stern and Constance stared at the tray, and at the envelope, of unmistakably military origin. They knew these envelopes, and their implications, as everyone did. There was a silence; then Stern said in a crisp voice, "You did quite rightly. Constance, we must return to the others. I will speak to Gwen. Someone must be with her. Maud. And Freddie—yes, it had better be Freddie."

Constance did as she was told. She watched everything happen at one remove. She saw Stern enter the drawing room and cross to Gwen. She saw Gwen's face lift, and her smile falter. She heard the conversation in that corner dwindle and saw the sudden jerk with which Maud looked up, to catch the warning in Stern's eyes. Gwen stood. The new tension in the room communicated itself to Freddie and to Steenie. They, too, rose; they followed their mother, Maud, and Stern from the room.

The door closed on them. There were some nervous whispers from the other guests, then a silence. *It can be only one of two people,* said a clear and precise voice in Constance's mind. *Either it is Boy. Or Acland.*

She turned and, moving away from the others, crossed to the long windows that overlooked the park. The day was fine and the park was crowded. Constance saw a woman carrying parcels, another woman dressed in unseasonable furs, with a bright little dog on a scarlet leash. A child with a hoop; a horse-drawn delivery van pausing near the gates. Constance saw these things, and these strangers, with that brilliant clarity which is the by-product of shock.

She rested her hands against the windowpane, which was cold. Behind her the other guests were beginning to speak once more. She could hear the hiss of their speculation, and because she knew that even those most sympathetic derived a certain glee from disaster, she would have liked to round on them, to scream at them, to act the savage, as she had done once before, six years before, when they had brought her father back to Winterscombe and she was still a child.

Instead, when it became unbearable to remain still a second longer, she turned to the door. She ran out upon the landing and stared down fearfully at a closed door at the end of the hall. They had gone into the morning room downstairs; she could catch the murmur of voices. Then, cutting through them and rising above them, came the sound of one long cry.

Constance ran to the stairs and hastened down them. She wanted to burst into the room, to demand to know—at once—what had happened, but when she reached the door, and heard the sound of weeping, she drew back.

She was excluded even now, even at a moment such as this. She was still the outsider. Did no one think to come out? Did no one think that she, too, ought to know? In a sudden rage of pain and fear, Constance turned back. She flung herself against the wall and covered her ears with her hands to block out the sound of Gwen's weeping.

After a long while the door of the morning room opened and Montague Stern came out. He paused, looked at Constance's tense body and bent head, then quietly closed the door behind him. He crossed to Constance, and when she did not turn, laid his hand on her arm. Constance at once swung around and clutched at him.

"Which? Which?" she cried. "Which of them is it? Tell me. I must know."

"It is Acland," Stern replied in a quiet voice, his eyes never leaving Constance's face. "I am afraid it is Acland. He is missing. Believed killed."

Stern had expected tears, but he was not prepared for the violence of Constance's reaction. At his words, color came and went in her face and she gave a sharp cry, stepping back from him.

"Oh, damn him, damn him. He promised me. Damn him for dying."

The vehemence with which the words were said surprised Stern. He made no reply, but stood still, watching her. He saw her eyes become vivid with tears, which she brushed aside with an angry hand. He saw her hands clench and her mouth move in a jagged grimace of pain. These things interested him, even at such a moment as that; he noted them, as he always noted the reactions of others, and then stored them away in his mind.

And perhaps, even in her anger and her grief, Constance saw the coolness of his appraisal, for her face grew tight with resentment. Then she made a spring and hit out at him.

"Don't watch me so! Leave me alone! I hate to be watched."

Stern did not move. He remained still while Constance's small fists flailed against him: a hail of blows against his chest, arms, and shoulders. When the force of those blows began to diminish, Stern made a sudden movement and caught hold of Constance's wrists. He held them in a tight grip while Constance writhed and struggled with a kind of impotent fury.

This seemed to enrage Constance even more, for she twisted against his strength; then, apparently for no reason, she became quiet and ceased her struggles. She looked up into his face as if she had decided to submit, although there was nothing of submission in her eyes. They looked at each other, and then Stern relaxed his hold.

He glanced back, once, over his shoulder, toward the closed door and the sounds of Gwen's weeping. Then he stepped forward a little.

"Cry," he said, and in a practiced manner he took Constance in his arms.

When, finally, they left Maud's house, it was in a sad procession: Steenie and Freddie supporting Gwen, who could barely walk, Maud fluttering at her side, Constance bringing up the rear. As Constance passed Stern on the steps, moving out into sunlight so bright it shocked her eyes, a small piece of paper was pressed into her hand.

Later, when she unfolded it, she found it contained the address of Stern's chambers in Albany, that separate establishment he had always kept up for the sake of Maud's reputation. It was a place that Constance had never visited.

Under this address he had written: *Any afternoon at three.* Constance stared at this missive for some time, then crumpled it and threw it across the room.

I shall not go, she thought to herself. *I shall not go.* But that night she rescued the scrap of paper and considered it again. It was—and this did not surprise her—both unaddressed and unsigned.

IV
MARRIAGES

From the journals

Last night I dreamed of Acland. He rose up from the ranks of the dead. He came to my room; he stayed with me there, all through the night. He had come to say goodbye—he would not come again.

I was not afraid. I told him all my truths. I confessed I had been to Jenna's room and read the letters—even that. Acland understood: He knew, if he had not died, I would never have done it. He said: All that was past now. He showed me why and how he had broken his promise. He died of a thrust from a bayonet; he showed me the wound below his heart; he let me rest my hand upon it.

Over a thousand men died the same day, he said: What was one more death among so many? Look, Acland said—and he showed me the place where he died. It was no place, barren as far as the eye could see. There was no grass, no bushes, no trees, no hope. It made me afraid, that place; I recognised it; I thought I had been there.

Acland said perhaps I had. He said it was a place we all knew, that it was inside each of us, waiting.

After that, we did not speak of death. He stayed with me, and untied all the knots, one by one.

When the dawn came, I wept. I knew he would leave me. Acland took a strand of his hair, which was as fine and red as Welsh gold. He bound it about my wedding finger; he made me his bride. We knew what we had always known, that we were one. We were: cut from the same rock, hewn from the same wood, forged from the same metal. We were closer than conspirators, than twins, than father and daughter. It was a fact. It had no end and no beginning. It was majestical!

Look, Acland said again. I turned my head. I saw the world in all its certainty and all its clarity. There were no doubts, paper, I promise you. In my dream there were no doubts. The world Acland gave me was made in heaven; from the smallest creature to the brightest star, I saw its symmetry.

But when I looked back, Acland was gone. It was a Sunday morning, and the bells were ringing.

Morning. Mourning. To wake. A wake.

Any afternoon at three. There is a lesser life to be lived, and Acland knows this. He understands.

Look, death, last night was my wedding. I still have the ring upon my finger. There it is, a circle of bright hair about the bone.

Shall I go, or shall I not go, every afternoon at three, any afternoon at three?

Acland understands, but on this he is quiet. He will not advise me.

Acland, please help. I am still young, and sometimes my mind is not as clear as I want it to be. I know you came to take your leave, but even so—when it is the right time, if it is the right time, will you tell me?

Jenna knew where the pain was: It was a specific ache, located between her stomach and heart, as identifiable as indigestion; she could have put her hand on it and said, "Look, there it is. That is my grief."

On the afternoon when Gwen and Constance were visiting Maud, and the telegram was brought, Jenna sat alone in her attic room and wrote a letter. She was writing to Acland, and it was the most difficult letter she had ever had to write, because she had to tell him she was expecting his baby.

It seemed to her that there must be, should be, a very clear and simple way to explain this to him, but if there was, she could not find it. She had already begun this letter several times before, and then torn up the pages because the words would not fall the right way. Now she was three months gone; she could not delay any longer.

Still, the letter would not be written. The sentences tangled; she became hot and muddled; the nib of the pen crossed; the words crossed; she made many blots.

She wanted Acland to understand that although she had known this was likely to happen when she went with him to the hotel at

Charing Cross (for she counted the days of her cycle, as she said), she had done it because she knew she had lost him, and she wanted to be left with a part of him that could never be taken away. She also wanted him to be quite clear: She did not intend to trap him; she did not expect marriage.

Two things, she said to herself, screwing up one page and beginning upon another; if she could just write those two things, it might be enough.

At once, though, her mind would fly off upon tangents. She would start doing sums; she would think of her savings—put by over a period of some twelve years—which amounted to seventy pounds. She would start to calculate how long such a sum could support a woman and a child—a woman who, once her pregnancy became obvious, would be both homeless and unemployable.

Then there was the morning sickness—she found she wanted to write about that, and how she hid herself away in the one bathroom set aside for the female servants, and ran the taps in the basin so no one should hear the sound when she was sick. She wanted to write about her skirts, and how she had let out the waistbands for the first time that week. She wanted to write about the room at the hotel, and the sad brown color of its walls; the dull look in Acland's eyes when he had lain on the bed and watched her.

These things were not the main things; she must leave them out, but they crept back in. The ink was low in the ink pot, too thick and powdery. The paper was cheap; it snagged the tines of her pen. The room, right beneath the slates, was very hot.

In the end, she finished the letter, sealed its envelope, and wrote with great care the mysterious digits of Acland's military address. The numbers could not be decoded, and she looked at them anxiously; she would have liked to write the name of a village, an understandable place. The numbers frightened her—so easy to put one digit out of place.

She pinned the envelope in her apron pocket. She always did this, because her great fear was that one of these letters would be dropped, and discovered. Then she crept down the back stairs. If the housekeeper saw her, she would invent a new task on the spot; if she did not, it might be possible to escape the house and post the letter at once.

Half an hour, still, before Constance was due to return, but the house was not quiet, as it usually was on such afternoons. There were doors opening and closing, footsteps, the sound of voices. Jenna went down into the kitchen, and it was there she came to understand: This letter would never be sent, for Acland was dead.

It was some while before this was clear to her. When she went into the kitchen, there was a hubbub. At the long deal table sat the cook (who was new; she had been at Park Street less than a month) and Stanley, one of the oldest of the footmen, whom Jenna had known when a child. Next to the table was a cluster of maids, eyes agog; in the midst of the maids, standing upon a stool, for he was short, was the boy employed by Maud to take messages. He was thirteen years old, and his voice was breaking. As Jenna closed the door he seemed just to have finished some momentous speech. The new cook had covered her face and her gray hair, which she set every night in curling papers, with her apron. As the boy stopped she lowered this apron. She drew herself up. She took charge. She, too, made a speech.

"Sit him down," she said. "Let the boy sit down. Draw up the stool for him, there, between me and Stanley. That's it. Now, Polly, fetch the lad a glass of milk. He's had a shock, too, the same as we've all had. Maybe a glass of the cooking brandy, Lizzie—you'll take one with me, Stanley, for medicinal purposes? I've the dinner to cook, and I don't know as how I'll be able, not after this. My boy Albert's out there, too, so it's only natural I take it hard. Just a small glass, Lizzie—well, maybe a drop or two more. I'm all of a jelly, so I am. Look, my hands are shaking. I ask you, how can I make them pastries, with my hands like this? You need a light hand for pastries, I've always said. A steady hand. There, child, you drink that up now, and then you'll feel better. Now, start again, nice and clear. Lizzie wasn't here the first time, and no more was Jenna. A telegram— out of the blue like that, and right in the middle of a tea party. Who'd credit it? Was he blown up, d'you think? That's what happens, my Albert says. 'Course, they word it like that to break it nice and gentle-like, but my Albert says they're blown up so small there's no way they know where one man ends and another's beginning. A man's head would fit in a matchbox, my boy says—that's the plain truth of it. They pick them up, when they can, but they're no more than joints of meat. Just like a leg of lamb, my boy says. A bit of scrag end, and you don't know but what it might be your sworn enemy or your best friend. 'It can't be Christian,' I says to him, and he says, 'Mother, so help me, that's the way it is.' "

Jenna heard this, but she did not understand. There was a background swell of sound, too, from the maids, which was how she imagined the sound of the sea, though she had never seen the sea.

Out of that murmuring there came a name, but she would not listen to it.

Then the messenger boy, refreshed by the glass of milk and perhaps sensing that his moment of glory would be brief, piped up once more. His voice pitched, sank, growled, then inched its way back up to the treble register. He was inclined to embroider now, and—seeing the rapt attention of the maids—began on a scene that he had not, in fact, witnessed.

"So," Jenna heard, "Lady Callendar, she gives this terrible scream. Then she bent up double just like someone punched her. Then she says, 'Oh, not Acland, not my darling Acland,' and the Jewish gentleman, he takes her hand and tells her to be brave. He says as how he died for his country, and when he says that, she straightens up and wipes her eyes, and . . . ."

Jenna did not stay to hear more. She left the kitchen and returned to her room. She opened her window. She thought she might burn her letter, but in the end she decided to keep it. She put it in the box where she kept all Acland's letters to her. She counted the letters. Acland did not write very often. There were twelve of them.

She waited three weeks. In those weeks she was very quiet and very methodical, just as she still was many years later, when I knew her. If she ironed a blouse for Constance, she pressed the iron on the material twenty-five times, no more, no less. Constance's hair received exactly fifty strokes. Clothes had to be folded in a certain way. She arranged the dresses in the wardrobes by order of function and color.

I think Jenna was like a child, counting the paving stones and avoiding the cracks. I think she believed that if she could impose order on the small things of the world, the larger things would become ordered too. I think she thought that if the little things of life could be set to rights, the wrong that was Acland's death could be righted too. I think she believed that if she worked hard, and the evening dresses in the cupboards were always to the right of the day dresses, then Acland would come back. In a sense Jenna waited for this, his impossible return, all her life.

She let out her skirts another inch in a methodical way. She was sick each morning at the same time. Then, three weeks later, when the sickness stopped and she knew the alteration in her figure must soon show, she wrote to Mr. Solomons and made (as she had promised Acland she would) an orderly appointment, for the following week.

Jenna was afraid of lawyers. She did not know the difference between a solicitor and a barrister. She expected Mr. Solomons to wear a wig and a black gown. She put him in the pigeonhole in her mind that she reserved for all figures of authority: teachers and policemen and magistrates. When she went to see him she wore her best dress, and she darned her gloves. She expected punishment or—more vaguely—reprimand. She knew what Mr. Solomons would think: He would think she was mercenary.

In fact, Mr. Solomons proved less fearsome than she had expected. They spent an hour together. Mr. Solomons did not wear a wig; his eyebrows bristled. He gave her quirky looks. His words were windy: There was a problem, he explained, a hitch. Yes, there was a will, and a very fine will it was, since he had drawn it up himself and, without vanity, could say he was a master when it came to wills, even tricky ones.

However, a will must be proved, and for a will to be proved, there must be a certificate of death. A telegram of the kind sent was not sufficient, unfortunately. This, he explained with another bristling look, was a recurrent problem these days, and a tragic thing, but there it was. There would have to be Communications with the Military Authorities, and although he saw no reason for the matter not to be resolved to the satisfaction of all parties, it would take time.

"How long?" Jenna said, when she had unraveled all this. She did not like to ask (it sounded mercenary again), but she had to ask. Her mind had begun on sums again. How long to live on seventy pounds? Where to live? She could not have told Mr. Solomons about the baby, for even though he did not wear a wig, he was a lawyer and a man, but the anxiety was making her hot and muddled again. Christmas, she thought, Christmas. That, more or less, was when her baby would be born.

"By Christmas?" she said, before she could stop herself.

"Goodness me, no." Mr. Solomons gave her a quaint look. "The law is a very cautious kind of animal—a very sluggish animal, if you take my meaning. Take the normal period of probate: Well, we should be thinking even then of a twelvemonth. In a case such as this, longer. A year and a half. Possibly two years. If I shake a stick at them, perhaps we might fine it down a bit. But more than a year, I'd say. That's the long and short of it."

Jenna walked home. She saved the omnibus fare and walked the three miles, looking straight ahead, one foot in front of the other. The sun shone. Acland was dead. Seventy pounds was no use to an unemployable servant with an illegitimate baby.

Back in her attic room she took off her best dress and her best hat and her darned gloves, and wrote a letter to Jack Hennessy. One page; no blots. It was easy to write, so much easier than the letter to Acland. When she read it through, she saw why this was: It was because it contained nothing but lies.

Jack Hennessy's regiment was being re-formed—a common occurrence then, when the losses at the Somme alone were so heavy. He was retraining in Yorkshire, and from Yorkshire he sent a reply, by return of post. It was a letter full of crossings-out and misspellings, but he replied as Jenna had hoped he would. He would stand by her. They would marry.

The letter was also full of arrangements, which surprised Jenna, who had expected confusion and reproach. No reproach—not a word of it. Hennessy told her he had found her a place to lodge, with Arthur Tubbs's mother—did she remember Arthur Tubbs, his good friend, now a corporal doing very well in supplies, who used to valet for Freddie? Mrs. Tubbs would be glad of the extra rent. As a soldier's wife, Jenna would receive an allowance of seventeen shillings a week; Mrs. Tubbs would accept six. Jenna would share a room with the eldest Tubbs girl, whose name was Florrie.

He had a wedding ring. He could get leave for the marriage, but it had to be arranged quickly before he returned to France. Arthur said a special license was required, since there was not time for the full banns, and so a five-pound note was enclosed with the letter. A special license cost three guineas.

This blotchy epistle ended, as all Hennessy's letters did, *You are my own Jen, and I send my love to you.* Jenna unfolded the large fine tissue which was the five-pound note. She looked at it for a long time. She read the letter once, twice, then again.

She was puzzled by the references to Arthur Tubbs; he and Hennessy might be in the same regiment, but it had never occurred to her that he and Arthur were good friends. Yes, it was the references to Arthur, she told herself, that made the letter seem so odd.

She read it a fourth time: lodgings, and banns, and special licenses. Her mind felt fuddled and hot. She did not know which church to go to; she had no idea where special licenses might be obtained, and Jack Hennessy did not tell her.

In the end, knowing she would need help, she was methodical once more. She considered Lady Callendar, who lay in her bedroom with the blinds lowered. She considered the housekeeper. She considered Constance. She considered Jane Conyngham, who was a nurse and who had always been kind to her, from that very first night when she dressed her hair for the party for the comet.

It was to Jane Conyngham that she finally wrote. She made an appointment to meet her at Guy's Hospital.

On the way there (she took an omnibus that time, and sat in the sun on the open top deck), she took out Jack Hennessy's letter and read it again. She knew then why the letter was odd. It was not the references to Arthur Tubbs that were so strange; it was something else.

No reproach, no questions—and not one single mention of the baby.

A week later Jane Conyngham presented Constance with a *fait accompli*. Jenna had left Park Street (Jane herself had spirited her away in a hansom). She was lodged south of the river, with Mrs. Tubbs, who lived in a small terrace house beyond Waterloo Station. The marriage to Jack Hennessy was arranged, and would take place the next day in a church (also south of the river) with which Jane had charitable connections. Jenna was expecting Hennessy's child, and that child would be born around Christmas.

Once Jenna was married it would be permissible for Constance to visit her, and Gwen had agreed to this, since Jenna had always been such a loyal and irreproachable servant. Jane hoped that Constance would do this, as she understood Constance would be concerned for her, and Jane herself might not be available, for she had decided—almost decided—that she would leave Guy's Hospital, and nurse in France.

Constance listened to this long explanation in silence. She watched Jane, who—on this occasion—spoke clearly and concisely and did not once break off or hide her face with her hands. Even when she mentioned the baby, Jane neither blushed nor faltered. She spoke (although Constance did not realize this) in the new way she was learning at the hospital: dispassionate, firm, and succinct. She did not judge Jenna; she emphasized the love between Jenna and Hennessy, the length of their attachment, and making no attempt to condemn her conduct (which surprised Constance very much), she seemed even to imply that Jenna's behavior was understandable, in time of war.

In fact, Jane spoke in this new and astonishing way for one very simple reason. She understood Jenna, because—and she was certain of this—Jenna was no different from herself. When Jane had learned the news of Acland's death (it had been brought her, by Freddie, at the hospital) she had thought two things. The first was when Freddie began, and said he brought bad news. Then Jane had heard a clear voice in her mind, and that voice had said: *Please. Let it be Boy. Not Acland.* The second had come later, when she prepared for bed that night in her neat room at the nurse's hostel. She had looked down at that narrow bed, with its coarse sheets and hospital blankets, and she had known that if ever the impossible had happened, and Acland had come to her and taken her to bed, she would have gone willingly, without question or hesitation. He had never approached her; she had never done so. The gap filled her with a wild regret.

The first of these thoughts made Jane ashamed; the second did not. There lay all the carefully constructed morality of her life, smashed at her feet. Small shards; she could look down on them and see them; she could trample them underfoot until they were nothing more than the finest dust.

Gone. She did not need them anymore; she was a nurse. She had loved Acland. She had cut her hair. She had new morals of her own, and because she had made them, patched them together from the dictates of her heart and the compassion of her mind, they had authority. No, she could not judge Jenna—she even admired Jenna. Love ought to be given when it could, for time was so short.

So Jane spoke to Constance in her new way. Her hands rested in her lap. Her eyes did not waver. Constance heard her out.

Constance, of course, did not know why Jane spoke in this way. She saw that she had, in the past, underestimated Jane, and she felt for her a new and wary respect. She also felt angry. She felt angry that Jane should be deceived. (Constance, that little spy, knew the baby was not Jack Hennessy's.) She felt angry that Jenna, who had had Acland, should now settle for a husband like Hennessy. She felt angry with Hennessy, who had carried her father's stretcher back to Winterscombe; Hennessy, who was so large, so massed, and so threatening—she had always hated him! She felt angry that Jane, who had once loved Acland and perhaps loved him still, should speak in this calm, cool way. She felt angry with the sun, which continued to shine, and the traffic of the city, which continued to flow.

Constance listened to Jane, and her anger mounted. She told herself they did not deserve Acland, any of them, and only she mourned him truly, so she was jagged with grief, and pain sprang out from her fingertips, from each hair on her head, like lightning.

Constance was afraid of these rages of hers. She could control them better than she did as a child, but she could not always control them well enough. They were like an epilepsy with her: They made her jerk and twitch and flinch. Her hands would not lie still; her feet moved—she could hear her heels drumming. She could smell burning, and taste bile.

Only I understand; only I was worthy of him, Constance cried to herself in her angry egoism, and, because she failed to quell this rebellion of her hands and her hair and her heels, she then behaved very badly. She behaved in a way Jane never forgot.

The explanations regarding Jenna were over. Jane and Constance sat alone in the Park Street drawing room; there was a hush in the house.

Then Boy came into the room. Boy had been granted a week's compassionate leave; he was due to return to France the following day. He was wearing uniform. He came into the room; in his hands was a large, black, leather-bound volume. This volume bore Acland's name upon it in gold letters, and the dates of his birth and of his death. In it were pasted the letters of condolence that Gwen and Denton had received on the loss of their son. His parents were constructing a memorial to Acland—such volumes were commonplace then. Boy, who had just left Gwen's room, had promised her to paste in the most recent letters. They, too, were there in his hands, a batch of black-edged envelopes.

When Boy came in, Constance rose to her feet. She inquired what time it was, for her watch was always slow, and—on being told it was almost three—began to edge toward the door. Boy did not greet her; he regarded her, Jane thought, in a hangdog way, his head slightly bent, his eyes averted.

Without warning, Constance sprang at him. To Jane's consternation she snatched the black album from his hands. She threw it upon the floor; the binding broke; black-edged letters scattered. Constance's face was as white as wax; there were two brilliant round spots of red in her cheeks.

"Oh, why must you read that thing? I hate it. It's morbid. This whole house is morbid. You can't breathe in this house—and Acland would loathe it every bit as much as I do. Leave them, Francis—"

Boy had bent toward the scattered letters. When Constance spoke his name, he flinched; he remained bent, hand still extended.

"Oh, for God's sake—do you think a lot of pious letters will bring your brother back? I've read them and I know—none of them write about Acland as he was. He's dull and sensible and painstaking and honorable when they write—all the things they think he ought to have been, all the things he never was! Those letters are lies, and your brother is dead. It's over. It's done with. I can't breathe here. I'm going out." She slammed the door behind her.

Boy lifted one hand to his face, as if Constance had struck him. Then he began, in a quiet way, to pick up the letters.

"She's broken the spine," he said.

"Boy, she didn't mean it." Jane bent to help him. "She's upset. She grieves, too, you know, in her way."

"I could try to stick it, I suppose. I don't know if it will hold." Boy straightened. "It will hurt Mama. She ordered this specially."

"Boy, leave it for now. Look—it's such a fine day. Why don't we go for a walk? We could go to the park. It would do us both good. I don't have to be back at the hospital yet—"

"All right." Boy continued to finger the album. He ran his thumb along the spine; he bent the torn leather forward, then back; he traced the gold letters of his brother's name.

"It won't mend." He shook his head—his new mannerism, which Jane found mildly irritating—as if he had water lodged in his ear. He set the album down on a side table.

"She shouldn't have done that. It was a wicked thing to do. I hate her when she's like that—"

"Boy—"

"All right. As you say. It is a fine day. Perhaps a walk in the park."

So, that afternoon in July (a time of year when, in peacetime, the Cavendish family would have avoided London) Constance walked in her direction, Jane and Boy in theirs.

Less than a mile apart. It was very hot. The air in the city was sticky and tight, as if the streets were a kettle, and the sky a lid.

Constance walked to Albany. She pretended to herself, at first, that she did not. She pretended to walk to Smythson's for Gwen's writing paper, a promised errand. Then she pretended she needed to examine the shop windows of the Burlington Arcade, and indeed she examined those windows with close attention, though she saw nothing of what they contained.

Then, in a casual way, a strolling way, her small handbag and her small parcel swinging from her wrist, she walked the short distance from the arcade to Albany itself. She looked up at that discreet and desirable building—a smart address. She wondered on which floor Montague Stern kept his rooms, whether he was still there, at half past three, whether he overlooked the place where she waited.

She could always walk in. She could inquire. She could leave a note. A lady might not be expected to do any of these things, but she could do them. Prudence? Reputation? She cared nothing for them. She could go in. She could stay here.

She swung her little handbag back and forth; she let the minutes tick by.

Constance had seen Montague Stern on several occasions since that day at Maud's, for he visited Park Street no less than three times a week. When he visited, and they met, Stern gave no sign of remembering what had taken place. The embrace, his note: they might never have happened.

It occurred to Constance that he might have put the matter from his mind; perhaps he was merely being discreet. On the other hand he might intend to pique her curiosity and her vanity. Which?

To meet, or not to meet? The decision was left with her, apparently. Constance swung her bag; she scanned bricks, glass.

She would not go in; she would leave no message. With a defiant air Constance turned and retraced her steps.

The air felt fresher; she increased her pace. Back toward Park Street, and Gwen, and a house where she could not breathe. Her home. As she approached it, she glimpsed the figures of Boy and Jane in the distance. They were arm in arm; Jane carried a parasol. They turned into the park.

Inside the house, Constance repented. She fetched glue, cardboard, a tube of Steenie's paints. She repaired the album for Acland. She strengthened the new join with the cardboard. She glued the spine back into place. She touched up the edges with the paint, so the frays in the leather should not show.

She tested her handiwork. The album was heavy, and the strain on the damaged spine considerable. Even so, she thought it might hold, for she had deft hands and had done the work well.

In the park they made for the Serpentine. There was a breeze there; the light was soft; people rowed on the water. After a while Boy led them toward a seat in the shade of a plane tree, and they sat down. Boy continued to gaze at the rowboats; he seemed morose and preoccupied, certainly disinclined for speech, but Jane did not mind this. It gave her time to prepare herself.

There were many things she would have liked to explain to Boy; some of them were small things, perhaps stupid things. She would have liked to tell him why she cut her hair, and how her hair made her feel brave. She would have liked to tell him about that mannerism with her hands, how she had noted it and decided to cure it. She would have liked to tell him about the boy Tom, who had recovered and returned home. She would have liked, above all, to make him understand what it had meant to her to be a nurse, and how—because of that, and because Acland was dead—she had decided: She was going to change her life.

There it was in her hands: a piece of clay. She could shape it. She would not be shaped by others any longer. She glanced toward Boy as she thought this, and saw he frowned, possibly daydreamed. She had half an hour at most. She must come straight to the point.

"Boy." She cleared her throat. Her hands jerked in her lap, and she clasped them.

"Boy. I brought you here because I want to ask you something. I want to ask you to release me from our engagement." There! It was said. Boy turned to her with a blank look.

"Release you?"

"I think we should end it, Boy. You know, in some ways we should never have embarked upon it. No, please listen, Boy, and hear me out. It's better if we are honest with each other. We like each other, I think. We respect each other. But we do not love each other, and we never did. It was an arranged thing." Jane drew in a deep breath. "You did it to please your father. I did it . . . because I was afraid to be a spinster. There! That's the whole truth of it, Boy. And look at it—look how foolish we've been. It's gone on and on, postponed until you finished Sandhurst, postponed again when my father died, postponed a third time when the war came. Boy, we'd go on postponing it forever if we could—you know that. All it does is make us both unhappy. So, please, Boy, may we not end it and be friends? You know—when the war is over—I feel sure you will meet someone else then, someone you love and truly wish to marry. Isn't it better to admit our mistake now—to be honest sooner, not later?"

"You don't want to marry me?" Boy was looking at her, Jane felt, in a most curious way.

"No, Boy, I don't," she replied, as firmly as she could. "And you don't want to marry me either."

"You're sure of this?"

"Absolutely sure. This is not an impulse."

"Well." Boy sighed. He gave a shake of the head. "If you put it like that, I suppose I have no option."

The alacrity with which this was said surprised Jane, who—knowing Boy to be stubborn—had expected more argument. There was also a lack of grace in the way he spoke, and this surprised her, too, for Boy had excellent manners. He was looking at her intently, his eyes fixed somewhere on the bridge of her nose. Jane had the impression he did not see her at all, but looked through her and beyond. Whatever he saw there seemed to evoke mixed feelings: Boy looked anxious, gratified yet fearful, and a touch smug. After a silence he turned back to the lake. Jane, expecting him to make a few conventional remarks about a continuing friendship, a continuing and unaltered esteem, waited. She felt she had done her part. Boy said none of the conventional things she expected. He seemed to ponder the matter, or possibly to count the rowboats. He remarked that it would be difficult to explain to his father.

"Would people need to know, do you think? Would they need to know at once? I go back to France tomorrow."

This, Jane had anticipated; she was firm. She would tell Gwen, but Boy must tell his father. He must tell him at once, that night. Only then could Jane continue to visit the house without hypocrisy or misunderstandings.

"Papa will be furious." Boy shook his head. He touched his ear, and wiggled it.

"Initially, perhaps. But it won't last. He'll come to accept it in time. Boy, you can't let him rule your life."

"It's just that he's so set on it. He always was."

"I know. Because of the estates, I think. He might have liked to see them joined." Jane hesitated. She reached across and laid her hand on his arm.

"Boy, if it will help, you can tell him that would not happen in any case. I've decided—I've almost decided—to sell."

"Sell?" Boy turned to her in astonishment.

"Oh—don't you see, Boy? Why not?" Jane tightened her grip on his arm. Her cheeks flushed. "I've been thinking about it so long. Why hang on to that huge house, all that land? I don't even want to farm it—I know nothing of farming. Boy, think: Do you know what that land is worth? Even now, with the price of land low, it's worth a great deal. Think, Boy, what I could do with that money! There are so many organizations crying out for funds. It could do such good! Clinics, for instance. Just the price of two fields would be enough to set up a clinic. Three fields, and you'd have a supply of medicines. Boy, some of the people I nurse—they have things wrong with them that have been curable for years. They have rickets, for instance, because they can't afford the right food. Or they contract tuberculosis because their houses are damp and cold. I know you can't cure their lungs, but cold and damp can be cured, Boy. You can cure them with money. . . ."

This was Jane's vision. It made her words race and her eyes brighten. She spoke of it with an excitement she could not disguise. It was some while, well into her speech, before she realized that Boy was regarding her with gentle distaste. Jane broke off. Her hand faltered to her mouth. Boy patted her arm.

"I say, you are worked up. Slow down a bit, don't you think?"

"Slow down? Why should I slow down?"

"Well, you're a woman, for one thing. Women are not usually endowed with a good business sense—they haven't had the training. Besides, it's a big step. A very big step. After all, your father loved that place—"

"Boy. My father is dead."

"And then you have to be practical. Clinics, medicine—that's all very well. I've nothing against them. But what about yourself? What about investments? Presumably you want to ensure you had something to live on—"

"When I'm an old spinster, you mean?"

"No, no, of course not. That wasn't what I meant at all. I just meant—well, that you must be practical. You ought to take advice—sound advice, financial advice . . ."

Male advice, Jane thought. "I already have. I discussed the matter with Montague Stern, as it happens. Just in a very general way. He advised me to wait, for the present. But he saw no reason not to sell in the long term. He said he was certain I could find a buyer, and at a more than reasonable price—"

"Oh, well, if you've talked to Stern." Boy sounded annoyed. "If you're prepared to take that man's advice . . ." He rose.

"Is there something wrong with his advice?"

Boy shrugged. "There are . . . rumors. There always were. You can't ignore his race. Shall we go back?"

He held out his arm. Jane rose. She took his arm, which made her angry with herself. They turned back toward the path.

One hundred yards in complete silence. Boy seemed unconcerned. He was back inside himself, protected by his uniform: male, mysterious, possibly anxious, possibly morose.

"Was it here?"

He spoke for the first time as they moved toward one of the park gates. The sudden question startled Jane.

"Was what here?"

"The accident to Constance's dog. Floss. You remember. Was it here?"

Jane looked about her. She gestured behind them, toward the sand track.

"Yes. Just over there. It was very quick."

"It always is."

Boy turned away. He began to walk again. His cap brim shaded his face and his eyes.

"Why do you ask, Boy?"

"Oh, I don't know." Boy jiggled at his ear. "I gave her the dog. She wrote to me about it, you know. And then she was ill. . . . No reason—I'd just like to picture it, that's all."

Boy was courageous enough in war, but he was afraid of his father; he told him of his broken engagement, but he took the coward's way out. He delayed the interview to the following morning. He timed it so that once the news was given, he would have to leave for the station and his train to the Channel port almost immediately. No time for rage. He faced his father in his father's study. Denton sat by a fire, with a rug across his knees. He seemed displeased to be interrupted; he was writing to generals and brigadiers.

These men—to whom Denton now wrote every day—were all old. They were history! They had served in battles now remote enough to be in schoolbooks: This one had fought in the Crimea; that one had lost an arm at Sebastopol; yet another had survived the siege of Lucknow and been a famous scourge of the Northwestern Frontier. These men had been Denton's father's contemporaries; he remembered them in all the splendor of their uniforms, when he was a small boy and they were the British Army's Young Turks. To Denton they were ageless. He wrote to them because he believed they still had power and influence. He wrote to them because he was sure one of them would make inquiries (at the highest level), write back, and reassure: There had been a mistake. There had been a typical army cock-up. They had sent the wrong telegram to the wrong family about the wrong man. It was all an error, and his son was still alive.

Many of these old men were dead; of those still alive, some replied. They wrote courteous, considerate letters from their retirement in Cheltenham or the English south coast. They regretted they could not help. Denton was not deterred. He crossed out their names and moved on. He was already exhausting generals. The brigadiers, Boy knew, were the first stage of his defeat.

In his father's study, Boy looked at these letters with a sense of despair. He had seen the war. He had seen men shredded. He knew only too well what was likely to have happened to Acland. It seemed terrible to him that his father should delude himself in this way; he felt a bitter anger against Jane, who had forced him to give his father this second blow—now, at such a time. Nevertheless, he had promised. The information was duly spelled out.

Boy then discovered that Denton would not accept the reality of the broken engagement; it was no more actual than the death of Acland.

"A lovers' tiff," he pronounced, and plucked at the rug. Boy found the room insufferably hot. "A lovers' tiff. Nothing to make a song and dance about. You'll make it up."

This sounded like a prophecy, or possibly a command. Boy had begun to sweat.

"No, Papa," he replied, as firmly as he could. "There was no quarrel. We remain friends. But it is decided. There is no going back."

"Time you left." His father picked up his pen. "Pass me the blotting paper."

Boy knew when he was dismissed. He left the room. He was agitated. He paced up and down the black-and-white flagstones of the hall. He looked up the vertiginous well of the staircase, past the four landings to the yellowish glass dome that surmounted it. Boy felt dizzy.

His bags lay packed in the hall; his father's ghostly Rolls waited outside the door to convey him to the station; his farewells to his mother and to Freddie were said. Freddie had already left for his ambulance duty. In Boy's pocket was a small leather box containing Jane's engagement ring, which, the previous afternoon, she had returned to him.

Boy juggled this box in his pocket; he shook his head and pulled at his ears. He did not know what to do with the box. Take it with him, or leave it here? It seemed a decision he could not make. He paced up and down twice more. He did a thing he had not done since childhood: He navigated the expanse of the hall one way on the white stones; he navigated it back on the black ones. Steenie came racketing down the stairs.

"Where's Constance?" Boy said. As soon as the words were pronounced he knew that was why he paced: The words needed to be said.

Steenie fluttered about the hall, gathering up letters, a long scarf, a walking stick with a silver head, a pair of gloves whose color made Boy shudder. He gave Boy a curious look, and a suspiciously pink smile.

"Connie? She's out."

"Out?" Boy felt aggrieved. Military engagements awaited him. His return to the war surely deserved more ceremony than an empty hall and a distracted brother.

"Boy, honestly! Your memory is like a sieve! Connie said good-bye at breakfast." Steenie fiddled with his gloves. He put them on. He smoothed supple yellow pigskin against his fingers.

"I need to speak to her. Out where?"

"*Aren't* these divine?" Steenie was still admiring the gloves. "I only bought them yesterday. Now, Boy, I must rush. No long farewells—I hate them."

Steenie hesitated. It occurred to Boy that, beneath the fuss with the gloves, Steenie was embarrassed. They looked at each other. Steenie tossed his scarf over his shoulder. He moved toward the door. Steenie had a new way of walking that Boy distrusted, a walk that resembled a glide, the hips advancing, the upper part of his torso at an exaggerated angle, leaning back. He touched the doorknob, turned back. He laid one yellow-gloved hand on Boy's uniformed arm.

"Boy, I shall think of you. And I will write. You know I always write. You will take care?"

Boy did not quite know what to do. He was touched, for it was true that Steenie did write, often; his letters were long, amusing, undaunted, decorated with drawings. Boy, who read and reread them in the trenches, had found—somewhat to his surprise—that they were comforting. Oblique—but comforting. He felt he might like to embrace his brother, but, in the end, he shook his hand. A military handshake; his eyes watered.

Steenie always fenced with emotion. He at once backed off. *En garde:* quick glittering blocking swishes of his foil. He made one, two, three inconsequential remarks: the weather, the waiting motorcar, his impending visit to a new gallery.

These remarks shamed Steenie, a little. Boy stood on a white stone flag; he stood on a black one: he saw himself and his brother from a distance, two figures on a chessboard, blocked. Boy could not say what he felt, because he believed it right to be manly; Steenie could not say what he felt, because he distrusted the spoken word. As he had said to Wexton, it was always too approximate. With this, Wexton did not agree.

"How absurd we are," Steenie said, foil glittering. Then, repenting, he made a rush at Boy and gave him a hug.

Steenie was wearing scent; Boy recoiled.

"I'll give Connie a message if you like." Steenie was repenting still.

Boy picked up one of his bags and inspected the label on it. "No. It doesn't matter. It was nothing important." Boy continued to inspect the label, as if it contained some secret message. It was addressed by rank and title, followed by numbers.

"Where is she anyway?" He straightened up.

"She's gone to Jenna's wedding. Boy—you know that."

Steenie knew he was about to burst into tears. When Steenie cried he made an exhibition of himself: The tears spouted; they smudged his mascara; they made runnels in the rice powder he applied to his cheeks. He distrusted tears as much as words; he knew he cried too easily.

Meanwhile it was possible—always possible—that he would not see his brother again.

Steenie made another rush, this time for the front door. He called his final goodbye over his shoulder.

"It was terrible," he said to Wexton some while later. "Boy can't say what he feels, and neither can I. What's *wrong* with us, Wexton? I do love him, you know."

Wexton smiled. "I expect he's noticed," he said.

The wedding was in a church. (Jane did not believe in registry offices.) The church was south of the river, august Victorian gothic, an island surrounded by slums. The church was cold: as cold as charity, Constance thought. An English summer could not be relied upon: Outside, the weather was squally.

The congregation was sparse. On the bride's side of the aisle sat Jane and Constance, side by side in a front pew. Constance's small feet rested on a tapestry hassock. She sat and flicked at the prayer book; Jane knelt and—presumably—prayed.

On the bridegroom's side of the aisle there was a better turnout. Hennessy's family was not present. He was represented by the Tubbs family, out in force. There was one large woman with a worn but kind face, and several girls of varying ages who must be Arthur Tubbs's younger sisters. There were five of them; the youngest was about four years old, the eldest about fifteen. The fifteen-year-old, Jane had whispered, was Florrie, with whom Jenna shared a room. Florrie worked nearby, packing shells in a munitions factory that was one of several south of the river owned by Sir Montague Stern.

Florrie looked thin and jaundiced; her skin was yellowish. Like the rest of the family, she wore serge. On her feet were buttoned boots, which looked several sizes too large. The youngest child wore woolen mittens with the fingers cut out. All looked excited. To the serge, they had pinned nosegays. Constance sniffed; she could smell poverty. It emanated not just from the Tubbs family but from the church itself, which had an air of keeping up appearances in grinding circumstances.

Once, perhaps, more prosperous families had worshipped here. Ranks of stained-glass saints and dragon-slayers celebrated their memory and their acts of piety; there were neat slabs commemorating them upon the walls. Constance could hear their ghosts, these merchantmen and their wives; she heard the men rustle the pages of their hymn books; their beards brushed her cheek.

Outside, the streets stank. The houses had a bowed, hopeless look, cramped in upon one another, seething. The children ran in the stinking streets in bare feet; they made toys from rubbish. These streets shocked Constance (who rarely ventured far south of the park, let alone the river). She felt they shocked the fabric of the church also, but in a different way. The church was affronted by this decline in the neighborhood; it reared up its black iron railings, the granite of its headstones; it slammed its great oak doors. It turned its back. It did its best; it smelled of incense, but also scrubbing buckets. There were two arrangements of flowers, provided by Jane. They stood either side of the altar, framing the backs of the bridegroom and best man. Dahlias, with large spiky heads and stiff stalks; they were orange and scarlet, acid-yellow and ineptly arranged. Constance looked at them with hatred.

Hennessy and Tubbs: they had both made an effort, that was clear. They had arrived on the overnight train from Yorkshire that morning; they would return on a train that afternoon. Jack Hennessy wore the uniform of a private; Arthur Tubbs, that of a corporal. Hennessy's uniform was spruce. His khaki jacket strained across the muscles of his back; the toes of his army boots were mirrors. The back of his neck looked raw—a severe army haircut; there was a shaving gash on his cheek. They made an incongruous pair: Hennessy so massive, Tubbs so shrunken. Tubbs was fluent as a weasel; his hair, parted in the middle, was smarmed with grease. He sported a new moustache; traces of the acne remained.

Of the two, it was Tubbs who appeared the more nervous. He fingered the wisp of moustache; he craned his head back and forth; he winked at his mother and his sisters; he shifted from foot to foot. Tubbs was a coming man (though Constance of course did not know that). Tubbs would do well out of the war: His expertise in supplies would become adroit; he would learn about markets, black and white; he would come to understand the poetry of supply and demand. After the war, Arthur Tubbs would rise; Jack Hennessy would not. Coke, and the boiler in the basement that ate pound notes, lay in wait for Hennessy, whose instincts were feudal.

Hennessy, meanwhile, was an impressive bridegroom. No sign of nerves: He stood ramrod straight; he did not turn once. A tree of a man, an oak of a man. Constance looked at his rigid back. Hennessy, who used to catch butterflies and put them in matchboxes. Once he showed her a stag beetle and pulled off one of its legs, so that it ran around in a circle. With such diversions Hennessy had entertained Constance Cross the albatross.

The asthmatic organ changed key; it made a new attack to herald the entrance of the bride. Still Hennessy did not turn around. Jenna was wearing gray, not white (Jane had paid for her dress). It was of soft material, gathered across the front to disguise the alteration in her figure. She came up the aisle on the arm of a small rusty old man, presumably another member of the Tubbs family, for as he passed them, the rusty old man winked. A steady pace. Jenna held her chin high; she looked neither to right nor left. She was carrying, Constance saw, a bouquet of violets.

Violets were cheap, easily available on any street corner, and perhaps therefore predictable. Nevertheless, they made Constance angry too. The ghosts in the church shifted and shuffled; they whispered about the violets; they snuffed at their scent of damp earth. Jenna had reached the altar rail. The priest drooped within vestments too big. Jenna faltered once as—for the first time—Hennessy turned.

How the anger sang! Constance knew she ought to clamp down on it now, quickly, but she did not want to clamp—she wanted to let it rip. There was lightning in her fingertips; her hair burned; she tasted smoke; her heels drummed. Acland's baby was being given away.

One person was missing from this congregation, and that person was Acland himself. Constance waited for him to join the other ghosts. She waited for him to stop this terrible ceremony. When he did not come (of course he would not; he had come once only, to her, to say goodbye) her anger rebelled. It made a chaos of this church: It took up the tiles from the floor and hurled them about in the air; it whistled and hooted its revolution; it made barricades of the pews and burned down the altar rails.

Constance looked up: up, up, up. Above the arches of the nave, above the clerestory windows, up to the spandrels and the curvatures of the roof. A dark place, full of words and whispers, they whirled with the most violent energy.

They brushed her skin. Constance gave a small cry; she would not stay. It was too wicked and too terrible. Easy to leave. Snap the prayer book shut. Kick the hassock. Tap the heels and the toes on the tesselated floor. Down the side aisle, past the monuments, past the poor box, past the font. The porch door was heavy. Its hinges screamed. Constance was outside on the steps. The rain still fell. The wind blew paper along the street. London wept.

Constance lifted her face to its tears. She breathed in great gusts of its air. She tasted salt and soot. She remained absolutely still—that was necessary—until the anger left her.

It did not want to go. It was like an incubus. It liked it inside her. It clutched and it clung. It insinuated itself into her veins. It pounded its fists in her head and made it ache. It drummed its heels up and down inside her lungs. It became soft, and the sponge of her lungs soaked it up.

It could be willed away; she had willed it away before. Constance closed her eyes and concentrated her mind. She gathered the ugly incubus into a bundle, a malevolent amorphous thing, a crafty thing, dwarfish and sly. It resisted being gathered, but she could do it. Tentacle by tentacle: there it was. She could feel it: It was lumpish. She forced it down, out, and away. It was like giving birth, getting rid of the thing. It stuck. Its lumpishness jammed her up. It clung to her.

"Get out, get out, get out." Constance said the words aloud. The thing gave a knotty and reluctant consent. It bunched, squirmed, clung, gave up.

It was gone. She could breathe again. Constance hugged her arms around herself. She began to see again. The city righted itself. The sky stopped weeping. She felt very pure. She was like an empty purse, a hollow shell; she rejoiced in the emptiness. It made her feel cleansed and perfectly light. A light, pure, clean, empty thing. Dry as a nutshell, light as a feather, capable of flight.

She stood very still upon the steps. No sound came through the heavy door of the church. She walked back and forth upon the steps in such a way that someone watching her might have thought she tried to come to a decision. Back and forth.

Then she stopped. Apparently the decision was made.

She carried an umbrella, which she then raised. Almost immediately she closed it again. She ran down the flight of steps. Acland told her to go on, so she sped along the wet pavements. Her feet pattered. Acland encouraged. The stones shone.

Along the street, around the corner, and she was on a bridge. She looked down and watched the Thames flow. A gray river, that day, deep and tidal. Farther up there was a landing wharf; the water was clotted with boats: a coal barge, two tugs, a ferryboat, a steam launch. Constance looked down at the river for a precise length of time: seventeen minutes, one for each year of her life. Stop, or go on.

A cab was passing. Constance, unused to hailing cabs, contrived to stop this one.

It smelled of hair oil and tobacco. There was a newspaper full of war left behind on the seat.

Constance climbed into the back without giving the driver directions. The engine idled; it made the vehicle shake.

She leaned forward and tapped on the glass partition. When the driver pushed it back she told him to take her to Albany, although she was quite aware it was morning still, and four hours till three o'clock.

When they came into the bedroom Jenna shared with Florrie—she and Jack Hennessy, alone for the first and last time that day—Hennessy said three things. They frightened her. He said: "Was it just the once?" He shook her when he said it, catching hold of her very suddenly and shaking her so hard it made her teeth clash. Jenna did not answer him. Hennessy seemed not to notice her silence. He said the next thing.

He said: "You done it before. It wasn't the first time. You've been dirty, you have. Dirty little bitch."

He took a gulp of air. He said the third thing. He said: "I know. I set that trap for him. When I heard he was dead, I thanked God. I hope he rots. I hope the rats get him."

He said these things very fast. The words were wet and hot, like his eyes; it seemed a physical effort for him to get them out past his teeth and his lips and his tongue. He shook with the effort; his skin glinted with sweat. The words seemed to give him pain, and pleasure; Jenna thought he looked like a man having sex. He grunted and turned away; his shoulders slumped. Jenna felt sick.

She knew she had to be careful—she had known that before they even came into the room. So she was careful with his words now. She edged away from him and, since there was no chair, sat down upon the bed. Her child moved in her womb. She looked at the words; she unpicked them; she stitched them together again. She told herself that they could not mean what she thought they meant; they must mean something else. A trap.

Jack Hennessy had begun to walk up and down in the small room. Its ceiling sloped, and he had to duck his handsome head to do so, but he seemed hardly to notice that. Back and forth, up and down. The floor of the room was bare scrubbed boards. There was one strip of coconut matting. Hennessy walked up and down this strip, like an animal in a cage at a zoo. He did not look at her. His hands were thrust into his pockets.

In her hand, Jenna held an orange. She looked down at it. She concentrated her eyes and her mind upon it, thinking that the orange might make his words go away. The orange had been provided by Mrs. Tubbs. It was a great extravagance, but Mrs. Tubbs said the children liked them; they always had oranges for Christmas, birthdays, and weddings.

They had also had, for the wedding breakfast, a bridal cake, round pies filled with steak and kidney, jellied eels, saucers of mussels and cockles doused in vinegar, a trifle decorated with crystallized violets, stout for the men, and a drop of gin for the ladies.

Jenna had eaten one pie, a spoonful of trifle. She had speared one cockle on a pin and swallowed it. It was rubbery and sour. The cake was rich and sweet; the icing pierced her teeth. Mrs. Tubbs was ribald—also kind. She knew there was something wrong with this wedding, and that made her kinder still. "Now, Arthur," she said, "let those two lovebirds alone. They've had enough of your stories. Give over. They want to be alone."

She had almost managed conviction. Jenna had been touched by that. She knew she did not look like a lovebird of any kind. They had gone upstairs obediently, and Jenna had taken her precious orange with her. It was wrapped in silver paper; when she eased the paper back and pressed her nail against the peel, the juice spurted. It was sticky on her fingers. It smelled tangy; it was as sharp as the sun.

She did not know Hennessy at all, of course. She had known that as soon as she walked into the church. There he was, familiar in every respect; she was acquainted with each hair of his head and each pore of his skin. She knew his voice, she recognized the deliberation of his hands, there were no surprises in his eyes—and yet he was a stranger. She was about to marry a man she had known since she was born, whom she had never met in her life.

She had almost wavered then. But her child kicked. She had walked on.

Jenna had been eight when her mother died, and Mrs. Hennessy, who had four sons and craved a daughter, had taken her in. The other three sons, all large like Jack, were boisterous. He was not. He liked to be on the edge. To sit at the edge of a room or the edge of a group. He always stationed himself near a door when inside, and when outside, would linger, delay, then—without explanation—peel off from the group. He liked to walk alone. He preferred to eat alone, when he could. He liked to drink alone, too, though this was never discussed. He went on binges, which might last for as long as two days, and then he would return and sit on the edge of the room again. He binged, and returned sullen.

He was slow. Some of the people in the village said he was simple. They would touch their foreheads in a meaningful way. Simple, but harmless, and a hard worker.

He could fell even quite large trees single-handed; he had been known to work eight hours in the sawpit. He liked to sand wood down, and he would do it religiously, rubbing, rubbing, rubbing until the surface was as silky as driftwood.

He smelled. He smelled now—of the sweetness of stout, of damp khaki, of sweat. Jenna thought that perhaps he knew he smelled, for he washed constantly—every morning and every night when he got back from work. His brothers might be lazy; Jack was not.

Washing was a performance: His mother had to boil water and carry it steaming out to the back scullery. Hennessy would strip to the waist. He immersed his head in the water; he soaped his thick arms, his huge shoulders, his chest, his back. He rubbed at his armpits. He sniffed at them. He splashed water all over the floor, which was earth, and left a muddy mess for his mother to clean up after him.

He would emerge: lean, muscled, anointed, gleaming, and his mother would hand him a clean shirt. He would stand by the door of the back parlor and button it up, slowly. His mother would make little rushing conciliatory movements, smoothing the sleeve, stroking out an invisible crease, and Jenna would sit by the fire and watch him. She thought Hennessy liked to be watched. She thought his mother was hurt when people said her eldest son was simple. She also thought his mother was afraid of him.

A hulk of a man. A man of few words, his mother used to say. When she was small, he fascinated Jenna: She could not understand how a man so large and so strong could also be so gentle. And he could be gentle; he was always gentle with her. He used to take her for walks. He held her hand and never crushed it. He picked flowers for her. He knew their names: lady's-smock; wake-robin; scarlet pimpernel; Queen Anne's lace. She liked him.

Going for walks, and walking-out. It was a crucial distinction. She and Jack Hennessy had passed from the one to the other without comment. She admired this reticence in him. He was teased by his brothers, who said he was gone on her. Hennessy ignored this, and she admired that too. Hennessy had dignity. He declared his affection for her once, and once only, when she was fourteen years old. Out of his habitual and brooding silence came a wellspring of words, which were not without eloquence.

He said she had him there in the palm of his hand, and always had, and always would do. He said he kissed the ground she walked on. He said he gave her his heart. He said he would die for her. He said, "You're mine, Jen. I always knew it."

His eyes swallowed her up. They looked hungry and anxious. They beseeched her and they commanded her. She knew people laughed at him. She felt sorry for him. He put his arm around her waist. It was the only time he touched her, ever; he said she was not like other girls, that she was decent, that was why—but all the same Jenna thought it was odd. She had expected him to kiss her.

She might have married him in any case—there was a part of Jenna that would not fight, a part that drifted, and clung to the familiar: to Mrs. Hennessy and the Hennessy house and the companionship of Hennessy's brothers. She might have settled for that. Then Acland happened.

After which, Hennessy was an alibi. She knew she used him, but she told herself she was scrupulous. She was kind to him. She talked to him. She never laughed at him. She was not required to lie—or, rather, she lied only by omission. Hennessy never asked her if she loved him, for he had always seemed to assume she must; there it was, weighty in his eyes: fate, destiny. Sometimes this made Jenna rebel. She resented the assumption and felt she wanted to slap it down and wriggle free of it. She never did. She let Hennessy assume—it was safer that way. It made for a better alibi.

Hennessy could not be hurt by what he did not know, Jenna had told herself then, as people do. She knew it was an evasion, and the evasion would set off small flurries of guilt. The guilt, in a way, made it worse—for when she was most guilty, she was also most kind.

And now she was married to him. There was a baby in her womb and a ring on her finger, and an orange in her hand.

Hennessy was still pacing the coconut matting.

Jenna examined the orange. She smoothed the silver paper. She unstitched Hennessy's three statements, then stitched them together once more. They frightened her very much. This stranger she had married was violent. He was not so simple, or so slow. He knew.

"Was it just the once?"

Hennessy said those words again. They came at Jenna out of the silence and the creaking of floorboards; they made her jump.

They did not fit with his other words, but they gave Jenna hope. She could see it in front of her face, opening out: the possibility of a lie.

Well, she had prepared a lie. She had coached herself. She had the words pat.

Hennessy lowered himself onto the bed near her. Its springs sagged beneath his weight. He sat upright, staring straight ahead. He seemed to be waiting for the lie, and so Jenna began on it. It was as close to the truth as she could make it (scrupulous again). There had been a soldier; it was her night off; she took one drink too many; it was . . . just the once.

A soldier—that was true anyway. Jenna did not find it easy to lie. She knew the fabric of the story was threadbare, and so, in an effort to make it stronger, she repeated the lie, once, twice, a third time: just a soldier, just a mistake, just the once. It was some time before she realized that, somewhere in this tangle of sentences, Hennessy had begun to cry.

He attempted to stop himself. When that did not work, he took gasps of breath, which made him shudder. He rubbed his knuckles in his eyes like a child. Jenna was shaken and appalled.

"Jack. Jack. Don't take on so. It makes me ashamed," she said. She moved closer to him and, in an awkward way, put her arms about his neck.

This seemed to quiet Hennessy. He became still. He took her hand in his and looked at it.

"I put that trap there. Did you guess? I put it there for him." Out came the words. He continued to stare at her hand.

"What trap, Jack?" Jenna said. She was very afraid.

"You know what trap. You know right enough. It wasn't in use. It was all rusted in one of the sheds—but it worked. I tested it. I thought . . . I don't know what I thought. I could see him in it. I could see that very clear—him, in his fine clothes, all torn. I wanted that. Only maybe I didn't want it, because I set it wrong, set it in the wrong place, caught the wrong man. I put it by the clearing. If I'd wanted him in it, really wanted it, I'd have put it where you met."

"Where I met?"

"Where you met him. In the birch grove. I'd have set it there. That's what I meant to do, I think. Only I didn't. I could have pushed him in it—easy. I could have done that. No more than smiting a fly. Killing a rabbit—as easy as that. He was tall, but he was thin. A gentleman. Not a lot of strength. I could have done it. I wanted to. I hated him, Jen."

He had gripped her wrists. The orange fell from her hand. Jenna watched it roll across the floor. When she spoke she was proud of her voice: It was steady.

"Who knows this, Jack?"

"No one. Only you. Mr. Cattermole—I think he guessed. Not many men could move that thing, not on their own. Maybe he added two and two and made five. Maybe. But he never said. He wouldn't know why, anyhow. Only you know that. I didn't mean harm—not by the next day, I didn't. I watched that comet. I saw you, sneaking off. I drank a lot. I don't remember that night. But I went back the next morning, first thing. I would have moved it. Only it was too late. That man was in it by then. Mr. Cattermole was there. The dogs were barking. He sent me up to the house."

He bent his head as he said this. He opened Jenna's palm and looked at the lines on her palm. He touched her palm with a finger, which was callused.

"I saw." He closed her fingers over his. "I saw. You and him. You didn't ought to have done it, Jen. Not you. Not when I loved you the way I did. So, you tell me now." He lifted his head for the first time and looked her in the eyes. "Don't you lie. You swear. Put your hand on your stomach. On the bulge. On its head. Swear by that. Is it his child? Is it?"

Jenna placed her hand across her stomach. Her baby rippled. Jack Hennessy's hand was now clenched in a fist. His face was clenched. His eyes were hot and wet. They struck at her. She could see him, striking her. One fist to the womb. A single blow would be enough.

"No, Jack. It's not his child." She was proud of her voice again. No wavering. "That was over. Years ago. I'm telling you the truth. It was a soldier. I met him in the park. He took me to a hotel at Charing Cross. I don't know why I went. I just did. We took a room for an hour. You can do that now. If the man's in uniform, they make allowances."

"You had a drink?"

"Yes. I had a drink. He bought it. A glass of . . . gin. And water. It went right to my head."

"You wouldn't have, otherwise—not without the drink?"

"No, Jack."

"Was it quick?"

"Very quick."

"I don't touch women." He unclenched his fist. "The other men do. Arthur does. They line up for them. They *queue*. I wouldn't do that. I wouldn't touch them. They're diseased. I told Arthur, but he won't listen." He stopped, cleared his throat. "I kept myself for you, Jen. I always did."

"Jack—"

"We'll be all right, we will. I had time, see, to think it all out, after you wrote. I couldn't get it quite straight in my mind, not first off. But I see it now. He's dead, after all. When the war's over . . . it will be all right then. We'll go back to the village, just the two of us, the way I always planned, and— "

"The three of us, Jack."

"You know that cottage? The one I always had my eye on, down by the river? They'd let us have that, I reckon. After the war. My father's getting on. I could be head carpenter a few years from now. We could make that cottage a pretty place. There's a nice bit of garden there—room for potatoes, runner beans, onions. No one living there in years. I always liked that place. You could be quiet there. I used to go down there and think. About you. You knew that, didn't you? You always knew you had me right there, in the palm of your hand."

As he said this, Hennessy took her left hand in his. Upon the third finger of this hand, there was now a wedding ring. It pinched. Jenna looked at the ring. She knew at once which cottage he meant: by the river, isolated—half-ruined, not inhabited for years. It was cold and damp in summer; in winter the road to it flooded. She hated that cottage. It was an unhealthy place. It was no place to bring up a baby.

"My granny's ring." Hennessy's hand closed upon it. His voice had become slightly hoarse. "My gran's. I kept that for you. I took it off her finger the day she died, and I kept it. Eight years, that is now."

She had hated his grandmother too. A bent woman, with gaps in her teeth. When she met Jenna, she used to pinch her cheeks.

"That's settled then?" Hennessy gave a sigh. "I want to get things settled before I go back. Then I can plan. You need something to plan, when you're out there. In the trenches. Waiting. It keeps you going. So, I'd like to be sure—"

"Sure?"

"My plans. The cottage. The bit of garden."

Jenna shifted under the weight of his gaze. She had not thought ahead, she said to herself. She had been so methodical and so careful, and she had never once thought where they might live.

"You do like it all right then? That cottage?"

"Oh, yes. Yes, Jack. Except—I don't remember it so well, but . . . it's right by the river, and come winter—"

She stopped. Hennessy's eyes had changed. It was there, then gone: something hard and triumphant, the gist of some pleasure.

He knew how she hated that place.

He hid it. The next second his eyelids were lowered. He wouldn't let her see the pleasure again. His face became tight with the effort of concealment. Jenna thought he might laugh, or he might cry again.

She was afraid of the gleam of pleasure. It frightened her more than anything he had said. Her mind swooped and darted; it tried to run away. *Oh, what have I done, what have I done?* she thought. She was terrified he might touch her. He was a handsome man, and he revolted her. His skin revolted her, his hair, his eyes.

"Before I go. Before I leave . . ."

Jenna thought he would touch her then. He would put a hand on her. He might stroke her. She drew back.

Hennessy did not touch her. He did not even look at her. He looked instead at his own hands, which lay on his khaki thighs: broad, square, capable hands. They were not without beauty.

"Before I go. Tell me again, Jen. It was in London?"

"Yes, Jack."

"Did you know his name?"

"Only his first name. It was . . . Henry. I think."

"He bought you a gin?"

"Yes. Yes. With water."

"A hotel by Charing Cross?"

"Yes . . . just . . . a small place. It was a brown room. You could hear the trains whistling."

"Was it quick?"

"Very quick."

On and on. He asked the questions, he listened to the replies, and then he asked them again.

At four o'clock Mrs. Tubbs knocked on the door. She made a great business of it. When they emerged she pretended to be coy.

She and Jenna stood in the front doorway; they waved; Hennessy and Tubbs walked away at a brisk pace. Their arms swung.

When they were out of sight Mrs. Tubbs shut the door. They went into the back parlor, a dark room. Mrs. Tubbs lit the gaslight. The light made Jenna's face blue; it stood out in peaks and shadows. Her mouth was slack with fatigue. Mrs. Tubbs gave her a long look. She took her arm. The pretense was over.

"Whatever it is, love," she said, "I hope you had the sense to keep it to yourself. Don't tell *him*." She gave a sharp jerk of the head in the direction of the front door. Mrs. Tubbs loved her son, but generally speaking she did not have a great opinion of men.

She fussed over Jenna. She had Florrie make a cup of tea. She tried to tempt her with trifle, with cake—she was eating for two, she reminded her. She fetched the last orange, divided it in two, offered half to Jenna and half to Florrie.

Jenna shook her head. Her baby stirred, then settled.

"Oh, well. Waste not, want not," Mrs. Tubbs declared. She spread her handkerchief on her lap and ate the half of the orange herself.

"Bless me!" she cried when the last segment was popped into her mouth.

Jenna had, while Mrs. Tubbs was eating her orange, removed her wedding ring.

In a deliberate and careful way she laid it down upon the hearthstone. She picked up the poker. She hit the ring with the poker. She hit it very hard, sure it would smash, but the ring did no such thing. The blow glanced; the ring sprang up, as if with a life of its own. It spun up in the air and came to rest upon the hearthrug. Florrie and Mrs. Tubbs stared at it.

"I hate that ring. It was his grandmother's. I hated her too." Jenna spoke in a reasonable tone of voice.

Mrs. Tubbs rose, retrieved the ring, and put it in her pocket. She looked at Jenna. She winked.

"Eighteen carat. I can tell by the color, see? A guinea, that's worth, maybe more. A guinea is two bags of coal. Two bags of coal is one fire for a week. Pop it."

"Pop it?"

"Pawn it, love. You can always get it back—and if you don't, well, just tell him you lost it. *He'll* believe you. Most likely."

Mrs. Tubbs sniffed. She was a direct woman, and so—despite the fact that Jenna was just married—she then touched her forehead.

"Slow," she said. "Good-looking, I'll say that. But not too quick on the uptake."

"You're wrong," Jenna replied. She rose, reached into Mrs. Tubbs's pocket, and extracted the ring.

She put it back again on her finger. She watched it wink.

"Well, Constance. That is interesting. A mystery solved." Stern paused. He moved to the window. "And when did you discover this?"

"This morning. I visit once a week, every week since her marriage. I am most religious in my concern. Poor Jenna! She looks ill. I took her some beautiful baby clothes. She broke down."

Constance, who had arrived in Stern's Albany chambers some fifteen minutes before, withdrew a large and glittering jet pin from her black hat. She tossed the hat upon a chair. One shake of the head, and her hair, only loosely pinned up, at once tumbled about her shoulders. Stern preferred it like this.

She eyed Stern, who had greeted her revelation about Hennessy in his customary dispassionate way. He looked out the window. Constance felt she could hear the filing cards click in his mind. Stern liked to be given information—Constance knew that, but she was careful to ration and to censor the information she gave: this, but not that!

"You see, Jenna once had a lover—this is years ago now—"

"A lover?" Stern looked back. "And who was that?"

"Oh, no one of any consequence—just some man from the village. Killed in the war, I believe, like everyone else. But Hennessy was jealous, it seems. Violently jealous. He knew where they met. So he set the trap for him—"

"And caught the wrong man?" Stern frowned. "It must have distressed you, Constance, to hear this."

"In a way." Constance moved off. She began, as she often did on the occasions when she came to Stern's Albany rooms, to pace about restlessly. She had been coming here for three months.

She paused behind a delicate table.

"However, it was a long time ago. The circumstances do not matter very much, when their effect is the same. It is too late now to do anything—I reassured Jenna of that. Let the matter rest. I had my suspicions before, in any case. Years ago . . . certain things Cattermole said. Anyway, I am not vengeful toward Hennessy. There was no time to think of myself. I was concerned, for Jenna—and her child. There is no one else she can turn to, now Jane leaves to nurse in France— and she looked so very drawn and thin. I was afraid for the baby—"

"You surprise me, Constance. I would not have suspected you of charitable intent."

"Oh, thank you, sir, for that estimate of my character." Constance gave Stern a pert look. "I have a heart somewhere, you know. It is a little hard, but it beats. But there—I would not expect a man to understand the closeness between mistress and maid. And you, of course, being unsentimental by nature, would have no concern for babies."

Stern gave her a cool glance. Constance moved away another pace. She took up her position behind a chair. She picked up from a table a small figure of jade, an exquisite thing.

"Besides," she went on in a thoughtful manner, "I discovered something interesting today about myself—that is why I tell you this story. Do you know why I forgive Hennessy so generously, Montague? It is because I understand jealousy. Oh, yes! It has crept up upon me, I think—yes, even upon me. Which is something I never expected."

She waited. Stern did not prompt her. Constance gave a small frown of irritation. He had kissed her hand when she entered this room; apart from that formal greeting, he had not yet touched her. He made her wait. Such a contained man! Constance turned the jade figure in her fingers.

"Tell me, Montague," she began again. "A jealous question now. Am I the first young woman to visit you here, or is this an established practice of yours?"

"Am I unfaithful to Maud? Is that what you're asking?" Stern folded his arms.

"I know you are not strictly faithful to Maud," Constance replied, with a dark look. "I have learned that these past months. But I wondered . . . if I was following a precedent. I find I might mind, if I were."

Stern gave a sigh. It sounded impatient.

"Constance, I have been faithful to Maud, as you put it, for some five or six years—with only a very few minor excursions. I am not a philanderer. I rather despise philanderers. I have not made it my practice to deceive Maud, nor do I like to deceive her now—"

"But you do?"

"Yes, I do."

"And I—am I just a minor excursion too?" Constance gave Stern her waif look.

"You, my dear, are more of a Grand Tour, as I'm sure you must know—"

"Oh, you are not just playing with me then?" Constance sighed. "You could be. Sometimes I feel that you are. I come here—I am so very careful about my alibis, no one suspects a thing. My heart beats so fast as I run up the street. And yet maybe I am no more to you than a game. I think that sometimes. I see you as a cat, Montague—a cat with very sharp claws—and myself as a little mouse. A pet for you. A plaything. You toy with me, but you wait to pounce—"

"What an unconvincing description." Stern smiled, but it was a fugitive smile. "I do not think of you in that way at all—as I am sure you must know. . . ."

"Ah, you say that, but is it true? How can I tell? I look at you and I see nothing at all, not a glimpse in the eyes of the slightest affection. You stand there with your arms folded so; you watch me, and you wait. I never know what you are thinking at all—"

"Am I so undemonstrative?" Stern said in a dry voice. "You surprise me, Constance. I thought I had given you the occasional indication—"

"Lust is something no man can disguise, Montague—not even you. In an embrace, its effects are obvious enough. So, I provoke that in you. It is not so very much—"

"On the contrary. It is not to be despised. Many women, of obvious charms, leave me entirely cold—"

"Oh, I see." Constance tossed her head. "In that case—"

"Whereas you—no, don't turn away, Constance—whereas you do provoke me, as you say. In many ways. Not all of them physical."

"Is that true?" Constance, who had made a pretty flounce toward the door, stopped. She looked back.

"But of course. My dear Constance, I have the very greatest respect for your intelligence, and for your willpower. I admire the deviousness of your approach. And I particularly admire the way in which you flirt. I find it charming and ingenious—"

"I hate you, Montague."

"I also find, just occasionally, that you protract it too long—which could make it tedious. Now, won't you stop this, and come here?"

Constance hesitated. There was a tension in the room, as there always was when they met, a tension partly sexual and partly combative. It drew her toward Stern with a force whose intensity she sometimes found alarming. She did not care for Stern to see how strong that pull was—and so, as he said, she would flirt and evade. Resistance! Constance loved these moments when they both delayed. They made her shiver with sexual expectation, as if she felt already on her skin the touch of Stern's cool and expert hands.

Expectation, however, needed to be tempered with caution. Constance might have felt happier were she surer of reading Stern's mind. Of this ability she was not certain at all. There was now in Stern's eyes (as there often was) an expression that made her wary. It was as if he knew, or understood, something that he kept from her—and that knowledge gave him the edge in their power struggle.

When Constance began these meetings with her pacings about the room, she sometimes felt she paced at the end of a silken tether. That tether was grasped firmly in Stern's hands. Constance resented this. Sometimes she feared it. Now, disobeying him, ignoring the tone of his voice—which alerted her body, which was like a note in her mind, clear and sharp as glass struck with a knife—she delayed. She consulted the small watch she wore pinned to the bosom of her black mourning dress. She remarked that the hour was late, her watch slow, that perhaps she ought to return home.

"Constance," Stern said again, cutting through these pretenses. He held out his hand to her. "Constance. Come here."

Stern rested his hand against her throat. He lifted her hair back from her shoulders and away from her face. At the touch of his hand on her neck, Constance gave one half-stifled cry, as if he had struck her.

She twisted into his arms and pressed herself against him. He was already hard. When she touched him, to confirm this, Stern—prudent even when aroused, circumspect even in desire—drew her to one side, away from the window.

He placed his hand upon her breast. He moved his fingers slowly back and forth across her nipple. He looked down into her face; when Constance could no longer disguise the excitement she felt, he kissed her.

Their tongues touched. When he released her, some five minutes more of their allotted time had passed. Constance was trembling. Her lower lip was swollen; there was a small cut—in the abandon of this embrace, Stern had drawn blood. He took out his handkerchief: clean, newly laundered white linen. He wrapped it about his finger. He pressed it against her cut lip.

When he removed it they both looked in silence at the small bright stain of blood.

"You make me bleed," Constance said.

She raised her eyes to Stern's face. They regarded each other. Stern, for once, was less than composed.

"No doubt you could make me bleed too." He turned away. "Given time. The right circumstances."

"Montague—"

"Look. I have bought you a present."

Ignoring the expression on Constance's face, and the tone in which she spoke his name (a tone she regretted, a second later, for it gave too much away), Stern put his hand in his pocket. He drew something out. Constance could not quite see what it was, but it glittered. Then, with deft fingers, he snapped it about her wrist.

It was a bracelet—a bracelet that, some fourteen years later, Constance would present as a christening gift. A most cunning, lovely, and intricate thing, this bracelet: a coiling snake of gold and rubies. It curled about her arm and the black material of her sleeve: once, twice, three times it curled. The blunt head of the snake, with its jeweled forked tongue, rested at the base of her palm, just above the pulse point. Stern lifted her hand and examined his gift.

"It would look better," he said at last, "against bare skin."

Constance gave a cry. She snatched her hand away.

"I cannot wear it. You know I cannot. It is too beautiful. Too costly. People would notice it. Even Gwen would notice it. They would ask . . . how I came by such a thing."

"No matter." Stern shrugged. "Keep it here. Wear it when you come to me. For the time being. And then—"

"Do you care for me?" Constance broke away from him. Her voice rose. "Do you? I care for you, I find. A little. More than I expected—more than I bargained for. I promised myself I should stay as free as air—and now, I am not so free. I don't say that you could break my heart—I'm sure no man could break my heart. But . . . there are things you do. Things you could do. I—"

She stopped. Her face becoming set, her eyes black and angry. Stern, who was used to these odd and sudden storms from Constance, said nothing. He waited, watching her—and that watchfulness seemed to perturb Constance even more, for she began to scrabble with the clasp of the bracelet, as if she might pull it off, as if she might—quite possibly—hurl it across the room. The clasp was tiny, and it defeated her. She gave a cry of anger and frustration. Stern took her hand quietly; he undid the clasp.

"You see? You may wear it or not, as you please. It is simply a *gift*, Constance—that is all."

"It is not simply a gift. Nothing you give is simple—"

"I'm sorry you dislike it so much. I thought it might please you."

Stern turned away. He put the bracelet down on a table. He walked away from her, about the room, moving an object here, an object there. Constance watched him, her heart beating fast. She had said too much: stupid, stupid, stupid! She must learn better control. She watched Stern pick up a vase and examine it. She told herself that Stern was a collector—he liked to acquire beautiful things; he liked to *own* them. She thought: *He will never own me!* Yet the idea of being in this man's possession—that idea drew her on even as she rebelled against it. Possession. She gave a small shiver. Stern, replacing the vase, looked back at her. There was now on his face an expression of unmistakable displeasure.

Constance found this displeasure exciting. She did not understand the reasons for this; she simply knew it was so. The threat of his anger was like a charge through the body; it gave her a sharp, slightly furtive thrill.

She met his gaze with her child's face, intimidated but slightly impudent.

"Oh, such an expression!" She gave a small pout, then hung her head. "I have offended you now—I have been rude and unkind, and hurt your feelings. Except you have no feelings to be hurt. See, Montague, I did not mean it. I am penitent. You may punish me at your will."

"I have no wish to punish you." His voice was cold.

"Are you sure, Montague? You look as if you would like to . . . smack me. Perhaps smack me quite hard."

"Really? It is not my practice to hit women." Curt now, he turned away.

"What then? I know I have made you angry."

"Not in the least. I had a mind to be practical. I thought we might discuss plans."

"Plans?"

"Plans. I am a methodical man, Constance, and plans need to be made. We cannot continue like this. Subterfuge. Alibis. Deception. It has gone on long enough."

"I don't see why." Constance, recovering now, gave another small toss of the head. "Besides, I hate plans. They confine one so. . . ."

"You did propose marriage to me once. Marriage might be described as a plan."

Stern's voice was now studiously polite. Constance, anxious to appear careless when she was most alert, began to move away.

"Marriage? Oh, I may have done," she began in a light voice. "That was months ago. So much has happened since then. Acland has died. I am in mourning now. I have been coming to you, I admit, but—"

"Was that another lie, then, your suggestion of marriage?"

Constance stopped. "Another lie?"

"Well, you lied to me about your mother, Constance," Stern said, politely still. "I wondered how else you might have lied, that is all." He moved toward her. "Constance, my dear, if you are to lie—and especially if you are to lie to me—then lie in ways that cannot be checked. Do not go into unnecessary detail—it is always a mistake, that, when lying." He paused. "No Jessica Mendl ever registered as a student at the Slade. In fact, I doubt there was any Jessica Mendl at all. Did you invent the surname? Pluck it out of a book?"

There was silence. Stern was now close. Their eyes met, and held. After a pause Constance began to smile.

"From a book," she replied. "One belonging to Acland, actually."

"And the real Jessica—was she Jewish?"

"She might have been. She was my father's secretary—when he could still afford secretaries. He married her when she became pregnant. He did not care for her, of course. He hated her—he told me often enough. If she *was* Jewish, she did not practice her religion—but then, of course, neither do you."

This was said with some edge, and Stern, who perhaps liked Constance best when she fought back, inclined his head, as if to acknowledge she had scored a point.

"So why did you lie to me?"

"Why? To make you notice me. You know that already."

"Did it occur to you I might investigate? Did you mind that you might be found out?"

"It did not occur to me then. I underestimated you, Montague." Constance scanned his face. The displeasure seemed to have gone.

"It did not occur to me," she went on, more slowly. "And I suppose that it should have. As for being found out—I am quite glad. I never claimed to be a virtuous woman. I prefer you to know me as I am."

"Oh, I prefer it too." Stern paused, then took her hand. This time, Constance did not snatch it away. "I prefer it, provided you understand one thing very clearly. It would be better—for us both, Constance—if you were not to lie to me again. Play games, by all means, but not with me. Then, after we are married—"

"Married? Shall we be married?"

"Certainly. And, after our marriage, let that be our pledge. Do you agree? No lies. I shall not ask anything else of you. I shall not ask you for declarations of love . . ."

Stern paused. When Constance did not speak, he frowned slightly, then continued, his manner stiff and (Constance found) rehearsed. "I shall not even ask you to be faithful to me. I am older than you, and I consider sexual loyalty to be of limited value. Other forms of fidelity concern me more. So—no lies between us. Our contract now, and our contract then. Is that agreed?"

Stern's face was serious; he spoke in a deliberate way, as if he intended her to remember this. Constance felt a rush of excitement. Also a certain wariness. Unsure why Stern should choose to propose in this way, she opted for a light, flirtatious reply.

"You put it very coolly, Montague. However, I agree. There! You have my hand, and my word upon it."

She sighed. She placed her small hand on her heart. "However, I do think, now it is your turn to propose, that you might do so with a little more passion. Contracts, indeed! We are not in the City now. You might betray a little emotion. Come now, Montague—won't you make me a declaration?"

"Very well." Stern seemed amused. "A declaration it shall be. A truthful one, according to our contract." He paused to consider.

"I do not love you, Constance—but I come closer to loving you than I have any other woman. I like you, Constance, despite your lies—or, more probably, because of them. I think we are alike. I think we have the . . . measure . . . of each other." He smiled, his manner becoming less tense. "Also, my dear, I think you would be an asset to me, as I would be to you. I think our . . . merger . . . might be turbulent, but also rewarding. And the dividends—the dividends should be generous. There, will that do? Is that declaration enough, from a City man? I find myself a little distracted. . . ."

During this speech Stern had touched her. When he spoke of assets, he began to undo her jacket. By the time he came to "turbulent," Constance's blouse was undone. When he reached "dividends," the palm of his cool hand cupped her breast.

His control was slipping, and Constance—who loved it best when he still tried to resist this weakening, who liked to tempt, see him struggle and then give in—caught his hand in hers and pressed it tight against the beating of her heart. She drew back just a little, her eyes bright with excitement.

"And do you know what I think?" She looked up at him. "I think, Montague, that we could make conquests together, you and I. I think we could be so powerful, and so rich, and so free that we should have the world at our feet. We could stamp on it, and disdain it, or stoop and pick it up—anything we pleased. Oh, we could be invincible—"

Here she broke off and became practical. She removed her jacket; she loosened her blouse. Then, when these now-customary preparations had been made, she turned back. She gave him a wicked glance.

"I also think it will be difficult. I hope you have it well planned. When people find out—when Maud finds out. Denton. Gwen. I am still under-age. There will be terrible scenes. Oh, Montague, there will be *mayhem*."

"I am sure you would enjoy that, Constance." Stern took her arm. "It might even amuse me. But as it happens, you are wrong. Now, where? Over here, perhaps . . ."

Stern had recovered some of his composure. He led her now to a small French armchair in a corner of the room. The armchair was upholstered in scarlet. It was positioned so that it faced a mirror. Constance allowed herself to be seated. She found she could not remember whether the chair had always stood in that position, or whether it had been moved in preparation for her visit. Moved, she thought—that excited her too.

She turned an expectant face to Stern, and Stern—as he liked to do—made certain preparations.

He removed her blouse. He adjusted her hair so that it lay in the way he preferred, its tendrils across her bared shoulders. He arranged her black skirt in such a way that the scarlet of the chair was still visible and her thighs were bared. When the composition satisfied his critical eye, he picked up the discarded snake bracelet and fastened it about her wrist. This time Constance did not resist. As he had predicted, the bracelet was more effective against bare skin.

"Tell me how I look to you," Constance said, gazing at their reflection in the glass. (This was something she often said to him.)

Stern looked toward the mirror with some seriousness.

"You look impure," he said, after a pause.

At that, Constance—who claimed she would like to be more impure; it was Stern who held her back—made a face.

"When?" she said.

"Oh, after we are married." Stern turned away. "You can lose your virginity only once—you might as well do so with some ceremony. Besides, I've told you, though I'm sure you already know, the sexual repertoire is limited. It is a great mistake to exhaust the variations too soon. So, today, when our time is brief, I thought—"

"Touch me." Constance caught his hand and drew it down against her. "Kiss me. Talk to me. Talk to me when you touch me. I like that. Tell me—tell me what will happen. Tell me why it will be easy. A man your age, my aunt's lover, and a girl young enough to be your daughter. Why will there be no scenes, no outrage?"

Stern moved behind the chair. He leaned forward. His eyes met hers in the mirror. His hand lay against her throat.

"There may be argument," he replied. "And I am sure there will be some outrage. That much is unavoidable. But I think you will find that no one, Constance, will put obstacles in our way."

"Maud?"

"I shall take care of Maud."

"Denton, then? Denton will never allow it."

"Denton is not your father. In any case, Denton will agree."

"Touch me. Oh, God, yes, like that. Denton? That is impossible. Why?"

"Why?" Stern bent forward. "Why? First, because Boy is no longer to marry an heiress. Second, because Denton owes me a great deal of money."

The word *money*, as he spoke it, seemed to carry some sexual charge. They both became still for a moment. Their eyes held.

"A great deal?" Constance leaned back. She rested her head against Stern's thighs. She rubbed her head gently back and forth.

Perhaps it was this action of hers, perhaps the cupidity in her voice—whichever the reason, Stern abandoned his pretense of control.

"Oh, a very great deal," he replied in a deliberate voice, and at that, a small shudder passed through both their bodies.

"Be quick," Constance said.

Stern adjusted the chair a fraction of an inch. Above the black silk of her stockings, Constance's thighs were very white. Constance fixed her eyes upon the mirror. She watched his touch, and his taste. When Stern bent between her thighs, she cradled his head; she began to speak. Salty and staccato rushes of words. Constance liked words, particularly those kinds of words; she liked the sweetness of their shock.

Words, and watching, the most reliable trigger of all: They had never failed her, so far.

Some weeks after this, as she had known was inevitable, Constance received a summons from Maud.

She went alone, at Maud's request. She waited alone in Maud's drawing room. She touched the furniture. I am afraid she first looked at the paintings and then counted them.

This would be the first time she had seen Maud since Stern had paid his visit to Denton, and the permission for their engagement had been obtained.

Stern, to Constance's irritation, refused to discuss his own conversations with Maud. On that subject, his discretion was absolute.

From Gwen, too, she had been able to learn little of Maud's reaction, although she had questioned her at length. Gwen was still sunk in grief for Acland. She roused herself sufficiently to plead with Constance. She suggested this engagement was unthinkable. Then, faced with her husband's inexplicable intransigence, with Constance's insistence that she must obey the dictates of her heart, Gwen had submitted. Unable to dissuade Constance, she avoided her.

So now, waiting for Maud (and my great-aunt kept her waiting some time), Constance felt a certain lively curiosity. She wondered how Maud would appear. Would she be tearful? Reproachful? Might she, even now, still hope to persuade Constance that this marriage could not occur?

Constance was learning to prepare for all the major scenes in her life as an actress might for a new role upon the stage. For this occasion she had composed a very pretty little speech. When my great-aunt Maud finally appeared, Constance was disconcerted. Maud entered her drawing room in her usual way, with an air of brisk efficiency and apparent good temper. She did not embark upon arguments or reproaches. She made no pleas.

Constance, taking a pause for a cue, then launched herself upon her speech. She reminded Maud of how much she owed her; she recalled Maud's kindnesses to her in the past. She made it clear that this indebtedness had, for a long time, caused her to fight her own feelings for Sir Montague. She had tried to ignore them; she had tried to combat them—but at length, when she came to realize his regard for her, she had been overcome.

She went on in this vein for some while; Maud heard her out. If, once or twice, Constance felt Maud's expression was scornful, she ignored it. She pressed on to the end. When she had finished, Maud remained silent for some while; both women were still standing.

"You did not mention the word *love*," Maud said at last, in a reflective way. She turned her gaze to the windows. "How odd. Neither did Montague."

Constance was annoyed by this. She felt *love* was a word Stern should have employed to give strength to his argument with Maud, even if he avoided it when with her. She frowned.

"I don't wish to cause any further hurt," she began.

Maud cut her off with a wave of the hand.

"Constance, please do not take me for a fool. You are perfectly indifferent to the hurt you cause, as I am well aware. In fact I sometimes think it goes beyond that. You have a positive taste for mischief, I suspect. In any case . . ." She turned back to Constance and gave her a thoughtful look. "I did not ask you here to question you, or argue with you, Constance. I have no desire to listen to pious speeches, so you can spare your breath." She paused. "I asked you here to tell you something."

"And what was that, Aunt Maud?"

"You are not my niece. Please to avoid that title."

"What was it, then?"

"You do not know Montague."

Maud moved away. Constance stared at her back. She made a face at it.

"Obviously I shall come to know him better—"

"Possibly. You do not know him now."

"Do you?"

At that, Maud turned. Constance had spoken in an insolent tone of voice; she perhaps hoped to provoke Maud, whose containment was beginning to vex her. If so, she failed. Maud looked at her for a while in silence. Her expression could be read as contemptuous; it could also be read as pitying.

"Yes, I do," she replied after that pause. "I know him perhaps as well as anyone can. I don't intend to meet you again, Constance, and so, before you leave, I thought I would give you a warning. Not that you will heed it, of course."

"A warning? Heavens—how dramatic!" Constance smiled. "Am I to hear some terrible revelation, because if so, you should know—"

"No revelations, Constance. Nothing so startling."

Maud was already moving toward the door. It became clear to Constance that this interview was over.

"Just one small thing. A vulgar phrase puts it most succinctly, I think. In selecting Montague—and I'm sure, Constance, it was you who did the selecting, not the other way about—in selecting Montague, you have bitten off more than you can chew."

"Really?" Constance tossed her head. "I have very sharp little teeth, you know. . . ."

"You'll need them," Maud replied, and went out, and closed the door.

V
IN TRANSIT

WEXTON TELEPHONED TO TELL ME he was in flight. From a biographer, on this occasion—or rather, from a would-be biographer, a young American academic whose persistence made Wexton shudder.

"He's after me," he said in lugubrious tones. "He's *interviewing* people. He's been to Virginia. He's been to Yale. He's even been to France. And now he's in Hampstead. Trying to flatter me. When that doesn't work, he tries threats . . ."

"Threats, Wexton?"

"Oh, you know. That he'll publish anyway. That he's sure I'd welcome the opportunity to set the record straight. He'll be going through the trash cans next. I know his type. I want to come to Winterscombe. I have to escape."

Wexton arrived a day later. He was carrying two enormous suitcases, both very heavy, whose contents he declined to explain. "Wait and see," he said. "My problem. Not pajamas and a toothbrush, I can tell you that."

I was very glad to see him. I had realized by then that embarking upon the past as I had, alone in a large house, was a mistake. My next commission (the one in France) had been delayed by the illness of my client; ten days spent working at my London offices had not, as I hoped, severed the links with the past. Winterscombe, Constance's journals, had tempted me back.

By the time Wexton arrived, his presence massive, sensible, reassuring, I was already beginning to see both these papers and the past zones as a trap. I was no longer sure of the balance of my own judgment. To my questions—and by then my mind thronged with questions—the dead returned dusty answers, answers I knew to be incomplete. In the case of Constance, the only reply was further questions and ambiguities. I felt confined in Constance's hall of mirrors, with its tricksy reflections. I saw, and I half-saw; I had begun to fear I might never get out. Yes, I was very glad to see Wexton.

On the day he arrived I told him about Constance's journals and the manner in which they had been given. I took him into the drawing room, expecting dismay. The room dismayed *me:* It was a mess, a clutter, a cascade of papers. It looked obsessional; it was obsessional. Wexton, I thought, would cure me. He would tell me to stop.

To my surprise, he did not. He ambled up and down, picking up a letter here, a photograph there. He discovered an old box of Steenie's Russian cigarettes, lit one, and stood puffing on it in an amused, reflective way.

"People can't resist it, I guess," he said at last. "Keeping all this stuff."

"This house is especially bad. Nothing was ever thrown away. I suppose there wasn't time, when my parents died and the war came. No time to sift, anyway. So everything was kept. It was just bundled into boxes and packing cases. No attempt to order things, no classification. There's so much *evidence.* Now, scarcely anyone writes letters—but my family never stopped. *And* diaries, journals . . . Who keeps diaries or journals now?"

"Statesmen. Politicians. They do," Wexton replied with gloom. "Still, those are different. Exercises in self-justification. Writing with an eye cocked for posterity. Juggling with the verdict of history. Except—no. Maybe all diaries do that."

"*Look* at all these letters. I can't remember when I last wrote a letter—a proper one, I mean, not a business one—"

I stopped. I could remember. I remembered then: the letter, weakly and cautiously phrased, to avoid betraying the fact that I still loved, and still hoped; I could remember the letter as vividly as I could the man to whom it was sent.

"It won't change," Wexton continued. "People love to record themselves. We're just in between methods right now. You wait. In fifty years someone in your position won't be sifting through a whole lot of letters and diaries, sure. But there'll be a substitute. Home movies instead of photograph albums. Computers! Imagine that. It'll happen. They'll store themselves away on machines. Great spools of tape. Do computers run on tape? People can't resist it, you see. It's the last vanity. Parting shots from the grave." He paused. "It's worth remembering that aspect when you go through all this. Not too many people in that situation tell the truth."

"You don't think so?"

Wexton shrugged. He picked up one of the black notebooks, then laid it down.

"Can you imagine Constance—on computer?" He grinned. "Or Constance's home movies?"

"Don't tease me, Wexton. It isn't as easy as that. This is my family. My parents. My past too. And I don't understand it. I can't tell lies from truth."

I explained then, as much as I was able. I brought Wexton up-to-date. I explained that Constance seemed convinced that her father had been murdered, and that when she came to name her suspects, it was members of my family who comprised her list. I told him, briefly, the truth as she wrote it, about her childhood. I told him how she had selected her husband, at her dance.

"Constance, Constance, Constance," he said, when I had finished. "That's an awful lot of Constance. What about everyone else? What are they? Bystanders? Spear carriers?"

"No, Wexton, obviously not. I *know* they're not. But even when I look for them, I can't find them. I can't hear them. Constance drowns them out. Look—"

I held out to him one of the black notebooks, the one I had just begun to read. Wexton shook his head.

"All right. Listen then. This is 1916. October 1916. I'll read you just a little bit. Then maybe you'll see what I mean."

"October 1916? So she's not married yet?"

"No, she isn't married yet."

"And it's before—?"

"Yes. Well before. That's 1917."

"Okay. Go ahead."

I read Wexton the following extract. Like many of the entries in the journal, it took the form of a letter. More than a diary, this was a one-sided dialogue—between Constance and a man she knew to be dead.

Poor Jenna [she wrote]. *I went to see her today, Acland, for your baby's sake. Don't you hope Hennessy is killed soon? I do. I hope some German gets him in his sights. For Jenna's sake, and mine. Acland, if you can, guide the bullet, will you? Nicely. Between the eyes, I think.*

What else? Montague is the very devil—but you know about that. Today I read him my latest letter from Jane, in my Jane voice. It was not very kind, perhaps, but it was very funny. Poor Jane. Do you know

*why she's gone to France? She wants to go to the place where you died.
Such a waste of time! She won't find you there, for you're somewhere
else—and only I know where that is. You're mine, not hers. We have a
pact, remember?*

*Oh, Acland, I wish you would come again in the night. Won't you?
Just once?*

"You see?" I closed the journal; Wexton made no comment. "It's
all so perverse. Writing to a dead man. *Montague is the very devil*—
what does that mean? I *met* Stern. Constance claims he never loved
her, but he did. He loved her very much."

"He said so?"

"Oddly enough, he did. It was not long before he died—maybe
he knew he was dying and that was the reason. I'm not sure. He told
me a story . . ."

I looked away. I could see Stern as I spoke, sitting in the
quietness of that room in New York, telling me how his marriage to
Constance had ended and giving me advice—advice I did not take.

"A story?"

"An episode. I found it sad—bitter, perhaps. He didn't speak
bitterly, though. He seemed to think of it as a love story. He avoided
that word all the way through, and then, when he had finished, he
looked down at his hands. He had very beautiful hands. He said,
'You see, I loved my wife.' "

There was a silence. Wexton turned away. "Well, yes," he said.
"I always imagined he did. Steenie used to say he was cold. I never
thought that—the opposite, in fact. Whenever I met them, here at
Winterscombe . . . He used to watch Constance, you know, all the
time. And when he watched her, his whole face changed. It was
like seeing a furnace door swing back. You couldn't look at it. It
burned your face. All that strength of feeling, held in check." He
paused. "A peep into the inferno, that marriage, I always thought.
People manufacture their own hells. Did Constance love him, do you
think?" .

"She claims not to. And he goes to great lengths to deny he
loves her—or so she says. You see? Just another thing I don't
understand."

"What exactly?"

"Love. These letters, these journals, all these papers—they're
all so filled with love. The more I see the word, the more I distrust
it. Everyone uses it. They all hijack it. They all mean something

different by it. Which of them is right? Steenie? Gwen? Constance? Jane? Or you, Wexton—you're here too. You know that."

"Yes, I know that." Wexton's face had become puzzled. He patted at his pockets in an absent-minded way, frowned at the fire.

"*Jane?* Why do you call her that?"

"Because that's what happened to me, Wexton." I turned away. "That's what I mean. I think of her in that way because I've read too much Constance. I know that."

"Your own mother?"

"Yes." I turned around angrily. "I was only eight when she died, Wexton—"

"Even so. You remember her, surely, as she was?"

"I don't *know* anymore, Wexton. Sometimes, when I read her diaries, I think I do. Then I go back to Constance's journals, and she slips away. She's Jane again. The heiress. The nurse. A kind heart. No imagination. A life of good works."

"I won't let that happen."

Wexton, I could see, was very distressed. He began to walk up and down the room in an angry way. He stopped and banged his hand down upon the desk.

"It's not *right*. That happens—to people like your mother. The good get wiped out. The bad get the best dialogue, the best plot lines. While your godmother was dancing about in London drawing rooms, there was a *war* on. I told you that. I told you to look at the war. Your mother was there. She was in the thick of it. She was a nurse. She *did* things. What did Constance ever do? Mess about with men. Set about snaring a rich husband—"

"Wexton—"

"Okay, okay. But it's wrong. You shouldn't let Constance get away with it. She's hogging the spotlight. But then that's not surprising. She always did."

I was chastened by this, because I knew Wexton was right. The outburst was fierce, from a man who was rarely immoderate except on the subject of literature. I listened, and I hope I learned.

Later that day I did return to my mother's journals; I followed her to the war. I followed her to France. Over the next two days, when I read, I read my mother's story exclusively. I listened to that quieter, very different voice. It was then, I think, that she began to come back to me for the first time. I saw her again as the woman I remembered. She emerged, to continue Wexton's metaphor, from the wings; there she was, in the lights.

Wexton knew, I think, that there had been a change in me, and that an unfair bias was in the process of being corrected. He apologized for his outburst, even claimed a bias of his own: Constance was not as trivial, and certainly not as one-dimensional, as he had claimed. "I overstated," he said.

One afternoon, returning from a walk by the lake, Wexton settled himself by the fire. We drank tea. Dusk fell. Wexton smoked some of Steenie's Russian cigarettes. We sat there in a companionable silence for a while, the air aromatic, the room comfortable, the house at rest. It was that afternoon that Wexton told me about the war, and my mother, as he recalled them.

"You know," he said, settling back in his chair, clasping his hands, stretching out his long legs, "your mother went out to France a month or so after I did. She was prickly, defensive, difficult to know at first. We remet in a town called Saint-Hilaire. It's still there. I revisited it once, after the war. Does she write about that?"

"Your meeting? Yes, she does."

"I remember it very well. It was the worst winter of that war. Maybe this is infectious—for once, I feel like talking about the past. About the war. Your mother too. Listen. It was like this . . . ."

Just outside Saint-Hilaire there was a narrow headland. It jutted out into the Channel. It was known locally as the Pointe Sublime.

It was not sublime in winter. It was cold. The wind cut. The view across the Channel was obscured by cloud. Jane ignored this. She turned up the collar of her coat and bent her head. She trudged along the narrow path above the dunes. She intended to reach the end of the headland, then walk back again.

Late afternoon; it was beginning to drizzle. The air was brackish; she could taste salt on her lips. When she reached the end of the headland, she looked back. She could see the cafés of Saint-Hilaire—their lights were being switched on. In one of the cafés an accordion was playing.

Next to the cafés was the larger bulk of the hospitals. There were five of them, and they had once been hotels. In that one—the third from the left—Jane now worked. She had been on duty there all night and all morning. There, on the first floor. She looked at the ranks of windows. They lit up, one by one. Her ward. It had once been the hotel ballroom.

The waters of the Channel were slick, oily. She watched them heave. To right and left the dunes were wired. She traced their lines: a zigzag of barbs. The beach below was more heavily fortified.

Impassable. She moved to one side, into the lee of the dunes. She wished she had worn a hat. The wind caught her smooth copper hair and blew it about. It whipped her face. Perhaps the wind veered, for she could no longer hear the accordion. She could hear the guns.

Heavy artillery, more than thirty kilometers away, a breathy reverberation.

Where was the war? Over there—always over there, where the guns boomed. And where was Jane? Always, she had decided, on the periphery; she was close, but she was not close enough.

She knew where the war was, in theory. If she had had a map, she could have traced it. The war was a snake, six hundred miles long. Its head was in Belgium, and the tip of its tail touched the border with Switzerland. The snake's spine meandered. It was patterned with trenches. It was a somnolent snake, and sometimes it shifted its position, making a new curve here, a new loop there. It accommodated advances and retreats; its position never altered greatly. It was well fed, this snake; after all, it ingested a daily diet of men.

There was the war, in theory. She could trace it on a map. She had traced it on a map. She did not believe her finger when it traced; she believed something more frightening. She believed the war was everywhere, and nowhere. She believed she had glimpsed this war long before it was ever declared, and would continue to see it long after any armistice. She believed the war was both an exterior and an interior thing. She believed it could transmute. She had never seen cells through a microscope, she had never witnessed their capacity to divide and subdivide, but if she had she might have said, "Yes, war is like that."

This made her afraid. What made her especially afraid was that she believed the war was inside herself. It had got in. She had let it in. It was there, and she might never get rid of it.

This belief seemed to Jane unreasonable, even mad. It was not a balanced way to think, and Jane told herself she thought in that way because she was tired. Because she ate poorly. Because her patients died, and their wounds were terrible. This happened. It was something all nurses must guard against. She must guard against it, too, for she had to be well enough to continue to nurse. That was it. Fix upon something simple. To continue.

That night, Boy would be passing through Saint-Hilaire on his way back to England. The letter from Boy, requesting a meeting (their first since she had broken their engagement), was in her pocket. Standing in the lee of the dunes, Jane took it out and read it again.

The rain spotted the pages and blurred the ink. The wind teased the pages and tried to twist them out of her hand. It was not a communicative letter, in any case. It was, as she had come to think of Boy, opaque. It resisted understanding. It began, as Boy's letters always had, "My dearest Jane." It ended, equally predictably, "Yours most affectionately, Boy."

Jane folded the letter back in her pocket. She would keep the appointment, although she did not want to. She turned to go back, and it was as she turned, glancing to her left, that she saw she was not alone, as she had thought. Not twenty feet away from her was a young man.

He was sitting in a shallow depression, on a shelf of sand and marram grass. He looked windswept. His hair stood up in curious quills and peaks. He wore around his shoulders an assortment of scarves, sweaters, and rumpled jackets. They were surmounted by a greatcoat, and gave him a hunched look. He was frowning. On his knees was a large notebook.

Whatever he wrote there seemed unsatisfactory. One minute he would write; then he would cross out. He would frown at the notebook, then at the sea, as if he blamed it in some way. Wexton. The American poet. Steenie's friend from London. She had met him outside the hospital in his ambulance the previous day. She did not want to meet him again today.

Jane edged away from the dune. He appeared not to have seen her. She had nothing against Wexton—who, whenever she had encountered him, seemed pleasant—but she preferred to be alone. She took a furtive step toward the path.

"Hello!" Wexton shouted. He shouted in a very loud voice, so it was impossible to pretend not to hear him. Jane stopped.

"Hello." He made an encouraging gesture. "Come and join me. Are you hungry? Would you like a sandwich?"

"I was about to walk back. I ought to go back."

Jane approached the square of mackintosh cape on which Wexton sat. She looked at him but kept her body turned to the path. Poised for flight.

"Me too," Wexton said cheerfully. He patted the cape. "Sit down for a minute. I'll walk back with you if that's okay. Have some of this sandwich first. The sea air always makes me hungry. Poems too. Here—it's cheese. French cheese, but it's not bad once you're used to it."

He held out to her a squashed baton of bread, and brushed away the sand that clung to it. Jane took the sandwich and bit into it.

Cheese, and mustard, and what might have been pickles of some kind—gherkins, perhaps. Jane did not usually like gherkins, but the sandwich was excellent.

"Have some coffee." Wexton was unscrewing a flask. "I put a bit of brandy in it. Just a drop. It's cheap brandy, but it perks it up a bit."

He handed her the lid of the flask, which was fashioned into a cup. Jane took a sip.

"Good?" Wexton was looking at her anxiously.

"Very good."

"Caffeine and brandy. It's unbeatable. Whisky's not bad either, but I can't get that."

This lack seemed to worry him, for he frowned, then turned back to stare at the sea. He seemed to feel no further need for conversation. Once or twice, making odd huffing and puffing noises, he wrote a few words in his notebook, looked back at the sea, then crossed them out.

Jane had always imagined that writing poetry must be a secretive and exalted process. She felt flattered that she should sit here and Wexton should continue to write. She took several more sips of the coffee. She stole a look at the notebook. She made out a list of words, most of them illegible. She began to feel relaxed—almost tranquil. The sandwich was good. The coffee was good. Wexton wrote a poem. He made no demands on her.

After they had sat in silence for perhaps ten minutes, she clasped her hands together in her lap. She cleared her throat.

"What is the poem about?"

To her relief, Wexton seemed unoffended. He sucked on the stub of his pencil. He poked his pouchy cheeks with the tip of it. Wexton, who was then twenty-five, appeared to Jane much older. He had been born looking forty-five, he used to say to me, and remained that way whether he was twenty or sixty. Jane considered his heavy cheeks, his furrowed brow; she thought he was as large and as ruffled as a bear, but that he also had the look of a hamster.

"It's about Steenie and me." He did not sound too certain. "I think. And the war, I guess."

He nibbled the pencil, spat out a splinter, and turned to look at Jane.

"I came to France to find the war, you see. And now I'm here, I discover it's someplace else. It's like trying to stand on the tip of a rainbow. I expect you find the same. Yes?"

He made this remark in a simple, direct, almost apologetic way.

The inquiry was cautiously optimistic. He sounded like a man hoping to retrieve a suitcase from lost-luggage.

"Over there," he went on before Jane could reply, pointing in the direction of the boom of guns. "I guess the war is over there. But you know, they sent me up to the front line last week, and even then . . ." He shrugged. "You know what I think? I think it's waiting. It'll wait a good long time, years maybe, until we're all back home—someplace else anyway. Then up it will pop. A jack-in-the-box. Here I am. This is the war. Remember me?" He looked back at Jane. "I'm not looking forward to that. Are you?"

"No. I'm not."

Jane was drawing in the sand with her finger. She looked down. She saw she had written the letters of Acland's name. She scrabbled them out, quickly.

"But you do know what I mean? I hope you do. I hope someone does. After all, it could just be me. I wonder about that." He turned upon her a beseeching gaze. Jane drank the last of the coffee. The wind blew her hair in her eyes, then made it stand up in points, a jagged copper crown.

"No, it's not just you." She made her voice very firm. "And I know exactly what you mean."

Jane was beginning a friendship that would last for the rest of her life. When she sat with Wexton on that headland, she had been in France two months.

The time could be measured. Day by day. Week by week. She measured and recorded it in her diaries. Those diaries allotted one page to each day. Sometimes she overran the allotted page. Sometimes she made no entry at all. When she read them back, time scrambled. On one of the pages, she found several weeks later, she had written one phrase, repeated three times. She could not remember having written it, but there it was. It said: *In Transit.*

She would remain in transit, no matter where she was posted, until she reached one particular place. That place (it was the location of a large Allied encampment, some thirty kilometers from Saint-Hilaire) was called Étaples. Étaples was the last place Acland was known to have visited. He had spent his last forty-eight-hour leave there; then he had been posted up the line (or down the line—she did not know which). Then he had died.

She had schemed to reach Étaples long before she left London. To ensure a posting there, she had written letter after letter. She had pulled strings without shame. The precise place where Acland had fallen was shrouded in military secrecy; if anyone even knew, it would be no more than a numbered square on a numbered map in the midst of a war zone. She could not visit that place. Acland had no grave. Very well, she would go to Étaples. Jane knew this had become an obsession, and sometimes she felt it was not a very healthy obsession. Even so, it remained. She told herself that if she reached Étaples, she would be able to relinquish Acland, to say farewell. She knew this was not the whole truth. In her heart she believed that, if she went to Étaples, she would understand his death. She would find him.

"Étaples?"

A young woman with a crisp upper-class English accent, an accent exactly like Jane's. Like Jane, she wore the uniform of a VAD (the Voluntary Aid Detachment). She stood next to Jane in a basement kitchen beneath a military hospital in Boulogne. Jane had landed the previous night. The journey had been slow; the Channel was mined. It was the beginning of her first day in France.

"Why there? Over here, one place is much like another, you know. Wherever you go there's confusion. Oh—and people dying. That too." She handed Jane a knife. "Sharpen it first. There's the steel. It makes it easier."

They stood side by side at a long deal table. It was five o'clock in the morning, still dark outside. The kitchen was cold. The young woman's breath made puffs in the air. In front of them, slapped down on the wood, were sides of meat. Jane had been told this was beef, but she suspected it was horse. Jane's task was to separate the fat from the meat. The meat would be used to feed patients and staff; the fat would be sent on to munitions factories. It was used to grease shells.

Jane looked at this meat. It was putrid. The fat on it was green; the leaner flesh was scummed. The smell of decomposition was very strong. She felt she might vomit.

"They won't let you nurse, you know," the young woman continued. She scraped out a maggot with the point of her knife, and speared it.

"Those Red Cross nurses may be angels to the men, but they can be absolute bitches to us. They've no time for VADs at all. You'll be lucky if you get to empty a bedpan. Not that I blame them, in a way. None of us is trained." She gestured to the other VADs at the table. "They shipped me out on the first boat. I can't change a dressing."

"But I have nursing *experience*. I was two years at Guy's, on a surgical ward."

"You can try telling them. They won't listen. Look—the best way to do it is this."

The woman pushed back a strand of hair with a greasy hand. She inserted her knife into the meat, gripped the meat, and levered. There was a sucking sound. A tranche of fat was freed.

"I shouldn't even be here." Jane poked at the meat. "I'm supposed to be in Étaples. I told Matron that. I told the sister—"

"They stood still long enough to hear? Well done."

"Maybe not. But I have letters from London. They state quite clearly: I'm to go to Étaples. It was all arranged."

"Letters from London!" The woman sounded impatient. "They aren't worth the paper they're written on. Not once you're out here. No one knows who anyone is, and no one much cares. You go where they decide to send you. When you arrive no one's expecting you. No one knows why you're there." She gave her piece of meat an expert half-turn, like someone making pastry.

"Do you know what happened to me last month? They sent me up to the front with a consignment of medicines. It turned out to be the wrong medicine. Quinine. It should have gone to Scutari, but the labels were mixed. I stayed one night; then I came back on the next train." She gave Jane a sideways look. "And I was glad. I was a coward, perhaps, but I could not have stayed there. You might think about that before you insist on another posting."

"Why couldn't you have stayed?"

Jane turned to look at her companion. Her face had taken on an expression with which Jane was familiar. Jane had seen it before—on Boy's face, on Acland's face, on the faces of numerous men. An absolute closing-off, which was perhaps tinged with contempt. The young woman shrugged. Jane realized she had irritated her.

"The smell. At least, here, the carcasses aren't human." The woman put down her knife. "Do you know what someone looks like when they've been in a gas attack?"

"No, but—"

"It burns the eyes out. They melt. Do you know what someone looks like when they've taken shrapnel in the stomach? When the man next to them stepped on a mine? Did they have that on the surgical ward at Guy's?"

"No, they did not." Jane's hands jerked. They wanted to hide her face. She forced them down. "No. But the people there were dying too. I saw . . . terrible things."

"Terrible things?" The woman's eyes were accusatory.

"It was a cancer ward."

"Cancer comes from God." The woman turned away. "He did not invent bombs or gas or shells or bayonets or bullets. Men did. I think that makes a difference. Maybe it makes a difference. I don't know anymore. It's better not to talk about it anyway. Talk is cheap. I have learned that." She stopped abruptly.

"We've met, you know. You obviously don't remember, but we have. You're Jane Conyngham—Boy Cavendish's fiancée? We met years ago. In Oxford—a party Acland gave. A picnic. We took punts on the river. I recognized you at once."

The river. The Isis. One of the canals behind Balliol. Jane could hear the slap of the water against the punt. The branches of a willow brushed her face. Acland lay back on the cushions opposite her. One of his hands trailed in the water. His face was lifted to the sky; light, then shadow upon his face. It was one of the few times she had seen Acland peaceful.

"Acland is dead," she said into the silence of the kitchen. The clatter resumed. A knife scraped steel. There was blood on her hands. The young woman sighed.

"I didn't know that. My brother went, in the first six months, and after that . . . I'm sorry. I was harsh. It was just . . . the way you spoke of Étaples, and the way I remembered you. I couldn't put the two things together. Obviously, you've changed. We all change—sometimes it makes one arrogant." She paused. "Listen, Jane—may I call you Jane? May I give you some advice? Forget Étaples for the moment. Speak to the matron again. Explain about Guy's. Insist you must nurse. There's a place called Le Tréport—you could mention that. I went there for a week. They have three hospitals. They're short of staff. The matron there is much younger—not so much the old guard. If you're still set on Étaples, she might arrange it. But it helps if you remember something, you know . . ."

"Remember what?" The woman's name had come to her. Venetia. Yes, Venetia. She was connected in some way—a niece, perhaps—with Maud's great friend Lady Cunard.

"You're in transit. We all are. Neither here nor there—somewhere in between."

"In transit?"

"Until the war is over." She turned back to the table. She picked up her knife. "It will be different then. I suppose."

* * *

"And so I went to Le Tréport."

Jane lifted her face to the wind. Beside her, Wexton wrote a word, then crossed it out.

"And after that?" He did not look up.

"So many places. They never let me stay anywhere very long. Back down the coast again. Then inland. Then north—a place called Trois Églises. That was close to the front. The guns were very loud. Then back to Le Tréport for a week. Then here, to Saint-Hilaire. They allowed me to nurse, in the end. But I still feel like a parcel, back and forth. In transit. Just as she said."

"You never felt you'd arrived?"

"No. Just that I was passing through. I think if I could reach Étaples as I planned, I might feel I had arrived then. Perhaps. I expect that is a delusion too."

"Why Étaples?" Wexton looked up. "You didn't say. Why that place more than any other?"

Jane hesitated. She did not discuss this—with anyone.

"Because of Acland," she heard herself say. "He was there just before he died."

She wanted to grab at the words, at once. Retrieve them quickly. She had the impression that they echoed, repeated themselves in the wind and the drizzle, shaming her.

"Acland?" Wexton said.

"Yes, Acland." Jane stood up. Brisk, brisk, brisk. She made a great business of belting her coat more tightly, turning her collar up. "I was very fond of him. Look, it's growing dark. I must go back."

Wexton made no comment. He stood. He gathered up his belongings, wound the numerous mufflers around his neck. The sky was darkening now, and he switched on a small flashlight produced from his pocket. They began walking, side by side. It was awkward, for the path was narrow and their shoulders kept bumping each other. The flashlight flickered.

"You sound ashamed," Wexton said when they had gone some way. "Is there some reason you're ashamed? I mean—why shouldn't you be fond of him?"

"I was engaged to his brother, for one thing."

"Were engaged?" Wexton sounded interested but noncommittal.

"Yes. I broke it off. Surely Steenie told you? After Acland died. It seemed the right thing to do."

Jane lifted her face to the wind. It buffeted her eyes. They watered. She was not crying—although sometimes she found now that she did cry, abruptly and without apparent reason. She was not crying now. It was simply the wind. They had almost reached the steps to the promenade. The lights of the cafés were close. She could hear the accordion again.

"Why?" Wexton paused. He shook the flashlight. Its battery was fading. Its light went off, then came on again. "Why did it seem the right thing to do?"

"I didn't love Boy, for one thing." Jane increased her pace. She could have hit him for this persistence.

"And you did love Acland?"

Jane stopped. She turned. "I did not say that—"

"No." Wexton had also stopped. "You said 'fond.' *Fond* isn't much of a word. It's kind of weak. *Love* is much better. Or it could be. Should be. If people didn't misuse it." He looked at Jane and perhaps understood her expression, for he seemed contrite.

"I'm sorry. I've overstepped the English mark. I do that, Steenie says. He says I'm a vulgar American." He paused. "I'll learn, I suppose. Not to ask questions. To be English. On the other hand, maybe I won't. Can you hear the accordion? I kind of like accordions. I go to that café sometimes when I come off duty. They do an omelette with potatoes in it, which is very good. I thought I might try to cook it sometime. I like to cook—did Steenie tell you? I'm teaching myself."

He had taken her arm. Jane kept that arm very stiff. They came to the steps and Jane marched up them. One, two, three: she jerked her legs like a marionette. She did not look at Wexton. She would not look at Wexton. She was displeased—with his Americanness, with his questions. Steenie was right. He had overstepped the mark.

Just as she thought this, they reached the promenade. It was lit with gas lamps; they paused in a pool of bluish light. Jane looked down at her own feet in her stout hospital shoes. She looked at the circle around them, the light, and the shadows beyond. She saw herself on a small island, marooned by her Englishness, marooned by her upbringing. Her circle; her mark. Wexton had indeed overstepped it. He stood in the same pool of light now, as she did. She stared at his feet. They were extremely large. He wore heavy shoes, encrusted with damp sand. The laces had broken and been knotted.

"You shouldn't apologize." She looked up at him. "I should. Why pretend? I was taught to do so as a child, I suppose. I go on and on doing it. I never say what I truly think. I try to, but I can't. And it's such a waste of time—I've learned that here, if nothing else. We have so very little time, all of us, and we ought not to waste it on evasions. So—you're right, you see. I know you're right. *Fond* is a feeble word. I was never fond of Acland. I loved him. I loved him for years and years. I never told him, and now he's dead. That's all. Please don't be polite—I couldn't bear it. I know what you must think. I know you'll go away and laugh at me . . ."

"Why should I do that?"

"Look at me! Just look at me!" Jane's voice rose. She caught hold of Wexton's coat in an angry way. She forced him around so that the light from the streetlamp shone on her face. She was shaking. Her face was streaked with tears.

"I'm plain. Not even something strong and definite, like ugly. Just plain. Dull. Invisible. I was invisible to Acland. I always knew that, and I loved him just the same. On and on, for years and years—loving him in that stupid, timid, shrinking way. I despise myself for it. I wish he had known. It probably wouldn't have mattered to him. He would have been embarrassed. You're embarrassed. I embarrass myself. But all the same I wish he'd known. I wish I'd had the courage to tell him."

She made a strangled, half-choking noise in her throat. Her face, which had flared at him a moment before, seemed to crumple, to disintegrate. She wiped her cheeks and her nose with the back of her hand. She caught Wexton's eye. She half-laughed, half-cried again. Wexton handed her a handkerchief. Jane blew her nose.

"I'm sorry." She took a noisy breath. "I must go back. I don't know why I began upon that. Once I began, I couldn't stop. I'd never said it before, you see. I'm tired. I was on duty all night. I expect it's that."

"I don't mind. No—keep the handkerchief." Wexton looked as if he were trying to decide something. He fumbled about with the flashlight. He shifted from one large foot to the other. "Would you like a cup of hot chocolate?" He waved his hand in the direction of the café where the accordion played. He smiled. "You don't have to be back yet. Come on."

They went into the café. They sat at a small round table by a steamy window. It was very hot. Wexton eyed the fat-bellied coke stove in the corner. In a cautious way he removed the greatcoat and one of the mufflers.

Wexton ordered two large hot chocolates. Jane concentrated on stirring hers. She stared at the table top. She knew that her face was blotchy and red. She could not quite believe she had said all those things. The warmth, Wexton's silence, the steam on the windows; she found that she was glad she had.

"I'm seeing Boy tonight," she said at last.

"Oh, really? You must bring him here." Wexton seemed abstracted. He was drawing in the steam on the windowpane. He drew first a bird, then a man, then a boat.

"I was writing about love." He made the announcement in a sudden rush. "When I saw you. It wasn't any good. It never is. I try. The words won't come right."

He pulled the notebook out of his pocket. He opened it at the page full of words and crossings-out. He tore out the page, scrunched it up in his hand, rose, crossed to the fat-bellied coke stove, lifted its lid, and stuffed the page inside. He returned to his seat. Jane put down her spoon. She was, she thought, being tested.

"About love?" she said in a high, careful voice. "You said the poem was about Steenie."

"That's right. I love Steenie."

Wexton put his elbows on the table and his melancholy chin on his hands. He looked at her.

"Did you know?"

"Not until now. No."

"I thought you might have realized." This, Jane knew at once, was a palpable untruth. He had never thought any such thing.

"In London. It always seemed very obvious to me. I thought everyone would know. Then I came out here. I thought I might understand it if I went away. I've been in love before, but never quite as badly. It hurt. I thought if I came here, it might stop. It hasn't, of course. It's worse, if anything. I try to write about it, and I can't. I try to write about the war, and I can't. The more I look, the less I understand." He came to an abrupt halt and blinked.

"Oh," he said, as if this had just occurred to him. "I've shocked you."

Jane looked down at her hands. Her face was on fire. The blush ran down her back. Yes, all right—Wexton was correct, she was shocked. But it was 1916; Jane was then twenty-eight. She had not been told the physical facts of life until she was eighteen. She had not known of the possibility of homosexual love until she was well into her twenties, when it was spoken of in terms of unnatural desires and even more unnatural acts. Sex, for Jane, was textbooks, read standing up in a hospital library, quickly replaced on the shelf. It was diagrammatic, yet furtive. In short, she was both innocent and prejudiced. So she blushed. Her hands made nervous crablike snatches at her cup.

However, she also knew she was being challenged. This announcement of Wexton's was deliberate. He perhaps returned the compliment she had paid him, and bared his heart. She could perhaps pretend to misunderstand, to assume he spoke of the kind of male friendship her dead brother had hymned, although she knew he did not. She could, she supposed, simply rise to her feet and leave the café. If she did so, she knew Wexton would not follow her. She doubted she would see him again.

She frowned. Diagrams danced up and down in her mind. She tried to relate the diagrams to Steenie and Wexton; she tried to imagine a man embracing another man. She risked looking Wexton in the eyes. He was waiting.

"Does Steenie love you?" The question was like a hiccup. It popped out before she could think. Wexton considered.

"He says that he does. I think it's true—in his way. For a while."

"It won't last, you mean?"

"No, I don't expect it to last."

"Does he write?"

"He used to write every day. Now he writes . . . less."

"Do you still love him—as much as before?"

"More, I think. It isn't rational. I know what Steenie's like, but I still . . . It grows. You can't stop it. Absence, I guess."

"And you don't . . . that is, you don't ever fall in love with women?"

"No." He paused a polite fraction. "Do you?"

There was a small silence. Jane's skin felt like glass. She could feel the blood rushing in to stain the glass a second time. She averted her eyes from Wexton's face, to look at the café. She saw it as a fixed, static place, inert as a photograph. Small round tables: two elderly Frenchmen, in blue working overalls and berets, playing dominoes. The curé of the town, who sometimes came to the hospital to administer the last rites; he recognized her; he lifted his glass to her. Jane felt a sense of sudden elation. Wexton tutored her, and her mind was quick. There were a few jagged shards of the old morality left, and if she could just crush them under her heel, grind them into well-deserved dust . . . She leaned across the table.

"Wexton . . ."

"Yes?"

"I'm not shocked. I was. But—it's stopped."

Wexton was drawing in the steam of the window again. He drew another figure, and another boat. He placed the figure inside the boat and added some sea beneath: three wavy lines. He did not seem surprised by what she said. He rearranged his mufflers; he hauled at the greatcoat; he drew back Jane's chair. They went outside. They walked back toward the hospital, arm in arm, at a brisk pace.

"You're back on duty at midnight."

They had come to a halt outside the hospital. Wexton's remark was not a question but a statement.

"You're on the ambulance run to the station," Wexton said.

"Am I? I thought—"

"You're assigned to my ambulance."

"Yours?"

"I fixed it."

"You fixed it?" Jane stared at him. "When did you do that?"

"This morning."

"How?"

"I bribed one of the other nurses. She swapped."

"You *bribed* her?"

"Yes. With a Hershey bar. I got a food parcel yesterday from home." He smiled. "It's thirty kilometers there, and thirty back. I thought we could talk. Besides, I had a hunch."

"A hunch?"

"I thought I would probably like you. I expected us to be friends."

Wexton wound one of the mufflers tighter around his neck. From one of his pockets he produced a woolly hat, which he pulled on. It was one of the most absurd hats Jane had ever seen: a balaclava with a bobble on top.

He lifted his hand in parting. He turned and shambled off in the direction of his hostel. He whistled in a tuneless but cheerful way. Jane watched him: Halfway down the street the battery of the flashlight decided to perform. The light came back on. Wexton gave a small but audible cheer.

"How was Boy? Did you try the omelette? Damn!"

Wexton swerved. This was not an easy journey. These were the reasons: The ambulance Wexton drove had solid tires, which would not grip; the road between Saint-Hilaire and the station inland was a minor one, intended for farm horses and carts, not the heavy traffic of hospital and military vehicles. It was December, and for the past two weeks there had been constant rain; the surface of the road was wet mud, across which the ambulance skeetered and slithered. In the mud were deep tracks in which it was sometimes possible to steer, so the ambulance trundled along like a train on rails. Occasionally these tracks led to deeper potholes filled with water and softer mud, where other vehicles had bogged down. It was difficult to avoid these; Wexton's ambulance was at the front of a convoy, and they drove without lights.

The authorities had decreed that the carbide lamps could be lit only for one small section of the road, when they were ten kilometers from Saint-Hilaire. They must be extinguished again ten kilometers before the station. This was because of German air attacks—of which, so far, there had been only one, some two months previously, when a German biplane had dropped explosives in the area of the road, missing it by half a mile. Wexton did not have great respect for biplanes or the authorities. He stopped the ambulance, climbed down and lit the carbides when they were five kilometers out. Jane climbed down to help him, and sank up to her calves in mud. It was raining again; the wind had strengthened. It took ten matches to persuade the carbides to light; once lit, they were unreliable. They illumined an area of ground for about five feet ahead, making the surrounding darkness a deeper black.

In the back of the ambulance, under a tarpaulin roof, was a group of Red Cross nurses from Lancashire, who sang as they slithered and bucketed. They were sheltered from the rain; Jane and Wexton were not. The front of the ambulance was unroofed; the windshield was low; the wipers tended to jam; mud sprayed. Jane was wearing two sets of woolen underclothes, three cardigans over her dress, a jacket, a coat, two scarves, two pairs of mittens. She was stiff with cold.

Wexton drove with erratic skill. He cursed a lot. He cursed the mud, the jammed wipers, the carbide lights, the potholes, the skid-marks.

When the Lancashire nurses sang "Tipperary," Wexton joined in, in a ringing baritone. The ambulance hit a rut. Wexton performed a skillful maneuver which was midway between a glide and a lurch. Somewhere in the middle of their journey he gave Jane her first cigarette, which made her cough. Farther on, he described Virginia. Farther on still, he discussed a book called *Buddenbrooks*. Another kilometer and he confided he was learning to knit. One kilometer more and they were discussing trains, for which Wexton had a passion. They bounced about in a companionable way from books to recipes, from his family (Wexton was one of eight) to hers (Jane had had only the one brother).

Jane enjoyed this. Yes, she was stiff with cold; every bone in her body ached from the jolting of the wheels. Her wet hair felt as if it froze to her face. Her throat was raw from the smoke of the cigarette. Nevertheless, she enjoyed it. She felt as if Wexton took her up in a balloon, fueled with his own unflagging benevolence, and showed her a world crammed with incident. Anything was possible!

One kilometer more—the station was approaching—and Wexton sang an American song. One kilometer after that, and, without warning, he switched to her meeting with Boy.

"Yes. We had the omelette," she replied at last.

Then, because Wexton did not prompt, and she liked that in him, she told him what had happened.

Since she had last seen him, Boy had been promoted. He had begun the war with the rank of lieutenant; by the time she broke off their engagement, he was a captain. Now, he was a major. Such rapid promotion was not unusual. The life expectancy of a Guards' officer at that point in the war was six months; men were in short supply. If the war went on this way, Boy said with an odd smile when she congratulated him on his promotion, he would end up a brigadier at the very least.

"Who knows?" He smiled a blank smile. "Even a general."

Jane did not believe this. She knew Boy did not believe it either. He made her sadder when he tried to make jokes. They sat at the same table she had occupied earlier in the evening with Wexton. As Wexton had advised, they ate the potato omelette.

Boy ate only half of it. He ordered a roasted chicken, took one bite, then set down his fork. He drank—Jane counted—one and a half bottles of wine.

Jane tried. She knew that during the previous two weeks Boy had been manning a dugout forward of the front-line trenches, in No Man's Land, under fire from a German machine-gun pillbox. The gun was eventually captured. She did not know the details. She did not know, for instance, that Boy would subsequently receive the Military Cross for this episode; she did not know that of the twenty men in his platoon, only three returned; she did not know that at one point Boy had been in the dugout, in four feet of water, under constant fire for a continuous period of fifty-six hours. She would not ask for details; you did not ask men who had been to Golgotha to describe the topography there.

She had not expected this conversation to flow, and it did not. It lurched. It jammed. It was punctuated by silences that embarrassed them both, silences that would end when they both began on precipitate speech at the same moment.

They discussed Boy's father's health, his mother's, Freddie's ambulance work, Steenie's forthcoming exhibition of paintings, and the astonishing news of Constance's engagement to Sir Montague Stern. Jane saw these events across a divide; once they might have seemed momentous; now they seemed petty.

Perhaps they seemed so to Boy also, for he spoke of them in a distanced way. He blinked. His hands described small jerky movements in the air. He looked deaf, and unhappy.

It was when, in some despair, Jane turned to the subject of photography that she knew something was seriously wrong. The moment she mentioned cameras, Boy's face took on a mulish expression.

"I've got rid of the Adams Videx."

"Got rid of it, Boy? You mean you sold it?"

"I smashed it up. I shan't take photographs again. I burned all the photographs I took in France. I broke the plates. When I go home"—he took a large swallow of wine—"I shall destroy all my photographs there as well. I hate photographs. They tell lies. Do you know the only thing worth photographing? A stick in the sun. A stick and its shadow. Yes. I suppose I wouldn't mind photographing that."

Jane was very shocked. To hear Boy denounce photography was like hearing a lifelong Catholic renounce his faith: It was a blasphemy. She looked at him more closely.

The war had altered his face; the war had improved his face. There was no sign of trench pallor. If you ignored the expression in the eyes, Boy looked as if he had just returned from an invigorating holiday—a spell by the sea, perhaps. His skin was wind-tanned; the rounded childish contours of his face, which had always made him seem younger than he was, were hardening into something older and more rigorous.

War was making Boy into a handsome man—there was an irony. Yet the anxiety in his eyes denied the new authority in his features. Boy looked like an actor who had forgotten his lines.

There was something Boy intended to say. First, though, it seemed he had to wind himself up. When he had finished the wine, he seemed to decide he was wound: levers and hairsprings. Boy cleared his throat. He shook his head to dislodge the imaginary water. He gazed at the condensation upon the window, through which Wexton's drawings of men and boats were still visible. He turned his head a little to the left and addressed a potted palm. He had come here, he said, to discuss Constance.

He began in a general way. He became fluent, as if this part of his performance had been well rehearsed. He explained at some length that most people (he included Jane) did not understand Constance, whereas he did. He said that what one had to remember was that Constance was still a child; she was vulnerable.

Jane did not agree. She considered Constance's engagement a disgraceful betrayal of Maud. This, she did not say; Boy gave her no chance. He was clearly not interested in Jane's opinion. The clockwork was in motion; once begun, Boy seemed unable to stop.

"This marriage of Constance's," he said, very distinctly, "this marriage must be stopped." There was then a great deal more. Boy said his father's behavior was inexplicable—permission to marry should have been refused. He said he found Maud's behavior inexplicable, also Stern's, Freddie's, Steenie's—even his mother's. Everyone's behavior was inexplicable, it seemed, except that of Constance. Constance's behavior Boy could explain. It was, he told the potted palm, a cry for help.

At this point in his speech Boy seemed to have reached some obstacle. He began to stammer, and the stammer was far worse than it had ever been. Boy's tongue stuck on the letter *C*. This caused him some anguish; it made it very difficult to pronounce Constance's name.

Having told the potted palm that Constance wanted help, Boy turned his anxious eyes back to Jane. He then explained the last thing, the thing that had brought him here that night, before he returned to England. Although he and Jane were no longer engaged, he had felt it correct that she should be the first to know his intentions. He intended to return to England. There, he would stop this marriage. That was the first thing. Then he would propose marriage to Constance himself.

"She must have been expecting it, you see." Boy leaned across the table. "She must have expected it as soon as I ended the engagement to you. When I did not ask, she did this. Do you understand?" He spread his hands and gave Jane a smile of great sweetness. "A cry for help. She knows that I love her, of course."

Jane began on this story to Wexton as they approached the railway station, where they would meet a train bearing the wounded from the field hospitals. The train was late, and they stood on the cold, black platform, side by side, shivering.

The story upset her. She found it difficult to recount in a coherent way, and kept rushing back and forth between the scene in the café and other scenes in the past. Gaps had opened up in a narrative Jane had presumed seamless, and these gaps worried her. She made little darts and rushes at them. She saw that she had never understood Boy, whom she had always thought so simple and straight-forward. There was a Boy in this story she did not know. Suddenly the past jostled with questions. She blamed herself. She had been blind. Obsessed with her own feelings for Acland, it had never occurred to her that Boy, too, might have a secret life.

She began to pace up and down the icy platform. She waved her mittened hands in the air.

"Blind, blind, *blind*," she cried—so the Lancashire nurses gave her a curious look. "I should have seen. I hate myself."

Wexton listened. He did not comment. There was a stanza of a poem in his mind. As Jane spoke, it began to take shape. He stood still, hunched in his scarves and jackets and coats. He held on to the poles and rolled canvas of his stretcher. The canvas was wet; a thin crust of ice was forming on its surface. He felt he had a crust of ice on his upper lip as well.

He stared downwind, along the rail lines, in the direction from which the train would approach. He listened to Jane; he listened to the poem; he also listened to something else. Distant, but growing more distinct, he could hear the throb of an engine. The wind distorted the sound. He thought, but he was not sure, that what he heard was the engine of the hospital train.

From the past, Jane had moved on to the future. She was trying to explain the expression on Boy's face: its gentle bewilderment, its unconvincing hope. This made Jane very agitated. She said she should have talked to Boy longer and tried to dissuade him. Turning back to Wexton, she began to explain that when she said goodbye to Boy she had had a premonition of misfortune.

It was then that Wexton's large hand hit her hard in the small of her back. He said: "Get down!"

The blow knocked the breath out of her. She fell painfully, flat on the wet paving, the stones skinning the side of her face. One leg twisted under her; Wexton's weight slammed against her back. The poles of the stretcher struck her across the head. Their bodies were a tangle of wet wool, canvas, mufflers. The air thundered, then lit. Wexton's elbow jabbed her spine. He rubbed her face on the wet pavement. Jane fought him off. She wriggled an inch, then lifted her head.

Wexton was insane. The platform was insane. What had been black was light. The edge of the platform was bitten off and furred with smoke. Flames ran up the poles of the station canopy. They fluttered like flags. They licked along the roof. The blackness was ecstatic.

Someone screamed. A Red Cross nurse ran by, her cape alight. Her hair was burning. Her mouth was jagged. Jane knew that she must stand and do something about this, but Wexton would not let her. She lifted her head and he crammed it down again. She could feel his fist on her neck. This made her angry, in the most violent way. She fought Wexton; she hammered at his hands; she tried to hit his face.

Wexton was too heavy for her and too strong. This was fortunate, for it was at that moment that the pilot of the Zeppelin airplane jettisoned his second bomb. He had been, in fact, off course. With a precision then rare, he hit not only the station but also the engine of the oncoming train.

The engine reared itself up. It flung itself sideways. It erupted hot iron and steam. Hot coals flew into the air. Shrapnel whined. The carriages behind careened forward, lost impetus, collided, and skewed. An iron snake, chopped into fragments; these fragments veered off, one to the left, another to the right. The fourth mounted the third; metal copulated. There was silence, then a buzzing like flies, then a scream.

Wexton had saved her. Jane knew this, finally, when she lifted her head, when Wexton, who was shaking, helped her to her feet. Just a yard from her, where they had been standing a few moments before, was a metal pole of some kind, part of the train, or a rail, perhaps once a part of the station roof. With the precision of a javelin, it now impaled a paving stone.

The carriages of the train were burning. The wounded men inside them burned too. This sight, and this smell, Jane and Wexton never described, although when I was a child, Jane would tell part of the story, would recount how her friend Wexton saved her life.

There were other incidents she left out, but which Wexton retold for me, all those years later, sitting together at Winterscombe. This was one of them. Toward the end of the night, when the sky was lightening and the horizon was no longer black but gray, Jane returned to the train. She returned to the last carriage; less severely damaged than those to the front of the train, it had been slower to burn.

All the men in it except one had been brought out. That man, whose leg had been broken under the wheel of a gun carriage some days before, could be glimpsed through the broken door. He lay beneath a sheet of twisted metal. He made no sound. He was thought to be dead. The carriage was beginning to burn as Jane approached it.

As she walked forward, the remaining glass in the carriage windows exploded. There was a burst of flame, a scatter of vicious confetti. Jane ducked her head. She clambered down from the platform and across the rails, which ran with hot grease. She grasped the wheel of the carriage and began to haul herself up. Wexton tried to haul her back. Jane clung to the jagged metal of the door. It was like grasping ice; her palms sizzled. She looked down and watched her skin peel back. Somehow, she brought the man out.

Wexton helped her, along with one of the Lancashire nurses. The smoke made them blind. They lifted; they dragged; they pushed. The man was extracted; he was bundled upon a stretcher; he was conveyed to Wexton's ambulance. There, her face blackened by smoke, her burnt hands hastily bandaged, my mother, Jane, attempted to dress his wounds. The man regained consciousness, but only briefly. Some three kilometers from Saint-Hilaire, he turned away his face and died.

That man—one of the Hennessy brothers, as it turned out—was the first of the Hennessy family to die. Two brothers were to follow him, one at the battle of Arras, one at Messines Ridge. Jack Hennessy was to be the sole survivor of the four tall sons who had once carried Edward Shawcross's body back to Winterscombe on an improvised stretcher, and Jack Hennessy—or so he said to me as a child—never forgot my mother's attempt to save his brother.

Shoveling coke in the basement, his instincts more than ever feudal, he would tell me war stories. He would tell me how, and where, he lost his left arm (an amputation that put paid to his ambitions to be head carpenter); he would tell me how, and where, his brothers died; and—undeterred by the fact that he himself had not witnessed it—he would give me this account of my mother's heroism.

Was it true? Wexton says that it was; my mother always claimed that Hennessy exaggerated. In her diaries she makes no mention of the incident—but Constance, in her journals, does. Its ironies amused her.

So, she wrote some weeks later, when the news reached her. *A Hennessy has died—assisted by Jane. The wrong Hennessy, alas, Acland. Still, I feel we both tried.*

Boy stood in the rain at the foot of the steps that led up to the Corinthian Club in Pall Mall. He looked up at the gray and august façade of the club. He was to meet there with Sir Montague Stern. It was evening, two days before Constance's marriage.

He had spent the day fasting; he felt he must prepare for this—a crucial meeting—in the correct way. He must be alert. He must not listen to the sound of guns he knew were the other side of the Channel. He must take his father's role, since his father had ducked out of it. He must behave like an officer and a gentleman—reliable and predictable rails, they ran dead straight.

He was confident. He was wearing uniform, a deliberate choice. He had a Sam Browne belt around his waist and, attached to that belt, a holster containing his service pistol. His cap felt like a helmet. Boy looked at the steps. He walked up them with firm strides.

Boy's choice of the Corinthian was an obvious one. His grandfather had been a member, as well as his father; Boy had been made a life member at the age of twenty-one. He might dislike the place, but he felt he had a right to it in a way Stern certainly did not. It was a mystery to Boy that a man like Stern had contrived to become a member at all. He expected Stern to look ill at ease and out of place.

At first, all went well. The club porter greeted him instantly by name and correct rank, despite the fact that it was years since Boy had been there. His greatcoat was taken, his army cap, his swagger stick. Several old men, deep in leather chairs, looked up as he passed and greeted him with a nod. His father's son.

Boy now felt safe only when playing a role. His confidence increased. This confidence was strong in the hall; it was strong on the stairs; it remained strong when he entered the smoking room. Then he glimpsed Stern: Stern was standing at the far end of the room, his back to the fire; a club servant hovered. To his left was an elderly duke; to his right was the Foreign Secretary. They appeared to hang upon his words. Boy was outraged.

It was then that everything began to go wrong. Stern greeted him with an easy warmth; he held out his hand, which Boy (who would have liked to punch him in the jaw) felt forced to take. The duke and the Foreign Secretary moved discreetly aside. Before Boy quite knew what had happened, he and Stern were both seated in leather chairs by the fire, and it was Stern, not he, who had placed the order for the whiskies. The servant returned with them speedily. Stern reached for a cigar case.

Boy focused his eyes first on Stern's waistcoat, which he considered monstrous, its colors loud. They moved on to the jacket Stern wore, which was too new and too aggressively waisted. They dropped to Stern's shoes, which were handmade but likewise too new. Boy stared at them, transfixed with loathing.

Boy, like his father and grandfather before him, despised new shoes. The point about shoes was that, once made, they lasted a lifetime. If new shoes were unavoidable, then they must be broken in first, boned and polished daily by a well-trained servant for at least a year before they graced the feet. Stern's shoes looked as if they had come out of their box that morning. His suit shouted money, which was unforgivable. His sleek hair, as tawny as a fox, was well cut and a fraction too long. His shirt cuffs were too white, the links on those cuffs too large. He was offering a cigar, and that cigar was a Havana. Boy took it, then almost dropped it; he felt his fingers burned.

The next moment Boy was glad of the cigar. He must remove the band, wait while its end was clipped, light it, puff at it; all these activities gave him time to think. He had already rehearsed what he would say; it merely remained to say it in the correct manner. Boy, aware that he was sitting on the edge of his chair, moved back. He crossed his legs, then uncrossed them again. He squared his shoulders. He ignored the nearby back of the Foreign Secretary. He attempted to fix Stern with the gaze he had planned, the same gaze he used when addressing his men before battle: the direct approach, man to man, no sign of fear and no need to insist on superiority of rank, for that superiority was innate, the essence of command.

He could not begin. He had squared his shoulders but he could not begin. His mind blurred and muddled: This sentence, or that one? He took a sip of whisky. One of Stern's well-shod feet tapped. At the back of his mind, in some recess that seemed never to clear, Boy heard the rush and reverberation of guns.

He set down the whisky glass with care. His hand shook somewhat, and he hoped Stern did not observe this. It was something that happened now, this shaking, and when it began, it was not always possible to control.

He eased his collar away from his neck. He was beginning to sweat. The room was too hot. It was too quiet. He was suddenly afraid that when he began to speak he would stammer. This happened, too; it had happened, once or twice in the past months, in front of his men—if he had missed sleep, if the events of the preceding day had been particularly terrible.

In France, when this happened, he had his sergeant to turn to: Sergeant Mackay, a Glaswegian, small, wiry, foulmouthed, and indestructible. Mackay could step in and interpret, if need be, when the words jammed on Boy's tongue. Mackay could . . .

Except, no. Boy did not have Mackay anymore. Mackay had been at his side, right through, until—three weeks before—he took a rifle-grenade in the jugular, and proved to be destructible after all.

Blood in the air. Mud in the air. Boy waved his hand in front of his face, as if to clear the cigar smoke. Subdued conversation; guns boomed. Boy set down his cigar and waited. He waited for the present to reassert itself—as it always did in the end. He pulled at his ear. The guns receded. Stern looked at his watch. Boy leaned forward. Clear and concise: an officer and a gentleman.

"This marriage," he said. His voice was too loud. He did not care. "This marriage," he repeated. "I have come here to tell you. It will not take place."

By then, Boy had been in England two days. He had shunted back and forth between London (where he saw Maud) and Winterscombe (where the marriage was to be celebrated). The phrase he used now to Stern—"This marriage will not take place"—was one he had already used, many times.

He had said it to his father, to his mother, to Maud, to Freddie, and to Steenie. Gwen wept. His father told him, brusquely, to mind his own business. Freddie said he could not help; he did not understand it either. Maud said that when Montague was fixed upon something, he was unswerving, and he was fixed upon this. Steenie had advised him to give in. "Stop this marriage?" He had raised his eyes to the ceiling. "Boy, you might as well try to stop an avalanche with a feather duster. Forget it, and forget it now."

Boy had ignored these remarks. He set off in pursuit of Constance. Constance, he feared, was avoiding him, and he did not track her down until late that afternoon. She was walking by the lake.

A monochrome day, frost in the air, the grass crisp beneath his feet, a skim of ice on the lake. Out of the pallor of the air, Constance glittered.

She was wearing a new coat, which was pale and impossibly expensive—even Boy could see that. This coat had a loose hood trimmed with white fox fur. The fur had stiffened in the cold, so that when Constance turned to greet him, with a laugh and a cry of pleasure, he found her face framed in a crown of tiny spikes, a halo of fox and diamonds.

Black hair, eyes blacker than he remembered, a brilliant mouth, tiny puffs of warm air as she cried his name. She took his hand. She pressed it between soft kid gloves.

She reached up on tiptoe. "Francis! You're here!"

She kissed his cheek. She danced toward him, danced away from him, displaying herself, displaying the small dog she had with her. A Pomeranian, snow-white, diminutive, absurd, and antagonistic. Boy could have killed it with one kick. The minute it saw him, the Pomeranian bared its teeth. Constance reprimanded the dog. She fastened its leash, which was scarlet leather attached to a rhinestone collar.

"My engagement present, from Montague!" Constance ruffled the little dog's fur. "Did you ever see a more preposterous animal—or a more vulgar collar? I love them both."

She danced toward him; she danced away from him. Boy had never felt larger or more slow. He pursued Constance, and dog, across the lawns. His feet plodded. They left large footprints in the frost. He explained (he was sure he had explained; he even felt quite certain that he had, as planned, proposed). Constance trickled through his hands; it was like trying to grasp water.

When he had pursued her as far as the terrace, she turned to him. She stood on tiptoe once more. She kissed his cheek once more.

"*Remember?* Darling Francis, of course I remember. I love you dearly too. I always have. I always will. You are my own special guardian and my brother. Oh, Francis, I'm so glad they gave you leave—I should hate to be married and you not there. I shall look for you in the church as I walk up the aisle. Do you remember the little ring you gave me once—the one with the blue stone? I shall be wearing that—something blue, you know, for luck. I want to be lucky. I shall wear it around my neck, so Montague may not be jealous—he can be *so* jealous sometimes." She shivered. "Quickly—it's cold, don't you think? Walk with me, Francis. Take my arm. No—let's run, shall we? I feel like running, and shouting and dancing. How good the air is! I'm so happy today."

She ran with him. She ran away from him. A small deft figure, the ridiculous dog at her heels. After that, she had managed—Boy was sure of this—not to be alone with him.

Which left him, as he had feared from the first, with Stern. Constance, who was a woman, and a child, could not be expected to deal with Stern. He should have seen that from the first.

"Will not take place?" Stern's face came back into focus. He was regarding Boy with a detached and urbane amusement. "The wedding is the day after tomorrow. My dear fellow, I leave for Winterscombe later tonight. I had thought we might travel down together. Is there some difficulty, Boy?"

* * *

"You are not a suitable husband for Constance."

A terrible thing was about to happen: Boy had no premonition of it at all. The sentences were flowing now. An officer and a gentleman. He never stammered once.

"Leaving aside the question of your age, and your . . . friendship with my aunt . . ."

"Leaving them aside?" A faint smile. "Boy, you surprise me."

"Leaving aside questions of your race, of the differences in background . . ."

On and on. The words were like one of the new tanks. He could see them churning up the mud, tilting, flattening. Boy approached his conclusion: He suggested Stern do the honorable thing and call off this marriage. He appealed to his instincts as a gentleman, while making it quite clear he did not consider Stern a gentleman and never would. Stern sipped his whisky. He drew on his cigar.

"Impossible, I'm afraid."

That was all. There was no mention of love, no attempt at justification. The arrogance of this stung Boy. He began to feel very hot. One gun boomed, then another. For the first time Boy began to feel afraid. He scented failure, and because of this he launched himself upon his last assault, one he had hoped to keep in reserve.

He raised the topic of Hector Arlington. Boy did not understand finance as well as he might have liked but he felt he understood this saga well enough. His voice rose. He became excitable.

"Hector and I were in the same regiment. We were very old friends. He told me how you'd advised his mother. Before he died—"

"Ah, yes. A tragic thing. I was very sorry to hear of it."

"You bled them white." Boy banged down his whisky glass. "You hypocrite—you've made a fortune out of this war. You sit there and tell me you're sorry—when it's your fault the Arlingtons went under. Compound interest—you inveigled yourself in there—used my father—used his house and his introductions. If Hector had lived—"

"If Hector Arlington had lived, there would have been only one set of death duties to contend with. Which would have altered the situation considerably. Boy—"

"Don't lie to me." Boy was now scarlet in the face. His hands would not keep still. They waved about in the air. The guns were there again, louder than ever, so loud the Foreign Secretary looked up.

"It's not just the Arlingtons in any case. There are others. I've heard. Your first partners—the ones who took you into their bank. What happened to them? One of them cut his throat—and why did he do that? Because you broke him; you set out to break him. Oh, I know what you'll say. You'll say those are old rumors—but some of those rumors just happen to be true. I've asked people. I've talked to Maud. I've put two and two together and—" Boy stopped. His eyes rounded. "That's it, isn't it? I've just realized. That's why my father is allowing this to happen. He owes you money. Of course. Everyone owes you money. He owes you money, and this marriage is a way of paying you back." Boy took a swallow of whisky to steady himself.

"Well," he continued, beginning to feel proud of himself—this indeed was how his father should have spoken. "I suppose that makes it simpler in a way. We can treat it as what it is: a financial transaction. How much to buy you off, Stern? Obviously there's a price. Name it."

Stern took some time to reply. He did not appear offended, which disappointed Boy. He sipped his whisky before he spoke.

"Oddly enough . . . " Stern looked away, into the middle distance. He sounded ironic, still amused. "Oddly enough, despite the fact that I am a Jew, there is no price. I feel . . . disinclined to be bought off, as you put it."

He glanced at his wristwatch as he said this, as if Boy no longer greatly interested him. Then he reached one of his narrow and elegant hands into the breast pocket of his jacket. He drew out an envelope. He rested that envelope on his knee, without comment. He looked back at Boy. He waited.

"I shall tell Constance," Boy burst out, trying to ignore this envelope. "And not just Constance. I shall . . . speak out. I shall . . . make the truth known. I shall, I shall . . . " He cast around wildly for something decisive that he could do, something that would expose this man for what he was: a moneylender and a profiteer. Money and munitions—how much profit per shell, per bullet, when there were so many bullets, and so many shells?

"Boy." Stern leaned forward. He regarded Boy with quiet eyes. "Boy, I think you are overwrought. No doubt there are reasons for that. You do not look well. Might it not be better if we forgot this conversation, and you left?"

"I won't do that." Boy's face became mutinous and stubborn. He could see Constance dancing away from him on the crisp lawns, with her appalling little dog. "I won't. You shan't ruin Constance's life. If I have to . . . stand up in that church and speak out, I'll do it. Just cause. Just impediment. You were my aunt's lover for years. You're old enough to be Constance's father. Constance does not care for you. She cannot—"

He stopped. Without a word, Stern had leaned across and placed the envelope on his lap.

Boy stared down at it. A small envelope, square, unaddressed and unsealed; there was something inside it, stiffer than a sheet of paper. Blood surged in Boy's head. Slowly—and his hands had begun to shake again—he opened the flap.

A photograph. He had no need to remove it from the envelope completely; just one glance down sufficed, for it was familiar enough. One of his own photographs, one of the secrets of his life: a young girl, Constance as a young girl. Innocence and experience. Her dress was wet.

"Where did you get this?"

The sentence jammed; it stuck on the letter *g*, which would not be pronounced. Stern did not answer the question, merely gave a small and perhaps disdainful gesture of the hand. There was no need for an answer anyway. From Constance herself—Boy knew that. From Constance, to whom he had given so many little presents: the ring with the blue stone, a collar of lace, a shawl of bright silk, a necklace of amber beads—bright magpie things, the hopeless tokens of his devotion. And (when she asked for it, and she asked for so little) the small silver key that opened the chest in his room, that opened the drawer where he kept . . . these photographs.

"I never hurt her. I never touched her. I give you my word on that." The pain was very great, but he had to justify himself, he found, even then, and even to Stern.

"I was looking for her. In my photographs. I wanted . . . to pin her down."

He said this, the best explanation he could give for something he had always seen as a quest, never a perversion. An impossible quest—he saw that now. Constance was not a butterfly, to be pinned, identified, labeled. She resisted categories, just as she had resisted his photographs. The remark, which Boy regretted at once, seemed to make Stern pause.

"I understand. I believe you. Nevertheless . . ."

Something flickered in Stern's eyes—a comprehension, possibly even a sympathy. Then his face became closed. He reached across, retrieved the envelope, replaced it in his pocket.

Boy stumbled to his feet. He felt the ground rock. The table holding his whisky glass tilted upon its tripod feet. No one looked up. Conversations continued. No one seemed to notice that Boy bled.

This confused him. He gave a small, inconclusive gesture of the hand. He turned, without addressing Stern, and navigated his way to the door. He weaved past tables and chairs, and might have been taken for drunk, for he was unsteady on his feet.

When Boy had left, Stern went out to the club's telephones. From there, sitting in a small paneled cubicle, the door closed, he telephoned Constance at Winterscombe. He knew she was awaiting the call.

"Did you do it?"

Her voice came and went on the wires; it had an odd note in it which Stern could not define, which might have been excitement or fear or distress.

"Yes. It was unavoidable, I'm afraid."

He gave her a brief account of the meeting, but Constance would not be content with a brief account; she must know the details. How had Boy looked? What had he said? Had he seemed hurt?

Stern cut these questions short.

"You would hardly have expected him to appear happy, I think."

"Did he cry? He does cry, sometimes. I've made him cry . . . before. Oh, Montague—"

"We will speak tomorrow."

Stern replaced the receiver. He returned to the smoking room. He turned his chair so its back was to the room and he might be left alone and undisturbed. After some while he took the picture out again. Stern pitied Boy, whom he had always liked; and this photograph of Constance he stared at for some time.

Constance wanted her wedding to be fast. She wanted it to be a dance, everything hectic, everything bright, everything quick. No time to think: a day of fragments, like a mesh of stars.

She would have run down the aisle of the Winterscombe church if she could—if Denton, at her side, had not been so slow, so out of breath, so limping from his gout. She felt as light as air; the cold air gathered her up from the huge car with its white ribbons. It gusted her across the churchyard, past the gravestones, which shone with thin hard snow. Into the porch, the nave. She was glad the floor was so cold; she danced over it in her thin satin slippers.

Tiny shoes trimmed with white ribbons, sent from Paris; war, to

Montague Stern, presented no boundaries and no obstacles. Gwen ordered these accouterments; Stern paid for them: slippers from Paris, white stockings of the finest silk fastened with blue garters, which cut her a little.

The dress—such a dress! Fifteen fittings at the House of Worth, *mousseline de soie*, Brussels lace. A long, long train fanning out behind her, a beautiful thing, looped, wired, flounced, embroidered with crystal flowers and stars—a triumph of engineering.

The tiniest of waists, cinched in, and cinched in again, her new maid hauling on the laces of her white corselet—*Pull it tighter*, Constance had cried—seventeen inches, sixteen and a half, sixteen. One span of Montague's fine hands—that was what Constance had intended, and that was what she had achieved. Impossible to breathe, almost, but today she felt she did not need anything as commonplace as oxygen; she was air itself: bright and invincible, like air, like a diamond.

There were diamonds around her wrists and diamonds in her ears; diamonds were strewn like tears in the artifice of her veil. The diamonds were a present from Montague; they lay on her wrists and, around her throat, like rain. They were her badge, the talisman of her daring.

Glancing to right and left, proceeding up the aisle, Constance felt she triumphed. What if the congregation was smaller and less distinguished than she might have wished? People feared scandal, that was all. Some who had been invited stayed away on Maud's account. So be it; Constance did not care. They would not ostracize for long; they would seek her out, all those who hesitated now. She would win them over. She and Montague would lay siege to them.

Lady Cunard was there, despite Maud. A woman who sensed the rising of a new star in the firmament; Constance gave her a little nod. Who else? Gus Alexander, the construction king, who once sent her a basket containing two hundred crimson roses. Conrad Vickers, who—in the face of Boy's refusal—was to take the wedding photographs. He flirted with Steenie. Three members of the Cabinet—they had come without their wives. Several prominent financiers. County neighbors, leaned upon by Gwen. Oh, it was enough, after all—this wedding was just the beginning.

Constance had reached the family pews. There was Gwen, her head bowed. There was Freddie; Boy, in full dress uniform; Steenie, who held her new little dog upon his lap—the dog had to be there, too; Constance had insisted, to the consternation of the vicar.

Poor little dog: she must leave him behind for her honeymoon.

Constance blew the animal a kiss. She smiled at Steenie, Freddie, Boy—who averted his face.

Twenty paces more; ten. There was the altar, decked with flowers, all of them white, as Constance had decreed: "White," she had said, "and no lilies."

There was the best man, some friend of Montague's—Constance did not give him a second glance. There was Stern, turning now, at last, as she approached. An even, level gaze; an unusual sobriety of dress.

Then—how slowly Montague Stern spoke the vows! Constance gave him an impatient glance. Why speak them so slowly and so weightily? If ever a man was an atheist, Montague was. "To have and to hold, from this day forward." Constance did not like the words at all; she refused to listen to them. Let them skip past, for they were full of traps, these words. Constance hated promises. Acland had promised her not to die; promises were air, and people never kept them.

When the ring was upon her finger she felt a great agitation, then the next second, a great security. There! It was almost done. Just a few more words and the whole thing would be over.

Quickly, quickly. Stern's hand touched hers. She was a married woman: Lady Stern. Constance stared at the altar. A cloth of white and gold. She tried out this new title on her tongue. Hard and bright and sure.

It was time for the bride to be kissed. Stern took her in his arms, as she had known he would, with an icy decorum. Constance turned her head. Her veil billowed. The veil spoiled the congregation's view. She laced her small arms tight about his neck.

Stern's eyes met hers behind the protection of that veil. His glance was as she had expected: cool, unmoved, watchful, and intent. As his lips brushed hers, Constance darted her tongue between them. She would ruffle this composure of his.

"Well, adversary," she murmured into his ear. She rested her cheek against his. This was a new term adopted between them. Stern's hand tightened over hers.

"Well, wife," he replied, with curious emphasis.

They turned. Constance shivered. The organ pealed: abrasive Bach.

The wedding photographs; the wedding breakfast. The photographs, which were to launch Vickers's career, were silver print, exquisite; Constance keeps them still.

The wedding breakfast, and a menu chosen by Constance, the first time she was to exercise her preference—which was for the rare, the expensive, and the small. Thimble-sized servings of caviar; quails' eggs in silver baskets; truffles as small as bullets, seasoned with a sauce of marrowbone; tiny woodcock perched upon fragments of toast.

Constance ate little. She was impatient to move on. One glass of Denton's pink champagne; one sliver of *foie gras*. The only person at the table who ate less than the bride was Boy.

There would be no dancing after the wedding breakfast; again, Constance had decreed. The honeymoon was to be spent at Denton's Scottish estate; the journey ahead of the bridal couple was long. Constance left the table at one; by one-thirty she was ready. She dismissed her new maid, who was slow, compared to Jenna. She surveyed herself in her glass. She pirouetted.

Not an ermine coat, after all. Constance had thought of ermine, then rejected it when she discovered that ermine was a species of weasel. Stern had provided sables. A cream traveling suit of silk and cashmere. (Scotland would be cold. Constance did not care. She would have welcomed even Norway, Sweden, Finland—the colder, the farther north, the better. Even if there had been no war, even if it had not been a winter wedding, Constance would have despised the idea of Italy or France. She wanted extremity.)

A cream traveling suit. Soft cream kid boots, which laced to the knee. A collar of pearls four inches deep, worn in the way Queen Mary had made fashionable. A hat with a veil—Constance had insisted upon a veil. She regarded her face in the glass, pleased with the way the veil obscured her expression.

So many goodbyes. The guests. The family. Gus Alexander, who, subduing jealousy, invited the couple most warmly to visit him in New York. A small drab lawyer named Solomons. Lady Cunard. Conrad Vickers, Denton, Gwen, Freddie, Boy, Steenie. Boy appeared to be drunk (in fact he was not; he was sober but looked dazed). As Constance kissed his cheek and bade him write to her from France, Boy pressed into her hands a small note. This irritated Constance. She put it, unread, into her handbag.

She flew to Steenie, whom she hugged. She pressed her little dog in her arms and kissed his nose and let him lick her face. She gave Steenie a rush of last-minute instructions. She kissed the dog once more; she clung to him; she allowed herself to be drawn away.

Into a great, stately car for the drive to London. Then, the night train north.

Her wedding night would be spent on the move. At that thought, Constance gave a laugh of delight. Turning to her husband, she kissed him, first chastely, then—as the great car gathered speed— more flagrantly.

Stern responded, yet he seemed preoccupied. This irritated Constance. She made a restless gesture. She drew back. Stern said nothing. Constance turned to the window; she rested her face against the cold of its glass.

In their compartments on the night train, they drank champagne. The attendant (this had clearly been arranged) brought them oysters.

"They smell of sex," Constance said, tipping back the shell.

Once the train whistled and jolted and the wheels' revolutions became rhythmic, Constance began to explore.

How intriguing these compartments were, how clever and luxurious! She looked around her with a childish delight: all this paneling and woolen padding, everything scaled down but as neat and snug as a ship captain's cabin. A small table that when lifted revealed a porcelain washing basin. Little cupboards with towels, fresh cakes of soap, and drinking glasses. Numerous hooks and shelves. So many pretty lamps, with pink silk shades that gave a flattering light: one by the basin, one by the door, one by her bed. A doll's house!

Constance inspected her bed, which had starched white pillowcases. The blankets were tartan. She frowned at these, for tartan rugs reminded her of her father's accident. For an instant, a bunk became a stretcher. She looked away. She sped off to the partition doors, which folded back, and found that the second compartment also had a bed, with similar furnishings.

"Two beds." She turned to smile at Stern. "I shall not call them bunks—they are far too splendid!" She paused. "Shall we take turns in them, do you think? It is such a long journey. . . ."

"We could do that." Stern had taken up a position by the door. He watched, arms folded.

"What I should like . . ." Constance eyed him. She unfastened her pearls and let them swing back and forth between her fingers, like a pendulum. "What I should like . . ."

"Tell me what you would like."

"I think I should like to lie on my furs."

"And?"

"Leave my stockings on, perhaps. And my pretty garters. And my wicked French boots. Yes, I might like that. You could pleasure me, Montague, with my boots on. Which is a kind of quotation, though I think it should be the other way about."

"Is it now?" Stern unfolded his arms. He began to remove his jacket. "Show me how you look then, Constance, on your sables."

At this, Constance tossed her furs across the tartan. Once its checks were invisible, she made a brief effort to undo her dress.

"I'm hopeless without a maid. Montague, you will have to help me."

She turned and offered Stern her narrow back. His cool hands glanced against her throat, then began upon the hooks and eyes. So many of them! Constance remained absolutely still. She closed her eyes. She opened them again. She listened to Stern's breathing, which was steady.

When the dress was undone and Stern had eased it from her shoulders, it fell to her ankles. Constance kicked it to one side. She did not turn to face him, but leaned back within the circle of his arms.

She caught his hands and drew them down, to prove that they would span her waist. She guided them upward again, so that they covered her breasts.

"Stroke me," Constance said. She looked down, to watch Stern's well-manicured fingers move across her skin. She bit her lip. She caught hold of his hand and pressed it tight against her lips. The train gathered speed. Stern's hand was dry and smelt faintly of soap, but not carnation soap. For a moment, this confused her.

Constance drew his hand back down to her breasts. She closed her eyes once more. The train rocked. She gave a small moan. She had known that she would do this, after so many inventive delays; she now began to believe that she could do this. She leaned back tighter within the circle of his arms. She felt his penis, like a rod against the small of her back.

Was he watching her? Constance believed that Stern always watched her. She bent her head. Stern kissed the nape of her neck; she felt his lips against her vertebrae. In a proficient way, with the air of some practice, Stern loosened her hair, then unlaced the corselet. The whalebone had left small scarlet weals across her ribs. Constance opened her eyes and looked down at these. She rubbed at them, as if she could rub them out. A lurch, then another gathering of speed. Constance gathered her will.

With one quick twist she slipped from Stern's arms, as slippery, as silvery, as dexterous as a fish. She threw herself back on her furs, looked up at Stern, who was removing the pin from his cravat.

Constance fixed her eyes upon the pin, then the cravat, then the jacket, then the waistcoat. She watched Stern fold these objects upon a chair. When he turned back to her, Constance reached up and switched off the pink light.

"Leave it on," Stern said. "I want to look at you."

Constance switched the light back on. Stern stood for a while, looking down at her. He moved to her side, then sat down upon the edge of the small bed.

This was the first time Stern had seen her completely naked. Constance had expected a swifter, more immediate response. She lay very still, counting seconds. Stern continued to look at her. He lifted his hand and ran one finger softly down the length of her body, from the hollow at the base of her throat to the black patch of hair between her thighs.

"You have beautiful skin."

He removed his hand. Constance found she could not tell whether he liked her nakedness or found it disappointing. Something seemed to perplex him. She had never seen his face more guarded than it was now.

"Shall we talk—for a while?"

This suggestion, made in an odd way, with some hesitancy, astonished Constance. She considered the idea of Stern as a shy bridegroom and rejected it at once. She sat up. She wound her small arms about his neck.

"Talk, now? Montague—we are husband and wife."

"Husbands and wives can converse on occasion, presumably?"

He might have been amused, but he disengaged her arms from his neck.

"On occasion, perhaps. But on their wedding night? Aren't there more pressing matters—"

"Nothing is pressing now. We have the rest of our lives, after all." He paused. "You understand the meaning of the word *know*—as it is used in the Bible?"

"But of course." Constance smiled. "Adam knew Eve. It means . . . fuck. I am not a child, Montague."

Her use of the word *fuck* seemed to annoy him. He frowned. Constance, who had been about to lay one small jeweled hand on his thigh, drew that hand back.

"And so? *Know*—very well, I understand its meaning. What difference does it make?"

"Just that I thought, before we know each other in that way, we should know each other more in others. You know very little about me, Constance, and in some ways, I know very little about you—"

"Montague, how can you say that?" Constance sat up. "Why, you know me through and through—everything that is important about me, I have either told you or you have seen for yourself. You see—look! Here I am, quite naked before my husband."

As she said this, Constance leaned back once more, so that her black hair fanned out upon the white pillows. She folded her arms behind her head, an attitude that lifted and displayed her breasts to advantage. She waited for this pose to produce the right effect, for Stern to forget this curious desire for conversation.

The pose did not produce that effect. Stern's face became set.

"Very well. If you choose to believe your nature is transparent to me, you must do so. It is not the case. And I thought you might want . . . There were certain things I wished to say to you—about myself."

There was a silence. Constance's heart gave a sudden skip. She looked more closely at her husband's face. A struggle seemed to be taking place between this silence and speech, between revelation and reticence. A secret, then! She was about to be told a secret—something, she felt suddenly sure, that Stern had told no one else. What could it be? Might it concern money, some dark event from his earlier life, an event that explained the swiftness of his rise? Or might it be a woman? Attentive now, Constance held her breath.

"I have never told anyone this before," Stern began slowly. "I shall never tell anyone again. But you are my wife now, and I would like you to know. It concerns my childhood."

Stern then told Constance a story. It concerned his childhood, as he said, a childhood that had been loving, but one of poverty.

As a boy, he said, the devout child of devout parents, Stern had worn a yarmulke. Provided he remained within the Jewish areas of Whitechapel, this was safe; it was less safe if he ventured farther afield. There, gentile boys threw stones at Jews. Certain streets were protected; others were not.

Once, returning from an errand for his father, an errand that had taken him beyond the Jewish quarter, he was first cornered, then set upon by a group of these gentile boys. He was alone, aged nine. The boys were older, larger, stronger, and there were eight of them. He was carrying a length of worsted cloth, expensive cloth needed for a special order, cloth his father could not afford to replace. This cloth was taken from him, ripped apart with knives, then thrown in the gutter while two of the boys held him pinioned and made him watch.

When the cloth was ruined, one of the boys had a further invention. They snatched the yarmulke from his head. One boy spat on it; another urinated on it; a third had the happy idea of then stuffing it into Stern's mouth. They told him to eat it. When Stern refused, they took turns at punching him, then kicking him. They broke his nose with a boot cap. They screamed obscenities about his mother and his sisters, kicked him again, grew bored, and then left him.

When he returned home, his mother wept. His father, who was a small man, in poor health, picked up a stick and went out into the streets to look for the boys, but he never found them. The incident seemed to weaken him. It was not long afterward that he contracted pneumonia and died. Stern's mother was left with six children, Montague being the eldest, and no means of support. Stern, with the backing of his father's brother, also a tailor, left school and went to work at his father's bench. Later, when he was thirteen, he was taken on as a messenger boy at a City merchant bank, where he received five shillings a week.

"And that was how I began in business," he said.

There was then a silence. Constance waited for her husband to continue. Surely, she thought, surely that could not be the whole story? Where was the revelation in that? Why, she could almost have guessed as much. After a while, when Stern still did not speak, she sat up, allowing the sheet to fall away from her breasts. She put her hand in his.

"I am listening," she said. "Tell me the rest."

"The rest?" Stern turned back to look at her, his eyes blank. "There is—no rest. That was what I wished to tell you."

"That was all? But, Montague, I don't understand. I knew something of that sort might have happened to you. There is prejudice, vile prejudice, and—"

"Something of that sort?" Stern rose. He stood looking down at her. Constance gave a small cry; she attempted to put her arms about his waist.

"Montague—don't look at me like that! You misunderstand. It is a horrible story—I can see. But still, I feel there is something *more*, something you still leave out. Tell me—please tell me. I shall understand, whatever it is—"

"There is nothing more."

"Dearest Montague, you can tell me. I am your wife. However

terrible—I shall understand. Look, I shall guess. You went after these boys—you knew who they were. You bided your time and then, maybe years later, you took your revenge. Oh!" She gave a small shiver; her eyes had become very bright. "I am right—I can tell by your face. By your eyes. You did something very . . . bad. What was it? Did you kill one of them, Montague? When I look at you now, I think you could kill. Did you? Did you?"

Stern released her hands. He took a step backward. His expression had become so cold that Constance was silenced.

"I never knew the boys. I never saw any of them, ever again. You have an overdramatic imagination, Constance—also an overactive one. You miss the point, my dear."

"Miss the point?" Constance was stung by his tone. "Well, no doubt I am being very stupid and slow. Today is my wedding day. I didn't expect to be carried back to Whitechapel on my wedding night. However, if I am to be—you had better explain. Spell it out, Montague, why don't you? What is the point?"

There was a silence. Some struggle seemed to take place within Stern.

"You look so very lovely. Your skin. Your hair. Your eyes." Stern stopped. He looked at Constance, who began to scent victory. She lowered her eyes.

"I thought you must find me ugly. Montague, that was why I was stupid and slow, I—"

"You are not ugly. I have never seen you more beautiful."

He laid his hand lightly against her throat. He lifted her hair away from her face. Constance thought he hesitated—Stern, who never hesitated. Then he moved away.

"I was damaged once—that is the point. My thinking was damaged and—some people would say—my heart. I wanted you to know that. If you are to understand my character—should you care to do so—it might assist you. The damage has been of great use to me, you see. I turned it to advantage long ago."

He paused. Constance began, for the first time, to see that she might have made a serious mistake. The tone he now used was so polite it chilled her skin.

"Whenever I find myself about to commit a precipitate action, or say something I will later regret . . ." He paused, looking her in the eyes. "And that does happen, even on occasion to me—I remember that episode. I think of it, and I find it checks me. It prevents my being rash. It prevents my trusting others—and that is a great advantage, both in business affairs and, I see, with my wife. Goodnight, Constance."

He opened the door to the next compartment. Constance sprang to the floor. She clasped his arm.

"Montague—what are you doing? Where are you going? I don't understand. What are you prevented from doing? What do you choose not to say?"

"Nothing, my dear. Go back to bed."

"I shall know—you shall tell me! What might you have said?"

"Nothing of any importance. Forget what I said. I'm sure you will."

"Montague—"

"My dear, I dislike to make love to you on a train—I think that is it. It has been a long journey this far, and a long journey remains ahead of us. It might be better, I think, if we were both to get some sleep."

He closed the dividing door. Constance heard the bolt drawn across. She began to feel cold; she began to shake. Her nakedness seemed foolish. She hated it. She gave a small angry cry, then wrapped herself tight, head to foot, in her fur coat. She stood quite still, listening.

It was hard to hear any sounds above the wheel's revolutions, but she thought she heard water run, the rustle of clothes or perhaps sheets. She stared fixedly at the band of light under Stern's door. After some while the light went off.

Constance considered. If she were to tap on the door or call her husband's name, she was sure he would come back to her—almost sure. She lifted a hand to rap the panels, then changed her mind and stepped back.

Plead, on her wedding night? Never!

For a while this mood of angry defiance sustained her. She paced up and down the small compartment. She considered what her husband had said; she turned it first this way, then that way. She prised his words apart, like a child taking a new toy to pieces. She reassembled the pieces. Some still did not fit; her husband's obvious anger remained a mystery—for what had she said to provoke that?

After some half an hour she was convinced: She, Constance, had hit on the correct solution. Only half the story had been told, and the second half, the untold half, was violent—just as she had guessed! Stern had committed some act of revenge, some dark, wicked, diabolical thing, and one day, later if not sooner, she would prise that secret from him. She wanted to know it, inside out!

There it was, she felt: the mysterious source of her husband's power. It lay in that capacity for violence which he hid from the eyes of the world. Beneath that controlled, polite, urbane exterior lay the secret husband, the predatory husband. Oh, it was dangerous to cross that man. He had the instinct for the jugular, perhaps even—yes— the capacity to kill.

This notion excited Constance. It excited her physically. Her skin prickled to be touched. Her nipples made hard points against the silk lining of her furs. She put her hand between her legs. She closed her eyes. She leaned back against the door that divided her from her husband. She rubbed one finger back and forth. A little beak of pleasure, there, just against her fingertip. It made her hot, also shivery; she could feel the blood rush about her head. To make love to a murderer, to make him spill himself and all his secrets into her, to swallow up all that hard male power—oh, the carnage, the rape and the pillage of such wicked, wicked sex. Who wanted tenderness when they could have this: a trip down a hot dark corridor, to the very darkest place? Constance moaned. She bit her lip. She wriggled and rubbed until her own little hand took her down there to that place she itched to reach. One sweet hot small moment of extinction: the *little death*, poets used to call it—or so Acland once said.

At once Constance felt calmer. All the anger and defiance had gone. She had no inclination now to tap upon her husband's door. Let him sleep—she could wait! She had no desire for sleep either; she knew that. But Constance was used to sleeplessness, which she preferred to bad dreams—and her dreams were often bad. She whiled away the time in unpacking her overnight case. She took out her new hairbrushes with her new initials: C.S.—the same as her old! She brushed her hair. She admired her wedding nightgown. She looked at the tartan blankets upon the bed, then pulled them off and stuffed them under the bunk where she need not see them. This done, her eye was caught by the sight of her small kid handbag, which she had hung upon a hook on the back of the compartment door. It swung back and forth with the rhythms of the train. Constance considered this pendulum bag; she considered Boy's note, which must still be inside it.

After a while, growing bored with her other diversions, she took the bag down and drew out the note. She gave a yawn. She slit open the envelope with her nail (no longer bitten—she had cured herself of that). Reproaches, she thought, *how dull*, and she unfolded her letter.

It was not so very long—just one page. Constance read it once; she read it again; she read it a third time. Then, because this letter made her feel cold, made her hands numb, made her body start to quiver and shake, she pushed the letter back in her bag, pushed the bag away, out of sight.

She would not look at it. She did not want to look at it. She pulled on her nightgown and crept between the sheets. She switched off the light. The letter pursued her into bed. It would not let her sleep.

What time was it? Past midnight. There was nothing she could do and no one she could tell.

Where were they? They stopped, sometimes. Every time they stopped, right through the night, Constance crept out of bed. She pushed back the stiff window blind and peered out. But the stations were too dark, or their signs sped by too fast. Birmingham? Manchester? Newcastle? York?

She had no idea of their route, and this frightened her. She hugged her arms tight about her chest. They were traveling north. They were in the dark. They were moving on, faster and faster, when just for once, all she wanted to do was stop.

It did not take long for the wedding guests to disperse. By three, the last of them were leaving. Only Conrad Vickers remained, but he would not stay long. Steenie found the absence of the guests disconcerting. The rest of Steenie's family seemed to feel this transformation, too, as if the house no longer fitted them. For a while they huddled around the fire in the drawing room, trying to make conversation. Steenie felt as if all the animation in the house had departed with Constance.

The conversation became desultory. It drained away. His father fell asleep. Freddie flicked the pages of *Horse and Hound* and stared morosely at advertisements for shooting clothing. Gwen sat alone by the window, gazing out toward the lake; her hair was gray, Steenie saw—grayer than he had noticed before. He knew she was not looking at the lake; she was looking at her dead son, Acland.

The other side of the room, on the chaise longue favored by Maud, sat Boy. He sat bolt-upright, his hands on his knees; he made cracking noises with his fingers. He looked as if he were waiting for the command to go over the top. Wherever Boy was, Steenie thought, it was not Winterscombe.

Had Wexton been with him, Steenie would not have minded his family's slump into this anticlimactic silence. But Wexton was not there, and Vickers was—smart, metropolitan Vickers, who took such clever photographs, who dared to wear his hair even longer than

Steenie's. Steenie was not sure he liked Vickers, though he wished to emulate him in certain matters—clothes, for instance. Also, Vickers flirted with him; there was no doubt about that, and Steenie found it flattering. Wexton had been away such a long time.

Vickers seemed quite prepared to ignore the heavy silence that lay upon the room. He was a great chatterer, and he chattered on now: a postmortem on the wedding. Vickers's intention was to dissect the rest of the guests.

While Steenie admired his clothes, Vickers went down the guest list. He came to Constance. He discussed her dress, her veil, her astonishing diamonds. He came to Stern. He said how surprising it was—for once the man seemed to have made an effort to display taste. No violent waistcoat—and Stern might have been capable of that, even in morning dress.

"Such restraint!" Vickers laughed again. He reached across the sofa and put his hand on Steenie's knee. "Tell me, is he reforming, do you think, or is it Constance's influence?"

"Oh, I shouldn't think so." Steenie considered Vickers's hand. The pressure of his fingers was not unpleasant.

"Connie adores him just the way he is. She says he's courageous —to be so consistently vulgar. She says he does it on purpose."

"No!" Vickers looked delighted by this minor revelation. "My dear, tell me more. I *long* to understand that marriage. Frankly, I have to say"—he lowered his voice—"I find him just the tiniest bit *sinister*. I can't *tell* you the rumors I've heard. My sister said . . ."

He continued with these rumors for some while. Steenie listened, then half-listened. He tried to think about Wexton. He tried to summon up Wexton's face. When this did not work, Steenie began to look at Boy—and what he saw alarmed him.

Boy was still sitting bolt upright on the chaise longue. His hands were still on his knees. His eyes were still fixed on the middle distance. His face was blank. Occasionally he shook his head from side to side. Once or twice Steenie saw his lips move: words, silent sentences. Boy was apparently now talking to himself.

Afterward, Steenie would never be quite sure whether it was concern for Boy or a desire to escape from Conrad Vickers that motivated him to propose the walk. Perhaps both: he felt that if he sat with Vickers any longer, he might be both influenced and coerced into some betrayal of Wexton; besides which, he could scarcely sit there and let his brother talk to the air. Any minute now and Vickers would notice. Steenie squirmed and then stood. He looked down at Constance's Pomeranian, curled in a resentful ball on the sofa next to Vickers, and inspiration came to him.

"A walk," he said rather wildly. "I ought to take Connie's dog for a walk. Boy, Vickers, won't you come with me?"

Vickers threw up his hands in horror.

"Walk! My dear Steenie—all that nasty wet mud? All that terrible fresh air? My dear, *no*. In fact, it's late—perhaps I ought—"

Boy had not reacted to Steenie's suggestion at all. He continued to stare into space. Steenie thought he might not have heard him.

With some haste he maneuvered Vickers out to the portico steps. Vickers was staying with other friends nearby; he remarked on this. He said Steenie must come over and meet them, *very soon*.

Then, pausing by his motorcar, he looked back to the house.

"I must say, Boy is awfully *odd*, don't you think? Whatever's the matter with him?"

Steenie blushed crimson.

"It's . . . the war," he began hastily. "France. You know. Acland was exactly the same. He'll be all right in a day or so—it just takes him a while to adjust . . ."

Vickers did not seem convinced by this. He pressed Steenie's hand. He kissed his pink-and-white cheek.

"Too sad. My dear, remember—if you feel too gloomy, if you need to talk, just *pop* over. I'm sure to be there . . ."

Steenie watched his car disappear down the drive. He turned back to the house with reluctance. Halfway up those steps he began to wish he had gone with Vickers there and then. At the top of those steps he encountered Boy, who seemed recovered.

Boy swung his arms. He took deep breaths. His voice was loud and jocular.

"A walk," he said to a portico pillar. "Jolly good idea. Just what we all need. Give the dog a run, eh?"

He gave Constance's Pomeranian, peeing against the pillar, a look of pure dislike. "Just go and change out of all this clobber," he said to the sky. "See you downstairs then, in a minute."

He reappeared some fifteen minutes later. Steenie had put on his London overcoat, his London scarf and gloves, and his London shoes. He did not like country clothes. Boy had put on his oldest tweeds, shooting stockings, brogues. He wore a flat cap, one of the Purdeys was under his arm, and the Pomeranian was at his heels. He looked, Steenie thought, ridiculous.

"Boy, what are you doing? We're not going up on the grouse

moors, you know. We're taking a very small dog for a very small stroll by the lake—"

"The lake? I thought we might go up to the woods, put up a few rabbits. It's a fine day—why not?"

"Oh, honestly, Boy. And I suppose you think that thing"— Steenie gestured at the Pomeranian—"that thing is going to retrieve? This I have to watch."

They set off for the lake. They took the path that wound around its shore and led toward the woods. Boy whistled. The air was clear and sharp. The Pomeranian pattered behind them. To his surprise, Steenie felt his spirits rise. Perhaps, he thought, he might just "pop over" to Vickers's the next day—Wexton could hardly object to that.

He fell into step beside his brother. Boy, too, was cheerful. He was in a nostalgic mood, but his nostalgia was brisk. That was the tree they all used to climb; he pointed it out. Acland had claimed you could see eternity from its top—which, of course, was typical of Acland. There was the old boathouse; did Steenie remember the punt they used to keep there, now rotten? Oh, and there, just upstream, was the best place to fish.

When they reached the wood, these memories continued. Steenie, too, became caught up in them. Yes, that was the place all four brothers had once made a camp. That was the tree on which they had all carved their initials, and the date. The initials were still there, cut deep into the growing wood. Steenie looked at the date: 1905. The last summer they had spent at Winterscombe without Edward Shawcross.

Boy had walked on a little way. Steenie paused, then ran after him.

"Not that path, Boy. I'm not going that way."

"What?" Boy turned. His face looked blank again, Steenie saw, as if he were having difficulty hearing.

"Not that way." Steenie tugged at his brother's arm. "It goes to the clearing. You know. Where . . . the accident was. I'm not going that way. I never do—not for all the tea in China."

"Oh, all right." Boy seemed not to mind the change of plan. He looked around him somewhat fussily, then sat down on a fallen tree trunk. He patted his pockets and drew out his pipe, then a box of matches, then his pouch of tobacco. Boy's pipe-smoking, taken up only recently, irritated Steenie. Such a performance! All that crumbling of the tobacco, the tamping down, the succession of matches, the reflective puffings and drawings. Maddeningly slow!

However, Boy did not like his pipe rituals to be hastened, so after a while Steenie sat down next to him and lit a cigarette. He watched Constance's dog patter back and forth among fallen leaves. He looked at his watch.

"Boy," he said, "the light will go in a minute. We'd better start back."

Boy had almost persuaded his tobacco to catch. He sucked at the pipe. The tobacco glowed.

"I killed him, you know," he said in a conversational way. "I killed Shawcross. I've told Constance about it. I've given her a note. I wanted her to know, now she's married. Do you think she'll have read it yet? Will they have reached the train yet? Maybe she'll save it and read it tomorrow."

Steenie became very still. He watched the dog. He considered what to do.

"Boy." He put his hand on his brother's arm. His voice squeaked. "Boy, let's go back now. You look awfully tired. I think—I think maybe you're not very well. Do you have a headache? Maybe, if we went back now, you could lie down, and then—"

"Headache? I don't have a headache. I feel fine. Why shouldn't I feel fine? This is a wedding day—of course I feel fine."

Steenie swallowed nervously. He tried to think calmly and clearly. Boy was mad. He was sitting here with his brother, on the edge of the woods, and his brother was mad. It was the war. This was what the war did to people. He had heard about it, discussed it once with Wexton. There was a name for this condition of Boy's: It was *battle fatigue*. Steenie tried to think of what Wexton would do in these circumstances. Wexton would do . . . something sensible. He would . . . humor Boy—yes, that was it: humor him.

Steenie sprang to his feet. "Goodness, it's so cold. I'm freezing. Come on, Boy—I can't sit here a second longer. Let's go back."

Boy did not move. He continued to puff on his pipe. He stared at Constance's dog, who, having had an energetic scratch, was now licking itself. Having licked, it curled up in a ball on a pile of leaves and prepared for sleep.

"I didn't push him into the trap," Boy went on, speaking as if there had been no interruption or pause. "I wouldn't want Constance to think I did that. I didn't know it was there, you see. But the thing was . . . Mama went to his room, and she shouldn't have done that. He shouldn't have done that. It was very wrong of him. It hurt Papa. It wounded him. I suppose . . . that Papa ought to have killed him. But I knew he never would. And I was the eldest—it was my job. I wasn't a boy any longer, you see. I was a man. I was engaged, that night. The timing was right."

Boy looked up at Steenie as he said this. His expression was anxious, as if he wanted Steenie to confirm what he said was right. Steenie knelt down. He clasped Boy's hands.

"Of *course* it was, Boy. I understand. Now, look—you don't want to think about that now. Take my arm. We'll go home—"

"I talked it over with Acland, you know. I did that first. I thought I'd better *consult*. He . . . I can't quite remember what he said. He thought it was a good idea—yes, I'm sure he said that. It might have been Acland who thought of the Purdeys—or was it me? How odd. I can't remember. It's the guns, you see. All those guns. The noise never stops."

He shook his head. He jiggled at his ear. Steenie had begun to cry.

"Look, Boy, please come back. Please don't talk about this any more. Boy—none of it's true. It's the war—the war makes you think like this."

"The war? What war?"

"Boy, you *know* what war. France, Belgium—the trenches. Please come home—"

"Oh, *that* war. I see what you mean. I thought you meant the other one." Boy stood up. He knocked his pipe out against the tree trunk. He put the pipe back in his pocket. His face brightened. "Anyway, I've explained to Constance now. I feel better having done that. I told her how it all went wrong. You see, I would have shot him. It would have been very quick and very clean, a good death. But the trouble was . . ."

He lowered his voice. He turned to Steenie with a confiding air. "Her father was a coward. I didn't tell Constance that. I thought it was better she didn't know. He—he broke down. He started weeping, pleading. He lost control. He—well, I can tell you this: He wet himself. That happens, you know, to some men. I've seen it. They're frightened of dying, and . . . they scream too. Shawcross screamed. I think he screamed. He tried to run away—and that was how it happened. That was the wrong thing to do, you see. He hadn't had the right training. What you should do is keep very still. Deep breaths—then your hands don't shake. You don't stammer. Nothing. You look death straight in the eye—for the sake of your men, you see. Oh, and you can shout. Mackay—Sergeant Mackay—he says shouting is the best thing. You know what he said to me?"

Boy took Steenie's arm. He leaned down to whisper. "*Shout, sir. That's what he says. Shout to freeze their guts. Louder, sir. That's it. Let them have it. Make them shit themselves. Fucking Kraut bastards.*"

Boy straightened. He smiled. "I don't approve of his language, of course. But that's the way he talks. And he's right. It works. Shouting works. Stops the shakes. But you see, Shawcross didn't know that. So he ran—like a rabbit. Straight into the mine field."

Boy stopped. He lifted his Purdey, broke it, tucked it under his arm. He whistled to the Pomeranian. He took Steenie's arm and set off toward the path.

"I've destroyed my photographs, you know," he remarked, still in an easy tone, as they reached the lake. "Thought I'd better do that. Just the ones in the bottom drawer. I told Constance that too. I wanted her to know. Why do you think she's marrying that man, eh? Why would she do a thing like that?"

They had reached the birch grove. Steenie's face was wet. He needed to blow his nose, but did not dare. *Just keep walking*, he said to himself; they could already see the lights of the house. Boy seemed to be waiting for a reply.

"Well, Boy," Steenie said in a bright and sensible voice, "I expect she likes him, don't you? She may even love him, you never know—"

"Oh, no. I don't think so." Boy stopped. He shook his head. "I think you're wrong there. No, no. It's me she loves. It always was. I'm her special brother. Her guardian. She told me so herself."

"Oh, yes—of course. I forgot." Steenie hesitated. On the terrace above them he could just see the figure of Freddie, wandering back and forth in a desultory way. Steenie waved his arms desperately. Freddie, looking the wrong way, did not see this wave. Steenie wondered if he dared to shout. No, perhaps it was better not to shout. It might startle Boy.

Boy was now staring at the trees of the birch grove. "Freddie's birthday," he said. "We had a picnic—do you remember? It was here, wasn't it? Yes. It was. I remember, I was sitting just over there, and Constance was behind me, under those trees—"

"Yes. That's right. We had champagne—pink champagne." Steenie squeezed Boy's arm. He edged away a few paces. He waved his arms again in the air; still Freddie did not see him.

"I know. Look, Boy, there's Freddie now. Just up by the house. Why don't I go and fetch him? Then we could all sit here for a while and . . . and remember the picnic, all Freddie's presents, what we had to eat. You'd like that, wouldn't you, Boy?"

"Good idea. You fetch him. I'll just sit down here and wait. Have another pipe, maybe. This is very good tobacco. I bought it in London. Not that terrible army-issue stuff . . ."

Boy sat down beneath a tree. The Pomeranian, bored now, also sat down. A small white puff of fur; it sat there, tongue lolling, looking out toward the lake. Steenie backed off a few more paces. He walked ten yards, looked back. Boy had his tobacco pouch out; he was beginning the process of stuffing the pipe.

Steenie began to run. He ran another ten yards. He waved his arms. He was half-blinded with tears. What was the *matter* with Freddie—had he gone blind? He waved again; he risked a small shout. Freddie looked up; Steenie gave a sob of relief. He increased his pace, his London coat flapping, his London shoes slipping on the grass.

"Freddie," he called. "Freddie, for God's sake."

Freddie began to walk toward him. Steenie stumbled, righted himself, ran faster still. His scarf fell off; he dropped his gloves. He waved his arms once more in a kind of wild semaphore, and finally— how long it took—Freddie seemed to pick up this signal of distress. He, too, began to run. Steenie cannoned into him a few yards below the terrace. He clutched at Freddie's coat. He had been running uphill and was panting so badly he could scarcely speak.

"Freddie—oh, Freddie, come—quickly—"

"What the hell is it? Steenie, calm down—"

"It's Boy. Freddie, please. Just come. It's terrible. He's sitting down there. He's probably talking to himself. He's mad—totally mad. Look, just come—I'll explain later. Oh, Freddie, it was horrible. He just keeps talking, on and on—he says these mad things. I've had to listen . . . It went on for hours. Freddie, please—"

"Where is he?"

"Down there, by the birch grove. He's having a pipe. I thought I'd never get him back to the house. He went on and on—Freddie, all these mad things. He thinks he killed Shawcross—"

"*What?*" Freddie, who had begun to run back down the slope, stopped.

"He does. He does. Freddie—it's the war. He doesn't know what he's saying. What's the matter?"

Steenie, running to catch up with Freddie, had just seen his brother's face.

"Oh, my God," Freddie said.

Steenie, turning, saw what Freddie had seen. It was there below him, a tableau: Boy, the gun, and Constance's dog. The dog, a tiny white spot from where they stood, was still sitting in the same place; Boy was not. He was standing perhaps twelve feet from the animal, his gun raised; it was clear, both to Steenie and to Freddie, that he had the dog in his sights.

"He's going to shoot it. Freddie, he's going to shoot it. Do something—do something quickly. Call to him, Freddie, attract his attention, wave—"

Freddie opened his mouth. No sound came out. He waved his arms. Steenie waved his arms. They managed, between them, a feeble cry. They started forward again, then stopped. They had heard the shout.

It was a great shout, a huge shout. It cracked the air, bent the trees, snapped the thin crust of ice on the lake. All the rooks rose up from the branches of the trees and swirled above the woods in a panic of smoke. Boy lifted his head; he watched them wheel, turn, settle. He had told Constance he would shout for her, and now it was done. The bayonet-charge shout—he had promised her that: the shout designed to curdle the enemy's blood, the shout so loud it could be heard in London, on a train north. That shout.

He bent his head again, shouldered the gun once more, set his sights on the dog. Above him, Steenie and Freddie saw him do this. The dog, a stupid dog, took no notice of the gun.

Boy had begun to shake. This happened now. The shakes were not always controllable, even after a shout. Boy frowned. He glanced up at the figures of his brothers, who were running and waving their arms.

"Go away," Boy shouted, so that he could get on with the business of killing the dog. He lifted the gun again. His brothers did not go away. They continued to run and wave their arms in the air and cry out. Boy turned his back.

He walked back a few feet, out of sight, to the place in which Constance had been seated on the day of the picnic. Ignoring the dog now, he considered this place, where the roots of the birches made ruts in the ground. He patted the pocket of his jacket, which contained the note to his mother: one note for Constance, one note for Gwen—that had seemed right.

He hoped he had explained it clearly enough in his note. He knew it was important not to make a mess of this—which sometimes people did, with the most horrible consequences. He did not want to blow his jaw off, or let the gun slip so he took a gut wound; his mother would be distressed by that. What he wanted to do—and he was sure he had explained it to her, very clearly—was blast his brains out of his skull with one sure clean shot, so there was nothing left. It was possible, of course, that if he went back to the trenches, the Germans would do this for him. That could not be relied upon, however, whereas this could.

His mother would understand. Boy leaned forward. He positioned the Purdey so the shoulder of the gun was wedged and firm in a rut. He leaned it toward him and looked down the barrels. He smoothed the silver mounts, engraved with the design his father had chosen all those years before. He opened his mouth and wriggled gently, so the tips of the barrels were wedged between his teeth and the roof of his mouth.

Constance's dog gave a small whine. Boy thought his brothers might be close now, because they had stopped shouting. It was not really fair to make them watch. Forget the dog—he had better be quick.

The gun tasted sour, of iron and oil. It made him gag, pressing down on his tongue. Steenie and Freddie, who had stopped short some twenty yards away, saw Boy retch. He repositioned the gun. Freddie took one step forward. He lifted his hand. Steenie found he could not move. He was sure it would be all right—even then. Boy was in such an awkward position; the gun might slip at any instant; it would be difficult to pull the trigger downward rather than back; Boy's hand was unsteady; Boy was, always had been, a lousy shot.

This is not happening, said a clear voice in Steenie's mind. (It was Steenie's first experience of shock.) He waited for Boy to drop the gun, straighten up. *He will jerk at the trigger, not squeeze,* Steenie thought. *He always does.*

Steenie opened his mouth to say Boy's name. It would not be pronounced. He stared at Freddie. He watched the muscles of his brother's face move. Freddie's mouth could not say the name either. It made an O of air. The same idea came to them, at the same moment: Steenie saw it form in Freddie's eyes; Freddie saw it form in his.

They both turned back to Boy at the same instant. The name that always made him alert, that had never failed to check him.

"Francis—"

They said it in unison. Their tone was exactly right. It was quiet, sensible, and firm.

Boy appeared to listen. Both syllables hung in the air. Steenie could still hear them, almost see them, when Boy (well trained, if not a good shot) squeezed the trigger, and the birthday gun went off.

VI
UNKNOWN SOLDIERS

From my mother's diaries:

General Hospital 1,
Saint-Hilaire,

March 21, 1917

It is six days since I lost a patient, but this evening the Canadian died. I want to write down his name. It was William Barkham. His family came from Devonshire, but sold up and went to farm in Saskatchewan, in a place called Fort Qu'Appelle. It is a very small place, and their farm's address is a box number. I have written to his mother there.

I knew that he would die: He had trench foot, and the doctors amputated badly. They had seared the wound with tar; he was then three days at the field station. The gangrene was advanced before he reached here. I knew there was no hope.

He talked to me for an hour before he died. He told me about that farm at Fort Qu'Appelle. They farmed wheat. They kept two cows, some bantams, and some chickens. The farm was near a lake; in the winter mornings, when he rose early for the milking, he used to walk by the lake and watch the sun rising. The ice was three feet thick; it stayed all winter, from November to March. When he was a child his father taught him to skate on that lake, and when he was a man he skated there with his girl. Except—I suppose he was not really a man. He joined up when he was eighteen. He was nineteen yesterday.

Each morning when he finished the milking, he walked back to the farm; his mother cooked him griddlecakes and bacon. He saw her at the end; he spoke her name when he was dying. There was something he wanted to tell her; he clasped my hand very tight; I could see the words in his eyes, but he couldn't speak them. He was in great pain, and being silenced. It made me very angry.

I wanted a miracle. I wanted to put my hand on him and feel the life come back. I prayed—but nothing happened. Nothing ever happens. There are no more miracles, and God does not listen to my prayers. Perhaps there is no God, and I had to come here to learn that. I think I prefer to believe that, than to believe in the God I see here every day, in the hospital wards, a God who turns his back on an only son, a boy of nineteen, a God who spares no one and never intervenes. Surely he could give some sign—is that so much to ask? Just one resurrection.

I thought I could not cry anymore—I could not even cry when they told me about Boy. Yet I cried tonight for William Barkham, and that made me angry too. Tears are useless. They give no comfort to the dying. Tears are an indulgence.

Some of the nurses take laudanum, for the tears. I will not do that. Wexton says that eventually you reach a place that is not beyond the tears, but in them. Maybe he is right. I am still waiting.

Yesterday Wexton brought me a present at the hospital. It was a haggis. He was given it by a Scotsman. We boiled it in a kettle on a primus stove, and shared it with the nurses on this ward. One slice each. I owe Wexton my life. I also owe Wexton my thanks. He has arranged for me to reach my destination after all: Next week, our transfer comes through. We leave for Étaples on Monday.

"Étaples. Didn't I tell you I could fix it?"

They stood outside the railway station; the train that had brought them was already steaming away into the distance. A crowd of people, still pushing through the barriers: several other nurses, some French and Belgian soldiers, an old woman dressed in black, carrying a crate of chickens. Jane turned, and there in the distance, just as Wexton had promised her, was Étaples, her destination.

A huge encampment, like a small city: rows and rows of Nissen huts, fields of khaki tents, a parade ground. Jane narrowed her eyes; she could just discern the figures of men, small as ants: They were drilling.

Part of her view was blocked by a large woman standing a few feet away. She was at least six feet tall, with the shoulders of a man and a bosom like the prow of a battleship. The woman wore an unfamiliar uniform, including belted greatcoat, jacket, and tie. On her head was a hat like a basin, pulled low over her eyes and cropped hair. Evidently she had recognized them, for as Wexton spoke, she stepped forward.

"Wexton," she barked.

Wexton jumped, as well he might, dropped both cases, and swung around with a beam of pleasure.

"Winnie!" He ignored her outstretched hand and kissed her. The giantess blushed scarlet. "Winnie, you've come to meet us! How kind. You must meet Jane Conyngham. Jane, this is Winnie. You remember, I told you? Winnie's a WAAC."

"How do you do?" Winnie extended her huge hand once more and grasped Jane's in a painful grip. "WAAC Clerical Division, actually. And as a matter of fact, *I* fixed it. Welcome to Étaples. Give me her bag, Wexton. Good Lord, is this all you have? It's as light as a feather."

"Winnie is a woman of influence." Wexton regarded her with pride. "Better watch out for her. How are you, Winnie?"

"In the pink. In the pink. Good to see you again, Wexton. Good to meet you, Jane. Do you like to be called Jane, or do you prefer surnames? I prefer surnames myself, so I'll call you Conyngham, I expect. See how things go. See if you last the course. See if I take to you. You may call me Winnie, though. Everyone does. I'm the controller, Regimental Base Depot Two—which is officer ranking, in case you don't know, but they don't give us fancy titles because the men wouldn't like it. If you need me, just ask for Winnie the WAAC—that'll find me. I work for Colonel Hunter-Coote. One of the old brigade. An absolute sweetie. Got him well trained. Eats out of my hand. So, any problems, any trouble with that matron, and you come to me. She and I have crossed swords already. On a number of occasions. Right—all ready? Off we go then. It's just over a mile. Shouldn't take more than ten minutes."

She turned and set off at a smart pace. Wexton and Jane exchanged glances.

"Isn't she wonderful?" Wexton gave a sidelong smile. "I'm mad about her. Étaples was my first posting. Winnie took me under her wing—which, as you can see, is a pretty large wing. I knew, if I wrote, that she'd fix it. Winnie can fix anything."

"I've never met a WAAC before," Jane said in a faint voice, trying to keep pace.

"Well, they're new, of course. But Winnie's not simply a

WAAC. Right now, Winnie's running the war. In my opinion. Hers too."

"She's very . . ." Jane stopped. It was difficult to think of an adequate word.

"English? *Isn't* she? What do you think of the voice?"

Jane hesitated. The voice, indeed, was formidable. The ring of the English hunting shires, overlaid with tones of the parade ground.

"It's loud. I suppose you could say . . . commanding."

"It's ridiculous." Wexton gave her a delighted glance. "It's ridiculous. And wonderful. I also love her moustache. In fact, I love everything about her. Oh, hang on . . ."

Ahead of them, Winnie had come to an abrupt halt on a small rise of ground.

"Look lively, you two." She turned. "Now, guided tour coming up. Pay attention, Conyngham, or you'll get lost. Right, behind us is the station . . ."

"We kind of noticed that, Winnie. We got off the train there."

"No lip from you, Wexton." Winnie shot him a fond glance. She pointed. "Now, there's the village—full of Frenchies. Watch out for them, Conyngham. Lot of old lechers, and they all chew garlic. Over there's the camp—mostly Tommies, some Aussies, a few Kiwi infantry at present. Rumors we *may* see the Americans, if they come in. Colonel Hunter-Coote says they will. We're still waiting, and my girls are *very* impatient. That's the hospital, over there—Conyngham, you see that big gray building beyond the perimeter? And the ambulance billets are just beyond that, so Wexton will be nice and close." She looked from Wexton to Jane as she said this, and smiled in a meaningful way. "Now look, over there—you see that building there, just past the parade ground? That's my depot, and that's where you'll find me. You'll both need a pass for the camp, but that's all taken care of. Meanwhile, *that*"—she stabbed the air with a large finger, and a note of pride entered her voice—"that little hut is our YWCA. We're setting up our own little club there. I fixed it with Hunter-Coote. I told him, straight from the shoulder: My girls are going to need a place to go to in the evenings. 'Cootie,' I said—I call him Cootie, by the way—'Cootie, my girls need a home away from home. You have the mess. What do we have?' So he put in a chit. Tablecloths, and china cups, too—none of that tin-mug nonsense, not for my girls. They won't stand for it. Everything tiptop quality, Army and Navy Stores, you know—I insisted. Fraternization with the men allowed." She fixed Jane with her eyes in a stern way. "My girls wanted that, so I hope you won't mind, Conyngham. All right by you, is it? By the way, there's a piano."

"Oh, of course. How nice . . ."

"We have singsongs. Of an evening. Then cocoa. Right. Off we go again. Come on, Wexton—what are you staring at?"

"That."

Wexton had put down his bag and was staring in the direction of the river below. The village of Étaples was set back between the river and hills so steep they were almost cliffs; the river continued down the valley toward the sea.

"That?" Winnie seemed reluctant to follow the direction of Wexton's eyes. "That's the river Canche. Over there, Conyngham, where the roofs are, that's Le Touquet. Nice beaches. Only one stop on the train. We go down on Sundays sometimes, for a swim. Hope you brought a bathing suit, Conyngham. If not, don't worry. I'll put in a requisition to Stores—"

"I didn't mean the river, Winnie." Wexton had not moved. "What's that?"

"Where those men are digging?" Wexton was now pointing, but Winnie still seemed reluctant to look in the right place. "That's the extension to the trenches. In case of air attack. Happened once or twice." Winnie sounded dismissive. "Didn't do a lot of damage. But you have to think ahead. Be prepared. Another week and the trenches will go all the way from the camp to the caves—"

"Caves?" Jane turned.

"Over there. In the cliffs behind the village. They're huge. Best possible shelter. It was Cootie's idea, actually. Evacuate through the trenches and into the caves. Put up the proposal weeks ago, but of course no one did a damn thing. Red tape, as per usual. Now—"

"I didn't mean the trenches, Winnie. Or the caves. I know about those." Wexton turned to face her. "I meant that. That yacht."

"Which yacht?" Winnie sounded irritable.

"There is only one yacht, Winnie. The large one, moored downriver. What's that? It wasn't here before."

"Evacuation yacht." Winnie sniffed. "Evacuation yacht, if you must know. For the VIPs. If the Allies have to evacuate northern France."

There was a silence.

"Evacuate? Surely not?" Jane said in a small tight voice.

"Lot of damn nonsense." Winnie shouldered Jane's case once more. "Alarmists in Whitehall. Now, shall we get a move on?" She set off; Jane and Wexton looked at each other.

"Oh, great." He bent and picked up his case. "That's the VIPs taken care of."

"It's just a precaution, Wexton." Jane looked back at the yacht. It was large and stately. For the first time it occurred to Jane that the Allies could lose this war. She began to walk, then quickened her pace; after some minutes Wexton caught up with her. Winnie, marching ahead, occasionally looked back. She appeared to have recovered her temper, for several times she gave them an approving nod.

"Why is she looking at us like that, Wexton?" Jane said when this had happened for the third time.

"She thinks you're my girlfriend." Wexton sounded nonchalant.

"She thinks *what?*"

"Well, I didn't actually say so. Not in so many words. She just kind of jumped to that conclusion. When I wrote. I didn't want to disappoint her. After all, you did want to come here. Of course, Winnie doesn't know about me. And I don't think she would understand if I explained. Winnie's led a very sheltered life—and besides, she's a romantic. She's madly in love herself."

"*Winnie?*"

"With Cootie. Didn't you gather that? And he with her. That's why she wouldn't look at the yacht, you see, and didn't want to talk about it."

"Why not?"

"Because if the balloon goes up, Cootie will be on the yacht and Winnie won't. Hunter-Coote is a VIP. Winnie, who damn near runs this place, isn't."

"I see."

Jane stopped, one last time. They had almost reached the camp. A group of men in Australian uniform were laying sheets of corrugated iron over the newly dug sections of the trenches.

Étaples. Acland had been here. He had stood, perhaps, where she stood now.

"So. If the balloon does go up"—she began to walk again—"if it does, where will Winnie be?"

Wexton gave her a gentle and ironic smile.

"Winnie? In the caves, I guess. Along with you and me and about a thousand others."

Wexton and my mother arrived at Étaples in late March 1917. It was the beginning of spring, after the most notorious winter of the first war.

Shortly after they reached Étaples, America declared war on Germany. Not long after that, Canadian troops, including the survivors of William Barkham's regiment, took Vimy Ridge. The third battle of Ypres, and Passchendaele, lay some months ahead.

Terrible battles, a year that marked the turning point in the war. I grew up with those names. They would come to me from the murmurings of grown-ups, when Wexton visited Winterscombe, or Winnie (who had by then married Colonel Hunter-Coote). It was years before I understood that these graceful, mysterious foreign words referred to battles. Passchendaele: I thought the word was *Passion Dale*, and I imagined a valley like Winterscombe, through which flowed the River Passion.

Wexton and my mother were to stay at Étaples only one month. It was there that Wexton completed the poems *Shells*, which he would dedicate to Steenie. It was from there that he wrote to Steenie, letter after patient letter to someone he still loved but was already losing.

Those letters haunted Steenie. Half a century later, when he was dying at Winterscombe, he would wait for a day when Wexton was absent; then he would read them aloud to me.

"Look," he would say at the end of a letter. "Look what I lost. Look what I threw away. Don't you ever do that, Victoria."

To two of those letters in particular, Steenie returned again and again. One concerned the caves at Étaples, and the curious event that would take place there. The other (with an earlier date) described the day in April when Wexton and my mother finally gave in to Winnie's invitations. They joined her and Colonel Hunter-Coote on an expedition to the beaches at Le Touquet—or, as they called it then, Paris-Plage.

It was a Sunday when they went by train to Paris-Plage. They had lunch outside, on the *terrasse fleurie* of the Café Belvedere. Wexton sat at a round table under a striped awning, overlooking the sea; it was the first warm day of spring; the sea glinted.

Next to him sat Colonel Hunter-Coote. Across the table, wearing civilian clothes that day, and a straw hat that shaded her eyes, was Jane. The air was a dusty gold. Wexton felt warm and well fed; he had the pleasant sensation that he had strayed into an Impressionist painting, and that the *joie de vivre* he experienced was not his but Renoir's. The war felt far away.

Below them on the beach, Winnie, with a group of her "gels," was preparing to swim. They were enduring what Winnie described as "the warming-up process." This procedure (Wexton felt sure it would be necessary; the weather might be warm but the water would be icy) involved the throwing to-and-fro of a large striped beach ball. Winnie, mountainous in a black woolen bathing suit that reached from neck to knees, worn with a frilled bathing cap that reminded Wexton of dairymaids, led this warm-up.

"*Jump*, Clissold," he heard her call in a commanding voice. "Oh, you silly gel. Not like that. *Higher*."

Colonel Hunter-Coote, a very small neat man with birdlike bones who, when next to Winnie, resembled an anxious sparrow, watched this performance with an air of pride. Only when the waiter approached did he turn. He then tried to interest Jane in the prospect of what he called pudding.

"Oh, but you must," he said. "One of those sort of cake things they have here. Winnie likes them." He eyed the approaching tea cart. "Why don't you let me choose for you? Now those, for instance. I can definitely recommend those. *Oui, garçon*. You're sure you won't, Wexton? *Deux*—er—*pâtisseries, s'il vous plaît, monsieur*. No, no, not the cakes. Those. That's it. Oh, jolly good. *Merci beaucoup*."

Jane, catching Wexton's eye, smiled. Her own French was fluent, as Wexton knew; Hunter-Coote's was execrable. He spoke it in a very loud voice, with an expression of profound embarrassment. It had obviously never occurred to him that Jane might speak French; she and Wexton had an unspoken pact not to disillusion him.

Jane ate the pastry, then, when the coffee was brought, accepted a cigarette from Wexton. She smoked occasionally now—something that would have horrified her a year before—but she smoked in the manner of a novice, taking small puffs, then letting the tube of tobacco lie between her fingers. She gazed out to sea. Wexton thought she was daydreaming.

She looked peaceful, contented; she was greatly changed, Wexton thought. When he had first met her, he had thought her more tense, more striving, more pent-up than almost anyone he had ever known—and this had interested him. Her nervous mannerisms had almost disappeared; this had interested him too. He liked Jane, had liked her even when he met her in London. He thought her . . . good. Or if not good yet, at least trying to be good. And that was interesting. Not many people bothered.

Jane had removed her straw hat now and was fanning her face with it; she turned in the direction of the promenade. From beneath the awning, one band of sunlight lit her hair. In this light it was as red as maples in the fall; the pallor of her skin against the flame of this hair was remarkable. Across her cheekbones and the bridge of her nose there was a dusting of freckles; Wexton found these, in their symmetry, pleasing. They drew attention to her eyes, whose beauty lay less in their formation than in their tranquil expression.

Jane possessed a quality he found difficult to define, but which was most apparent when she nursed. Now, she no longer used that quick bright blank voice they had taught her at Guy's; she did not need it. She might lay her hand on a man's arm, and Wexton could see a mysterious process of transference take place: From Jane to the man, there was an intense outflowing of energy. This energy calmed. And yet *energy*, too, seemed the wrong word for something so serene. For want of a better word, Wexton would have said Jane possessed *grace*.

That term, a hangover from his Episcopalian upbringing, fretted him a little.

He leaned forward in his seat so that he might also see what had caught her eye on the promenade at Paris-Plage. Not Winnie and her gels—though they had the loyal attention of Colonel Hunter-Coote, and Winnie seemed to be preparing to swim. Jane looked away from the beach. She looked toward a now-familiar sight.

There, on the promenade below them, was a group of Red Cross nurses pushing wheelchairs; they lined the chairs in a neat row, so that their occupants faced out to sea and the warmth of the sun was on their faces. The nurses arranged red blankets across their knees; they fussed over them briefly; they withdrew.

Such expeditions were judged remedial for these special patients, whose wounds were invisible. These men were explained by various euphemisms: They had "neurasthenia"; they had "battle fatigue." At the camp they were restricted to a certain wing of the hospital and were nursed only by the most experienced of the Red Cross. There, too, they were brought out into the sun; someone presumably had faith that fresh air and sunlight might heal them.

Wexton, who had carried some of these patients in his ambulance, doubted that. If they had damage to their bodies—and some did—that might be cured; he doubted even time would heal the damage to their minds.

The men with broken minds: they embarrassed people. They were shipped here first, then—once the doctors were sure there was no malingering—they were shipped back to England. They were sent to special hospitals in remote parts of the countryside, in order that they might have peace and quiet. That was the official line. Wexton doubted that too. He thought the relevant authorities pre-

ferred to hide them away; they were more than an embarrassment—
they were an accusation.

The men with broken minds; the men who had seen the unspeakable; the men who had been driven quietly—it was usually
quietly—mad. For some time now Wexton had believed that it was
these men only who were sane.

Jane watched them, he saw, with a fixed concentration, and
when she finally turned back, Wexton saw that her eyes shone: with
tears, he thought, and then realized that it was not tears. Jane was
angry.

"Oh, I say!" Colonel Hunter-Coote rose to his feet. Jane and
Wexton moved with him. They moved to the edge of the terrace,
with its pots of geraniums, and looked down at the beach. Hunter-
Coote cheered.

"Keep it up, Winnie. Jolly good." He turned to Wexton and to
Jane, his small brown eyes irradiated with love. "*Isn't* she the most
remarkable woman? Nothing daunts her, you know. Absolutely
nothing."

Some way out, the figure of Winnie could be discerned. She
advanced upon the sea, head high; she gave the waves a quelling
glance. She flapped her arms. An impertinent wave splashed her
face; it engulfed her to the armpits. Winnie waited for it to subside
and then launched herself upon the swell of the next. Once the small
tidal wave created by this attack had diminished, Winnie swam. Her
teeth were clenched. Her chin crested the water. Her frilly mobcap
bobbed. It was some while before Wexton realized why this intrepid
progress looked so odd. Then it came to him: Winnie was swimming
doggie-paddle.

Jane perhaps realized this at the same moment, for she began to
smile. She glanced at Wexton and her smile broadened. She did not
look back again to the promenade and the lines of wheelchairs.

At the end of the afternoon they began the walk back to the
station. Hunter-Coote and Winnie walked in front; Jane and Wexton
followed them. The sun was warm. The road was dusty. Their feet
kicked up white dust as they passed. Wexton whistled. Jane stopped,
removed her hat, and lifted her face to the sun.

"Maybe it's wicked. Maybe I shouldn't"—she took Wexton's
arm—"but I feel happy. I feel at peace."

"Acland?"

"Yes. I can feel him. Just as I hoped. He's very close." She
looked up at Wexton anxiously. "I know he's dead. But I can still
feel it. Do you think I'm imagining it, Wexton?"

"No, I don't." Wexton's creased face was sad. "Steenie was close—and I knew. He isn't anymore—and I know that too. You can't explain it. Maybe it's a sixth sense. Or an eighth. Or a tenth. It's there, anyway."

"I'm sorry, Wexton." Jane took his arm. "Was it Conrad Vickers?"

"Well, Vickers was available when Boy died—and I wasn't. Steenie had witnessed a terrible thing. He would have needed someone to talk to—"

"But it wasn't just that?"

"No. I don't think so. It might have happened anyway, sooner or later. Steenie's very young. He's very impressionable. He likes . . ."

"Fashionable things?"

"Kind of. And I just read and write all the time. I can see it's pretty dull."

Jane made no comment. Wexton looked at the white road, at the decorous but affectionate figures of Winnie and Colonel Hunter-Coote. He looked at the flowers by the wayside, the small train that puffed into the station just ahead. Jane's hand lay on his arm.

He felt energy flow from her hand; the loveliness of the day and the serenity of the valley beat in upon him. The sky was azure; there were small puffs of white cloud. He felt the surprising perfection of the moment. He would change nothing—not the clouds, not the sky, not the shape or disposition of the houses, not a blade of grass, not even the faithlessness of Steenie. The knowledge of that was part of the day's composition. It pained him, but the pain gave sharpness to the beauty around him. A poem, just there, hovering at the outer edges of his consciousness.

"I'm all right," he said finally. "Steenie too. He's moved into his own studio. He's having that exhibition of his paintings soon. All that will help."

"Are they good—Steenie's paintings?" Jane turned to look at him.

"Some of them are good."

Jane stopped once more. She sniffed the air. "I believe in God—today. Yesterday I didn't. Today I do. I didn't expect that to happen. Maybe it's the sun . . . and the air. I can't feel the war today—maybe it's that. Never mind anyway." She gave him a rueful smile; she took his arm once more. "Forget my religion. Tell me yours. Tell me about words, Wexton."

"A poem, you mean?"

"Yes. Tell me a poem."

"All right," Wexton said.

He started on a sonnet, one he knew by heart, one that fitted the day and the walk and the white road and the station just ahead and the steam of the train hissing.

Fourteen lines: by the time he reached the end, they had reached the platform. Winnie was fussing: The train was two carriages short.

"Just tell me," she was saying to an aged French porter. "Just explain. Are we to sit in the luggage racks? This is a *disgrace*. There is no room for my gels."

Later that April my uncle Steenie did have his first exhibition of paintings. It was also to be his last exhibition, although Steenie did not know that then, of course. It was, in social and even critical terms, a success. In later years Steenie liked to recall his moment of triumph, but Steenie was no fool; his triumph had also been the occasion of self-discovery. "I found out I was a *dabbler*," he would say.

The circumstances surrounding that exhibition were to prove memorable: It was held late in the war; it was some three months after Steenie and Freddie had witnessed Boy's death; and it was on the very day of Steenie's preview party that the strangest event in my family's story occurred.

We will come to that event in due course. (News of it reached Steenie and others late that night.) But even before this news was broken, it was—according to both Steenie and Constance—an important day. "A day of reckoning!" Constance said.

Constance and Steenie spent that day together; they had spent many days together in the six weeks since Constance had returned from her honeymoon. That morning, Constance had visited Jenna and her baby, a son born the previous Christmas, named Edgar. Constance seemed to Steenie oddly obsessed with this child, whom he had never seen. She would dwell at length on the charms of the child, his quietness, his green eyes, the minute details of his babyish progress. Steenie found this tiresome and suspected insincerity. Constance was now full of plans for poaching both Jenna and the child from the Cavendish family. According to her, Jenna had no wish to take up marital life with Jack Hennessy once the war ended; there was no reason why Jenna had to go back to Winterscombe to live as a head carpenter's wife; there was every reason (Jenna was the best maid she had ever had) why Jenna and child should take up residence with Lady Stern and her husband.

There were, Constance had admitted, one or two minor problems. In the first place, she and Stern still did not have a permanent residence. Since their return from their honeymoon they had spent a great deal of time inspecting houses both in London and the country, but despite the fact that money was no object, they seemed unable to settle on one they both liked. Constance became, Steenie found, oddly evasive on this subject. (In fact, Steenie had the impression she was keeping something back; whatever it was, he could not worm it out of her.) Meanwhile, they were renting a series of houses in London, each more magnificent than the last.

Apart from this difficulty, there were other problems regarding the hiring of Jenna; Constance tended to dismiss them with a wave of the hand, but they seemed to Steenie serious. In the first place, Jenna herself was opposed to the idea. ("She's frightened of Hennessy, that's all," Constance would cry. "She need not worry—I will deal with *him*.") Also, the idea was opposed by Montague Stern—with vigor.

Steenie found this odd. Why should Stern care whether his wife had one maid or another? What possible difference could the baby make in a household that was bound to be a large one? Constance did not explain her husband's opposition. She said, in a dismissive way, that Stern thought she fussed too much about the baby; she would, however, talk him around. Steenie, privately agreeing with Stern, doubted Constance's husband was the kind of man to be "talked around"; he was wise enough not to say so.

Constance's frequent visits to Jenna and her child always seemed to leave her in a pensive and uncommunicative mood. The day of Steenie's preview was no exception. But then Steenie had found that these moods of Constance's were more frequent now—and they did not always seem to be caused by visits to Jenna. He would catch her staring off into the middle distance when he was in mid-anecdote, clearly not listening to a word he said. She had changed since her return from her honeymoon; she was quieter, more subdued, thoughtful. Even her movements, always so swift, had become slower. There was a new quality to her beauty which Steenie had never seen before: It had lost its hard-edged defiance; it had acquired a stillness and a repose previously lacking. Steenie had wondered once or twice if she might be expecting a child; when there seemed no evidence of this, he assumed that her husband had wrought this change in her—and that made Steenie curious. He would dearly have liked to know more on the subject of Constance's married life, her attitude to her husband, indeed the circumstances of her honeymoon in Scotland. But when Steenie asked how the time in Scotland had been, she gave what he felt was a very odd reply. The telegram giving the news of Boy's death (in a shooting accident—that was the official line) had been there, awaiting Constance and her new husband when they first arrived at Denton's shooting lodge.

"So my honeymoon began with a death," Constance said. And then she changed the subject.

At the time Steenie had been glad she did. He did not want to be reminded of Boy's death. He had been discovering, those past three months, just how remorseless memory can be. No matter how hard Steenie tried to suppress what he and Freddie had witnessed, the memory stalked him, then pounced. It insinuated itself into his dreams and his daily life; no matter how fast he ran (and, those three months, Steenie had been running very fast indeed) it caught up with him. *I understand now what the Greeks meant by the Furies,* he wrote in a letter to Wexton, one he never sent. The letter was unposted because Steenie had some self-respect left; he knew he had no right, now, to turn to Wexton for help—he was too deeply embroiled in his new love affair with Conrad Vickers. *I have betrayed you, Wexton,* he wrote in another emotional letter, also unsent, but he knew that was not the whole truth, for he added a postscript: *Worse, I have betrayed myself.*

So, the night of his preview, both Constance and Steenie were tense. They had spent the afternoon at the gallery, Constance on the telephone, making sure that everyone on Steenie's ambitious guest list would be coming that night; Steenie checking that his paintings were advantageously hung. They were. The lighting could not have been more flattering. The framer's handiwork was irreproachable. The surface prettiness of his paintings, their pleasing coloration, his own gift for line—all this was still apparent to Steenie. So, unfortunately, was the paintings' irrelevance. They were decorative, charming, oversweet; they were the visual equivalent of a diet of Turkish delight. Steenie thought of Boy. He thought of what had happened to Boy's head. He looked at the paintings again.

Glucose and rosewater, Steenie thought, and fled.

He and Constance returned to his new studio. His splendid new studio. Steenie, fencing with emotion as always, refusing to raise the subject of Boy, pretended to himself and to Constance that his greenish complexion, the fact that his hands shook, were entirely due to nervousness. The preview. The party. The guest list.

"It's going to be ghastly," Steenie said. "No one will come. No one will buy. They'll slink off, making polite noises. I think I might be sick."

"Don't be feeble, Steenie," Constance replied, staring off into the middle distance once more. Then, as if repenting her absent-mindedness, she became kind. "Why don't you have a drink? Just a little. That will help. Where's the champagne I sent you?"

"In the bath. Keeping cool."

"Then open a bottle."

As Steenie gave his attention to the champagne, Constance prowled about; she moved a chair a few inches; she rearranged a heap of cushions that might have been found in a seraglio; she switched on, then off, a lamp she had provided. She seemed totally absorbed.

This was the first occasion, Steenie would later say, on which he truly noticed Constance's obsession with rooms, her desire to dictate to the inanimate. It did not occur to him then that Constance might wish to order a room because other aspects of her life were in disorder. All Steenie could see was that Constance, three months a wife, was *certain*—about everything.

Steenie was not. His capacity to make any decision veered as wildly as his moods. He felt he could not control his own life, let alone the details of his environment. One moment he would think of Boy; the next, Wexton. He would vow never to see Conrad Vickers again, then rush off to meet him half an hour later. Everything was in flux—whereas Constance exhibited an unfailing tenacity. This was the only material for the curtains; that sofa was unthinkable, this the perfect one. The result was a studio that was eclectic, dramatic, resonant, and unconventional. It made Steenie very uncomfortable. It was, he thought as he poured champagne, Constance's room and not his.

This he could not say. Constance would have been offended; besides, he was being foolish. After all, this studio had been much admired. Conrad Vickers had said, in high fluting tones, that he simply couldn't *begin* on his new flat unless Constance advised him. Lady Cunard, whose taste was more conventional but whose instinct for innovation was acute, was also now claiming that Constance simply *must* help her with her new country house. Constance's future career (although Steenie did not know that then) was in the process of being launched.

Steenie handed Constance her glass of champagne. She did not drink it. Steenie drank his very fast, then poured another. Constance was now rearranging an amusing group of objects on a side table. She moved a small porphyry column a fraction of an inch. She frowned at the flowers—Steenie's one contribution to the room. They were large, heavily scented white lilies—expensive lilies; they had used up one whole week's worth of Steenie's meager allowance.

Steenie began to feel sicker still. There was another reason why this room made him uneasy: Most of the contents had been paid for by Constance—and, since Constance had no money of her own, that meant they had been paid for by her husband. Constance was generous with Stern's money. It acquired things Steenie could never have afforded himself, since his father had been, Steenie felt, remarkably ungenerous over the whole matter of his new home. With grumbling reluctance, Denton had stumped up the money for the lease; he had refused—in an extremely graceless way—to stump up any more. Steenie had been expecting an advance against his trust fund; it had been refused. Constance, waving a checkbook, had stepped into the breach. Considering she had been married such a short time, Steenie thought she had learned to spend her husband's money very fast. He had risked one such observation, and Constance had given him a wry look.

"Man and wife are one flesh," she said. "One bank account, too. Remember that, Steenie."

If it had not been for Constance, this studio would have been furnished with castoffs from his parents' homes. He would have been surrounded by memories. Constance had saved him from this. Nevertheless, Steenie felt he had been dictated to; he also felt he had been compromised. A specific indication of that fact confronted him that very evening: The guest list for his exhibition preview, which of course included Constance and her new husband, accordingly excluded his aunt Maud. Maud, when told this by an embarrassed, squirming Steenie, had behaved with dignity, decorum, and (Steenie felt) a magnificent unconcern. She said she *quite* understood; she would make her own, private visit to the gallery at a later date. Would Steenie perhaps keep back for her one small painting which she had always liked? Steenie had agreed. The painting in question was now the only one in the gallery bearing a small red sticker to indicate it was presold. Looking at this sticker, Steenie had loathed himself.

Steenie downed his second glass of champagne. He hesitated, then decided to risk a third.

"Lady Cunard *is* coming?" His voice came out in a squeak.

"Of course she's coming, Steenie. I told you. She promised me."

"And Stern—do you think he'll be able to get away?"

"Montague? Oh, he'll come. I shall meet him there. He has some meeting first, I think."

Her tone was careless, as it often was when she spoke of her husband. Steenie, who knew that tone of hers, and knew Constance used it to disguise strength of feeling, looked at her closely. As always, her face revealed nothing.

"Oh, well, I'd like to know what he thinks of them. If he doesn't make it, I shall understand. I know how busy he always is—"

"Busy?" Constance seemed to find this amusing. "Oh, he is always busy. But he is also very organized. Meeting after meeting, right through the day—yet he fits marriage into his schedule, Steenie. He is very good about that."

"Fits it into his schedule?"

"Of course." Constance gave an odd smile. "Do you know, he returns to me every evening at exactly the same time? Six. Six-thirty, at the very latest. I could set the clock by the turn of his key in the lock. I wait for him upstairs—well, downstairs sometimes. Do you know what we do then, Steenie? We go to bed."

Steenie was startled. It was unusual for Constance to be so frank. He took nervous refuge—as he had begun to do—in a passable imitation of Conrad Vickers.

"*No!* Constance, darling, *every* night—always the same time? Too impressive. Such ardor—"

"Every night. Always the same time. Other times as well, of course—but always then. From Downing Street to bed. From war to his wife. It's strange, I find. Tell me truthfully now, would you ever have suspected such a thing?"

"From Stern? No. I suppose not. He always seems so very controlled. . . ."

"I know." Constance gave a small shiver. She appeared to hesitate. Steenie flung himself down on the sofa Constance had chosen and Stern had paid for. He adopted an artistic pose.

"Darling!" he said, throwing up his hands. "It's too riveting. I have to admit, I *had* wondered. Is he . . . I mean, when you—"

"I shan't be indiscreet." Constance's face became closed. "I have no intention of telling my marital secrets to you, Steenie."

"You mean there are secrets?"

"Perhaps. One or two. Montague is—"

"The most incredible lover." Steenie giggled. "The stuff of

every woman's dreams: masterful, dominant—I can imagine that. Connie, my sweet, I feel positively envious."

"I could love him, Steenie."

Constance put down her champagne glass. She turned away. Steenie stared at her in astonishment.

"*What* did you say?"

"I said I could love him. I come . . . very near to loving him. That was something I never expected. *Like* him, yes; admire him, even, or respect him—I expected all that. But not love. I hadn't calculated on love. I used to think . . . Well, never mind what I thought. I'm probably wrong in any case. It's just a passing thing— being a new wife. . . ."

Steenie began to regret the champagne he had drunk. It was clouding his mind and slowing his responses, just when he wanted to concentrate. For a moment he forgot about being Conrad Vickers.

"Connie, I don't understand. You sound so resentful. He's your husband. Why shouldn't you love him?"

"Because I don't want to love *anyone.*" She turned back to Steenie in an angry way. "Is that so hard to understand? I don't trust love. I don't believe in it. It weakens people. It makes them dependent—stupid little puppets, with someone else pulling the strings. I don't want to be like that—I never did. Most women can't wait, of course. Love, love, love—they think of nothing else. They speak of nothing else. It's a disease with them. Well, I don't want to catch that disease. I'd sooner have malaria, typhus, tuberculosis —anything. . . ."

"Connie—"

"It's true! I'd rather my lungs rotted than my mind—and that's what happens when someone loves. Their mind goes. Their thinking goes. Their *self* goes. I've seen it often enough—"

"Connie, stop this." Steenie found that her remarks came too close to him for comfort. He stood. "You're working yourself up for no reason at all. You don't mean half you say—"

"Oh, but I do," Constance replied more quietly. "I have thought about this very carefully. My husband does not love me, you see. He was never even *in* love with me. He made that very clear. He has spelled it out to me, several times, face to face."

"Connie, don't be foolish." Steenie stared at her in consternation. "Listen—if Stern said that, he cannot have meant it. He . . . is playing a game, that's all. People do. Conrad does it with me. Stern just doesn't want you to be too sure you've made a conquest. You're a woman. Women are bored by easily available men—you especially.

If Stern threw himself down at your feet, languishing with love, you'd hate it—you know you would."

"Perhaps." Constance turned away. "I might respect him less. I might think his judgment poor. I am not worth loving—I always knew that. Still, I might have liked to be loved, just once."

"That's ridiculous." Steenie stared at her in astonishment. "You know that's not true. Lots of people love you. I love you. Look at all those men, following you about, before you married—they were besotted with you—"

"Ah, but they did not know me."

"Well, Stern must know you."

"No. He does not." Constance shook her head. "He would like to, I think sometimes. I intrigue him, you know—like one of those clever Chinese puzzles. He would like to take me apart, put me back together again—and then he would lose interest at once. So, I am very careful. It would be a bad idea, don't you think, if he knew how I felt? I shall never tell him, Steenie. Not if we are married for fifty years. I shall never let him be sure who I am, whether I love him or not. The politics of love, you see? I intend to keep a balance of power."

"That's absurd. No one can live like that. Besides, what's the point? If you love someone, why not trust them and say so? Why turn it into a stupid war? Wexton always said—" Steenie stopped, coloring. "Well, anyway, it's just false pride that makes you say these things—"

"No, it's not. It's experience."

"Why experience?"

"Because I loved my father. I loved him very much, Steenie. I used to tell him how much I loved him. I'm sure you can remember the result." She looked back at Steenie over her shoulder, then gave a small resigned shrug. "He hated me. He resented me. The more he saw how I loved him, the worse it was. I shall never make that mistake again. Once is enough."

Having said this—and she spoke in a flat tone, with no sign of bitterness, as if stating an obvious fact—Constance walked away. The conversation, begun without warning, now seemed to be closed. Steenie hesitated. The last person he wanted to discuss was Edward Shawcross.

"Connie," he began awkwardly, after several minutes of silence, "are you unhappy? Is your marriage making you unhappy—is that what you're trying to tell me?"

Constance seemed to find this question strange.

"Unhappy? No. Why should you think that? You're quite wrong. I like being married to Montague. He is changing me. My new life is beginning. I think I just wanted to tell you—" She broke off. "You are my only friend, Steenie."

This was the closest Steenie had ever seen Constance come to admitting any kind of weakness. He was touched by it. He blushed, hesitated again, made a rush at her, and gave her a hug.

"So I am. And you're *my* best friend too. Oh, Connie"—he drew back—"I feel such a mess. All these nerves—it's not just the party and the invitations—"

"I know that."

"It's Wexton, you see. I miss him terribly. Then Conrad likes to make me jealous. I can't talk to Freddie anymore. Mama never goes out—she won't even come here, you know. Father's so old and so crotchety. He goes on and on about money. And I know it's because of Boy. I know it's broken them, and none of us can say what's really wrong. When we talk it's awful. It's like tiptoeing around a mine field. We can't mention Acland. We can't mention Boy. Everyone pretends they believe all that stuff about a shooting accident—and no one does. Even Freddie pretends. I *told* him all those terrible things Boy said—but he won't listen. He just says it was shell shock, the war talking—and I *know* he's right. Part of me knows he's right. But there's another bit that won't lie down. I keep asking questions. I think, what if . . ."

Constance, he saw, was watching him; no staring off into the distance now. Her face was intent and concentrated. When Steenie turned away and sat down, Constance followed him. She sat next to him. She took his hand.

"Steenie," she began in a hesitant way. "Steenie, tell me. All those what-ifs of yours—do you mean what Boy said to you about my father's death?"

"I suppose so." Steenie concentrated on his hands. "You see, I know he wouldn't have done that—all those things he said. I know he wasn't sane when he said them. But he was so very *definite* about it. He went on and on in this awful reasonable voice. How he took the guns. How he discussed it with Acland. And so I think sometimes—well, *something* must have happened. Why else would he invent all that? Where would the idea come from?"

"I understand. He was very definite in his note to me as well." There was a pause. Constance was about to say something to Steenie that was of the very greatest importance. Steenie would later explain to Wexton that what she told him gave him not only relief but a sense of release—although what she told Steenie did not have that effect on me when I read it.

"Steenie," she began in a tired voice, "I don't really want to talk about that night anymore. But if there was something I could tell you—about that night, and about Boy, which would put an end to all your doubts . . . if you could be sure that it was just the war talking when you sat there with Boy—would that help?"

"Yes. It would. You see—" Steenie paused. "I did love Boy. I can understand shell shock, at least. But I can't bear to think of Boy as a murderer."

"He wasn't a murderer, Steenie. If you think about Boy, and remember him as he was, you'd know that anyway. The point is: he could not have been involved in my father's death. Not in any way. It's the one thing that's impossible, and he must have known I would know that."

"Why? I don't see—"

"Oh, Steenie." Constance squeezed his hand. "Because the night of the comet, I was with Boy. I was with him all night."

Steenie's parents did not attend his preview party; their absence was not remarked in the melee. The reception began at seven; by seven-thirty the gallery was so crowded that guests had spilled out onto the pavements. Steenie, plotting the guest list with Constance and Conrad Vickers, had been worried that it might prove divisive. He feared a kind of social apartheid, with the older, grander, richer friends ("The Cunard contingent," as Vickers called it) on one side of the room, and the younger, poorer, more artistic element on the other. To Steenie's great surprise and growing delight, lavish quantities of alcohol broke down social barriers. There was a brief period of suspicious social sniffing ("Like dogs! Only more decorous," Steenie cried later); then resistance was overcome.

Conrad Vickers and Steenie swooped from group to group, and if Steenie paid marginally more attention to potential patrons than impoverished poets, his friend Vickers made up for it, scattering his "dah-lings" far and wide with a generous lack of discrimination. More and more red stickers were appearing; more and more people, it seemed, did not consider this work glucose and rosewater—or if they did, preferred art that was so palatable.

Montague Stern, who did not—and who was the one figure at this gathering who remained, cautiously, on its margins—was the person (Steenie later claimed) who started this rush. Arriving punctually, he reserved three paintings at once; where Stern led, others followed.

Constance, seeking her husband out some half an hour later, gave him a kiss.

"That was kind of you, Montague. I know they are not to your taste."

"I like Steenie. Perhaps his paintings will grow on me."

"I doubt that."

"He seems to be enjoying it all anyway." Stern watched Steenie sweep down on a new guest. "He looks happier than he has in weeks."

"Ah." Constance gave her husband a sidelong glance. "That is partly my work. He has been worrying about Boy, as you know. He finally explained. And I was able to tell him something that set his mind at rest." She paused. "It is something I must tell you, too— and I will later. When we escape. I should have told you before—I see that now. When this is over, may we go home and just sit quietly together, like an old married couple, and talk?"

"I should like nothing better, my dear. But for the moment, you should circulate. It might be an idea, perhaps, to rescue Lady Cunard from that parlor pink."

Constance was not anxious to tackle this man, a famous sculptor. (The last time she had done so, he had lectured her first on Marx, then on free love. Constance thought free love a contradiction in terms.) However, he was becoming louder, and possibly more drunk; Lady Cunard was beginning to look trapped by his arguments and his bulk. Constance did her duty.

Lady Cunard moved off fast; the sculptor lurched.

"Constance!" He gave her a scratchy kiss. "My muse. Where have you been hiding yourself? How was the honeymoon?"

Constance recoiled sharply. Before she could stop herself, out came the phrase, the same one she had used to Steenie: "Oh," she said. "My honeymoon. Well, it began with a death."

That honeymoon. Stern and Constance had finally arrived at Denton's shooting lodge late in the afternoon, after a long and arduous drive, the nearest station and town being some eighty miles away. *Lodge* is a misleading term: The house in which she and Stern were to begin married life (a house that Stern was later to purchase) was a huge mock-baronial castle, an extravagant but bogus piece of architecture built by Denton's father. The road to it, narrow and rutted, wound up through a pass in the surrounding mountains, then cut down through outcrops of rock and heather toward the coast and an invisible sea. The house itself, at the neck of a remote glen, was constructed out of blood-red sandstone.

They saw it first, the view opening out before them, as they came through the pass. Stern asked the driver to halt; he climbed down from the car and stood for a few moments facing into the wind. Constance refused to leave the car; she shivered and clutched the traveling rugs around her. They faced west. The sun was setting; beyond the red bulk of the house the sky was a conflagration; the clouds bled. Constance averted her eyes. She had visited this house before, but only in the summer months; bleak magnificence, in winter, made her afraid. Was this the extremity she had sought? You could see the hand of God in this landscape. Even the trees were poor and stunted things, shrinking from the violence of the elements. The mountains were sharp as teeth against the sky; the bones of rocks broke from the ground all around her. A wild, desolate, and deathly beauty. Constance thought, shivering again, *Oh, why did I agree to come here?*

When they entered the house they were greeted by the steward, and by a telegram. Constance, who had not mentioned to Stern the note Boy had given her, knew what that telegram was likely to say. She sank down into one of the enormous chairs in the huge and vaulted hall. Her eyes rested on the vastness of the room, on windows some twenty feet tall, on a massive fireplace that burned eight-foot tree trunks. Her small feet rested upon a tiger skin; the beady eyes of dead stags looked down at her from the walls. She clutched her little handbag very tight. She felt that her husband, who saw everything, saw through the leather of the bag, saw through the vellum envelope, and read the contents of Boy's last letter inside it. Stern gave no sign of anxiety as he opened the telegram; as he read it his expression did not alter. Looking up, he said with perfect calmness: "Boy is dead. A shooting accident. I will telephone Winterscombe."

It took time to make the connection; once it had been made, Stern dealt with the situation with his customary imperturbability. He expressed shock, regret, condolences; a perfect readiness, if it would help, to curtail this honeymoon and return to Wiltshire. In view of the lateness of the hour, he suggested the decision be made the following morning.

"I don't think that it was . . . an accident," Constance said in a small voice, once they were alone.

"I imagine not. In the circumstances," Stern replied.

He said nothing more. The question of suicide was not discussed; there was no examination of his own culpability or his wife's; no reference to the photograph shown to Boy in the Corinthian Club. Constance found his composure alarming; in an odd and furtive way, she also found it thrilling. *Schadenfreude:* as she had on the train north, she found all instances of her husband's ruthlessness thrilling. *A secret man—death is his familiar,* she thought. She felt a quick nervous excitement. What would this husband of hers do next, when they were upstairs in the bedroom?

What he did was disappointing. With a cold politeness Stern escorted her to her room, summoned her maid, informed her that he understood she must be both exhausted and shocked, and then left her to rest and to recover.

Constance did not want to rest. She spent a sleepless night. The wind howled outside. It rattled the great doors and windows. The next morning Stern came into her room and drew back the curtains. The light was bright and unnaturally white.

"It has snowed during the night," he said. "Heavily. I'm afraid there is no question of returning to Winterscombe, Constance." He turned back, his face expressionless. "We are cut off," he added, and then he left her.

Cut off indeed: they were marooned, Constance discovered. Snowfall had made the one road to the house impassable. No one could reach the house, and no one could leave it. The telephone lines were down. It seemed to Constance that her husband was pleased by this; he exulted in this enforced isolation.

Constance did not. Despite the vast fires burning day and night, she was always cold. The rooms and the corridors echoed. The view from the windows was of loneliness.

"What can you see, Constance?" Stern said to her some five days later, when the snow remained but the storm had abated. They sat in the great hall, Stern by the fire, Constance curled up on a window seat.

She pressed her face to the glass. She dug her nails into the palms of her hands. For five nights she had slept alone; for five nights her marriage had remained unconsummated. No explanation.

"What can I see, Montague?" she replied. "Why, twelve thousand acres of white. The same view, from every window."

The next day, Stern gave instructions to the steward. His wife, he said, found the house confining. Estate workers were dispatched to dig a path through the snow. When the work was complete, Stern drew Constance to the doorway. Smiling, he displayed to her this path, cut for her benefit. A glittering pathway, just wide enough for two people to walk side by side, it led straight from the door to a balustrade. This balustrade marked the boundary of Gwen's unsuccessful attempt at a garden. Below it, the ground fell away to a viewpoint overlooking a Highland wilderness. Constance looked at this path, at the bright sky without clouds, at the high sun. The air was icily fresh, with a tang of salt in it. The glitter of the air tempted her; Stern smiled.

"You see?" he said. "Freedom."

Every day for the next three days, morning and afternoon, Constance and Stern took the air. They would walk along this path, arm in arm and side by side: a slow progress, from the house to the wilderness, from the wilderness to the house.

"A little like exercising in a prison yard, don't you find?" Stern said once as they paced back and forth. He glanced at Constance as he said this, as if the remark amused him, as if it held a meaning he would like her to understand.

"A little," Constance replied, clasping his hand. Gloved fingers; a slight and reassuring pressure; she decided the remark had no edge.

"Shall we walk to the wilderness?" Stern would say in the same tone of amused irony, and walk to the wilderness they would. One hundred paces each way; sometimes Constance would say to herself that when they had taken fifty, or a hundred, when they reached the balustrade, she would speak. It shouldn't be so hard, after all, to turn to him and ask why he left her still to sleep alone, her husband.

One day, two days, three days. She never did. The words would stick in her throat, the way thanks did when she was a child.

By the afternoon of the third day, she had decided: No matter what, the words would be said. No more hesitation. She would pronounce them the very second they reached the balustrade. One hundred paces, Stern accommodating his longer strides to her smaller steps. She clenched her gloved hands tight, rested them against the stone of the balustrade, opened her lips to speak, looked at the view, and was silenced.

Such a majestic view and, to human beings, so diminishing. All color was bleached out: The peat bogs, the heather, the outcrops of rock—all these were invisible beneath the snow. Snow upon snow, in the distance the white bones of mountains and then, below them, ringed by them, the flat black water of the sea-loch.

This loch had a deathly and forbidding air. The sun rarely reached its waters; protected from the prevailing wind by its flanking mountains, its surface was without ripples. In the distance, some three miles away but clearly visible in this crystalline air, she could discern the point where the waters of the loch flowed out into the open sea. Two black sheer rock faces fronted this boundary, making a narrow channel through which, at high and low tide, the water sucked and hurtled. A dangerous stretch of water this, notorious for its currents. Constance, who could not swim and was afraid of water, had always hated it.

"How deep is it?" she had asked Acland once when she was still a child. Acland, indifferent, had shrugged.

"God knows. Very deep. One hundred—two hundred fathoms."

No, she could not speak. The loch would not allow her. It trapped the words on her tongue. With a sense of fear and despair Constance looked up at her husband.

He had not spoken for some while. Now, as he gazed out across that landscape, she saw it again on her husband's face, that expression of exultation.

Stern, she saw, did not shrink from this place, as she did. He gloried in it. For a moment, watching him, she thought he was engaged in a silent battle of will with the savagery and desolation of this landscape; it was as if he matched himself against it, as if he challenged its dangerous beauty. He seemed oblivious to her presence, locked in that private struggle of his own. Constance was humbled by this. It was on that occasion, in profile to her, his face fixed and pale, etched against the sky, that she saw for the first time how little she had understood her husband. Stern the Machiavelli, Stern the power broker, exercising his influence in clubrooms, corridors, drawing rooms—that was how she had thought of him, and she had been wrong. *Today, I saw Montague's soul*, she was to write in her notebook. *It was in that terrible, beautiful place, in that loch, in those mountains.*

After a little while, when Stern still did not speak and seemed to have forgotten her presence, she stole out her hand and laid it upon his arm. She would have liked to tell him what she had seen in his face, but the words would not come out correctly. She said only that his liking for this place surprised her; she would not have expected it. Had she been asked to describe a location that matched his character, she would have selected the very opposite of this place.

"A classical house, and a classical park—I should have chosen that," she said. "Somewhere a little austere, a place men had tamed for generations."

"I can like such things," Stern answered in an absent way, his eyes still fixed on the horizon. "But I prefer this. I never came to Scotland before."

There was a silence. Stern continued to look out over the snow. His eyes traced the line of the crags against the sky. In the far distance a bird—an eagle or a buzzard, great wings outstretched—soared upon the thermals.

"Shall we have this?" Stern turned to Constance suddenly, startling her. He gripped her hand. She saw his face unmasked, freed from all his customary restraint, naked to her gaze for the first time, his eyes lit with a dark excitement.

"Shall we?" His grip on her hand tightened. He gestured toward the landscape before them. A wide arc of the arm: rocks, mountains, water, sea.

"We could, Constance, if you wished. We could have all this. It could be ours. We could . . . claim it."

"This place?"

Constance was drawn to him. Stern offered her all this, and more. Such recklessness! For a moment the air sang in her lungs; she, too, was lifted up on those invisible thermals. There the world lay before their feet; one word and it was theirs. No, not even a word, for her husband bent toward her now; all she had to do was kiss his mouth.

She looked into his eyes; she reached up for his kiss; his arm tightened around her waist. At the very last moment, one tiny second of time, she shivered. She was afraid. She shrank back.

She gave a small and hopeless gesture of the hands; tiny kid gloves against the elements. She looked at the ring of mountains, the water of the loch beneath. Did she think of her father? Perhaps, perhaps.

Too far north, after all, she said to herself. Too cold, too extreme. She turned away with a hateful little shrug, a pout of distaste she despised but could not suppress.

"This place? It's well enough in August—if you like to kill animals. But in winter?"

She stopped, appalled at what she had just said. When she turned, the light had gone from Stern's face. *One more chance,* she wanted to cry out: *just one more chance.* Instead she said, "Why do you ask?"

"No reason," Stern replied, turning away his face. He took her arm. "Shall we return to the house?"

"Montague—"

"You're cold. We'll discuss it another time," he said in a curt voice.

Constance felt that voice shrank her; it shriveled her up. One hundred paces back to the door. By the door, Constance lingered. It was unbearable to go in. If she went in now, if she did not speak, it would be an end. But how to speak? She bent and picked up a handful of crisp snow. She crushed it tight in a ball between her fingers.

"Over dinner tonight," Stern said in an indifferent voice. "We can discuss it then."

He opened the door. Constance did not move. She did not believe him. They would not discuss it over dinner. This was not something that could be . . . discussed. She crushed the snow tighter in her hand.

"Montague . . ."

"Yes, my dear?"

"Do you ever feel confined? Shut up, closed away—so—so you cannot breathe, so the air is like a prison, so you reach out your hand and all you touch is bars—" She stopped. Stern was watching her now with attention.

"Yes," he began in a cautious way. "I have felt this. I imagine most people have—"

"You could let me out," Constance cried, clasping his hand, scattering the snow. "You could. Oh, I feel sometimes that you could. If I dared just a little bit more. I think then—I should be so free. So marvelously free. And you might be too. We might free each other. Oh, Montague—" She raised her face to his. "Do you understand me? Do you think I'm right?"

Stern looked down into her face, which was lifted to his, which was imploring. His own expression became gentler. Drawing her to him, he kissed her brow, then traced, in a tender, yet regretful way, the lines of her face.

"That is why I married you," he replied quietly. "Did you not realize that?"

"When we return to London, Constance," he began, after dinner that night, watching her down the length of the table, "we shall have to decide where to live. Do you have a preference?"

"Somewhere in London. And a place in the country, I suppose." Constance spoke with care; she knew Stern was leading up to something. "Then, after the war, I should like to travel. I don't care to feel too settled."

"I know that."

Stern looked down. He gave his attention to his wineglass. He moved the glass back and forth in an arc across the dark polish of the table. The servants had withdrawn. Between Constance and Stern was a monstrous pyramid of fruit, an epergne, flanking lines of silver candelabra some two feet tall. Constance looked about the room with a sense of despair. Massive chairs, vast banners with tattered heraldic emblems, great mauve paintings of Scottish glens. *Everything in this house is too big*, Constance thought; *even the chairs dwarf me.*

"I could have Winterscombe within the year—if we wanted it." Stern spoke suddenly, without looking up. "The house is security against my loans. I can call those loans in at any time. I see no possibility of their being paid back."

He looked up. Constance stared at him.

"I could have Winterscombe," he continued in an even voice, "but not just Winterscombe. Did you know I owned the Arlington estate?"

"No, Montague."

"I bought it, after Hector Arlington's death. I also own Richard Peel's estate—you remember Peel, Denton's old crony, who was quite happy to take investment advice from a Jew, rather less happy to have that Jew eat at his table? He died last autumn. I bought his estate from his executors. He had no children."

"The Arlingtons' and Peel's *and* Winterscombe? Those estates adjoin."

"Obviously. And then there is the question of Jane Conyngham's land. She has the largest holding of all. She tells me she intends to sell."

"And her land borders the Arlington land." Constance watched Stern closely. "You could take four estates and make them one?"

"I could." He seemed almost bored. "This place, too, perhaps. I like it here."

"If you did that, how much land would you have?"

"Fifteen thousand acres—discounting the twelve here. Together with four houses—which would give us four to choose from. Winterscombe is not greatly to my taste, though it may be to yours. Jane Conyngham's house is fine. Peel's is even finer. We could look them over. If you disliked them, we could build." He gave a dismissive gesture of the hand. "Houses do not greatly interest me. I have owned several. I feel obliged to fill them with things, and once they are filled, they rather bore me."

"You mean it is the land that interests you?"

"Yes. I suppose that it is."

"Why is that, Montague?"

"I like space." Stern rose. He stood, looking down the table at her. "When I was a boy I dreamed of space. The house I grew up in had only three rooms. You could never be alone in it. However—you do not like to discuss Whitechapel, as I remember."

Stern turned away. He moved to the windows, drew back the heavy curtains, and looked out. There was a full moon; Constance could just glimpse it over her husband's shoulder, riding high in an unclouded sky. The stars were ice in the dark. She looked at their patterns. She looked down at her plate.

"Is that the only reason, Montague—your love of land?"

"Not the only reason. No. I have always wanted—this may surprise you—I have always wanted to have something I could pass on. You said once that you thought the subject of children did not interest me. You were wrong. I should like . . . a son. I should like to pass my land on to my son. Perhaps I have dynastic leanings." He paused. "I have a dream, a recurrent dream, which I've had for many years. In that dream I see my son quite clearly. His face, his hair, every feature. We walk together, through our estates. We—survey them, perhaps. And we know, as we walk, that they are virtually limitless. We could walk all day and still not reach our boundaries. Sometimes we stand in the center of all that land. We look at it. And I say to him: 'This is yours. Take it.' " He broke off. "My son is different from me, of course. He is freer than I have ever been. Anyway. That need not concern you. It is just a dream."

"I would have thought it might concern me," Constance said in a low voice.

"But of course. I'm sorry. I did not intend any slight—"

"Are you always alone with your son in the dream, Montague?"

"Yes."

"I am never there—even now?"

"Not so far, my dear. I'm sure that will change, and you will make an appearance. My mind takes time to adjust, perhaps, to our marriage."

"I'd have liked to be there." Constance continued to stare at her plate.

"You manifest yourself in my dreams, Constance—you have for some time."

"You're sure?" She turned to him anxiously and held out her hand to him.

"But of course." His tone was gentler now. He took Constance's hand, then bent to kiss her.

"Such a sad face." He drew back, tilted her face up to look

at him. "Such a very sad face. Why is that? Have I made you unhappy?"

"A little."

"Tell me why. It was not my intention."

"I'm not sure. I might not want to live at Winterscombe. Or anywhere near Winterscombe. It reminds me too much of the past. Of my father—"

"Then we will forget that idea and build our little empire somewhere else. Think about it for a while, and then, if that is what you decide, we will change our plans." He paused. "I think . . . it is not just Winterscombe, is it? There is something else?"

"I suppose so. I . . . Do you like me, Montague?"

"Such a question, from a wife to her husband! Of course I like you, Constance. I like you very much." He frowned. "Perhaps I do not express myself very well. It's my nature to be indirect. I have tried to make you see—" He stopped.

"Could you . . . almost love me, Montague?" Constance darted out her hands and caught his in an impulsive and pleading way. "It would be enough, I think—if you could almost love me."

"Shall I tell you something?" Stern drew back. "It may answer your question. I've been certain—of my interest in you, of my concern, for a long time. Would you like to know when it was that I first noticed you?"

"Yes."

"When we went to the opera, to see *Rigoletto*. And we stood in Maud's drawing room. You told me what it was you thought happened in the opera—after the curtain went down."

"Then?"

"Oh, I think so. The device about your mother, and her race—none of that was necessary, you know. I knew that I would marry you some months before you proposed."

"I don't believe it! You're making fun of me." Constance sprang to her feet.

"As you like." Stern shrugged. "You are wrong. I would not risk making fun of you, nor would I want to. I'm telling you what I thought. That we would marry. That we might have children—in due course."

"But you were still with Maud then—"

"Even so."

"You made a decision—just like that, so coldly?"

"It did not feel cold at the time, though decisions are best made in such a frame of mind. I imagine you calculated your assault on me quite coolly. You see? We are two of a kind. If you would learn to trust me a little—"

"Do you trust me?"

"I try."

"You won't make me . . . live at Winterscombe?"

"No. I shall try never to make you do anything against your wishes." He paused. "I had thought—obviously I was wrong—that you had an attachment to the place."

"To the house? No."

"To someone in it, perhaps?"

"No. Not now."

"To Acland, for instance?"

"Why Acland? Why should you say that?"

"No particular reason. It was just an impression I had."

"Oh, Acland and I were old enemies. He was my sparring partner, that is all. I do not think of him now. Acland is dead. I have a new antagonist, Montague. Look—I wear his ring upon my finger."

"You wear a great many rings on your fingers," Stern replied, examining the small hand Constance displayed to him.

"Only one of any significance."

"Is that true?"

"Of course. I am a wife now. I am . . . almost a wife."

"Shall we make you a complete wife?"

That was Stern's reply, and it is there that Constance's account of that particular night, and of her honeymoon, breaks off. There is a gap—literally a gap, of half a blank page. Then the following sentences, written in a hand which is almost illegible:

Montague was so good, so kind and patient and gentle. No games now, and no words. I did not manage very well. I bled. I waited. I thought he would say I was scrawny and clumsy, but he never did. I thought his eyes would hate me, but they didn't. I think this confused me. I did a terrible thing. I cried out your name, Papa—three times.

I have managed better since. Montague never questions me. He is considerate at all times. When he touches me, I feel dead. He cannot wake me up. I want want want to wake up. We have to keep trying, both of us; we can't stop. If I stand next to him, I have to touch him.

I shall have to tell him. I'm afraid to tell him. All those secret stories. All those little boxes. Shall I open them all—or just some of them?

"Tell me then, Constance," Stern said to her.

It was still the night of Steenie's preview party; Constance and her husband had returned home to the latest of their opulent rented houses. It was ten in the evening, and the telephone call that would so change their lives was still one hour away.

Stern sat by the fire, and Constance, her face set and concentrated, paced about the room. Punctilious in such matters, she was wearing half-mourning for Boy—a dress of advanced cut, made up in a muted lavender-colored material: a compromise between chic and the conventions of grief. There were signs, even so, that Constance rebelled against these strictures, for in her hands she held a most beautiful scarf, of the brightest colors: indigo, vermilion, violet. As she paced back and forth, she passed this scarf through her hands, sometimes winding its colors about her fingers and her rings.

She prefaced her explanation by saying that part of it had been told to Steenie earlier that evening, but, not wishing to hurt him, she had given him an edited version.

"And am I to have the uncensored account?" Stern asked in his dry way.

"Yes," Constance replied, winding her scarf about her hand. "But even if you are angry, you must not interrupt. I see now that you have to know everything. I should have told you before. You see, Boy liked to photograph me—you know that. What you do not know, no one knows, is that Boy also liked to touch me."

Constance then told her husband the following story. Since the only other witness to that story was dead, I have no way of knowing whether the story was true or whether Constance—unable to tell her husband the whole truth, even then—invented it. Perhaps parts of it are true; perhaps it is all true; perhaps it was a complete fabrication. Constance was not an ordinary liar, and she often used fiction, as a storyteller does, to convey a deeper truth.

You judge. One thing is sure: Constance's role in all this is unlikely to have been as innocent as she made out. Remember how she posed for Boy's photograph, in the King's bedroom? Remember Freddie? If there is a hidden tempter in this account, a serpent carefully disguised in the long grass, I very much doubt that it was Boy. To portray herself as a victim would have been accurate had Constance been telling Stern the story of her father—but a victim of Boy? That I cannot believe. My reaction, however—and even yours—is less important than Stern's. The question is: did Stern believe her?

It began with talking, Constance told him; talking developed into a series of games. The first game had clear-cut rules: Boy was the father and Constance the daughter. She was required to call Boy

"Papa," and when she visited him in his room, she was required to confess to this "papa" all her childish misdemeanors. Sometimes this new father was benevolent: He would say that her small crimes—rudeness to her governess, a torn skirt, a quarrel with Steenie—could be forgiven, and he would give her an absolving kiss. On other occasions (for no clear reason) this new father would decide the crime was more serious. "Inattention in church," he would say. "Now that is very serious." Or: "Constance, your reading of the book is slipshod. You must pay better attention to your lessons." He would pause, frown. "Constance," he would say, "I shall have to punish you." The method of punishment was always the same. Boy would lean her across his lap and administer several stinging slaps. When this happened, a change would take place in Boy which, to begin with, Constance did not understand. His eyes would become fixed and glazed; he would stammer; the timbre of his voice would change; he would also have an erection

She did not, then, know what an erection was, Constance told her husband; all she knew was that when Boy played this game, when he pressed her down across his lap, she would feel something stir, then thrust against her rib cage. This seemed to make Boy ashamed; after the spankings he would never look at her.

Some while after this, Boy invented a new game, a form of hide-and-seek—an odd form, since they both hid and there were no seekers. In his bedroom at Winterscombe, Boy had a very large wardrobe, a huge mahogany affair. Inside, it was lined with fragrant cedar wood. It was like a small room—even Boy could stand upright inside it. In the game they both climbed into this wardrobe; then Boy pulled the doors closed. It was one of the rules that they must both be absolutely silent.

Inside, Constance would be as quiet as a mouse. She would be pressed up against evening cloaks, tweed jackets, the fine khaki of Boy's officer uniforms. Boy, a poor performer at this game, always breathed heavily. There was no light. Constance, stealing her hand out, found she could not see it. She would start to count, and tell herself that when she reached fifty, Boy would end the game. She would pray to be let out; she could not breathe in there.

One day, or one night, perhaps the third or fourth time they played this game, Boy whispered: He said they might hold hands in the dark, because he knew she was frightened. He held her hand for some while; then he made a strange noise, which was somewhat like a sigh and somewhat like a groan. He guided her hand so it touched him.

There was that strange thing again, as stiff and hard as before; it made a bulge beneath his trousers, and Boy made her hand into a cup shape, so it fitted over him snugly. He moved about, twisting a little from side to side so that he rubbed against her hand. His movements became urgent; he rubbed faster, in a surreptitious and frantic way, never speaking—until suddenly he gave another groan, and a tremor ran through his body. He released her hand at once. When he lifted her out of the wardrobe, he gave her a little kiss on the corner of her mouth. He said this was their secret; they could play this game because Boy was her papa and her brother and he loved her.

They played it in this way for several weeks, never speaking once they were inside the wardrobe. Then Boy began to introduce variations. One day he unbuttoned her dress; another day he knelt and stroked her ankles. A third day, inside the wardrobe, there were shuffling and fumbling noises; then, when he guided Constance's hand, she found the bulge thing had been unbuttoned. She could feel it, standing up in the dark like a big stick. It felt warm and damp, and Boy told her to stroke it, but the instant her hand closed around it, Boy shuddered convulsively.

Constance was afraid of this thing, but she was also fascinated by it. She was not sure whether Boy produced it out of love, as he said he did, or whether it was an instrument of punishment.

As the weeks passed, Boy grew bolder. Now, they did not always go into the wardrobe, and into the dark. Sometimes Boy would produce this thing when he took her photograph. He liked to pose her, load the film, set up the camera, and then—before he took the photograph—sit opposite her with this thing in his hands.

He never looked at her face when he did this. He liked to stare at the small slit between her thighs. Constance hated this part of her body, her own secret place, but Boy would stare at it and stare at it while he stroked. Then he would close his eyes. Sometimes he would groan in a way Constance hated. Afterward, he would wash. He always washed next. The soap he used smelled of carnations.

Finally, a long time after this first began, Boy introduced his final variation. One last game: it was called "caving."

This game was always played in the same way and in the same position. Boy would sit down; Constance would sit astride his lap. Once, Boy kissed her on the mouth, but he never did that again. He did not like mouth kisses. Boy would put his hands around her waist, and he would raise her and lower her.

When he reached the cave—he always called it reaching the

cave—Boy's face would contort. This game hurt Constance, and she thought it must hurt Boy, too, because whenever he reached the cave, he looked like a wounded man. She could not understand why he liked this game so much, when it hurt them both, but Boy would never explain.

When it was over, he would help her dress. He was always very kind and gentle. He might give her a kiss or a small present. Once he gave her a ring with a blue stone; another time he showed her a box in the corner of the room, and there, fast asleep under a rug, was a tiny tricolored spaniel, a puppy. After the present giving she would leave his room. She would have to be very careful never to be seen—and for a long time she was not. Then, one day in that long hot summer when war was first declared, and Boy was on leave from his regiment, she was caught.

It was a Sunday morning, and just as she crept out onto the landing, there was Acland at the top of the stairs.

He stopped. He looked at her. Constance knew he could see into her. He never said one word to her, but he went into Boy's room, and from the far end of the landing she heard the sound of voices raised in anger. Something must have happened; no one explained, but the visits ended then. No more photographs; no more hide-and-seek; no more caving.

Acland had rescued her, and Constance was grateful for this. She was no longer a child by then; she knew the games were wrong. She did not exactly blame Boy—she thought he really had loved her—but all the same, it was a sin, and sometimes she hoped Acland had punished him.

This was her secret, Constance said, turning back to her husband and winding the bright scarf tight about her hand. It made her ashamed. She felt sullied.

"Do you see?" she said. She was trembling. "That is what was done to me. I cannot always forget. It has made me into a circle of air, a nothing. I cannot be like other women. Boy locked me up in that wardrobe of his, and I am trapped in there, with no air to breathe. It killed Boy, and now it is killing me. Even now. You are the only one who can release me." Constance began to weep as she said this: one of her sudden and violent storms of emotion. She covered her face with her hands.

Stern, who had been sitting silent all this while, rose to his feet. He did not go to his wife at once, but walked back and forth in the room. When Constance looked at him, she saw his face was white with anger.

"It's as well for him that he killed himself," Stern said. "Had he failed, I would have done the job for him."

Constance, looking at her husband, did not doubt for one second the truth of what he said. There was no bluster in his voice; he spoke coldly, with decision. As she had before, once or twice in Scotland, she glimpsed some extremity in her husband, an ability, a willingness to step over the edge. As before, it excited her: Constance was drawn to people who allowed violent emotion to take them beyond the boundaries of civilized behavior. She liked it out there, in bandit country—and perhaps she liked it even more when she knew the crossing of the frontier had been provoked by herself. Stern, her avenger: more deadly than any such fictive creature in a novel or a play, more satisfying, too, for this drama was real and her life was the plot. Her tears stopped. She gave a shiver. Stern, who had turned away from her, turned back.

"Boy gave me his word. That day in the club. He said he never once touched you."

"What would you expect him to say?" Constance cried. "He was scarcely likely to confess then—and to you, of all people—"

"But the way he said it. I thought I understood—"

"Believe him then!" Constance began to cry again. "That is always men's way. They will always trust another man's word against a woman."

"No. No. It is not that. Constance, don't cry. Of course I do not doubt you. No one would say such a thing unless . . . Come here." Stern put his arms around her. He drew her close, tight against his heart. He began to stroke her hair. He kissed her brow. "Constance," he went on, in a different voice, a gentler voice. "I wish you had told me this before—I would have behaved very differently. I blame myself now. If I had known, I would have . . . Constance, when did this begin?"

"The night my father died." Constance clung to her husband. He stopped stroking her hair. Constance wound her arms tight about him. "That makes me even more guilty—do you see? My father was outside, and he was dying, and I never even knew. I was inside. I was with Boy—I was with Boy all night. From the end of the comet party until almost five o'clock in the morning. I sat in his room with him and we talked. That's all it was then, just talking. But that was the night it began. And that was what I told Steenie tonight. Not the other things, the later things. Just that we talked. I wanted Steenie to understand that all those things Boy had said to him were lies. It wasn't Boy who killed my father."

Constance stopped. Stern's hand rested against her shoulder. She could feel a new tension in his body and, when she looked up, saw a new alertness in his face.

That was when he drew back from her, all signs of anger gone. He held her hands. He looked down into her face. A clock in the room ticked. Several minutes of silence went by.

"It was not Boy?" He frowned.

He drew her toward a sofa. They both sat down. Then Stern said to her: "Constance, explain."

Explaining anything to her husband, Constance was later to write, could be difficult. It was like explaining a sequence of events to a barrister, under cross-examination. As she spoke, Stern would from time to time interject questions. It was then Constance began to sense that all these details he requested—time, place, circumstances —were being cross-checked against other information already stored away.

"You see," Constance said, "Boy had already taken my photograph that day—the first picture he ever took of me alone. It was in the King's bedroom, that morning. I had never paid much attention to Boy before then, but that day—I could see—he was trying to be kind to me. Then, later that night, Steenie and I were allowed to stay up. We watched the comet. Nanny put me to bed, but I knew I wouldn't sleep—I was far too excited. I used to pry in those days— I've told you that—but that night I just wanted to watch the party. I wanted to look at all the beautiful dresses. I crept downstairs in my nightdress, and I hid in a place where Steenie and I used to hide from Nanny Temple. It was in the conservatory, behind a high bank of camellias. You could see into the drawing room from there."

"That was how you witnessed the famous proposal?"

"Yes. Jane was playing the piano, and the music made me a little sleepy. I was just going to creep back out to the hall and go to bed, when the music stopped and Jane and Boy came in. He proposed—well, you know that part of the story. He did it very badly, and I used to make fun of him for that. Steenie and I even made it into a play once, and acted it for Freddie. I wish we hadn't now. It was unkind. You see"—she turned to look at her husband—"I don't hate Boy, Montague, no matter what he did. I do . . . pity him. He was his father's victim. He knew he would never be the man his father wanted him to be. It made him very unhappy."

"It made him into a child molester—is that what you're saying?"

"Don't be harsh." Constance looked away. "Boy was afraid to

grow up. He was afraid of adult women. When he was a child he was sure of his father's love, but the older he became, the more he felt he failed him. I could understand that—wanting to remain a child. Wanting to remain the same age you were when you were happy."

"Could you?"

"Oh, yes. And Boy knew that. It was why he felt safe with me. I *was* a child, for one thing, and I was a horrid, unattractive, sullen child as well—*no one* could feel himself a failure next to me, not even Boy. He was always being pitied—and he hated it. I could understand that too. So, there was an alliance between us. We were friends."

"Very well. I understand."

"Do you?" Constance gave him a sad glance. "I would like you to, but I can see it is difficult. You don't know how hateful it is to be pitied. No one would dare to pity you."

"I am not as invulnerable as you think." Stern took her hand. "But never mind that. Go on."

"Very well. After Boy and Jane left, I was more excited than ever. A proposal! I wanted to wake Steenie at once and tell him the news, but when I went back to the nursery, Steenie was fast asleep. I thought I had better not wake him. It must have been about midnight by then, perhaps a little later. Anyway, I could hear the guests beginning to leave. You know where the nurseries are at Winterscombe? They're on the second floor. Just along from the day nursery, there's a landing, then a corridor where Boy and Acland and Freddie had their rooms. The landing overlooks the hall below—so I went to sit there. I had a bird's-eye view. The hall, the main staircase, everything. I peeped through the banisters. I watched the guests leaving. Then I watched the houseguests go up to their rooms. I saw Maud go up." She gave a small smile. "I even saw you go up, Montague. I saw Boy escort Jane to her room. Jenna went in to her; then Boy went upstairs to bed. He looked so very miserable! After that, the house became very quiet. I was just about to go back to the nursery when Boy's door opened and he came out." She paused. "I think he was looking for Acland, because he called his name in a low voice, then opened the door of Acland's room—but he can't have been there, because Boy came out again almost immediately."

"He was looking for Acland?" Stern's question was sharp. "What time was this?"

"I'm not sure. Late. I had no watch. Everyone else was in bed, even the servants. It must have been about one, perhaps a little later."

"One o'clock—and Acland wasn't there?"

"No."

"Do you know where Acland was?"

"I asked him once." Constance turned away. "He said he was with a woman. All night."

"A woman?"

"Yes. All night."

"Did you believe him?"

"Yes. I think I did. Anyway, Acland is beside the point. The point is, Boy came out onto the landing and he saw me. He asked me what I was doing, staying up so late, and I explained about the comet. He smiled. He said he used to watch the grown-up parties when he was my age, from just that place. He asked if I still felt wide-awake, and when I said I did, he said I could come and sit in his room. We'd have a talk."

"A talk?"

"That was what he said. I went in, and Boy sat me down by the fire. I only had my nightdress, no dressing gown, so Boy fetched a rug to wrap around me. He gave me a glass of lemonade and some biscuits. He showed all his collections—the birds' eggs, the lead soldiers. It was fun! Then we talked. I think Boy was very unhappy—he needed to talk to someone, and I was there."

"You talked. For how long?"

"A very long time. It didn't feel long. Then, eventually, Boy said I must go back to bed. He took me back to the nursery. That was when I looked at the clock. It was a minute or two before five—I remember because I was surprised it was so late. I crept into bed, and as I lay down, I heard the church clock strike."

"You're quite certain of all this?"

"Absolutely certain."

"What time was the accident discovered?"

"Six-thirty. Cattermole always said around six-thirty."

"How strange."

"Why strange?"

"Because, as you say, Boy could not have been involved. Why should he claim to Steenie that he was? Was he shielding someone else, do you think?"

"Shielding someone? Do you mean his father?"

"That's one candidate. There is another."

Constance rose. She shook her head. "I'm sure that wasn't it. I think he was just . . . confused. Our marriage made him unhappy.

He was shell-shocked. It was the war making him speak in that way—that was what I wanted Steenie to see—"

"You seem very anxious to believe that."

"I want to forget all this—perhaps that's why. Oh, Montague, don't you see? It used to obsess me so much. I used to say to myself that it was not just an accident, that one day I would know the truth. I used to try and patch it together, piece by piece. I don't want to do that anymore—"

"Why not?"

"Because it *was* an accident. No one was to blame—except Hennessy. He put that trap there, and the wrong man was caught by it. It was seven years ago. I want to forget it, leave it all behind. Please, Montague, don't you see?" She turned to him and caught at his hand. "I want to begin a different life—with you. This is the last time we ever need to talk about the past. I want us to find somewhere beautiful to live—"

"Not Winterscombe?"

"Not Winterscombe—not anywhere near Winterscombe. Don't you see now how impossible that would be?"

"Yes. I do see that."

"And then—oh, I want us to be happy. I want to give you your son. I want us to begin conquering the world together, just as we planned. I want—"

"Do you still want Jenna as your maid?"

"Yes, yes. I should like to save her and her baby from that horrible Hennessy. I should like to look after them. But that is just a small part of my plans—forget that. The important thing is us. Oh, Montague, I want us to be so very close—"

"Is Hennessy that baby's father?"

"How should I know? What difference does it make? Jenna says he is—presumably she knows! Forget them. Listen to me, darling Montague. I told Steenie something else today, something that concerns you. And now—"

"No. You listen to me, Constance." To her surprise, Stern interrupted the rush of words. He laid his hand across her lips to silence her. Constance would have pulled that hand away and pressed on, but she was silenced by the expression on his face. She gave a small cry.

"Oh—so grim and so sad! Why do you look at me like that?"

"Because there is something I want to tell *you*. Something I have just understood. An answer to an old puzzle. There were always pieces missing, but tonight you put the last piece into place. Now I can see it, the whole pattern—and I think you could, too, if you would look closely enough. It is really very simple—so obvious I should have seen it long ago."

"I don't understand."

Stern sighed. Whatever he was about to say, he seemed to find it difficult to begin. He took both her hands in his.

"Constance," he began gently. "You should look at this, just one last time. You can never leave it behind you otherwise, and, perhaps, neither can I. Listen. Ask yourself. Was it an accident? Wasn't there someone in the house that night who might have had good cause to harm your father? Someone who felt betrayed by him, someone who might have seen him as a trespasser, someone who knew of his affair with Gwen?"

"Denton? Do you mean Denton?"

"Well, Denton is an obvious candidate, of course. But no, I do not mean Denton." Stern paused. Again he seemed reluctant to go on. "You forget, Constance—I was there that night. I have considered this too. I ruled out Denton long ago. By the end of dinner he was so drunk he had difficulty in standing, let alone walking. Peel and Heyward-West and I helped him as far as the library. He passed out almost at once. We left him to sleep it off."

"That's where he was?" Constance frowned. "Boy was looking for him, you know. He never found him. He wanted to tell him about the engagement—"

"Well, that is where he was. I saw him there before I went up to my room. He was out cold."

"Then there is no one. Don't you see? No one."

"Oh, but I think there is, Constance." Stern released her hands. "You seem very reluctant to examine this. Ask yourself. Of all the alibis, whose is the weakest?"

"Oh, I see." Constance gave a small angry gesture. "I see what you are driving at. I see what you are trying to make me say."

"Do you?"

"Yes. You're accusing Acland. I won't believe that. It can't have been Acland. He told me where he was that night—"

"Constance—"

"I shall not listen to this! Acland is dead. He can't defend himself. It's wrong to speculate—you have no right. You never knew Acland, and I did. I knew him through and through. You're jealous of Acland—I see that now. You're always mentioning him, always questioning me about him. Well, I won't have you speak of him in this way. Acland could not lie to me—"

"Ah, but you could lie to yourself, Constance. Think about that." Stern rose. He looked down at her. "You could believe what you wanted to believe. We are all capable of that, especially if it helps us to avoid an ugly truth. Don't you see?" He looked at her with great sadness. "When a truth is painful, and it concerns someone we love, none of us wants to look it in the face. We shield ourselves from the knowledge. We also shield the person we love."

"You think I love Acland?" Color mounted in Constance's cheeks. She stood. "Is that what you mean?"

"The possibility had occurred to me. Among others." Stern moved away. "You were certainly greatly distressed by his death. I remember that."

"You think I am shielding him?"

"I think you are shielding yourself. I think you refuse to confront the truth."

"Very well then, I'll tell you." Constance's voice rose. She crossed to her husband. "I believed Acland when he said he was with a woman, because I know who she was. He was in love with her then—he spent every moment he could with her. That night he met her in the stable loft. It's true, what he said. I won't tell you her name, but—"

"You have no need to tell me her name. I know who she was."

"You can't possibly know."

"Oh, but I can." Stern turned back to her. He took her arm with an expression of regret. "I told you before, Constance, I am not easily deceived, and I dislike to be misled. The woman was Jenna. Her lover was not some man in the village, as you once said to me, but Acland. It was Acland that trap was set for, by Hennessy, who was jealous of him. I imagine Hennessy will remain jealous, and suspicious, despite the fact that Acland is dead, since Jenna's child is almost certainly not her husband's. That, I suppose, is why you take such a proprietary interest in the child. It is Acland's, is it not? You might have said so. But then there are a number of other things you might have said, and did not. You still edit the truth, you see, Constance—to me as well as Steenie. I sometimes think you also edit the truth to yourself."

"How do you know this?"

"Partly through observation. Partly through information. When Acland enlisted he made a will. It was completed not long before he was killed, by a lawyer I recommended to him. In that will, he left what money he had to Jenna. Oh, and it might interest you to know—you were not forgotten. He left you his books."

"You know the contents of wills?"

"Some wills. I happen to have read this one."

"I hate you for that. Spying in that way. It's the most despicable thing I ever heard—"

"I doubt that. In my position you would have done exactly the same thing. Neither of us has the least concern for social niceties—"

"I shan't listen to this." Constance turned away angrily. "It simply proves my point, in any case. If you know about Jenna, then you know why I believe Acland. His alibi is not a flimsy one—"

"All night?"

"He was in love."

"Oh, I'm sure he was devoted—at the time. I'm sure he met her in the stable loft, just as you claim. Perhaps he remained there— who knows? But we can be certain of one thing. Jenna did not. You yourself saw her, shortly after midnight, going in to Jane Conyngham's room."

"Oh." Constance gave a small start. "Yes, I did. I had not thought of that. Oh, God." She bent her head.

Stern crossed to her. He put his arm around her. "Constance," he said, "even that proves nothing—don't you see? If Acland's alibi is flimsy, so are the others. Yes, Denton was drunk, and passed out—but perhaps he recovered. Perhaps you were mistaken about the time, and you stayed talking to Boy less long than you thought. We could argue this a thousand ways." He sighed. "Maybe you were right, and the whole affair was an accident."

"Ah, but you don't believe that, do you? I can tell."

"No, I don't." He turned Constance to face him. "I think I know exactly what happened that night—and I think you know too. But it is painful, and you will not examine it."

"Acland could not lie to me!" Constance's eyes filled with tears. "And besides, he is dead now. Don't you see, Montague, it does no good to resurrect all this. We should draw a line under it all, you and I, and begin again."

"Very well. We shall never speak of it again." Stern bent, as if to kiss her. As he did so the telephone rang.

He straightened, an expression of annoyance on his face. He picked up the receiver and listened.

At first, Constance paid no attention to this call, which she expected to concern business affairs. Then Stern's manner—the change in his face, the oddness of the questions he put—alerted her. She turned to watch her husband. She approached closer and tried to identify the voice on the line, a woman's voice. When Stern replaced the receiver, she made a dart at him.

"Was that Maud?"

"Yes."

"Did you give her this number?"

"No. Gwen must have."

"How dare she call!" Constance gave a small stamp. "What's wrong? Something must be wrong. She wouldn't call otherwise."

"Something has happened—"

"Well, it doesn't seem to please you, whatever it is! Is it money? Is she ill?"

"No." Stern turned away and sat down. He did not speak. Constance stared at him in growing consternation. She made a rush to his side, knelt down by him, and took his hands in hers.

"Oh, Montague, I'm sorry. I'm being stupid and jealous. What is it? Has something terrible happened? Oh, tell me—tell me quickly. You make me afraid."

"Something strange has happened."

"A bad thing?"

"I'm not sure."

"Does it concern me?"

"I fear that it does."

"Tell me."

"Oddly enough," he said, "it has to do with caves."

Jane liked the caves at Étaples. The air attacks, once they began, always came at night; they took refuge in the caves, always at night. And the caves, stretching back into the hillside, a labyrinth of limestone caverns and corridors, fascinated her. In the deeper caves no light penetrated, and no sound. To stand in them was to lose all sense of time and place. It might have been midnight or noon. The air was chill; winter or summer, the temperature scarcely altered. Without a flashlight, and some degree of care, she would have become lost within minutes, wandering through fissures of rock. This danger she also liked. Sometimes she would walk back into the hillside; then, when she reached a large cave, she would switch off her flashlight. She would lift her hand in front of her face. It was invisible. She would listen. There was no sound but her own breathing and the drip of water: the liquefaction of centuries. Sometimes she would make herself count to twenty, then fifty, then a hundred, before she switched on her flashlight once more. Her skin would prickle with fear. She liked to remind herself in this way of the caves' silent power—and, benign or malevolent, they possessed power; she was sure of it.

Winnie felt no such thing and once, when Jane tried to explain, became irritable. Winnie disliked the caves. She said they were confining, despite their size. She complained of the cold. She complained of the hardness of the rock on which she was forced to sleep. She became, in fact, quite bitter on the whole subject of the caves— and there was a reason for this. Colonel Hunter-Coote remained with his men in the camp: Winnie, who considered WAACs military personnel first and women second, resented this separation. "Our place is down there, gels!" she would cry, standing at the mouth of the caves. She would point down through the darkness to the camp, where the guns lit the dark.

Once the exodus to the caves became a regular occurrence, however, Winnie began to enjoy herself. Her considerable powers of organization came to the fore. For Winnie, a night in the caves was intolerable without a great many solaces: She must have a blanket, a small inflatable rubber pillow, a pump to aid the pillow's inflation. She would not leave camp without a length of string, a flashlight, a box of matches, a penknife, a book, writing paper and pens, spare batteries, and candles. "If we can't sleep we'd better eat," she would declare; neither she nor her gels ever set foot in the caves without flasks of cocoa, tinned fruit, and hefty packages of sandwiches wrapped in grease-proof paper.

After some three or four nights of this, Winnie observed the habits of the French villagers, who, within days, began to turn the caves into homes. First of all, they selected the best cave, the warmest and the driest and the one that provided the finest view of the activities below, since it overlooked the guns.

Having established this cave as their territory, they marked it out with piles of belongings, which would be left there in readiness until the next raid. Mattresses appeared; one very old man even toiled up the hill hauling a sagging armchair. Children carried up baskets of food and bottles of wine; grandfathers brought accordions and harmonicas; one grandmother brought her goat, on a string. She sat in the mouth of the cave and milked it.

"Typical—absolutely *typical*!" Winnie pronounced jealously, after visiting this cave. "Do you know what that woman was doing— the one with the goat? She was frying chicken on a paraffin stove. In the middle of a battle. The French really are the absolute *end*." The night after this, Winnie produced a primus stove, which she set up with a flourish. The night after that, she used it. Being English, she did not fry chicken; she heated up tins of thick oxtail soup. The next night, she promised, there would be deviled sardines.

"Sardines at midnight—amazing, Winnie," Wexton murmured.

In fact these sardines never made their appearance, for that night the German aircraft scored a direct hit. They missed munitions, they missed the parade ground and the Nissen huts, but one bomb fell, fair and square, right on the top of Winnie's YWCA club. No one was injured, but the Winnie who made her appearance in the caves the following night was a changed woman.

"Gone, all gone!" she announced with a stricken look. "All my lovely tins of condensed milk—and I'd waited *weeks* for those! The china, the tables and chairs—matchsticks! Even the piano, utterly smashed. They knew—I'm certain the Huns knew. Munitions? They weren't attacking the munitions dump; they were attacking our morale."

Winnie was determined to be inconsolable. She even refused cocoa. She hunched herself under her blankets and began, after a while, to emit noises that might have been snores or groans. When they were sure they were snores, Jane and Wexton left her.

Jane checked the cave where her own patients lay, then joined Wexton at the mouth of the caves, overlooking the camp. They stayed there some while, talking to the sentries, peering out into the darkness, listening for the drone of approaching planes. Wexton sat down. He lit a cigarette and took out his notebook. Jane left him, and turned back.

The cave with the French—she could see the grandmother and her goat sitting side by side. The grandmother was knitting. She passed on to a deeper, larger cave, where the wounded lay sleeping in rows of camp beds. She went farther into the hill and looked into the cavern where the men who suffered from battle fatigue were stationed. This cave was the innermost of those in use; here, the sound of guns and explosions was muffled. The men seemed to sleep peacefully enough. One of the Red Cross nurses, a woman Jane had met at Winnie's club, sat watching over them. There was a book on her knee and two candles at her side. The light of the candle flames leaped against the walls and danced devils upon the nurse's face. Seeing Jane, she glanced up from her book and smiled. Jane walked on.

Deeper and deeper into the hillside; the silence was absolute now. Some of the caves were small, little more than spaces below shelves of rock; others were caverns so high that the beam of her flashlight could not penetrate to their roofs. The light made the seepings from the rock gleam; it lit the phosphorescence of stalactites.

Jane did not pause to look at these. She quickened her pace. There was one cave she wanted to reach, one she had explored before, a cave that was as high, as wide, as echoing as a cathedral. At the entrance to this cave there was a hollow of rock as smooth as a stoup. It contained water. When she reached this cave, she felt for the rock. She dipped her hand into the ice-cold water and splashed it against her face. Holding her flashlight tightly, she walked forward, first five paces and then ten.

She stopped. She listened. Far above her, something stirred, a leathery rustling, almost certainly bats. Jane was afraid of bats. She imagined them tangled in her hair. She hesitated; then she knelt.

Jane came to this cave to pray. She came to it because it gave her total privacy. But sometimes, even here, Jane felt her prayers were small things. They knotted and twisted and doubled back.

That night, her prayers began in this way. The cold rock cut her knees and distracted her. There was still that leathery shuffling high in the roof space. She tried to pray for Boy, who, she believed, had killed himself, although his parents claimed it was a shooting accident. Water dripped. She tried to pray for her aunt Clara, who was dead, and her father, who was dead, and her brother, Roland, who was dead in a different war. The darkness stifled the prayers. She sat back on her heels. She felt her stockings tear at the knee. It was perhaps wrong, she thought, that she always seemed to pray for the dead. She ought to pray for the living.

She then did a very strange thing. Later, when she tried to describe it in her diary, she could not account for it at all. It resisted the net of her sentences. There was no conscious decision. One moment she knelt; the next, she lay full-length on the rock, flat against the limestone, arms extended.

All the words were gone; the rock drew them out of her. Anger and pain, war and the pity of war, faith and its obstructions; no more contradictions—they clung and then were gone. Such lightness, being lifted above the words; how small their anguish seemed as she rose above them. A space traveler, gifted with pinions, she looked down on the words and they were as small as a star, inexorable as a planet, distant and lovely as a moon—the good and the bad, the hope and the despair, all the opposites, moving in a sure equilibrium.

Faster than light. She looked down at the woman she had left behind in the cave; she looked down on serenity and on battles; she watched the rhythms of death and birth, of extinction and regeneration. The beauty of this patterning was blinding; its exactitude and justice dazzled her eyes—and the woman in the cave below her cried out.

Over in an instant, lasting beyond a lifetime. Once the brightness of vision was gone, the darkness of the cave was absolute. She lay there, resting in the darkness; then she began to be afraid. She stumbled awkwardly to her feet; the flashlight dropped from her hand. A moment of pure fear then, a vision of being trapped in that labyrinth of passageways. Then, bending, she found the flashlight at once. Her hand closed over the metal casing; the battery rattled. She heard that leathery shuffling in the roof space again; then the beam of light came back on.

Jane trained the light against the rock face. Had she entered this cave by the slit in the rock there, or the one a little farther to her right? Should she go through the near opening or the far one? Which way?

She turned in one direction. She turned back. She stared down fearfully at the ground where she had lain a few moments before. She was no longer sure that she had lain there at all. She might have imagined it. This frightened her more. There was a power in these caves, a power she had sensed from the first; she now began to believe it was malevolent. These caves meant her harm. They meant to lose her.

Something brushed against her face. Jane cried out. The rock caught her cry and threw it back at her. The beam of the flashlight wavered, then strengthened; at once she felt calmer. She looked first to her left and then to her right. She was sure—almost sure—that she had entered this cave by the small opening to the left of her; she considered this fissure, then turned away from it. A few paces; a narrow gap, a shelf of rock, and then a passageway, its floor rising sharply.

Not the way she had entered this cave, but the right way to leave it. She edged through the gap, then began to walk more quickly, now certain of her route; an Ariadne, she thought, following an invisible string. This way. She stumbled, then broke into a run. She was almost there. She stopped at a point where the passageway widened and three paths joined. The bombing had begun again; muffled by stone, she could hear the reverberation of guns. The cave where Winnie slept was to her left; the cave where Wexton sat with the sentries was straight ahead; the cave she must find was to her right.

She ran forward a few paces. As she reached the right cave, a

gun stuttered. When she entered, the Red Cross nurse set down her
book. She yawned, stretched, smiled. Her two candles were almost
burned down. She picked up two more, lit them, fixed them in a
pool of soft wax. Their flames wavered, then strengthened. "How
long the night is," she said.

Jane looked from the nurse to the beds. She counted them.
There were twenty-five men here. She shone the beam of her
flashlight along the rows. Most of the men slept, huddled figures
beneath their blankets. One man, caught in the light, sat up in his
bed. He counted and then recounted the fingers of his hand. Two
beds along, a man moaned, a low, monotonous crooning. Next to
him, a man touched himself; the blankets lifted, then fell, up and
down, a remorseless jiggling. His eyes rolled back. He opened and
closed his mouth. He sighed. Then he began on the jiggling and the
jerking again.

"Best to leave them." The Red Cross nurse looked across at this
man. "They don't mean any harm. Just like children, most of
them—and besides, if it keeps them quiet, why not?"

Jane looked back at the beds. The man who had been moaning
was growing restless. He began to thresh back and forth in the bed.
He leaned back and banged his head against the rock.

"Oh, that one—he's one of the difficult ones, he is." The nurse
stood. She gave Jane an assessing look. "Some of them are quiet as
mice. Never say a word. But that one . . ." She clicked her tongue.
"Once he starts, there's only one way to stop him. You want to see?
You won't say a word? We all do it, and it settles him just nice—but
the sister wouldn't like it, not if she knew—"

"Please. They are your patients."

Jane turned away. She looked at the candles. She watched
shadows move against the rock. When she turned back, the nurse sat
on the edge of the moaning man's bed. She bent over him. She
smoothed his forehead. She gave a quick, precautionary glance toward
the entrance to the cave. She loosened the front of her uniform
and drew out one plump breast.

"Here you are, love. Here. There now. There now."

The man's eyes were still tight-shut; at the sound of her voice,
his wails diminished. The nurse took his hand and guided it. It
closed on the pale globe of her breast and clutched at it. He began to
make smacking noises with his lips. The nurse leaned forward, cradling
him. She slipped her nipple between his lips. The man sucked.

She sat there, nursing him, for perhaps two or three minutes.
Then she laid him back, stroked his brow, refastened her dress.

"Quiet as a lamb now, poor thing. He'll sleep now, you'll see. It's a comfort to him, and what is it, after all? No more than you'd do for a baby if it cried. Better than morphine, not as addictive, and quicker too."

"Does he talk?" Jane still stared at the line of beds. "Does he think you're his mother?"

"I couldn't say, dear. He moans a lot—like you heard. Never says much. Not actual words. I think . . ." She hesitated. "I think he won't make it back, not that one."

"Do any of them talk?" Jane turned back. "I mean, do they ever talk—about what made them like this? What it was they saw?"

"Some of them." The nurse gave a sigh. "Usually it's just one little thing, something they fix on, and they will go over it again and again. And then, others—like him—they never speak at all. They just look right through you. There's some don't even have a name. We don't know who they are, and when they bring them in, we give them a number. I don't like that, so I give them a name anyway. I say to them: Right, you're Bill, or Johnny. They seem to like that. They can't remember a thing, of course. It's all blanked out."

"Names?" Jane turned back to the beds. "Why wouldn't they have names?"

"A hundred reasons. Blown up. On the wire. Half-buried alive. In a dugout with dead men for five days before they get to them. It happens all the time. Some of them still know who they are, some of them can be identified, and some of them can't. They sort it out, I expect, when they get them back to England. Oh, Lord! Look at that one. I'll have to stop him. I won't be a sec."

She pushed her chair back. She crossed to the man whose blankets had jiggled and jerked. His blankets had now fallen from the bed. His trousers gaped. Between his pumping hands was a strip of anxious hooded flesh, scarcely erect. Jane averted her eyes. There was a sound of a slap. The man groaned. When Jane next looked back, his blankets were in place. The man's eyes were closed. His thumb was in his mouth.

"No peace for the wicked." The nurse paused by his bed. She switched on a flashlight and shone it along the line of beds, first to the right and then to the left. Her patients were quiet. She looked up.

"Do you fancy something warm to drink? I've a flask here with some warm milk and a spot of something stronger. Would you like some, dear? I'd be glad of the company. We'll be here hours yet."

"In a minute. I should just like to . . ." Jane walked forward.

She edged between the beds. "One of the men you checked just now—when you shone your flashlight. Something just caught my eye—"

"Which one?" The nurse flicked her flashlight again, up and down the row. "This one? He's quiet tonight. He's another won't make it back, I think."

"No, not that one. Over there."

The nurse directed the beam of her flashlight the other way. It shone on gray blankets and averted faces, closed eyes, grown men curled as tight as a fetus.

"What, that one?" The beam hovered, then was still. "Oh, he's one of the numbers. I don't know much about him. They only brought him in—what?—two days ago. Three. There was an exchange of prisoners—at Arras, I think. Then they shipped him up here. Isn't he thin? Half-starved. And he's had a horrible wound—it's healed now, but it's still horrible. Look."

She leaned across and drew back the blanket.

"Oh, don't wake him. He's asleep."

"He won't wake." The nurse gave her a sidelong glance. "And if he does wake, he won't speak. He's catatonic. I only give him a week. Look—just look. You tell me. How does a man get a wound like that and still live?"

The man's jacket was unfastened; his shirt was loose. The nurse pushed them to one side. She directed the flashlight.

The man had taken a bayonet wound in the chest. The bayonet must have glanced across his ribs before penetrating just below the heart. The wound had been poorly sutured. It had left a livid scar, a cicatrice the shape of a crescent moon. The marks of stitches were clearly visible. Around the man's throat was a thong and a small leather medallion.

"One-nine-three?"

"That's his number. His hospital number." The nurse began to sound impatient. She pulled the blanket back into place.

"Did you not give him a name?"

"This one? No, I didn't. I don't know why. He hasn't been here long, and I haven't nursed him that much. Also, he scares me. Some of them do, you know. The look they get in their eyes. As if they wanted to kill you. He has that. Cold eyes. They look right through you. And they're a funny color."

It was as if the man heard her. He stirred, turned, opened his eyes. He lay on his back, staring straight up at them without blinking. He must have seen them, but he gave no sign. He might have stared at a wall.

"Why don't we have that milk?"

The nurse turned away. Jane did not move.

"Come on. I've some cigarettes, too, if you'd like one. Shouldn't, not when I'm on duty—but the night's so slow, don't you find?" She shivered. "I hate these bloody caves."

"Yes. Very slow."

Jane knelt beside the bed. She took her own flashlight from her pocket and switched it on. She shone it carefully to the side of the man's face, so it would not blind him. A thin face. The reddish stubble of a beard, perhaps four or five days of growth.

Why had no one shaved him? she thought. She felt a sudden spurt of anger. Why had no one done this for him, if he could not do it for himself? And his hair was unwashed, as well as uncombed. She lifted her hand to smooth it; the man's hair was alive; his scalp crawled. Jane jerked her hand away. She almost dropped her flashlight.

"This man has lice." She swung around accusingly.

The nurse shrugged. "I'll make a note of it. They can deal with it tomorrow."

"It should have been dealt with at once. At *once*."

Jane stopped. The man had turned his head. He regarded her face with a still cold gaze. His eyes turned to her hair, to her cap. He looked downward toward her mouth and chin, then back up to her eyes. His eyes had the vacancy of the blind.

"Look, do you want some of this milk or don't you?" The nurse sounded impatient. "Leave him alone. Let him get some sleep. I don't want trouble."

"I know him," Jane said. "I know him."

She leaned forward so that her own eyes looked down into his. The man continued to stare straight ahead, as if he looked through her into the dark. His eyes were green, the left a perceptibly different color from the right. Jane took his left hand and held it between her own. Once he had worn a signet ring on the little finger of this hand, though he wore none now.

"Acland."

She spoke his name very quietly, so only she and he could hear. There was no flicker of response.

"Acland. Can you understand me? It's Jane. Look, touch me. I'm a nurse here. I've cut my hair since you last saw me, but I'm sure if you look you can recognize me—"

Jane's voice broke. She felt confused. Her vision blurred. Hair? Why was she talking about hair? How could she be so stupid?

"Look." She lifted his hand so that his fingers rested against her face. His hand remained stiff and inert. "Look, I'm crying, Acland. Tears—can you feel them? I'm only crying because I'm so happy, Acland. I thought I'd lost you, you see. But you're not lost. You're found. Acland—can you hear me? Oh, please, can't you see me?"

The man below her gave no sign he heard her voice. His hand remained stiff. There was no answering pressure from his fingers, no trace of response in his eyes. Jane thought: *I was always invisible to him; I am invisible still.*

"Acland, please, let me help you. You will be safe now. I shall look after you. I shan't let anyone hurt you. I'll take you home— Acland, think: Winterscombe. You'll see Winterscombe. It's spring there now—"

Jane stopped. She dropped her own hands and drew back a little. Acland's hand remained as it had been. He did not lower his arm. Jane had begun to shake. A bomb breathed in the distance. The air moved. She tried to force this upraised arm back down against the blankets, but it would not be forced. It was as stiff as the arm of a day-old corpse. She swung around.

"What is wrong with this man—what is it?"

She put the question angrily. The nurse took offense.

"Wrong with him? What do you think is wrong with him? The same as is wrong with all the others. And you're wasting your time trying to talk to him. Maybe he can hear—but if he can, he doesn't listen. And he never speaks. Look—come and have a drink. Have a cigarette." Her voice became conciliatory. "Come on, dear. It's best to leave him. He's mad."

VII
LAZARUS

"WEXTON," I SAID, "will you read this?"

I held out one of Constance's black journals. Wexton, who had refused to look at any of them before, took it with obvious reluctance.

"Please, Wexton. I want you to understand why they disturb me so much."

"After the caves?" He put on his reading glasses.

"Five months later."

He moved to the window, where the light was strong. A clear, cold autumn day; outside, the sun shone on the gardens at Winterscombe. He bent his head to the page, and, in silence, he read the following entry. Constance had written it in this house, in October 1917.

Full circle. We are all assembled here again. It was Gwen's idea. The family home, the family circle—Gwen believes this will cure Acland, five months in London and six most distinguished doctors having failed.

The weather is fine. There is a bright new window in the church, Denton's memorial to Boy. Gwen took Acland to look at this yesterday, against Jane's advice. He sat in his wheelchair, facing the window. Perhaps he saw it; perhaps he did not. Needless to say, he did not speak. Then, last night, his nightmares returned; his screams were so loud they woke me. I ran out onto the landing. I thought my father had come back.

I stood there listening. People scurried to and fro. Even Montague woke and came out of his room. He saw me standing there; he put his arm around me. He offered to stay with me, but I sent him away. I do not need him now, not for the present. I need you, Acland. I am going to bring you back from the dead.

Now listen to me, Acland, my dearest Lazarus: I've been patient, but I shan't be patient anymore. You'll get no loving kindness from me—let Jane supply the sops and the prayers. Kindness will not bring you back. They've wasted five months on kindness. You need harsher medicine than that: truth, for instance, not the consolation of lies.

You think you're wounded, Acland? Just wait—I can wound you in ways you wouldn't believe. Stab, stab, stab. Whatever the Germans did to you, I can do worse.

Shall I tell you about Jenna? Would you like to hear about your baby son, Edgar, whose eyes were exactly like yours—and who died three weeks ago, of a pleurisy? There's plenty more.

You see? Truth hurts. Words bruise. Time does not stop, Acland, and you cannot ignore that, any more than I once could. Remember that, next time you look through me.

I need to be alone with you. Not for long—an hour would do, but even an hour is difficult, for Jane guards you ferociously. However, Jane is tiring; you are wearing even her optimism thin. So, I shall have my hour soon enough. Tomorrow, or the day after.

Then, when you know how it really feels to have a mind full of rocks, and those rocks grinding, grinding—you can choose. Die if you want. After all, we both know death is the last best secret.

But if you die, at least make it a glorious death, not this miserable dwindling away. Spit in the eye of this trumpery world; go out on a tide of triumphant blood. I'll help you. What would you like? A gun? A razor?

Or live—if you feel angry enough. Wager yourself against the world. It can be done. I do it. But make no mistake—you must be angry first, and you must keep that anger with you, forever and ever.

Jane will promise you the old solaces: faith, hope, charity—can't you just hear her? She will tell you there is a valley, and it is a quiet place, a restful place; it is just ahead; you can reach it. Don't believe her. There may be a valley, but after that there is always another mountain range, and then another, and at the very end, when you have climbed them all, there will be one last precipice, one last stretch of black, black water.

My husband is at the door. Acland, I shall stop writing now and lock this away. Don't worry, I keep you secret; I still protect you. He is clever—so I have to be careful. Oh, Acland, do you remember the night you came to me and showed me your wound? You made a ring of bright hair and bound it about my finger—dear dead Acland, how alive we were then!

Wait for me now. I shall come soon, I promise. I shall bring you two presents: death in my right hand, and life in my left. Dexter or sinister: think about it, Acland. I shall kiss you, and then you can decide.

Wexton closed the notebook. There was silence.

"Do you see, Wexton?" I said eventually. "She was in love with my father. I think he was in love with her. Always. Everything she says there, she did. Do you see, Wexton? It wasn't my mother who brought Acland back to life. It was Constance."

"Odd." Wexton did not appear to be listening. He pulled first at his earlobes, then his hair. He frowned. "Odd." He turned. "I can't remember. Is Constance right-handed?"

"What? Yes. Yes, she is. But—"

"*Dexter or sinister.* I kind of like that. Except"—he paused— "most people, unless they were left-handed, they'd offer death with the left hand and life with the right—don't you think? She reverses it."

"I don't see . . . It doesn't seem very important—"

"Oh, I think it is. A mirror image. It's pretty clear which one she wanted him to choose. The razor hand. Was it a razor?"

"Yes."

"A cutthroat, huh?" Wexton smiled. "But then a safety razor— apart from the fact it wouldn't do the job as well—it doesn't have quite the same ring."

"Wexton, please don't make fun of this. I can see—the way she writes. But she always writes like that. She means what she says."

"Oh sure, I realize that. And I'm not making fun of it. It's highly colored, but better than I expected. I wouldn't mind reading a bit more."

"Wexton, this isn't literary criticism. This is my *father*—"

"Was she always that in love with death?" Wexton stood.

"What? I don't understand."

"Sure you do. Think. This is a love letter, right?"

"I suppose so. In a way. One of many. Those journals are full of them." I turned away bitterly. "And they're all addressed to my father."

"Oh, I don't think so. She's writing to death. She just happens to call him Acland."

"A love letter—to death?"

"That's how it seems to me. I could be wrong, of course." He frowned. "You know the line in Keats? *And, for many a time I have been half in love with easeful Death?* Only in her case she isn't half in love—it's a full-blooded romance. And death isn't too easeful. In fact, as lovers go, he sounds pretty vigorous, wouldn't you say? *Stab, stab, stab . . . Go out on a tide of blood?* It's full of sex. Death as the ultimate sexual partner."

He stopped, as if an idea had just occurred to him. His face, alert and interested just a moment before, clouded. He shook his head.

"I wonder . . ."

He seemed about to say something more, then thought better of it. He was looking toward the future. I know that now, but at the time I misinterpreted his reaction. I thought there was a very good reason why Constance might have associated Acland with death, and it concerned the accident to her father. If Wexton had also made that connection—*Acland, don't worry, I keep you secret; I still protect you*—it was not something I wanted to discuss then. I wanted those suspicions to go away; I was not ready to confront them yet.

"Wexton," I said, "you remember India—you remember the day I went to Mr. Chatterjee?"

"Yes."

"You remember what he said about two women?"

"Uh-huh." Wexton's expression became guarded.

"It's not that I believe in clairvoyance, exactly. Obviously, I don't."

"Obviously." Wexton smiled.

"But two women—they are here, do you see? Constance and Jane. Constance and—my mother. He said I would have to choose between them. And I feel as if this is the place. Right here."

"One of them cured Acland, you mean? That story?"

"Yes. I grew up with that story, Wexton. I still believe it."

"So do I."

"You see, if I could just be sure . . . which of them it was. Constance always claimed she did it."

"That sounds pretty typical. What did your mother say?"

"She said it was God."

"I can imagine that. I mean, Jane—well, she would say that."

"It was all so *strange*, Wexton. If I could just be sure."

"You can't. That's the point, I'd say."

He hesitated. He crossed the room; he patted my hand in an awkward, affectionate way.

"Can you hear your mother's voice now? Constance isn't drowning her out anymore?"

"No. Not so much. I hear her—I think I hear her."

"Then think about it. Trust your instincts. Weigh one against the other and decide." He paused. "And no, don't ask me. You know what I think, anyway. But then, I'm hopelessly biased—"

"You think it's obvious?"

To my surprise, Wexton shook his head.

"Oh, no. I don't think it's obvious at all. I've never underestimated Constance's powers. I certainly don't now." He gestured toward the journals. "As women, she and your mother were at opposite extremes. It was a duel of angels."

That phrase surprised me even more—Wexton was not usually given to exaggeration. He saw my surprise, and it seemed to amuse him. His face crumpled into his benevolent smile.

"Why not? Life isn't ordinary. It is extraordinary. I've always believed that."

"Truly, Wexton?"

"Of course. But then I don't like the prosaic—never did. It's why I write poetry, not prose."

Having made this pronouncement, he settled himself in a chair by the fire. He lit one of Steenie's aromatic cigarettes. He gave every appearance of an elderly man preparing for a pleasant midmorning doze.

I returned to Constance, my mother, and my father: a love triangle, at Winterscombe.

When I was a child, my father's recovery was my favorite bedtime story. "Please," I would say to my mother, "tell it to me again." And she would: She would tell me about the caves, and her certainty that once she found the right one, she would also find Acland. She would tell me about the journey back to England, the long months in which Acland's illness seemed incurable, and the night when, finally, he spoke. I knew what came next, of course—they married—and I knew what happened subsequently: They lived happily ever after, as people do in the best stories.

I can't remember how old I was when I first realized that there was another part of this story, a part my mother left out.

Certainly, by the time I was twelve or thirteen, I understood that as far as the credit for my father's recovery went, people were divided in their verdict.

Great Aunt Maud, for instance, definite in all things, was most definite in this, no half-shadings: My mother nursed my father back to health. She was Acland's good angel, Maud would declare, and she brought him back from his underworld with the undramatic gifts of common sense, coddled eggs, fresh air, and serenity.

Wexton, too, a more reliable witness, supported Jane. He would bring out that Episcopalian word *grace* to bolster his argument. Steenie, on the other hand, was all for Constance. Constance, I learned, had also visited Acland on the day of his recovery: Constance, according to Steenie, was the dark angel who nipped in between my father and death. My uncle Steenie had had a classical education. In his—more lurid—version of events, Acland had already been rowed across the Styx; he shook hands with Hades. To spirit someone back from that place, Steenie claimed, required something a great deal more dramatic than common sense, or even love: It required daring, guile, bravado, and excess. All these qualities, Steenie argued, Constance possessed—in trumps.

"Make no mistake," he would cry, on his second bottle of Bollinger. "Constance shocked him back to life. I don't know how, but she did it!"

Steenie would wink when he said this. I disliked that wink—it made me nervous. Inevitably, I asked Constance to explain, and—equally inevitably—she never did. "Me—and a little black magic," she would always say, then change the subject.

Her journals were less reticent. There in front of me, blow by blow as it were, were all the details of Constance's resuscitation process. As with much of what she wrote, they had a dreamlike clarity. I think I believed them then; I think I believe them still. One thing is important: Constance and my mother saw Acland on the same day, within a few hours of each other. Dark angel or not, Constance was a fast operator. Two days after she wrote the entry in her journals that Wexton had just read, her chance came: Jane left Winterscombe to spend the day in London.

Two women; two accounts; two diaries on the table in front of me. My mother was good, also an innocent—and one of the penalties of innocence can be blindness. Before she left for London, Jane asked Constance to spend a little time with Acland in the course of the day. She did not like him left alone for long periods. She suggested Constance might read to him. She had believed Constance disliked sickrooms and expected reluctance. *But I misjudged her,* she wrote: *Constance can be kind. She agreed without hesitation.*

*   *   *

Jane had two reasons for this visit to London: She was to see Jenna, and then, before catching her train back, she was to see Maud. The first of these visits was urgent: Jane was anxious for Jenna, who had lost her baby; Jenna, whose health was poor.

There was, however, another reason for this journey, although it was one she was reluctant to admit. It would be the first time she had left Acland's side since she brought him back from Étaples, and she needed that day's space; she hungered for it.

Acland's condition was almost unchanged. His physical health might have improved—he ate, provided he was left alone to do so; he slept, after a fashion; he consented to be moved, from a bed to a wheelchair—but these were the limits of his cooperation. He still looked through, rather than at. He could not be cajoled, or tricked, into speech—although he screamed words that were recognizable when he had nightmares.

At this compromise, this half-life, Jane rebelled. She could feel the rebellion drumming away at the back of her mind when she boarded the London train. It churned with the revolution of the train's wheels, a gathering and metallic momentum, more insistent with each mile that passed. Jane argued with herself. She reminded herself of all the appropriate medical and ethical points, one, two, three, four: It took time for a man's mind to heal; it required patience, tenacity, perseverance, and faith. These it was her wish, and her duty, to provide. She looked out the window. Fields raced; hedges sped. She rebelled against such pieties. There it was, at the back of her mind. What Acland did was *wrong*.

This she would not confront—yet. She would not deny it either. She would let it rest, there at the back of her mind, and as the day passed, she would travel toward it. By the end of the day, she might be ready for the confrontation. She believed this; it gave her an odd sense of freedom and exhilaration. She alighted at Paddington; she took a taxicab to Waterloo; she walked through mean streets, past the church where Jenna had been married, past the cemetery where her baby son was buried. Rebellion crept up on her. She lifted her face to the city sun. She thought, *close, close, close.*

Six weeks after the birth of her baby, while Jane was still in France, Jenna, in need of money, had taken work. The job, although Jenna did not know that, had been procured for her by the lawyer Solomons, who had spoken to Montague Stern. Mrs. Tubbs was left to look after the child. A reluctant Jenna joined Florence Tubbs at Stern's munitions works—a well-paid position, much sought-after. Jenna received twenty-four shillings a week; she packed shells.

This work had left its mark upon her. One of the chemicals used in the shells was tetrachloride. Handling it produced side effects in the women at the works, including dizziness and acute nausea. It also affected the skin, turning it a jaundiced color; the shell-packers, for this reason, were nicknamed "canaries."

The Jenna who opened the door to Jane Conyngham that October morning was greatly changed: Poverty and grief had aged her; her youth had gone.

"Please." She took Jane's hand, then pulled a shawl about her shoulders. "I want to go straight there. I want you to see it. It's so fine. I could never have . . . I'm grateful."

She began to walk very fast, catching Jane by the arm and pulling her along beside her. She turned down first one side street and then another. They came to a lodge and a pair of tall iron gates. These Jenna leaned against before starting to walk once more, even faster this time, so Jane half-ran to keep up with her.

It was a large cemetery, one of the largest in South London, and it is there still. You could retrace the path Jenna took that day, even now: past the stone angels, the carved urns, the stone catafalques of the more prosperous dead, to the smaller, more closely packed tombstones of the poor.

Here, in a corner shaded by a yew, Jenna paused. There, up against the wall of the graveyard, overgrown with brambles and rank grass, was a line of small wooden crosses no more than eight inches high, some leaning at an angle, some bare of all inscription, some inked with initials and dates already fading from sun and rain. These, too, are still there, although they are very overgrown now, and most of the crosses have rotted. They were the paupers' graves. Jenna looked at them with indignation.

"He was a lovely boy. I was proud of him. I didn't want him lying there. I hate those graves. I couldn't have rested, not if he'd gone there. The money you gave me—you see, look. It's Welsh slate. It takes the carving well, the man told me."

She turned and drew Jane back, beneath the yew. There was a small mound, newly turfed, a stone vase containing violets, and a tombstone of blue slate. It bore the name Edgar—no surname—and the dates of the baby's birth and death. Beneath it was the inscription: MUCH LOVED AND MUCH MISSED BY HIS FATHER AND HIS MOTHER. REST IN PEACE.

The letters curled across the slate. A most violent anger and pity rose up in Jane's mind. Money could do this much, she said to herself; money could do this little.

"I wish you'd seen him," Jenna went on. "I understand. I know it wasn't easy for you to come, and then, when he was ill, it was very quick. He was a fine baby—everyone said. He never cried. He'd grasp my finger—he could hold on so tight! And he'd smile. He knew it was me, when I came back from work. I'd take him in my arms, and . . . I think maybe he should have cried more. Babies do. Maybe I should've known, when he was so quiet. Maybe he wasn't very strong, right from the first. He took his milk, though—he always took that, right up till the day before. And then we thought it was just a cold—just a cold, nothing serious. The house is damp, you see, and we couldn't always get coal. Florrie ran for the doctor, but he was busy, and so I wrapped Edgar up in this shawl, and I ran with him down to the clinic. It's only five streets away, and I ran as fast as could be, but it was raining, and it was getting dark. Maybe I shouldn't have done that. Maybe I should have stayed in. And waited. But his mouth was blue. He couldn't breathe. I don't think he could breathe—so I thought I must. He still felt warm—when I reached the clinic, he still felt warm. But he'd gone. He must have gone then—when I was running. And I didn't even know. I didn't . . . I would have liked to . . . speak to him. Kiss him perhaps. Just one last time. I'm sorry. This helps—it does help. To know he's here, with a proper stone, that it's done right. I do thank you for that. It's just . . . I'll be all right again. In a moment. Yes. Yes. You're very good."

Jenna knelt. She bent her head. Her body shook as she wept. Jane remained standing. It had begun to rain, a fine drizzle from a sky pale as milk. The rain spotted the leather of her gloves. She looked down at these gloves, which were modest, plain, serviceable kid. One pair of these ordinary gloves cost two weeks of Jenna's wages. Jane regarded them. They looked unjust.

After a while, with a sudden impatient gesture, she pulled the gloves off and screwed them into a ball. She threw them down into the long grass. She removed her hat also and threw that down too. She lifted her face and her hair to the rain; she took in deep breaths of the damp and sooty air. She thought of all her estates, of her houses, of her money, which lay in a bank, and her investments. Meaningless stupid things, as unneeded as those gloves.

With the rain on her face, and Jenna's stooped figure at her feet, she listed one last time all the factors that had caused her to delay: convention, and her own timidity; Boy; then nursing; then, finally, Acland.

At this, the rebellion sensed upon the train came back to her.

She ran to meet it; it flooded her mind with a light of the most brilliant intensity. She shook back her wet clipped hair and felt its assurance. Her hands trembled a little with the strength of the emotion welling up in her, and she pressed them tight together, so the knuckles showed white. She bent down and helped Jenna to her feet. She put her arm around her shoulders and walked back with her, more slowly this time, to the house.

She stayed with Jenna two hours; then, as promised, she crossed the river to see Maud. The time seemed to Jane both very slow and very fast. It was necessary to pass through it; she was also impatient to reach the event that lay on its other side.

My great-aunt Maud was fretful; deserted by several friends, including Lady Cunard, she was perhaps lonely.

"Do you know the latest thing?" she asked over tea, in a tone nicely balanced between disdain and outrage. "These paintings" —she waved her hands at the walls, at the pictures Constance had once found it so useful to admire—"they were a gift, and now it seems *she* would like them returned. Quick-smart. I have been sent, if you please, a list."

This, from Maud—who was usually very careful of her own dignity, who considered it ill-bred to exhibit either pain or jealousy— was a major indiscretion. She perhaps regretted it almost at once, for having flapped the offending letter, she pushed it aside. To Maud's great surprise, Jane did not change the subject, or exhibit tact. Instead she sprang to her feet, and in the most impassioned way she clasped her hands together and looked at Maud with flushed cheeks.

"Oh, but don't you see?" she cried, in what seemed to Maud the most immoderate tones. "That's exactly what you should do. Send them back. Send it all back—you would feel so much freer, so much better!"

"My dear. What a delightful notion. I could live like a gypsy. Of course."

Maud—aware that if all Stern's gifts were returned, as recommended, she would be without a roof over her head—poured tea and changed the subject. She found herself a little irritated with Jane, who was displaying a romanticism and an emotionalism that were most unexpected.

"You've been working too hard, my dear," she said in a reproving way, when Jane took her leave. "Your eyes look very bright, and you are still quite flushed. Do you think you could have a fever?"

"No," Jane replied, in a way Maud found peremptory. She took

Maud's hand and, smiling, pressed it against her forehead, which indeed felt cool.

"It was good of you to come, Jane. I'll remember what you said . . ."

Maud felt quite at a loss. Her eye strayed to the cool brown lines of a Cézanne landscape, which hung close to the door. From certain angles it represented a place; from others, it took on an abstraction Maud had never liked. She thought about these paintings. She thought about Montague Stern, whom she missed greatly.

"Perhaps you are right," she said thoughtfully. And then, because the question would not be held back: "How is Monty—well, I hope?"

Jane considered this. She frowned. "Unhappy, I think," she said at last, as if the thought had just occurred to her. "Yes. Well. But unhappy."

Such frankness, at that juncture, was too much for Maud. She embarked upon a flurry of farewells. Jane, distracted again, scarcely listened to these.

She found herself impatient to be outside, impatient to reach the street, the train.

As the door of the house closed she looked at her watch. It was three-thirty in the afternoon. If she caught the right train, she would be home shortly after six. Acland waited for her. It made no difference whether he replied or not. For once, Jane knew exactly what to say to him.

Constance reached Acland first. Even so, she was delayed, which made her angry.

First, Gwen insisted that she, Gwen, must spend most of the morning with Acland, wheeling him up and down the terrace outside, then returning him to his room, where she read to him. When Gwen finally departed, Denton puffed his way up the stairs to spend half an hour with his son. Then Freddie and Steenie must look in. When they withdrew, the hired nurse insisted her patient must rest. Miss Conyngham had left explicit instructions.

By the time this rest was over, luncheon was served. After luncheon, Montague Stern—to Constance's fury—insisted she accompany him on a walk. He took the route she most disliked, past the lake, through the woods, and down to the river.

Constance was afraid that her husband, who watched and saw everything, might know what she intended to do. She was therefore at great pains, first to accept the suggestion of a walk, then to appear unhurried.

So, as their walk began, she chattered. She hung upon her husband's arm; she fixed her gaze upon his face; she teased and provoked. Stern perhaps enjoyed this display; he gave no sign of suspicion or displeasure. He walked at an even pace, his eyes on the landscape ahead; from time to time, when Constance was droll, he smiled.

Constance was encouraged. Although he was silent, and there was a brooding quality to these silences of his, Constance had grown accustomed to them. Once, they had made her cautious, but with familiarity, she began to grow more careless.

When they had walked just over a mile, they crossed the river by a small bridge and strolled to a rise of ground near the boundary of the Winterscombe estate. From there, looking west toward the house and east across fields, it was possible to survey the extent of the Cavendish land, marking the point where it joined the rougher country which had once been Sir Richard Peel's estate. Stern liked this view. Releasing Constance's arm, he walked a few paces farther and leaned against a gate. He looked out over fields and hedgerows; he turned his eyes in the direction of the Arlington estate, farther north, and then toward the hill where the Conyngham land began. Since his back was turned, Constance looked at her wristwatch; it was almost three.

"Montague—"

"Yes?"

Stern did not look around. His gaze, Constance saw, was now fixed upon a long avenue of chestnut trees and, beyond them, on the gray bulk and slate roof of a house. Peel's house, once upon a time, and now in Stern's possession.

Constance hesitated, and then—seeing that this ill-timed walk might be turned to advantage after all—she advanced a step or two. She laid her arm on the sleeve of Stern's coat.

"It is a beautiful house." She glanced up at Stern. "Jane's may be grander, but Peel's is the more perfect—even I can see that. An eighteenth-century house—"

"In an eighteenth-century park." Stern smiled.

"Restrained. Classical. An Adam façade. Gainsborough painted it, you know, with one of the Peel ancestors in the park."

"So Peel never tired of saying."

"The ancestor was rather plain. But she had a charming dog. A spaniel, like my Floss."

"Well, well." Stern gave a gesture of irritation. "It is just a house."

"One you own. One you like, I think. An austere house. It suits you, Montague—do you remember? In Scotland, I once said—"

"I remember." Stern looked away. "I took it for one of your pleasantries. An austere house? Why should that suit me, when my fame is for being vulgar?"

"Ah, but you are not vulgar at all." Constance crept a little closer, then closer still. "You pretend to vulgarity. Perhaps it amuses you to do so. But you do not fool me with your waistcoats and your white cuffs and your new shoes. I know your mind, and a little of your heart. You are not a vulgarian. Won't you kiss me, Montague? It is days since you kissed me."

"I might—since you ask," Stern replied. He took her in his arms. His embrace ruffled Constance. She felt as if all the boxes in her mind, so neatly stacked a second before, now wavered and shifted and threatened to collapse.

She took a step back.

"That was a passionate kiss."

"Abstinence has its advantages."

"Don't sound bitter."

"I was not sounding bitter. I was simply stating an obvious truth."

"Montague . . ."

"Yes?"

"I might have changed my mind, you know."

"You change your mind frequently. It is one of the more charming things about you. Changed it about what?"

"About the estates. Where we should live—all the things we discussed in Scotland." Constance came closer once more. She rested her gloved hands against Stern's chest, then insinuated one of those hands beneath coat and jacket, so it lay warm against his heart. She bit her lips so that they reddened. She looked up into Stern's eyes.

"I could perhaps live near Winterscombe after all. I feel less violently now. I begin to let the past go, after all. We must live somewhere—we cannot rent houses forever and ever. I think I could live in Peel's house, if I lived there with you."

"You flatter me."

"Nonsense, Montague. I would not dare. I am just being practical, that is all. We must settle the matter. Now that we are back at Winterscombe—together—I find I cope with it quite well. It has pleasant memories for me, as well as uglier ones. Besides, we should not be here—we should be nearby. So, it is worth an experiment, surely? Then, if we find the Peel house does not suit us, we can move. What could be simpler? It is not an irrevocable thing. As you say, it is just a house."

"Indeed. What you say is very sensible."

Constance was encouraged once more by this lack of opposition. She looked up at her husband's face, at the heavily lidded eyes, which disguised his expressions, at the tawny hair, brushing against the white linen of his shirt collar. She reached up her small hand and fondled a strand of his hair. She coiled her arm once more through his.

"Say yes, Montague. Please do. I'm bored with moving from place to place. I'm bored with looking at houses. Think what fun we could have—we could redecorate from top to bottom. Your paintings—they would look very fine in the library there, don't you think? We—"

"What made you change your mind?" Stern turned as he interrupted her. He fixed upon Constance his most even gaze. Constance gave a vague wave of the hand.

"Nothing in particular. I told you. We have been married almost a year. Things change. I—"

"Is it because of Acland?"

"Acland? Of course not. Why should that be?"

"When you believed Acland dead, you had no wish to live here. With Acland alive, you change your mind. Perhaps you like the idea of him as a near neighbor."

"What a ridiculous notion!" Constance drew back. "How you harp on Acland. Besides, he won't be a neighbor, will he? You can have Winterscombe any time you decide. Call in your debts, Montague—"

"Now?"

"Well, perhaps not immediately—not when he is still so ill. That might look a little . . ."

"Vulgar?"

"Rapacious." Constance smiled. Reaching up on tiptoe, she kissed her husband's cheek. "Well, you can be rapacious—and so can I. We both know that. But it might be prudent, for form's sake, not to appear so. A little patience—you see, Montague? You have taught me how to wait. The end of the year, perhaps—call in your debts then. After all, in his present condition—and that is unlikely to change—Acland will not even know what is happening. Winterscombe, or a nursing home somewhere—it is all one to him. Speaking of which"—she glanced down at her watch—"I promised Jane most faithfully that I would sit with Acland a while this afternoon. You know how she fusses! I am to read to him, from one of his dreary books. We had better go back."

"Of course. Take my arm. The path is a little slippery here."

"Thank you, Montague."

Constance, who was sure-footed, nevertheless clung to her husband's arm. Feeling that quickening and gaiety she always experienced when she succeeded in getting her own way, she began the walk back in high spirits.

"Do you remember, Montague—" she began, and then launched herself upon a wave of memories, incident after incident from their brief married life. She left out all the occasions when their encounters had been difficult or pained, and concentrated upon those that could be considered joyous. The kiss by the altar, their walks in Scotland through the snow.

"Do you remember that, Montague?"

"I think of it religiously."

"It was so cold—and then so warm when we went inside. You liked it there. You should take that house, too, you know—after all, it has special memories for us. We could renew our honeymoon there, every year."

"We could."

"And then, that day in London. Oh, Montague, I often think of that! Do you remember—I came in from the park, and you listened to your precious Verdi, and you did not even realize I was there—"

"Wagner."

"Wagner then—no matter. You surprised me that day. You took me—by surprise. That is why you suit me so well, I think. Because you can always surprise me. So cool and contained one moment, and so . . . forceful the next." She tightened her grip upon his arm. They had left the woods and begun the approach to the house.

"Do you remember, Montague, the night in Scotland, when you told me about your estates? When you told me your dream about your son? Did you think I had forgotten that? I have not, you know. Those words are very precious to me. Your holy words—that is how I think of them. It was then we became truly married, I think. And do you know, I feel quite sure that if we were to be settled, if we move to Peel's house, it might happen then. Our child." She pressed one small hand against her heart. Stern's pace slowed.

"Child? What am I saying?" Constance came to a halt. "Why should we stop at one child? I should like us to have a whole tribe. Four boys and four girls. Would you like that, Montague? Peel's house is the most perfect place for children. All those attics and passages to explore. That huge garden—Montague, what is the matter? You're hurting me."

Stern had stopped. As Constance chattered on, he took her wrist in his hand. As she continued to speak, his grip tightened. He bent her hand back, so that for a moment Constance felt her wrist might snap.

She gave a small cry of astonishment and pain. Stern released her hand. He looked down into her face.

"*Don't.*" He said the word with considerable force. Then, thrusting his hands in his pockets, leaving Constance standing on the path, he walked on alone toward the house.

The unexpected violence of Stern's reaction alarmed Constance somewhat. When she ran into the house and reached the stairs to Acland's room, she considered it. Was her husband jealous? He always sounded jealous when she mentioned Acland. This idea—that Montague might be capable of jealousy—pleased Constance, who found all reminders of her own power gratifying.

At the head of the stairs she paused. Of course she had been insincere, but Stern could surely not have known that? No, jealous, she decided, and that remark concerning abstinence had certainly sounded bitter. How long since she had slept with her husband? Several weeks. Since the news of Acland's discovery in France, her need for him had diminished.

To allow her husband to see that was perhaps incautious. Should she ask him to stay with her that night? Constance hesitated. What she was about to do was a betrayal of her husband. It would certainly be a mistake for Stern to discover the extent of her planned disloyalty. On the other hand, to provoke her husband out of his habitual composure, whether through anger or jealousy, excited her. So, of course, Stern must never find out what she did this afternoon—that was far too dangerous. But to encourage him to think of Acland as a rival, just with the smallest hints—there could be no harm in that.

So, thinking of her husband, Constance approached Acland's room. His nurse was seated outside, in a small anteroom. Constance dismissed the woman and sent her downstairs with instructions to walk her dog, Box, for at least one hour in the park. Once she had left, Constance picked up the book currently being read to an unresponsive Acland: *The Antiquary* by Scott. Constance had always found it tiresome.

She bent its spine back and forth, then tossed the book down. Rather wishing that her husband was there to witness this intended infidelity (let him try and be composed then!) Constance opened the door to Acland's room. She passed through, paused, then—on consideration—locked it.

For his return to Winterscombe, Acland had been assigned a large guest room, his old bedroom on the second floor being judged too small and too remote. Facing south, it had a bay window overlooking the gardens, lake, and park.

Acland, when Constance entered, was seated in this bay in his wheelchair. He was washed, shaved, dressed—these niceties Jane insisted upon. His thin hands rested on the arms of the chair. His thin face was turned to the window. An angled light, from a declining sun, gave radiance to his hair.

Constance did not greet him. She picked up a chair and set it down directly in front of him, its back to the window. Having made sure the chair was in his field of vision, and that his eyes, if unseeing, were open, she pushed the curtain to one side and looked out at the view.

"A panorama," she began. "You can see the woods and the lake. You can see the birch grove. That was where Boy killed himself, you know. It was not an accident, as they pretend. He blew his brains out with one of the Purdeys. Freddie and Steenie witnessed it. Before he did that, he confessed to Steenie. He told him he killed my father. I know that was not true. I think—I could be wrong—that you know it, too, Acland."

Constance sat down. She looked at Acland closely. Neither his face nor his hands had moved. His eyes remained fixed upon the window. Constance gave a small gesture of distress.

"Do you hear me, Acland? I believe that you do. Why do you try to hide from me? Why do you close yourself off? You cannot succeed. We are too close for that. I know you, Acland. Everything you've ever done, everything you've ever been—I see it. I look down to the bottom of your soul. I hear your thoughts. I watch your dreams. You cannot hide from me, and I cannot hide from you. Please, Acland—can't you understand? I don't judge you—I could not judge you. It would be like judging myself. If you have done bad things, seen bad things, I have too! I know how it feels to want to die. Please tell me—was it the war, Acland, that made you like this? Or was it something else, something you did a long time ago, and the guilt crept up on you, and up on you, over the years? Guilt can do that, I think. Oh, Acland, please tell me. I find this so very hard—"

Constance broke off. She waited, her hands trembling slightly.

The silence of the room rested upon her. Acland remained immobile in his chair.

"Won't you look at me, just once? I know you want to look at me," Constance said, and then, when Acland still did not turn, she gave a small sigh. She reached up and began to unpin her hair.

"Very well," she went on in a low voice. "I don't care. I shall not give up. Watch, Acland, and listen. I shall show myself to you. I want to see how dead you really are."

She shook her head so that her hair fell about her shoulders. Then, in a slow and careful way, as if she were alone in the room, she began to unbutton her dress. A crucifix, one of Stern's presents, given on a whim by an irreligious man to an irreligious wife, swung between her breasts. Constance pressed her hands against it, then rested them against her bared skin. She gave a small shiver, a small sigh.

"Oh, I am quite alone now. No one sees me. No one watches me. I hate to be watched. It is so good to be quiet, to be secret with myself. Do you know, it makes me sad sometimes, to lie, to act, to pretend to the world? And when it does, this is what I do. I come here. I come inside this little circle. Ah, I see it now! There it is."

Stretching out her foot, she drew a small arc upon the floor. "You see, Acland? An invisible circle. You can see it; I can see it. No one else can. A circle with walls of glass. They are very strong. No one can touch us in here, and when we are inside it, we can do anything we like, everything we like. Shall I show you what we do? We touch the darkness away.

"Listen," Constance said, and she closed her eyes, because she was sure, now, that Acland saw her; she could feel his vision brush against her skin. "Listen," she said, "and I will tell you the story of Constance and her lover. His name is Acland. He is the only man she has ever loved or ever wanted. This is how he is: He is her enemy and her friend, her brother and her deliverer. Which of his stories would you like? There are so many to choose from. He comes to her in so many guises. When she was a child, he came to her in the shape of a bird, a great white bird—such a free creature! Then he lifted her upon his wings and they surveyed all the world together. That is one story—I could tell you that. Or I could tell you how he came as a man—and he did that very often. Oh, night after night. He would touch her: first her hair—he loved her hair—then her throat, then her breasts, then her thighs. Once, they lay down together in the snow, and he made her body weep. Once they went to the woods, and once they lay down on the stairs, and once they hid—yes, they hid together, in a closet, pressed up against the coats in the dark, and his hands were very violent. That time when she touched him, he was as hard as a rod, and when she tasted him, he tasted like a god.

"That was how it was. That *is* how it was." Constance halted. She gave a small moan. She wrapped her arms tightly about herself. "It went on and on, for such a long time—year after year, whole centuries. It was unbearable to be apart. It felt like dying, to be apart. But then, not so very long ago, a terrible thing happened. He came to her room one night. He held her in his arms, and he said he had come back from the dead. He told her how it felt, to cross that boundary. Such a secret! He opened his shirt, and he showed her the wound he had, just below the heart. Then he made a ring of his hair, his bright hair, and he bound it about her wedding finger. She was his bride, and also his widow. She knew he would leave, you see. And he did leave. He stayed with her all night long, and then he left, when it was morning.

"*You* left." Constance lifted her head. She opened her eyes and looked directly at Acland.

"You left. You went away. I thought you would never come back. I thought that was the end—my punishment and my sentence, always to be alone." She paused. "If it is, I can survive in my way. I shan't die—not directly. But I should like to be sure—whether you have gone or whether you could come back. Will you keep very still? I need to touch you."

Constance rose as she finished this story. Her feet were unsteady; the room made her dizzy. She took one step forward, then another. Bending toward him, she looked into Acland's eyes. She unbuttoned the front of his shirt, then slipped her small hand beneath it. The scar there was familiar to her; she rested her hand against it.

> *What I wanted was to be a sorceress* [she writes]. *I wanted to be Acland's very own Circe. So I told him our love story and I showed him myself. If he didn't respond to my words, then he might to my body. Men are like that. I think they like my skin, and also my stories.*
>
> *My lips were so close to his they were almost touching. Acland was not so very dead—I could see that. I could have touched him, to prove my point—and I wanted to touch him, very much. But I wouldn't. I was determined he would give me a sign, and—in the end—he did.*
>
> *He lifted his hand. I thought he was going to touch my breast—I*

think he wanted to touch my breast. But he didn't. He touched that crucifix Montague gave me instead. His palm brushed my skin. He held the cross in his hand very tight. He could feel my heart beat, I think.

I waited. The corners of the room whispered to us, and the air brushed us, and then, I decided. It was enough. I was almost glad he did not touch me! I don't want us—ever—to be ordinary. I went on to the next scene. All those facts he needed to know. There was only a little time left, and I had to be quick. I had to be practical.

I buttoned up my dress. I sat down on my chair. Then, when I was quite sure he was looking at me, and not through me, I dealt out the facts, slap, slap, like a deck of cards. Boy; Jenna; Jenna and the baby. (I told him I would have cared for his baby.) I explained about the money that his father owes to Montague. I explained how Montague wants Winterscombe. I stopped then—just for an instant. I had to. Acland's face was so very white.

I thought, perhaps he is guilty. Perhaps he feels guilty about Jenna and the baby—he might. I wasn't sure, then, what to say. I think I understand the principle of guilt, but I am not sure I ever feel it. I can't manufacture it—I couldn't, not even when Boy died. That part of me was left out when I was made. But Acland is different—I know that. So I tried to explain: Guilt is a useless emotion. He couldn't undo the past, I said, but it was in his power, if he wanted, to influence the future.

I stood up, and I walked to the window. I pointed at the gardens and the lake and the wood. I said that I wasn't sure if these mattered to him, or if he cared for them at all—but if he did, if he wanted to preserve them for himself, or his brothers or any children he might have, they could be his. Even now. Montague might have set his heart on this place, I said, but even Montague could be outmaneuvered, if Acland would only listen to me. All Acland needed to save his home was a rich wife—and who, I added, was richer and more available than Jane Conyngham?

I sat down again. I counted off all Jane's advantages. "Jane," I said, "is excessively rich. Why, she could pay off your father's debts, save Winterscombe, and scarcely notice the difference!" I reminded him he owed Jane a debt. After all, she did save his life, and she has nursed him with more patience than I care to think of.

I pointed out to him that Jane loved him, and had for years. I think that surprised him—Acland can be oddly obtuse. Since she loved him so much, I said, to marry her would be one way of repaying the debt he owed her. And then, if he found my scheme too mercenary, no doubt he could hit on a way to repay the money. He is not without talents!

I thought Acland looked unconvinced. His face was so set, and his eyes so cold. So I tried even harder. I said I could quite understand that he might not find the idea very attractive, but, after all, Jane would make an excellent wife, and in time an exemplary mother.

"Think, Acland," I said. "She is clever. She is brave. You have many things in common. She has seen the war at first hand. You like the same music. You even like the same books.

"Of course," I went on (and here I was a little sly), "there are certain imbalances. I cannot imagine you find Jane very exciting. But if, after some years of married life, you felt in need of new stimulus—well, you might not abstain, but I'm sure you would be discreet. You would never hurt Jane, as another man, with fewer scruples, might. So, you see—you could make her an ideal husband!"

I thought Acland seemed to be growing tired by this time—I could see the strain in his face—and I thought to myself: He won't do this; he'll choose the razor. I rushed on to the end.

"Finally," I said, "I have left out one thing. Just a small one. If you married, and lived here, then I might see you from time to time. After all, if I live in Peel's house—and I shall—you and I will be neighbours. We co..ld—"

I stopped then. I didn't want to say all the things we could do. I know Acland knows them. I know he dreams them. I think I expected him to speak then. When he did not, it made me anxious. My hands jerked about, and my gestures would not stay still. I tried to explain—that that was how I wanted us to be, near and far, distant and close, both at the same time. We mustn't ever touch, I said, but we could speculate. That kind of love is the best kind; it always stays perfect.

It made me angry to have to explain, and spell it out in this dull way. I know he understands this, and always has. I know he sees the things I see.

Our secret love. Being angry made me shake a little. I could smell the anger burning. I knew I had to be quick. It was time to give him his two presents. I went across to his chair, and I knelt down beside him. I had the razor in my pocket and I took it out. I held it very tight, in my right hand.

I leaned forward. I looked him in the eyes. I felt so glittery! I rested my lips against his. I tasted him. I let him kiss me.

"Look," I said. "Here are your presents. Death in my right hand and life in my left. Choose, Acland."

Acland looked at the razor for a long long time. It seemed to surprise him, though he must have known I'd bring it to him. To help him decide, I opened it up. It was very sharp. I drew the blade across my palm. It sliced the skin open. All the blood came gushing out. I held my hand out to him. I said:

"Taste it, Acland. I know you are familiar with the taste and the smell. There. That is the taste of the way out. Is that what you want? Because if it is, take it. I'll help you, I promise you that. Your wrists or your throat. I'll help you guide it, and I'll wait here until it's over. The door is locked. I promise you I won't scream or cry out—I'm not like other women. I know I can do this, and if you want me to, I will. Choose, Acland."

His fingers closed around my wrist. I think he jerked my hand. The razor flew up into the air. It arced across the room. It came to rest on the Turkey carpet, just at the foot of a cabinet.

Acland said: "You are an extraordinary woman. You are the most extraordinary woman I have ever met."

I think he said that. After he had chosen.

I picked the razor up. I put it back in my pocket. That was that. I wanted to tell Acland that the woman he loved wasn't so extraordinary. She was . . . an accident. A little freak. Someone with too many pieces crammed in the wrong way. She had been born like that—or maybe she was made to become like that. I didn't say it, though; I knew I did not need to. Acland loves me for my opposites and my variety. He knows I can be every woman, and any woman—just for him. I can be his little virgin or his little whore, his little saint, his little sinner. And he is my impossible man, who has been to death and back, who would kill on my behalf. Acland, my deliverer—there is no end to his daring!

I walked across to the door, and I put my hand on the light switch. Outside it was growing dark, and the room was dusky. I switched on the light. I switched it off again.

"Look, Acland," I said. "Here I am. And here I am not." Then I left him.

I went back to Montague. We made love, rather roughly. I liked that. I like to be . . . manhandled, occasionally. I cannot come, still, if he's inside me. I asked him, in a careless way, if he'd had other women like that—and he said yes, one or two; it could take time; I mustn't let it worry me.

He was half an inch away from pity, I thought, and I didn't like that. Next time I shall pretend, I think; I shall give him an ecstasy.

"Did you read to Acland?" he said, when he was changing for dinner.

I said I had. I said the book was <u>The Antiquary</u>. *I said the plot was incomprehensible, but I read very beautifully.*

It was past five o'clock when Constance left Acland's room. It was an hour later when Jane went in to him. The nurse, thinking he slept, had left him in his wheelchair in the bay window. Jane, seeing his eyes were open, paused in the doorway. She thought: *He is looking at the war.*

Her return from London had been as swift as she could make it. Running into the hall below, she had glimpsed Gwen sitting alone in the drawing room. She sat in the twilight, her head stooped, her attitude one of grief and misery.

The sight spurred Jane on. She knew how Gwen grieved; she knew the effort it cost her to go every day to Acland's room, talk to him, read to him, remain bright and cheerful. Jane ran up the stairs; she was filled with anger and humiliation. Her heart beat fast. It might go against all her training as a nurse, but she intended to speak out. She thought: *I will not let him inflict this on his family anymore. I will not. It is selfish.*

Running across to him, she knelt down by his chair and grasped his hands tight. Dusk was falling. Shadows grayed Acland's face. Even so, she could see: He had been weeping.

It still shocks me when men weep [she wrote], *and my heart went out to him. I loved him so very much. My whole body ached with it. I'd planned what I would say, and all the arguments I would use—but when it came to it, all the love and the anger and the indignation mixed up. I think I did not speak very clearly.*

I wanted him to see that no matter what had happened in France, no matter what he did there, or what he witnessed—he had <u>survived</u>. *He had been given the most precious gift of all, life. How many thousand men—how many million men—had been denied that gift? They would never come back. Time would pass, the battles would be recorded, but the men, the individual men, they would be forgotten.*

They will build their war cemeteries, I suppose, when this war finally ends—and people will visit them. The anniversaries will be marked. But will we remember them? Every one of those graves, a man; every cross, a life story. Those who loved them will remember, but when they are gone, too, what will be left? Anonymity. People forget wars very quickly.

I think I began to cry then. My voice shook. I could not steady it. I wanted to make him see that what he did was wrong. It was more than a waste—it was a <u>sin</u>. God gave him his life—and he was throwing that gift back in His face.

That was a stupid thing to say—I knew that at once. Acland does not even believe in God—unless the war has given him faith, and that isn't very likely. I tried to begin again. I tried to be coherent. To be given so much, to have had every advantage in life, to come back from the war whole, not maimed, to be here where he has every comfort, more than any man could need, to be with his family, who love him—I couldn't go on. I felt so strongly, but I knew I must sound banal, trite, stupid.

That made me angry with myself—and so I told him. I said, I love you, Acland. I've loved you for years and years, for as long as I remember.

He did not move. He did not turn his head or shift his hands. Nothing. I was sure he could hear me. I was sure he could understand what I said. But he didn't care enough to give me the smallest sign. Oh, I felt such a bitter anger and regret.

I let go of his hands. I stood up, and I told him what I had decided. I said that if I could not help him, there were other people to whom I could be of use. I had a life to live. I can remember exactly what I said then, because what happened next was so amazing.

I walked past him to the window. It was dark outside. An owl hooted from the woods. My ribs felt too tight, and my throat hurt to speak, but I felt strong. I knew I was right—and that doesn't happen often. I said: My life, Acland. I do have one. I shall stop nursing you. I love you, but I shall stop. I would help you to live if I thought I could. But I won't help you to die—not when there is no need for it. I despise you for this. I hate what you're doing to your mother and the rest of your family. There are people out there far far worse off than you are. You know what that wheelchair is—and that silence? It's cowardice.

I did not look round. I stared out at the dark. I thought: I am twenty-nine years old. I thought about houses and money and trying to do good. I heard a small sound. I wasn't sure, at first, what it was. Then I realized. It was Acland's voice. He was saying my name.

He said her name three times. Jane turned, and Acland held out his hand to her. He said:

"I can speak. And walk. And think. And feel. You make me —very ashamed."

Jane gave a low cry. The light was very poor. She could just make out the shape of the wheelchair, and Acland's figure. The pallor of his face was indistinct. For a moment she was almost sure she had imagined this, his figure was so still; then she knew she had not. Tears sprang into her eyes. She took a step forward, then another. She looked at the hand held out to her. Then, clasping it, she knelt down.

"You've cut your hair."

Acland's fingers brushed her throat. He rubbed a strand of hair between finger and thumb. Jane looked up.

"I recognized you. In the caves—at Étaples." His voice was slow. It hesitated at the consonants, as if it distrusted them. Something flickered in his eyes, Jane saw; then his face became still and concentrated again.

"I recognized your voice. Long before you came across to my bed. I could hear your voice. I could hear all the things I thought I had lost. England. This house. Something more than that—something much more important than that. I wanted to call out, and I could not."

He bent his head. In the half-light his hair was bleached of all color. He sighed. Slowly, Jane reached up to touch his face.

"I always thought of you—" He stopped, then went on. "I thought of you as my brother's future wife. I—couldn't see you—"

Jane drew her hand back. "It's all right, Acland," she began. "I know that. I understand that. But we were always friends."

"No. You don't understand. You don't understand at all. I feel so terribly tired. I don't think I can explain. If you would just look at me—"

It was then Jane began to hope. She tried not to hope; she told herself not to hope—but it was impossible. There the hope was; it would not be denied. She looked at the pallor of Acland's face. She looked at his eyes, whose disparity of color had always perturbed her, whose resonance she had always loved. The expression in these eyes was one she had never seen before, and had never expected to see.

"Acland—" she began.

"I know. Isn't it strange?" His hand tightened over hers. "I would never have predicted this. And yet, it is so very strong. When you spoke just now. When I look at you. I think—perhaps it was always there. Just out of sight. I think I have—glimpsed it. Once or twice."

He lifted his hand. He rested it against her cheek. He traced, with one finger, the line of her brows.

"Your eyes are full of light." He let his hand fall. "And your hair—your hair is like a helmet. You sounded so fierce just now." He hesitated. "It was brave, to say those things. Were you always brave? Why did I never notice?"

"No. No. Not brave," Jane said quickly. "Not brave at all. If I have changed—"

"Come over here."

Acland stood. He drew her with him, toward the window, where they stood looking out over Winterscombe. Jane watched a cloud move across the face of the moon, the light darken, then shine.

Then he looked down at her. "You've changed? When did you change? Why did you change?"

Jane thought: *I am not invisible to him, not now. I might never be invisible to him again.* "My work, perhaps," she said. "And growing older. And the war—"

"Ah, the war," Acland replied, and he took her in his arms.

When I had read this account of my mother's, I left Wexton slumbering in his chair and I went out into the gardens. I walked down toward the lake, and the birch grove; I walked through the view that had been there, outside that bay window, on the night of my father's recovery.

I heard my mother's voice, that day, more clearly than I had for thirty years. It made me a child again. I could see her as she used to be: a quiet presence, and a secure one. For the first eight years of my life, she had never given me cause to doubt her love and her concern, for me and for my father. She did not become angry (as Constance did) at trivial matters, a dress the wrong shade, a haircut that failed to please. She was without vanity. Lies might make her angry; injustice certainly did. There was my mother. I could feel her force now, and her strength. A good woman; and how had I repaid her? With disloyalty.

I had allowed her to slip away from me; I had allowed myself to forget; I had allowed Constance to usurp her place. I knew I could make excuses for this. My mother died young; the living almost always usurp the dead. Goodness is, perhaps, not the most vivid quality—the good are not the people who first draw attention in a room. Goodness lacks charisma. Goodness can seem dull. Oh, there were plenty of excuses. I despised myself, even so.

I sat down by the lake. I thought of married love, which can seem dull, too, I suppose—although I believe it can bring the very greatest fulfillment. I sat by the lake, and I knew what I wanted to believe: I wanted to believe my mother's account. I wanted to believe in her love for my father, and his love for her. I wanted to believe that it was her love that had restored my father first to speech and then to health. We are all children, I think, in this respect—that we have a continuing need to believe in the love that brought us into the world, long after we have reached an age when we know that need may be irrational. Enduring love, that happily-ever-after of the bedtime stories: I passionately wanted to believe that in my parents' case it had been true. But there were doubts, of course. Constance had planted them.

I came close to hating Constance then, the closest I had ever come. I hated her for the sublime confidence with which she wrote, her blithe assumption of the bond between herself and my father, her unshakable conviction that it was she who contrived my parents' marriage, that it was a mercenary affair, a marriage of convenience.

Nothing I remembered of my parents together would have suggested such a thing; I would have thought that, to my father, such an idea would be anathema. But there were doubts even so, and they would not go away. The father in these notebooks had already treated Jenna shabbily. The volatile iconoclast of the prewar years was not the father I remembered; the bearded figure in the caves at Étaples, the silent figure in a wheelchair—all these were strangers to me.

By the time I turned back to the house, I was sure that Constance's gift of the past was malevolent in intent. I looked at her journals with suspicion and dislike. Wexton, waking from his doze, yawned and stretched.

"So," he said, "what happened next?"

I already knew, to some extent, for I had read a short way ahead. I had read (it had better be admitted) with a certain malicious pleasure.

"Constance gets her comeuppance," I replied.

"Oh, *good*," Wexton said.

When the news of Acland's engagement to Jane reached Constance (and there was a delay of several weeks before even Acland's immediate family were told) she danced about her rented drawing room in London. The news came to her from Gwen; Constance tossed its pages in the air. She let them scatter upon the carpet. She picked them up. The power of her own will was extravagant, irresistible. She kissed the pages one by one.

She hugged her knowledge to her all day. She stored it up until her husband returned. Even then, she kept it a while longer to herself. When should she break the news? How should she break the news? The pleasure—Constance loved to nurse secrets—was intense.

All through dinner she said nothing. She performed for her husband as an actress might upon a stage. Her eyes were brilliant; her cheeks were flushed; her tiny hands made jeweled circles as she spoke. She wore her hair loose, as her husband preferred. She wore a new, vivid, and beautiful dress. Her snake bracelet coiled about her arm: once, twice, three times. *I have outwitted him this time*, Constance thought.

After dinner she hung upon her husband's arm. She kissed first her little dog, then him. She played one of her favorite roles, that of the childish coquette. She reminded him, with a little sideways glance, that there was a party they had promised to attend; she suggested, with a small caress, that it might be more amusing to stay at home.

At ten she drew him toward the stairs, with kisses and whispers. At ten-fifteen, first coy then bold, she undressed. At ten-thirty she drew Stern into her bed. She climbed upon him. She linked her small arms behind his neck. She wound her legs about his waist. *I shall give him an ecstasy*, she said to herself—*and I shall tell him after that.*

There was a mirror behind her marital bed. Constance watched herself perform. She rose and fell. Her skin was the color of roses. Her hair was long and very black. Her lips were as red as blood. "Talk to me, shock me," she whispered: "I like that."

When it was over, she lay for a while in her husband's arms. She acted languor beautifully. She pretended, briefly, to sleep. She bided her time, eyes closed. How long should she wait, fifteen minutes? Ten? And then, having revealed the engagement, should she mention living in Peel's house at once, or wait? No, she could not bear to wait. She would reveal the engagement, then—stressing Acland's newfound devotion to Jane—raise the question of the house.

Constance sat up. She gave a pretty little yawn, then a stretch. "Montague," she began, "I have some news—"

"One moment, my dear." Stern rose from the bed. He crossed to his desk, unlocked it, then turned. "A present for you, Constance," he said.

Constance was diverted at once. She took a childish delight in all presents—and Stern's were always generous. This was an odd present though: two envelopes. With a politeness that at once made her wary, he placed them in her lap.

Constance opened the envelopes. She considered their contents for some while. The skin prickled on the back of her neck. In her hand were two tickets for an ocean liner: single tickets, from Southampton to New York.

"What are these?" she said at last in a tight voice.

"Why, reservations, Constance. One for you and one for me. Look, our names are upon them."

"I see that." Constance kept her head bent, her face hidden. "I see the date too. It is next month."

"December. Yes. By Christmas, my dear, we shall be in New York."

"New York? How can we be in New York? There is a war on."

"Even so, these liners still sail. The journey is in no way impossible."

Constance knew that even and imperturbable tone of voice. She risked a quick look at her husband. He was seated beside her, regarding her with equanimity, a slight smile on his lips.

"And how long shall we stay there, Montague? A month? Two months?"

"Oh, longer than that. I thought we might stay there . . . for good."

Constance did not like the tone in which this was said. A certain icy triumph could be discerned beneath the surface politeness. She risked a small wail.

"For good?" She drew her husband closer. She coiled her small arms about his neck. "Dearest Montague, don't tease me. How can we live in New York? All your work is here. The bank. The munitions factories—"

"Oh, I have disposed of those," Stern replied easily. "Did I not mention it? The intervention of the Americans in the war has been decisive, I feel. It cannot last much longer. I sold—for a better price than I would get a year from now."

"But, Montague, the bank—"

"I have partners who can run the bank. It has links with Wall Street, in any case. Surely you remember. I have mentioned it."

"I don't remember at all." Constance drew back with a sulky expression. "You never mentioned New York. Or America."

"Perhaps you did not attend. Does the idea not please you? I thought you would be delighted. You always wanted to travel, my dear. You like change. New York is a city of change. It will make London seem very dull—"

"I don't want to live in London," Constance burst out. "I told you. We discussed this. I want to live in Peel's house—"

"In Peel's house?" Stern appeared surprised. "But, Constance, that is no longer possible. I have sold it."

Constance became perfectly still. Color mounted in her face.

"Sold it?" she began slowly. "When did you do that?"

Stern shrugged. "My dear, this week, last week—I forget the exact date. Constance, you change your mind so very often. I thought your wanting Peel's house was just a passing whim. It never once occurred to me—"

He stopped. It was now clear to Constance that her husband was lying. Never occurred to him! Why, she was perfectly certain he knew how much she wanted Peel's house—and worse still, might even have known why.

Constance bit her lip hard with her small white teeth. Tears pricked behind her eyelids. To have been so close, for every one of her plans to have fallen obligingly into place, and then to be outwitted by this husband of hers.

Devil, devil, devil, she said to herself. She clenched her small hands into two tight fists.

"Darling," Stern said (Stern, who scarcely ever used such endearments). He leaned forward to embrace her. His voice (how she resented his acting ability) was contrite. "Constance, my dear—you seem distressed. If only I had known. An offer came up, to buy both Peel's house and the Arlington place. The price was good—"

"Oh, I'm sure it was," Constance muttered. "I'm sure it was."

To her fury one small angry tear ran down her cheek. To her greater fury, her husband kissed first the tear, then her lips.

"Constance," he went on, putting his arms around her. "Think a little. In Scotland you were very definite. Not Winterscombe, nowhere near Winterscombe—you said that. And besides, our little empire—you remember we spoke of that? That empire has been shrinking these past weeks. Peel's house has few attractions, don't you think, without the Winterscombe land or the Conyngham estate? And those, I fear, I shall never acquire—not if these rumors I hear are true—"

"Rumors? What rumors?"

"That Denton's debts may be miraculously repaid. That Acland and a certain heiress are much in love. Those sorts of rumors, my dear."

"Acland and Jane, do you mean? In love?" Constance struggled free of his arms. She tossed her head. "I never heard anything so silly in my life."

"More than in love, or so I hear. Devoted." Stern rose.

"Devoted—and engaged to be married," he added, with some emphasis.

Constance lay back upon the pillows. Since she was very angry, she knew better than to speak. Malice, she told herself, in that last remark of Stern's—or, if not malice, an unmistakable desire to wound. Worst of all, since she was supposed to be indifferent to Acland, she could not show that hurt.

She should, of course, have been more careful, more subtle—she saw that now. Maud had warned her; she herself, in the early days of their courtship, had been well aware of Stern's skill as an adversary—and yet what had she done? She had schemed and, while she did so, had forgotten the possibility that her husband might scheme too.

A foolish mistake. Constance considered her husband. If he felt triumph at outwitting her, he disguised it well. She watched as, with his customary composure, he returned the liner tickets to their envelopes. As she watched him, she felt her anger first abate, then transmute into admiration. *More than a match for me*, Constance said to herself, and, since it pleased her to be combative, she began to scheme anew. Stern had won this battle, yes—but to win a battle was not to win the war. There was a small but discernible gap in her husband's defenses.

"Montague . . ." she began in a thoughtful voice.

"Yes, my dear?" Stern replied, somewhat warily.

Constance held out her hand to him and drew him down beside her. She gave him her most innocent smile; her husband, she noted, tensed.

"Montague," she began, "tell me the truth now. Have I made you angry?"

"Angry?" Stern replied, somewhat stiffly. "Of course not. Why should that be? Besides, I am rarely angry. I was blessed—or cursed—with a cool temperament. To be angry wastes time."

"Does it?" Constance said, with a small sideways glance. "Are you never angry then?"

"Occasionally." Stern's eyes met hers. "I do not like to be crossed, Constance."

"Crossed!" Constance made a little face. "Heavens! I'm sure no one would dare to cross you—I certainly would not. How strange. It cannot be anger then. Yet I thought, looking at you, when you gave me those tickets—"

"A present, Constance. A surprise."

"Oh, and a lovely surprise, of course. But still I wonder. If you were not angry, were you jealous? Do you know, Montague, I suspect that you were! Ah, there!" She raised her eyes. "I see it in your face. I have hit upon it. You *are* jealous—of Acland. That is why you dispose of Peel's house so conveniently, why you spirit me off to the other side of the globe. I suspect, Montague, that you want me a long way away from the . . . temptations of Winterscombe."

To Constance's irritation, Stern took this suggestion with an urbane and unruffled amusement.

"Constance, my dear, I hate to disappoint you. I know women like to attribute such motives to men. It is part of their feminine thinking. But in my case, alas, you are wrong. I have many failings. Jealousy is not one of them."

"Truly, Montague?"

"I regret, but it is true. Acland is nothing to you, my dear. I know that, because you have told me often enough. So the sad truth is, my motives were purely financial."

"Have you never felt jealousy then, Montague?" said Constance, who did not intend to give up.

"Not so far as I recall," he replied shortly. "I try not to be possessive."

Constance, sensing at last a vulnerability insufficiently disguised, gave a little frown. She lay back upon the pillows.

"Of course, I remember now," she said, in a meditative voice. "What was it you said? That you did not set great store by physical fidelity—yes, that was it. Goodness, you are so very high-minded, Montague. I am not like that at all—"

"Are you not, Constance?"

"Never!" Constance cried, sitting up again and clasping his hand. "I am as jealous and possessive as could be. If you so much as looked at another woman, I should begin to die inside. If you went to bed with her . . . Oh, Montague, how horrible it would be! I should feel cut into little pieces, with sharp little knives—"

"Constance. Don't say such things." Stern's hand tightened over hers. "You must know—there is no danger—" He checked himself. "There is no immediate danger of that. I am . . . content with you. I have no desire for other women."

Constance gave a small cry. She pressed herself against him. An admission, she thought, as she clung to him: an admission, at last. She felt a rush of triumph and then, almost immediately, a flurry of more contradictory emotions. To be embraced by Stern, to feel his hands stroke her hair, to feel his lips against her brow, these provoked in her rebellious truthfulness. To be truthful was to be exposed, however, and that she would not risk—with Stern least of all. She drew back.

"So, there we are," she said in a calmer voice. "I have a jealous nature, and you do not. Though I cannot quite believe you are as cold as you claim. Suppose I were to take an interest in another man . . . Suppose I were to take a lover. I never shall, of course—but if I did? You must mind then? A little? Not to do so would be inhuman, Montague."

"Very well. If you insist." Stern gave a small gesture of annoyance. "I would not be without feelings, obviously, in such a case. But I would try to contain them. I told you. There are other forms of faithfulness between a man and a woman which seem to me of greater importance. When I said that—"

"Yes, Montague?"

"I was . . . looking ahead many years. I was thinking of the disparity in our ages. I was trying to be . . . realistic. After all, you are very young." He hesitated. "When you are thirty, Constance, I shall be approaching sixty—"

He stopped. Constance watched him carefully.

"Oh, I see," she said at last, in a small voice. "I understand. You were speaking of the future, not now?"

"Obviously. Constance, we have been married only a year, less than a year—"

"A year?" Constance gave an odd little cry. "Is it only a year? It feels so much longer than that. You make me happy, Montague. When I am with you, I have no sense of time. I feel . . . you change me—" Leaning forward in an impetuous way, she began to cover his face with quick kisses.

"I do! It's true. If I were with you all the time—if I were never alone—I might change even more, I think. I could become—" She stopped. "Still, never mind that. That is not important. I just wanted to say: I'm glad you bought those tickets, Montague."

"Is that true?" Stern tilted her chin, turned her eyes to his. He looked at her with some sadness. "Is it true? With you, Constance, I find I am never sure. Perhaps you mean what you say. Perhaps you would like to mean what you say. Perhaps you simply pretend—"

"It is true. I do mean it. I mean it now. Of course . . ." Constance lowered her eyes. She began to smile. "Of course, I cannot speak for the future. What I mean now I may not mean five minutes from now, or five years. . . . You see? I am honest, Montague. I know my own nature. I give you . . . little snatches of sincerity—and that is a great deal more than anyone else ever receives at my hands. So: the truth. When you gave me those tickets, I was not so very pleased.

But now—I am. I think you have been clever, and wise—and I think we shall be happy in America. Just think . . ." Kneeling up in the bed, she put her arms about his neck. "A new world for us to conquer, just as we planned. Who cares for London and Winterscombe and all the people in them? We can leave them behind. We can begin again. Oh, I wish we were leaving tomorrow! You'll see—I'll be such an asset to you. Why, I shall toil and scheme—we shall have all the best parties, all the best guest lists. The whole city shall be at our feet! I shall be . . . a splendid wife for you! You'll look at me and you'll think: Constance is indispensable. . . ."

"But my dear, I think that already," Stern said in a dry voice.

"You will think it *more*," Constance cried, rushing on, missing the implications of the compliment; and she began, as she liked to do, on a flurry of plans: where they should live, how they should live, detail after detail.

Stern, listening with some amusement, was touched by this. Constance's optimism, on occasion, could be as artless as a child's—and as poignant. Stern did not expect that this excitement or optimism would endure, yet he found that he was wrong. His wife's spirits remained unflagging, her affection toward him undiminished, throughout the following weeks.

She besieged her friends; she telephoned; she lined up addresses and introductions. She shopped for new clothes, new jewelry. Every night when Stern returned, she would display her small triumphs for him.

Stern warned her, once or twice, that these social triumphs might be more complex than she envisaged: His race, he explained, might well close many doors to them in New York.

Constance pushed such suggestions aside. She tossed her head. She said that if they encountered prejudice, they would disdain it; they would treat it with the contempt it deserved.

"No one like that shall come to *my* parties," she proclaimed.

"Constance, they wouldn't come in any case. That's what I'm trying to explain to you."

"So much the better then," she cried, "for I shan't want to know them!"

This energy and excitement faltered only once, and this was when they were aboard ship. The crossing was rough, and Stern enjoyed it. Constance teased him for liking to pace the decks, for standing at the rails overlooking the space of the Atlantic. The water was the color of lead, the sky a wash of gray; by day and by night, there was always a narrow band of light at the horizon.

Stern tried to persuade his wife on deck, and she went once, their first evening. He showed her the finger of light the moon made upon the waves. He led her to the stern of the ship, so she might watch the wake churn. He spoke of the power of the turbines.

Constance looked at these things and shivered. She hated the sea, she said; it frightened her. She returned belowdecks and remained there for the duration of the voyage. She played bridge every evening, for high stakes, usually winning. She made many acquaintances who would later be useful to her in her advance upon New York society. She flirted with one of them in particular, a young man from one of New York's oldest families who was returning, on honorable discharge, from the war.

On the day they landed, Constance's spirits were high. She looked at Manhattan with love and with expectation. Standing on the deck, she kissed her husband with some passion. The face she lifted toward him was dazzling.

"Darling," she said (she had begun to call him this on the voyage). "Darling Montague. You have made me very happy. I can't wait to be ashore. I am a land creature, you see." She gave him a teasing glance. "I like pavement under my feet. That way—I run faster."

It was at this point in the journals that, for some time, I broke off. It was strange to read a story with a combination of hindsight and foreknowledge, and when I reached the point of that Atlantic voyage, I felt uneasy. I knew what happened next; I *almost* knew.

Do you see? A pattern was being fixed. It was a pattern that was to remain fixed over the next twelve years, a span of time that divided 1918 (when the war ended, and my parents married) from 1930, the year of my birth.

During that time my parents lived at Winterscombe. My father, for a few years, took work as a partner in a merchant bank in London—in an effort, I imagine, to repay some of the financial debt he owed Jane. It was work he disliked, for which he had no aptitude—his quick mind, his keen intelligence, his gift for abstract argument, his interest in literature, history, and philosophy, did not adapt well to the stringencies of finance. In this respect he was, perhaps, a prisoner of his class: The pursuit of profits made his lip curl.

Once his father died (it *was* an apoplexy, or as we would say, a heart attack; the year was 1923) my father gave up the merchant bank to devote himself full time to Winterscombe. He became caught up, increasingly, in my mother's many charitable projects, particularly in the architectural design of orphanages. He wrote several pamphlets on the subject and even, at one point, campaigned energetically for parliamentary reform regarding the care of the destitute in society. He came to believe that the actual design of institutions (not just orphanages but also prisons) had a profound effect on the mentality of those confined within them: If you caged people, he said, then obviously they would behave like animals.

In many of these arguments—that prisons for minor offenders should be more open; that orphaned children should be placed with families and not institutionalized—my father was far ahead of his time. I think he knew his schemes were a lost cause, but that did not deter him. He liked lost causes. Lost causes cost money; Winterscombe cost money; over the next twelve years a number of my mother's charitable schemes would come to successful fruition—but successful or less successful, they ate into her capital. She was, I think, somewhat easy prey to con men and charlatans, at least in the early years. Certainly some of her investments (and all these projects were being funded by investments) were unwise. Year by year, idealism inched my parents toward that genteel poverty of my childhood. I was proud of this, and I am still—but I could see the pattern ahead of me as I read. At Winterscombe, idealism and financial decline; across the Atlantic, pragmatism and an inexorable advance toward worldly success.

In New York, Constance and Stern prospered. Stern was to become as feared on Wall Street as he had been in the City; Constance danced her way to dominance in New York drawing rooms. "The meek shall inherit?" she liked to cry. (Constance was never averse to mild blasphemy.) "What nonsense! The meek *go under*."

Every year, once a year, these two factions met, when Stern and Constance traveled to Europe, to England, and to Winterscombe. The last such visit was made in 1929, the year of the Wall Street crash. The following year I was born, and Constance attended my christening without her husband. It was her last visit. She was then banished from Winterscombe.

Something happened then; something happened to interrupt that twelve-year pattern. I still did not know what it was, but I did know one other fact: 1930 was also the year in which Constance's marriage to Stern ended.

Do you see my predicament? I knew something of the past and something of the future—and it seemed to me that the link between the two had become obvious. Constance's obsession with my father was a small time-bomb; it ticked away for twelve years. At the time of my birth, presumably, it exploded. For me, many years later, the detonations continued.

And so one night, about a week after Wexton arrived at Winterscombe, I decided. I would not continue. I was afraid to continue—and you will see exactly why, shortly. I did not admit that to myself at the time. I simply packed all those letters and diaries away. I packed up the past and confined it to desk drawers and packing cases.

Wexton made no comment. I think, in fact, that Wexton had already decided where I needed to go next and was waiting for me to catch up with him. He took the disappearance of all those disorderly papers in his stride.

"I've booked us some seats for Stratford," he announced one morning at breakfast.

We went the next day. For that day, and several afterward, we edged away from the past.

The play we would see was Shakespeare's *Troilus and Cressida*, one of Wexton's favorite plays, and one that reflected his current obsession with war.

We drove to Stratford-upon-Avon that morning, had lunch, walked about the town, saw the play in the evening, and then drove home, on dark and peaceful country roads, to Winterscombe.

I think this visit was a kind of pilgrimage for Wexton, part of his process of saying goodbye to my uncle Steenie. We had often made expeditions to Stratford before, but always with Steenie making up the party. It was the first time Wexton and I had ever been there alone. Wexton never mentioned this, of course. He never once showed the least sign of melancholy. We ate lunch at Steenie's favorite riverside pub. After lunch we strolled about the town, Wexton deciding which of the numerous Olde English Tea Shoppes would be the one we would patronize later. Having selected the worst of the half-timbered places on offer (it provided an Anne Hathaway cream tea—Wexton was delighted), we took the route I knew we would take, because we had always taken it with Steenie: along Waterside to Holy Trinity Church, where Shakespeare is buried.

Wexton never visited Stratford without paying his respects to Shakespeare's tomb. This must have been our twentieth time there.

We made our way into the church. We approached the tomb. Wexton appeared blind to the school party (bored) on one side of him, and the Japanese businessmen on the other (disappointed; inside the church, they were not allowed to use cameras).

He stared down at the inscription on the gravestone for some time. Later, he struck up one of his instant friendships with a Japanese businessman, with whom (walking back from the church) he discussed charabanc outings, the meaning of *Hamlet,* and the likelihood of Anne Hathaway's having provided cream teas for her husband.

When we had finished that tea, Wexton (happily oblivious to the nudges and stares from across the café—there were students there; he had been recognized) lit a cigarette. He smiled at me amiably. His thoughts, obviously, were still back at Holy Trinity Church, and the inscription on the tomb which he had again been reading.

Good friend, for Jesus' sake forebare/to dig the dust enclosed here.

"Excellent advice," Wexton said. "Got it right, as usual. When we go back to Winterscombe, let's have a bonfire."

The next day, we did. I discovered the contents of those two mysterious suitcases with which Wexton had arrived at Winterscombe: Inside them was a mess of papers. Wexton dumped them in a great pile. Neither he nor I was allowed to examine them.

We had selected a place not far from the lake. Wexton's preparations were meticulous. "A funeral pyre," he said cheerfully. "We have to build it properly."

There was plenty of kindling, plenty of dry timber. We lugged logs back and forth. We made a fine bonfire. Wexton tipped out the contents of the suitcases: There were certainly letters there; I think there were also poems. Then, when it was all arranged, Wexton lit the first match. The funeral pyre burned beautifully. The paper caught; the dry sticks crackled; the breeze fanned the flames, and the flames licked and mounted.

The heat became intense. We had to step back from it. Occasionally, when some scrap of paper threatened to flutter out from the pile, Wexton—using a long stick as a poker—would shove it back in again. He was—there was no doubt in my mind—enjoying this very much.

I was more hesitant . . . at first. I felt I ought to have argued more, dissuaded more. It was one thing for Wexton to consign letters, his private life, to the flames—that was his choice—but I hated to think he was also consigning poems to oblivion. Wexton, however, took such pleasure in the whole enterprise that I was caught up in it too. Fires produce a certain excitement; a pyromaniac lurks in all of us. Within a very short time we were both feeding the fire energetically. At one point, when the flames gushed, Wexton (normally slow-moving and staid) almost capered.

"That's it," he said finally. "That's everything. Up in smoke. I feel *much* better. *That'*ll show that vulture at Yale what I think of him."

I hesitated then.

"It isn't the whole lot, Wexton," I said finally. "There's still all your letters to Steenie. They're here, in the house. Do you want me to fetch them?"

"No," Wexton said firmly. "Those belonged to Steenie, not me. Now they're yours. You decide what to do with them."

"You're sure?"

"Oh, yes." He gave me a sidelong glance. "I'd kind of prefer them *not* to end up at Yale—or Austin. Austin's getting really terrible, you know. Every writer's graveyard. But you decide. Make another bonfire sometime . . . or don't. It's up to you. I trust you. Oh"—he paused—"and this wasn't a hint to you, if that's what you're thinking. I'm not suggesting you make a bonfire—or not yet anyway."

We stood for a while, watching the fire burn down to bright spars of wood. Then, as dusk fell, we walked back to the house, my godfather and I.

Wexton was quiet over tea, and thoughtful. There was a brief interruption, when an almost-excited Gervase Garstang-Nott telephoned to say that he had finally pinned down his corporate raider/ property developer, who had, it seemed, finally stopped shuttling between the Cayman Islands and Switzerland. He was now in London. He had agreed to come down to Winterscombe.

"Strike while the iron is hot!" said Garstang-Nott, uncharacteristically. "He wants to come down the day after tomorrow."

An appointment was agreed upon. I felt faint stirrings of optimism, which I tried to clamp down on. I knew the corporate raider was likely to prove as lukewarm in his interest as the previous potential purchasers who had visited. Still, I felt a certain hope. And, as it turned out, I was justified. The corporate raider did not buy Winterscombe, but his visit was to prove important.

Wexton, still quiet and thoughtful after his bonfire, did not take a great deal of interest in the advent of the corporate raider. I was full of plans for making Winterscombe look enticing; Wexton did not listen. He helped me prepare dinner, but did so inattentively.

"About those journals," he said finally, when dinner was over. "About Constance and your father—"

"Yes, Wexton?" I replied, tensing.

"Something's bothering you. Something more than you said. Something you haven't told me."

"Yes, it is. Wexton, I don't want to think about it—"

"Well, you'll have to, sooner or later. It won't go away. If it's any help, I can guess what it is. It used to bother me, too—and Steenie." He paused. "The accident to Shawcross—it's about that, am I right?"

"Yes," I said, somewhat cagily. I hesitated. "You had a theory about that, Wexton. I know, because Steenie mentions it, in one of those letters he never sent. He said you'd discussed it, and he'd decided you were both wrong." I stopped. "I . . . wondered what it was, Wexton. It seemed odd—that you'd never told me."

Wexton shrugged. "It was just a theory. Probably wrong. I don't want to discuss it now. It wouldn't be right."

"It might upset me?"

"Yes. It might." Insofar as he could, Wexton began to look evasive.

That evasiveness in Wexton alarmed me. I began to feel a little sick. I pushed the rest of my meal aside, unfinished.

It was steak, I remember that, because Wexton—more sanguine than I was—continued to eat with every appearance of good appetite. When he finally set down his fork, he smiled his benevolent smile and leaned forward. He mentioned Tibet. He made a further suggestion, an obvious one, I suppose—certainly one I should have considered.

The next morning, I acted upon it. After all, there was a professional solver of puzzles in my own family. I also happened to be very fond of him. And while I had no wish to upset him with my questions, he was, apart from Constance herself, the one person still alive who had been there, at Winterscombe, on the night of the comet party.

FOUR

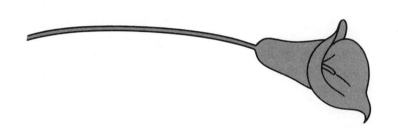

I
CUI BONO?

MY UNCLE FREDDIE WAS THEN PAST SEVENTY. He still lived in the house in Little Venice where I visited him for tea as a child. The house had, however, been smartened up: The sweep of a new broom in Freddie's life could be detected the moment you entered the front gate. This new force was responsible for the gleaming brass mailbox and knocker, for the hedge, which was cut with military precision, and for a garden pond, installed since my last visit, which lay squarely beneath the windows. It was decorated by a fat and pugnacious cherub.

"Newts!" said Winnie as she opened the door to me and clasped me to her battleship bosom. She pointed at the pond with pride. "They're our new thing. Absolutely fascinating."

Winifred Hunter-Coote had been widowed in the mid-1950s, when I was living in New York. Winnie mourned her husband, Cootie, greatly, and still tended to wear black in his honor, but she was a sensible woman with a great zest for life, and widowhood did not suit her. Once she realized this, which took about two years, she set about the business of finding a new husband.

She cast around the circle of her acquaintance, hit upon my uncle Freddie, and carried him off within three months. The courtship was, I think, entirely on Winnie's side. She had remained friends with Freddie after my mother's death, and when she was casting about for a husband, she came here, to Little Venice, for tea. She looked around her, saw that Freddie was both unhappy and disorganized, and decided.

The deciding factor was Uncle Freddie's detective novels. With these books (he had stuck to them; unlike his other enthusiasms, they never fizzled) Freddie had had steady and growing success. To his great astonishment, for Freddie was modest, a publisher had accepted his seventh attempt at the genre, and had then seemed inclined to accept its successors. Even more astonishingly, people actually went out, paid money, and bought them. Uncle Freddie knew this because they sometimes wrote to him, which he liked very much, and because he read the figures on his royalty statements.

The arrival of these statements, twice a year, was a time of great celebration. "Look," Freddie would say. "Look, Victoria! I've sold three thousand, four hundred, and thirty-six copies! Isn't that the most astonishing thing? I wonder who they all are, these people? I wonder how many guessed the murderer? It was the secretary, you know. He used a special poison—I had to read up on it. It was very interesting. . . . Now where did I put that poisons book?"

He generally could not find it—the poisons book, or the gun manual from which he had taken details of the pistol used, or the railway timetable that allowed the murderer to double-back and be in two places at once (one of Uncle Freddie's favorite devices). He could not find it because Uncle Freddie's house was the most terrible mess.

Winnie took this in with one glance, that day she went to tea. She looked at the fluffy crumb-strewn carpet, at the brass table with its cobra base, which no one had cleaned in years. She looked at the posters for German cabarets and at Mrs. O'Brien's carpet slippers when she brought in the tea. She looked at the ink pot on the table in the window at which Freddie wrote, at the piles of papers, books, timetables, manuals, library tickets, filing cards—and she came to her decision. Uncle Freddie needed organization.

"Who types up your novels for you, Freddie?" she asked in a stern voice.

"Oh, some girl. Different girls. When they're finished, I wrap them up and take them 'round to an agency."

"An agency!" Winnie was deeply shocked. "Do they correct your spelling? Your spelling is terrible."

"Well, no, they don't." Freddie looked sad. "I don't think they spell terribly well either. And I did ask them once to have a look at the punctuation—you know, commas and those colon things—but I don't think they were a great success. However"—he brightened—"I have a very nice editor. A very sound man. He does it."

"I can type, Freddie," Winnie said in a meaningful way. Since she was merciful, she forbore to say that her spelling was also excellent and that she was a hotshot at grammar. She became thoughtful.

Later that afternoon, when Freddie proudly showed her his filing system, she became more thoughtful still.

"Look," Freddie said. "You see, Winnie, I have it all organized. Pink cards for the suspects, blue ones for the clues. Then I can't get muddled. Oh—and three murders per book! I make that a rule. Three murders—that's the ticket."

Winnie examined this filing system. At first the drawers stuck. When persuaded to open, cards flew out like confetti. Picking them up, Winnie found a suspect on a blue card and a clue concerning cream cakes on a pink one.

Inclined now to show less mercy, she pointed this out to Freddie.

Freddie sighed. "Oh, I know," he said in a defeated voice. "I get so carried away. The plot, you know. I suppose what I really need is a secretary."

Winnie gave him a firm glance. Privately, she had reached her decision: He needed not only a secretary, but also a wife.

Winnie was installed as his secretary within a week; after that the marriage was inevitable. Freddie, who had never been known to act hastily, used to boast of this.

"Winnie is a very determined woman," he would say with obvious delight. "She took one look at me and swept me off my feet."

They made an excellent, if unconventional, couple. My uncle Freddie, so ebullient as a boy, had lost his way through life at some point—perhaps because of Constance, perhaps because of the death of Boy, perhaps because of some flaw in his own character. For years he had been adrift. With the advent of Winnie, he discovered not just a sense of purpose but also a new and surprising energy.

He had been accustomed to write one detective story every two years; with Winnie, his literary output first doubled, then trebled. He invented a new detective, Inspector Coote (named in tribute to Winnie's first husband). Inspector Coote, whose character was influenced, I think, by long conversations with Winnie, became a great favorite with Uncle Freddie's readers. Freddie's sales mounted. His royalty figures soared. He began to be published in America, where they liked his country-house settings; in Germany; in France. Freddie's great strength was that the world he wrote about never changed. It was, basically, the world he had known as a boy. His books might be set in the present day, but Inspector Coote remained an energetic forty-five, and none of Freddie's central characters could have contemplated life without a butler.

By the time I came to visit them that morning, Winnie and my uncle Freddie had been married for about ten years. They were inseparable. They were devoted. They were profoundly, demonstrably happy. They lived a life of undeviating regularity, in which Winnie organized everything and Uncle Freddie did as he was told. This suited them both. They had discovered the charms of routine.

At nine forty-five on the dot, Uncle Freddie was at his tidy writing table in the window of the sitting room, pen in hand; Winnie was at a very neat desk, of advanced design, at the other end of the room. Winnie typed; Uncle Freddie wrote.

They took a break for a snack (coffee, hot chocolate, and digestive biscuits) at eleven, a further brief break for lunch (served on trays by Mrs. O'Brien, who—like the house—had been smartened up). At three they took a walk together for half an hour, by the canal, always following precisely the same route. In the evenings, when work was over, they ate supper—again on trays—and watched television. Quiz shows, plays, soap operas, snooker, football, documentaries, reruns of *I Love Lucy:* whatever came on, they watched, with a contented lack of discrimination. Uncle Freddie was addicted to the controls. Since he liked people to look healthy, he adjusted the color tuner so everyone's face was bright orange.

From this routine, Winnie and my uncle refused to depart. It was interrupted only once a year, when, in a sudden burst of intrepid energy, they took a two-week holiday of an adventurous nature. These grew more ambitious each year. They had already been up the Nile in a felucca. They had visited Angkor Wat. They had ridden camels into the Sahara. Most recently they had walked in the foothills of the Himalayas, and made that flying visit to Tibet.

When I visited, the brochures from which they would select the next year's jaunt were already on the table. We sat in the workroom/ sitting room drinking coffee. Uncle Freddie's inkwell, blotting paper, and pen were laid out in readiness. Winnie's typewriter sat waiting across the room, paper already inserted. Next to my mug of coffee were bright pictures of temples and pyramids, remote mountains and dangerous rivers. Winnie and Freddie were not yet decided, but they thought next year they might fly to Australia and camp in the outback. This was explained. The Himalayas were described. Then there was a pause. I began to feel guilty. I was interfering with the routine.

When I said this, they both became very kind.

"Nonsense," Winnie trumpeted. "You look peaky. Something's wrong, isn't it? Better get it off your chest, whatever it is. Come on, speak up. Is it a man? You can tell us, if it is. Freddie and I can't be shocked. We're very broad-minded. Come on—speak up. A problem shared is a problem halved. What is it?"

I hesitated again. They both waited. In the end, it seemed foolish to have gone this far and then to stop, so I said, "Well, it's about Constance."

Their reactions were swift. Winnie harrumphed. Uncle Freddie (who had, finally, been cured of Constance) raised his eyes to the ceiling.

"Don't tell me you've seen her again, Vicky. You *know* she's a troublemaker."

Winnie gave a huge snort. "I've met her, you know. Before your mother died. At Winterscombe. She used to wear very doubtful hats. Very doubtful indeed. I wouldn't trust that woman one inch. I didn't then, and I don't now." She gave me a magnificent glance. "Freddie *knows*," she added, with great dignity, "what *I* think of her."

A certain glance passed between Winnie and my uncle—a meaningful glance. I wondered then just how much Freddie had told Winnie about his own involvement with Constance. Given Winnie's determined nature, I thought probably quite a lot. I could not imagine secrets between them.

There were pitfalls here, however, so I was careful. I explained about my visit to New York, about my search for Constance. Winnie tended to interrupt. At one point she made a hot speech in which she referred to Constance's age (she added five years to it). She referred to gossip columns. She made a number of remarks about, first, maneaters and then nymphomania.

This word, on Winnie's lips, surprised me very much. Winnie, seeing this, gave an airy wave of the hand.

"Oh, Freddie and I know all about things like that. We keep up, you know, Victoria. We saw a *very* interesting program on the question just the other night, on television. *Most* revealing. I told Freddie, he could use it in one of his plots. Handled in the right way, of course."

There was then a pause. I noticed that silent messages were being exchanged between Winnie and Freddie. Winnie was rolling her eyes at him in a most peculiar way. She nodded in the direction of the mantelpiece (why the mantelpiece?), whereupon Freddie cleared his throat.

"You didn't see *him*, by any chance, when you were in New York?" He blushed. "I just wondered, after all this time, if you might have—"

"No. I didn't see him."

"I think about him now and again." Freddie looked embarrassed. "Winnie and I—we'd like to see you settled, you know. We both thought . . . you seemed so well suited. I liked him very much. He was—"

"*Is,* Freddie, *is.* He is . . . an exceptional man. A fine man."

"Winnie—" I began.

"And what's more, he's still unmarried," Winnie continued. "Freddie and I still take an interest. We follow his career. Of course, I always knew he would be a success. You could see—the drive, the dedication. Do you know, there was an article about him in *The Times,* just the other day. Now where did you put it, Freddie? I clipped it specially—"

"Please, Winnie, I'd rather not read it," I began, but protests were useless. I just had time to feel grateful that neither Winnie nor my uncle had mentioned his name (it still made me agitated; it still hurt me) when the newspaper clipping was produced. It had been in readiness, just beneath that brochure for the outback. A reprint from a profile in *The New York Times:* the headline was A CONQUEROR OF INNER SPACE.

The accompanying photograph was large and had been taken at the Scripps-Foster Institute. It had been taken, I saw, by Conrad Vickers, and Vickers—that chronicler of our times, that recorder of the beautiful, the fashionable, the gifted, and the damned—photographed very few scientists.

Dr. Frank Gerhard was by then a very eminent scientist, a leader in his field, but that was not the reason Vickers had accepted the commission—I knew that at once. No, Vickers would have wanted to photograph this man for the quality of his face—an arresting face, and one it pained me still to look at.

Vickers had photographed him in that celebrated laboratory, surrounded by the impedimenta of his profession. His right hand touched a microscope; he was leaning forward; Vickers had caught him, I thought, in mid-speech.

Impassioned speech—I could see that. Dr. Gerhard would have been speaking of his work and Vickers had caught upon his features a look I remembered well: a poise between intensity and reticence, conviction and melancholy. Dr. Gerhard had a *driven* face.

I did not read the article then—indeed, I think I could not have read it, for the words would not lie still upon the page. Isolated phrases sprang out at me; I saw that the cancer research work continued; I saw that the journalist described this research as a quest, that he wrote of the charting of new worlds, that he (but not Dr. Gerhard) touched on the possibility of cures.

A scientist with priest's eyes, Wexton had once said of him. I looked at his eyes, his hair, his hands. His features were dear to me still; I could not look at them with equanimity. My hands shook. I folded the clipping in half. I thought: *I have no future that matters to me anymore.* I handed it back.

"Not married," Freddie said. (Winnie was telegraphing again.) "You see? Not married. It says that."

I looked away. I said, "It doesn't make any difference. It's over. You know that."

"Don't see why." Freddie, still encouraged by Winnie's eyebrows, sounded truculent. "You're being obstinate, that's all. You can be obstinate, you know, Vicky."

"So could he, Freddie."

"Yes, I know. I know. But there were reasons for that. Winnie and I thought if you were just to—"

"Freddie, please. I don't want to talk about this—" To my surprise, and my relief, Winnie interrupted.

"Leave it, Freddie," she said. "Victoria's right. This isn't the moment—"

"But, Winnie, you said—"

"Freddie!"

Winnie had obviously decided on a tactical withdrawal. Perhaps she had noted my distress. Whatever the reason, she leaned forward, her voice brisk.

"Now, my dear," she said, "let's keep to the point. We were discussing that woman. You had something to tell us, I think?"

"Well," I began, "I looked for Constance, as I told you. But I didn't see her. She gave me a present instead."

"A present?" Uncle Freddie began to look uneasy.

"Her diaries."

"Diaries? I never knew Constance kept a diary." Freddie had again blushed red.

"Well, it's more like a journal really. She didn't write in it every day. I've been looking through them—and I've also been going through some of the other papers at Winterscombe. They made me think about the past. They raised questions. Questions I thought you might be able to answer."

Freddie's face had taken on a hunted look. Winnie was staring at the tray in front of her.

"What sort of questions?" Uncle Freddie asked, after a long pause.

"Well, mainly about her father's death," I began in a firm voice. An expression of immense relief came upon Uncle Freddie's features.

"What, that? That was an age ago. Long before you were ever born. I can't see how that could matter to you, Vicky."

It was Winnie who asked me to explain, and so—in a careful and edited way—I did. Freddie and Winnie listened attentively. As soon as I mentioned the word *murder*, they both sat up very straight, then leaned forward with a keen professional look in the eyes. When I had finished, however, Winnie gave one of her snorts.

"Typical!" she said. "Absolutely typical. That woman likes to make a drama out of everything. If she ironed a shirt it would turn into a three-act tragedy. Murder? I've never heard such rubbish in all my life. I've heard that story hundreds of times. It's perfectly simple. Her father was a bad egg. A very *shifty* type, and he suffered an unpleasant accident. That's all there is to it. I should forget this at once, Victoria. It has absolutely *nothing* to do with you."

Uncle Freddie seemed inclined to be more thoughtful. He drew a doodle on his blotting pad. He crossed it out.

"If she thinks it was murder," he said eventually, in a slow voice, "then presumably there was a murderer. Is that the problem, Vicky?"

"Yes, it is," I said, looking at my hands. *Should I risk it, or not?* I decided to risk it. I looked up at Uncle Freddie. "You see, Constance seems to think . . . it was my father."

My father might have been dead for thirty years, but Freddie still loved him. He grew heated in his defense. Winnie—and I could not help noticing this, for it was unusual—was quieter. I had expected loud dismissals, more trumpetings on the subject of Constance's unreliability. None came. It was then, I think, that I began to wonder for the first time if Winnie—such an impassioned champion of my mother, Jane—was perhaps less enamored of my father.

As Uncle Freddie drew to the end of his confident, rambling, but eloquent speech on his brother Acland's behalf, Winnie stood.

"I am going to cook us some lunch," she said briskly. "It's one of Mrs. O'Brien's days off. I shall do us something with fish."

I, too, rose. "Winnie, I'm sorry. I'm keeping you both from your work. I'll go now."

"No, you won't." Winnie placed a large hand on my shoulder, pushing me back down in my chair. "You will talk this out with Freddie. The work can wait. This has obviously upset you. Now—

you listen to Freddie, and he'll sort it out. Your uncle, Victoria, is a *very* wise man."

"Oh dear," Uncle Freddie said when Winnie had left the room. "I'm afraid I'm not, Vicky. Not wise at all. I wish I were." He looked very sad, even crestfallen. Because I felt sorry for him, I hit on a way that might help us both.

"You see, Freddie," I said, "Constance never spells it out. Once, when her husband suggested to her that my father was involved, she denied it fiercely. But the more she denies it, the more afraid I am. I tell myself it must have been an accident—then the doubts creep back in. It's like one of your books. I feel I have to prove my father's innocence. I feel I have to solve it. And so I thought: What would Inspector Coote do in a case like this?"

Uncle Freddie brightened at once.

"If it *was* murder, you mean?"

"Yes."

"Ah, well"—he rubbed his hands together—"now that's interesting. What *would* he do? Well, he'd interview everyone who was there, of course, at that party. All the guests. All the family. All the servants."

"And then?"

"He'd examine the question of timing very carefully. He's a fiend for timing."

"And after that?"

"You know his watchwords, Vicky. M.O.C. Motive. Opportunity. Character. Those are the key things. *Cui bono*, Vicky—that's the thing you must never forget."

"*Cui bono?*"

"Literally, 'to whom the good?' In this context, who benefits?" Uncle Freddie, launched now, gave a broad smile.

"In your books, Uncle Freddie, all the suspects benefit—that's what makes it so hard."

"Ah, of course, red herrings!" Uncle Freddie chortled. Then he frowned. "But in this case, looking at it purely speculatively, no one benefited, as far as I can see. Absolutely no one."

"Freddie, that's not true," I said gently. "I know some of what happened. There *were* people who might have wanted Shawcross out of the way. My grandfather, for instance. Wasn't he jealous?"

"Of Shawcross?" Freddie began to look evasive. "Maybe."

"And my father. He obviously resented Shawcross. I think he hated him—"

"It's possible." Freddie waved his hands about. "But you don't want to exaggerate. *Hate* is a strong word. My mother . . . Lots of married women had these special friends then. No one thought much about it. Acland never liked Shawcross, that's true—but then, none of us did. I couldn't stand him. And I didn't murder him, if that's what you're thinking!"

"Of course not. But, Freddie—"

"If you look at it purely from the point of view of a detective story"—Freddie was beginning to cheer up again—"and now I think about it, it might make quite a good plot: the motiveless murder! Yes, I like that! Then you'd have to say: who hated, but hid that hate? Was there someone in the house that night who had a secret link with him—a financial one, perhaps? Maybe one of the guests *knew* Shawcross already? And then—this is important—you'd have to consider: who was strong enough? Shawcross was reasonably fit. You couldn't just follow him into the woods and say: 'Here's a trap; would you mind stepping into it?' He'd have to be pushed. Or threatened. Hmmm. Interesting."

This seemed to me to be leading us back toward my father—which was not what I wanted. I leaned forward.

"Uncle Freddie. If this upsets you, stop me. But you see, I know about Boy. I know what Boy told Steenie the day he killed himself. And I know it can't have been true, because Boy was with Constance. But in that case, who took those Purdey shotguns? Someone did. They were missing by the end of dinner—and that must be true. It's in my mother's diaries."

Freddie sighed.

"Poor Boy." He shook his head. "I still think of him, you know. He was a good sort. Wouldn't have hurt a fly . . ." He hesitated. "If it helps, I don't know who took the guns. But I do know who put them back. It was my father."

"Denton? Are you sure? Freddie—"

"I remember it very well. I was passing the gun room and I saw him lock them back in their case. Shawcross wasn't even dead. He was upstairs, dying. I thought it was odd—what was father doing with Boy's guns? Of course"—he brightened again—"that makes my father a prime suspect. Is that what you're thinking? Well, I'm afraid you're wrong. He couldn't have done it. At least, I don't *think* he could have done it."

"Why not, Uncle Freddie?"

"Because I saw him, you see—the night of the comet. He wasn't wandering 'round the woods after Shawcross. He was in the house."

"In the house—how do you know, Freddie?"

Freddie blushed. "Well, the thing is, that night . . . I drank rather too much. They let me stay behind for the port—it was the first time I'd done that. I had three glasses. Then I had some champagne. By the time I went up to bed, I felt ghastly. I had this valet—forget his name now—"

"Tubbs. Arthur Tubbs."

"That's it! Clever of you." Freddie beamed. "Well, I sent Arthur away. Then I felt too ill to undress. The room was going up and down—you know how it is. So I just flopped down on the bed. I fell asleep for a bit—but not for very long. When I woke up, I had a raging thirst. My head felt as if it'd been kicked by a horse. Port does that, you know. Far too acid. I never touch it now—"

"Freddie—"

"Sorry. Keep to the point. Anyway, I got up to drink some water. Walked about a bit. Then I thought some fresh air might help. So I went downstairs. I went out on the terrace, took some deep breaths. That seemed to do the trick. Most people were in bed by then, but there were still lights in the billiard room. I could hear voices. So I toddled along in there. Wanted to be one of the men, I suppose—I was only fifteen then. Anyway, in I went—"

"And your father was there?"

"Well, I'm pretty sure he was." Freddie frowned. "You see, it's so long ago—and at the time it didn't seem important, who was there and who wasn't. Also I was still a bit tipsy. The room was full of cigar smoke. There was quite a crowd in there—my father's cronies. They used to like to stay up. Let me see—there was a man called Peel, Richard Peel. He was there—I remember that. And there was another chap, something to do with the City—"

"George Heyward-West?"

"That's right. I say, you have gone into this, haven't you? George Heyward-West, that's the man. I remember him because he and Montague Stern were having some kind of contest. They were both very good at billiards, and I watched them play for a bit—"

"Montague Stern? He was there? Freddie, he can't have been—"

"Why not?" Freddie began to look irritated. "He certainly was. It was the first time I met him. I remember it distinctly. He and Heyward-West were getting on like a house on fire. Stern used to wear these terrible waistcoats, and he was wearing one that night. Crimson, with gold embroidery. They'd both taken off their jackets and rolled back their sleeves, and—"

"Freddie, what time was this?"

"Heavens, I don't know. I've no idea. Two? Three? Pretty late. Anyway, the point is, my father was there too. He was sitting over in the corner, in a wing chair. Every so often he'd wake up; then he'd go back to sleep." Freddie stopped. "I don't remember it all too clearly. There were a lot of people in there. At some point someone gave me another drink, and I could see what they all thought, so I thought, *I'll jolly well show them*—and I drank it. It was whisky. I'd never had whisky before. It was definitely a mistake. I remember, Acland had just given me one of his cigarettes—I used to pinch them from his room sometimes, I'm afraid. Anyway, he'd just given me one, then I drank the whisky, and then I thought: *Oh, God, I'm going to be sick*. Acland got me back to my room. Somehow. And the funny thing is, I used to think Boy helped him. Except Boy wasn't there, of course, so it must have been someone else. George Heyward-West, probably. He was a nice chap. Always used to give me a tip when he stayed—never less than a sovereign . . ."

Freddie stared off into the middle distance. He sighed. A silence fell.

I considered all this. I considered the fact that if this were true, and not just a fabrication of my uncle Freddie's well-trained and comfortable memory, Montague Stern had not remained with Maud; he had been downstairs. Denton had been downstairs. Most important of all, *my father* had been downstairs. The timing might be vague (I was sure it would not have satisfied Inspector Coote) but my father had been there. No one could commit murder and then return to a house and play billiards, surely?

I stared past my uncle at the view from the window: an ordinary street, an ordinary day. I felt the greatest relief. Of course the death of Shawcross was an accident—and I should never have doubted that. Constance had been unbalancing me, I thought, with her fictions.

I think Uncle Freddie must have guessed what I thought, because he smiled. He, too, became brisk and sensible.

"In any case," he said, "if you go back to where we were—if you think of it from Inspector Coote's point of view—you can see it can't have been murder, anyway. It's obvious. It's impossible."

"Why, Uncle Freddie?"

"Think. Shawcross *didn't die*—not immediately. It took three days. Now, as it happens, he couldn't speak during that time—he was too ill. But a would-be murderer couldn't have known that. After all, Shawcross might have been found earlier. He might not have been so badly injured. He might have been able to speak—and then he would have identified his killer! It's a very chancy way to bump someone off. The murderer would have to be sure he couldn't be recognized—and that's impossible. There was a moon that night. There would have been a struggle." He paused. He patted my hand. "You see? You're upsetting yourself about nothing, you know. You really are. I've had fifty-eight years to think about this, and I know I'm right. An accident—and if Constance is suggesting otherwise, I'd ignore it." He hesitated, his expression kind but veiled. "She's not the best person to trust, you know. She . . . likes to make trouble. You know that."

Winnie had come in during the latter part of this speech. She brought with her a tray. We ate an excellent lunch. We discussed recipes and cooking methods. Once or twice I tried to bring the conversation around to 1930, my christening, and the mysterious quarrel between Constance and my parents, but Freddie and Winnie seemed unwilling to take the bait, and having risked the question of Shawcross earlier, I had no wish to upset them more.

Some weeks after this lunch, a period during which there were great changes in my life, my uncle Freddie began a detective story based on that accident in 1910. He called it *Inclined to Murder*. It was to become one of his greatest successes, being reprinted many times. It is still in print now, and you could read it. You would find the setting, and many of the characters, recognizable. The solution Uncle Freddie reached was not my solution—but then, his version was fiction, whereas by that time mine was fact.

Although Uncle Freddie's account of what happened differs from mine, there was much in what he wrote—and much in what he said on that day in Little Venice—that overlapped. Talking about a murder that day, I can see that he came quite close to the truth; it was just around the corners of his words, obvious, yet neither of us saw it.

There were reasons for this. Uncle Freddie was prejudiced, as I was. There were certain things, for reasons of love and loyalty, that both of us preferred not to see. Nothing significant happened until I came to take my leave. We had finished lunch. Winnie began to look in a loving way at her typewriter. I said that I would go.

Uncle Freddie, anxious to resume work, remained at his writing table. I saw his eyes stray in the direction of the mantelpiece again; I saw Winnie give him a small and mysterious nod.

Winnie showed me out. She closed the sitting-room door firmly. She looked back over her shoulder, motioned me along the passage to the front door. Her color was high. When she was sure we were out of earshot, she gripped my arm.

"Victoria. There's something else, isn't there, dear? You haven't told us everything, I think."

"Well, no, Winnie. Not absolutely everything. It doesn't matter. I feel much better. You've both been a great help."

"Listen to me." Winnie brushed these assurances aside. "What Freddie said just now—as I came in with the lunch. He was absolutely right! That woman is a troublemaker. Still is, always was." She paused. "In my opinion, she once did Freddie a great deal of harm. There's no need to go into the details—the details don't matter. What does matter is what it did to Freddie. All his confidence went. He couldn't settle. It took years and years to heal, what she did to him. She poisoned his mind—against certain members of the family—and it took a long time for him to recover. I shouldn't like to see that happen to you."

"I won't let it, Winnie."

"That's all very well to say, and I'm sure you mean it. But is it true? At lunch, when you asked about your christening, the rift—was that an accident?"

"No, Winnie. Not altogether."

"I *knew* it!" Winnie's manner became heated. "She's put some idea in your mind, hasn't she? About her and your father?"

"Sort of."

"Well then, let me tell you"—Winnie turned me around to face her—"I was *at* Winterscombe for your christening. It's not an occasion, unfortunately, that I care to recall. However." She sniffed. "I was there. I know *exactly* what happened—"

"She had an affair. With my father," I said in a flat voice. "It's all right, Winnie. I worked it out weeks ago. Either it was just before I was born or just after. The details don't matter. I'm sure he loved my mother—but he loved Constance too. And she certainly loved him. Things like that happen—I know that. I'll get used to it—"

"Stuff and nonsense," Winnie snapped. "It wasn't like that at all—and if she suggests it was, she's lying through her teeth. What happened was very simple. She turned up—at your christening, if you please!—she set her cap at your father, and he turned her down. She went back to New York in a fine temper. I told you, she thought she was irresistible to men—even a man like your father, with a happy home and a wife he loved and a newborn baby. She couldn't stand that, of course. She wanted to smash it up." She paused.

"You'd understand that, surely? You know what she's like. She did the same thing to you."

There was a certain challenge in the way this last remark was said. I did not reply.

"Hell hath no fury like a woman scorned!" Winnie trumpeted. "Do you see? I've *always* believed that. When Constance left Winterscombe, she was perfectly *livid*. In my opinion, she'd always wanted to get her talons into your father—and having failed, she'd turned to you instead. I've always said to Freddie, that woman is a damaging influence. He should have put his foot down. She should *never* have been your guardian. You should never have gone to live in New York. If I'd been married to Freddie then, it would certainly never have happened."

"Winnie. She was kind to me. For many years. More than kind—until we quarreled—"

"Ah, but *when* did you quarrel?" Winnie asked on a note of triumph. "When she thought she was losing you. When she thought you'd found happiness. Just as she did with your father—do you see? When I *think* of the scene she made that last night at Winterscombe, the lies she told. In front of everyone. Wexton was there. You can ask Wexton if you feel the need. He'll confirm what I say. I told your mother at the time—exile! Exile wasn't enough. What one needed in Constance's case was *exorcism*."

Here Winnie came to an unexpected halt. Her cheeks were still scarlet from her outburst, but her expression changed: She began to look simultaneously kind and furtive. She fumbled in her pocket, thrust a card into my hand, and maneuvered me toward the door.

"Something we wanted you to have, Freddie and I. Don't look at it now—you can look at it later. We can't go, you see, and so we thought, perhaps you . . ."

She opened the door. She propelled me out onto the steps. She suddenly seemed in a great hurry for me to leave. "Inspect the newts on the way out," she cried, somewhat wildly. "There's one big brute we're very fond of. By the lily pad on the left, usually. That's his den."

The door shut, hastily. I inspected the newt, mystified. He was where Winnie had said he would be: a fine, fat, warty specimen. I reached out to touch him, but he was wily. When my hand was still three inches away, he plopped back out of sight under his lily pad.

When I was half a street away, I unfolded the card Winnie had given me. I then understood the glances toward the mantelpiece (where Winnie propped invitations). I also understood the embarrassed and surreptitious way it had been pressed into my hand. A benign conspiracy. The card was an invitation to a lecture two days away. The lecture was being given, in London, by Dr. Frank Gerhard.

There were a great many letters after his name. I stood on the corner and counted them. Freddie's and Winnie's names were in the top left-hand corner: the writing was Frank's own. Since I still loved him, since—for what it is worth—I had never stopped loving him, I was tempted. I thought: *I could go.*

However, I had spent eight years training myself to be sensible, and those eight years slammed in my face. Reunions after eight years may occur in fiction; they are rare in real life.

I walked to Paddington Station. I bought four newspapers, because I wanted to read and not think. It was the end of October by then, and the papers were full of war: the Vietnam War, in which a halt had just been called to the American bombing. I read the same story, in four versions, over and over again. I did not understand the words or the sentences, but I stared at them with blind concentration all the way back to Winterscombe.

The next day I had the distraction of that potential purchaser— for which I was grateful. There was not a great deal that could be done to improve Winterscombe's appearance at that point, but what little there was, I did. I spent the morning arranging flowers. The corporate raider, whose name was Cunningham, was due at eleven o'clock.

It was not raining, which was fortunate; in rain, Winterscombe did not look its best. It was a clear, cold, bright day. At nine, returning to the house from the winter garden with an armful of the last late roses, I stopped and looked up at the house.

The morning sun shone on this, the east face of the building; it softened the house's architectural assertions and mellowed the color of its brick. A beautiful disarray of creepers advanced upon the windows; I turned to look back across the lake, toward the autumn woods. There was a faint mauve mist over the water, no sound except birdsong. I remembered the phrase Franz-Jacob had once used to me, thirty years before: *Ein Zauber Ort*—a magical place.

I felt a great welling of affection for the house then—for the house, its past inhabitants, their lives and their secrets. I could, this morning, sense their ghosts. A magical place. I wondered, would a corporate raider sense this?

When he arrived (on time, in the back of a chauffeur-driven

Corniche; Garstang-Nott and I were waiting for him) he did not look the kind of man who would enter "magic" in the credit column when he accounted the pros and cons of a house. He stood frowning at the façade. I was sure his eyes rested on the inadequacies of the guttering. His expression was that of a man who senses the invisible fungi beneath the floorboards. I took him to be in his mid-sixties. He was actually a good bit older, I learned. He was spruce, slightly built, well got-up, deeply tanned. His clothes were expensive and a shade too carefully conservative. He emanated a wiry, impatient air of cocksure energy. His accent was mid-Atlantic. His first question, as soon as he was inside the door, was whether he might use the telephone.

I was familiar with businessmen who suffered withdrawal symptoms when deprived of a telephone for more than an hour. I think Mr. Cunningham experienced this; I also think he wanted to emphasize his own importance. He took the call in the next room, door open, voice loud; large figures were bandied about in some detail. Garstang-Nott's expression became pained. He pursed his lips. He winced. When Cunningham finally returned, bristling with new confidence, he and Garstang-Nott exchanged a challenging glance. It was clear that their detestation of each other was immediate, that neither was very inclined to disguise it. Garstang-Nott spoke in a patronizing manner acquired at his public school, a manner he had had many years to perfect; Cunningham responded with new-money aggression. Garstang-Nott implied he found it very odd indeed that a man such as Cunningham should aspire to such a house; Cunningham, by gesture, stance, and remark, implied that times had changed, buddy—the public-school man was a flunky and he himself was now cock of the walk. Class hatred sparked; the air was dense with its smoke.

We began the tour of the house. Garstang-Nott's theory—it might sound perverse, but I, too, had encountered the phenomenon and knew he was right—was that the very rich were not interested in acquiring perfection. They did not *believe* in perfection. Even presented with a house faultless in every respect, there would be niggles. They *liked* niggles. They itched to find something to alter, something to correct.

Winterscombe, of course, was far from faultless—and as we proceeded from room to room, Garstang-Nott, obeying his theory, enumerated its disadvantages with zest: dry rot, wet rot, drains, guttering, roofing, wiring, heating. He gave the now-silent Cunningham a pale glance. Undersell: Garstang-Nott proved a master at it. I had a precise idea of how much money it would cost to restore Winterscombe properly; Garstang-Nott coolly doubled it.

"As a *minimum*," he drawled. "That's leaving aside, of course, all question of redecoration."

The implicit suggestion, conveyed by accent and general air of unassailable superiority, was that Winterscombe was well beyond Cunningham's means. The corporate raider rose to the bait.

"*So?*" he said with considerable aggression. He turned his back on the real-estate agent. He advanced on the fireplace, where the original bellpull for the servants was situated. He yanked it. "These work, do they?"

I said yes, they still did. He smiled, in an odd, slightly malicious way. It was then, as we moved on to the next bedroom, that I began to realize something. He seemed familiar with the geography of the house, and—Winterscombe being so large—that geography was complex. He seemed to expect stairs, to see around corners—and it occurred to me he might have been here before. I wondered if it had been during the war years, if he could have been stationed here in the period after the army requisitioned the house.

We went from room to room. Cunningham made little comment, but within an hour I could tell he was not going to buy. He was palpably losing interest. He looked around him with an air of resentful irritation, as if he had expected much and the house failed him.

I was hurt by that, and angered too. I was still old-fashioned enough to feel he could have made an effort to be polite. I thought that if Winterscombe had the absurdities of its era, it also had its strengths. I felt partisan. I pointed out the views: the lake, the trees, the woods. He glanced briefly, looked away. He kicked a wainscot. He glared at the parquet. Behind his back, Garstang-Nott made a rude face.

We trudged around the stables, the coach house, the old laundry buildings, the abandoned dairy. I stood, for the first time in many years, in that converted dormitory used every summer by the orphanage children. This was the end of the room where my friend Franz-Jacob had had his bed; this was the very window from which he had flashed Morse-code messages to me, thirty years before. I closed my eyes. I saw the letters flash. I opened them again and looked around with a sense of despair. Was nothing in this house ever thrown away? The long room was still stacked with the old iron-frame orphanage beds.

I knew I was wasting time—all three of us were. As we walked back toward the house I was just about to suggest we recognize that fact, and curtail the inspection, when Cunningham stopped. Still ignoring the estate agent, he turned to me.

"I know this place," he said.

I hesitated. The admission seemed made reluctantly. His air of cocky energy was gone.

"I thought you did. Was it during the war?"

"What?"

"Were you stationed here, during the war? I thought—"

"Stationed here?" He gave an odd smile. "Oh, no. I used to *work* here. They sent me down from the London place when I was fifteen years old. Your family trained me." The smile became a slight sneer. "I was valet to your . . . uncle, would it be? Your uncle Frederic? Writes now, I believe. Detective stories, that sort of stuff?"

I stared at him, astonished. "You're Arthur—Arthur Tubbs?"

Because my mind was still full of the past, I saw him as a boy, a thin, acned boy bursting into Freddie's room, drunk on disaster, the morning of the accident. I thought of him as Constance described him—nervous-weasely, the best man at Jenna's wedding. A bit player, now center stage. I wanted to say: *But you were peripheral.* I wanted to say: *Oh, but you're real.* Fortunately, I said no such idiotic thing. I noticed that at the mention of his name (probably unexpected) he had flushed beneath his tan.

"Yes, well, I don't use that name now. I changed it. For business purposes, see? I'm Cunningham now. I've been Cunningham for forty years."

I thought: *Conyngham/Cunningham.* I thought: *There is another story here, one I shall never know.* He had turned back, meanwhile, to the house.

"It's weird." The mid-Atlantic accent, which had wavered, was now firmly in control. "I wanted this place. I waited for years for it to come on the market. I knew it would, in the end. I thought, when it does, see, I'll buy it. Only . . ."

"Only now you don't want it?"

"No. I don't." He turned back to me. He gave a shrug. "Can't say why exactly. It doesn't . . . measure up."

"Well, the house is run-down now," I began. "I know that. It needs restoration. But—"

"Oh, it's not *that.*" He gave me a scornful look. "I'd want to do it over, in any case. I had thought, maybe you—I've seen your work. Anyway. No point in discussing that. It doesn't suit. Time is money. No point in wasting either. I have to get back."

He set off at a rapid pace, to the front of the house and his waiting car. His driver climbed out. He doffed his cap. He opened the rear door.

"Well trained." Tubbs/Cunningham gave a small tight smile. "But then, I was well trained. I know how things are done."

He glanced back at the house one last time. I began to see why he might have considered employing me to redecorate this house—a decision that would have had nothing to do with any skills I might have as a decorator. The server, served. I realized for the first time that Garstang-Nott was an irrelevance. It was me that Cunningham disliked.

"You know how many indoor servants there were then?" He gave me a cold glance. "Fifty. Who knows? Maybe that's what I miss. All that bowing and scraping. Yes, my lord. No, my lady. Three bags full, my lady. You know what I used to be paid to pick up clothes? A pound a week."

"*With* room and board, I imagine," Garstang-Nott put in, none too politely. "And it *was* rather a long time ago."

They exchanged glances of cordial hostility. Cunningham climbed into his car. He made—to me—one last remark before it pulled away.

"Jumped-up little creep," said Garstang-Nott. "Made his first pile as a black-marketeer, I believe. Rather a crook, didn't you think?"

I made no reply. I did not share Garstang-Nott's political or social certitudes; neither did I agree with them. I thought Arthur Tubbs more interesting, and more complex, than that. To be exploited, then to wish to exploit; to seal a business career by purchasing the very house where you once served—I could see the sad logic of that.

I looked at Winterscombe with new eyes. I saw its capacity to transmute, to be valued, in many different ways by many different people. For Arthur Tubbs the house was a revenge for years of servitude; for my grandfather, escaping the taint of trade, a way of obliterating all memory of factories that made bleach. For Montague Stern it had represented freedom and power, a dominion where the outsider could rule, a bequest to a dream-son. To Constance it had been a house of secrets; to my father, an elegy; to me, a shrine to a lost childhood. All of us, I thought, in our different ways, had looked at bricks and mortar and created a chimera.

I could see the danger. I think it was then, looking at Winterscombe, that I determined, truly determined, to let it go.

"It's not . . . *as I remembered it*," Cunningham had said to me, before he rolled up the car window. I was struck by that. Chance remarks can often lead one around a necessary corner.

"Wexton," I said, when Garstang-Nott had departed and I had gone inside. "Would you mind if I went up to London tomorrow? I want to go to a lecture."

"Sure," Wexton replied, in a way that made me immediately certain that he knew which lecture, given by whom, and that he, too, was included in Freddie and Winnie's benign conspiracy.

Going to my room that night, knowing I would not sleep, I thought of all the versions of the past I had been given: There were as many possible versions as there were people. But there remained one version still unexplored, and one story so far excluded. My own: the past as *I* remembered it.

It was territory long avoided. Only one person, I think, could have persuaded me back there, and it was he who waited for me there, obscured by the practiced evasions of the last eight years.

Oh, yes, I knew where this route led. It led backwards, but also forward, to that man in the laboratory: my American, Dr. Frank Gerhard.

He *cured* people. That was his profession. After taking his medical degree at Columbia, he moved on to Yale, then the Scripps-Foster Institute, where he pursued his biochemical research. His special field was the transmutation of cells, the anarchy or—if you like—the internal wars that disrupt the human body's equilibrium. He was a biochemist; I was a decorator. You will see now, I hope, why a parting eight years before had easily remained absolute. To meet again required decisive action, on his part or on mine. There was no likelihood of chance encounters. The paths of biochemists and interior decorators do not often cross. He worked in America: I avoided that country. We were both, perhaps, excessively careful; even in the same city accidental meetings would have been unlikely. I regretted this. There had been many times, those past eight years, when (not believing in destiny) I had wished some such force might have intervened and given us—a nudge.

On the other hand, had it done so, I might have been obstinately blind to it. I could be blind—I had been blind when we first met. I met Frank Gerhard through my work, and through my friendship with his mother, the impossible Rosa. I was to meet him again, on several occasions, over several years. That first time I met him, at

Rosa's house, he said two words to me: "Hello" and "Goodbye." Behind the greeting and the farewell, I thought I sensed indifference, even dislike—for which there seemed no very obvious reason. Five minutes in my company (and that first meeting was as brief as that) seemed enough to make him dismiss me. This rankled. I resolved to ignore his reaction, and him; since he continued to make his dislike plain whenever we met, this was not always easy.

The first time I was unable to ignore him was in 1956. It was early spring. Constance and I were in Venice. Yes, it was the occasion on which Conrad Vickers (part of Constance's entourage) took that photograph outside the church of Santa Maria della Salute.

Frank Gerhard was in Venice on an errand of mercy. His father, Max Gerhard, a professor of linguistics at Columbia, had died some months before. The visit to Venice had been planned by Frank and one of his brothers (the Gerhards were an enormous family) in an attempt to help their mother, Rosa, through a difficult bereavement. Rosa, grateful and brave but not a good actress, was trying to pretend, I think, that this plan had been a success.

Rosa, attacking grief with her customary energy and with an air of bewildered defiance, was dressed in red. Guidebook in hand, she had just been conducting her family on an exhaustive, very Rosa tour of the church, buttress by buttress.

Constance, Conrad Vickers, and I, together with several other Constance acolytes, had—predictably—been engaged on more frivolous pursuits. The acolytes included Bobsy and Bick van Dynem (then in their early thirties and dubbed the Heavenly Twins by the gossip columns, on account of their fortune and their dazzling good looks); we had just been to visit some distant connection of the Van Dynem family, and were going on from this principessa's house to Harry's Bar.

The two groups, one gaily frivolous, the other sadly exhausted, chanced upon one another in the sunshine of a perfect Venetian afternoon. Constance, catching sight of Rosa in the distance, said, "Oh *no*. Too late for evasive action." Rosa, who had not known we were in Venice, gave a cry of pleasure. She embraced me. She greeted Constance warmly. I drew aside and looked out over the water. The reflections of a beautiful city bent upon its surface; the light was as gold as a Veronese.

"Hello," Frank Gerhard said to me as, some five minutes later, we lined up for one of Conrad Vickers's impromptu photographs. My friend Rosa, glad to be rescued from culture, I think, was talking to Constance, whom she had known for many years, Constance's firm having decorated all of Rosa's many houses. Vickers fussed and rearranged the group; there was some horseplay between the Van Dynem twins with a Panama hat. Bobsy put the hat on my head and ruffled my hair—I remember that. I removed it and said, a little sharply:

"Don't do that."

Constance, who like to pretend that Bobsy van Dynem was a suitor of mine, made a knowing face. Bick van Dynem complained; he said he wanted a drink. Conrad, still fussing, rearranged his group. He placed me first on the edge, in the shadow of the church, then pulled me out into the sunlight again. I found a silent Frank Gerhard by my side. I looked toward the church. The shutter clicked.

I expected Frank Gerhard to say goodbye at once; to my surprise, he did not. He gave the Van Dynem twins a dismissive look, yet he seemed inclined to linger. He edged me away from the rest of the group.

We exchanged brief notes on our respective activities in Venice. Escaping from Constance's endless round of cocktails and parties, I had visited the Accademia the previous day. Frank Gerhard had been there as well. We must have missed each other by minutes.

This coincidence—not so remarkable in itself—seemed to make him thoughtful. He gazed down at the waters of the Grand Canal. Light, then shadow, reflected by the water, moved across his face. He seemed troubled. I ventured some faltering and inadequate remark about his father. He acknowledged the remark in a brusque way. I risked a few more stilted words; I was, in those days, painfully shy. They elicited little response. I looked at Frank Gerhard in his black suit; I told myself that, no matter the circumstances, he was difficult, brooding, impolite, and (I had noticed this quality in him before) abstracted.

Rosa, meanwhile, was discussing houses with Constance—a subject Constance had initiated. Could she have forgotten that Rosa was newly widowed? It was possible; Constance could be careless about the details of other people's lives.

"Well, Rosa," she was saying, "and when is the next move to be? You know, sometimes I think you move house the way other people pack suitcases."

"Oh," Rosa said, in a quiet voice, "I won't move again. Not now. You know—because of Max."

She gave as she said this a small gesture of distress. She turned away. Behind her back Constance caught Conrad Vickers's eye; she made an impatient face. When Rosa rallied and began to speak again, Constance interrupted her hastily.

"Yes, yes," she said. "But don't let's talk here. Bick will expire for want of a drink. We're going to Harry's Bar. Come with us, Rosa. We'll have Bellinis." Rosa's kind face at once lit up. She had always liked Constance, and probably believed the invitation generously meant. She accepted with some alacrity. I felt sorry for her and furious with Constance. My godmother was socially ruthless. Once at Harry's Bar, I knew, Constance would find some pretext; Rosa and entourage would be unceremoniously dumped.

Frank Gerhard, too, had seen that glance exchanged between Constance and Vickers. I saw him move across to his mother and speak to her quietly.

"No, no," Rosa replied. "I'm perfectly fine, not tired at all. Harry's Bar! I've never been there. Thank you, Constance."

Frank Gerhard spoke briefly to his brother, drawing him aside. The brother took Rosa's arm. The group began to move off. Only Frank Gerhard and I remained by the church; the gap between us and the Bellini contingent widened.

Frank Gerhard, frowning after them, seemed to come to an abrupt decision. To my astonishment, as I moved to follow the others he took my arm. He said:

"We don't have to join them."

"I just thought—"

"I know what you thought. Rosa will be all right. Daniel will look after her. Would you like a drink? There's a place near here, a quiet place. . . ."

He scarcely waited for an answer. Still keeping hold of my arm, he steered me down a narrow street. We went through a maze of passageways, at a fast pace; we turned through an arch, crossed a bridge.

Neither of us spoke. Finally we reached a small café situated in a courtyard. It was shaded by the branches of a magnolia tree; water fell from the mouth of a stone lion into the shallow basin of a fountain. We were the only people.

"I found this place the first day I came to Venice. Do you like it?" He seemed oddly anxious that I should.

"I like it very much. It's beautiful."

He smiled as I said this, and his face was transformed; it lit with an infectious, irreverent amusement.

"You don't like Harry's Bar then?" I said, as he drew out a chair for me.

"No, I do not like Harry's Bar," he replied. "I do not like Harry's Bar at all. It is the one place in Venice I would avoid above all others."

"And you don't like Bellinis?"

A glint of mockery had come into his eyes: I knew that it was the company he was avoiding, not the bar or the Bellinis, and I think Frank Gerhard knew I knew that. He made no comment however, merely shrugged.

"The painters, yes. The drink, no. However, I've earned a drink, I think. This afternoon, at Santa Maria, I believe I saw every window, every statue, every pavement, every altarpiece. I could recite the *Guide Bleu* comments by heart. It's a very large church—a very large church *indeed*. Very beautiful, too, of course, but after the fifty-sixth buttress . . ."

"Rosa is indefatigable."

"She is." He looked at me solemnly, still with that glint of amusement in his eyes. "However . . ."

"It helps her?"

"I think so. I hope so," he replied shortly. "What would you like? Do you like Campari?"

When the Camparis arrived, the rims of the tall glasses had been sugared. I remember that. The drinks were the color of liquid rubies. There were rivulets of condensation on the outside of the glasses, and I fixed my eyes upon these as we talked. I was shy, as I say—used to Constance dominating any social situation, and clumsy at making conversation. I had never been alone with Frank Gerhard before, and I found him intimidating. He had then recently completed his doctorate at Yale (I knew this from Rosa, who was fiercely proud of him) and, for a while I tried to ask him about this, about his work, about New Haven.

My attempts at conversation were stilted, probably; Frank Gerhard's replies were mechanical, and I had the impression his mind was neither on my questions nor on his own replies. He seemed to be watching me; I could feel his eyes upon my face. He also seemed oddly tense. From time to time, when he glanced away, I stole a look at him.

I was then twenty-five; Frank Gerhard was twenty-seven or -eight. He was very tall and, for his height, thin. He had a narrow and intense face, very black hair, which fell forward across his forehead, and eyes of so dark a brown that they, too, could appear black. He was an observer, by training, as all scientists must be; he was also one, I thought, by temperament. His gaze, first intent, then impatient, missed little. I knew him to be very bright; in the past I had also judged him arrogant.

That day, I was less certain of my verdict. Having brought us here in that impulsive way, he seemed as uncertain as I was how to proceed. Our conversation continued like a poor tennis match between two hesitant players: a series of lobs across an invisible net. My replies became duller by the second. Hating myself, wishing I had been gifted with Constance's wit and verbal pyrotechnics, I could feel myself miserably dwindling into monosyllables. It was at this point that, having glanced away, he turned back. He did so suddenly, giving me no time to avert my gaze. Our eyes met.

I saw him truly then, I think, for the first time. Having done so, I could not look away—and it seemed he could not do so either. I think he said my name, and then broke off. His hand, which lay on the table close to my own, gave an involuntary movement and then lay still. I could see in his face no sign of boredom or preoccupation or indifference or hostility. This confused me. His expression seemed at first tense, then inexplicably joyful, then grave. He seemed to be waiting for me to speak; when I did not, I saw his face change.

You know the expression *to read a face?* I thought of it then. It is an odd phrase, for a mysterious process. When we read in that way, what grammar do we use? What sentences do we trace? His features did not move; he did not speak; he made no further gesture. Nonetheless, I could read the change in his face. Some dulling in his gaze; a transition from concentration to sadness, and then an attempt to disguise that sadness with a brisk *froideur*. I read all those things in the second or two that passed; then he began to speak.

He had been about to say one thing, I felt—then changed his mind and embarked on a different topic. I cannot now remember what it was. It is not important. He spoke for the sake of speaking, his words a barrier between me and his thoughts. As he spoke, I listened—not to what he said, but to his voice.

He spoke, first, in a stiff, then rushing way, and with a trace of an accent that sounded very like that of his mother, Rosa. Rosa Gerhard was by birth a Catholic, her family a branch of the minor south-German aristocracy. Her father, losing both his lands and his money by the end of the first war, had emigrated with his family to America. There he amassed a considerable fortune. Rosa, an only and a pampered daughter, educated at a restrictive and exclusive Catholic girls' boarding school, kicked over the traces at eighteen when she met, and shortly afterward married, Max Gerhard, also of German descent, born in Leipzig and—to the horror of her parents—a Jew.

Rosa, with exuberance and determination, converted to her husband's religion, embraced his politics (radical), and having inherited a good deal of money, proceeded to marry the bourgeois to the academic life. As a child on the Upper East Side, she spoke German at home; she spoke German at home as a wife. She was impossible to classify; she could not be pigeonholed by nationality, class, religion, or race. She was, she herself would cheerfully say, a hybrid—and this mixture of influences could still be detected in her voice.

They could be detected, also, in her son's. Listening to him that day in Venice, I could hear both Europe and America, a prewar voice, and a modern one—two cultures, and two eras, wedded in one voice.

I liked this; I would come to love it. I was thinking this and trying to remember: Frank Gerhard reminded me of someone, but I could not place who it was. Then I realized he had asked me a question—a question I had not heard. His elbows were on the table, his eyes intent on my face.

"I'm sorry?"

"The war. I was asking you about the war. Were you in England then?"

"Oh. No, I wasn't. I left in 1938. After my parents died. I went to live with Constance then."

"Do you go back? Have you been back?"

"Where? To England?"

"Your home. England. Yes."

"Not to my home. We go to London sometimes. Not very often. Constance prefers Italy, and France."

"And you? What do you prefer?"

"I'm not sure. I like Venice. I love France. Usually we go to Nice, or Monte Carlo. But there was a place we stayed one year, a very small place, a fishing village near Toulon. Constance took a house there. I liked that best. I used to go to the open-air markets. Walk along the beach. Watch the fishermen. You could be alone there. I . . ."

"Yes?"

"Oh, it's not very interesting. It was just a place. We didn't stay there long. Constance found it dull, so—"

"Did you find it dull?"

"No, I didn't." I looked away. "Anyway. We left. We went on to Germany. I wanted to go there, and Constance knew that, so—"

"Germany?" This seemed to interest him. "Why should you want to go there?"

"Oh. My parents' death. The accident—I'm sure Rosa must have told you about that—"

"Yes." He hesitated. "I believe she did."

"It was never explained, you see. What happened. I used to think, in Berlin, somewhere, there must be records of some kind. I might be able to find out . . . how the accident happened. No, not that. *Why* it happened . . ."

"And you didn't?"

The gentleness of his tone surprised me. I had never spoken of that grim journey before, to anyone—and I regretted doing so now. Sympathy brought me closer to tears than indifference would ever have done. I looked quickly away.

"No. I didn't," I continued in a brisker voice. "The records had gone—if there ever were any. So that was that. It was foolish to have gone, in any case. Constance warned me, and I should have listened to her. The records were irrelevant. It's just that I felt—" I stopped. I said, in a bright polite voice: "Have you ever been there? Have you visited Germany?"

There was a silence. His face hardened.

"Have I visited Germany? No."

He drew back from me as he said this. His voice was curt. A moment before, his hand had been lying on the table, very close to my own. A few inches between them, only. Then, abruptly, the hand was withdrawn, and his attention as well. He began to look about for the waiter. I had obviously offended him in some way. Foolishly, I attempted to make amends.

"I just thought—perhaps you might have gone there. Since the war. With Rosa, or with your father. I know Rosa once said—"

"Hardly. You know my father was Jewish. If you think about it, I'm sure you can see: jaunts to postwar Germany were not too high on his list."

I blushed scarlet. Frank Gerhard rose and paid the bill. He gave no sign of repenting this reprimand, or the harsh way in which it was made. Indeed, he seemed anxious to be rid of my company as soon as he decently could. We left the restaurant and set off at a fast pace. I said I would rejoin Constance's party; he said he would return to his hotel. There was a river-bus landing stage near Harry's Bar; he would walk back with me as far as there. This he insisted upon; miserable, confused, I had no heart to argue. We walked along in silence. At the end of the street that led down to the bar, he stopped.

In the distance, with their backs to us, I could see the figures of

Constance and her acolytes. Conrad Vickers was talking and gesturing; Constance laughed; the Van Dynem twins, decorative and indolent, lolled against a wall. Rosa was not with them. As we stood there, waiting for the *vaporetto* to arrive, fragments of Conrad Vickers's conversation drifted to us on the air.

It was at once horribly apparent that he was discussing Rosa.

". . . thirteenth house," we heard. "Tell me, dah-ling, how can you *endure* it? That dress! Like a big red mailbox. An ambulatory mailbox. Terrifying! I thought you said she was a widow? She *can't* be a widow. Is she a *merry* widow—is that it?"

I tried to edge us both out of earshot, but it was obvious that Frank Gerhard had heard the comments on his mother. He turned away, walked a few paces, then swung back, his face stiff.

"Shall I tell you why she wore that dress? That red dress?" His voice was tight with anger. "Today happens to be her wedding anniversary. Red was Max's favorite color. So today she wore a red dress—"

"I understand. Please—"

"You do?"

"Of course."

"Are you sure?" The sarcasm was now undisguised. "After all, that man is your *friend*, isn't he? Conrad Vickers. The Van Dynem twins. Your constant traveling companions. Your close friends—"

"I travel with them sometimes, yes. They're really Constance's friends. That is—"

"Bobsy van Dynem—he is your godmother's friend?" The word *friend* was said scathingly. I was not sure whether my godmother's relationship with Bobsy was being queried, or my own.

"Well, not exactly. He's my friend too. And I've known Conrad since I was a child. I know he sounds affected, but—"

"Affected? Oh, yes. Also malicious."

"He is a fine photographer. Frank—"

I stopped. I acknowledged to myself (and for the first time) that Vickers—whose praises Constance was always singing—was a man I disliked very much. I could have said so, but I did not. To dissociate myself from Vickers might be tempting, but it was cheap. Besides, I could see it was pointless. By their friends ye shall know them: It was clear from Frank Gerhard's expression that as far as he was concerned, Conrad Vickers and I were tarred with the same brush.

He was staring back down the street, one hand clenched, a dark flush of anger on his cheeks. For a moment I was afraid he was going to walk back, confront Vickers, possibly even strike him. Then, with a look of loathing and an angry shrug, he turned aside. The *vaporetto* approached.

I know now that his reaction was far more complex than I understood, that jealousy was involved, and that not all of his anger was directed against Vickers. I did not know it then. Already confused and distressed, feeling I was losing something that mattered to me but which I could not define, I started forward. I said his name. I think I held out my hand. The motorboat drew alongside. Frank Gerhard turned back.

"How old are you?" he said.

When I replied that I was twenty-five, he made no comment. He did not need to; I knew what he thought. At twenty-five, I was more than old enough to exercise my own judgment.

Grow up: he might just as well have said the words. He said a chilly but polite "Goodbye," instead. I could have told him then (and some years later, I did): I was trying. But it was difficult to grow up, hard to break free. Constance had loved me as a child; Constance liked me to remain . . . a child. Even physically—and that had long been absurd.

"Stop *growing*," she would say to me as, in my teens, I mounted to that five feet ten inches at which I would (mercifully) stop.

"Don't grow so *fast*," she would cry, half-mocking, half-serious—and I, desperate to retain her affection, would have stopped if I could.

"Oh, you make me feel a *dwarf*," she would complain. "It's horrid. I hate it. I shall never catch up."

"You're so tall for your age."

It was one of the first things she ever said to me, the day I arrived in New York. My first day with my godmother. My first day in a new world. I was quick to be enchanted.

We were standing in that hall of mirrors, looking at our reflections, while Jenna waited silently to one side. I had been on an ocean liner for several days. I had just been in an elevator for the first time. I still felt in motion; beneath my feet, the carpet was waves.

"How many Victorias can you see?" my new godmother said. She smiled. "How many Constances?"

I counted six. I re-counted and found eight. Constance shook her head. She said we were infinite. "How tall you are for your age," she said. I looked at our reflections. Aged eight, I already reached almost to my godmother's shoulder. She was very perfect and very tiny. I wondered why my height should be a cause for regret.

She had sounded regretful. She took me by the hand; she led me through the hall into a very large drawing room. From its windows I could see the tops of trees. I thought: *We are in an aerie.* The floor of the aerie rippled.

"You must meet Mattie," Constance said, and Mattie, wearing a white uniform and white shoes, came forward. She was the first black woman I had ever met. There had been no black people in Wiltshire in 1938. There had been none in first class aboard ship. I stared hard at Mattie's skin. There was a purplish hue to this blackness, like the skin of a hothouse grape. Her cheeks were round and taut; they looked polished. She was enormously fat. When she smiled, her teeth were whiter than white. The room hefted me about.

"Like as two peas in a pod," said Mattie mysteriously. "Just like you said."

She gestured as she spoke. There, on the table next to her, was a photograph of my father. I knew this photograph; the very same one always stood on my mother's desk. There was my father, in some long-ago time: He looked careless; a croquet mallet swung in his hand. I stared at this photograph. I thought about my father, and my mother, whom I had left behind at Winterscombe; who were dead.

A large black bear came into the room; he licked my hand. This was Constance's latest dog, a Newfoundland of profound gentleness. This was Bertie.

Three thousand miles. I was still traveling. I felt the air lift me up and propel me toward something very obvious, but something I had had to travel across an ocean to discover. There I was, eight years old, tall and skinny, with bones that stuck out. I had a high bridge to a thin nose. My muddy-green eyes did not quite match, one being greener than the other. Three thousand miles, and I could see a new Victoria. There she was, receding into a tricksy infinitude, a girl who looked exactly like her father.

I began to cry. I had promised myself I would not do this, but once I began I could not stop. I wanted my father back; I wanted my mother back; I wanted summer and Winterscombe and my friend Franz-Jacob. I said so. Once I started talking I could not stop that either. Out it all came, on a tide of misery too long suppressed: my parents' death, my own terrible guilt, the boast to Charlotte, the prayers morning and night, the enormity of penny candles lit every Sunday to speed a wicked prayer to heaven.

They were all very kind, but my strange godmother was the kindest of all. She put me to bed, in a room so luxurious it made me weep again, for the plainness of Winterscombe. My godmother sat down. She took my hand. She made no attempt to be soothing, and because of that, the tears finally stopped.

"I am an orphan, too," she said. "Like you, Victoria. I was ten when my father died. It was an accident, a very sudden thing—and I blamed myself, just as you do. People always do that when someone dies—you'll understand that when you're older. We always think: but I could have done that, I could have said this. You would still feel like that, even if you had never made up those stories, never said those prayers." She paused. "Do you believe in God, Victoria? I don't—but do you?"

I hesitated. No one had ever asked me this before. Belief was assumed at Winterscombe.

"I think so," I said at last, in a cautious way.

"Well, then." Constance's face became sad, so I thought it must make her unhappy to be an atheist. "If you believe in God, and He's a good God, you can't believe He would play a trick like that, can you?"

"Even if He wanted to punish me—for telling a lie, to Charlotte?" I looked at her anxiously.

"Certainly not. He would make the punishment fit the crime, don't you think?"

"I suppose so."

"I know He would." She looked down. She pleated the sheet between her fingers. She looked up. "It was a very little crime, Victoria, I promise you that. Why, it was so small—a speck of a crime! He has much bigger ones to worry about. Imagine—He has to think about killing and theft and war and hate. Really big things. All the monsters! You told a little lie, out of a great deal of love. He would never punish you for that."

"Are you sure?"

"I am totally, three hundred percent, absolutely sure. I give you my word on it." She smiled. She bent forward and kissed me. She stroked my forehead with a small hand crammed with pretty little rings.

I believed her. I felt a sudden certainty that she saw into the mind of God, this strange godmother of mine. If she said this, if she gave me her word, it was true. The relief was very great; the loss was still there, but the guilt lessened.

Constance seemed to know this—perhaps she could read my mind, too—for she smiled again and held out her hand, palm upward.

"There. It's almost gone, hasn't it, all that guilt? Is there any left? Just a bit? Right, give it to me. That's it, put it there in my hand—all of it now! Good. Oh, it likes it here—I can feel. It's tickling my palm. It's running up my arm. It's joining up with all the other guilts—it has lots of friends, you see? There!" She gave a wriggle. "It's in my heart now. That's where guilt likes to live, you know. It's settling down nicely. You don't need to worry. It will never come back to you."

"Is that where guilt lives—in the heart?"

"Definitely. It skips about sometimes, and people think: *Oh, I have palpitations!* It isn't, of course. It's just the guilts, limbering up."

"And you have lots of them already?"

"Lots and lots. I'm grown up."

"Will I have them again—when I'm grown up?"

"Some perhaps. And regrets, too—they can be nasty. We'll make a pact, shall we? If you feel them creeping up on you, give them to me. Really. I don't mind. I'm used to them."

"I might go to sleep now."

"I thought you might. Did you sleep on the ship? I never could. I don't like ships. And the sea—all that sea. The sea is horrid."

"Shall I call you 'Aunt'? I thought I might."

"Aunt?" Constance made a funny face. She wrinkled up her nose. "No, I don't think I would like that at all. *Aunt* sounds very old. It smells of mothballs. Besides, I'm not your aunt, and Godmother is a terrible mouthful. Do you think you could call me Constance?"

"Just that?"

"Just that. Try it out. Say 'Goodnight, Constance,' and see how it feels. Actually, it's the middle of the morning, but we shan't mind that."

"Goodnight . . . Constance," I said.

Constance kissed me once more. I closed my eyes and felt her lips brush my forehead. She stood up. She seemed reluctant to leave me. I opened my eyes again. She looked both sad and happy.

"I'm so glad you're here." She hesitated. "I'm sorry if we upset you. That photograph—it was very thoughtless. Did you not realize how like your father you are?"

"No. I never did."

"Do you know, when I first met him, he was thirteen years old, almost fourteen. He looked exactly as you do now. Exactly."

"Truly?"

"Well, he didn't have braids, of course." She smiled.

"I hate the braids. I've always hated them."

"Then we shall banish them," she said, to my great surprise.
"Unbraid them. Snip them off. Whatever you like."

"Could we do that?"

"Of course. We'll do it tomorrow if you want. You decide—
they're your braids! And now you must go to sleep. When you wake
up, Mattie will make you some pancakes. Do you like pancakes?"

"Very much."

"Good. I shall tell her to make a great stack. And look, while
you sleep, Bertie will guard over you. You see—here he is. He'll lie
down like a great rug at the end of your bed, and he'll snore. Will
you mind that?"

"No. I think I might like it."

"He dreams, you see. When he snores, and scrabbles his paws, it
means he's having his favorite dream. He dreams about Newfoundland,
you know, and swimming in the sea there. He loves to swim. He has
webbed feet. He swims in his dreams, and he sees . . . oh, such
marvelous things. Great caverns of ice, and polar bears and seals and
walruses. Green icebergs, as tall as Everest. And sea birds—he sees
those, too, when he dreams. . . ."

I was not sure when she left, not sure when she stopped
speaking. The words became Bertie's snores, and the snores the
yelp of gulls. The room became very watery, and as I swam it,
I thought my godmother was astonishing. She could banish braids
without a second thought. She lived in an aerie. She gave me
my father back—there he was in my hair and my skin and my
eyes—and if he was so close, my mother must be there, too,
just behind him, just to one side, where the seas began, in the
elevators.

I slept for a long time: hours and hours of the morning and
afternoon. When I woke I ate five pancakes; Mattie introduced me
to maple syrup. I sat at the kitchen table and Mattie told me her life
story. She had run away from home when she was twelve years old
and had many adventures. Mattie had once sung with a dance band,
washed sheets in a Chinese laundry, learned to pick pockets, and
scrubbed floors in Chicago.

"Can you still pick pockets?"

"Sure can. Nothin' to it," Mattie said, and demonstrated.

The next day my godmother kept her promise. The braids were
unwound. It was a great ceremony. I stood on a sheet in the middle
of the drawing room. Mattie encouraged. Jenna watched.

Snip, snip, snip: Constance cut my hair herself with a pair of silver scissors. She cut it to a more manageable length, so it just touched my shoulders.

"Now! See how pretty you look," Constance cried when it was over. I stared in the glass. Not pretty—I would never be that—but a definite improvement. Even Jenna said so. Then Jenna frowned, and I thought perhaps she was upset, that she thought it too soon to make changes. I looked back at Constance uncertainly. She was an orphan, like me. When guilt sat in the palm of her hand, it tickled. She owned a dog with webbed feet who dreamed of icebergs. She was very small and very beautiful.

Snip, snip snip: hanks of red hair on a sheet, a sheet laid out on a flowery carpet. I did not care if it was too soon. I needed someone to love, and I loved Constance there and then. I loved her the way an orphan does, which she would understand: at once, unreservedly.

I think Constance knew. She did not say a word. She held out her arms to me. I ran into her arms and she hugged me tight. When I looked into her face it shone at me.

I thought then that she looked so happy because she loved me too. I still think, even now, that that might have been true. On the other hand (reluctantly, with an adult's hindsight) I can see something else. Constance liked to make conquests. Maybe I was loved; maybe I was a pushover. I still do not know.

This is what we did, every afternoon I remember. At three o'clock, no matter how busy her schedule, Constance would return home. She and I would walk Bertie. We would sail down in the elevator, cross the avenue, walk up Fifth a way, and take Bertie to explore the smells of Central Park. We would walk into the entrance near the zoo, which sometimes we would visit, because Constance loved the animals, though she hated to see them locked up. With the bears and the marmosets, we would mourn their imprisonment, and then we would walk to the stream. Do you know that part of the park? There is an ornamental lake with a fountain. There is the bandshell not far away. Once Constance and I went there in January. There was snow. A white Manhattan circled the park. We were the only people.

Bertie liked the snow and he liked the New York winter. But he had a thick coat—a waterproof coat, with a thick, oily underfur—and he hated the heat of those wartime summers. They made him listless and miserable. To begin with, Constance and I used to persuade him into the kitchen, and sit him by the refrigerator with the door open. This was fine for Bertie, less good for the contents of the refrigera-

tor. The servants complained; Constance bought Bertie an air conditioner. This he liked very much. We would turn it on full power, and
Bertie would sit there, facing into the blast with his ears blowing.

The other expedition we often made—and went on making for
years and years, until I was well into my teens—was to a pet shop
located on the corner of Sixty-second and Lexington. It was a smart
pet shop, catering to the smart clientele living nearby on Park Avenue, and many of the pets it sold were exotic. There were talking
parrots and angora rabbits; there were pythons who had to be anointed
every day with baby oil to prevent their skins' drying. There was
every description of dog—shaggy ones, smooth ones, large ones,
small ones. There were also cats and kittens.

Given the proximity of Park Avenue, these cats, too, were rare
of their kind. There were no ordinary tabbies or black-and-whites;
there were somnolent, aristocratic Persians, bluepoint Siamese,
Burmese; above all, there were Abyssinians. These cats I loved.
They were elegant and restrained; they surveyed the world from
their cages with a disdainful air; their fur blended caramel with
black. They were the cats of Egyptian tombs, though I did not know
that then. All I knew was that I wanted one.

I wanted one the more, I think, because I knew it was an
impossibility. The only pet animals Constance disliked were cats.
When we went to the pet shop she avoided their cages; nothing
would have persuaded her to stroke one. "No cats for us," she would
say. "And besides, we have Bertie."

It was on our return from one of these visits to the pet shop that
I first asked Constance about her other dogs, Bertie's predecessors.
We were turning west toward Fifth. Constance smiled. We swung
along at a brisk pace.

"Heavens! Well, the very first was called Floss. Your uncle
Francis gave him to me. He was the prettiest dog, brown and black
and white, with a tail like a feather. Then there was Box—someone
else gave me him. He was white, fluffy, very obedient. He came with
me to live in New York, and he lived to be fifteen years old and
rather fat. Then, let me see . . . I had a Pekingese for a while, then
a pug—I loved my pug! Then, when he died, I decided to change.
All my dogs had been little dogs, you see. I thought I would go to
the opposite extreme. I met Bertie."

"Why did you want to change—from such little dogs to such a
large one?"

"I just did. Let me see . . . Bertie is six. I was changing. I do
that every so often. I change quite radically. I slough off my old skin

and grow a new one, like those snakes at the shop. Yes, that was it. I changed, and I bought Bertie to celebrate. It was the right decision. Bertie is noble. And very wise. But you know that."

"Do you love him very much, Constance?"

"Yes, I do. I think I love him the best of all. If he died—and big dogs don't live so long, you know, as little ones—well, I don't want to think how horrible it would be. Bertie will be my last dog. I owe it to him. I've decided."

"Truly, Constance?" I was very impressed. "Your last dog? You wouldn't have another?"

"Faithful unto death." Constance checked her stride. "Yes. Bertie is my better self. I make a solemn oath, right here, on Sixty-second. I swear it."

"Of course, you did love the others, too," I said as we turned onto Fifth. "Floss especially. He was the first, and—"

I was about to add that Uncle Freddie had told me the sad story of Floss's death, and how ill Constance had been with grief afterward.

"Oh, Floss, yes," Constance said, interrupting. "He caught tetanus, you know. It was terrible. He died at Winterscombe."

I knew what tetanus was—one of my father's horses had died of it. Tetanus was not the same as being trampled in Hyde Park, but I did not like to say so. I was brought up to be reticent; reticence was polite.

We entered our apartment building. The elevator bore us up. Constance had just told me the first of her lies, but I did not know that. I thought that my uncle Freddie, who could be vague, had been wrong.

It was 1939, shortly after the declaration of war. I was beginning the second stage of my childhood, which would end, as you will see, with the 1945 armistice. *Tetanus*, I said to myself—and I kissed Bertie, who came bounding up.

Every day during those war years I wrote letters. Letters kept me in touch.

Once Jenna returned to England, I was often alone, left with Mattie or one of the other servants, or with what became a series of governesses; Constance would be at work, or would be making one of her brief impetuous visits to friends out of state, and I would stay behind in that aerie of an apartment, sometimes doing lessons, more often reading or writing letters with Bertie lying at my feet.

I wrote long blotchy epistles: I wrote to Great-Aunt Maud, to my uncles, to my godfather Wexton, to Jenna; twice a week, without fail, I wrote to my friend Franz-Jacob.

My family were generous: I received bulky, regular replies. Every morning Constance would bring my letters in and lay them beside my breakfast plate, like a present. Every afternoon, on our way out to walk Bertie, we would mail my letters in the smart brass box in the lobby. It was from these letters that I learned the most about the war.

Aunt Maud, still too ill to write herself, dictating to a newly hired secretary, told me about dogfights over London, barrage balloons in Hyde Park, and the (very rude) things she would have said to Von Ribbentrop, had she the opportunity. Steenie wrote from Conrad Vickers's new villa on Capri, then from Switzerland, where he remained ("a cheerful coward," he said) for the duration of the war. Uncle Freddie told me about enrolling in the Fire Service, and writing his detective novels during the Blitz. Wexton, whose work was of a more secretive nature (involving coding and decoding, I think), stuck to uncontroversial subjects: He wrote a lot about rationing.

"He's a spy," Constance said, reading one of these letters. I could tell, even then, she disliked Wexton.

Jenna, who had been left some money by my parents, had gone to work as a housekeeper for a retired clergyman in the North of England. Her husband had not gone with her—but this did not surprise me. Even at Winterscombe they never spoke; I used to forget they were ever married.

Constance, when I once mentioned this, was brisk.

"Jack Hennessy?" she said. "That horrible man? She's well rid of him. He was a bully and he drank. He hit her, you know, once too hard and once too often! He gave her a black eye. You had just been born—that was when Jenna moved back into the house." She frowned. "Your mother kept Hennessy on. I can't think why. I suppose she felt sorry for him."

I was writing a reply to Jenna when she said this. I dropped my pen in astonishment. It was a good ten minutes before I was calm enough to continue. Hennessy the boiler-stoker was a bully. He drank. My Jenna had once had a black eye. Men could hit women. A whole world tilted on its axis, wobbled and realigned. I passed on this riveting discovery about Jenna and her husband to my aunt Maud in my very next letter. Her response was immediate.

"No, I did *not* know about Jenna," Maud wrote. "And had I known, it would not have been discussed. I *abhor* gossip! Such matters, Victoria, are *beyond the pale*. They are not part of *polite*

588 · SALLY BEAUMAN

conversation. And, since their source was your godmother, they are to be taken with a *large pinch of salt*! Your godmother was always *most* inventive with her stories. . . ."

Fond though I was of Aunt Maud, I did not believe her. She was an avid gossip, for one thing—so that part of her letter was untrue. I dismissed the rest. I liked, and believed, Constance's stories.

Constance, by then, had become my ally. In many ways she used to behave as if she and I were the same age, two children ganging up in a conspiracy against those spoilsports, the grown-ups. "Now," she would say, "I'm going to park you at the office with Prudie. She is all bark and no bite—don't let her boss you." Or she would return to the apartment, where one of the ill-starred, short-stay governesses would be attempting to teach me.

"Lessons over for the day," Constance would cry, and whisk me away for lunch in a grand restaurant or a drive into the country to a house she was decorating. She was firmly against schools, dismissive of learning, snapped her fingers to all imposed discipline. One of the better governesses, a stern Bostonian who made me quake, was dismissed for the large wart on her chin. Another, a tutor, male this time, young and good-looking, seemed greatly in favor and looked set to endure—but he, too, was fired in due course, although I liked him.

That dismissal caused an angry scene. From the other end of the apartment I heard raised voices, then the slam of a door. Constance shrugged off the reasons for his dismissal: She said she didn't like his taste in neckties; she said he was unimaginative; she said he was a bore.

Constance and I against the diktats of the rest of the world, the adult, responsible, dreary world—that was the scenario. What child would choose Latin verbs when the alternative was blinis and caviar at the Russian Tea Room? Where was the point in struggling with that detested algebra, when I could go with Constance to the Aladdin's cave of her Fifty-seventh Street showrooms? Constance dazzled me with her anarchy.

But she was also my ally in a different way—a way that increased my enchantment. Although Constance would sometimes behave as if she were my age and we were children together, she could also behave as if I were her age and we were both adults. From the very first, when I joined her at work she consulted me—and she appeared to listen to my opinions. "Which yellow, do you think?" she would say, holding up two pieces of material. I would select one, on blind instinct, and Constance would nod approvingly.

"Good," she would say. "You have an eye. Good."

I had never been greatly praised before for any aptitude, and I was flattered. I was also flattered that when I confided in Constance, she always listened. If I asked a question, she gave a direct answer, as if I were not a child but a woman.

My aunt Maud did not seem to like her? That was easily understandable: My aunt Maud had once been in love with the man who became Constance's husband. What was his name? Why, Montague Stern. Where was he now? They never saw each other, but Constance believed he lived alone, in Connecticut. Why had they parted? Because he had wanted children and Constance could not have them. Had she prayed for one? Yes, she had, in her own way: She had willed herself one—and here that child was now with her godmother.

At the time, these explanations were only half understood. Even so, I accepted them. They reassured me. They told me I was wanted.

Since Constance told me so much, I told her much in return. I opened my heart to her. Within a very short time of my arriving in New York, I told her one of my most important stories. I explained about my great friend Franz-Jacob—and it was in this respect, the search for Franz, that Constance became, above all, my ally.

Franz-Jacob, as you know, never wrote to me. At first, as the weeks went by, I blamed the mails. I was writing to the orphanage my mother had helped to fund; I began to believe it was not the fault of the mails, that I must have the wrong address. But even if my letters did not reach him, that still did not explain Franz-Jacob's silence. How could he promise—and then not write?

Distance is of no object between the hearts of friends. I would think of the ship, and the quay, Franz-Jacob's gold box of Viennese chocolates. I still kept that box! I began to be afraid. I thought: Franz-Jacob is ill.

Constance was very kind about this. I had already told her the story of Franz many times. She never became impatient when I told it again. I told her about his ability at mathematics, about his sad European eyes, about his family. I told her about that strange and terrible day when Franz-Jacob, with his magical powers, had smelled blood, and war, in a wood.

I described the way we had stood, pale and shivering in the clearing, listening to the greyhounds crash through the undergrowth. And Constance, listening to this story, would become pale too.

"That place," she said, the first time I told her. She put her arms around me. "Oh, Victoria. We must find him."

It became our joint campaign. I badgered Freddie and Aunt Maud to intercede, to question the orphanage. When these efforts produced no conclusive news, Constance telephoned the orphanage authorities herself. It was a fiery conversation, followed by an even more fiery letter, concocted with Miss Marpruder at the office. Constance and Prudie between them composed such imperious paragraphs, such insolent reproaches, such an assault on the inadequacies of bureaucracies, that at last we made a breakthrough.

We were passed on to another organization, in London, that dealt with evacuees. For several weeks we were buoyed up in the belief that Franz-Jacob had been moved, as so many children were, to the countryside, away from the bombing. Then came the news: Franz-Jacob was not an evacuee. Two months before the declaration of war, at his parents' request, he had returned to Germany.

I remember Constance's face as she showed me the letter, the quiet and gentle way in which she spoke. I was nine by then; all I understood was that if Franz-Jacob had returned home, it was dangerous. Very dangerous: I could tell that from the sadness in Constance's eyes, from her refusal—for once—to be frank. I knew what that expression meant on an adult's face; I had seen it before. It meant there was something bad here from which I had to be shielded. I became, for the first time, truly afraid.

Constance shielded me—but she could not shield me forever. Certain facts became inescapable. Eight when the war began, I was fourteen when the war finally ended. Franz-Jacob was a Jew.

I knew then why he never wrote. I knew what had happened to Jews in his homeland.

I mailed my last letter to him on V-E day. I had continued to write, into a void, throughout the war years, and Constance, who must have known those letters would never be read, understood and respected my need. When that last letter had dropped into its box, her eyes filled with tears.

It was I who comforted her. I said, "It's all right, Constance. It's the last letter. I understand now. I know he's dead."

A stupid English girl: *ein dummes englische Mädchen*. It had taken six years for me to catch up with him, six years to understand that on a hot prewar afternoon, in the woods at Winterscombe, it was his own death Franz-Jacob had sensed.

A coded message, six years later understood: one last flash of Morse. I wished I had been quicker. I wished I had understood then, but at least I understood now.

The understanding, I felt, was our final pact. Across loss, and death, I clasped hands with Franz-Jacob. Distance—even that last distance—was of no object between the hearts of friends. *Dear Franz,* I wrote solemnly in that last letter, *I shall always remember you. I shall think of you every day for the rest of my life.*

Oddly enough (fifteen-year-old girls may be sincere, but their most heartfelt promises get forgotten in the rush of life) I kept my word to Franz-Jacob. I never forgot him, nor that private promise to a lost boy.

But it was a *private* promise. I did not tell Constance, then or later. I kept it to myself.

It was because of Franz, I think, that I first took an interest in Rosa Gerhard, also of German parentage, also—by conversion—a Jew. In such ways, perhaps, the dead continue to influence the lives of those who survive them.

I first heard Rosa's name when I was twelve or thirteen years old and the war was continuing.

That day I had been whisked away by Constance from the man who would prove to be the last of my teachers. This man, a lugubrious White Russian émigré, down on his luck in New York, was one of Constance's lame-dog friends. Constance made a specialty of relics, and her weekly parties were always leavened by imperious, impecunious aristocrats whose influence was long extinct: Serbian grand dukes, now on their uppers; impoverished marchesas; the Gräfin von this, the Duquesa de that. History stalked Constance's parties; you could hear its anguish in the anteroom.

The Russian who tutored me was named Igor; his nature was indolent, his technique hit-or-miss. In a burst of enthusiasm, his first week, he taught me many vital things: how to distinguish sevruga from beluga, how to curtsey when I met a Russian grand duchess. I learned the name of the headwaiter in the best prerevolutionary restaurant in Moscow (a restaurant blown up some fifteen years before). I learned that Igor loathed the Bolsheviks.

This was a first burst; by the second week (I could tell) Igor was losing interest. Occasionally, rousing himself from his ruminative melancholy, he would read to me in Russian. When he realized I did not understand a word, Igor was mortally offended; he considered it bad manners, I think. He switched to French, winced at my plodding replies, and gave up. He suggested, with a wave of languid exasperation, that I should read.

Read I did; that was how we passed our lessons. I, liking to read anyway, would sit with Bertie in a corner with a book; Igor, liking to dream, would sit in another, sipping vodka. This arrangement suited us both. There was only one problem: Constance's apartment, so opulent in every other respect, was not well endowed with books.

"You're like your father, you see," Constance said one day. "Acland was always reading, reading. Victoria, what happened to all his books? They are yours now. Think of that library, at Winterscombe—"

"I imagine they were packed up, Constance," I said. "When the army moved in. Daddy's books, and Mummy's. My grandparents' books too. They'll be in the attics, I expect."

"I shall send for them!" Constance was roused. "Prudie shall write to those doddering trustees. I shall insist!"

The books took months to arrive by sea mail, and during those months Constance made a shrine for them. Her apartment was large; one room was made over for a library. Constance designed the room herself, right down to the smallest detail. I was not allowed to look.

The day came for the unveiling. Igor, Bertie, and I were proudly led to a resplendent room. All four walls, floor to ceiling, were lined with books.

I was very touched that Constance should go to such trouble, such expense. Even Igor pronounced himself impressed. We walked from shelf to shelf. Igor patted the Shakespeares. I stroked the long flank of Sir Walter Scott. Then, gradually, I began to realize something odd. The arrangement of titles was careful, yet their disposition strange. All my mother's books were on the right of the room, all my father's on the left. The same authors had been divided: A literary apartheid had been imposed.

I made no comment. I did not want to offend Constance. Igor, whose sense of self-preservation was strong, said nothing either. Constance left us. Books to the right of me, books to the left of me: my lesson began.

It was in this curious room that I worked every day—if to read novels can be described as work—and it was from this curious room that Constance whisked me away on the day I first heard of Rosa Gerhard.

That day, I was reading *Persuasion;* I might have liked to go on reading *Persuasion,* but Constance's demands, however capricious, were always obeyed. I was ferried down to Constance's showrooms on Fifty-seventh Street. I was consulted on the color of a piece of silk, and then forgotten. This happened. Every so often Miss Marpruder would look up; she would jangle her beads, give me a wink, a jaunty wave. Telephones shrilled, Constance prowled: I liked being there, to watch, to learn, to listen.

The assistant nearest me, an elegant, impressive woman, was the one who took Rosa Gerhard's call.

"Oh," she said, "Mrs. Gerhard." And a silence fell.

Everyone stopped to eavesdrop. Glances were exchanged. The assistant, I noticed, held the receiver some three inches from her ear. Her part of the conversation was minimal. Squawks and wails issued from the earpiece. When the receiver was at last replaced, Constance counted out loud—to ten.

"Don't tell me," she said. "The yellow bedroom?"

"No, Miss Shawcross. Worse. She's *moving.* She's bought another house."

The assistant lit a cigarette as she said this. She inserted it in a holder. Her hand shook as she did so. Rosa Gerhard, I was to learn, affected people like this.

"Is that the seventh?"

"No, Miss Shawcross. The eighth." She shuddered. "I could *try* to get rid of her."

"Get rid of her? You *can't* get rid of her. Rosa Gerhard is a fact of life. You might as well try and put a hurricane in a Hoover. *I* will deal with her."

"Shall I get her on the line, Miss Shawcross? She said—"

"I think you'll find that won't be necessary." Constance gave a tight smile. "Wait. About another twenty seconds, I should say."

We waited. Twenty seconds ticked by; a secretary gave a nervous laugh. Thirty seconds passed; a telephone shrilled. Constance picked it up. She held it at arm's length. A shriek could be heard.

"Ah, *Rosa* . . ." Constance said, when a minute had passed. "It is you? How *lovely* to hear from you at last . . ."

Rosa Gerhard was like Thanksgiving: She came 'round once a year. Rosa was in pursuit of the perfect house; she found it, every year. I could have ticked off the years of my childhood, house by house: 1942, 1943, 1944. Rosa was on her eighth, her ninth, her tenth perfect environment. When she reached the tenth, I remember, we opened a case of champagne.

I thought Mrs. Gerhard was a mystery. I thought there were a number of mysteries in Constance's life, and—unlike Mrs. Gerhard—not all of them concerned her professional life. If Rosa Gerhard was so impossible, why didn't Constance simply refuse to work with her? Why did she not steer her toward another decorator—the famous

Sister Parish, for instance? I said this, one day, to Miss Marpruder, who had taken me home to her apartment. I lived in hope that Prudie would one day *explain.* I used to look forward to these visits to Prudie's home, as—years before—I looked forward at Winterscombe to my uncle Steenie's visits. Any minute now, I would think, and there will be a revelation.

Now, Prudie gave a sigh. She fiddled with the telephone. She adjusted its lace mat.

"I think she amuses your godmother, honey. I think that's it."

"But Mrs. Gerhard makes her mad, Prudie. And every time she gets mad at her, she says she'll never speak to her again. And then she does."

"It's just her way, honey."

That was what Prudie always said. Constance's "ways" explained everything. They explained her moods, which could be unpredictable. They explained her (often sudden) absences. I thought this was inadequate. When Constance took off (she had just done so; she had been away two days) I would think to myself: *why?*

"Prudie," I said in a careful way, "have you heard of the Heavenly Twins?"

I knew she had; everyone had heard of the Heavenly Twins. Their exploits were in the gossip columns every day. Their real names were Robert and Richard van Dymen, but—as you know— they were always referred to as Bobsy and Bick. Bobsy and Bick were, as we might say now, *seriously* rich. They were heirs to an unassailable East Coast fortune, but (and this is a tribute to their looks) they were even more famous for their beauty than their wealth. Bobsy and Bick would later come to sad ends: Bobsy killed in a sports car in the late 1950s, Bick studiously drinking himself to death not long afterward. But that was later. In 1944, Bobsy and Bick were twenty, two blond-haired young gods in the full flush of a golden youth. They were not, perhaps, particularly intelligent, but they were immensely good-natured. They had always, both of them, been very kind to me, as had their father and their uncle, also twins, also fixtures at Constance's frequent parties.

"Sure. I've heard of them," Prudie replied, still fiddling with the lace mat.

"Does Constance *stay* with Bobsy and Bick, sometimes?" I asked. "Is she with them *now*, Prudie?"

This put Prudie on the spot. She always knew where Constance could be reached, and she knew I knew that.

"What—their place out on the Island?" Prudie shrugged. "Why should she? She has her own place."

"Yes, but Constance isn't *there*, Prudie. She said she would be, but she isn't. I tried to phone her, Prudie, last night."

"You shouldn't do that." Prudie became red. "She doesn't like it. You know that." She paused. She rearranged some cushions. "She must have been out," she went on. "At a party. Dinner someplace."

It was possible. I wondered if I should tell Prudie that, if so, the party had gone on very late. I had rung Constance's East Hampton house at three, then again at four. She had not been back. I decided not to say this.

"Why Bobsy and Bick?" Prudie said in a sudden way. "Why hit on them? There's hundreds of places she might be—why them?"

"Something I heard Bobsy say to Constance once. They arranged to meet. Then, the next day, Constance never mentioned him. Or Bick. She said she went somewhere else."

"Changed her plans, I expect." Prudie became arch. "*And* it's none of your business, little Miss Pry."

"I know, Prudie. And I didn't mean to pry. But I would like to know—sometimes. . . ."

Prudie's face softened.

"Look," she said, "your godmother likes to get about. You know that. I know that. She can't travel so much—not with the war. But she likes . . . to see people. To have a good time."

"Prudie," I said, in a rush. "Prudie—did you ever meet her husband? Did you ever know Montague Stern?"

"No," said Prudie in a gruff voice. "I did not."

"Do you think she loved him, Prudie? Do you think he loved her?"

"Who knows?" Prudie turned away. "But I know one thing. It's none of my business. Or yours."

That was it, a brick wall. We hit it that day; we hit it others. I thought Prudie knew a great deal more than she said. I thought Prudie knew about Montague Stern, *and* Bobsy and Bick—and she did not intend to explain to me. I thought she knew the reasons for the absences. I thought she could explain the other things—the flowers that would arrive for Constance at the apartment whose cards would be torn up; the telephone calls curtailed if I came into the room; the way (observed at parties) in which Constance became friends with certain men very fast. Prudie could explain why Constance's face changed when she spoke of her estranged husband. Prudie could explain why my father's books were at one end of a room, my mother's another. Prudie could explain, I thought, about *love*. I knew love was involved in all this, lurking there in the margins. I recognized the signs, and the hints; I'd seen them—in novels.

But Prudie would not explain—and neither, I was beginning to see, would Constance.

"Love?" Constance would toss her head. "I don't believe in love, not between a man and a woman. Just attraction, and a lot of self-interest." Then she might kiss me or give me a hug. "I love you, of course," she would say. "I love you very much. But that's different."

I was too young to be told about love, it seemed, at thirteen. I could read and imagine and dream (which I did), but I could not ask questions. Questions about her past marriage, her absences, and love—all these could make Constance irritable. So (I was obedient) I stopped. But I did continue to ask questions about some of Constance's more intriguing clients, including Rosa Gerhard.

"What is she *really* like?" I asked Constance one day. (It was the spring of 1945. I was fourteen. My last letter to Franz-Jacob was still weeks away. We were walking in Central Park, with Bertie. Bertie, defying predictions as to his longevity, was eleven.)

"Well, let me see. She's rather grand by origin, and rather eccentric by nature. She was brought up a Catholic, converted when she married Max. She goes to the synagogue every week; she also goes to Mass. She sees no contradiction in that. That's the kind of woman she is."

"Is she still married to Max?"

Constance smiled. "Heavens, I forget. You know how she collects houses? Well, she collects husbands too. And children."

"Husbands?" I stopped. I had no idea then that I was being misled. "You mean she keeps getting divorced?"

"Goodness, no. I rather think they die. That's it—they keep dying on her. I'm sure Rosa loves them very much, but she wears them out. Do you know how a car sounds when it's done eighty thousand miles? That's how Rosa's husbands sound. The record-holder was Mr. Gerhard, I think. I believe he lasted a whole decade."

"And the children?"

"Ah, the children. Well, do you know, I don't think I've ever actually met any of them. They tend to flee. But they are numerous. Nine, ten, maybe a dozen? I know all about them, though. Rosa tells me. Let me see, there's the movie director, the senator, the mayor of New York, the attorney—he's moving fast. There's the daughter who just won a Pulitzer. Oh, and I forgot. The son with the Nobel Prize."

I stopped. We had just reached the stream.

"The mayor? A Nobel Prize?"

"Yes." Constance smiled. "Now, was it for physics or medicine? I forget. This was some years back. He was about thirteen at the time."

"You mean they aren't . . . all those things?"

"I mean Rosa is a mother. That is her profession. She is also an optimist. The most sublime optimist I ever met in my life."

"Do you like her, Constance?" I asked as we followed Bertie down the steps. Constance stopped.

"Funnily enough, I do. I don't know why, though. Rosa is the only woman I have ever met who can change her mind about a piece of material thirty times in thirty seconds. Not even I can do that. However, I do like her. She is a *force de nature*. She is also entirely without malice—and that, Victoria, is *extremely* rare."

We walked on. We paused by the lake. I forgot about Rosa Gerhard. I was not to encounter her firsthand for another five years, except very briefly at parties. That afternoon I had something else on my mind, something far more immediate than Mrs. Gerhard.

I was watching Bertie. He moved more slowly now. When he ran, he would sometimes cough. I wondered if Constance had noticed this too. I thought she had, for when we returned to the apartment she was unusually quiet.

She sat down with Bertie on a rug. She looked afraid. She told him she loved him. Then, stroking him, she began to tell him the stories she believed he liked. She whispered into his ear, about icebergs, seals, white gulls, and the cold seas of his Newfoundland.

The following summer, the summer of my fifteenth year, was a sad one, and a busy one. Those two facts were connected: I was sad because I had recognized the truth about Franz-Jacob, because my mind and heart teemed with all those questions about life and love which no one would answer. Both Constance and I were saddened by Bertie; we could see (though we denied it to each other) that he was weakening.

"*Work!*" Constance said. "We must work twice as hard, Victoria."

This was Constance's solution, always, to any form of unhappiness. Work, she taught me, was therapy.

So, that summer, the touchy, vodka-drinking Igor was given his notice, and all further pretense at education for me ended. Europe was still out of the question. ("You wait," Constance said. "After the war, we'll make such journeys.")

We decamped, as had become our practice, to Constance's East Hampton house, but once there, Constance refused to settle. She was in one of her jittery, restless states; not even the presence nearby of Bobsy and Bick could console her. *Work*, she cried, watching Bertie pant listlessly in a patch of shade—and so, work we did. It was that summer Constance truly initiated me into the mysteries of her art.

I already knew a little. I had listened to Constance talk. I had sat in the corner of those showrooms. I had been allowed to run errands and take messages. I had been consulted on the colors of snippets of silk. I was now allowed to prepare sample boards. I could already (Constance said I was quick) measure a room by eye, and I began to understand a little of proportion—but I was an acolyte, only. It was that summer, the last of the war, that Constance admitted me to the rites of the temple.

She had been commissioned, earlier that year, to redecorate an enormous and very beautiful house, with its own private beach, some ten miles from her own house at East Hampton. The owner was in California. Constance had won the commission against stiff competition. Having won it, her interest had flagged—as sometimes happened. Now, it revived. "The Hope House," Constance called it; she said if we worked hard enough there, there would be no room for sadness.

We went there every day, just the two of us. Constance owned a Mercedes coupé then, which she drove fast and dangerously. Every day Bertie would be installed on its inadequate rear seat, and off we would set. Constance wore dark glasses. Her bobbed hair, which I always thought of as Egyptian, would blow in the wind; Bertie's ears would flutter. Once we arrived, Bertie would be installed in the high, cool, stone-flagged hall, and Constance and I would set to work. Shape, light, color, proportion, form: Constance gave me a crash course. I thought the drawing room was beautiful; look at it again, Constance would insist, and I began to see: Its dimensions were imperfect.

"The doors—they're too tall, and they're not aligned," Constance said. "And the windows are the wrong style for the period. Do you see?"

Yes, I began to see. And some weeks later, when the workmen

arrived, I began to see more. I had known for a long time that I wanted to be a decorator. It was at Hope House that I started to become one.

I was learning the pile of velvet, the ductility of silk. Constance showed me color. She taught me that color, like truth, is not a fixed thing but a fluctuating one. Color changes—with lighting, with texture, with position. Take a piece of cloth; it is green, you say? A clear sharp green, like emeralds? Put it against white and perhaps it is—but try it against black; try it against plum, or cobalt, or apricot. You see? Its hue changes.

You want yellow? Which yellow do you have in mind? Lemon? Chrome? Ochre? Crocus? Saffron? Sulphur? Whichever you want, I can give it to you—but I can also make it shift, transmute. Do not trust your eyes—I was taught, that summer, how to trick them.

Constance also taught me about shape, proportion. She took the fixed; she gave it a new guise. All things were possible: Make a large cold room seem warm and intimate; make an enclosed space open out. Take a room that is badly built; raise, lower, divide, subdivide—any space can be transformed by the duplicity of decorators. Decorators bend space. Look, they say, at the ugly angles of this room; give me light, give me color, give me money—and I will give you symmetry. Out of angle and ill-proportion, I will give you Palladio, the restfulness of the perfect double-cube.

A summer in which I learned sorcery; a summer in which I learned disguise. Constance (that inventive storyteller) was a born decorator—she taught me patiently, and well.

We stayed at Hope House all summer. And it was there, on the long veranda overlooking the sea, in a house I have never revisited, that Constance gave me, at last, her version of what it was that had happened at my christening.

The account was unprovoked. I had asked no question. It came out of the warm stillness of a summer afternoon, a salt breeze from the ocean, and—perhaps—from the bracelet I was wearing that day on my arm. My snake bracelet; my christening present. It had arrived in New York at the same time as my parents' books. Constance liked me to wear it, even in daytime.

"Ah, Winterscombe," she said. She leaned across and touched my wrist. She looked at me with a sad regret.

"How lovely you are today. You're growing up. You'll be a woman soon. You'll leave me behind. You won't need me then, your little godmother."

Then, still with her small hand on my arm, and her eyes on the sea, she explained: why she had been banned from Winterscombe.

I was disappointed, I think. I read all those novels, as you know: I was beginning my father's favorite Walter Scott. No doubt I expected something very dramatic: some ancient feud, a mistaken identity, an illegitimate birth, a hidden love affair.

No such thing, it seemed. It was money.

"Money." Constance gave a little sigh. "It often is. You're old enough to know that now. I forget the details, but your parents borrowed; I fear my husband lent. He was a fine man, Victoria, in many ways—but it was not a good idea to be in his debt. There was a quarrel. A rift. Unforgivable things were said on both sides. I had a foot in both camps. It was sad, looking back. Your father was a brother to me. I loved him very much. I loved Montague, too, in my way. Ah, well, it was a long time ago. I miss Winterscombe though, sometimes, even now. Even here. It's growing late. Bertie is tired. Shall we go? We can call in at the Van Dymens' on the way back."

A few days after this, Constance and I returned to New York. Late September; the war had ended. I had written my last letter to Franz-Jacob. I thought about love, and how you might recognize it when it happened. I thought about kinds of love, and how—in different ways—you might love a friend or a brother or a husband.

I also thought about death. I had to; I had lost Franz-Jacob; within a month of the end of the war, in Europe I also lost my aunt Maud. She suffered her final stroke sitting upright in her chair in her once-famous drawing room. I would never see her again. Maud and I, it seemed, had said goodbye seven years before. Quick-smart, no more letters.

Sorrows *can* come in battalions: That was one of Constance's favorite misquotations—and that fall, they did. Bertie, too, began to die. You could see it happening. He did so slowly at first, running down like an old clock. Each day he walked less far, more slowly. He coughed when he walked. He became crotchety, then resigned, then sad. He was malodorous; I think he knew this.

We could not perk him up. Constance cooked him chicken, tiny pieces of his favorite fish. She tried to feed him from her hand, but Bertie would look at her heavily, with reproach in his eyes, then turn his great head away. I think he knew he was dying—animals do—and he wished to do so privately, with dignity. A wild animal, knowing it will die, finds a secret place, a hole, a gap under a hedge.

Bertie was in a New York apartment. He began to lie only in corners; he panted; we could see his heart beat.

Constance became frantic. She summoned vet after vet. She canceled all appointments. She gave no parties. Once it was clear that Bertie was fading, she would not leave his side.

One Tuesday—it was a Tuesday, and quite late—Bertie rose from his place in his corner. He stretched. He lifted his head and sniffed the air. Constance, with a cry of delight, sprang up. Bertie had turned to his air conditioner. He looked at it. His tail gave a wag.

Constance turned it on; a low setting. Bertie stood there, nose to an electrical breeze. His ears blew. Then, rejecting the air conditioner, he moved in a stiff way to the door.

"He wants to go out! Victoria—look! He wants to go out. Oh, he must be better, don't you think?"

We took him out. It was a warm autumn evening, late enough in the year for the air to be fresh, not clammy. We walked up Fifth, into the park, past the zoo, Bertie leading the way. He inspected the fountain. He inspected the stream. He peed on all his favorite verticals.

He snuffed the air, then turned for home. I promise you, he was very noble, just as Constance had said. Bertie's farewell to the smells of Central Park. He did not cough once. When we returned to the apartment he found a new space, behind the sofa, next to a screen, obscured by a chair. A fine and private place. Bertie lay down. He went to sleep. He began to snore. His forepaws scrabbled. Constance stroked his webbed feet.

I knew he was dead as soon as I woke the next morning. It was very early; I could hear the sounds of Constance, keening.

When I went in, Bertie lay with his head on his paws. His sides did not rise and fall. His huge tail, which could sweep a whole table of china to the floor with one wag, was curled under him. Constance lay on the floor by his side. She had not been to bed, and was still fully dressed. Her arm was around Bertie's neck. Her small jeweled hands, with their magpie rings, rested in his fur. She could not weep, and she would not be moved. She stayed there like that for another two hours, and if I was to have only one memory of Constance, it would be that, of my godmother saying goodbye to the last and the best of her dogs.

Her detractors were not right about Constance, do you see? Winnie was not right; Maud was not right—and I have not always been right either. Disloyal, perhaps; unjust, certainly. Those who disliked Constance saw only a part of her—a part that was there, yes, but they did not see her whole. They did not understand . . . well, let's just say they did not understand about the dogs.

Bertie had a good funeral. He was buried in that well-tended pet cemetery. The tombstone was designed by an orchidaceous young man who had made a name with his sets for ballet. As you know, it was supposed to be an iceberg, and—if you look at it from the right angle—it does resemble one. But it is difficult to convey in stone the simultaneous opacity and transparency of ice; the tomb, even Constance acknowledged, was arresting, but scarcely a success.

The orchidaceous young man claimed a triumph—but then, he was full of praise for his own sets. Constance lost her temper; she said it was a lump of badly carved stone, an insult to Bertie's memory. The designer, quivering, told her to grow up. Yes, Bertie's funeral was seemly, but his wake was not.

Constance did remain true to her promise. She never acquired another dog. But the death of Bertie altered her greatly. For several weeks after Bertie's death she sank into the blackest depression. She would not leave the apartment. She would not work. She scarcely ate. One day when I returned from her showrooms, I found her with her head sunk in her hands, her face without makeup, her Egyptian hair disordered.

She said there was a bird in the room. She had opened the window and the bird had flown in. She could hear its wings beat. It was trapped. It made her head ache.

I could hear nothing. To placate her, I searched the room. Like all Constance's rooms, it was crowded. I had to peer behind screens, look under tables and chairs, move flowers, lift every one of a hundred objects. There was no bird, of course—but in the end, to satisfy her and settle her, I pretended the bird had been found. I cupped my hands around air. I opened the window. I told Constance the bird had gone, and this seemed to revive her.

It was after this—about three days later—that an extraordinary thing happened.

I had been at Constance's workshops, still trying to cover for her absence. Commissions and orders were falling behind. There were decisions that had to be made, and only Constance could make them. One of these decisions involved Rosa Gerhard, who, after a lull, was about to move again. She had wanted, insisted on, a blue bedroom for herself. Then she had thought no, pink or lavender might be better. Similar changes were being suggested for all the other rooms in a very large house, rooms for which the color schemes were already completed.

That day, Rosa Gerhard had reverted to the idea of blue for the main bedroom, but could not decide which of two fabrics was the perfect one for the curtains. Knowing that if there was any further delay those two would swell to fifty, I took her call; I said I would seek Constance's opinion.

I returned uptown, two bolts of material under my arm. I rushed into the lobby. I soared upward in the elevator. I hurried into that hall of mirrors, and stopped.

There—apparently just about to take his leave from a radiant Constance—was a tall elderly man.

I thought, from his clothes, his stance, that he was another of Constance's erstwhile aristocrats. Another Rumanian or Russian. Certainly he looked foreign; the cut of his clothes would have been fashionable thirty years before.

A tall man, of erect carriage, with strong features and thinning tawny hair. He was wearing a black coat with an astrakhan collar. He held a homburg hat in one hand, a silver-topped cane in the other.

I stopped. He stopped. We regarded each other. I saw Constance move amidst our many reflections in the mirrors. She said nothing. One small quick gesture of the hands.

"This must be Victoria?"

The man had a deep voice, an accent I could not place. Central Europe, I thought, somewhere. He gave a slight formal bow, an inclination of the head.

"Enchanted," he said.

He passed out of the doorway. The gates of the elevator opened and shut.

"That was my husband," Constance said.

Stern had come, she told me, to express his condolences for Bertie's death. Constance seemed to find nothing odd in the fact that a husband she had not seen for fifteen years would return to commiserate for the loss of a dog.

"He's like that," she said. "It's the kind of thing he would do. You don't know him. He was always punctilious."

I could understand that—just. I did not understand, however, how Stern *knew* about Bertie's death. Constance was quite capable of announcing that death in *The New York Times*—but she had not done so. Constance required no explanation.

"Oh, he would know," she said carelessly. "Montague always hears everything."

From this moment, Constance began to recover. A lingering sadness remained, but the black depression lifted. She returned to work, and for several months worked with great energy.

I hoped secretly that this meeting would begin a rapprochement between Constance and her husband. I was disappointed. Stern made no further visits; Constance seemed to forget him. Her life became increasingly frenetic.

The end of the war meant she was free to travel again. These were the years of the planes, boats, and trains, the hectic visits to a postwar Europe, the little rushes from Venice to Paris, from Paris to Aix, from Aix to Monte Carlo, from there to London.

These visits, as time passed, became arbitrary. Constance might decide at midnight to leave for Europe in the morning. Her work was abandoned—let the clients wait! At first I made these journeys with her, but as time passed, Constance seemed to prefer to go alone. I was left, as she put it, to mind the shop. "Please, Victoria," she would say. "You're so good at it."

I was slow to see that there was another, obvious reason why Constance preferred me to stay behind. I was sixteen before I realized she did not travel alone; she went with, or to meet, lovers. Even then, I imposed my own form of censorship. I would not call them lovers, these men who passed through Constance's life at the speed of light, taken up one day, banished a week later. Her *admirers*, I said to myself, at sixteen. I was eighteen before I admitted to myself that not all these admirers were so transitory, and that as a permanent fixture they included those twins more than twenty years Constance's junior, Bobsy and Bick.

I knew better than to make any comment. Constance's temper, always on a short fuse, grew more fiery with the passing of time. She could be imperious and irascible; she became furious if she thought she was being questioned or watched.

Constance liked me less, I used to think sometimes, as I grew older. She would return from those journeys, a mock-scowl on her face; she would say, accusingly, "You have grown *another inch*." At other times she would overwhelm me with affection or shower me with gifts. When I reached twenty-one, she would make me her partner, she said. Meanwhile, this commission—such a lovely house— might I like to work on it? I could begin at once. She would call me, to check on the details, from her hideout in Venice, Paris, or Aix.

It was in this way, in 1950, late in the year and not long before my twentieth birthday, that I set off one day for Westchester County. Rosa Gerhard awaited me in her twelfth house. Constance said she had decided to throw me to the lions at last; she would be leaving for Europe the next day. She thought the whole affair hilarious.

So did Miss Marpruder, the assistants, the secretaries, and the rest of the staff. They gave a small party for me to speed me on my way. They gave me, as a good-luck gift, a pair of earplugs.

"Just be absolutely, totally, three hundred percent *firm*," Constance said as I was leaving.

The secretaries collapsed against their desks. They moaned with laughter.

"Remember to ask after the children!" one wit called.

I gave them a cold glance. I told myself they were being juvenile. Being twenty, optimistic, still inexperienced, I told myself I could cope. Yes, Rosa Gerhard was difficult—but she could be handled. All clients could be handled. I just had to hit on the right technique.

I returned home ten hours later. I was wrecked.

"Please, Constance," I said, "please. Don't do this to me. I like her, but I can't work with her. Don't go to Europe. Stay. Better still, give her to someone else."

"Oh, she loves you, too," Constance replied. "She's already telephoned three times since you left Westchester. She thinks you're wonderful. Sympathetic. Intelligent. Beautiful. Original. She's *wild* about you." Constance smiled. She was enjoying this very much.

"I'm dead," I said. "As far as Rosa Gerhard is concerned, I'm dead. I've done eighty thousand miles. Like the husbands. I'm finished. I'm worn out." I stopped. "Oh, and by the way—you were wrong about that. The husbands, I mean. There was only one. *Is* only one. The survivor. Max."

"Was I wrong?" Constance gave me an innocent look. "Ah, well, it made a good story. The fact remains: if you can cope with her, you can cope with anyone. Mrs. Gerhard is yours. So are the husbands—sorry, the husband. So are the children. Do tell me, did you meet any of them?"

"Yes, I did. One." I hesitated. "Only briefly. On the way in and on the way out."

"I told you. They flee. They're rare birds. But you had a sighting. How thrilling! Which one?"

"One of the sons."

"And? And?" Constance leaned forward. "What was he like? I want *all* the details. You're not being very communicative. . . ."

"*He* was uncommunicative. There *are* no details. He said hello and goodbye. That was it."

"I don't believe it for a second. You're hiding something, I can tell."

"No, I'm not. I told you—we were introduced, we shook hands—"

"Did you like him?"

"I didn't have time to like or dislike. Though he seemed to dislike me—"

"Impossible!"

"Very possible. Maybe he's allergic to decorators. Under the circumstances, I could understand that."

"Well, yes. Indeed. I suppose so." Constance gave a little frown. "And which one was this?"

"The second son, I think. Frank Gerhard."

"Handsome?"

"Memorable. Obviously very bright, from what Rosa said." I turned away. "Not that it matters, but he's the Nobel Prize one, I think."

II
FRANK

THE NOBEL PRIZE ONE: Frank Gerhard. On that first day I met him, years before our encounter in Venice, he might have been uncommunicative, but Rosa Gerhard was not.

In the course of the ten hours I spent with her, we made little progress on the designs for her house, a great deal of progress in other respects. By the time I left I had had Rosa's family history from her great-grandparents downward. I could now see exactly how Constance, embroidering as usual, had misled.

She was right about one thing only: There were a round dozen children. Nine were Rosa's own, and three were the children of her husband's brother, taken in by Rosa after this brother's death. Max, the only and enduring husband, was absent—Rosa suggesting, with a smile, that this was a practice of his. Even when not lecturing or teaching, it seemed, the professor found it hard to work at home. He could not, Rosa said fondly, concentrate on his books. This was understandable: Children—a bewildering number of children—ricocheted through the house.

Rosa took this in her stride. The children seemed to range in age from five to the early twenties. Taking me on a tour of the house, the chaotic house, Rosa would pause in mid-anecdote; she would attend to a cut knee, arbitrate in a squabble, assist a ten-year-old who had punctured a football, or an anguished teenager who could not find a clean shirt. She did so excitably, throwing herself into their predicament with energy, then returning to the subject at hand without missing a beat.

"How about this carpet? You like this carpet? I hate this carpet, but Max likes it—so it stays, yes? Do you think blue with it? Or no, maybe yellow? Or green? This is Daniel. Daniel is fifteen. He writes. Poetry. All the time—also he loses shirts. You want the blue shirt, Daniel? How about the white? Okay, okay, the blue. It's in the chest in your room—*Lieber Gott,* it is *so* in the chest in your room. The second drawer on the left. Did I sew on that button? Yes, I sewed on that button. Maybe if we moved the carpet—put it downstairs? Would Max mind that, do you think? I sometimes think that all he sees is his books. Still, men can be like that. Ah, through here, Victoria. More introductions. Are you keeping count? This is Frank."

Frank Gerhard, a handsome man, rose to his feet as we entered this room; it appeared to be his study. He had been reading a book, which he put down politely enough. We shook hands. Rosa launched herself on a lengthy speech, first on the subject of Frank Gerhard's accomplishments, and then on mine. There followed a highly embarrassing list of my gifts as a decorator, and a warmhearted but equally embarrassing explanation of the sympathy Rosa had felt toward me, the instant we met.

Frank Gerhard listened to this recitation in silence. I could see that he doubted the accuracy of the praise and considered the sympathy precipitate. He made no comment but simply stood there, arms folded, until Rosa came to the end of her speech.

Toward the end of it, even Rosa seemed to sense that there was something wrong, an undercurrent of unease, for, in a way uncharacteristic of her, she faltered, began again, lost impetus, and then hurriedly ushered me from the room.

Our meeting was not, as you can see, quite the way I described it to Constance. Frank was not the only son I met; it was not a hurried exchange, on the way in and the way out. Perhaps there was something in that encounter, even then, that I wished to keep to myself. Certainly I continued to be puzzled by it, and so, I think, did Rosa, for when we went back downstairs for tea, she returned to the subject of this son.

"He works so hard," she said, "and we interrupted him. He has his finals soon at Columbia—I think that was it. He is a perfectionist." She stopped, shook her head. "Frank is not . . . I wouldn't like you to think . . . He is working too hard—such long, long hours. I think that is it. Last night, for instance, he stayed up all night, not a wink of sleep. He came down, ate no breakfast, nothing. His face was white. I told him: Frank, you'll make yourself ill with all this work. There are other things in life. I tried to tell him about the house, about you, how you were coming over—well, he knew that. But no. He wouldn't listen. Back to his books. I thought he looked pale—when we went in—didn't you?"

I agreed he had looked pale, though his pallor was not the chief thing I remembered of that encounter. After some further discussion of this son, his dark good looks, his dedication to medicine, the honors being forecast for him, it was possible at last to steer Rosa back to the subject of this house.

For a while, with animation, she told me of her plans, but we did not stay on the subject long. I think in some ways that Rosa was never truly interested in houses. She dreamed of a perfect, an ordered environment, a setting for her family life: a room for every child, space for everyone in a huge family to enjoy both community and privacy, punctual meals, exquisite planned rooms. Yes, I think she dreamed of these things, but she never achieved them and, had she done so, would have hated it. As it was, the constant moves, the color schemes, the purchases, all these served to absorb some of Rosa's prodigious energy. But the houses were never her main concern, as I quickly realized that day; that concern remained, in all the years I knew her, her husband and her family.

That day, to my relief, we returned to that topic very quickly. Rosa, on color schemes, was exhausting. Rosa, on the subject of her family's dramas and characters, was interesting.

Consider: I was an only child. I had never been to school. I had very few friends of my own age; from my childhood in England through my years in New York, I had spent my time almost exclusively with those much older than I. I lived, with Constance, in an apartment that was the antithesis of this house, an apartment in which every object, every piece of furniture, every painting had its perfect, its inviolable place. To come to the Gerhards' was to take a journey to a foreign country. Sitting there, listening to Rosa, I felt an unspeakable loneliness, a passionate wish that I, too, had grown up with brothers, sisters, disorder, friends.

Perhaps Rosa sensed this. She was one of those women who, by sheer warmth of personality, invites confidences from others. She also had the directness and determination that breaks down reticence. She found me very reticent, she said—and then, when she had discovered more about my background, laughed.

"Ah, but you are English, then," she said. "The English are like this. They make friends by millimeters, don't you think? A very little, then a little more. After sixty years, maybe you can say you are their friend. Not before. Never before. Whereas I—sixty minutes. Sometimes, sixty seconds. If I like someone, I like them. I always know. At once."

Rosa was right about this, right about me anyway. I had become too wary and too reticent. I longed to be different. I longed to be as fearless as Constance, as open and impulsive as Rosa. I used to think, sometimes: *I am marking time. When does it start: my life?*

For that reason I tried to open up to Rosa, both on that first day and at our subsequent meetings over the following months. As a result of this, Rosa knew a great deal more about me than anyone except Constance, and I failed to resist when Rosa's questions steered me closer and closer to the subject that was closest to her own heart: romance.

Rosa was, as you may imagine, a convinced, a flagrant, an evangelical romantic. She had already told me, many times, the story of her meeting with Max, their courtship and their marriage. She had also regaled me with the love stories of her parents, her grandparents, her maternal uncle, several cousins, and a woman once encountered on an uptown bus.

Rosa told these stories very well. We had first meetings, we had *coups de foudre*. We had parental opposition, misunderstandings, hopes, temptations. All these stories, so far as I recall, were alike in one respect: They had happy endings. No divorce, no death, no quarrels, no adultery; like the novels my great-aunt Maud had liked when I was a child, all Rosa's stories ended with a ring and an embrace.

It was some while before I understood: These tales were also cues. I became aware that they would be followed by silences, by looks, by hints. Rosa was waiting for *my* story, my romance. There was none—a fact I bitterly regretted. When, under onslaught, I admitted this, Rosa became very knowing indeed. English reticence again, she suggested. Well, well, she understood. In time, I would confide in her perhaps. No, no, she would be good, not another word; she would ask no more questions. . . .

She asked another question, next breath.

"On the other hand—a special friend?" We were sitting in her drawing room. I had silk samples spread out at my feet, a plate of superb Sacher torte on my lap. Sweet tea, sweet cake, sweet confidences. "I feel sure"—she looked at me wistfully—"a lovely girl like you, so young, all her life ahead of her—there must be *someone*. You wait for him to call, yes? Your heart beats faster when you hear his voice? He writes perhaps, the way my Max used to write to me, and when you get his letters—"

"No, Rosa," I said, as firmly as I could. "No calls. No letters. I told you—no special friend—"

I stopped. Frank Gerhard had just come into the room. He asked his mother some question, then, without a glance in my direction, left.

"Such a blush!" Rosa said as the door shut. She gave a smile of maddening complacency. "You're hiding something. Ah, well—you'll tell me in time."

Rosa was right: I did tell her in time. By the time that confession came, many months later, the work on Rosa's house in Westchester had long been completed. That work, which continued for some eight months, cemented our friendship, though it often did so via quarrels.

I should explain that Rosa's taste was very odd indeed. Rosa's rooms, like Rosa herself, were a hybrid. From her own family she had inherited a great deal of fine, though somewhat heavy, furniture and some excellent paintings. There were tapestries that might have suited a *Schloss* but which looked unhappy in Westchester. There were antique black oak German cabinets, towering ecclesiastical candlesticks. These were expected to complement the furniture Rosa herself had acquired, much of which was florid.

Rosa loved gilt and curves. She worshipped the rococo. She had a weakness for buhl. She had a whole collection of costly (and, I suspected, fake) Louis Quatorze chairs. Room had to be made for a collection of Steuben glass animals on the one hand and, on the other, for some exquisite Meissen. Finally, there was the influence both of Max and of those numerous children. There were books, stacks of pamphlets, a creeping tide of papers, records, musical instruments, toys, sports equipment, academic journals. Order, in this house, fought a losing battle with clutter. I might have liked to *be* there, but to *work* there was to abandon all my own principles.

I tried to explain this from time to time to Constance, but Constance merely laughed. "Oh, don't be such a purist," she said. "Finish the work and forget it. Then you need never go back."

But I would go back—I knew that. Rosa drew me back; her family drew me back; step by step I was being taken into her family circle. I would return for a family supper, for tea with Rosa, for discussions on the next set of rooms—and I would find that the work I'd done had already been destroyed. Rosa wore down each room within a week of its being completed.

One of the ubiquitous frilly lampshades would reappear, then some truly terrible piece of cut glass. (Rosa loved anything that glittered.) A Meissen figure would inch back in—and that was fine, except Rosa put it next to a Steuben glass pelican. I would look around at a once-beautiful room and see a rash of *things*.

"Rosa," I would say, "what am I *doing* here? What on earth is the *point?*"

I have a hot temper; Rosa had a hot temper also: these arguments would flare up into loud, prolonged, impassioned fights. At least twice I walked out, saying I would not work with her again. At least twice, Rosa, shaking with indignation, clutching to her bosom the offending glass pelican or cushion or lampshade, would fire me. It made no difference. She always rehired me the next day; I always went back.

Toward the end of the eight months, when the house was almost completed, we were both beginning to realize, I think, that we half-enjoyed these rows. That did not prevent our having another—a truly major one on this occasion, one that left us both out of breath and scarlet in the face.

It was of such splendor, volume, and length that it drew witnesses, although neither Rosa nor I realized that at the time. I would later discover that several of Rosa's younger children, drawn by the hubbub, were watching from the safety of the doorway, convulsed with laughter. I would also learn that they were caught there by their elder brother Frank and shooed away—as a result of which he overheard the end of the row, the part when I said nothing and Rosa a great deal, the part that left me chastened.

"I know what you think!" Rosa was saying—or, rather, shouting. "You think I have no taste. No, worse than that! You think I do have taste and it is horrible! Well, let me tell you: Not everyone wants to live in a museum. You know what's wrong with you? You have *too much* taste. *Lieber Gott!* A perfect eye, yes—you have a good eye, I admit that, but no *heart*. I have to *live* in these rooms. My children, Max—they live here, too, you know. This isn't a shop window. It isn't a photograph. It's my *home*—"

Rosa stopped on a high and indignant note. Then, quite suddenly, she began to laugh.

"Look at us, will you—the two of us? Eight months—and still shouting. Listen, and I'll explain. When you finished this room, I looked at it. It was so simple, so lovely—and I thought: *Rosa, you will reform. Learn from Victoria. Try.* But then, you see, I sat in here, and it seemed so very empty! I missed my little things. I *like* my pelican you hate so much—Max gave me that pelican! I like to see Frank's books, Max's pipes, all the children's photographs. All those fat cushions—my mother embroidered those cushions. When I look at them, they bring her back. So"—she crossed the room and took my hands in hers—"we'll never agree—do you see that? We look at the world different ways. If we continue like this, we'll say something we both regret—and that will be that, phut! I shall lose a good friend. I don't want that. So, now, listen to me, yes? I have a suggestion to make. . . ."

The suggestion—that we sever our professional relationship in order to preserve our personal one—was a good one, and we acted on it. I decorated no more rooms for Rosa; we became closer friends. Rosa had taught me something that day. If I am less autocratic as a decorator now, and I hope that I am, it is because of Rosa. It was she who showed me something very simple and very obvious, something missing from Constance's tuition: A house is a home.

A home. Shortly after this I began to understand: Perfect rooms in a perfect Fifth Avenue apartment did not constitute a home. Much as I loved Constance, I had had no true home since Winterscombe—and I wanted one.

Constance sensed this, and it made her irritable.

"There, *again?*" she would say, when I was leaving yet once more for Rosa's. "Is there some special attraction in Westchester that I don't know about? This is the second time this week. Anyone would think Rosa had adopted you."

In a sense, I suppose Rosa had. Constance was often away; for all her virtues, she had never been motherly. Rosa was. Perhaps I went to her house so often hoping she could fill a gap I was only just beginning to realize existed. Perhaps I went simply because the evenings I spent at her house, the noisy family dinners, the games, the arguments, were such fun—and so different from the hard-edged, somewhat brittle chic I found with Constance's friends. Perhaps I went in order to see Frank Gerhard.

That may have been it; if so, I did not admit it then. Besides, by that time Frank Gerhard had completed his medical degree and moved on to Yale for a further doctorate in biochemistry. He was rarely in Westchester—never, I noted, if he knew I had been invited. On the few occasions on which I did meet him there, he watched but rarely spoke to me.

Once I partnered him at bridge—at Rosa's insistence—and played very badly. On another occasion, at a party for one of his sisters, he was persuaded—to the accompaniment of much raillery—to dance with me; a smoky room, smoky music, an improvised space so crowded it was impossible to do more than shuffle; one dance, performed from a clear sense of duty, grip firm, head averted. On a third occasion, at his father's suggestion this time, he was prevailed upon to give me a lift back into the city, and on that drive, to my relief, he did unbend a little. It was spring, a beautiful evening; I remember feeling a sudden exhilaration, a wish that the evening might continue in his company. Approaching Manhattan was like approaching a future; I could glimpse its towers and its avenues. They beckoned through a haze of inexplicable happiness—to me, not (it became clear) to Frank Gerhard.

I had been, at his prompting, talking about England, and Winterscombe; we had reached Fifth Avenue and were driving south. As we passed that entrance to the park where I used to take Bertie for walks, Frank's manner changed with a startling abruptness. His face became closed once more, his manner formal and distant. Yet again, it seemed, I had done or said something to reawaken his hostility. I was dropped off at Constance's apartment with chilly politeness; his car was already halfway down the block before I entered the building.

Mystified, it was shortly after this that I tackled Rosa; I wanted to understand what I could have done to provoke this dislike. Rosa was dismissive. It was, she said, nothing to do with me. Frank was difficult, she said; just now, he was impossible. He was moody, preoccupied, short-tempered—even his family found him so. There was a reason, however; an obvious reason. Frank Gerhard was in love.

With one of his colleagues at Yale, it seemed: a woman scientist. She was—Rosa had met her—very beautiful.

I can remember when we had this conversation—over tea that June. I can remember, all too clearly, the consequences. Rosa described this woman at some length. The more her virtues were enumerated, the more I disliked her. Dark hair, Rosa said; dark eyes; a brilliant future. I was filled with a most unreasonable detestation.

Yes, in love, Rosa continued in a thoughtful way—she was almost sure of it. It had been going on, she saw now, for some time. Frank was displaying all the symptoms. Of course she was pleased; she was also anxious. Frank, she said, was the kind of man who could not love lightly.

"An idealist," she continued, a little sadly. "He never learned to compromise. So obstinate! With Frank, it is all or nothing."

This seemed to me a virtue. Rosa was less sure. It could be, she said, dangerous. Supposing Frank was putting his trust in the wrong woman?

There was a silence after this. I leaned forward.

"Rosa—the symptoms. What are the symptoms?"

Rosa duly listed them. They made being in love sound like a case of the flu.

"You'll know them when you feel them," she said.

"Are you sure, Rosa?"

"I am a woman!" This, on a note of triumph. "Of course!"

It was at this point, in a sudden fit of rashness, that I told Rosa about Bobsy van Dynem.

There was, in fact, very little to tell. That, I'm afraid, did not stop me.

As you know, I had been friends with the Van Dynem family for many years; of the younger twins, I had always liked Bobsy the better.

That summer, when I made my confession to Rosa, Constance was in Italy. I suspect, looking back, that Bick van Dynem, drinking increasingly hard, was with her. Certainly Bick was absent from Long Island, and his parents kept the reasons for his absence vague.

Without his twin, Bobsy van Dynem seemed easily bored. His spirits flagged; his taste for pranks diminished. He seemed to tire of the attentive girls, the tennis parties, the competitive games that made up the Van Dynem family summers.

He seemed inclined to talk—and inclined to talk to me. I was invited to the house one weekend; I went a second. Bobsy liked to walk with me along the beach, where he would take up his position, staring in silence at the ocean. He liked to drive fast at night, in his new car (a Ferrari, but not the one he would later die in). Sometimes he would park by a jetty not far from his house, and sit there with me, dance music drifting downwind; he would talk about Bick, sometimes about his friendship with Constance, often in a roundabout way, as if there were a mystery here and it puzzled him.

On one of those evenings, parked by the jetty, he had—after a long silence—kissed me.

It was a sad, gentle, and regretful kiss, but I did not know that then; I had little experience of kisses.

I might have forgotten the incident (I'm sure he had done so) had it not been for my visits to Rosa, had it not been for those long, foolish, and inflammatory conversations. Those conversations made me *want* to be in love; from wanting, from being anxious to experience at last all those sublime and terrible feelings that I read about in novels, it was but a step to believing I *was* in love—particularly with Rosa on the sidelines giving advice and encouragement.

Fictions—both those I read and those Rosa provided—urged me on. Invited to the Van Dynems' again, not long after that first discussion with Rosa, I threw myself at Bobsy van Dynem in a way it still shames me to recall. My efforts were probably inept; they were certainly confused and desperate; they were successful.

Bobsy, easygoing, not too highly principled, and (I see now) deeply unhappy, obliged. I flirted with him; he flirted with me in return. We drove more often to the beach; we sat more often by the jetty. There, by the ocean, some weeks later, Bobsy kissed me once more. He said, in a weary way, "Oh, why not?"

By the ocean: that was where it began and where it ended, my first affair.

It was brief. If I was anxious to persuade myself I was in love, Bobsy was desperate to be diverted. I was gauche; Bobsy was immature. Neither of us understood, at that point, very much about the processes of self-destruction. Bobsy continued to drive his fast car too fast; he tried hard to be debonair and gallant. I tried hard to ignore the widening gap between reality and expectation.

For some weeks we played our respective roles. We would dance cheek-to-cheek to Frank Sinatra records. We would go for those long nighttime drives. We would walk along the beaches by moonlight. We tried hard to obey all the conventions, and at the end of the summer, when we both knew it was not working, the affair ended.

I was fortunate in that I was not hurt as much as I might have been by someone less considerate. Bobsy began the affair with kindness; he parted from me with grace. We extricated ourselves in such a way that we remained friends until the time of his death, some years later—and it was during the years of that friendship, not the brief weeks of our affair, that I finally came to understand the obvious. I was not an accidental choice of distraction; I was a substitute, the nearest thing Bobsy could get, that summer, to Constance.

Rosa, I think, never understood exactly what happened. I knew she would have disapproved of my actions (these events were not as she would have scripted them) and so, in a cowardly way, I did not enlighten her. Rosa, benevolent and in many ways innocent, believed that a romance (not an affair) had begun. I did not tell her when it ended. It was becoming a rather *long* romance, she would hint sometimes, but no doubt there were reasons. Once or twice, long after the affair was over, when I saw Bobsy only as a friend, Rosa would hint that I let things run on too long, that it was time the Van Dynem heir made up his mind. She would mention weddings. By then, it was useless to protest that I was not in love. Just good friends. Rosa would listen to those protests and smile; she would not believe me.

I had become one of her stories; I had entered her repertoire of fictions. Rosa (I was later to learn from Frank Gerhard) confided her hopes for me to her family. A brilliant match! She would expatiate upon it at length, seek the advice of her husband and children as to how best she might promote it.

As a result, when Bobsy van Dynem accompanied me to Rosa's house, as he did both that first summer and on later occasions, our visits were accompanied by a chorus of smiles, knowing looks, and meaningful silences. Bobsy found this amusing; I did not. And on two occasions, when Frank Gerhard was present, he made it very clear that he both disliked and despised Bobsy van Dynem.

Poor Heavenly Twin! We would sit at that noisy supper table of Rosa's, surrounded by her clever and argumentative progeny, and Bobsy, with the confidence of his class, would put forward his inherited ideas, his ill-formed political opinions. Often he would lose his way mid-sentence. Although he had charm, he did not possess wit, nor was he gifted at analysis. I knew that several of Rosa's children—not children now, but young men and young women—found Bobsy foolish. At least they had the manners to disguise what they thought; that was not true in the case of Frank Gerhard.

He would sit opposite Bobsy, frowning, watching him intently. Once or twice, when Bobsy had made a particularly asinine remark, Frank would come back at him with a quick wit and an insolence of phrase that emphasized Bobsy's inadequacies.

Bobsy's background had bequeathed him a thick skin; I think he scarcely noticed these episodes. Had he done so, they might not have worried him, for Bobsy had the complacency of his class. They did worry me. They made me protective toward him. I knew Bobsy's failings, but I also knew his virtues: He might be foolish and indolent, but he was also capable of kindness and solicitude. I was also beginning to understand how deeply unhappy he was. An Adonis, courtesy of Brooks Brothers, who had lost his way through life. I hated Frank Gerhard for his sarcasm; I thought him rigid and arrogant.

Bobsy, for his part, liked—as he put it—to "get along with" people. Once or twice he made attempts to overcome Frank Gerhard's cold reserve, to engage him in conversation. I remember the last time Bobsy tried, late one evening, when he had taken my arm and we were both leaving. In the doorway he asked Frank about Yale. (Bobsy's father was a Yalie.) I stood at his side. I looked at these two men, one so tall and fair, the other so tall and dark. Bobsy's easy charm was not being well received; Frank Gerhard looked ready to punch him.

"Awfully weird" was Bobsy's verdict, but then Bobsy thought people who read books were weird; his definition of eccentric was lack of interest in tennis.

"Awfully weird. What did I say? What did I do? I asked him about Yale, and did you notice? He looked as if he could kill me."

It was not long after this dinner that Max Gerhard became ill. The illness was sudden and brief; he died that winter. I saw Frank Gerhard at the funeral, and I saw him again—as you know—the following spring, that chance meeting outside a church in Venice.

After that debacle, I could scarcely expect him to seek me out; it came as no surprise that a long time passed before I next met him. I heard of him only at second hand, from his brothers and sisters or from Rosa. Shortly after that Venice meeting, it seemed, he had accepted an offer from an Oxford college of a visiting lectureship. The decision to go to England had been made abruptly, Rosa said, and it was undecided how long he would remain there. His motives in accepting the fellowship, Rosa hinted, were not solely professional. It was an honor, obviously, but one he had intended to refuse. He had left, she hinted, in order to forget: That paragon of a woman scientist had, it seemed, disappeared from the scene. Now, Rosa never spoke of her.

I think, then, that I did not expect to meet Frank Gerhard again. I thought that time and change would take him further and further from my orbit, and that I would hear of him only as I did then, via others: small reports, the stations of a stranger's life. He was in this country; he was in another; he advanced in his career; he married.

Out of my ken. I felt an odd and nagging regret at this, a sense of inconclusiveness. But I did not examine those feelings too closely; I hid them behind other changes that took place during that time, small adjustments and alterations, a general sense that my life was awry.

Twenty-five, twenty-six, almost twenty-seven: I could see my life ticking past, the clock gaining. I worked, and was judged a success at my work, but work did not fill every available minute of every available day, no matter how hard I might try to make it do so. Sometimes I would feel a great but indeterminate impatience, a reaching-out to something only vaguely perceived. I would line up appointments and tasks; I would despise myself for wanting something that remained nebulous.

I did not know it then, but my life was poised just this side of decisive change. I was to meet Frank Gerhard again, and that strange meeting, which came about in a circuitous way, lay not far ahead of me. It took place at the very end of 1957, in New Haven.

What brought that meeting about? Innumerable things, but one of them was scandal.

The scandal concerned my uncle Steenie. Steenie, then fifty-seven, was living by that time at Winterscombe. His finances were precarious, but his way of life remained exuberant.

Steenie had, with the passing of time, become more promiscuous. The young man who once declared his undying love for Wexton in a tea shop had developed a taste for briefer, colder, easier liaisons. He had, more specifically, developed a taste for soldiers.

Guardsmen in particular. It had been Steenie's practice to proposition these sturdy young men in Hyde Park, then invite them back to his London apartment. On one occasion, earlier that year, he encountered a soldier who, well used to such approaches from elderly roués, suggested that it would be quicker, more practical, easier all 'round, to go behind a bush.

This, Steenie had never done before. Explaining himself—and he felt a constant need to explain himself—he said it had been deliciously *furtive*. He and the soldier ducked into the shrubbery. When matters reached a compromising stage, two plainclothes policemen popped up from behind a neighboring bush.

"I put up an argument!" Steenie cried. "An eloquent argument!"

The eloquence, however, was insufficient, and the current state of British law against him. The soldier was discharged; my uncle

Steenie went to prison for six months. When he came out of prison his friends did not want to know him. Conrad Vickers found that his house on Capri was full for the whole summer. Steenie might never have hidden his homosexuality, but he had now committed the unforgivable sin: He had been caught, publicly.

Constance at once invited him to New York. She not only took Steenie in, she also took him out. She put him on public display, at concerts, art galleries, restaurants, parties. Those of her friends who balked at meeting a homosexual jailbird were dropped. I would like you to remember this: Constance could be loyal; she had never lacked courage.

Steenie, ensconced in the luxury of Constance's apartment, put a brave face on things; however, he suffered. He alternated between peaks of brave, defiant gaiety and troughs of acute peevishness. He was inclined to burst into tears; he was inclined to harangue life at unpredictable moments. His fondness for wee tots and quick nips increased. His behavior, even Constance admitted, was alarming.

Late in December, when the news came that Wexton would be giving a memorial lecture at Yale and that both Steenie and I were invited, Steenie was overjoyed. He said it was years since he had seen Wexton; that a long talk with Wexton was just what he needed, that Wexton would set him right.

I doubted this. Constance, not included in the invitation, was scornful. Steenie pleaded, and in the end it was agreed: We would go. I decided, before we set off on this expedition, I would banish the silver flask. Damage control: I could see we were in for trouble.

Two days before we were due to go, my premonitions deepened. I was visiting Rosa in Westchester, as I had done every week that past year. Rosa had been much changed by the loss of her husband. I was used to finding her sad, reflective; that day, greeting me, she was radiant.

"Such news," she said, clasping my hand. "Frank is home—"

"Home? You mean he's here?"

"He flew back yesterday. He's out now. You'll see him before he leaves for New Haven. He asked after you. Well, he always does, of course. When he writes, in his letters from England, he never forgets. He always says: How is Victoria? I told him about the lecture, about your godfather. Such a great man! Frank will be at the lecture, and—"

"Frank will be there?"

"Of course. He loves your godfather's work. Nothing would make him miss it. He's hoping, I think, that you might join him—after the lecture, after the dinner? Drinks in his rooms? It's your first visit to Yale—I know he wants to welcome you—"

"Rosa, I'm not sure if that will be possible. You see, my uncle will be with me, and—"

"Your uncle, too—you must all go. Frank was most insistent." Rosa talked on. I sat in silence, only half listening. The reappearance of Frank Gerhard agitated me; the issuing of this unexpected invitation made me very nervous indeed. I tried to imagine an encounter between the difficult, taciturn Dr. Gerhard and my uncle Steenie, with his dyed hair, his makeup, his lavender cravat.

This reaction would have hurt Rosa; it had to be hidden. She had never met Steenie; it would have been inconceivable to her that I should go to New Haven with that great man, my godfather, and not introduce him to that other great man, her doctor son. Hospitality was involved, too. No, I could not let Rosa see my reaction, and so I sat quietly while she continued to talk of this particular son.

Once past her initial excitement, the flurry of news, her manner did become quieter, her sentences slower. There was, gradually, a return to that reflectiveness and residual sadness marked in her since her widowhood. She was watching me, I saw, in a considering way.

"I wish sometimes that Frank . . ." she began.

"Wish what, Rosa?"

"Oh, foolish things. Foolish things. I'm getting older. Since Max died . . . He shielded me—I can see that now. When I had worries, before, I could talk it over with Max. My Max was a wise man! But now . . ."

"You can talk to me, Rosa."

"Of course. Of course. But not about everything. You're too young, and . . . Still, forget this. Switch on the lamp. How dark it is outside! I hate these long winter evenings." She paused while I switched on the lamp, closed the curtains.

"My children," she said, half to herself. "Max always said I fussed too much. Mothers do, I said to him. I can't help it. I want them to be happy. I like to see them . . . settled."

"Rosa—"

"You, too, Victoria." Rising, she took my hands, then kissed me. She looked at me closely, her face thoughtful. "You've changed, do you know that? This past year, two years—"

"I'm older too, Rosa."

"I know. I know." She hesitated. "I want to ask you something. You know how we used to talk? Bobsy van Dynem—it is all over, isn't it? I knew it was, I suppose."

"It's over, Rosa. It's been over for ages. Bobsy and I are friends, that's all."

"And there's no one else? I did think, once or twice—"

"I thought so too. Once or twice." We smiled. "It never came to anything, Rosa."

At that, Rosa rallied. As I took my leave of her she gave me one of her lectures. She said I shouldn't talk like that, like an old woman—and I shouldn't think in that way. It was a waste.

I was touched by that. I left her there, in her cluttered and comfortable sitting room, and passed out through the hall. There was no sign of Frank Gerhard; children's voices floated down the stairs. I put on my coat; I buttoned up on melancholy.

It was raining outside. I stood on the steps of the house, watching the rain fall and the sky darken. The light was almost gone; it would be a long, slow drive back to Manhattan.

I had borrowed Constance's convertible. Fumbling for the keys, I dropped them. It was only as I bent to pick them up in the circle of light in the gravel that I realized I was not alone. Footsteps; then someone else bent for those keys; a man's hand closed over them.

I think I must have started and drawn back, for when Frank Gerhard gave them to me, he took my hand. He said, "Don't go. Wait. There's something I wanted to say to you. . . ."

I turned to look up at him, alerted by the tone of his voice. It was the first time I had seen him since he stepped onto a *vaporetto* in Venice all that time before, but he spoke as if we had parted yesterday.

His face was pale, his coat and his hair wet from the rain. He looked tired and strained, much older than I remembered. Some battle seemed to be taking place within him. I saw then, for the first time, that he had pride and that it was pride which now made it hard for him to speak.

"I wanted to thank you," he went on, "for coming here as you have. For seeing Rosa. It has been difficult for her—"

"Rosa is my friend. Of course I came. Frank, you don't have to thank me—"

"I . . . misjudged you." He gave a sudden angry gesture. "When I last saw you—in Venice. Other times. I do that: make wrong judgments. Hasty ones. Arrogant ones. It's a fault in me—"

The acknowledgment of this weakness seemed to cost him dearly. The admission was made in an impetuous, angry way; then he broke off. His look became wry.

"However. I imagine you noticed this some time before I did."

"Yes." I smiled. "I did. Once or twice."

"You see, I wanted you to understand—I wanted to explain—"

"You don't have to explain. It doesn't matter. It was a long time ago—"

"I know this. You think I don't know this? I could tell you exactly how long it was. How many months, days, hours—"

"Frank." His air of urgency and agitation had increased. "In Venice—You don't have to apologize. If I'd been in your position I might have done the same thing. There were reasons—Conrad Vickers, Constance. The way they behaved to Rosa."

"They were not the only reasons."

I looked at him with confusion. He had spoken, suddenly, with great firmness. His face had become set. He looked directly into my face.

"They weren't?"

"No. They weren't."

There was a silence. We looked at each other. He lifted his hand and—very briefly—rested it against my face.

I felt the warmth of his skin, the wetness of rain on his palm. I suppose I knew then; certainly, although very little more was said before I left, it was agreed that we would meet in New Haven.

Wexton's lecture went well. He stood at a lectern, hunched over a microphone like a great eagle. He peered into the spotlight, looking simultaneously blind and farsighted. He spoke of time and mutability. He concluded by reading extracts from poems, including some of his own. He ended with one of the sonnets from *Shells*, that collection of poems written in the first war, dedicated to the young man who had once been Steenie.

Dr. Gerhard sat several rows in front of us. Steenie sat next to me. He wept silently and copiously. When the lecture was over and the applause began, he took my hand.

"I used to be different, you know," he whispered. "I really did."

"I know, Steenie."

"I wasn't always an old reprobate. I might have been something, once. I had lots of energy. Lots and lots. Then it went. I frittered it away. Wexton might have stopped me, if I'd let him. But I didn't. It's too late now, of course."

"Steenie, it isn't. You've changed once—you can change again."

"No, I can't. I'm stuck. Never let that happen to you, Vicky. It's terrible." Steenie blew his nose in a silk handkerchief, noisily. He wiped his eyes.

"It was Vickers's fault." Steenie seemed somewhat recovered. He rose to his feet, clapped his hands very loudly, shouted an embarrassing "Hurrah."

We went on to the formal reception and dinner, at which Steenie became quietly drunk.

"Tight as a tick," he announced when we finally escaped the dinner. "Tight as a tick."

He weaved about from side to side. Ahead of us Wexton ambled along, and Frank Gerhard, our host for what remained of the evening, walked at a fast and determined pace. We passed gray stone colleges, ivy-clad walls; Steenie, unimpressed by this close resemblance to Oxford or Cambridge, said it was all unnatural. "A stage set. No, I won't be quiet, Victoria."

Frank Gerhard's rooms, overlooking a college courtyard, were untidy. They were full of books. There was a microscope on a chair. Wexton (it resembled one of his rooms) looked about him with pleasure. I stared at Steenie fearfully. His face was greenish; I was terrified he might be sick.

I did not dare to look at Frank Gerhard, who, having brought us this far, might well be regretting he had done so. When I had quelled Steenie, which I did by pushing him unceremoniously into a chair, I risked a glance. Frank Gerhard looked from face to face: a distinguished poet, an elderly roué much the worse for drink, and me. His face betrayed no reaction, though I think I saw a glint of amusement in his eyes when Steenie attempted to sing us all a brief song and I quelled him again.

Some conversation was attempted, but at that point Steenie fell asleep and at once began to snore. Perhaps sensing an undercurrent of tension in the room, perhaps taking pity on Frank Gerhard, who seemed to be finding coherent speech difficult, Wexton—spotting a chessboard with the pieces laid out—suggested he and Frank Gerhard might play chess.

Frank did not seem to hear this suggestion the first time it was made. The second time, he did. He asked if I would mind. When I said that no, I would not, he paced up and down the room, remembered no one had drinks, and then poured them. He did so in a distracted way. Wexton later said that his was neat gin. Mine tasted like whisky and tonic.

The game began. I sat across the room and watched them play. Silence; I was glad of that. The evening's events would not lie still. I waited to be calmer; I also waited, I suppose, for Wexton to win.

Wexton played chess exceptionally well. I remembered the ease with which he used to beat my father—and my father was a very good chess player. Half an hour passed; an hour; if Wexton was winning, it was taking an unusually long time. I leaned over to examine the board. Wexton was playing his usual tight and defensive game; his pawns were well deployed but his queen looked precarious.

I am not good at chess, however, nor am I a good judge of the progress of a game. It was at this point, safely invisible to everyone in the room, that I began—as I had wanted to do from the first—to look at Frank Gerhard.

I rested my eyes upon his face. Either I had been blind or his face was translated. Where I had judged him brooding, preoccupied, and censorious before, I now saw a man whose face conveyed both gentleness and strength. Where I had recited defects, I now recited virtues: intelligence, loyalty, humor, resolve. Was he proud? Yes—but I was glad he was proud. Was he arrogant? Possibly, but I could forgive arrogance, once I saw it as a defense. Was he obstinate? Yes. I thought once or twice, when he glanced up at me, that he looked very obstinate indeed, almost fiercely obstinate—and at *that* type of obstinacy, I rejoiced.

The minutes ticked by. I heard them tick, for there was a clock above the fireplace; it was half an hour slow; I liked this. As I sat I began to experience a curious and heady sensation: that time both continued and stopped, that we were in this room, all four of us, and that at the same time we were somewhere else. In that place, wherever it was, the air was animate, busy; its molecules rushed back and forth. They whirled about. They made me giddy.

Perhaps Frank Gerhard felt this too. If he did, it did not seem to affect his ability at chess; he continued to make his moves with speed and decisiveness. Nevertheless, he was affected, as I was. I knew this, first, through my nerve endings, then through an action—a strange action—of his.

He did not look up from the chessboard; in the game, it was his turn to move. He was playing white. I thought he would probably move his knight, or possibly his castle. Whichever piece he chose, Wexton's position looked perilous. Without turning his head or, apparently, breaking his concentration in any way, Frank held out his hand to me. I rose and clasped it. His grip tightened. I looked down at his hand. I considered past years, past meetings, past words, past sentences. Goodbye and hello: the sentences were immaterial.

Frank Gerhard moved his bishop in a deep diagonal, the width of the board. Wexton parried, but was fenced in. Frank Gerhard continued to hold my hand. I continued to hold his. Some five minutes later Wexton resigned. An ingenious checkmate. The game was over.

I think Wexton left the table at that point and went to rouse Steenie. I remember that he disappeared. I remember Steenie's protesting that it was too soon to return to the hotel, and I suppose Wexton must have insisted, because both of them certainly left, and on his way out Uncle Steenie managed to knock over the microscope.

I suppose that more must have been said; it must have been agreed, for instance, that I would follow them later. I have a vague recollection of Frank Gerhard's saying he would walk me back. But it was all very brief. My uncle Steenie was too drunk to see what was happening; if Wexton saw (and I am sure he did) he was too wise to interfere or comment.

I remember the door closing. I remember Steenie, in the court-yard outside, caroling. But such things were peripheral. I continued to hold Frank Gerhard's hand; I continued to look at him.

He had risen—I think when the others left. Despite my height, he was considerably taller. I looked up at him; he looked down. He looked at my face in a strange way, as if he quantified the features there, perhaps measured the length of my nose or the space between my eyes. I felt quite blind. Happiness stole upon me; it made his face a haze. I remember wondering what the source of this happiness might be, and deciding it was the grasp of his hand.

I continued to stare. The clock continued to tick. The features of this face were delightful to me. He frowned. I thought that frown a marvelous thing. I intended to look at that frown forever.

"Seventy-two," Frank Gerhard said.

I was concentrating so deeply on the frown that speech was unexpected. I jumped.

"Seventy-two," he said again, in a stern way. The frown deepened. "You used to have seventy-two. Now you have seventy-five.

There are three more, all on the same side, under your left eye. Freckles, that is."

I suppose I must have said something; perhaps I just made another startled and incoherent sound. Whatever it was that I did, it appeared to make him impatient, and joyful. An expression that was familiar to me came upon his face.

"It's perfectly simple," he continued, and I could see the effort it cost him to speak in this reasonable way:

"You had seventy-two freckles. Now, you have seventy-five. I didn't mind them then, and I don't mind them now." He paused; the frown deepened. "No, this is wrong. The truth is: I *love* them very much. Your freckles, and your hair and your skin and your eyes. Especially your eyes—"

He stopped. I said:

"Franz-Jacob."

"You see, when I look at your eyes . . ." He hesitated; he was struggling. "When I look at your eyes—it has been hard, so very hard, not to tell you. Not to say, and to do, so many things. I—What did you say?"

"I said: Distance is of no object between the hearts of friends."

There was a silence. Color came and went in his face. His hand lifted, then fell. He said:

"It mattered to you? You do remember?"

I began to tell him, then, how much it had mattered, and how many things I remembered. Such a strange list: greyhounds and algebra, Morse code and waltzes, Winterscombe and Westchester, the children we had been and the adults we were now.

I did not progress very far with that list. When I had reached greyhounds, or perhaps algebra, Frank said:

"I think I have to kiss you. Yes, I have to do it now, at once—"

"No algebra?"

"No algebra, no geometry, no trigonometry, no calculus. Another time, perhaps—"

"Another time?"

"Possibly." A determined look had come into his eyes, tempered by amusement. He put his arms around me. I knew I would not finish that list.

"Possibly. On the other hand, maybe I won't care very much if your mathematics goes to the dogs. Maybe I am indifferent to your progress, or lack of it, in mathematics—"

"You're sure?"

"Not quite. I am, however, very sure"—he drew me closer—
"very sure *indeed*, about this." He paused one last time before he
kissed me. He looked into my eyes; he touched my face; when he
spoke, he did so very gently:

"*Versteht du*, Victoria?"

"*Ich verstehe*, Franz," I said.

That was how it was. There you are. I felt: all the equations
came out. Q.E.D.—in my life, this was the arithmetic.

I stayed with him all night; we talked all night—or most of it.
Frank said:

"Two of Rosa's children are adopted. Daniel came out from
Poland. I came out from Germany. We never speak of this. It would
hurt Rosa if we did. Rosa never speaks of it, to anyone—well, you
know this. We are all . . . her children. That was her choice. I had to
decide . . ." His face became closed.

"Either I could be Franz-Jacob, with no family, or I could be
Frank Gerhard. I decided to be Frank Gerhard. I admired her
husband, Max. I came to love them both. It was a way of thanking
them for what they had done."

"And now, which are you? Frank Gerhard or Franz-Jacob?"

"Both, of course. I never tell Rosa that."

"And which shall I call you?"

"Whichever you choose. You see, it does not matter. As long as
you are there, nothing else matters. Names least of all."

He had turned away from me as he said this. Turning back, he
took my hands and held them tightly.

"Do you know how many letters I sent you? I wrote once a
week, every week, for three *years*. To begin with they were short
letters, very dry, full of sums—that was the kind of boy I was. I
didn't find it easy to express what I felt. I still don't, even now. I can
want, so much, to speak from the heart—and then, I don't. I fail. A
scientist, you see." He shrugged, in an angry way. "Poor with words.
English words, anyway." He paused. "I can be a little more eloquent, occasionally, in German."

"I find you very eloquent. You are eloquent—to me. Words
don't matter, not when I look at you." I stopped. "Frank, tell me
about your letters."

"Very well. They were . . . boy's letters, to begin with. What
was happening then, when I went back to Germany—I couldn't
describe it. So I wrote about other things. I was twelve then. I
imagine, if you'd ever had those letters, you would have found

them very dull. You might have said: 'This friend Franz writes like a timetable, a textbook. . . .' Those letters, anyway. Not the later ones."

"The later ones were different?"

"Very different. Very . . . desperate. I was fourteen, fifteen by then. I poured out my heart to you. I had never done that before. I have never done it since. I said . . . Well, it doesn't matter now what I said."

"It matters to me. It will always matter to me."

"It was a long time ago. I was a boy still—"

"I want to *know*, Frank."

"Very well." He rose and turned away from me. "I said that I loved you. As a friend—but also not just as a friend. I said that."

The admission was made with the greatest reluctance, in a stiff way. I said gently:

"You sound ashamed. Why sound ashamed? Is that such a terrible thing to have said?"

"I am *not* ashamed," he replied fiercely. "I won't let you think this. It is just—"

"I said it, too, you know. I expect, if I could read now what I wrote then, I'd find it embarrassing. Does that matter? I meant what I said."

"You said that?" He stared at me.

"Of course. In very bad prose. Too many adjectives. Adverbs everywhere."

Frank had begun to smile. He crossed back to me. He said, "Tell me some of these adjectives. And these adverbs . . ."

I began on some of them. Like my earlier list, it was a brief one. I might have reached *dearly*, or perhaps *passionately* or maybe (I'm afraid) *eternally* before I was silenced.

Some while later, Frank took my hand. I was too dazed with happiness to think very clearly, but I could see that despite everything, he was still troubled.

"I still cannot understand. All these letters—your letters, my letters. Where could they have gone?"

I think that even then, at the very beginning, it was that question above all which I wanted to avoid. I said, the letters were gone; I said, now it need not matter.

"But it *does* matter. The logic of it matters—you must see that. You wrote throughout the war. How many letters was that?"

"I don't know."

"I know how many I wrote. Once a week, every week, for three years. Work it out! That is one hundred and fifty-six letters. To the correct address. In war, maybe one letter might be lost, five, ten—but one hundred and fifty-six? That is against all laws of probability."

"We know now, what we said—"

"That's not the point! Don't you see the consequences? You might have believed *your* letters went astray, but what about mine? What did you think, when I had promised to write and I never did?"

"I thought you were dead."

"Oh, my darling, don't cry. Please, listen. Look at me. Try to imagine: You thought I was dead—what did I think? I knew you weren't dead. I knew you were alive. I knew where you lived. Listen." His voice became more gentle. "You haven't asked me one obvious question. You haven't asked why I stopped writing when I did."

"It makes me afraid. That's why—"

"Don't be afraid. There's nothing to fear now." He paused, looking across the room. "It was the middle of the war, late in 1941. I was in New York by then. I had been with Rosa and Max a few weeks. And one afternoon I crossed town. I knew where you lived— such a very grand address! I stood outside that apartment building, trying to summon up the courage to go in. And while I was standing there, across the street, you came out, with your godmother. You were arm in arm. You had cut your beautiful hair. You had a dog with you—a huge dog, like a black bear—"

"Bertie," I said. "His name was Bertie. He's dead now. You were there? You can't have been there—"

"I watched you walk up Fifth Avenue, arm in arm. You were laughing and talking. You walked very fast. I saw you go into the park. I followed you, as far as the zoo. It was a fine day—there were a lot of people. You never looked back. It was easy to do."

"And then?"

"Nothing. That was the end. I stood there in the park, and I decided. I would never write to you again."

"You made up your mind—just like that? I couldn't have done that. If that had been me, I would have rushed after you and caught you by the arm, and—"

"Would you?" Frank turned me to look at him. "Are you sure? I thought . . . You can imagine what I thought."

"Tell me."

"I thought you had forgotten me, obviously." His face stiffened. "I thought that . . . you couldn't be bothered with that friendship of ours. That our promises meant nothing to you. A little death of the heart." He shrugged. "I did not think so well of you then. I said: one hundred and fifty-six letters; enough. I went home. I shut myself in my room. And I worked. When I was unhappy, that was what I did then."

"You worked? Oh, Frank."

"Mathematics, I think. Sum after sum. It was effective, up to a point. I still find it effective, even now."

I looked away. I thought of a boy, shut in a strange room in a strange house in a strange city, a boy who had already lost a family as well as this friend. I could understand, now, how that boy could grow up into the man who sat next to me, a man who found it difficult to trust and painfully hard to admit the strength of his feelings. All those episodes from our more recent past fell into place, incident after sad incident. I reached for his hand.

"Frank, if I had recognized you, that first day I came to your house—would it have been different then?"

"It would have been different for me. I hope I would have behaved better, then and afterwards."

"And in Venice—you almost told me then? You were about to tell me—and you stopped?"

"I might have told you. I wanted to do so—very much."

"Were you jealous?"

"Oh, yes." That glint of amusement returned to his eyes. "I can be intensely jealous. This is another fault of mine."

"I don't mind it. I don't mind it at all—"

"It is not so very easy to sit opposite a woman you love, to find you are not recognized, to think—even if you were, it would make no difference. It is especially not easy when you also know you are being touchy, and arrogant, and very, very obstinate—"

"You could have—"

"Oh, I'm very well aware of what I could have done. I could see the possibilities, very clearly, while I did the very opposite. So . . . I left. I went to Oxford. I thought I could teach myself to forget—"

"And you didn't?"

"No. That lesson, I cannot learn." He gave one of his shrugs. "For better or worse, that is the kind of man I am."

I hesitated. I looked toward the window, and saw that morning began. I said:

"But you did change your mind. You must have changed your mind. Why? *When?*"

"When I was away. When I asked you to come here. And tonight, I think. Yes, when I was playing chess with your godfather—"

"*Then?* Why then?"

"I had had enough of opening gambits. I saw the next move. It was a risky one, perhaps—"

"You thought it was risky?"

"Oh, yes. Very much so. Until I took your hand—"

"And then?"

"I knew," he replied. "It was not just the correct move—it was the *only* move. I saw that then."

Wexton and Steenie and I traveled back from New Haven by railroad. On the train, I babbled. I babbled to Wexton, who was trying to read, and who occasionally smiled. I babbled to the train windows, to the air, to the paper cups of watery coffee. I babbled to Steenie, who had a hangover. He winced. He groaned.

"Love? Vicky darling—*please*. My head aches. There are these furry little spots dancing up and down in front of my eyes. My left leg could be paralyzed. I don't think I can bear to hear about love. Besides which, you're repeating yourself. People in love are not only egotistic, they're the most terrible bores."

"I don't care. I'm not going to stop. You're going to listen. I love him. In a way, I've always loved him. Steenie, please listen. He isn't Frank Gerhard—well, he is, but he's also Franz-Jacob. You must remember Franz-Jacob."

"I don't remember anything. I'm not sure I recall my own name. What were we drinking last night? Was there port? Or was it brandy?"

"Never mind all that. Did you like him?" I tugged Steenie's arm. "Steenie, did you like him? What did you think of him?"

"I thought him . . . a most alarming young man." Steenie gave a sigh. "He had a wild look in his eyes. Also, he walks very fast. He walks at an immoderate pace."

"But you liked him—you did like him?"

"I can't remember if I liked him. I went to sleep. He keeps microscopes on chairs—I do remember that."

"You were drunk," I said. "You were tight as a tick—you said so yourself. If you hadn't been drunk, you'd have noticed how wonderful he is. Wexton, did you notice?"

"He plays very good chess."

"And? And?"

"He can hold hands with you and checkmate me in three moves—I guess that's impressive."

"Wexton, you're teasing me."

"Not at all. I wouldn't think of it."

"You are. Both of you. You and Steenie. You've forgotten how it feels—"

"I resent that," said Steenie strongly. "I resent that very much. I remember how it feels *exactly*. Don't you, Wexton?" A glance passed between them, affectionate, a little wry.

"Sure," Wexton replied. "Now and again."

"Though on the whole . . ." Steenie felt about in his pockets. He produced another silver flask, twin to the one I had confiscated the day before. He took a restorative nip. "On the whole, I prefer *not* to remember. It's too exhausting. Being in love is all very well at your age, Vicky my sweet—but it uses up so much *energy*. Look at you, fizzing away. It's very charming, my dear. In fact, it suits you. But it makes me feel beige. Washed out. Washed up. Besides which"—he sighed—"I see rocks ahead. I advise you not to fizz quite so much, Vicky dear, when you tell Constance."

"Constance? Why not?"

"I don't know. Just a feeling I have."

Steenie tapped his nose in a ridiculous way. He took another nip. Wexton closed his book, opened it again, then put it away.

"Constance will be pleased," I said into the silence that followed. I leaned forward. "Steenie, why should Constance mind?"

"I didn't say she'd *mind*," said Steenie. "I just advised you not to fizz. Try to look a fraction less happy. Constance can find other people's happiness very irritating. She's allergic to it. It makes her want to scratch."

I thought this unfair. Considering Constance's recent kindness to Steenie, I thought it disloyal as well, and said so. Steenie sighed.

"Vicky darling, you do flare up. Calm down. It was just a remark. You're probably right, anyway—I'm thinking of Constance as she used to be, years and years ago. When she was a child."

"Steenie, that isn't fair, either. Constance is the same age as you. You said last night that you had changed. Well then, Constance must have changed too."

"I'm sure she has. I'm sure she has." Steenie made pacifying noises. He lit a cigarette. He inserted it in a long holder. He puffed in a contemplative way.

"One hundred and fifty-six letters," he said at last as we approached the dereliction of outer New York. "One hundred and fifty-six. That's an awful lot. And to disappear like that. It is odd, wouldn't you say, Wexton?"

Once more he and Wexton exchanged glances. Wexton looked at me in a worried way.

"Well, yes," he said finally. "I would say it was . . . odd."

Constance said: "Tell me everything! Begin at the beginning and go on to the end. I want to hear it all. Life is so strange! I love it when it plays tricks like this. Tell me. Tell me."

To hear my story, Constance had led me into that library once designed for my father's books. Books to the right of me, books to the left of me. I told her. I tried not to fizz.

"But I don't understand." Constance shook her head. "He wrote—to the right address? You're sure he wrote?"

"Yes, Constance."

"Every week—just as he promised to do?"

"Yes, Constance."

She gave a small frown. "But how could that happen? Your letters to him—I can see they might have gone astray. But his to you? It's impossible. Tell me again where he went."

I told her again the story Frank had told me. At least, I told her parts of it: the return to Germany, where his father had been assured by a highly placed official that for a scholar of his eminence an exit visa was merely a matter of time. The conviction of his mother that the family must remain together. And then the inevitable: boots on cobblestones, a night arrest.

"They took his father. Just for questioning, they said. No one was allowed to see him. Frank's mother panicked. She refused to leave, herself, but she decided she had to get the children out. There were five of them. They still had no visas. She knew they'd never escape in a group, so they were split up after all. His mother tried to make it into a game, for the sake of the children. They drew lots, who should go—to which friend, to which uncle or aunt. Frank drew a cousin in Karlsruhe—not far from the French border. He stayed there a week. Then they heard: His mother had been arrested too. They were moving his parents east—the cousin was very afraid. She had a friend in Strasbourg, and that woman had a friend in Paris. He was put on a train, just one small paper parcel. When they got to the border, he hid.

"They got him out, Constance, just in time—into France, and then back to England. He was passed on, to a refugee organization. There were children being evacuated to Australia, Canada, America.

He came here. He was put in a camp in upstate New York. He had to wear a label with his number around his neck. Rosa and Max found him there."

"Oh, my God." Constance stood up and began to pace the room. "And his family? What happened to his family?"

"He didn't find out for certain until the end of the war. They were all dead. In different camps."

I stopped. Constance's face was white. She continued to move restlessly about the room. I said:

"Constance. It happened. It happened to hundreds of children. Frank was one of the fortunate ones—he knows that."

"Fortunate? How can you say that? Fortunate, to be orphaned in that vile way, to be in a camp with a number around his neck?"

"Constance—he did live."

"Oh, if only we'd known! I was so very sure he must be dead! It pained me so much, to see you go on writing, go on hoping—" She stopped abruptly. "Except, wait—there's something I still don't understand. When he came here, to New York, he knew where you lived. Why didn't he contact you then?"

I made an evasive reply. I did not want to tell Constance the story of that afternoon when Franz-Jacob followed us to the park; it was private between us. I think Constance noticed my evasion, and was hurt by it, for she cut my explanation short.

"Well, well," she said, "it doesn't matter now, I suppose, since you have found him again." She paused. "How odd. Franz-Jacob was lost, and now he is found. It's quite like your father." Her face grew thoughtful. "So . . . you love him, then?"

"Yes, Constance. I do."

"Oh, darling, I'm so very glad! I can't wait to meet him. Meet him properly, I mean. How odd—that time in Venice, I remember noticing him then: such a handsome man! But I never thought . . . Well, well, so it's happened at last. I suppose I shall lose you—you'll leave me, leave home. Oh, don't look like that. It will happen. I can tell." She hesitated. "He didn't mention . . . you didn't talk about future plans?"

"No, Constance."

"Ah, well, all in good time. I'm sure he will." She paused again. "Is he that type of man?"

"What type of man?"

"Decisive, of course—you know what I mean. Some men aren't. They will shilly-shally about, deciding which way to jump. I hate men like that."

She frowned at the books on my father's side of the room as she said this. When I replied that, yes, I thought Frank decisive, she seemed scarcely to listen. She began to pace up and down the room again.

"He must come here at once!" she cried. "As soon as possible. He must come down from Yale—and I'll give a party for him. Shall I do that?"

"No, Constance—he'd hate it, and so would I. Not a party."

"Well, a little lunch then, so he and I can talk. I want to get to know him. Oh, I feel I almost know him now, from your stories. I can see him, at Winterscombe, with his sums and walking the greyhounds . . . that day you went to the woods together. Such a strange little boy, a little boy with second sight! And now he's a man, and you love him—"

She broke off and turned to look at me.

"Did you tell him that, by the way?"

"Constance, that's my affair."

"Oh, all right, all right!" She laughed. "There's no need to be so defensive. Keep your secrets. It's just that . . ."

"What, Constance?"

"Oh, nothing. But you can be a little direct, you know—for a woman. You're much too trusting—you always were. You will pour out your heart to people—"

"Do I? I wouldn't have said that."

"When you like them you do. And when you love them, you certainly do. And it's very charming, and I admire it—but you should remember, with men it's not always a good idea. They like the thrill of the chase. They like to *pursue* a woman. Don't let this man of yours be too sure of you, too quickly—"

"I want him to be sure of me."

"Oh, very well, very well. But you're making a mistake—if you want to marry him."

I blushed. Constance at once was repentant.

She gave me a kiss and an embrace.

"Darling Vicky, I'm so sorry. I shouldn't have said that. I always rush ahead much too fast. Now, not another word! I'm going to plan this lunch. Come on—let's consult Steenie and Wexton."

"Frank!" A tiny figure, an impetuous rush across that large and exquisite drawing room. Flowers on every table; the light refracted from mirrors; small high-heeled shoes pattering across the garlands of an Aubusson carpet. An eddying scent of ferns, with a hungrier undertone. Constance in a dress of verdant green, eyes sparkling, hands gesturing.

First meeting: she clasped his hand, laughed as she looked up at him. She reached just to his heart. She looked searchingly at his face, then drew him down so she could kiss first his right cheek, then the left one.

"Frank," she said again. "Oh, I'm so very glad to meet you at last. I began to think I never should—and now you are here. Let me look at you. Do you know, I feel we are friends already? Victoria has told me *everything*. Oh, I feel we met long ago! I feel quite uncertain— should I call you Frank, or Franz-Jacob?"

Frank took this with an equanimity that surprised me. Constance, twirling that matador's cape of her charm, either dazed men or discomfited them. Frank, however, gave no sign of being ruffled. If he did not embrace her in return, he did not flinch from her embrace either. His reply to her final question was an even one.

"Most people," he said, with great politeness, "call me Frank."

"Not Francis?" Constance still hung on his arm, looking up at him.

"No, never Francis, so far as I recall."

"Oh, what a shame! I rather like that name. One of Victoria's uncles was called Francis, you know. His nickname was Boy, and he hated it. So I always called him by his proper name. We were such friends, that Francis and I. He's dead now, of course." Constance scarcely paused for breath. "Now," she continued, drawing him forward, "you'll know everyone, I think? You don't? Well now, this is Conrad Vickers—"

"Ah, yes. We met briefly once, in Venice."

"Of course you did! And that is Steenie, over there, skulking by the brandy bottle. Bobsy van Dynem I know you've met— this is Bobsy. On the other hand, it might be Bick. Now, who else . . ."

There were other guests present that day, but you will get the picture, I think. Constance had, as she put it, dredged up some other friends and acquaintances of hers who, she claimed, might be interesting for Frank to meet. There was, I remember, an ancient Gräfin von something, one of Constance's erstwhile aristocrats, a sweet woman who happened to be profoundly deaf, and who was placed next to Frank at lunch. There were one or two New York socialites, who looked bewildered to be present and who regarded this young scientist in a wary way. Yes, there were other guests, but they are unimportant; the starring roles had been assigned to Vickers and the Van Dynem twins, the three men of Constance's acquaintance guaranteed to cause Frank most unrest.

Why didn't I stop this? you will say. Surely it would have been easy to prevent?

The answer is that until I walked into that drawing room, ten minutes before Frank arrived, I had no idea who was invited. Constance, planning this lunch, which had been postponed and postponed again (Frank seemed reluctant to attend it), behaved just as she had done all those years before, assembling the library for the Winterscombe books: "A surprise!"

At the time, when I walked in and saw who was present, I felt dismay, yes, but nothing more. I had said nothing to Constance of Frank's dislikes—she knew nothing of his reaction in Venice to Vickers or the Van Dynems. At least, I believed that then. So, as that appalling first meeting began, and then continued over an equally appalling, embarrassing, ostentatious lunch—a lunch in which everything, from table settings to food, was of luxuriant vulgarity—I believed that my godmother, in her anxiety to make a good impression, had made a painful, almost pitiable faux pas.

And it was pitiable, to me then. When the champagne was poured and Constance boasted loudly of the vintage; when the caviar was brought in, in a silver bowl the size of a bucket; when the caviar was succeeded by foie gras and Constance made some terrible remark about Strasbourg ("Oh, but of course you were there, Frank, weren't you, during the war? Did you see the famous geese? Poor little geese!"); when she did all these things, I might have wanted to die from shame and mortification, but I pitied her.

For the first time I could ever remember, she was showing her age. She had applied too much makeup; the scarlet lipstick was garish. Her dress might be couture, but it was far too elaborate for a luncheon. Constance, to make such a mistake, to deck an already unflattering gown with too many overlarge brooches, when her fame was to be understated—yes, I pitied her for all this. I pitied her for the terrible, bright, and artificial way in which she spoke, for the vapidity of her comments, the triviality of her subject matter. No sign, that day, of Constance's abrasive wit. An aging woman, once a beauty, she presided over her table, whipping the conversation along without tact or sensitivity, interrupting, not listening—oh, I was ashamed, but I still pitied this.

"Oh, God, oh, God," Constance would say to me later that day. "What a disaster! I was so nervous, you see, so determined to make him like me. The more I tried, the worse it was. Oh, Victoria, did he hate me, do you think?"

"Of course not, Constance," I said, as robustly as I could. "He understood. I'm sure Frank was nervous too—"

"He wasn't! He wasn't! He took it all in his stride. He's amusing, Victoria, and he can be charming—I never expected that! Somehow, you made him sound . . . I don't know, reserved, a little unapproachable, but he was so good to the dreadful old Gräfin. Deaf as a post! You see, I thought they might talk about Germany—how was I to know she'd come without her hearing aid?"

"Constance, she never had a hearing aid."

"Nonsense. I'm sure she does. It's large and plastic and very pink—I remember it distinctly. In any case, it doesn't matter, because your Frank handled her brilliantly. She adored him! Helping her into her coat, going down to her car with her, listening to all those incomprehensible and utterly boring stories of hers—"

"It's all *right*, Constance. Frank *liked* her. He didn't find her boring in the least."

"But the others!" Constance gave a small wail. "I feel sure he loathed them. Vickers scattering those awful *dah-lings* of his like confetti. Bobsy making those asinine remarks about the Russians and Hungary—you realize he hasn't the slightest idea where Hungary is? And then Bick—oh, God, what on earth persuaded me to invite Bick? How could I have done such a stupid, stupid thing? I hadn't realized how bad the drinking had got. Do you remember"—a mischievous look came into her face—"after lunch, that terrible moment when he went to sit down, and missed the sofa? He seemed to go on falling forever and ever—and I wanted so much to laugh. Eyes as round as an owl—it *was* funny, but it was also absolutely ghastly—"

"Constance, truly, you don't need to worry. Frank has seen drunks before. We all have."

"Well, that's it. Bick's never coming here again—and neither is Bobsy. I've had more than enough of both of them. In fact, after this I may well cease to entertain altogether. You can tell Frank, I adore him but I shall never inflict another luncheon on him again. He shall come to tea—just the three of us, Victoria—and I'll try to make amends."

"Constance, you don't need to worry. He liked you. I'm sure he liked you—"

"Did he say that?" Constance replied, somewhat quickly.

I considered what had happened after we left. I had said, in the lobby:

"Frank, can you forget that lunch? Every ghastly minute of it? Constance was so anxious to impress you—that was why it all went wrong. She wants so much for you to like her, you see."

"Really? I thought the reverse. I thought she set out to make me *dislike* her."

It was said drily; given the circumstances, I interpreted it as a joke.

Not, however, a joke that it would be tactful to pass on to Constance now.

"He told me . . . you more than lived up to your reputation—"

"*Did* he?" Constance said, becoming quiet and looking thoughtful. "Well, I like him too. I see now—he's a very clever man, your Frank Gerhard."

"Tell me, Frank," I had said after we escaped from that lunch. "Please tell me—what did you think of her?"

"She more than lives up to her reputation," he replied, and increased his pace, so I half ran to keep up with those long and, as Steenie put it, immoderate strides. We were walking across town, to an undisclosed location.

"A mystery tour," Frank had said when we left Constance's apartment building.

It was a clear day, late spring, with a cold wind. Frank had turned up the collar of his coat; he faced into the wind, which caught his hair and made around his face a black halo. His grip on my arm was tight.

Now that we had escaped from the apartment, the details of that dreadful meal seemed less important. Even at the table they had been made bearable by Frank, whose ease of manner had astonished me, and whose eyes—at the worst moments—had met mine with a look of dry and amused encouragement. Social debacles of that kind were survivable, provided we could laugh at them together. We had reached the far side of the park and turned north. As we passed the Dakota apartment building, and I was admiring those gothic pinnacles outlined against a cold blue sky, Frank said abruptly:

"I know her husband. I haven't mentioned this."

I stopped in astonishment. "Constance's husband? You know Montague Stern?"

"Yes. I've known him some time."

"You can't! Why didn't you say? Frank, what is he like?"

"One, I don't see why I can't know him. Two, it didn't seem relevant—I don't know him that well. Three, as to what he's like, I'm not sure. He's . . . a formidable man." He paused. "I love it when you ask questions in threes, do you know that? All at once, in a rush. Now why should that be? Not logical at all. You see what you've done? A man of reason, vanquished."

"Don't try to change the subject," I said as we walked on. "How do you know him? When did you meet him?"

"I met him first about four years ago. Through the Scripps-Foster Foundation. There was a project I was working on at Yale, and they funded it. Stern is one of their trustees—and a major benefactor. I was being head-hunted. I met him then."

"And you've met him since?"

"Yes, several times. I suspect he may have been behind my appointment at the Institute."

"You mean, the research department they're giving you—he was behind that?"

"He was one of the board members who interviewed me. I expected them to appoint an older man. He's interested in my work." He shrugged. "He may have had a hand in it. The decision wouldn't have been one man's in any case—"

"They *all* wanted you. Of course they did. A unanimous decision—they couldn't have done anything else."

"Darling, you're very partisan, but things don't work quite like that. Anyway, the point is: I don't know, and Stern would certainly never bring it up. He keeps his own counsel. I like him—very much."

"And you see him, apart from your work?"

"From time to time. Not often. We have dinner once in a while."

"Where does he live? Not in New York, surely?"

"No, outside the city somewhere—"

"Connecticut? Constance said he lived there."

"No, not Connecticut—at least, I don't think so. Nearer the city, I think. When he's here, he stays at the Pierre. He keeps a suite there. If we have dinner, it's there in his rooms, served very formally by his own manservant. It's very odd indeed, very slow, very, very dignified. Like being in a men's club. With the clock stopped around 1930."

"1930?" I halted. "Does he . . . ever talk about Constance?"

The wind gusted; Frank braced himself. He drew me closer to him and increased his pace.

"God, it's cold. Let's hurry. It's not far now. Constance? No, he doesn't—never, so far as I recall."

I had the sense that this might not be entirely true, and that Frank was keeping something back from me. The next minute I forgot all that. Frank had come to a halt outside a shabby apartment building, between Amsterdam and Columbus.

"Anyway," he said, "you can meet him sometime if you want. I'll arrange it—but never mind that. Can you face the stairs? There is an elevator, but it usually doesn't work."

Do you remember that apartment—the one I revisited, when I was searching for Constance, the one that had a fire escape and washing hanging on a line, the one I looked up at, thinking *They live there now, some other couple?*

It was that apartment. A bedroom, a living room, a tiny bathroom, and a kitchen. It was clean, empty, and had been painted white. From the window you could watch Manhattan by day or night.

When we entered it, I could see that Frank, having brought us here at that fast pace, now seemed tense. A look had come over his face that I grew to recognize: a closed look. The formality of his manner and his speech at once increased.

"Do you like it?"

"Yes, Frank, I do." I hesitated, mystified. "I like . . . the view. The view is wonderful."

"It's very small. I know this."

"This room isn't so small. And the kitchen—the kitchen is ingenious. It's very neat."

"The elevator does work, sometimes. It worked last week." This was said a little mournfully. Through the silence that followed came, loudly and unexpectedly, the note of a trumpet, silver and pure. I jumped.

"That's the apartment below." Frank's manner was now very guarded. "A man called Luigi lives there. He plays the trumpet. In a dance band. He has five children. He's . . . very nice."

"I'm sure he is, Frank." I turned back and, beginning to suspect the truth, put my arms around his waist. "Whose apartment is this?"

"It's mine. I leased it last week. When I begin working at the Institute, I'll live here. I'll walk to work. It's rather a long walk—"

"Frank. It's nearly forty blocks."

"I thought that would be good for me." His face had become a mask of obstinacy. "To walk. Then to come back here, and . . ."

He was floundering—I could see that. With a lurch of sadness and of disappointment, I understood why he had brought me here. In the months that had passed, while he finished his work at Yale and I visited him there, or he came down to New York, he had never once mentioned, as Constance would have put it, the future. So, now, the future was explained. He would live here. Alone. I made my voice as bright, as careless as I could.

"Oh—it will suit you very well, Frank. Look, there are bookshelves for your books, and when it is furnished, you—"

"Furniture. I hadn't thought about furniture."

"Well, you'll need it, Frank. Even you. You can't sleep on the floor. You need a table, a chair, and . . ."

I could not go on. I was furious with myself. I knew that it had been wrong to hope, to tell myself that, once he left Yale, Frank would ask me . . . ask me what? To marry him, as Constance seemed to expect? To live with him? Simply to be with him? Something, anyway: I had never spelled it out to myself, but I had allowed that moment to be ahead of me, bright with hope.

"Oh, I'm a fool. I've done this all wrong. Always, always I do this!" Frank turned me to look at him. "You're crying."

"I am not. I . . . had something in my eye. It's all right."

"I love you. Will you listen to me?" He paused, and again I could see that struggle in his face. "You see, I should have explained. About the money. About the *lack* of money. I . . . am not rich, Victoria."

"I know that. You think that matters to me?"

"No, I don't. Of course I don't. I know you don't add up the world this way. But the fact remains . . ." His face tightened. "When I came to this country, I had nothing. The clothes I stood up in—isn't that what they say? Max and Rosa took me in. They paid for my upkeep, my schooling—for a very long and protracted education. Since Max died"—he paused—"Rosa is not as well off as she thinks she is, Victoria. Max didn't leave a great deal. She can be extravagant, or has been in the past. She has the younger children still to finish schooling. So, you see, before I can think of myself, I must pay Rosa back."

"Pay her back?"

"Darling, universities are not free. Research fellows are not that well paid. Some of the money I've repaid already, but there is more.

Once I'm at the Institute it will be easier, if I live in a modest way, like this—like a scientist monk, just for a short while—"

"Not too much like a monk, I hope."

"Perhaps not in every respect like a monk." He smiled. "Eventually, when this has been done, then I'll be in a position . . . I'll be able to . . . we can . . . I hope that . . . I would want nothing more than—"

He stopped. He broke into German, in which language he swore volubly and at length. Frank Gerhard was not a man given to swearing, in any language. I began to smile; my heart lifted, with the very greatest happiness. Frank, who had stopped swearing, regarded this smile with suspicion.

"You find this funny? I can assure you it's not funny to me."

"I find *you* funny, Frank. Why don't you finish what you were going to say?"

"I'm not in a position to do that. I was trying to explain, but I see now it was foolish to begin. I wanted you to know that one day—one day soon—I'll be able to ask you something that I am not able to ask you now. Because if I were to ask you now, it would be—"

"Be what, Frank?"

"Wrong."

"Wrong?"

"Dishonorable."

There was a silence.

"Frank. What year is this?"

"It is 1958."

"And what country are we in?"

"We are in America. Obviously."

"Then don't you think, maybe, since we're not in England or Germany, and it's not—I'm not sure when, possibly 1930, possibly 1830—that you might be worrying unnecessarily? That you might be just a little out-of-date?"

"I know I'm out-of-date. But I wish to be. It's because I respect you. Also"—he hesitated—"I saw today . . . the way you're used to living. A large apartment. Servants. Caviar for lunch—"

"Frank, couldn't I live here with you, in this apartment? I would like to, you know. I would like it very much—"

"You would?" This seemed to astonish him. For a moment his face lightened.

"Yes, I would. Surprising as it may seem, I think I could live very happily without lots of rooms and servants. I could certainly live without caviar. Frank, think"—I crossed to him—"you remember Winterscombe, how shabby it was? No money. Holes in the rugs."

"There was a butler." This was said on an accusing note.

"There was William, who was very old. A cook who gave notice once a week. And Jenna. That wasn't so extraordinary, not in 1938."

"It was a large house."

"Frank, will you stop this? You are the most obstinate, obtuse, inflexible man I ever met. Why can't I be here, if I love you, if I want to be? Or is it that you don't want me here? Is that it?"

"You know that's not true," he burst out. "I want you with me *always*. I want to live with you, think with you, talk with you, sleep with you, wake with you. When you're not there—it's like the song. I die a little. However." He stopped short. "You cannot live here. It wouldn't be right. When I'm in a position to support you, when I have the right, then—"

"Frank. I *work*. I can support *myself*."

"Even so," he replied stiffly. "I must be in a position to . . . allow you to stop working. I am not so old-fashioned as you think. I can be modern, too, proud that you work. But"—he hesitated—"sometimes a woman cannot always work. If she is having a child. If she has children. I—"

He broke off once more, and put his arms around me.

"I'm making a mess of this," he said simply. "I was afraid I would. But you see—it's not for so very long, and I love you so very much. When I say this thing, when I can say it, with a good heart and a clear mind, I want it to be the *first* time I say it. It will be important. I want it to be . . . perfect, so we will always remember it, and"—he paused—"I will say the right thing then, I hope, in the right way. In English. I will make you the speech you deserve. I've been working on it, at night."

"You've been working on it? Oh, Frank."

"I'm on the third draft." A glint of amusement had returned to his eyes.

"The third?"

"*Natürlich*. I expect five or six drafts. That may get it right."

"You're making this up."

"A little bit. Not all of it."

"You're teasing me."

"Why not? You were teasing me, I think."

"You are a very strange man, and I love you very much. One thing, though."

"Yes?"

"Does your very strange and rigid code permit me to visit you here? Will my reputation be safe then, if we're very discreet? Do you think I might, just occasionally, be smuggled in and smuggled out?"

"I'd die if you were not," Frank said.

"To 1959! A very *special* year," Rosa said—and, being Rosa, then became flustered, kissed all of her family, kissed Frank, kissed me, talked a great deal, then stopped, then wept.

She had looked toward Frank and me as she pronounced it a special year, and then—since Rosa never hinted lightly but preferred good weighty hints, solid as a brick—she drew me to one side and said, "Look at Frank."

Frank was, at that point, entertaining some of his nephews and nieces, for Rosa was by then a grandmother several times over, and this new generation of Gerhards had been allowed to stay up, to see in the New Year. In the middle of Rosa's crowded room, they were in the process of erecting a tower of bricks—no, not simply a tower, a Taj Mahal of bricks. Frank was on his knees, assisting in this process. He was demonstrating some law of advanced physics while constructing a small bridge. He did this with tact, never placing the bricks himself, but allowing smaller hands to do so. From time to time he made modest but vital suggestions as to where a brick might go without destroying the entire edifice; from time to time he would make an obviously bad suggestion, and be pounced upon with scorn. Four-year-olds and five-year-olds explained to him patiently why the brick could not go there; Frank took this with great humility. Rosa said, "You see—how good he is at this!"

She did not stop there, of course. She told me, in some detail, with obvious happiness, what a good father Frank would make.

I knew she was right. I also thought, though, that Rosa did not entirely understand this adopted son of hers. Rosa, even since being widowed, shied away from the darker side of life. She did not like to look toward the shadows, and so the portrait of Frank she gave me was loving, but inexact.

I may wrong her in this, but I think she did not see in Frank a darkness that was certainly there, and was deeply engrained in his character. He had suffered much as a child, and he had lost much; those losses, and the manner of them, he never forgot. They were there with him even when he was at his happiest: those *Gespenster*, his private ghosts. They influenced his moral code, which was stern and eschewed compromise; they also affected his willpower, and that (I was learning) had a tensile strength. Once he believed in something, he pursued it with tenacity.

He was, in a sense, out of tune with the age in which he lived, and would have been even more so during the decade that followed, the 1960s. To Frank, changes in social customs or attitudes were meaningless; a moral loner, he had evolved his own code and his adherence to it was rigorous. I tell you this because it may help you to understand a factor in our relationship that was of central importance—and that was his attitude to Constance.

Frank Gerhard had plain beliefs, held passionately. He believed in truthfulness, hard work, marriage, fidelity, children, and the importance of family life. Constance, therefore, represented everything that was anathema to him. This, he never said.

By this time, when we attended Rosa's New Year's party, he had been in his small white New York apartment since the summer. I had been visiting him there—although sometimes, despite his old-fashioned concern for proprieties, those visits had been prolonged— for some six months. During that time (and this is important in view of what happened next) he never criticized my godmother once. He never praised her either—he did not find it easy to lie—but he never spoke a word against her. Constance would frequently suggest to me that he must. "Oh, he doesn't like me," she might cry, or "He disapproves of me, that man of yours. I know it! He does!" Whenever she did this, I could reassure her—but I did so, as time passed, with an increasing sense of unease.

Frank did *not* like her—I sensed this for all his stubborn refusal to say it. Indeed, what he felt toward her, I feared, was much deeper than mere dislike. Sometimes, when we were together at Constance's, I would surprise on his face an expression of implacable hostility. Several times I noticed that when I spoke to him of Constance, his face would take on that closed look, and I would suspect he knew more of her than he ever said. I had wondered, once or twice, if Montague Stern might have been his source of information, though from what Frank said of him, that seemed unlikely. I also noted that I still had not properly met Stern, who was apparently not well; several meetings had been proposed, then abandoned.

On other occasions it would seem to me that Frank did not possess any special information about Constance, and that his reaction to her was a curiously primitive and instinctual one; he *drew back* from Constance as if there were in her something he could not bring himself to touch.

That night, driving back from Rosa's, in the warmth of the car, Frank was quiet. He seemed preoccupied. He kept his eyes on the road ahead. He drove fast but with precision, just this side of danger; we were—and this was unusual—well over the speed limit.

We were due back at Fifth Avenue, at Constance's New Year's Eve party—which, she had announced gaily, would go on all night. It was already almost two o'clock. I was sleepy. I watched the rain on the windshield; the rhythms of the engine and the wipers lulled me. I had no wish to go on to this party, but Constance could be jealous of Rosa; it was important to be evenhanded. These past months Constance had been complaining of my absences.

Frank did not like to give Constance ammunition for these complaints. If I had suggested we skip the party, he would have said no, you promised to go. We must be there.

"Was it ever explained," he said, out of a companionable silence, "why your parents quarreled with Constance, why she never went to Winterscombe again? Do you remember, when we were children you used to talk about that?"

"Oh, yes." I yawned and snuggled further in my seat. "The oldest reason of all. Nothing very dramatic. Money. My parents borrowed from Montague Stern. Maybe they didn't repay quickly enough, or the rate of interest was very high—I don't know exactly. But there was a quarrel. Constance says it wasn't a very good idea to be in his debt."

"I can imagine that. Yes. Damn this rain."

Frank slowed, then accelerated again.

"It seems odd, though, don't you think, to quarrel so finally about something like that? After all, she had known your father since childhood. She grew up there. You'd have thought—"

"Oh, I don't know. People do quarrel about money. Money and love—those are the divisive forces. That's what Constance says."

"You quote her a lot—do you know that?" He glanced toward me.

"Do I? Well, she can be quotable. You know that."

"I didn't mean her words so much. Her ideas. You quote them."

"No, I don't." I sat up indignantly. "Constance is very different from me—"

"I know that."

"I disagree with her about a thousand things. She does things I wish she wouldn't do, things I hate—"

"For instance?"

"Oh, men, I suppose." I hesitated. "Bobsy and Bick, for instance. I like them, and I wish she'd leave them alone. She says she will, and then she never does. And they're equally hopeless. They quarrel with her, but they always go back. They *depend* on her—I've never understood that."

There was a silence. Frank appeared to hesitate.

"They're more than twenty years younger than she is," he said at last. "Also, they are twins. Also, they are both her lovers. So—"

"What did you say?"

"I think you heard me."

"That's not true! They are *in love* with her—I realized that, eventually. But they're not her lovers. That's a ridiculous idea. People gossip—I know that. But people always gossip about Constance. If she goes to the theater with a man, they gossip. Most of it is lies. I do live with her. I know."

"So they are not her lovers?" Frank frowned. "It is . . . what? A platonic friendship?"

"No—not exactly. It's a flirtation. I know that—I'm not blind. But Constance flirts with all men. It doesn't mean a thing."

"Does she not have lovers then?" he asked in a quiet voice.

I looked away. "Yes. I know she does. From time to time. But not nearly so many as people say. She likes to make conquests, I think. It's vanity as much as anything—and loneliness as well, sometimes. It doesn't hurt anyone—"

"Oh? The wives are not hurt? The children? Or does she confine her attentions to unmarried men?"

I was astonished that he should speak in this way. It hurt me, and since I knew what he said was true, it made me angry.

"Why do you say that? You never discuss Constance—ever—and then suddenly you say something like that. You shouldn't judge her—you don't have the right to do that. I owe everything to her, and I love her—"

"Darling. I know that."

"When I first came to New York—if you'd seen how she was then. How kind to me she was. How she could make me laugh. Oh, a million things—"

"Tell me some of the things." He looked toward me. "I want to understand. Tell me."

"Well," I began, "she can be . . . the greatest fun, just to be with. She can take a day, the dullest day, and light it up. When she tells you something, she turns it inside out and upside down—like a juggler, like a conjuror. She's so very quick and . . . startling. She won't let your mind be still. She shakes it about, so you can't be dull or predictable or complacent. And she changes: One moment she'll be happy, funny, laughing—and then, suddenly, terribly sad. This great welling-up of sadness, from inside—you can see it in her eyes. You see"—I hesitated—"you never saw her with Bertie. You don't know about the dogs."

"Tell me about Bertie."

So, as we drove on I told him that story, and I told him others. I had not spoken to him very often of my New York childhood, and once I began, episode after episode crowded into my mind. His quiet attention, the hiss of the tires, the sense of being cocooned in the car, traveling through time, not space—all these things drew me on.

Because I was so anxious to convince him, to *convert* him to Constance, I told him for the first time how she had joined in my search for him, how she had telephoned, and written, on my behalf.

"She wanted your letters to arrive almost as much as I did, Frank. Every morning when the mail came, she used to bring the letters in to the breakfast table. People were very good—there used to be lots of letters. Maud, Steenie, Wexton, Freddie—they all wrote. Constance knew their handwriting, of course. So she knew your letter wasn't there. She was so gentle. She would put the pile beside my plate. Sometimes she'd kiss me, or shake her head. . . . Frank, what are you doing?"

"Nothing, sorry. Those headlights blinded me. I'll slow down. Go on."

"There's nothing more, especially. It's just . . . Oh, I want you to see her. As she really is."

"I see her better now."

"Do you really? I want you to like her, Frank."

"Go on. What else did you do?"

"Well, we walked Bertie—every day, as you know. Unless Constance was away, of course. She'd come back from work and fetch me, and we'd go out. Oh, and we'd stop on the way and mail all my letters in the lobby. Then we'd go up to the park and—"

"Such a routine!" He smiled. There was a fractional pause. "And was she often away? Who brought you your letters then? Who mailed them? What did you do, without all these rituals?"

"Oh, I can't remember." I yawned. "I'm getting sleepy again. One of the servants would bring in the mail—Mattie, I think. There was a maid called Mattie, who knew how to pick pockets. I liked her. She left at the end of the war. And as for Bertie, I wasn't allowed to walk him on my own, so one of those governesses would come with me. Just the same: mail the letters in the lobby, walk to the park. It was dull without Constance."

"You must have been lonely. That huge apartment. Maids, governesses who came and went—"

"It didn't feel lonely. I used to read a lot. Frank, it's getting terribly late. It's well past three. Where are we?"

"Almost there." He slowed the car. He frowned at the road ahead.

"When we get there," he said in a casual way, "show me the mailbox in the lobby, will you? I'd like to see . . . where you sent the letters from. Imagine you there." He paused. "Oh, and show me that library, will you? That's interesting too. I'd like to see that."

I showed him the box in the lobby—but I did not show him the library, not that night. I had said, as we left the elevator and approached the apartment door, "It's a very *quiet* party. Do you think we're too late?"

It was quiet, because there *was* no party, and all the guests had left some hours before. All the guests except one. When we came into the drawing room, Constance sat alone with Bick van Dynem. For once in his life, that twin was stone-cold sober. It was he who told us: Bobsy was dead.

"People are going to say it's suicide," Bick said in a flat and reasonable voice. "That's not true. It was an accident. He was here tonight. I talked to him. He couldn't kill himself. He's my twin. I know that."

If it was not suicide, it was a strange kind of accident. Bobsy had attended Constance's party, left around ten, hit one hundred on the Long Island Expressway. He outdrove three patrol cars, made for that jetty where he had once liked to park, and aimed the car at the ocean, full-throttle. He was wearing no seat belt. The car's doors were locked and all its windows were open. When it was recovered, no trace of alcohol was found in his blood. He had not drowned, but had died as the car hit the water, his sternum pierced by the steering column.

The Van Dynem family were to close ranks after that accident; Bick was to set about drinking himself to death, succeeding within two years. I never saw him again. My last memory of him is as he was that night, standing in the middle of Constance's drawing room, white-faced, rooted to the spot, saying over and over again that it could not have been suicide.

Frank watched him with a stony face; then I saw his expression change to one of compassion. Speaking gently, he crossed to Bick.

"Shouldn't you be with your parents?" he said in a quiet voice. "They'll need you now, Bick. Don't you want to be with them?"

"I don't have a car." Bick turned to Frank with an expression of bewildered, childlike woe. With a shock I realized that Frank Gerhard, who seemed immeasurably older than Bick, was actually four years younger. "I'm not allowed to drive, you see," Bick went on. "They've already gone out to the Island. I would go, but I don't think I'll get a taxi. It's New Year's Eve. You can never get cabs on New Year's Eve. . . ."

I looked down at the floor. Constance's car, I knew, was downstairs. I said:

"How long ago did this happen, Bick?"

"I'm not sure. I think . . . maybe around midnight. That's when they called. Or was it one?" He cleared his throat. His beautiful and patrician face looked blindly around the room. "Actually—I'm not too sure what I ought to do. I suppose I ought to do something. I do want to be there. I used to have a car. I can't quite remember . . . when they took it away from me."

"That's all right," Frank said. "I'll drive you."

"All the way out to the Island?" Constance spoke for the first time, sharply. She rose. Her face, too, was white. She clasped her tiny hands very tight. "At this time of night? Bick's in shock. He should stay here."

"I think his parents will need him. And I think he will need them," Frank replied. "It's all right, Constance. I'll take him."

Across the room I could sense it: a brief, bitter struggle of wills. I think Constance was about to protest further, but Frank's expression deterred her, as did the tone of his voice.

For a second there was discernible on Constance's face an odd, blanched anxiety. I realized she did not want Bick van Dynem, in shock, alone on a long drive out to the Island with Frank Gerhard.

"Victoria will stay with you," Frank said as he drew Bick to the door. "Victoria, it might be a good idea to call a doctor."

"I don't need a doctor." Constance's voice rose. "I'm not ill. I'm perfectly all right. Bick—"

Bick had reached the door. As Constance said his name he hesitated.

"Maybe I shouldn't go?" He looked at Frank pleadingly. "My parents—they might want to be alone. I can't leave Constance. She's upset—"

Something very disturbing happened then: It was a tiny thing, almost imperceptible; I have never forgotten it. There were Frank and Bick van Dynem, by the door; there was Constance, standing rigidly on the far side of the room. She was looking at Frank with an expression of unmistakable hatred. As I watched in consternation she turned her eyes to Bick. She inclined her head: a small nod of permission. Bick left the room at once.

Not a word was said; the nod was given with something close to contempt for that Heavenly Twin.

I shivered. I suppose it was then, in that fraction of a second, that I began to understand, at last, about Constance.

Constance may have sensed this—we *were* attuned to each other. She may also have sensed that I kept something from her. When I saw Frank the next day, he told me little of what had happened on that drive, and nothing of what Bick had told him. That came later. But I could see his anxiety and his concern. He said only: "You do realize—we are going to have to talk about your godmother? Talk properly? It cannot wait much longer."

He would not do so then; he knew the death of Bobsy van Dynem had left me deeply shocked—that may have been the reason. Instead, taking my hands, he said, "I must arrange that meeting with Montague Stern. He's better now. You should meet him— properly this time, not in a hallway. One thing though"—he paused— "Stern would prefer it, I think, if you did not tell your godmother."

I did not. Constance perhaps sensed this evasion of mine, as she also sensed that I had begun to draw back from her. She went on to the attack: She began to make it very clear that, since Bobsy van Dynem's death, she had taken strongly against Frank Gerhard.

What followed, I can see now, was a steady campaign, carefully waged over several months. It began with that drip technique of nuance, suggestion; it became gradually more overt.

"Do you know," she might say, "I'm not so sure of this man of yours as I used to be, Victoria. Does he ever intend to make up his mind? After all, it's been over a year now—and even I am not sure what's going on. Are you living with him? No, not quite, not exactly— yet you disappear for days at a time. I gather he has *not* proposed.

Darling, you will be careful, won't you? I would hate you to be hurt. . . ."

That was a favorite tack; there were others, more subtle. "I wonder," she would say, frowning. "Now I think about it, it worries me, that link from your childhood. Are you sure you're in love with Frank Gerhard—or is it Franz-Jacob? You're sure you're not harking back to that childhood of yours? You see, you could think you love him, because you connect him with Winterscombe. You always made that house into a kind of shrine, darling—and I understand that. But it isn't healthy. And the same could be said of him. He lost his home, his family, so what did he do? He developed this fixation on a friend—a friend who never wrote to him. Both of you are in love with the past—not each other."

When this did not work, she tried another approach. She began to suggest that Frank did not understand me.

"You see, darling, there are all these disparities! Think— what does he earn? What do clever scientists earn? Not nearly as much as they deserve—we both know that. Whereas you and I are rather grossly overpaid. I'm afraid he resents that. He is so old-fashioned in some of his views—I see his frowns! When you went out of town on the Gianelli job, he wasn't too pleased—admit it."

"Constance, we had to change plans we'd made, that's all. You said you would deal with the Gianelli house—"

"Well, I can't handle everything! Doesn't he understand? This isn't the kind of work where you can keep office hours."

"Constance, he *does* understand that. He doesn't keep them either."

"I hope you're right. But I have to say, he doesn't seem to understand our work at all. He's visually blind, for one thing. So unworldly! He couldn't tell the difference between this Aubusson and a Bokhara. . . ."

"Constance, will you stop this? I don't understand *his* work. *I'm* visually blind when it comes to science. I may try, but I know nothing of the structure of cells, and—"

"That's another thing!" Constance cried. "It's very important for a man and a woman to have things in common. Not for an affair, maybe—but in marriage it's vital! Your parents, for instance—think. They liked the same music, the same books. Montague and I—"

"Just what did you have in common with Montague Stern, Constance?"

"We *thought* the same way!"

"Maybe Frank and I think the same way—has that occurred to you?"

"Of course—and at first I thought you did. Now I'm not so sure. He's very wrapped up in his work, and he's very clever. Now you're clever, too, in your way—not everyone may see that, but I do! But it's a *different* way. He's analytic; you're intuitive. Maybe what he really needs is someone who *does* understand his work, someone with the same background, the same training. There! I knew it! That idea has passed through your mind, hasn't it? I can tell from your face. Oh, darling, don't look sad—it makes me so *angry*. *I* know how talented and gifted you are, and if he can't see that . . .''

And so it went on, day after day, month after month. Once, when I could no longer face the thought of that apartment, and those suggestions, I stayed away for almost a week. When I returned, Constance wept. She said she had known this would happen. Frank Gerhard hated her; he *wanted* us to quarrel.

"That's not true, Constance," I said. "He never speaks against you. You're getting stupid and paranoid. I stayed away because I'm sick of this. I won't listen to it anymore. Either you mind your own business and stop talking about Frank, or I'll move out altogether."

"No, no—you mustn't do that! He'll think you're trying to force his hand, make him marry you—"

"Constance, I'm warning you. From now on, we don't talk about him. Anything else, but not Frank. This is making me miserable, and you miserable, and it must stop. I love him. I won't listen to him spoken of in that way. Not once more. I mean it, Constance."

"Very well. I won't mention him at all." Constance drew herself up. "But I will tell you one last thing. I love you, and I think of you as my daughter. I loved your father, too, very much, and I've been trying—yes, trying—to take his place. I keep asking myself, what would Acland do now? What would happen if you had a father to protect you? I've been trying . . . to be that father; and all the things I've said to you I've considered very carefully. I'm not a fool. I know you don't want to hear them. I know they may turn you against me. Even so, I say them—because I have your best interests at heart. And because I know, if Acland were here now, he would say the very same things. The *very same* things. I'd like you to remember that, Victoria."

It was Constance's great gift: her instinct for the Achilles' heel of others. Did I reject out of hand all those things she said? Some of them, yes—but not others. They seeped into my mind; I hated the way they stained my thinking.

That spring I finally met Montague Stern. It was during what Constance called our "cold war" period, in which all comments on Frank Gerhard were banned and an uneasy truce was being observed between us. It was May 15; I can remember the date, just as I can remember every other detail about that evening.

I met Frank at his apartment. He was late arriving, held up at the Institute, where he was completing a report to be published in a medical journal. One of the assistants had been late in assembling certain data.

"Darling, I'm so sorry," he said. "I couldn't get away—and I may have to go back later. We'll be working on this half the night by the look of it. I may have to leave you with Stern—"

"Would it be better if we called it off?"

"No, no." He seemed abstracted. "It's too late. It would be rude. Besides, we've put this off several times before, and his health is poor. If we cancel now . . . No, we must go. I want you to meet him."

"Is he seriously ill?"

"Darling, he's over eighty. Come on, we should leave."

I noticed, as I had noticed before, a slight evasion in his manner, and also a tension. I might have been more concerned with this had it not been for the fact that I, too, had worries. During the past month Constance had coolly doubled my workload. That afternoon, equally coolly, she had announced a new commission, one we had been hoping for, for months: the restoration of a large château in the Loire owned by a family with one of the finest collections of furniture in Europe. "Darling," she said, kissing me, "it's ours. We've got it. More precisely, it's yours. I want you to do it, Victoria—you deserve it. Do that and you'll be made. Oh, I'm so glad, darling."

I was not glad. The commission was tempting indeed; it would also involve at least three months away in France.

"Frank," I began as we walked along. "Frank, would you mind if I asked you something? It's about my work—"

"Ask away, darling, but do hurry. Damn these cabs—we're going to be late—"

"Does my work seem very stupid to you? I think it must, sometimes. After all, you go down to the Institute, you study disease, you try to find a cure—and what do I do? I choose shades of paint. Select fabrics. Fiddle about with colors."

"Fiddle about?" He frowned. "You don't fiddle about. It's

interesting, what you do. I may not understand it very well, but I'm trying to learn. Do you remember that time in the workshop, when you were mixing those glazes, experimenting with the colors? That was very interesting."

I thought about that time: I had been trying to create for a client a red room—not the same red Constance used so often, the one she called Etruscan, but another. It could be achieved only by a base color overlaid with many tinted glazes. Each glaze, transparent and glowing, modified the color beneath: vermilion over carmine; rose madder over magenta; Venetian red; then a final wash of raw umber, to knock the color back and to age it. It was slow and, to me, fascinating, experimenting with these glazes on the sample boards; the capacity of color to modulate I saw as magic.

"Like truth, you see?" I had said, looking up at Frank as I completed the final layer. "That's what Constance says. There's always another layer. You could go on adding to it, and each time it would change the layer beneath."

"Like truth?" Frank frowned. "I don't agree. Truth cannot be changed. Truth is—one and indivisible, isn't it? I've always thought that truth was very simple."

He had spoken with a certain impatience then, that closed look returning to his face. Seeing that it had been a mistake to quote Constance again, I said no more. I would have liked what he said to be right, but I did not agree with him.

Now, walking south, still with no free cabs in sight, I took his arm. I thought of that commission in France; of his work in a laboratory.

"It's just that I think sometimes," I went on. "I think that there're so many differences between us. Your work is vital, and mine is a luxury. I know that. I do it because I like it—and because it's the only thing I can do well. But it must seem trivial to you. And sometimes . . . sometimes I think . . ."

Frank stopped. He turned me toward him and cradled my face in his hands. He forced me to look at him. "Is this serious? Darling, tell me what you sometimes think."

"Well, I think . . . that you must want someone who understands your work better than I do. Someone with whom you could discuss it. Look at me. I never went to school. As far as science is concerned, I know nothing. I can't play chess. I'm lousy at bridge. I'm not even a good cook—what can I cook, except spaghetti? What can I do? Decorate a room. It's not an awful lot, is it?"

"Anything else that you can't do?" He looked at me with gentle amusement.

"Give me time. I'm sure I'll think of a few other things—"

"No, you won't. Instead, I will tell you a few of the other things you do well. You can be kind—well. You can show understanding—well. You can talk, and think—well. You can touch—well. And you can love—well." He kissed my forehead. "Not so very many people have those gifts, especially the last. Don't you know that?"

"Frank, you do mean that? You are sure?"

"Sure about what?"

"Sure about me. I mean, I would understand. In time, if you found that what you needed was, well, a different kind of woman. A scientist, say, someone like that—"

"Oh, you would understand that, would you?"

"No. Well, I might understand it. I'd bloody well hate it, but—"

"That's better. Now. Take my arm, and as we walk along I shall tell you about my ideal woman, yes?" He turned. "Now, let me see . . . Well, she is a nuclear physicist, I think. She explains where Einstein went wrong while she cooks my breakfast eggs. Eggs Benedict perhaps—she cooks them very well, but then she is a *cordon bleu* chef. She took lessons, when she was also learning Russian—"

"Russian?"

"Oh, of course. Also Chinese, I think. Such a woman! Bobby Fischer learned from her, at chess. And then she is very beautiful. . . ."

"She is?"

"She looks like . . . Let me think, what does she look like? One of those very strange women you see on the covers of magazines. She has skin like china and an expression of haughty surprise. In bed she is a tiger and a seductress—"

"Will you stop this?"

"—famed on three continents for her charm. In fact, there is only one thing wrong with this woman, with this ridiculous woman." He stopped and turned me once more to look at him. We were, I saw, outside the Pierre Hotel at last. Frank's manner was now absolutely serious.

"She is not you—you understand? And it is you that I love. Never say that to me again—never, you hear? I know who put those thoughts in your head. I know who it is who likes to make you think you are inadequate—and it is going to stop. We draw the line, you see, here, outside this hotel. Now, come in. It's time you met your godmother's husband."

*　　*　　*

Stern's rooms were much as Frank had described them. They were paneled, dimly lit, their quiet atmosphere that of a gentleman's club. Looking at the worn leather chairs, the gleam of leather bindings, the fine rugs, at the masculinity of them, at the elderly manservant, I felt that Frank had been wrong about only one thing. Yes, the clock had stopped here, but long before 1930.

I was wrong—I know that now. Frank had been accurate in the date he selected. Then, I felt I had been transported back to the time of my grandfather, and that the room I entered, like the man who rose courteously to greet me, was Edwardian.

Stern's figure was now a little stooped. He moved slowly. Constance had once described his loud taste in waistcoats, but he wore nothing of that kind; his clothes, including a dark velvet smoking jacket, were dated but not vulgar. Approaching me, he bowed over my hand; when he spoke I could still hear that accent I remembered: English, but with traces of central Europe.

"My dear. I am so glad you were able to come. I have looked forward to meeting you. I must apologize—I regretted the postponements. At my age they are a fact of life, I am afraid. I cannot always plan ahead, as I used to." It was said in a dry way, almost as if the thought amused him.

With urbanity he took command of the situation; he seemed to be playing the role of the practiced host, conducting two much younger people on a journey back to a former era. There, conversation proceeded at a measured pace, gently steered by Stern so that each person in turn should have the opportunity both to speak and to listen. Indeed, there was only one thing odd about this conversation: It was entirely impersonal.

Neither before dinner, nor during it, was my godmother mentioned. Whenever the conversation might have ventured in her direction—when there was mention of shared friends or of my work as a decorator—Stern would give it, I noticed, the gentlest of tugs: The subject would be changed, and the reins of the conversation remained in his hands.

Frank did not attempt to forestall this polite evasion—indeed, I sometimes thought he assisted it. This surprised me. I had expected that Stern would speak of Constance, at least ask after her; I had even assumed that it was because of my connection with her that he had wished us to meet.

Toward eleven, when the meal was over, Frank took his leave. The problems at the Institute had been explained earlier, and Stern showed no sign of disappointment that his dinner was being curtailed in this way. Thinking he might be tiring, I suggested that I, too, might leave, but Stern insisted I remain a short while longer.

"Please, my dear. I hate to take my coffee alone—and it is very excellent coffee. Won't you stay and keep me company? I generally allow myself a cigar after dinner. You wouldn't object? My doctors do, I fear—but then, that is the function of doctors, don't you find? To make objections long after they are useful."

It was clear to me that this invitation, made with some charm, was not to be refused. I could feel the force of Stern's will, palpable across the table.

We remained there while the manservant brought us coffee. Stern lit a cigar and drew upon it with evident pleasure.

"Such a pity," he said, "that Frank had to leave us. I admire him—I would like you to know that. There was a time, once . . ." He paused. "I would have liked to have had a son. Unfortunately, that never happened. Had I done so, I would have liked a son like Frank Gerhard."

There was a pause. "However," he continued smoothly, "I'm sure I have no need to recount his qualities to you. I know you will be aware of them. I am very glad, my dear—very glad that he has found you. There was a time, some years ago, when I first met him, when I feared he would not be so fortunate. However, that is past. You must tell me about yourself. What has happened to Winterscombe? I have the very happiest memories of Winterscombe."

I told him what had happened to the house; I mentioned my uncles Steenie and Freddie. As I talked I noticed that Stern's marked reserve was diminishing. He became more inclined to match story with story, anecdote with anecdote; he relaxed, I thought, and it seemed to give him pleasure to speak of the distant past. He encouraged me to speak of my childhood, and even of my parents.

"So you see," I said. "I feel that in some ways I almost know you. Aunt Maud often spoke of you, and of course—" I stopped just in time. I had been about to add that Constance, too, often spoke of him. That admission, I felt sure, would have brought a swift curtailment to the evening.

"Yes?" Stern said. "Do continue."

"Oh, nothing. I was just about to say: it is so curious, when you know someone at second hand, via others. After all, it might have been so very different. If it hadn't been for the quarrel with my parents, I should have met you long ago, at Winterscombe, and—"

I stopped again. Stern's eyes rested on my face; he was watching me now, I saw, with marked attention.

"Quarrel? And which quarrel was that?"

I was blushing. Having stepped into that particular pit, I could see no way of extricating myself. I looked at my watch.

"It's getting very late. I was just thinking, perhaps I ought to go."

"My dear, you were thinking no such thing. What quarrel?" It was said politely, but again I could feel the force of his will.

"You're right. I'm sorry. It's just that it wasn't the most tactful thing to have said—I can see that."

"It was untactful? And why was that?"

"Because you don't want to speak of Constance," I replied in a rush. "I can see that, and I respect that, and I didn't intend to mention her—"

"You did not mention her. You mentioned a quarrel."

"Yes, well, I know about that. There was a . . . disagreement about money, between you and my parents. It was why you and Constance never returned to Winterscombe. Constance explained all that to me. I understand. I'm sure it's a bad idea, to borrow money from friends. It always leads to disagreements—"

I stopped for a third time. Every addition to that embarrassed explanation was making things worse. Stern was now frowning with some displeasure.

"But you are wrong," he said in a cold voice. "I quite agree with you that to borrow from, or lend to, friends can be unwise. However, I never lent to your parents. Nor was I asked to. In fact"—the frown deepened—"I cannot recall having quarreled with them, on any occasion. I simply ceased to see them, after the end of my marriage."

I had risen to my feet. As he said this I sat down again. I said, in a miserable way:

"Oh. I must have misunderstood. I am sorry."

Stern continued to look at me, his face thoughtful. He extinguished the cigar. He allowed the silence to continue, and then, as if coming to a sudden decision, he leaned forward.

"Is something wrong, my dear? You look unhappy. What you have just said hardly justifies that expression. Whatever is wrong is rather more serious than a conversational faux pas, I think. Won't you tell me? Wait." He held up his hand and smiled. "If I am to be treated as a father confessor—and at my age I am quite used to that—then I must first have a brandy. You, too, my dear. No, don't argue. You will like it. It is very good brandy."

It was very good brandy. It hit the back of my throat and

warmed my stomach. I stared at the glass, wondering whether to speak or not.

"If it helps you," Stern began quietly, "consider my age. Consider my . . . position. I think you will find that there is very little you could say to me that would surprise me. Also . . ." He hesitated. "Frank speaks to me, you know. I am not unacquainted with his hopes—and with some of his worries."

"Frank confides in you?"

"There is no need to look so fierce, my dear. Frank Gerhard, as I'm sure you know, is both loyal and—for his age—very discreet. He has said nothing to me about you, or anyone close to you, which he would not say to your face. However, I can draw certain conclusions of my own. So why not tell me what is worrying you? You need not be concerned—it will cause me no pain or embarrassment, should you wish to speak of my wife."

That last remark, I think, was not true. I am sure that it did cause Stern pain when I spoke of Constance—I could see it in his eyes. Nevertheless I did so. I hope I was not disloyal, but I was desperate for his advice. In many ways I can see now that the question I was asking him was the same question I had been asking all my life: Who *is* Constance, and what is she?

I did not tell him the story of the Van Dynem twins or that moment of revelation in her drawing room. I can see now that I did not need to. What I said centered on Constance's capacity for fiction. I tried to explain her interventions between Frank and me; I tried to explain her gift for turning truth inside out. I tried to explain the central issue: When I was with Constance, I did not know myself.

Stern heard me out to the end.

"You see," I said finally, "I love Frank very much. I also love Constance. And I can see—she is going to make me choose between them. She will force a confrontation. And I'm afraid—I'm so very afraid—of that."

"I understand," Stern said after a long silence. He looked across the room in an abstracted way, as if trying to decide something. The silence went on so long it seemed he had forgotten I was there. Then, just as I was about to suggest that I should leave after all, he roused himself.

"Listen, my dear," he said. "I shall tell you a story."

That story was about an apartment in New York, and I will tell it to you in due course. It was about the apartment where, all those years later, Constance would leave me her journals, with her little note: *Here I am.*

I am certain it was a story Stern had never told before and would never tell again. I think he told it for his own sake as well as mine, as if it held a truth that he had to examine one last time. He did not say that. When he had finished, he made a dismissive remark about his wish that history should not repeat itself. I thought for a moment that he regretted having spoken.

Then he leaned across the table and took my hands in his. His dignity remained unimpaired, but the composure had gone; his face was marked, almost scarred, with the deepest emotion.

"That was how, and why, my marriage ended," he said. "I tell you this because I admire your friend who has just left us, and because, as far as he is concerned, you should not hesitate. If it comes to a choice, that is the choice you should make." He paused. "And I tell you this for one other reason, because our predicaments are alike. No matter the circumstances, despite everything, I have always loved my wife."

Later the same evening I returned to Frank's apartment. There, I told him the story that Stern had told me; he listened in silence, his back to me, looking out at the night sky from the window.

"I knew he loved her," he said when I had finished. "He rarely speaks of her. I still knew."

"She has lied to me, Frank. I can see that now. Not just little lies. Big ones. Lies that matter. Lies that go right to the heart of everything. She's lied about my parents, about Winterscombe, the quarrel—"

"Did Stern explain that?"

"No, he didn't. But she did lie. It was nothing to do with money—I can see that. She's lied about her marriage, about Stern. She's lied about herself. I feel I don't know her anymore. I don't know how to speak to her, how to trust her—"

"I think . . . you've known that for some time." He came back to me. "Darling, haven't you?"

"Perhaps. Half-known. Didn't want to know. Refused to admit. All those things."

"Can I say something to you, something important? About her, and about those lies?"

He sat down next to me and put his arm around my shoulders. "It has to be said. Sooner or later. I had hoped . . . but I see now we cannot evade this."

There was a silence.

"She took our letters," he said at last, with a quiet reluctance.

"Darling, you must know this. You must have realized. If she has lied to you, that was the worst lie of all. Are you listening to me? I know I'm right. She took the letters."

I stared at the floor. When had that possibility first occurred to me? When had I first acknowledged it? I knew the answer to that: It was the night Bobsy van Dynem died, when she gave that small dismissive nod to his brother, and I had understood—Constance liked to break people.

"I've thought of it," I said. "I even thought of asking her. But she would only deny it. It's not something that I could ever prove."

"I know she took them." He hesitated, frowning. "In some ways, I think I've always known, from the very first moment I met her. When she kissed me, that first day—do you remember? Then I told myself I was wrong—it was impossible. But it isn't. It's feasible, and . . . it's in character."

"I can't believe that—I still can't believe that." I turned to him imploringly. "She does love me, Frank."

"I know that. I don't doubt it for one second. But what she loves, she destroys." He stopped. "You do understand—she will destroy you, if you let her? She'll break you down, and break you apart—step by step. And she'll do it so skillfully, so sweetly, you'll never feel it happening until it's too late. That's what will happen—if you let her."

"That isn't true." I stood up. "You shouldn't say that. It makes me sound so weak."

"You are not weak." He sounded resigned. "But she has one great advantage. You went to her as a child. You know what the Jesuits say? Give me the child, and I will give you the man."

"That's not true either. I am not her woman—"

"No, you are not. But a part of you belongs to her. When you doubt yourself, that is Constance, who wants you to doubt. When you know something to be true, and you doubt—that is Constance. When you doubt us, when you doubt me—that is Constance also."

I knew what he said was true, and the sadness with which he said it cut me.

"Is it so wrong to doubt?" I said at last.

"Sometimes. Very wrong. I think so. Maybe *I* am wrong—" He broke off. "But I believe, when we all have so very little time, maybe we shouldn't waste too much of it. On doubts. Or on delays. And there I am at fault—I know that."

There was a pause. I saw him look around the apartment; then he turned back. "I thought we should wait—until circumstances were perfect. Until I could give you the things I thought you should have. I can see now that was wrong. I said I would make a speech— but now I think I won't make this speech. I love you, and I want to marry you, Victoria."

One month later, and a few weeks before the date set for our marriage, Montague Stern suffered a heart attack; he died shortly afterward. I learned the news in a long, distracted, and emotional call from Constance. I was in France, and Frank (to Constance's vexation) was with me, taking two weeks away from the Institute. When I told him, it was a Friday morning; we were sitting on a hotel terrace, over an early breakfast. A most beautiful summer's day, the sky unclouded. The house I was decorating lay across the valley; the river Loire lay below us, snaking into the distance, mile upon mile. The movement of the water was invisible.

When I told him the news, Frank rose and turned away from me. There was a long silence.

"When did it happen?" he said finally.

"During the night." I hesitated. "Frank, she's terribly distressed. She was not acting. I shall have to go back."

Frank turned his face away toward the river. He said carefully:

"She hasn't lived with Stern—she's virtually not spoken to Stern—in nearly thirty years. But she is so distressed that you have to go back? You will fly three thousand miles, interrupt your work— after all that has happened?"

"She is his *widow*. They never divorced. That one time he came to the apartment, after Bertie died . . . Frank, if you'd seen her face then . . . In *her* way, she loved him."

"We've discussed the results of her love." His face stiffened. "Stern deserves to be mourned—but not in her company."

"I promised her I would go. The funeral is Sunday. It will be Orthodox. She begged me to be with her, and I agreed. Frank, whatever she's done, I cannot just turn away from her. She's losing everyone. She's lost Stern; she's losing me—"

"Is she?" he said sharply. "You are marrying me. That does not mean she's losing you."

"*She* feels she is. And it's true, in a sense. We are not close, as we once were. Frank, please—she's asking for my help. She just wants me there a short while, a week—"

"She is asking for your help?" His face darkened. "Very well, then so will I. I ask you to stay here. I ask you not to go to her."

"Frank, *why?* What harm can it do now?"

"I'm not going to discuss this."

I think I had never seen him so angry. I watched him fight that anger, and his face—passionate a moment before—became closed. He stood looking down at me. Then, in a cold voice, a voice he had never used to me before, he said: "Very well. You will go back, and I will go with you. I should attend the funeral in any case. I would like to be there. Assist your godmother through her period of distress. I don't imagine it will be a long one."

He was wrong. Constance's grief was deep. It also lasted for months.

She insisted, when I arrived, that she would attend Stern's funeral the next day without me. "I am going alone, in my own way," she cried angrily when I tried to dissuade her. "He was *my* husband. Why should you be there? You never knew him."

Her manner was imperious and agitated. I knew that if I told her then that I had met Stern, it would have provoked a scene. The next morning I tried to explain that Frank had known Stern and would be at the funeral. I am not sure she listened, or that she heard me. She was pacing up and down the room, dressed in black from head to foot, brandishing a letter sent by Stern's solicitors. I had already been made to read this letter, which gave the preliminary details of Stern's will. The bulk of his estate went to charity; his properties, which were numerous, had been left to Constance.

"Look at this letter! I hate this letter! I hate lawyers! I hate the words they use! Houses—how dare he leave me houses! Especially *these* houses. Scotland, the house where we spent our honeymoon— he's left me that. How could he do something so cruel? I know what he was trying to do—make me think, make me remember. It won't work. I'll sell it. I'll sell all of them."

I had promised her that I would wait at her apartment for her return. That return grew later and later. The funeral, I knew, would be over by midday. It was late afternoon when Constance made her appearance.

The black clothes drained all color from her skin. Her face was ashen. She would neither sit nor stand still. She paced up and down, up and down, beginning a sentence, breaking off.

"I hate time!" she cried out at last, in a violent way. Her eyes looked black, as they always did when she was angry. Her black-gloved hands shook.

"Why can't we stop time? Why can't we wind it back? It

marches over us—can't you hear the sound of its boots? I can." She covered her ears with her hands. "Tramp, tramp, tramp. It deafens me. It makes my heart ache. I want it to stop. I want it to go back. Oh, I wish I were God!"

She dropped her hands and began to pace again.

"You know what I'd do, if I were God? I'd do everything so differently. No one would grow old. No one would die. There would be no sickness, no madness, no accidents, no nasty little tricks. And no *memories*. Those least of all. We would all be little children, forever and ever. Very small children. Too young to be afraid of the dark. Too young to remember yesterday. That's how it would be—if I were God."

"Constance," I began, but I doubt she heard me. She scarcely seemed to see I was there.

"Oh, I feel such regrets. I ache and I ache with them. I want my life back. Where did my life go? I want it back, and I want it *different*. I don't want to be alone. I can't bear to be alone. I want Montague. I want the baby I lost. I did love him. I *almost* loved him. And he was always so cold. When I think of him, do you know how I see him? Walking through the snow, in Scotland, on our honeymoon. Back and forth. Back and forth. He used to take my arm. Exercising in the prison yard—he called it that. 'Shall we walk to the wilderness?' he would say. Well, now I'm *there*. Oh, God. It kills me just to think of it—"

"Constance, please don't. I'm sure you're wrong. I'm sure he wasn't cold. I'm sure he loved you—"

"What do you know?" Constance rounded on me. "What do you know about love? Nothing. Stupid little pieties. You sound just like your mother, do you know that? You think love is happiness. Love has *nothing* to do with happiness. Love is being on the rack."

"Constance, please sit down. Try to be calm—"

"Why should I? I am never calm. I hate to be calm. Do you *know* who was at that funeral? That man of yours. Black suit. Black tie. Why was he there? Why is he everywhere I turn, following me about, spying on me—"

"Constance. He *knew* Stern—through his work. I told you he would be there."

"No, you didn't. You never said a word. I know what you thought, both of you. You thought I might not notice him, there were so many people—hundreds of people. Well, I did. I saw him, and I thought: I'll wait. If I have to wait here a year, I'll wait until I'm the only one left. I am Montague's wife. It is my *right*. So I waited in the cemetery. It rained and it rained. He came over to me, that man of yours. He tried to persuade me to leave. But I wouldn't. I shouted at him, I think. Maybe I shouted. He went away, anyway—they all went away in the end. I stood there all alone—and it was horrible, horrible. All the graves were so white. Why are they like that, Jewish graves?"

She covered her face. She turned away to the window, then turned back. She stopped pacing and stood still, staring in a blind way across the room.

"Do you know, I never understood Montague? I discovered that today. I did not understand his paintings. Or his music. I tried, but I never did. Wagner. *Tannhäuser*—that was the opera he liked best. Yes, *Tannhäuser*. Why that?"

She gave a small shake of the head. "The funeral service was in Hebrew. They spoke Hebrew by his grave. I stood there. I listened and I listened. It made me feel so ill. I was a stranger there. I was a stranger to him. The rain poured down. There we were together, my husband and I. I thought, if I listened very carefully, I would understand. One word, one phrase—but I couldn't, Victoria. Oh, it was horrible. I think Montague did it deliberately. He did it for me—one last little irony, one last little reminder. I couldn't speak his language—do you see?"

"So there it is. Nothing but emptiness."

It was over an hour later. Constance was still talking. Nothing I could do would make her stop.

"We bring nothing into this world, and we take nothing out of it. Montague and I—we planned such conquests. Where are they now, all those victories? I have nothing and no one. I am a child again. You see—my black dress, just the same, and my black shoes and my black hair. Everything black. Why is that bird in the room?" she cried out. "Victoria—make it go away. Catch it. I know you want to leave me. You want to talk about me—behind my back. You mustn't do that. Not yet. You must catch the bird first. Quickly. Put it out of the window. Now."

She began to cry again as she said this, covering her face with her hands. She still wore her gloves. She still would not sit down. And she was still crying out, about the bird, some ten minutes later when Frank arrived.

Looking at her from the doorway, he said brusquely, "Call her doctor. Call him now."

Then he disappeared. When I got off the telephone and went in search of him, he was in the kitchen. A frightened maid was in the act of collecting all the knives and locking them away in a cupboard.

"Frank, what are you doing?"

"The doctor will inject her with a sedative. Sedatives wear off. You'll have to clear the apartment—no knives, no barbiturates, no kitchen bleach, no razor blades." He paused. "Does she take barbiturates? I imagine she does."

"Yes, Nembutal sometimes, if she can't sleep. Frank—"

"Make sure you remove all of them. Go through her drawers, all the closets. Check clothes, and the pockets of clothes. Everything."

"Is that necessary?"

"Oh, I assure you it's necessary. You'll see. Do it now, and while you do it I'll sit with her."

It took me a long time, going through all those rooms, all those cupboards, drawers, and hiding places. Constance had never encouraged visits to her own rooms, treating them as her lair, her domain. Now, standing in her dressing room, flanked by closet after closet, I could see the extent to which Constance hoarded the past. Dresses she had not worn in twenty years, rack upon rack of shoes, box upon box of gloves, all meticulously color-coded. Even her wedding dress was there, that legendary creation, looped, embroidered, scattered with seed pearls, the material as brittle as paper. It was packed away in a box. To open it made my hands shake. This was trespassing. I felt like a thief.

By the time the job was done, the doctor had been and gone; Constance had been put to bed. I stood alone in her room, looking down at her. She lay there as still as death, her face as white as the pillowcases.

On the dressing table I had lined up Constance's secret armory of weapons. They had been stockpiled, just as Frank said—stuffed inside shoes, wrapped within underwear, concealed in pockets, at the back of drawers, one little lethal container after another. Different doctors' prescriptions, different dosages, different dates; some of these pills had been prescribed that year; others were older—much older. The most ancient of these pills had been prescribed in 1930.

There was also something else—one final discovery, also small and lethal. I found it in the pocket of a coat long discarded. The envelope was ripped; the stamp was American; the letter inside was brief.

My dearest Victoria [it said]. *My heart is heavy as I write. I have been thinking that you have forgotten your friend. Do you know how much it hurts, when you do not write? I think perhaps I have made you angry, with all that love I wrote, so today I say—I ask only to be your friend as before, so that we may walk and talk as we did. Look, I send another sum to you, just as I promised. Not too hard, this sum. If you cannot do it, I will help—this I promise! I try to make a joke of this, you see—but it is very hard, to speak and never to be answered. I think if you will forgive me, this will be the last letter and the last sum I send to you, Victoria. If you do not write this time, then I shall know for sure that you have forgotten—*

your friend, Franz-Jacob.

I read that letter again, then, standing at the end of Constance's bed. I read it and reread it, until tears made further reading impossible. I was still standing there when Frank came into the room.

I saw his eyes take in the stacks of pillboxes, then the tears, and finally the scrap of paper in my hand. Without a word he took me in his arms and held me close while I wept over this evidence of love, and of treachery.

Frank said we must be careful. He said that twenty-four-hour-a-day nurses were not necessarily enough; he said we might have removed that stockpile of sleeping pills, but there were always other methods, other weapons.

"If she wants to die," he said, "she will find a way to do it."

In this, he was correct. The day before our wedding, Constance smashed a glass and slit her wrists.

The wedding was canceled. On the afternoon when it should have taken place, I sat with Frank in his apartment. He said, "Victoria, listen. If someone wants to succeed with that particular method, they do it behind a locked door. They cut lengthways, up the artery, not across—and they do not do it in their bedroom, in the certain knowledge that a trained nurse will return within ten minutes. This was not a genuine attempt at suicide. It was a message to you. It was a warning."

"Can you be sure of that?"

"Not entirely. I don't doubt that your godmother is ill—and has perhaps been ill, in that way, for many years. But I think she has reasons to stay alive, however much she flirts with death. She likes to fight. She is . . . rejuvenated by battles. As long as she believes that she can take you away from me, she will not kill herself. Not Constance."

"But *why*, Frank—why?"

"I have no idea. It is the way she is," he replied simply.

It was the way she was, and the way she continued to be. Time passed, month after month of it. Summer became fall; Constance's condition fluctuated.

Assisted by tranquilizers, by rest and good nursing, she would seem to make progress. She would leave her bedroom one day; the next, she would announce that she felt strong again—she could go out. The day after, she would feel able to see friends; the day after that, she would insist on returning to our showrooms. During these periods, her appetite would return; she would seem lucid, calm—and repentant. She would apologize in a humble way for all the anxiety and trouble she was causing me, for her failure to take on her share of our work, for the postponement of my marriage.

"I can see now," she said to me quietly one day, "I was right about Frank to begin with. I don't know why I took against him like that. He's been very good to me, Victoria."

I did not trust her then, when she said this—but I did begin to hope. I would think: *another few weeks, a month at most* . . . and I would be wrong. As suddenly as she had seemed to recover, there would be a relapse. Sometimes these were gradual, a terrifying slow seeping-away of all that regained energy—a process I would watch with dread. Sometimes the relapse would be very sudden, without warning.

This cycle, from health to illness, from hope to despair, left me with a dragging fatigue. At work I would try to cope with a mounting backlog of commissions, some postponed, like the château in France; some canceled by furious clients; some in a state of chaos caused by Constance's telephoning nervous assistants, interfering, complaining, countermanding instructions I had given.

I felt I could never escape from her: If I was with a client, she would telephone; if I was with Frank, she would telephone. She might call at three in the morning, then again at four, then again at six. "Why are you there?" she would cry. "Must you be with him now? Victoria, I *need* you."

To begin with, I coped with this because of Frank. He was there always to reassure and to support me. But as the weeks passed, and then the months, I could see that he, too, began to change. He would no longer discuss my godmother's progress, or lack of it, in any detail. His face would harden into a mask of impatience when I did. We were more often apart, as I spent longer and longer hours at work, trying to hold things together, and Frank retreated to the laboratory. On those occasions when the mounting barriers between us seemed about to fall, Constance would interrupt. She seemed to have an intuitive sense for the right moment. On one occasion, when the telephone had rung ten times and I finally reached out in weary resignation to lift the receiver, Frank slammed it back in its cradle.

"Leave it," he said angrily. "Just this once—for God's sake. Leave it."

We quarreled that night—it was our worst and most painful quarrel, accusation and counteraccusation. The next morning we sat opposite each other in silence across the kitchen table. I stared at coffee cups, at pots of marmalade. I felt a sense of despair, and of misery. Frank did also; I knew that. Finally he reached across and took my hand. He said:

"You see what this is doing—to us both? We are never alone. We can never be together. This is what I have done: We have our license. The arrangements are made. We will marry next week. I want your word that this time—no matter what happens—we will not postpone it. Do you promise?"

I said yes; I promised.

That same day, Constance came down to the Fifty-seventh Street showrooms, looking well and contented. All morning she worked with her assistants in her old manner, imperious but amusing, inventive. Around twelve some prospective clients were due to arrive, and this made me nervous—but once they were there, she behaved impeccably. Rooms were discussed, color schemes, preferences, schedules. By twelve-thirty Constance and I were leading these clients, a husband and wife, both deeply conservative, around the showrooms. There was, Constance said, a particular table she wanted to show them, a fine piece, Irish Georgian. Approaching this table, Constance stopped. She said, in a quiet voice:

"Victoria—who put that mirror there? I thought I made it clear. I *said*: no mirrors."

The mirror, an eighteenth-century one, French, heavily carved and gilded, was fixed to the wall. Constance looked at it for some while. Next to her was a large and very valuable Chinese vase. Without another word she snatched up this vase and threw it straight at the mirror. Both smashed. Shards of glass flew in all directions. Someone—the client, I suppose—said:

"What in hell is going on here?"

Constance, having smashed both vase and mirror, began to pick up other objects. She hurled them about the room, a violent cascade of things: boxes, candlesticks, vases. Turning to an antique chair, she grabbed a shard of glass and began to rip its silk, then the muslin underlining, and finally the horsehair stuffing.

She ripped the chair apart; she disemboweled it. The clients had left, of course, long before the chair was demolished. I knew they would never come back. This story—they were influential people—would be all over New York by evening.

Constance was taken home to the apartment, to the full-time nurses. A new doctor was summoned. Two days passed; three. Finally, afraid, I confessed to Frank what had happened. I tried to explain the craziness of the scene. He heard me out, grim-faced, until I had finished. Then he took my arm.

"Get your coat," he said. "I want to show you something. Come with me, to the Institute."

"I want to show you your godmother," he said, leading me into his laboratory. "One last time—I want to try to make you understand.

"Look." He forced me down into a chair. In front of me were two microscopes. "Look at these slides, and tell me what you see."

One last time: those words made me afraid. I could see the strength of emotion in his face, feel it when he touched me. That laboratory made me afraid, too, with its medical smells, its bluish influorescence. The floor tiles were white, each twelve inches square. Every object had its function; every slide, every test tube, its label. Precision instruments, all around us. I was afraid of laboratories, yes—those places where no inconsistencies except those of aberrant cells were permitted. There were no fine shadings here, and there could be no interpretation of facts: Either something was so, or it was not so. I could understand why Frank would say to me: *Truth is simple.*

Reluctantly, I looked in turn down the two microscopes. Frank stood behind my chair. He said:

"These are both blood samples, magnified many thousand times. The slide on the right contains a sample taken from a healthy body. The round shapes you can see are white cells; the ones like small sticks are a virus. You see how the white cells move? They are pursuing the virus, attacking it—disarming it, if you like. In a healthy body, there is this kind of war. It continues all the time. Whenever a virus, a germ, any source of infection enters the body, the body marshals the white cells to its defense.

"Now, look in the left microscope. The sample in this case was taken from a person who is dying of leukemia. The cancer is advanced. What has happened, among other things, is that the body's defense, its immune system, has broken down. More than that—it has defected. The white cells, which should be defending the body, are attacking it instead. The body is self-destructing."

He stopped. I straightened. He said, more gently:

"Do you understand? I show you this because it is the only way I can explain. To me, that second slide is Constance."

"That's a monstrous thing to say."

"I know. But it is what I believe. I am not as hard as you think—I can pity her, up to a point. I know there must be reasons why she is this way." He stiffened. "I do not believe in the idea of pure evil. I think I do not. Nonetheless, I see her as evil—if not in herself, then in the effect she has on other people. I saw it in Montague Stern. The van Dynem twins. And I see it in us. At that point, I draw the line—and I do it now. I must do." He hesitated, then continued: "I know you will not agree with this—but it is what I believe. You may blame my past, if you wish, but I think it is a mistake to imagine you can compromise with evil."

There was another silence. I could hear in his voice a plea, also pride, also the inflexibility of the idealist, an inflexibility deeply ingrained in his character. I thought: *I suppose we had to come to this. It was inevitable.* I measured those white tiles with my eyes: twelve inches, then another twelve inches.

"May I say one more thing?" He leaned toward me. "In med school I worked with people who were dying, with people who wanted passionately to recover and to live. Young children. Men and women in their twenties or thirties—people who had families to support and protect. Fathers who wanted to survive, for the sake of a wife and a child. They were desperate to live. And I had to face them, knowing they would die. So you see, I do not react quite as you do when your godmother slits her wrists. She is not physically ill. She has every advantage. She has your love. She could have everything to live for. If she *chooses* to die—after a certain point—that is her decision. And it will be caused by the malignancy of her will."

"She *is* ill, Frank. What you say is not entirely true. Her *mind* is ill—"

"Possibly," he said shortly. "Sometimes I believe that. Sometimes I doubt it very much. There is some true weakness, and a great deal of pretense. I think she has now taken some grief—genuine grief—and developed it, nursed it into a major breakdown. She will continue to do that as long as it's effective. We set a date for our marriage—she cuts her wrists. She throws vases and breaks mirrors. It is a little convenient, don't you think, this great illness of hers? Its cycles are becoming quite predictable. I found it very strange this evening, when you described that dramatic collapse. It happened . . . two days ago? Yet when I had lunch with her today, she seemed in excellent health and spirits."

"You had lunch with Constance today?"

"Yes. At her apartment. She invited me, and I went. She said she wanted to talk to me urgently. That was not the case. She wanted to give me this."

He held out to me a piece of paper. It was, I saw, a check, a check for a terrifying amount of money. It was made out to the Scripps-Foster Foundation. The ink was black, the strokes of the letters bold. I counted the zeroes.

"It is a bribe, of course." He gave a small shrug. "She suggested that the time had come for me to set you free. She explained we were unsuited, that I made you unhappy, that I interfered with your career, and that for a scientist, you would make an unsuitable wife. She suggested you would not like to live in a modest way, that it was something you had never had to do—and that it was selfish of me to expect you to do so. She said she knew my real priority was my work, and advised me, for my own well-being, to concentrate on that. This check was designed to help me do so. It will be honored when and if she sees results. You see—it is dated one month from now."

"She would . . . donate all this?"

"So she said. She was perfectly lucid when she did so. However, now that you have seen it, I will tear it up. It is something I do not like to touch too much, this check, so you see, we will tear it up very small, into hundreds of pieces. There."

He scattered the fragments of the check upon the bench. Then he turned back to me.

"Then—I am going to ask you one more thing." He looked at me sadly. "Will you still marry me this week? Or will you want to postpone it again? I think you were about to suggest that, earlier this evening. I could see it in your face. No." He made a gesture of the hand. "Don't answer me, not yet. You should know, before you do answer—there is a condition attached."

"A condition?"

"I will never—under any circumstances—see your godmother again. She took our letters. She wrote this check. She has behaved toward you in a way I will never forgive. Never. So—I draw a line. That is it."

"You will never see her again?" I stared at those floor tiles.

"I will not see her. I will not have her in our house. If we have children—and I hope with all my heart—" He stopped himself. "I would like us to have children, and I would not wish them to meet her either. I would not feel safe, if they did."

"You're banishing her," I said slowly, still staring down at those tiles. I looked up. "You're banishing her, Frank—just as my parents did. Do you realize that?"

"Of course. When I was trying to decide . . . what to do . . . I thought of that. It made me feel sure I was right. I am doing this for you—as I suspect they did."

"And this condition"—I paused—"would it also apply to me? Am I not to be allowed to see her?"

"You think I want to impose rules, restrictions?" He flushed. "You are unfair to me, I think. You must decide whether you will see her or not. I would ask . . . that you do not."

"Ask? Oh, I see. I do have some choice, then?" I stood. "That's very good of you, Frank—to allow me free choice when it comes to seeing the woman I think of as my mother. The woman who brought me up—"

"She is *not* your mother. The fact that you think of her as one—that is part of the problem." He turned on me angrily and caught hold of my wrist. "She has behaved like a mother to you, has she? What kind of mother takes the letters two children write to each other? What kind of mother tries to buy a husband off? What else does she have to do to you before you find the courage to break from her? When you look at her, you're *blind*—do you know that?"

"You're wrong. I am not blind." I shook my wrist free. "And it's not a question of courage. I won't be . . . lectured like this—"

"Lectured? This is a lecture?"

"Brought in here, like a child, told to sit down like a child, made to look through a microscope. Told that you will marry me, but now there are *conditions* attached. Conditions—when it comes to marriage? I hate that. I *despise* that."

"Victoria, wait. You misunderstand. Listen—"

"No. You listen. Constance is right in one respect. We *are* different. We don't think alike—and we don't *feel* alike. For you, it's clear, precise, just like your work. Black and white. Right and wrong. It's not like that for me. It doesn't matter to me, you see, not in the final analysis, whether Constance is good or bad. Whichever she is—and she is *both;* she can be *both*—I love her. I can't stop loving her because I disapprove of her—it doesn't work like that. Morality doesn't enter into it. No matter what she's done, or been, I love her—*unconditionally,* the way a child loves a parent, or a parent a child. I can't choose to stop because you tell me to do so. And I won't marry someone who asks me to do that."

I stopped. Frank's face had become white and set.

"Ein dummes englische Mädchen," I went on, more quietly. "Oh, Frank, can't you see? You said that to me once, and there's a part of you that still thinks of me in that way. It makes you impatient—I see it in your face. You think I'm being slow, stupid, that I won't confront the obvious—but you're wrong. I know I'm not clever in the way you are, but sometimes I understand things that you don't. I'm *not* always blind. Sometimes, I do see things."

"And I do not? Is that what you mean?"

"I mean you simplify. You try to make people conform to your beliefs. You fit them into categories: This one comes up to your ideals, or your principles, and that one fails."

"I love you," he said, and I saw the shutters come down on his face. He turned away. "I love you—unconditionally. I thought you understood that."

"But you won't change your mind? About Constance."

His back remained turned. There was a silence, of struggle and hesitation. Eventually he said:

"No. I want our marriage to endure. I will not change my mind about that."

"You think Constance would endanger our marriage?"

"I know, without a doubt, that she would."

There was one last silence. We both knew, I think, that we had reached an impasse. I looked at the particularly bleak cul-de-sac. If Frank had turned back to me then, or spoken or touched me, I know that I would have weakened and given in. I would have agreed to anything then, in order to stay with him. I am sure he knew that. For that reason, with a scrupulousness that was also a part of his character, he did not turn or touch or speak. It was my decision, and Frank, who counted ethics when he computed love, allowed me to make it as an adult should—on my own terms, in silence. Eventually I said:

"Very well. That is that. I will go away. That would be best."

"Go away?" He turned then. I could not look at his face.

"Go to France. Finish that commission. Concentrate on the European work for a while. I can do that."

"Work? I suppose there is always that." He picked up one of the microscopes, then set it down in a hopeless way. "I suppose I can do that too. Work." He paused. "I would give almost anything to prevent this—you do know that?"

"Almost anything? Not your principles, Frank?"

I regretted saying that the moment the words were out. He paled and turned away.

"Well, my principles are rigid and inflexible—you have already told me that. I don't want to argue. I don't want to part from you with an argument—"

"I'll go then," I said.

I waited a few seconds more. I fiddled around with stupid but useful female accessories: gloves, a purse. Frank had turned away to the window. He did not look back. After a while, when silence had become distance, and that distance not traversable, I walked to the door.

The last thing he said to me as I stepped out into the corridor was either a command or a plea. He said: "Don't write. I'd rather not hope. Don't write."

I went straight from the laboratory to Constance's apartment. She was expecting me, I think. I could feel the electricity of that expectation crackling in the air.

She had been eating dinner alone; when I came in, the maid was dismissed. Constance was beautifully and formally dressed, her face perfectly made-up. There was no sign of her illness. She ate, as was her custom, small things: a sliver of toast, a fragment of cheese, half a biscuit, a few purple grapes.

It was the last meeting I was to have with her (I had already decided that) and it was brief. I sat there in that overcrowded, overburdened, lacquered room, a Chinese box of a room, while Constance chattered away: inconsequence, this and that. I scarcely heard a word she said. I thought of her, and of Frank. The two people I most loved in the world, both attempting in different ways, and for very different motives, to force me to make a choice. Either/or. In choosing neither, I felt no sense of achievement, no renewal of confidence. I felt numb, and I felt bleak.

"Constance," I said, when I could bear the chatter no longer, "why did you take our letters?"

A little color rose in her cheeks. I might have expected denials and protestations, but I should have known—Constance was better than that; she was quicker than that.

"You found one? I know you went through my things." She paused. "I should like to say—I opened only one. The last one. I destroyed the others, unread."

"Constance, that doesn't make it any better. It was a wicked thing to do. It was cruel."

"I know that."

"Then why did you do it?" I paused. "I'm leaving, Constance. I'm leaving you, and Frank. I will never come back here, and I won't see you again. So before I go, I want to know: Why would you do such a thing as that?"

"I'm not sure." She seemed to consider the matter. "I have always found it difficult to account for my own actions. Other people always seem so very sure. They did it for this reason; they did it for that. I always feel there are a multitude of reasons—and they may change from day to day—"

"Constance, I've heard all that before. Why did you do it?"

"Well, I think I did it for you. Also for myself—I would not deny that. I was jealous, perhaps. But mainly for you. I was looking ahead—to the future, you see. You set such store by that friendship, and I said to myself: *Oh, that is very sad.* Poor Victoria. She will be let down by this great friend of hers. He will grow bored by this correspondence, or he will forget her, or he will die—she will be disillusioned in time, and disappointed, as women are always disappointed by men. I wanted to spare you that. You see . . ."

She began to gesture, with those tiny glittering hands. There was a slight return of agitation.

"You see—you had put all your trust in him. I could see that. And that is *always* a mistake. Never do that, Victoria. It's like shutting yourself in a prison, throwing away the key. The more you care for someone, the more—in the end—they disappoint you. Men are better at knowing this than women. They spread their bets. Whereas we—all for love. It is our greatest failing."

"Constance, I was a *child*, writing to a friend, in wartime—"

"Ah, but an unusual friend. A friend with unusual powers. A boy who could smell blood, and war, in a wood. Maybe it was that which made me take against him."

"Why should that be? You liked that story. You told me."

"My father died in that place." She turned away her face. "I *never* liked that story."

I knew there was no point in pursuing it further. All I would get would be more ingenious explanations, explanations that would spiral away, advance, then double back. I stood up. Constance at once became alert.

"What are you doing?"

"I told you, Constance. I'm leaving."

"You can't leave. We need to talk."

"No. You talk too much. You always did. I don't want to listen anymore."

"You can't go. I'm still ill. I'm not well yet."

"You'll have to get well without my assistance, Constance. I'm sure you can. Oh, and you should know: Frank tore up that check."

"How high-minded of him! But then he is high-minded, and it does rather show. Was that why you decided not to marry him?"

"No. I admire him, and I love him, Constance. It had nothing to do with that. I'll go now."

She gave a sudden gesture of alarm; she rose to her feet. "You're not really going? You will come back?"

"No. I won't come back."

As I turned toward the door, she began to move toward me. I saw her with Frank's eyes: swift, decorative, mesmeric, dangerous, absorbing others into the force field of her own destructiveness. She seemed, for a moment, dismayed. Her tiny hands gestured in the air. Her little rings glinted. She made one of her rushes at me, as a child does, demanding in an imperious way some confirmation of affection. My godmother, who had never grown up.

She rested her hand on my arm. I think she tried to kiss my cheek. Her hair brushed my face. I smelled that scent she always used, ferns and civet.

The kiss missed. I walked through the doorway. Constance caught at my arm. "Oh, stop—please stop. You're leaving for good—I understand now. That is it, isn't it? I can see it in your face. Oh, please don't go. Stay awhile. You can't leave me alone. I'm not strong. Come with me. Look, Victoria, look at all these rooms, all these memories. That was where you stood, just there, in the middle of the carpet, when I cut your hair. Do you remember the braids—how you hated them? And Bertie—think of Bertie. When he was old and ill, that was where he lay—in that corner there. You loved me then. The books—don't you remember all your father's books? Please stop. Just here. Look at this hall. Don't you remember, the day you arrived, and you came in here—such a solemn little thing! You counted your reflections—you must remember that! You counted six Victorias, then seven, then eight. Look again. Look now. Count again. You see how stern and tall and moral you look? And I look so sad and so small? Look, can you see the tears? I'm so sad. My heart hurts. Constance and Victoria. Mother and child. How many of us can you see? Nine? Ten? There's more than that. Please, Victoria, I don't want to be alone. Don't leave me. Don't go. . . ."

I did leave. I did go. I walked out the door and into the elevator. I left Constance in her hall, with all those reflections of herself to keep her company. Until the moment the door closed, I'm sure she thought she could persuade me back, for she was good at persuasions. Think of all the others who had loved her, the practice she had had.

For a few weeks Constance continued to pursue me by telephone. I saw Frank several times before I left for that commission in France. There were arguments, pleas, then a sad diminuendo, over suitcases; hurried meetings in which each of us found it difficult to meet the other's eyes.

He saw me off at the airport; he insisted on that. Neither of us could find anything to say. I think we both regretted his decision to come. I passed through passport control; I looked back, for one last view of him.

It was cold outside. He was wearing a dark overcoat. Passengers pushed past him and pressed about him on all sides. He looked distraught, dispossessed. He reminded me of refugees, photographs of refugees, on the border between nowhere and nowhere.

I wanted to go back, but I picked up my suitcases, rounded the screen, boarded the plane. I drew a line under the sum, just as he had.

Some time after this—I think it must have been about three years later—I came across him, but at one remove.

Time was devoting its lead story to the new generation of American scientists; there, on its cover, were photographs of the ten people who, according to *Time*, led the field in their disciplines. An astrophysicist; a nuclear physicist; a biochemist. The biochemist was Dr. Gerhard. I wrote to him then, to congratulate him on the progress of his work; I received in reply a letter very like my own, guarded, polite, noncommittal.

Some two years after that, when I was working on a project in California, I saw him again—and again at one remove. One night, alone in a hotel room, I switched on the television and there he was. It was a documentary, a series commissioned by NBC, designed to make medical research comprehensible to the layman. Frank fronted this program. He did it very well: He made science and the painstaking pursuit of disease into a quest that was moving and understandable.

He looked to me unchanged.

This series, and a second that followed it, made Frank Gerhard famous. It made him that rare thing, a public scientist. I almost wrote to him then, but his new fame deterred me. I did not write, though once, when his program came on, I was weak—I touched the screen. I touched his hair, his face, his eyes, his mouth. An electronic pulse. The glass was warm. I missed him very much.

He wrote to me too. It was about six months before my uncle Steenie fell ill, before I went to India. He, too, it seemed, kept in touch at one remove. He had read an article about my work in an American magazine; there were photographs of a sixteenth-century house in the North of England, now a museum, which I had helped to restore.

He complimented me on this work, in a formal way. It was a short letter, which I reread countless times. I carried it everywhere with me. He had signed it as he used to sign those childhood letters. It ended: *your friend, Frank*.

When you love someone, there is always the compulsion to see a secret message, to decode; you read into words meanings you would like to find. I knew that. I understood that love has its links with espionage.

I considered the term *friend*. On the one hand, it was a powerful link with the past, a word that for me—as Frank must have known—was charged with emotion. On the other hand, *friend*, from a lover, from a man I had once looked upon as a husband—that could be read as a polite demotion.

If Frank had given me one more sign, one small and secret indication, I would have answered him. As it was, I hesitated; I delayed; I procrastinated. My uncle Steenie became ill. I did not write an answer to a letter I hoped might be an overture; I was too afraid I might be wrong.

Instead, I let time catch me up and propel me along. I returned to Winterscombe to help Steenie die the way he wanted to die. I listened to him read from Wexton's letters; I listened to that voice of love and sanity. Perhaps, if I am honest, the change began then.

These were the stations of that change: I arranged a funeral; I went to India; I went to America; I looked for my godmother; I returned to Winterscombe. I read. I searched for Constance—and in the process, if I found Frank Gerhard again, I also found myself.

Then, that October evening, I drove from Winterscombe to a London lecture room. It was a large lecture room, and it was packed. I sat in the back row, next to a student whose denim jacket was weighted with badges. The badges proclaimed the defiance of a new generation: MAKE LOVE, NOT WAR.

I can remember the moment when Dr. Gerhard was introduced and came onto the platform. I can remember the moment when the lights dimmed. I can remember that the lecture was highly technical and was accompanied by slides. I can even remember some of those slides, the cells they showed, the vision they opened up of our invisible, active, interior universe. I cannot remember what was said; it afflicted me too deeply to hear the sound of his voice.

Once, I felt almost sure he had seen me. His gaze was directed toward the back of the hall; in mid-sentence he halted, then continued. He spoke without notes; it was the one moment of brief hesitation.

When the lecture was over, the speeches of praise and thanks complete, Dr. Gerhard left the room. There was to be a reception, I knew. I watched the students in the audience file out; I watched older, professorial figures close ranks.

I did as I had planned to do. It was a London university lecture hall; I had a note for Dr. Gerhard, already written. I entrusted it to a porter, and left.

It was ten by the time I reached Winterscombe. Wexton had gone to bed. He had written me a note. It said:

Your godmother called. She wouldn't leave a number. Or a message. She said she might call back.

I stared at this note for some time. The fire was dying down. I threw some more logs upon it. I watched them catch, and the flames leap. Until then, Constance had been remote from my thoughts; it was not her call I was concerned with that night.

I sat down by the fire and put the telephone on the table beside me. I forgot Constance almost at once. I willed the telephone to ring. I tried to calculate how long that reception might continue, at what point Frank Gerhard might receive my note. At ten? At eleven? And, when he had received it, would he telephone at once, or the next day, or not at all? An hour passed. I had an excuse, a reason, for

every one of those silent minutes: The reception continued; the
porter forgot the note; the note was delivered, but left unread.

By eleven-thirty I had other reasons for that silence—and less
innocuous ones. The imagination, at such times, is always vigorous. I
saw how foolish it was, after such a gap of time, to assume Frank
thought of me as I thought of him. Then, at one minute after
midnight, the telephone rang. My heart leaped. I picked it up; I
listened, for some seconds, to silence. Not quite silence: it was a
bad connection, and I could hear on the line a soughing and a
whispering, a sound like the sea heard in a shell, a sound like
the wind, shifting leaves and branches. When a voice finally
spoke, it was distorted by distance; it advanced and was clear, then
receded.

"Victoria," Constance said.

The disappointment was acute. I could not speak. There
was another silence, a sighing along the lines; then she spoke
again.

"Have you read my present?"

"Some of it. Not all of it. Constance, where are you?"

"At a station. I'm calling—from a station."

"Constance—"

"You didn't cheat? You did begin at the beginning? You haven't
skipped to the end?"

"No—"

"I knew you wouldn't. Did you like the flowers I left for
Bertie?"

"Constance—"

"How sad it all is! Other people's lives. They're never quite
real, don't you think? Just a little blur on the side of the picture.
The focus wrong, or maybe someone moved at the wrong moment.
Did you solve the murder? Did you discover who was killed? I have
to go now—"

"Wait—"

"Darling, I can't. There's someone with me. He's calling,
gesturing—I'm afraid he's getting rather impatient. You know how
men are! Better not keep him waiting. I just wanted to be sure my
present was safe. Goodbye, darling. Love and blessings."

She had replaced the receiver. I listened to the line hum.
Constance's voice worked inside me: Even after a gap of eight years,
it still had power.

I am still not sure if it was Constance alone who conjured
me back into the past, one last time. I think it was partly her,

partly the man I loved, partly the fact that to sit and wait was unendurable.

I wanted to act. Instead, I read. I opened the drawer and once again took out Constance's journals. I laid them on my mother's writing table. I stared at them for some time. I feared those plain black covers. Yet inside them, eventually, must be Frank and myself.

They had been given to me in chronological order. I had kept them that way. I cheated. I reached for the notebook at the bottom of the pile. I had no wish, then, to read of putative murders, or distant family history. I wanted to go forward. I wanted to understand missing letters, Constance's view of my own missed opportunities.

I opened this last notebook at the first page. I read:

I have decided this marriage must end.

For an instant I thought I had found the right place, first try. Then I saw the date for the entry: *December 1930.* The writing blurred. I began to turn pages in a frantic way. I came to the last entry: *January 1931.* After that, the pages were blank.

I dropped the notebook. I rummaged through the others, first one, then another. This made me anxious, confused. In the end, when I was certain, I rearranged the notebooks in a stack. I saw, as I might have guessed, that Constance was the one who did the cheating.

Her story stopped too soon. She abandoned it, very soon after I entered its pages.

I was angry then. If I could not hear Frank Gerhard's voice, I would have liked to read his name. Instead, Constance's last journal concerned my christening.

For a moment, I hated those journals. I wanted to throw every one of them on the fire and watch them burn. I almost did so. Then I paused. I still held that last notebook in my hands. It was open at the final entry.

There, I read something that shocked me to the heart. I stared down at a sequence of words. Words became sentences; sentences, paragraphs; paragraphs made sense. There, on those pages, was a solution to a mystery, and an explanation of my past.

I read the last, brief journal then. There were not so many pages. When I had finished, I understood why Constance had given me this present. I understood the letter she had enclosed.

At last all the pieces of the puzzle fell obligingly into place. I knew what had happened in 1930, at the time of my christening; I knew what had happened twenty years before that, in 1910. A death and a birth: it was all spelled out. There before me at last was the name of the victim, the identity of the murderer, the nature of the crime.

I had missed certain clues, in my earlier reading. In some ways I had been hoodwinked; in others, I had been willfully blind. Were you quicker than I was? I wonder. Perhaps you were. All I can tell you is that I read with surprise, with remorse, and—finally—with a sense of release.

Constance had me hooked, yes—but by the time I finished reading, I knew: I was hooked for the last time.

THE
FINAL
ENTRY

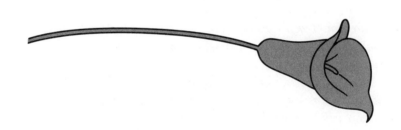

From the journals

I have decided this marriage must end.

Acland had his child today. When the cable came, the words made Constance itch. I don't want distance anymore. The Atlantic is too wide, after all. Acland—I want you close. Acland—I have decided to come and claim you.

Montague knows, I think. Such a frown when I said I must go to England! He was not fooled by talk of christenings. I hoped he might forbid me to go. I will be truthful, Acland—I did. He is so very controlled! He even takes the lovers in his stride—which disappointed me, a little. He keeps to that bargain of his, you see. And so I did wonder—what would he do, my husband, if I broke the rules? Ordinary lovers are one thing; you are quite another. Montague knows that. He believes you killed my father.

Do you know he has never said he loves me? Not once. Not even—in extremis. Don't you find that extraordinary? I do. We have been married all these years, and I am still not sure. Sometimes I think he cares for me; sometimes I think he is indifferent. Once or twice, I have sensed a tiredness and even a disgust. I'll be honest. That alarmed me.

So, you see, I shall come to England, Acland—but I am not quite sure: who am I coming for? I think it is you. I am almost certain it is you. But it might be my husband.

This is your fault, Acland. I'm not sure now how faithful you are to me. Sometimes, now, when I draw my little circle of glass for us, you won't come.

You leave me all alone in there—and that makes me shake. It makes my head ache. It makes the traffic say horrible things. It distorts all the patterns in the sky. I don't like it.

I wish I had a child. There was one—did I tell you, Acland? I had it scraped out. I said it was wicked, but Constance said it wasn't. She said I'd know for sure then whether Montague cared. We both looked in his eyes. She said he hurt. I said he didn't. After that, the doctors said no more children would grow. I minded. Yes. I minded for a while. That little baby haunted me. I don't know what they do with them, dead babies, but it came into my dreams at night. Its eyes wouldn't open. It was worse than my father.

I minded. But today, I don't mind. Today you have a child for me. A girl. Does she look like you? Does she look like me? I shall like to be her godmother—I shall insist on it. Godmother is better than mother, don't you think? It sounds more powerful.

Today—do you know what I did today, while your baby was being born? I made a room. A room that was silver and black and red. I always wanted a room like that. Today I made it. It is perfect. Every single thing in it is in the right place. Half an inch to the right with one thing, and you'd spoil it. That was what I did today.

Acland—you are there? You are listening? Speak up. Speak up. Your voice is so quiet sometimes. It's such an ordinary voice. I hate it to be like that. Speak up. Shout. Shout louder. Acland, please. Constance can't hear you.

That afternoon, when Stern looked into his wife's sitting room— the room she had just completed decorating; it was red and silver and black—Constance was writing.

She sat at her writing table, head bent; her fountain pen scratched. She gave no sign of hearing Stern enter. When he spoke her name she gave a start. She covered with her hand the page on which she wrote. As Stern approached she closed the black cover of the notebook in a hasty, furtive way.

Stern was faintly irritated by this pantomime. It had been performed before. It was designed, he suspected, to awaken his interest in these notebooks. In the early days of their marriage, the existence of these books (diaries, journals, whatever they were) had been more carefully protected. But time had passed; the notebooks had been, first, revealed (as if by mistake), then flaunted. Once they had been locked away; now, from time to time one would be left out, as if Constance had forgotten it. Stern understood the reason for this: His wife wished him to spy on her, as she spied on him. Accordingly, he was careful. He never touched these notebooks.

"My dear." He leaned forward. He placed a light kiss on her hair. "Don't look so anxious. I respect your privacy."

This annoyed Constance. She made a wry face, attempting to disguise her displeasure.

"How moral you are. I can never resist other people's secrets. I used to be a great reader of other people's letters, you know."

"I can imagine."

He looked around this new room of his wife's. The walls glowed. Lamps were lit, such daylight as there was almost obscured. A coromandel screen—a fine one—hedged off a corner. The lacquered walls glowed a dull red; Stern, for some reason he could not define, found this color, though subtle, confining. The room was over-crowded, he thought—as were most of the rooms his wife designed. He found it . . . fortified.

"The room is a success? It pleases you?"

He had not meant to make the remark a question. The fact that he did seemed to irritate Constance more. She was very thin-skinned about criticism.

"I like it. It suits . . . me."

Her tone was defiant. Stern looked out the window: a winter dusk; snow was falling. He turned back to his wife, who was now fiddling with pens, paper, envelopes, as if impatient he should leave.

Constance's head was bent. The lamp on the table made a circle about her. In its light, her black hair shone. It was cut in an angular way, across her forehead, flaring out in a wedge shape either side of her delicate jaw. It gave her an Egyptian look, a look much admired, much copied. Stern, who could see that the effect was beautiful, missed the old hairstyle. He had preferred the suggestivity of that long and abundant hair, which, when the pins and combs were removed, could tumble about bared shoulders. This, he knew, was the Edwardian in him. His tastes were old-fashioned.

Constance fiddled with one of the many bracelets she wore. She smoothed the skirt of her dress. Stern's gaze seemed to make her uncomfortable. The dress, made for her by one of her French designer friends, was a dramatic, an electric blue—a color few women could wear. Its skirt was short, the cut of the shoulders somewhat mannish. Stern, able to see that the effect was elegant, disliked the dress. He still could not accustom himself to high heels, bared legs, the seams of stockings, the assertiveness of a painted face. He felt a moment's regret for the fashions of the past, for clothes that revealed less and promised more. He was, he thought, growing old.

"You're going out?" Constance put her notebook in a drawer.

"My dear, yes. That was what I came in to say. Not for long. An hour or so. You remember the South African I mentioned—the one from De Beers? He's staying at the Plaza. Just passing through. I have to see him."

"Oh, there's always someone you have to see." She made another face. She rose. "You know what I wish sometimes? I wish you had lost all your money last year—like other people. I wish you had gone *phut!* in the crash. Then we could have gone away, just the two of us, and lived somewhere very simply."

"My dear. You would dislike that very much, I think. I apologize for not going *phut,* as you put it. I was always prudent, as you know."

"Oh, prudence. I hate prudence—"

"I did make some losses, in any case. Everyone did."

"Did you, Montague?" She gave him an odd, fixed look. "I can't imagine that somehow. Making gains, yes. Losses—no."

"We all make them occasionally, Constance."

Something in the way Stern said this seemed to disconcert her. She gave a toss of her head.

"Maybe so. Maybe so. Well, if you're going, go—I don't want to make you late. For your South African."

"I'll be back around seven, Constance."

"Fine. Fine." She sat down again at her writing table. "We should leave for the party at eight—you hadn't forgotten?"

"No. I shall be back in good time."

"I'm sure you will. You were always punctual." She consulted her small wristwatch. "Two hours, for your South African? He must be important. On a Saturday too."

"It may not take so long. I'll be back as soon as possible."

"Oh, don't rush on my account. I have plenty to do. You must give him your full attention."

Stern went out. He ignored the edge in her voice. He closed the door. He paused. As he had expected, Constance at once picked up the telephone.

A small click as she raised the receiver. She spoke in lowered tones; Stern did not stay to eavesdrop. He knew who it was she would be calling—his wife, that self-appointed spy in the house of love. She would be calling the latest firm of private investigators.

*   *   *

Outside the house—which was located close to the apartment building on Fifth Avenue where I later lived with Constance—Stern paused. To reach the Plaza Hotel, and a nonexistent appointment with a South African useful to him the previous year but now safely in Johannesburg, Stern would have turned left and walked south. Instead, glancing up and down the avenue, he turned right and headed north.

He walked at a leisurely pace. The sidewalks were crowded; people had begun their Christmas shopping. Women with shopping bags, and children in tow, pushed past. The sidewalks were slushy. Dirty snow lay in the gutters. It made him think of Scotland, and of his honeymoon, thirteen years before. *Shall we walk to the wilderness?* Stern braced himself, turned his face to the cold wind blowing down Fifth. He had the sensation, though alone, that his wife walked with him.

The apartment he visited was some ten minutes' walk away. Located on Park Avenue, on the fifth floor of a new building, it was the apartment he spoke of to me shortly before he died; the same apartment I would visit all those years later, in my search for Constance. It had been purchased by Stern in a false name, through one of his companies. Stern had been careful to make the trail that connected the apartment to him a devious one, but one it was not impossible to disentangle.

The investigators his wife employed would have traced the connections by now, he knew; they had had over a year in which to do so. They had followed him to the apartment from the first, of course. Considerate to their needs, he had selected one whose windows overlooked the avenue. With the lights left on and the shades raised, the man who followed him—who always took up his position on the far side of Park—had an excellent view.

Stern had become fond of these investigators. These spies reassured him of Constance's jealousy; their presence reaffirmed the possibility of her love.

Stern, considerate to these hard-working men, did not hurry. The man usually fell into step behind him around the junction of Park and Seventy-second. Only when the man assigned for that day did so, at precisely this place, did Stern quicken his pace.

The apartment had been purchased in the name Rothstein. The porter greeted him by this name, as he always did. Stern took the elevator to the fifth floor. He let himself in. He switched on the lights in the living room, which overlooked Park Avenue, and moved once or twice in front of the window. When he was sure he had given the watcher sufficient encouragement, he sat down, out of sight.

The woman he awaited would be punctual; he paid her, among other things, to be so. There would be, as there always was, fifteen minutes of solitude before she arrived. On this, from the first, Stern insisted.

When Stern first bought this apartment, he had for several months left it unfurnished. He relished its emptiness and its anonymity. In those days, when the deception first began, an empty apartment had been enough; he had felt no need for furnishings, or for the woman. To begin with, his visits there had been brief, intermittent; then, as the weeks passed, more frequent. In this apartment Stern sought release that he could not always find at work, in his office building on Wall Street. He certainly could not find it at home. Here, in empty rooms, he did.

After some months it occurred to him that the investigators, eager to earn their employ, might not content themselves with watching. They might secure entry to this love nest—it would not be difficult. Porters, after all, could be bribed.

Thinking that the investigators might find a love nest without carpets, chairs, or bed somewhat odd, Stern had furnished it. He had done so, to his own surprise, with great care. He constructed that environment I would see, unchanged, almost forty years later; he constructed an environment without memories.

The rooms had a bleached look: white walls, white furniture, white carpets. Snowy rooms, pristine, their contents the height of modernity. You remember? Bauhaus brutalism, an apartment in which nothing was older than yesterday: an environment made for the machine age. Stern, looking around him, knew that he had achieved what he set out to achieve: a place devoid of memories, an urban empty space.

Several months after he first came here, realizing that as far as the investigators were concerned, there was one element still missing, he had hired the woman.

The woman, he felt, matched the room. Her real name he was about to discover that afternoon; her stage name, the one she always used, was Blanche Langrishe. An absurd and artificial name, a name only an innocent could ever have selected: *Blanche*. Yes, this girl fitted this white apartment.

She was a singer. The first time Stern ever saw her, she was in the front line of the chorus of the Metropolitan Opera. The second time, at a friend's house, she sang lieder after supper. She had a high, clear soprano voice, still needing further training but possessed of an extraordinary purity and range. Stern, drawn by the voice, had spoken to her. He discovered something else: Blanche might have an angel's voice; her instincts were those of a showgirl.

She came from Queens. She had made it to the Metropolitan, which she despised, and to Manhattan, which she did not. She was taking dance lessons. She saw herself moving on from opera to the Broadway musical. One day, she would say, her name would be there on the Great White Way, up in lights.

Stern thought this possible; the girl had drive, surprising common sense. When, some weeks after that first meeting, he had outlined his proposal, Blanche considered, then, without argument, agreed to his request.

She did not ask questions, but she liked to talk. She had short platinum-blond hair, a pert and pretty face. The antithesis of his wife. She fitted this apartment. Sometimes Stern, looking at her lying back on the sofa, long legs against white leather and chrome, felt he had chosen the furnishings for her before he met her.

He paid her, for two visits, two hundred dollars a week.

Five minutes to go. Stern did not need to look at his watch. He could compute time as it passed, without the aid of instruments.

Rising, he crossed to the window. He adjusted the shade; he gave his watcher hope. He returned to the white leather chair. He sat down. He thought.

About his marriage, as he usually did. Once, he had been able to divert himself from this topic. The ramifications of his business dealings, the intricacies of finance, the consideration of music or art—all these subjects had had the power to banish thoughts of his wife. That was less true now. At work, at the opera perhaps, sometimes in a gallery, Constance could be drowned out still, but these occasions became rarer as time passed. Constance invaded his mind's space; she took up a vantage point there. Stern hated and resisted this. Often, he disliked his wife; he could not understand why he continued to love a woman he did not respect.

He considered her duplicities: the smaller betrayals, then the larger ones. He considered her lovers, a long list of them. He considered a baby, lost in a miscarriage—Constance claimed—the previous year. He was not convinced that all of the lovers existed. He was not even convinced that the baby had existed or, if it had, whether an abortion or a miscarriage had taken place.

"Hold me, hold me, hold me," Constance had said, lying in

bed, her face waxen and strained. "I've been trying to tell myself it was for the best. I wasn't sure if you were the father. . . . Oh, Montague, don't be angry. I know I've been careless. I'll never be careless again."

Stern rested his face in his hands. He saw that he had forgotten to remove his fine leather gloves, that he still wore his overcoat. He removed them. He folded the coat on an aggressive chair. He sat down again. *I shall never have a son. We shall never have children.* He said this to himself; he knew it was true, and he wondered, in a distant way, when it was that he had accepted this fact.

He looked around the brightness and cleanliness of the room; he found it thronged with figures, all of them men. Some of the lovers were men he knew; others were merely names to which he attached shadowy faces. Constance did not like this; she wanted her lovers to be very clear to him. She wanted Stern to *know* them.

"But, Montague," she would say, clinging to his arm, "I only obey you. I stay within the limits you set! You said sexual fidelity did not matter. You said that as long as I told you everything, and there were no secrets between us—"

"Constance, my dear. Keep the details to a minimum. By all means say when you begin an affair, and with whom. Feel free to tell me when it ends or when you embark on another. But I really have no interest in what you do in bed."

"Don't you? Don't you?" She clung tighter to his arm. "You sound very sure, Montague—and I don't believe you at all. I think you want to know, very much. This new young man of mine—well, he is a great deal younger than you, so I can't help but make certain comparisons."

Her animation, at such moments, was always very great. She would look up at him with the confiding air of a child, her lovely face flushed, her eyes bright. Stern might try to stop her; once or twice, when the anger and pain were intense, he came close to violence— which delighted her. Sometimes he would leave the room, telling himself he would also leave his wife. At other times, despising himself, he listened—because, of course, his wife was right. He did want to know: every painful detail.

There was a part of his mind that insisted on knowing—all the gyrations, all the cries and exertions. Was this voyeurism on his part? Sometimes, when he found the accounts arousing—and that happened —Stern feared that it was. At other times he felt no perversion was involved. It was simply that he had to understand the geography of betrayal; he wanted to chart the terrain of the worst.

Did these events his wife described truly occur? Stern was never sure. But, real or imagined, he watched these lovers. He saw their sweat. He saw also (she insisted he see) the degree of his wife's response: greater, she claimed, than with him. That was the next, and inevitable, wound. He had expected it; he had awaited it. When it came he was calm; he wondered, in a distant way, how she would contrive to torture him next.

There was always a new twist. The previous year, a child which might or might not have existed, which might or might not have been his. This year, he thought: *Acland*. Acland, a weapon kept so long in reserve, would be the next.

The lovely ambiguities of lies; the unfailing seduction of the half-truth; the allure of an enigma, of a riddle without a solution— these were the things he loved. He retaliated with deceptions, with riddles of his own, with a secret apartment and a hired woman. Stern grasped the chrome arms of his chair. His hands felt dry and cool, yet some residual dampness in the skin left the print of his fingers on the metal. He lifted his hands. He looked at a pattern, the unique whorls of his identity, printed on the arm of a chair. The air dried them; even as he looked, they evaporated.

Destruction was a great absorber of energy, he thought in a tired way. So much time, so much agonizing, yet he began to see that both he and Constance were imprisoned by their marriage.

He thought: The only way we can reach each other now is through pain. There is a conspiracy between us, the complicity of the tortured and the torturer. The hostage and the hostage-taker need each other. No closeness, he thought, is closer than that.

He picked up his overcoat, half intending to leave. He heard a punctual key turn in a hired lock. *This is what I have allowed myself to become*, he said to himself. Was change possible, even now? He laid the coat down, then, as the singer came into the room, rose to his feet.

Blanche Langrishe wore a pert hat. A small spotted veil disguised the serene china-blue of her eyes. Her high heels tapped on the parquet floor. She moved straight to the window.

"Poor guy. He's there. Right across the street. He looks as miserable as sin. It's freezing out there."

She removed her hat in a businesslike way. She tossed her coat across a chair, shook her blond curls into place.

"He's got a notebook, I'll bet. At least, I've never seen it, but I'm sure it's there. You know what? I think it's time we gave him something to write in it. A new development. What d'you say?"

"What had you in mind?"

"Oh—you *can* smile." Blanche gave him a sideways glance. "I was beginning to wonder, you know?" She sighed. "Well, what about a kiss? We could give him a kiss—for a start."

"You think a kiss would encourage him?"

"Sure. I can think of a few other things as well, since you ask—but a kiss would do for openers." She looked back at Stern again. She gave him a considering glance. "I like you, you know. You're handsome. I like the way you dress. How old are you, anyway?"

"My dear." Stern was not listening. He moved to the window. He adjusted the shade. "My dear, I am ancient beyond belief. I think of myself as very old, especially when I am in the company of such a charming young woman as yourself—"

"How old?"

"I am . . . fifty-seven," Stern replied.

This was the truth, and it surprised him.

"You don't look it." Blanche took his arm. "You could pass for forty-eight, any day of the week. Come on, don't look so sad. Cheer up." She paused. "Wouldn't you like to kiss me—after all these weeks? You never have."

"I suppose I could."

Stern moved forward. He took Blanche Langrishe in his arms. Her height was surprising to him after the tiny stature of his wife. Her skin smelled milky, powdery, sweet.

"You don't mind the lipstick?"

"No. I don't mind the lipstick."

"Flamingo pink. That's what they call it. I ask you—what jerk thinks up those names?" She took a step to the side. "Come a little closer. He can't see us there. That's it."

Stern kissed her. It was fourteen years since he had kissed any woman other than his wife; the kiss felt odd, unorthodox, a matter of mechanics. He put his arms here, his lips there. Blanche Langrishe tasted cosmetic, a not unpleasant taste.

"Well, I don't know about him"—Blanche gestured to the window; she smiled—"but I liked that. I knew I would. Want to do it again?"

"Perhaps not. We don't want to overexcite him."

"How about me?" Blanche made a face. She moved away from the window. She threw herself down, in a decorative way, on the white leather couch. She kicked off her high-heeled shoes. She examined the symmetry of her stocking seams. She flexed her small pink toes. She gave him a measuring look.

"You know what I thought today? I thought: two hundred bucks a week to sit on my butt and talk. Am I giving value for money? That's what I thought. I could give you a whole lot more, you know."

"That's very generous of you, but—"

"No, huh? Okay." She sighed. "I thought you'd say that." She sat up. "Look, why don't you level with me? I won't talk. But I get kind of curious—I mean, this whole setup . . . You're fixing up a divorce, right?"

"A divorce?" This surprised Stern. Such a possibility had never occurred to him. "No." He looked away. "No. I'm not contemplating a divorce."

"But you are married, yes?"

"Yes. I am married."

"Okay. Okay. End of inquisition. Except"—she hesitated; she drew a small circle on the parquet with one stockinged toe—"except, I do think—you know what I think? She must be crazy, your wife."

"She's very far from that."

"Oh, yeah? She makes you miserable. She's losing you. There's a lot of women in this town who—"

"I don't want to discuss my wife, Blanche."

"Sure. Sure. Off limits. Okay. You're loyal. I can understand that." She hesitated. To Stern's surprise, she blushed. "I wish you'd *look* at me, sometimes, that's all. Maybe it's that."

"I do look at you. We . . . talk."

"Oh, sure. We talk. You look—except you don't see. I might as well be invisible. I am *here*, you know. I am real. Blanche Langrishe."

"That's not your real name."

"No. But then Rothstein isn't yours either. I know that."

"Do you know my real name?"

"Sure." Blanche gave him a defiant look. "I asked around. It's okay—I won't say anything."

"Would you tell me your name—your real name?"

"Mine? You really want to know?"

"Yes. Oddly enough, I do. Perhaps today—" He looked away. "I would like to know who you are. Who I am."

"Okay." She had not caught the last part of that remark, said in a low voice. She hesitated. Color mounted in her cheeks. "It's

Ursula. I mean, can you beat that? Ursula. I hate it. Sounds like a nun or something. Sister Ursula. Ugh!" She wrinkled her nose in distaste. Stern smiled.

"It suits you," he said gently. "It suits your voice—your singing voice."

"You think so?" She looked confused by this. "Well, I guess it doesn't matter. What's in a name, right? I was Ursula. Now I'm Blanche—"

"Oh, I don't agree." Stern had risen. He moved toward the window. "The name one is given at birth—it's important, I think. Part of one's identity. Have you ever been to Scotland?"

"What?" Blanche was staring at him. "*Scotland?* You must be joking. I never even went to Europe—" She broke off. "Why do you say that? Why there?"

"Nothing. No reason." He still had his back to her. "I went there once, that's all. When I was first married. It was wintertime. There was snow—in fact, my wife and I, we were marooned for some while by the snow. When I was there—" He stopped. There was a little silence. Blanche could see the tension in his body.

Leaning forward, she said, "Go on."

"When I was there—it was a desolate place, I suppose, though I did not find it so. When I was there, I felt . . . the very greatest exhilaration. The world seemed filled with possibility. My marriage seemed filled with possibility. A promised land—" He stopped once more.

Blanche said gently, "A promised land? Do you mean the place—or your marriage?"

"Oh, both," he replied. "The place, and my marriage—at that point they felt to me connected. I believed. I hoped—a promised land. My wife—" His voice broke.

Blanche saw him bend his head, then cover his face with his hands. She watched him break, this man whose composure had never previously faltered. He did not speak again. She could see that he tried to silence the sounds of his grief. Tears came to her eyes; quietly she sat there, letting him weep.

Some while later, when he was calmer, she rose to her feet. She knew he would not want to look at her, and that it would shame him to know she had seen him like this, exposed, and vulnerable, all the waste of the years in his face.

She touched his arm gently.

"Stay there," she said. "Stay by the window. I'm going to sing to you. You like it when I sing." She hesitated. "It's why I'm here, I guess—I see that now. Because of my voice. I'll sing you lieder—the way I did that first night."

Standing in the center of the room, she drew in her breath. Her voice moved, up and then down the octaves. She tossed back her showgirl curls and began on the lieder, in her angel's voice. Unquestionable purity. Stern, facing a window and a lighted city, neither of which he saw, listened to the notes: high, clear, sweet, pure, true. He saw himself, and his wife, walking through the snow along a narrow pathway. They came to a balustrade rail and looked out at a beautiful wilderness. *We could have all this.* . . . And so they might have once—he believed that still. But not now; now, too many years had passed, and too many wrongs had been committed. By himself, he knew, as well as by his wife. If their marriage had become a prison, a kind of hell, he, too, was to blame.

Lack of trust on his part; pride; a will so trained he could not let his heart speak. Might it have been different, had he not feared to express love? Perhaps, he thought sadly—but no more than perhaps.

He could feel the music now, opening out, offering to him the consolation of art, welcoming him, note by pure note, to a finer place. This, at least, he had still; this at least remained undestroyed. He thought, with a sense of surprise, there was another world; its promise was here, in this music and in this voice. With this realization he felt the sense of the greatest release, as if the door of his prison swung back, and there at last—beyond the figure of his wife—was the freedom he sought, the peace, and the refreshment as well as the loneliness of an isolated place.

When Blanche had finished her singing, he embraced her once. She knew, he thought, that they would not be meeting here again. She accepted it, as he had known she would. He pressed her hands, thanking her for the gift of her voice. He left.

Leaving the apartment building, he crossed the avenue. This he never did, and the departure from a settled routine caught his watcher off guard. In a hasty way the man turned to fix his eyes on a shop window; Stern, as he passed him, gave a courteous bow and raised his hat.

That night, when he and his wife returned from the dinner party, they sat together for a while. Stern held a glass of whisky; Constance played with her two small dogs. One was Box, now old (and indeed, as Constance had said, grown fat); the other was a pug, a recent acquisition. Their conversation was at first desultory; Stern lapsed into silence. He sipped his drink. Constance, kneeling on the carpet, toyed first with this dog, then with that. She seemed to Stern both in high spirits—as she often was when new mischief was afoot—and curiously tense.

She spoke of her forthcoming visit to England; of a christening; of Acland. Acland she mentioned with some emphasis. Stern made no comment. He was listening to the lieder as sung to him that afternoon. Inside the lieder he was safe.

"Well, Box, what do you think?" Constance said, picking up her Pomeranian and kissing him on the nose. "Shall I go to England? Shall I make Montague very, very cross? Shall I make him jealous? He gets very jealous indeed when I talk about Acland—have you noticed that? Oh, you have—what a *clever* little dog! You're not jealous, are you? You don't mind whom I love—"

"Constance, don't be childish." Stern set down his whisky glass. "You pet those dogs too much. You're turning them into lapdogs."

"They like it." Constance gave him a sulky look. "Don't you, darlings? You see? They do. Box just gave me a kiss."

"Constance, it's late. I'm going to bed."

"Don't you want to talk about England? I think you do, really. I can tell from your face."

"There is nothing to discuss. I have asked you not to go—"

"Asked me?" Constance put Box down. "Oh, you always *ask*. It's so boring. Why don't you *tell* me not to go? Forbid me? That's what you'd like to do, after all. You can't bear the thought of my going. Every time I mention Acland's name—such a black look!"

"You exaggerate. I have no intention of forbidding you to do anything. You must make the choice."

"I've made it—I've told you. You can't stop me. I will go. It just might be amusing if you forbade it, that's all. Then I could see whether I dared to defy you—"

"Constance, stop playing foolish games. If you want a husband who behaves like a tyrannical father, you should have married someone else."

"Should I indeed?" Constance, all movement a moment before, became very still. She turned upon Stern a set and calculating glance. Stern, married long enough to know that this expression would be followed by theatrics, by an outburst of some kind, stood up.

"Maybe you're right. I should have married someone else," she went on in a thoughtful voice. "Maybe I should have married Acland. I could have, you know. A snap of the fingers! As easy as that."

"Do you think so? I rather doubt that."

Stern, moving toward the door, paused, then looked back. Constance remained crouched on the floor. Her eyes glittered. With a sense of exhaustion, Stern watched her anger gather. He could see it coiling in her body, tight as a spring.

"What do you know? Nothing." One of her small hands clenched, then unclenched. "You're unimaginative, Montague. You'd never be able to understand Acland and me—all you know is that Acland is a threat."

"A threat?" Stern frowned. "To me, or to you?"

"To you, of course." Constance sprang up. "How could Acland be a threat to me?"

"Oh, when we invent people, they are always a threat. I know that. I learned the lesson firsthand."

"Invent? Invent? You think I invent Acland? What a fool you are." Constance tossed her head. "How dare you say that. You're dull. You understand making money—nothing else. Acland and I are close. This close!" She pressed her two hands together. "We always were. Like twins—no, closer than twins. Shall I tell you something— something I never told you before? You know why I am bound to him? Because Acland was the *first*."

Stern considered this piece of information. He had expected it, or something similar; it was part, he supposed, of the next twist.

"Yes. Well, Constance, it's a little late for such dramatic revelations. I shall go to bed."

"You don't believe me?"

Stern looked at his wife. Anger, as always, increased her beauty. It made her eyes shine; it brought color and radiance to her face.

"No, my dear. I don't believe you."

"It is true!"

"I think you would like it to be true. Wishing does not alter facts. I imagine that if you had consummated your relationship with Acland, you would have tired of him, as you tire of everyone else. As it is—"

"Sex? You think it's a matter of sex? How stupid you are! A vulgarian, after all, with a mean little imagination."

"Possibly. On the other hand, you pursue sexual gratification with considerable energy, and I suspect you find it remains elusive. Despite your claims. I warned you once, of that."

"I pursue what I cannot find with you—that's natural enough."

"My dear. There is no point in hurling accusations back and forth as to my virility or your frigidity. Let's just say I am sorry to

have disappointed you in that respect. However, it is late, and we
have had this conversation before, many times—"

"And if I loved Acland—what then?" Constance took a step
forward. "That would spoil all your careful bargains, wouldn't it?
Lovers are permitted—but not love! Only you could think up a
contract like that and imagine it was workable. You always wanted
me bridled. You always wanted me on a leash—"

"Constance, you are mixing your metaphors."

"You set down all the provisos, and you expect me to abide by
them. Why should I? They stifle me. They close me in so I can't
breathe, so I can't be myself. But if I loved someone—I'd be free of
you then. There! Just like that! One might tire of a lover—not of
someone one loves."

"Do you think so?" Stern looked at her, a certain regret in his
voice. "I disagree. I think it quite possible—to tire of someone one
loved."

The quietness with which he spoke seemed to disconcert Constance. She stepped back from him. She bent down, picked up one
of her dogs, and fondled it. She kissed it on the head. She looked up
at her husband. She gave a small, tight smile.

"Did you fuck Blanche Langrishe today, Montague? You were at
the apartment quite some time, so presumably you did. More than once.
You can't have imagined I believed in that South African, surely?"

"I was not very concerned whether you believed or not."

"Oh, but I thought we had an agreement—no secrets between
us! Yet you have been seeing that woman for months, and never
mentioned it once."

"My dear, you know all my secrets. I knew it was only a matter
of time before you found out."

"Well, indeed. A little singer, with dyed hair, who comes from
Queens. Not what I would have expected from you, Montague—a
man of your refined tastes. Still, I expect you find her gratifying in
bed. A cheap little whore with her eye on your wallet. What is it you
like about her, Montague? I long to hear. It can hardly be her
intelligence, I think. What is it? Her chorus-girl legs? Her tits? Her
ass? Or is she simply very good in the hay?"

Stern still paused by the door. An expression of distaste came
upon his face.

"You should not speak in that way," he said in the same quiet
voice he had used before. "The words—you choose such ugly words.
Cheap ones. I have always disliked it when you speak in that way.
The words . . . don't suit you."

"Oh, I'm so sorry. I forgot. You have such gentlemanly tastes. A woman is not supposed to know such words, let alone use them. I mustn't say *fuck*, is that it, Montague? Oh, no, of course I may say it—but only to you, in bed. That's a little hypocritical, don't you think? After all, it's a perfectly good verb. It's what you do. You go to your apartment, and you fuck your little whore, twice a week. Then you pay her off, I suppose. Or do you just give her presents—vulgar presents? Yid presents? Like the ones you give to me?"

Constance advanced on him as she spoke. Stern watched her approach. The closer she came, the smaller she appeared. His tiny, angry, hurting, vulgar wife. Her anger pulsed in the air; it snapped in her eyes, flew out from her hair. Her voice had risen. The pug, always terrified of such scenes, fled for cover. It crouched under the legs of a chair, then peeped out.

"You're frightening the dogs, Constance," Stern said in a polite voice. "Don't shout. The dogs dislike it. I dislike it. And the servants will hear you."

"Fuck the servants. Fuck you. Fuck the damned dogs. I hate both of them, anyway. You gave them to me, and I hate them. A rhinestone collar and a red leash—only you could choose something like that. You have East End taste, did you know that? Common taste. And you are common, too—oily manners, stupid foreign affected bows. Do you think you can pass yourself off as European, a gentleman? People laugh at you, Montague, behind your back—and I laugh too. You know what I say? I say, 'Oh, you'll have to forgive him. He can't help it. He knows no better. He grew up in a slum. He's a common little Jew.' "

Constance had never before made such a taunt. Perhaps she knew she had gone too far. Perhaps something in Stern's expression—a hardening of the features, a contempt in the eyes—frightened her. She gave a cry. She covered her face with her hands.

"Oh, God, oh, God, I'm so unhappy. I hurt so much. I wish you'd hit me—why don't you hit me? I know you want to. I can see it in your eyes—"

"I have no desire to hit you. None."

Stern turned toward the door. Constance clasped his arm. She attempted to drag him back.

"Please—look at me. Can't you understand? I don't mean all those things. I say them to hurt you, that's all. It's the only way I ever reach you, when I hurt you. You're so cold—at least when you're angry there's some response. It's better than nothing. I'm jealous, that's all. There—does that please you? I'm sure it does.

You want to hurt me too. And you do. I can't bear to think of it. It's so unlike you. It's so sordid and predictable and small. Taking an apartment, lying about appointments, and that girl! Such a cheap girl. Such a cheap name. Blanche—I hate her name. At least I showed some discrimination with my lovers—in a way, they're a compliment to you. But you—you pick up a cheap little tart off the streets—"

"She is not a tart." Stern opened the door. "And Blanche is only her stage name. Her real name is Ursula."

"Ursula?"

For some reason, this seemed to distress Constance very much. She stepped back from her husband and looked at him with an expression of childish woe.

"Ursula. Ursula. Ursula what?"

"That need not concern you."

"It does, though. It does concern me. It is a good name—as good as Constance. I feel as if . . . as if it erases me."

"My dear. I should forget it. Go to bed and get some sleep."

"No, wait, just tell me one more thing—"

"Constance. I dislike these scenes. They are pointless. We both know that. Most of this has been said before. Many times."

"Oh—I am becoming predictable then." She gave a sigh. "Does that bore you, Montague?"

"It can be tedious, yes."

"Oh, dear. What a death sentence." She turned away with a small sad smile. "I might have known you'd pronounce it like that. So coolly. *Tedious*. Ah, well."

Despite himself, Montague paused. He watched his wife changing before his eyes. As always, the transformation was chimeric, swift. A moment ago, a virago; now she was quiet. She looked back at him in a forlorn way, a way that would once have brought Stern back to her side. When he did not cross to her, she pressed one small jeweled hand against her heart.

"Oh, I ache so. You've changed, Montague. I see that now. When was it—that you changed?"

"Yesterday. Today. A year ago. I have no idea."

"But you have changed? No, you don't need to answer. I can see that you have. Ah, well, I should have foreseen it. Maud warned me once, you know."

"Maud is an astute woman. Not an infallible one."

"Maybe. Maybe. Montague, before you go—before you're quite gone—tell me one thing. No, please don't look at your watch. I won't be crude and coarse and horrible. Your mistress—You see how polite I am? What is it that you find with her? What is it I cannot give?"

Stern hesitated. "Her voice, I think. Yes, that. I like it when she sings. She has a very beautiful voice."

"Oh, I see." Constance's eyes filled with tears. "I see. That hurts. I cannot compete with that."

"You are still my wife, Constance," Stern said in a stiff way. He could see the trap of his own pity. He still found it difficult to turn away from her tears.

"Still? Still your wife?" Constance gave a small grimace of pain. "I don't like that 'still.' It frightens me."

"Constance, it's very late." Stern put his arm around her. "You're tired. Go to bed."

"If I said"—she looked up at him—"if I said that I did love you, Montague, loved you very much—would that make a difference? What would you say then?"

Stern considered. He looked at what his response might have been once, a year ago, an hour ago. Gently, he disengaged his arm.

"My dear," he replied, his voice regretful and kind, "I think I would say that you had left that particular confession too late."

"You're sure?"

"I'm afraid so."

"I will go to Winterscombe then." She clasped at his arm.

Stern gently loosened the grip of her fingers.

"My dear," he said, "that is your right. And your choice."

Constance did, as you know, come to that christening of mine. The hope that her action might provoke some crisis with Stern clearly encouraged her; I am still not sure whether she would have gone had Stern forbidden her. Probably it would have made no difference; the more something was forbidden, the more Constance wanted it. She was addicted to brinkmanship. Anyway, she left New York at the beginning of the new year, 1939. The christening was held in the middle of January.

Her decision to attend the christening, the fact that Acland had agreed she should be one of my godmothers, provoked trouble. It would have delighted Constance to know that Acland and Jane, who rarely quarreled, came close to quarreling over that.

My mother, Jane, had come through a difficult birth, which had left her weak. Her opposition to the choice of Constance for god-mother was there, in the background, for weeks; it did not surface openly until the day before my christening, the day before Constance was due to arrive.

All morning she said nothing, although her anxiety, and a sense of impending trouble that she could not explain, were very great. That afternoon—the doctors insisted she must rest in bed each afternoon—she decided finally she must protest. Her timing was bad: Acland, having helped to settle her in bed, was about to go for a walk with Steenie and Freddie.

The bedroom was quiet. A fire burned in the grate. The cradle in which her baby slept was at the end of her bed. The room was the same room—with the bay window—in which Acland had stayed during the months of his illness. Jane, returning to Winterscombe as a bride, had selected it for that reason.

Her baby had been born in this room. In this room—defying the conventions of their era and their class—she and Acland slept. The room was filled with their marriage. Acland slept on the left side of the bed, Jane on the right. If ever he was away, she found it difficult to fall asleep without the reassuring warmth of his body. Their separate identities fused in this room, in this bed.

Jane looked at the bay window, at the cradle, at the red coals in the fire. Acland bent forward to kiss her. Knowing it was entirely the wrong moment, and far too late, Jane began on rational objections, knowing she felt an irrational unease. She said the idea of Constance as a godmother worried her. The whole point of godparents was that they should be Christian; if they were not, then the ceremony was meaningless. Constance, she said, pleating the sheet between her fingers, was a self-proclaimed atheist who, the last time she visited Winterscombe, had flatly refused to attend church.

"Acland," she said tiredly, "oh, Acland, why did you agree? I cannot understand it."

Acland, who was not sure why he had agreed (except that Constance had insisted and it had seemed easier not to argue) and who wished he had not done so, became irritated. Their baby was to have two godfathers and two godmothers, he pointed out. My godfathers would be Wexton and Freddie, neither of them noted for Christian zeal.

"Freddie goes to church," Jane said. "When he's here he goes to church."

"Darling, for God's sake! He does that to be polite—because we go. And Wexton never joins us—so where's your argument?"

"Freddie is a good man. So is Wexton. Wexton is the most religious man I know—in his way. Oh, Acland, I can't explain it."

"Darling, I know you can't. It's not reasonable, that's why. I think the truth is, you dislike Constance. Why not be honest and say so?"

"That's not true. I don't dislike her, exactly. I just think she's the wrong choice. She won't understand it—the whole thing will be meaningless to her. And besides, what shall we do about Maud?"

"I've *told* you. Maud has agreed to come."

"I can't believe she will. Not with Constance here. And if she does, Maud will cut Constance dead, right across the font."

Acland smiled. "No, she won't. She's promised me. She'll be on her best behavior. Besides, she's a godmother too. She'll cancel Constance out, if that's what's worrying you."

"It's horrible. I hate it. A christening ought to be joyful. A celebration, a giving of thanks, a promise—and now it won't be. Maud hates Constance, and Constance hates her. The whole church will be full of hate and anger and resentment, when it ought to be filled with God. We're supposed to be promising something for our baby's future, and all we'll be doing is raking up the past. Old scores to settle. Acland—please."

Jane struggled up against the pillows. She took Acland's hand.

"Please, Acland—even now—can't we change it?"

"Darling, it's done. I can't change it now. Constance's ship docked yesterday. She's in London now. She'll be here tomorrow. What am I supposed to say to her? Sorry, but you've come three thousand miles for nothing—we've changed our minds? You're not a suitable godmother? Darling, I can't do that. If you think about it, you wouldn't ask me."

"Not even for me?"

"No. Not even for you."

"Not even for Victoria?"

"Not even for Victoria." He leaned forward and kissed her brow. "It won't matter to Victoria, darling—you fuss too much. I can hardly remember who my own godparents were; they certainly never did anything useful. I imagine they produced the traditional christening present, and that was that. I'm perfectly sure they never concerned themselves with my spiritual welfare."

"I wish you wouldn't mock." Jane released his hand.

"I'm not mocking. It's just that you can be a little solemn sometimes."

"It matters to me. Is it wrong to be solemn about something that matters?"

"No. Perhaps not. But it's not very charitable either. Just because Constance doesn't go to church is no reason to exclude her. I thought there was more rejoicing in heaven when one sinner repented—"

"Stop it, Acland."

"Well, maybe Constance will repent. You never know. The christening might effect some good upon her. A bolt of light, a vision on the road to Damascus. She might turn into a model godmother after all."

"You think that's likely?"

"No, my darling, I think it's extremely *unlikely*. However, the Lord God moves in mysterious ways His wonders to perform. You never know."

"You frighten me." Jane turned her face away. "Sometimes you frighten me. You used to do it—years and years ago—"

"Do what?"

"Oh, make jokes. Jokes that sound close to blasphemy—"

"I don't believe in blasphemy—perhaps that's why." Acland stood up. He made an impatient gesture. "I've *seen* blasphemy. Blasphemy is what people do—not what they say. You know that. You saw it too."

There was a silence. Acland moved away toward the windows. Jane wondered if he looked at the woods and the lake—or at the war. She knew he still looked at the war, as she did, often.

It was a bright cold day outside. Acland, with the light striking his face, still looked very young. Jane had passed forty; Acland still had that difficult birthday to come. Sometimes it seemed to Jane that the disparity in their ages grew more marked with each year that passed. Why should the gray show in her hair and not in his? Acland's face showed the past: She could see there the strains of his illness, the memories of the war, the difficult passages of their marriage, two babies lost, increasing difficulties with money, employment Acland had loathed and since left.

Yes, those marks of the past were on his face when her husband was tired and dispirited. At other times, though, when Acland had some new project to engage him, such as the estate or plans for a new orphanage, these marks might almost disappear. He would move with his old speed and impetuosity; he would talk with the old racing fervency. Then, he looked simultaneously young and middle-aged. Jane found the combination poignant. She would think sometimes: He is a young man, tied to an aging wife.

This filled her with an acute despondency. Leaning back against the pillows, she closed her eyes. She tried to force back the tears.

She hated and despised these tears, which she saw as chemical, and alien, forced upon her at unexpected moments, a bodily reaction she could not control. It did not help that the doctors said, briskly, that such despondency was predictable at her age, after a difficult birth.

"Darling." Acland had seen the tears. He came back to the bed. He took her in his arms. "My dearest, don't cry. I'm sorry I spoke in that way. Listen—if it matters to you so much, I'll do as you say. I'd sooner hurt Constance's feelings than yours. The hell with Constance! Look, I'll call her in London. I can reach her tonight. I'll put her off. I'll tell her not to come. Winnie will be here—let's have Winnie as godmother instead."

"No, Acland. Leave it as it is." Jane sat up. She dried her eyes. She made a rueful face. "Forget what I said. You're right in any case. I am being stupid and uncharitable. I feel old—I think that's it. Old and crotchety. A thoroughly disagreeable woman. I'm sorry. Go on—you'll be late for your walk."

"Old? You don't look old." Acland gave her a little shake.

"Oh, Acland—don't lie. I have eyes. I can use a mirror."

"You look beautiful. Your hair shines. Your skin is soft. Your eyes are full of light. Look, I'm going to kiss your eyes, because I love them and I hate to see you cry. There, now, you see? You look very nearly as lovely as your daughter."

Jane smiled. "Acland, she doesn't look lovely at all. We both know that. I love her with all my heart, but the fact remains—"

"That's better. What fact remains?"

"The fact remains that she has very little hair. In fact, she's almost bald. Also rather red in the face, especially when she cries. And scrawny. Admit it, Acland. We have a scrawny daughter."

"I'll admit no such thing." Acland stood up. He crossed the room and looked down into the cradle.

"She's not crying now. She's not scarlet in the face. She has ears like the most delicate shells. She has nails on her fingertips. She can grasp the finger of my hand—which I won't encourage her to do, because then she might wake up. And bawl. Furthermore . . ." He bent.

"Furthermore, what?"

"She is going to have freckles. On her nose. Like you. And red hair."

He crossed back to the bed. He took Jane's hands.

"Promise me you won't cry again."

"I can't. I'm sentimental. I'm bound to cry at the christening."

"All right. You're permitted a few more tears, then. But only a few. Then no more until . . ."

"Until when?"

"Oh, her wedding, I suppose. That's when mothers cry, don't they—at their daughters' weddings?"

"That might be twenty years. More."

"That's right."

"That's a long time, without tears . . ."

"Twenty years? Twenty years is nothing. Think of all the time we have. Thirty years. Forty. Give me your hand."

Acland placed a kiss in her palm. He closed her fingers over the kiss. He looked up.

"Do you know what I thought, when she was born?"

"No, Acland."

"I thought"—he hesitated—"I thought of all the things I had failed to do. All the things my family expected me to do. I thought of my mother, and how I disappointed her—"

"Acland, you never disappointed her—"

"Oh, but I did. And it doesn't matter. Don't you see? None of that matters. Whatever failures there may have been, I did two things right. I married you—and we were given *her.*"

He gestured toward the cradle.

"It's not such a great thing, I suppose—other men have children, after all. But it felt a great thing to me. I had achieved something . . . lasting. Do you know, I'd rather have her than build a city, paint a picture, rule a kingdom. I'd give every one of Wexton's poems—good though they are, they're nothing compared to her. To us. Which is just as well, I suppose, because I shall never write, or rule, or make a great impact on the world—not now." His hand tightened over hers. "I hope you don't mind that. Do you? Maybe you do. Maybe you'd prefer a more ambitious husband."

"There's no other husband I'd prefer. Ever. None. You know that."

Jane gripped his hands. Acland, seeing the old fierceness in her face, a strength he sometimes felt he no longer possessed, bent his head. He rested it against her breast. Jane stroked his hair. The coals in the fire shifted. Acland thought: *I am at peace.*

After a while he straightened up. He kissed his wife. "I'd better go, I suppose. Freddie and Steenie will be impatient. We're going on a long march—to the top of Galley's Field. Promise me you'll try to sleep. Shall I ask Jenna to come in and sit with you?"

"Yes. I like it when she's here. She knits. I can hear the needles click."

"You and she—you're very close." Acland looked at her, his expression puzzled.

"She's my friend, Acland. I feel that. I'm glad she's here now. I hated it when she had to live in that cottage—"

"Yes. Well. Maybe you're right." He hesitated. "I'll ask her then, on the way out."

"Thank you. Oh, I feel so sleepy. Look, my eyes keep shutting. I can't stay awake. . . ."

"I love you." Acland kissed her once more. "I love you," he said, "and I hate it when we quarrel."

Of the three brothers, Acland walked the fastest. Slightly ahead of them as they passed through the woods and crossed the bridge, he gained a greater distance when they reached the hill beyond. He walked ahead; the gap between them widened. Steenie strolled behind him, gazing about him with a bemused air, as if he found the country startling. Freddie, by then rather stout, brought up the rear. He was already puffing.

Steenie was wearing a preposterous coat, two silken mufflers, and a pair of pigskin gloves very similar to the ones that had so offended Boy, years before. Steenie had just flown in from Paris, where he had had another of his perennial fights with Conrad Vickers. He complained, volubly, first about the defects in Vickers's character, then about the flight.

Freddie was trying to decide whether Steenie's walk would be better described as a mince or a glide. It somehow contrived to be both. Freddie frowned at the yellow gloves. (He disapproved of them as strongly as Boy had.) However, his silent criticisms of his brother were mild. Freddie liked family gatherings; he liked to return to Winterscombe when he could.

Toward the top of the rise, Acland paused. He waited for his two brothers to catch up. He looked, Freddie thought, both happy and carefree, much fitter than Freddie had seen him for years. His face was tanned from outdoor work on the estate; he walked with long strides. With great enthusiasm, he had begun to discuss cows.

Freddie was pretty sure that, two years before, it had been sheep. And he was pretty sure the sheep had not been a great success. Freddie did not mind that. Bouts of misguided and often short-lived enthusiasm were something he understood; he himself was currently between engagements. When Acland spoke of cows, Freddie nodded in a sage way. He felt a kinship with his brother.

Steenie did not. Steenie was quite happy to accept funding—his own money having been used up years before—but funding Steenie's expensive tastes (and Acland must do that, Freddie assumed, since no one else did) was no way to gain protection from Steenie's tongue.

"For God's sake, Acland," he said when they had stopped near the top of the hill. "Do we have to listen to this? You sound like a farmer."

"I am a farmer. I try to be a farmer. Something has to be done with all this land." Acland climbed onto a fence. He lit a cigarette.

"Well, it doesn't suit you. You don't know what you're talking about, I'm sure. And you're far too optimistic. Proper farmers are never optimistic. They are men of unremitting gloom."

"I can't be gloomy. Not today. I'm a father. Freddie understands —don't you, Freddie?"

"Give me one of those cigarettes. A father?" Steenie inserted the cigarette in a holder. "I can't imagine why you should sound so smug about that. Lots of men are fathers. Most men are fathers. Where's the distinction in that?"

"Nevertheless. That is what I feel. I shall . . . halloo her name, to the reverberate hills." Acland, standing on the fence, did so. "Victoria," he shouted. "Victoria."

As Acland shouted, the woods called back. The hills resounded to a name. Acland, embarrassed by this, knowing his gesture had been extravagant, climbed down from the fence and leaned against it. He narrowed his eyes. He measured the dimensions of his fields. He felt he loved these fields. They were no longer something to grapple with, sullen, difficult places that never produced an adequate crop, fields that resisted his flocks. They were something to pass on. He wondered whether he might say this, and—catching Steenie's cold blue eye—decided better not.

"Papa liked this place." Freddie, too, rested against the fence. "He liked to stand just here. I came up with him, once or twice."

"He would. You can see the whole estate from here. It looks big. He liked that—being kingpin."

"Shut up, Steenie. He was all right in his way. He wasn't such a bad sort."

"Did I say he was? I just said he liked to be kingpin, monarch of all he surveyed. Which happens to be true. I loved him too, Freddie. He drove me 'round the bend—however, I did love him. Just a bit. Well, more than a bit." Steenie sighed. "I don't think he noticed. My hair distracted him. I don't think he liked it so blond. I think its *exceptional* blondness distressed him. Still, there you are." He drew on his cigarette. "When does Wexton arrive? It will be nice to see Wexton again."

"In the morning." Acland did not look around. "Constance is coming then too. And Winnie. Maud motors down separately. She comes to the ceremony, then goes straight back. It might be quite a good idea, Steenie, if you didn't remark on that."

"Would I?" Steenie gave both brothers a look of injured innocence. "I can be tactful, you know, when I want to be. Deeply tactful. I shan't mention Montague once."

"Oh, it'll be all right," said Freddie in his comfortable way. "It was ages ago. Maud will be fine. She always is."

"Darling, I'm sure Maud will be dignity personified. It's not Maud I'm worried about. It's Constance. Constance *adores* scenes. She's bound to do something perfectly ghastly. It's probably why she's here—"

"She's here to be Victoria's godmother. She insisted, and I agreed. She's not staying long, anyway. Two days, three at most. And you exaggerate, as usual, Steenie. Constance has stayed here umpteen times. She comes over every year, and there has never been a scene."

"Ah, but that was with Stern. He keeps her in check. And Stern isn't coming."

"Her husband is not the only person capable of keeping Constance in check." Acland sounded irritated. "I can do it, if need be. Freddie will help—won't you, Freddie?"

"I suppose so." Freddie did not sound confident. "I'll try. But I haven't seen her in years. I'm not sure I remember what she's like."

Steenie made no comment. He smiled in an enigmatic way, perhaps intended to irritate. He leaned on Freddie's arm as they returned downhill. Freddie puffed in the effort to keep up with Acland.

By the time they reached the bottom of the rise, the light was failing fast. They crossed the river, took the path that led past Jack Hennessy's cottage, back toward the village and the woods.

The garden of Hennessy's cottage was very overgrown: Weeds encroached on the path and the walls. Its roof sagged. Its uncurtained windows were dark.

"What a beastly dump," Steenie said, once they were safely past. "Acland—wait for us. Does Jack Hennessy still live there?"

"Yes. He likes it." Acland glanced back. He shrugged. "He asked for it, when he came back from the war. It seems to suit him. You know, he's not quite normal. He's something of a recluse."

"But what about Jenna? Is it true he hit her? Hennessy the wife-beater! Well, I'm not surprised. He always gave me the creeps."

"He hit her the other week. I don't think it was an habitual thing. There's only trouble when he drinks. Anyway, Jane dealt with it. Jenna will live in the house now—she'll look after Victoria. It's convenient, all 'round. Come on." Acland began to move off.

"You ought to do something about that place, Acland," Steenie said, trotting to keep up with him. "It'll fall down on Hennessy's head one of these days. And these houses, too." They stopped. They had reached the village green. Steenie peered about him. He gave a sigh.

"It does look a mess, Acland. Maybe it's just that I haven't been back for a while, but it looks so horrid. Half the houses look empty."

"Half of them *are* empty." Acland gave a gesture of annoyance. "Would you like to know why, Steenie? They're empty because half the work force has left. Because I can't afford the wages of men to live in them. No one wants to buy them, you know—"

"Well, *someone* must want the houses, surely? Writers, painters, poets—those sorts of people. Potters! Potters love places like this. You could do the houses up. I remember how it used to look. It was particularly charming, in a feudal sort of way. There were vegetables. Lines of runner beans, and hollyhocks—"

"Jesus Christ, Steenie."

"Well, there *were*, Acland! I'm just remarking. It's true. You've let the place go downhill."

"Steenie. There was a *war*." Acland gave a sigh of exasperation. "Do you understand that? I wonder sometimes if you do. Just try and think about it, will you? All those men who worked here, who planted the runner beans and the hollyhocks—do you know how many of them ever came back? No, you don't, of course. You're too busy gadding about." He turned away. "There's a memorial in the church. You can look at it tomorrow. Count the names of those who never came back. Work it out for yourself, why don't you?"

"Oh, the war, the *war!*" Steenie's voice rose. "I'm sick of the bloody war. You harp on about it. Jane harps on about it. Even Wexton harps on about it. For God's sake, the war's *over*. It's been over for twelve *years*—"

"Over? You think it's over?" Acland turned back. He caught hold of Steenie's arm. He turned his brother back, in the direction of dereliction. "Just look, Steenie. And think for once. The war didn't end in 1918. That was just the beginning. Look at your village, Steenie. Go on, look properly. You know what it is? A little war zone, all of its own, right in the heart of Winterscombe. You know what kept this place going? Investment income. Low taxes. Cheap servants. Ridiculous, misplaced, feudal loyalties. All that has changed. I'm even glad it has changed. And yet, I can't let it go. I keep propping it up, trying to make it work again. My wife provides the money, and I provide—I try to provide—the energy. It gets harder and more expensive to do so every year. And you get more expensive too. You might remember that as well, Steenie."

"That's not fair!" Steenie gave a wail. "I hate it when you talk like that. You sound so quiet and so grim. I try! I said I'd economize. I try to economize. If Papa had managed things better, I'd have been all right. How was I to know half the money would disappear? Mama always said . . ." Steenie's voice hit a high note. It cracked. Tears spouted suddenly from his eyes. They plopped down his cheeks. "Now look what you've done! You've made me cry. Oh, *hell*—"

"You cry very easily, Steenie. You always did."

"I know I do. I can't help that." Steenie blew his nose. He wiped his eyes. He gave both Acland and Freddie a dignified look.

"It's my nature to cry. When people are beastly to me, I cry. There's not a lot of point in my trying to be manly, is there? And the tears are sincere. If you want to know, I'm crying for the hollyhocks, and an idyll that never was—"

"And yourself, Steenie—don't forget that."

"All right, myself as well. I know I'm weak. But it isn't awfully nice, being a remittance man—"

"Steenie, you're impossible." Acland's voice had softened. He gave a small shrug, as if to shake off the last of his anger. He turned. "We'd better go back anyway. There's no point in arguing. Come on—it'll be dark in a minute."

"Say I'm forgiven." Steenie hurried after Acland and caught his arm. "Go on. Say I'm an idiot and a horrible social butterfly and selfish and impossible—and you forgive me."

"You're a pain in the backside."

"And I'm your brother—"

"Oh, all right." Acland sighed. "You're a pain, and my brother. And I forgive you. Why not?"

"Say something nice too." Steenie put his arm through Acland's. "Say . . . Oh, I don't know. Say you like my yellow gloves."

"Steenie. I cannot tell a lie. Your gloves are bloody awful."

"*That's* better." Steenie gave a chirrup. "I feel quite cheered up now. Come on, Freddie. Look at the three of us, marching along! Three brothers! *Isn't* that nice?" He gave them, in turn, a mocking glance. "What shall we do now, do you think? Go back to the house for tea—or talk about Moscow?"

Freddie's theatrical tastes had never run as far as Chekhov. He did not grasp the reference, but knowing a further quarrel had been averted and animosity healed, he began to grin, then whistled. He disliked contention. He began to dwell on the question of tea.

"Shall we cut through the woods?" he suggested as they came to a fork in the paths. "The quick way—through the clearing? Let's. I'm starving."

At this, to his surprise, both Acland and Steenie hesitated.

"It's not that much quicker . . ." Acland began.

"It is. It's a good ten minutes quicker. What's wrong?"

"Nothing." Acland hesitated. "Nothing really. I don't usually go that way—"

"The vengeful ghost of Shawcross!" Steenie gave a somewhat nervous giggle. "I *hate* going that way. I don't mind admitting it. I'm a terrible coward—especially when it's dark. That part of the woods is distinctly creepy—"

"Don't be ridiculous." Freddie turned down that path. He considered toasted crumpets. A warm fire. Tea—perhaps cake. "For God's sake, what's the matter with you both? I don't believe in ghosts, and neither do you. Come on, hurry."

He set off down the path to the clearing. Acland followed, with reluctance. Steenie let out another affected wail, which made Freddie jump.

"Wait for me," he called. "Wait for me!"

When they reached the clearing where Shawcross had been trapped, they all—by unspoken consent—slowed. In the middle of the clearing they stopped.

"You see what I mean?" Steenie peered at the bushes. "It is creepy. It gives me the shakes."

He took out from his pocket his silver hip flask. He took a large nip. He offered it to Acland, who refused it with a shake of the head, then to Freddie, who took a swallow.

The brandy kicked in his stomach, then exuded a pleasant warmth. Freddie handed back the flask. He looked about him.

Ridiculous though it might be, Freddie felt that Steenie was right. In the twilight the trees and the bushes pressed close. Outlined against the graying sky, the bare branches of the trees reached out. The undergrowth, hummocks of brambles and holly, piled with dead leaves, took on a threatening look. Freddie peered about him. He wondered exactly where it had been—that trap.

Over there, he thought, somewhere in that undergrowth. He gave a shiver. When Steenie handed him the flask again, he took a second swig. He looked at his brothers. Acland was staring at the undergrowth, his face fixed and pale.

"It was over there." Acland spoke so suddenly that Freddie jumped. He pointed to a hummock of brambles.

"Just there."

"Are you sure?" Steenie peered. He shivered.

"Yes. Just to the right of the path."

"How do you know that?" Steenie's voice had risen sharply. Acland, shrugging, turned away.

"The thing had to be moved—afterwards."

"I thought Cattermole did that—"

"I came down with him. With some of the men." Acland's voice had become terse. "I forget who. The Hennessy brothers, I think."

"Ugh. How horrible." Steenie gave a shudder. He stared at the spot Acland had indicated.

"Yes, it was. There was a lot of blood. Torn clothing. It wasn't a pleasant job."

Acland moved off a few paces. He stood with his back to his brothers. There was another silence. Having reached this place, Freddie felt it exercised a peculiar power over them. None of them had wanted to stop, and, having stopped, none of them seemed able to leave. Freddie told himself that on a bright sunlit day the place would hold no terrors. It was the gathering dusk that made it sinister. He said, in a voice less firm than he would have liked:

"Let's go back."

"Do you remember what Mother said—when she was dying?" Steenie put the question. He seemed not to have heard Freddie's remark. He glanced toward Acland.

"Yes, I remember," Acland replied shortly.

"Remember what?" Freddie said.

He had been in South America, flying his mail planes, when Gwen died several years before. Her illness—pneumonia—had been brief. Freddie, alerted too late, had arrived at Winterscombe the day after her death. This had hurt him at the time, and hurt him still. Steenie and Acland had been with her; Jane had been with her. He had let her down.

Freddie looked from brother to brother; he stared back at the undergrowth in a miserable way. There was a wound in his own relationship with his mother which antedated her death by many years. It had never quite healed. He would have liked to tell his mother, before she died, that he loved her. Yes, he would have liked to say that.

"What did Mama say?" he prompted again.

Acland did not reply. Steenie gave a sigh.

"Well, at the end"—he hesitated—"she talked about Shawcross. It was rather ghastly. She talked about him a lot."

"Oh, God." Freddie bent his head.

"She wasn't distressed, Freddie," Steenie said, taking his arm. "Honestly. She was quite calm. But I think . . . I think she thought Shawcross was there in the room. Don't you, Acland? She seemed to. She spoke to him."

"You said it was easy," Freddie burst out. "You both told me that. You said it was easy—you said she just . . . slipped away."

"It was. Sort of." Steenie frowned, as if trying to fix the memory. "She seemed glad to go. She didn't protest. But then she never did really, about anything. She'd raise objections, and then she would give in. Oh, God—I wish we hadn't come this way. How did we start on this?"

"I want to know. Acland"—Freddie grasped his arm—"what did she *say?*"

"Nothing." Acland shrugged off his hand. "She talked about Shawcross, that's all. As Steenie says. The drugs they prescribed made her drowsy. She didn't know what she was saying—"

"Yes, she did." Steenie turned back. "She said that when Shawcross was here, the night of the comet, he heard her call. He told her, before he died. It was the last thing he ever said to her. Then, when she was dying, she remembered. It was very strange—"

"Strange? Strange in what way?"

"She became awfully agitated—didn't she, Acland? I think she knew we were there. It was as if she wanted to tell us something—and then couldn't. It was as if she was afraid."

"She was very ill," Acland said in a curt voice. "There's no point in resurrecting all this, Steenie. She was confused." He hesitated. "She slept after that. It *was* peaceful, Freddie, in the end. She was . . . tired. I think she was glad that it was all over."

Steenie drew in a shaky breath.

"That's true," he said. "Really, Freddie. Once Papa died—she missed him, I think. She needed him, and once he'd gone . . ."

"She stopped fighting." Acland's voice was flat. "Well, at a certain point we all do that."

"Oh, God, I'm so miserable." Steenie clasped Freddie's arm. "I hate this place. I wish we'd never come here. It brings it all back.

Look at us. We all disappointed her, in our different ways. She made all those plans—and now look at us. Acland, trying to pretend he's a farmer. Acland is a failed aristocrat. I'm a failed painter. Freddie is—"

"Oh, I'm the worst. I'm a failed everything." To the surprise of his brothers, Freddie made this pronouncement in a robust, quite unbitter way. "There's no point in wallowing in it, Steenie," he continued in a sensible voice. "Anyway, it's not totally true. Acland keeps this place going—against all the odds. That takes courage of a sort. You may not paint now, but you keep going too. You make people laugh. You are what you are. You don't apologize for it—and that takes courage too. And I—well, I muddle along, just as I always did. I don't do much harm, anyway. At least I try not to. We could be worse. I think we could be worse. We're still here. We have each other—"

"Oh, Freddie." Steenie began to smile. He put his arm around his brother's shoulders. "You are totally absurd, do you know that? Only you could give us a homily like that—"

"I don't care," Freddie replied stoutly. "I know I'm not a brain-box. It's true what I said. We're like everyone else. A mixture of bad and good. Just . . . ordinary."

"And hungry," Acland interjected, turning. He smiled. "Don't forget that, Freddie. Come on—we're all becoming maudlin, and Freddie is right. There's no point. Think of all the things we could be thankful for." He turned. "I miss my wife. I miss my baby. I want my tea. Come on, let's go back to the house."

Freddie at once felt cheered. They began walking, first slowly, then at a brisker pace. They left the woods behind; the shadows lessened; the undergrowth retreated. He felt a sudden welling of affection for his brothers. There it was, a large warm thing, situated in his heart. He could have put his hand on the exact spot. They would not have disappointed his mother, he thought, in this.

"We beseech thee," began the priest.

Constance's hat came into his view (the hat Winnie had pronounced doubtful, a hat that dismayed the vicar, a hat the color of Parma violets). He averted his eyes. He cleared his throat.

"We beseech thee, for thine infinite mercies, that thou will mercifully look upon this Child; wash her and sanctify her with the Holy Ghost; that she"—he paused—"being steadfast in faith, joyful through hope, and rooted in charity, may so pass the waves of this troublesome world, that finally she may come to the land of everlasting life, there to reign with thee, world without end, through Jesus Christ our Lord. Amen."

"Amen," replied Constance in a quiet voice.

"Amen," replied Acland and Jane, exchanging a glance, and then a handkerchief.

"Amen," replied Wexton, looking toward Steenie.

"Amen," replied Freddie, looking up at the memorial window to Boy.

"Amen," replied Steenie, thinking of the war memorial—where, as instructed by Acland, he had counted forty-five names.

"Amen," replied Maud, looking down at the baby.

"Amen," replied Winifred Hunter-Coote, glancing at Freddie.

"Amen," replied Jenna from a pew behind, where she sat with William, the butler.

"Amen," replied Jack Hennessy, who sat alone at the back of the church, one empty sleeve pinned neatly to the front of his best jacket.

The vicar proceeded with the prayers. It was the same vicar who had married Constance some thirteen years before; he had not forgotten that occasion, or Constance. The woman who had insisted her pet dog should attend her wedding. He had a clear memory of this animal, seated on Steenie's lap, panting during the prayers, yawning during a hymn, and sniffing in a threatening way at one of the pews on the way out.

He had protested.

"He is one of God's creatures," Constance had replied.

He had given in.

This he had resented at the time, and he found he resented it still. Indignation intruded between him and the words of the service. Constance was looking at him in a way he found unyielding, and inappropriate. The vicar averted his eyes. He fixed them, instead, on the large and benevolent, the rumpled figure of Wexton, whose poetry the vicar greatly admired. A wise godfather, he said to himself; the meaning of the words returned to him. He proceeded.

There is a point during the Church of England service of baptism when, since the baby cannot speak, the godparents make vows on its behalf. It had been previously agreed that when this point was reached, Freddie and Maud should stand on one side of the baby, Wexton and Constance on the other. Acland had already rehearsed them in this tactful arrangement.

When the moment came, however, something went wrong. Wexton, abstracted and vague, walked the wrong way. He stationed himself next to Freddie, leaving Maud to flank Constance. To the dismay of everyone, the vicar launched into the next part of the service with two godfathers on one side of the baby, two bristling godmothers on the other.

Maud, less dependable than Freddie had said, behaved with provocative decorum. Clutching her prayer book to the breast of her superbly tailored suit, and hitching the furs she wore around her neck, she contrived—with every air of accident—to elbow Constance to one side.

Maud was tall. Constance was not. Constance's view of the baby was obscured by Maud's shoulder, and by the mask of the fox fur draped around Maud's neck. Right on a line with Constance's eyes was a small, pinched, beady-eyed, triangular, dead fox head.

"Dearly beloved," began the vicar, pressing on.

"I am so sorry," said a small clear voice. "I am so sorry, but I seem unable to see."

The vicar coughed. Maud did not move one inch.

"All I can see," continued the voice, in a tone of patient reason, "is a shoulder. And a dead fox. I *am* a godmother. I should *quite* like to see the baby."

"Ah, Constance, is it you?" cried Maud. "Are you there? I must have missed you. I forget . . . how small you are. There—is that better now?"

She moved six inches to the right.

"Thank you so much, Maud."

"Perhaps the veil obscures your view, Constance? Might it be an idea, to lift the veil?"

"Oddly enough, Maud, I see through the veil. That is the purpose of veils."

"Yes. Well, this is hardly the moment to discuss hats."

Maud turned back to the priest. She had no respect for priests whatsoever. Her brother had endowed this church; its living had been in his gift, as it was now in Acland's. As far as Maud was concerned, the vicar was a hired man. She gave him a firm look.

"Proceed," she said.

The vicar gave a sigh. He proceeded.

He completed the initial prayer. He came to the godparents' vows. He addressed four faces.

"Dost thou," he asked, "in the name of this Child, renounce the Devil and all his works, the vain pomp and glory of the world, and the carnal desires of the flesh, so that thou wilt not follow, nor be led by them?"

"I renounce them all," replied three voices. Freddie and Maud spoke firmly, in unison. Constance more slowly, a little behind the others. Wexton did not speak at all. He was looking at Constance in a preoccupied way. The vicar cleared his throat. (Great poets were allowed, perhaps, to be absent-minded.) Wexton came back to attention.

"Oh. Sorry. Yes, I renounce them, too, sure."

Wexton blushed. The vicar continued with the vows. He inquired whether the godparents believed, on the baby's behalf, in God the Father, in His only-begotten Son, in the crucifixion and the resurrection, in the Holy Church, the Communion of Saints, the forgiveness of sins, and life everlasting.

"All this I steadfastly believe," the godparents answered.

It was at this point in the service (or so he decided later) that Acland noticed that Constance, despite all predictions to the contrary, was moved. Throughout the vows she stood still, her hands clasped before her. Her eyes never wavered once from the priest's face; she seemed to hang upon his words, her face composed, sad, intent.

The baby was baptized; the sign of the cross was made. Acland, looking up from the font, saw that Constance wept. She did so silently; two tears, then two more ran down from beneath the veil. Acland, deeply moved himself, was touched by this. He thought: *Constance is more than she seems.*

"Victoria Gwendolen," Constance said to him afterward, as they walked through the churchyard, back to the waiting cars. She took his arm, then released it.

"Victoria Gwendolen. They're lovely names."

"Her two grandmothers' names—"

"I like that. It links her to the past." She glanced up. Ahead of them, Maud waited by her car.

"I'll go back to the house now, with Steenie." Constance gave a little smile. "I know I'm in the way. I just wanted to say thank you, Acland, for letting me be her godmother. It means a great deal to me. I'm so happy—for you and for Jane."

She said no more. With admirable discretion, she avoided Maud, climbed into the first of the waiting cars with Steenie. The car drew away in the direction of the house. Maud watched it depart, her expression haughty. She turned to Jane, then Acland. She kissed them both.

"I shall come back," she said, "when that woman has gone. No, Acland, I shall speak my mind for once. I have to say that I find your selection of her as a godmother quite inexplicable, and deeply unwise. I cannot understand, Jane, how you, of all people—"

"It was my decision, Maud," Acland said in a quiet voice.

"Yours? Then I can only say it was foolish." Maud drew herself up. "She has not improved—in fact, if anything, she is worse. That hat! That hat, in my opinion, was a calculated insult—"

Behind Maud, Winifred Hunter-Coote, who concurred with this view, gave a loud snort.

"Quite unsuitable for a christening," Maud went on. "But then, she must always draw attention to herself. She feeds on it. I am glad to say I thought the hat most unbecoming—far too young for her. She is beginning to show her age."

"Maud. Could we stop this, please?" Acland interrupted her. "It's unkind and unnecessary. It's upsetting Jane—"

"Jane?" Maud gave him her coldest look. "Jane is not the one who is upset."

"Maud, I think that's enough."

"Did you see how she looked at my poor fox? She gave it a most *malignant* glance—"

"It was in the way, Maud."

"It was *intentionally* in the way. I'd prefer her to look at my fox like that, than your baby—"

"Maud, *please*."

"Very well. I shall say no more. I shall return to London." Maud, somewhat flushed, adjusted the contentious fox. She glanced grandly to left and to right. It did not escape her notice that Freddie, listening to this exchange, was trying hard not to laugh.

"I shall say only one thing—and no, Freddie, it is not a cause for amusement." She paused. "That woman is ill-bred. And what is more, it *shows*."

"I'm in disgrace," Constance said that afternoon, after lunch. Wexton and Steenie, she and Acland were walking down by the lake. Jane had retired to rest; Freddie had fallen asleep over a new novel by Dorothy Sayers; Winnie, with a quelling glance in Constance's direction, had refused to join them. She was, she said in a meaningful way, retiring to her room, where she would write to her husband, Cootie.

"Winnie thinks I should be writing to Montague." Constance made a wry face. "I have a sneaking impression she thinks I'm a less than dutiful wife."

"She's in Maud's camp," Steenie said, with an air of glee. "She disapproves of you violently, Constance. I think she took exception to your hat."

"How unkind! And I took hours choosing that hat."

"Maud said it was a calculated insult," Steenie continued cheerfully, ignoring Acland's warning look. "Do you know what Maud calls you? She calls you 'that woman.' She said you gave her poor fox fur a most *malignant* glance."

"So I did," Constance replied with spirit. She took Acland's arm. "I must say, Acland, it is nice to come three thousand miles, to my old home, and be made to feel so welcome."

"Oh, Maud doesn't mean half she says," Acland replied in an unconvincing way.

Constance gave him a little glance. "Oh, she does. I know she does. I can just hear her saying it: 'That woman is a bad influence. I cannot *think* why you should select her as a godmother. Did you *see* how she looked at my poor fox?' "

Constance smiled. It was a brilliant piece of mimicry: Constance had Maud's voice to perfection, its swoops, its glides, its exaggerated emphasis. For a moment, tiny though she was in comparison to Maud, she even contrived to resemble her, drawing herself up in just the way Maud had done, outside the church. Acland smiled; Steenie laughed; Wexton gave no reaction. Constance, reverting to her own self, gave a sigh.

"Oh, well, I cannot blame her. She once loved Montague, and she will never forgive me. I regret that. I always liked Maud, very much."

She gave a shake of the head; they walked on for some way in silence. Acland wondered if perhaps Constance was more hurt by Maud's remarks than she acknowledged, for there had been a certain defiance in her tone—a defiance he remembered from long before, when Constance, as a child, had used it to deflect the dislike she seemed always to expect from others.

They came, after some ten minutes, to a division of the paths. There, Constance paused.

"Do you know where I'd like to go? The old Stone House. Is it still there? Do you remember, Acland—your mother's favorite place? I haven't been to that part of the grounds for ages."

"Oh, it's still there. It's not in very good repair—like everything else—but it's still there."

"Shall we go and look at it now? May we? Steenie, Wexton, will you come? I remember it so well. Gwen used to keep her watercolors there, and her flower press. Boy took our photograph there one morning, I remember. Let me think—Gwen was there, and you, Steenie. Oh, and my father."

She stopped. She made a small gesture. She turned away, then walked apart a few steps.

All three men stared at her back. Seeing that Acland was puzzled, Steenie mouthed the word *comet*.

"We were in the Stone House that day," he said in a low voice. "The morning of the comet party. I think it might not be a terribly good idea to go there. You know how she is when she remembers—"

"I'm going back to the house in any case," Wexton announced abruptly. "It's cold. Are you coming, Steenie?"

To Steenie's surprise, Wexton—who usually ambled along—set off for the house at a smart pace, without a backward glance. Steenie, who was anxious to tell Wexton all about his quarrel with Vickers, but who was also filled with a sudden unease, hesitated. He looked at Constance's back. He looked at Acland.

"You go on," Acland said.

"You're sure?"

"Yes. Go on. We'll catch up." He lowered his voice. "It's all right, Steenie. She's obviously upset. Give her a minute or two."

"Oh, very well."

Steenie turned with apparent reluctance. He began to walk away, hesitated, glanced back, then ran to catch up with Wexton. Once Steenie was at his side, Wexton slowed. Both men paused to look back; Constance and Acland were now out of sight.

"My dear," Steenie said with a sideways glance. "Ought we to leave? I'm not entirely sure Acland's safe. . . ."

"Nor am I. However, it's his problem, don't you think?"

"I wouldn't like to see him hurt—or Jane, for that matter." Steenie hesitated. "It's *probably* all right—after all, it wouldn't be terribly apposite timing, would it? Just after the christening. On the other hand, with Constance—"

"Quit meddling, Steenie. Come on. Let's go back to the house."

"You're sure?" Steenie sighed. He turned with some reluctance. "Maybe you're right. Maybe she was genuinely upset. I have seen it before—when something brings her father back. She did love him, Wexton."

"Oh, yes?" Wexton did not sound convinced. "You remember that story you told me once—her father's novel, the nail scissors?"

"Yes."

Wexton shrugged. "If she loved her father so much," he said simply, "then how come she cut up his books?"

*　　*　　*

"Do you want to go back?" Acland said when they had reached the Stone House.

"No. No. Truly—it's all right. I'm glad we came. Not all my memories hurt, you see. I always liked this place. You can watch the woods and the lake from here. Do you remember, Acland—your mother used to have a table here. And her watercolors and her easel—over there. And then there were her books—on these shelves. My father's novels. He had them bound in vellum, especially for her."

Constance wandered about the small room as she spoke. She seemed oblivious to the damp of the building, the chill of its stone floor. She touched the pillars of the loggia outside, which fronted toward the lake, then retreated into the building's one room, gesturing, touching.

Acland stood watching her in an uncertain way. Despite what she said, he felt it had been unwise to come here. He hesitated, half in the building and half out, leaning against one of the loggia's pillars. He lit a cigarette. One of the black swans moved across the lake, then disappeared behind a clump of sedge. *Alone,* he thought, *and palely loitering.* He was unable to remember the rest of the poem.

Constance seemed reluctant to end this exploration. He watched her move back and forth, her breath making small white clouds in the cool of the air. She drew off her gloves and ran her hand over the bookshelves. Her rings glittered. Acland thought she looked small, delicate, lovely, and solemn: an odd exotic creature to find at Winterscombe. She wore no hat. Her Egyptian hair framed her face. Her expression was forlorn, almost disconsolate, as if—now the others had left them—she could drop the defensive mask of mockery and gaiety.

She wore a soft coat of some dark-gray material—an unusually somber choice, for Constance—which gave her a religious air, reminding him of a nun, a nurse, some quiet and ministering female influence. Beneath this coat he could just glimpse the whiteness of a blouse, its collar crumpled against the stem of her throat. As he looked at her, Constance, unconscious of his gaze, unfastened her coat. It swung back as she reached up to touch the place where a picture had once hung. She traced the mark it had left on the plastered wall. Beneath the pale silk of her blouse, the line of her breast was clearly visible. Acland could see the jut of the flesh, the outline of the aureole. Startled, even shocked by the lack of underclothing, he looked away.

When he looked back once more, Constance was sitting on an old wooden bench, a bench once placed on the loggia outside. She seemed to have forgotten his presence completely. Her head was bent, her hands clasped, her gray coat wrapped around her. Once again Acland was reminded of a nun, a penitent. He smiled to himself—it was an unlikely image for Constance. She is lovely, he thought to himself, and, remembering the time when she had been ill, when he had gone to her room in London, he felt an old affection welling up, distant and yet strong, like the memory of a perfume. She looked, he thought, very young; fragile, vulnerable, costly, highly finished—the kind of object a person might glimpse through the glass window of some expensive shop. They would stop, look at it, think *That is lovely, but not for me*—and then pass on.

"I shouldn't have come to Winterscombe." Constance looked up at him, her face sad and pinched. "I shouldn't have come. I shouldn't have asked to be Victoria's godmother. I've put you in an impossible position, I know that. You've been very kind, and gallant—but it wasn't fair. I'm sorry, Acland. All I've done is irritate everybody. Even Jane. Why do I do that? I don't mean to—yet I can see it happening. Oh, I wish I'd never worn that stupid hat. . . ."

"It was a very pretty hat." Acland smiled. "I liked it."

"Oh, Acland—such a gentleman! That's not the point, anyway. The hat is trivial—I know that. It's me, not the hat. I don't belong here, and I never did. It was wrong of me to force myself on you. And yet, I'm glad I was there. I'd never been to a christening before. The words—the words are extraordinary, don't you think? 'Steadfast in faith,' 'joyful through hope,' 'the waves of this troublesome world.' You see?" She smiled. "I have them by heart. Waves—I understood that. I hate the sea. And the world is troublesome."

"The words are moving—even if you don't believe. They have a power of their own." Acland walked into the Stone House. He looked at his mother's bookshelves. He sat down.

"They make you believe, I think. While they're being said." Constance gave a small shiver. "They make you believe in impossible things. Redemption, change . . . I don't know. I did mean it, you know, when I made all those promises this morning. Such solemn ones! I know no one else will think that I could—but I did mean them. I want you to know that." She shivered again. "It's cold here, Acland."

"Shall we go back?"

"No, not yet. I want to stay—just a while longer. It's only my hands that are cold. Will you hold them, Acland? Yes, like that. Rub them a little bit. The fingertips. Oh, that's better. They felt freezing. I think the circulation had stopped."

Acland held her hands. He chafed them between his own, as she asked, until they felt warmed. Then, since there seemed no reason to release them, he continued to hold them. He looked down at them; he rested her right hand, then her left, across his palm.

"So many rings. You always wear so many rings."

"I know. I don't know why. I like them. I'm greedy for rings. Just little ones. They remind me of people. You see that one there, with the blue stone—Boy gave me that, when I was fourteen. Montague bought that one. The opal came from Maud—before I fell out of favor."

"You cried today, in the church. I saw you."

"I know. I'm sorry. I thought no one had seen."

"You were very discreet. Just two tears, then two more."

"Crocodile tears, Maud would say." Constance smiled. "That's not true either. I don't cry very often. Not like Steenie. I save the tears up, perhaps. No, that's not true. They have a will of their own. I cried when my dog Floss died—but I couldn't cry when I lost my father. Isn't that strange?"

"Not necessarily."

"Acland, may I ask you something? Something I've always wanted to ask you—and never have?"

"If you want."

Constance hesitated. "You won't be angry? It's about my father."

Acland released her hand. He drew back a little. Constance looked at him in an anxious way. He, too, seemed to hesitate, perhaps be about to refuse. Then he shrugged.

"Ask away. I expected you to ask—one day."

"The night of the accident"—Constance fixed her eyes upon his—"did you think it was an accident—as everyone said?"

"It's twenty years ago, Constance."

"Not to me. To me it is yesterday. Please, Acland. Tell me."

Acland sighed. He leaned back against the bench. He turned away. He looked out across the grass toward the lake and the woods beyond. He rested his eyes upon the trees and the deepening gray of the sky. After a silence he said, "No. At the time—I didn't think of it as an accident."

"And now?"

"Now?" He frowned. "Now—I'm not sure. Time changes things. It alters the memory. It makes some things stand out and others recede. Sometimes . . . I try not to remember, perhaps. In any case, my ability to concentrate—on anything—is not as good as it used to be."

"Because of the war?"

"Perhaps."

"Do you think that, because of the war, you erase certain things?"

"It's possible."

"Acland." Constance stole out one small hand. She rested that hand over his, in his lap. As she did so, her coat fell open once more. Again Acland glimpsed the curve of her breast, taut under the silk of the blouse. He looked away. The sky on the horizon was turning mauve, streaked with pewter. He thought: *It will grow dark soon.*

"Acland. Answer me truthfully now. I think I know the answer anyway, and I promise you that nothing you say will distress me. But I want to hear the truth, from you." She paused. "Did you take those guns, Acland?"

"The guns?"

"Yes. Boy's guns."

"The Purdeys." Acland turned back to look at her. His gaze, distant, calm, composed, rested upon her face. He showed no sign of emotion.

"Yes." He sighed, as if suddenly realizing he was tired. "Yes. I took them. The day of the party, we had tea outside on the terrace—do you remember? Your father was angry with you. He sent you inside to wash and change. Jane went with you."

"I remember."

"After that"—Acland hesitated—"I walked down to the lake with Boy. He was very distressed. He'd just seen them, you see—your father and my mother—for the first time. He saw her go into your father's room—" He paused. "Boy was a strange person. He always seemed so quiet—but underneath . . . His reaction was very violent. He had a very simple view of the world, and it had suddenly been overturned. I listened to him for a long time. Then he went back to the house. I went into the gun room. I told Boy what I was going to do."

"You took his guns?"

"Yes. I don't know why. They were the best guns in the house—my father's pride and joy. I think that was the reason. Anyway, I took them. I hid them in the cloakroom—the one by the side door, you remember? The one we used to call the hellhole? I'd been in there that afternoon, to fetch some galoshes for Jane. The place was always such a mess. It made a good hiding place. I put them under a pile of coats. I thought they would be easy to fetch—later."

"Tell me what you meant to do with them."

"Something harmful, obviously. To your father, of course."

"Because you hated him?"

"Yes. I hated him." Acland paused. "I was seventeen then. I think I've never felt such pure hatred for anyone, before or since. I loathed him for what he was, and for what he did. For what he'd done to my father—and my mother. For what he'd done to Boy. I thought . . ."

"Tell me, Acland."

"I thought the world would be a better place with him dead."

There was a silence. Constance rested her hands on her lap. She looked at her rings. She counted them.

"Tell me what you did, Acland," she said at last. "I have to know. With the guns. Tell me what you did—later."

She leaned forward as she said this. Acland heard her voice falter, felt her breath against his cheek. He could smell spring, and earth, in the scent she used. Her proximity distracted him. He looked at the curve of her throat, the line of her chin. Her lips, scarlet as always, were slightly parted. Her eyes rested anxiously upon his face.

"Constance—I'm not sure I want to go on. I'm not sure it's right to go on. It was so long ago. Can't we both forget?"

"I can never forget. And I must know. I've waited so long to know." She shook her head. "Please, Acland. Tell me. I guessed some of this. When did you go back for the guns? You did go back, didn't you? Was it after you went to the stables, after you left Jenna?"

"Some while after that. Yes."

"Tell me."

"Very well. It was eleven—about then—when I left the stables. I didn't want to return to the party. So many people. I wanted to stay outside, in the gardens in the dark. I wanted to think. How could I do it—when I could do it. Then, when I was standing there, I saw your father come out. I saw him take the path to the woods. I knew he would be going to meet my mother. One of their assignations. I knew that."

"Did you follow him?"

"No. Not at once. I waited. I heard the guests leave. I might have left, myself, gone to bed, given up the whole idea—I was almost ready to do that. Jenna had calmed me, a little. But then . . .

my mother came out. She saw me on the terrace. She called to me. She touched my coat, I remember, and said it was damp. She told me to go inside. She sounded so insistent. I knew why. She had been delayed. She was about to leave, herself, to meet Shawcross. She didn't want her son to see her leave. He might have asked her . . . why she went for a walk in the woods at one o'clock in the morning.''

"Oh, Acland." Constance gave a small sigh. "It was just as I thought. Were you very angry—did you hate him then, very much?"

"I suppose I must have." Acland frowned. "I went back for the guns. I selected one of them. I set off down the path to the woods. Halfway down the path, I loaded the gun. Both barrels."

"Both barrels?" Constance shivered.

"I wanted to be sure. One shot might have missed him. I was clear what I would do. I thought: *I will walk down this path, and when I find Shawcross, I'll fire the gun.* In the head. In the heart. At close range. I wanted him to be dead—instantly."

"That gun would kill him—at close range?"

"Oh, yes. Have you never seen the results of a shooting accident?"

"No. I never have. Please hold my hand, Acland. Don't let it go. I do want to know. I want to understand. But it frightens me. Look. Put your arm around me—yes, like that. Now you can tell me, very quietly and very simply. You see how close I am? We never had secrets between us—except this one. You are my brother—no, closer than a brother. You saved my life once. Please, Acland, tell me. You loaded the gun. Both barrels. You walked on down the path. . . .''

Constance rested her head against his shoulder. She had drawn Acland's arm around her. He could feel the tension in her back. Her soft coat seemed very thin. Where his hand rested upon her upper arm, he could feel—brushing against his fingers as she moved—the curve of her breast. A woman's breast: Acland found this strange, unaccountable; Constance was so like a child: as small as a child, as breathless and agitated as a child. He thought of her as a child still, and yet this child possessed breasts. He shifted his hand higher, so it rested upon her shoulder. He turned his gaze to the lake outside, and to the failing light. Two evenings in succession, he thought, in which twilight summoned the past.

"Constance. This is difficult to say. . . .''

"Say it nonetheless."

"You want to hear this?"

"I want to hear this."

"Very well. I loaded the gun. I walked on down the path to the woods."

"Did you know about the trap? Oh, God, Acland—did you?" She pressed closer to him. She had begun to tremble. She shivered inside her thin coat. Acland stroked her arm. He continued to gaze at the lake.

"No. I didn't know about the trap. Man-traps were illegal. My father might rant about using them, but I didn't take that seriously. I had no idea it was there. In any case it makes no difference, because I stopped."

"You stopped?"

"Just stopped. In the middle of the path. I came to my senses— I suppose that's what people would say. I looked at myself, walking along a path, carrying a gun, intending to kill someone. I saw . . . how ridiculous it was, I suppose. Not wrong—it didn't feel wrong. Just ridiculous."

"Killing someone you hated? That seemed ridiculous?"

"Constance, is it so hard to understand? I looked at my actions from the outside—and they seemed absurd. A seventeen-year-old boy's idea of melodrama. Avenging his mother's honor. And I was right. It was absurd. So—I went back. I put the gun back under the coats. I went into the house and played billiards." He paused.

"But the next day—after the accident—when they brought your father back to the house. Something happened then."

He turned to look at her. "It was you, I think, Constance. The way you cried out. The way you looked at me. I felt as if you read my mind. I felt you knew—what I'd intended to do. I felt like a murderer then. It was just as if I had killed him. You . . . shamed me."

Acland sighed. "There's nothing more really. The next day, I went to my father. I wanted to confess to him. Surprisingly enough, he was very good to me. He was understanding, even strong. I never told him why I wanted to kill Shawcross. I never mentioned my mother. He knew, of course. I could tell from his face. He had dignity, you know—in his way. He wasn't as stupid as he could seem. I showed him where I had left the guns. He returned them, I think. That day. Or the day after."

There was a silence. Constance gave a small convulsive shudder. She drew back. She pressed her hands tight against her forehead. She stared out in a blind way at the trees, the lake, the gathering twilight.

"I thought you had killed him." She spoke with a tone of

regret. "I did see it in your face when they brought him back. I looked at my father lying there on that stretcher, with those horrible tartan rugs. Then I looked at you. It was as if I recognized you. I was sure—so sure! It was like an arrow in my mind. I've believed it ever since. I never told anyone. Twenty years. You see, if it was you—it all made sense."

She reached for his hands, then clasped them between hers. "Acland—you wouldn't lie to me? You promise you wouldn't lie? Will you look me in the eyes, and say it—just once. Say: 'I didn't kill him.' "

"I didn't kill him, Constance. I wanted to kill him. I even meant to kill him, for . . . what? Six hours? Eight hours? But I didn't do it. I had to be trained by the army to kill—and even then I was never very good at it. To be good at killing, it has to give you pleasure, I think. Or you have to be very afraid. One or the other."

Acland said this in a quiet voice. Constance cried out. She pressed her hands against his face. She covered up his eyes.

"Oh, don't look like that, Acland—don't speak like that. I hate to see you like this. You look so tired—and older, a little bitter. You look so very different—"

"I am different."

"I do believe you." She stood up and began to move back and forth in an agitated manner. "I believe you. You can't lie to me. But I don't understand. Someone else must have killed him then—they must have. It was not an accident, Acland. I know it was not. Pleasure? You say people have to feel pleasure, to kill well? Or, what was the other thing? Fear. Yes, that's it. Fear. But who could have felt that, Acland? To do such a horrible thing. Not your father, not Boy, not you—there's no one. Oh, I wish I'd never asked. I felt so sure, and now I'm back again, with all the questions, all the questions! They rush about so in my head. They make me ache, all those questions. Twenty years, Acland—and they won't go away. They rush, and they . . . bite. It feels as if they bite. They make everything so black. It must have been an accident then—just as everyone said. I wish I could believe that. If I could, I could rest. I could. I think then that I could—"

"Constance, don't do this to yourself. We shouldn't have come here. We shouldn't have begun on all this. Wait—Constance . . ."

Acland had risen. Her distress, the distracted way in which she spoke, the fact that she was still shaking—these things alarmed him. He took her arm, and when Constance attempted to push him away, he drew her gently toward him. He could feel the agitation in her body. She was jerky, angular with distress.

"Constance, I'm sorry. Leave it—can't you leave it?" he began. He pitied her, and because he pitied her he drew her closer, then began to stroke her hair. Her hair was springy, resilient to his touch. He had forgotten the feel of that hair, yet the moment he touched it, it was familiar to him. He rested his hand against her skull. He stroked downward, gently, feeling the curvature of bone beneath the hair's vitality. This seemed to quiet Constance. She made a small sound, part gasp, part sob.

"How kind you are, Acland," she said in a low voice. "I never thought of you as that. I used to think of you as angry, scathing—hard, perhaps. But you can be kind. You have changed. Oh, I'm so cold. I can't stop shivering. Hold me close—please, warm me. I'll be all right in a moment, and then we can go."

She gave another shiver as she said this. She burrowed against him for reassurance. As she did this, her coat slipped farther back from her shoulders. Somehow—Acland was not sure how—he found that his arm now encircled her waist beneath the coat. Her waist was tiny. He could have spanned it with his hands.

This made him feel awkward, even compromised. He stopped stroking her hair. When he attempted to move back, Constance clung to him.

"Please hold me. Just a while longer. I'm so unhappy. Look, I'm crying. I'm making your jacket all wet. I hate that jacket. So thick and scratchy—like a horrible hair shirt. Tweeds—why do Englishmen always wear tweeds? There, that's better."

Acland found that his jacket was undone. Constance nestled against him. She gave a small, contented sigh. The scent of ferns and damp earth rose from her skin. He felt the dampness of tears against his shirt. The scent of her hair slowed his mind; it was acrid and hypnotic. One of Constance's small jeweled hands rested above his heart. Her breasts pressed against him in an insistent way. He felt her nipples harden.

Years of marriage to a very different kind of woman had perhaps slowed his instincts. One part of his mind was still arguing that this insistent pressure was an accidental eroticism, when Constance moved. She touched him in a way he could not misinterpret.

Acland at once released her and stepped back.

Constance regarded him with an air of patient, almost sad tolerance. She shook her head in a reproachful way. She bit her lips so that they reddened. "Such a very married face." She smiled. "How silly. Oh, Acland."

"It's no use running away," Constance said as Acland moved toward the doorway. "You cannot run away from me. I am not in the least taken in by demonstrations of marital devotion."

"I'm not running away. I am going back to the house, and back to my wife. I prefer her company."

"Her company?" Constance followed him to the door. "How very dull. I could make you forget the pleasures of companionship in five minutes. Less. Kiss me, Acland—and then tell me how valuable companionship is. I think you might find it became less valuable then. Not negligible—I would never say that—but not something you need too urgently."

"Constance, I love my wife."

"But of course you love her. I never doubted that for one moment. After all"—she gave a small impatient gesture—"I promoted your marriage. I told you she would suit. You need her, just as I need Montague—up to a point. However, you also need me. You want me. You always have. If you touched me, you would know that. You don't dare to touch me—and that's why you're running away so fast." She shrugged. "It's quite useless. You can't leave me. I'll be there in your mind. You'll consider, speculate, wish. Just as you always did. Just as I always did."

She spoke with an air of absolute certainty. This arrogance angered Acland.

"Do you believe that?" he said in a quiet voice.

"Of course. I've never doubted it."

"You're wrong. I could touch you—and feel nothing at all. The point is, I have no desire to touch you."

At this, Constance gave a small cry. It seemed to Acland too perfectly timed, that cry, and the gesture of apparent pain she gave, too contrived. From arrogance and certitude a moment before, she switched to vulnerability. This seemed to Acland mechanical. Constance used these shifts, he thought, like ratchets. Obedient to the leverage of her will, they were designed to manipulate speech into a scene, a scene upward to the peaks of drama, or melodrama.

"Look, Constance," he began in a reasonable voice. "Think a little. I am married. You are married. You came here for my daughter's christening. A moment ago we were talking about your father's death. You were distressed, and I tried to comfort you. That's all. Nothing more. If you misinterpreted my actions—I'm sorry. Now, can we stop this, and forget this, and go back to the house?"

"You saved my life, once—" Constance gave another cry.

"Constance, that was so long ago. You were ill, and perhaps I helped, in certain ways, in your recovery—"

"You promised me not to die." Her eyes had again filled with tears. "You swore to me. And you didn't die. You came back."

"Constance, I know all those things. I don't deny them. They were before my marriage."

"Oh, before your marriage! You make your marriage sound like some horrible barrier. A great wall." She clasped her hands together. "How can you speak like that—in that dismissive way? All those sacred things. And you wave them aside. I believed in you. I believed in us. It's the only thing I ever have believed in—in all my life."

"Constance, I'm not dismissing them. I'm just saying they are over, that's all."

"You are! You are! You're denying them!" She gave another cry. She covered her ears with her hands. "I won't listen. I can't bear to listen. It's like Saint Peter, and the cock crowing, three times. It's hateful. It's sinful."

"Constance—stop this. Listen—"

"I won't." She dropped her hands. She took a step back. Acland realized he was no longer certain whether she was acting or was sincere. All color had left her face, which had a blanched, stricken look. She was again trembling with the force of her own emotion.

"You loved me. I know you loved me. There was something there, between us. It was alive—so alive. And now you're trying to kill it. You've changed. You wouldn't have done that once. You're less than you used to be, Acland. You took risks once. Now, you won't even admit the risks are there. You pretend they don't exist—it's safer that way! Oh, Acland. When did you decide to make yourself an ordinary man?"

Acland turned away. He looked at the lake, the darkening sky. The woods were now invisible, a shadow beyond the water.

"Is it ordinary," he said slowly, "to love your wife, and your child? Is it ordinary—to value a marriage? Perhaps it is." He shrugged. "Very well, then. I am . . . ordinary. That is . . . what I have become."

There was a silence. When Constance next spoke, her voice had changed. She spoke slowly, in a considering way: "I wonder," she said. "How strange. Maybe you always were. Maybe no change was involved. Perhaps . . . I invented you. Montague suggested that.

Yes, I see now. It could be that. I made you, Acland—into such a fine creature. A hero. I looked at you—and do you know what I saw? A unique man. No, not even a man. An angel. Your hair was like fire. Your eyes could strike me dead. You were invincible—one of the immortals. All that power, and I gave it to you! I coined it, in my mind. I breathed it into you, year after year. I made you so strong. I looked at your two hands, and do you know what I saw? I saw death in the one hand, and life in the other. My redeemer, and my deliverer. The creature who could save me, the creature with the courage to kill my father. So much then, and so little now. Ah, well—"

"Constance—"

"I am not so small, after all. I see that now. I seem small sometimes, even to myself. I look at myself, and I shrink before my own eyes. But now—I'm not so sure. Perhaps I am . . . considerable." She gave a sigh. "Does it make someone considerable, do you think, if their imagination is large?"

"Constance, we should not have come here. You're not well."

Acland turned back to her. She was standing stiffly, her hands clasped in front of her, looking out toward the darkening water of the lake. She had spoken as if to herself, as if she did not see Acland at all.

"Come back to the house." He took her arm. "Constance, can you hear me? Listen. It's late. It's cold. Come back. Come back now."

"I'm braver than you are. I understand that now. I begin to understand it." She turned upon him a blank gaze. "I shall never forgive you for that, Acland."

"Don't talk anymore. Look, take my arm and we'll walk back to the house. You should rest—"

"I don't want your arm. I shall never rest. What a fool you sound! Leave me alone."

"Constance—"

"You know the only courage worth having? The courage to kill. And I thought you possessed it. How stupid I was! You loaded your gun. Then you turned back. God, I despise you—"

"Constance, stop this. You don't know what you're saying. Look—sit down. Try to be quiet." Acland looked about him in a helpless way. Constance did not move.

"Shall I fetch someone?" He turned back to her. "Steenie— perhaps if Steenie came down? He could talk to you, and then, when you feel calmer—"

"Oh, but I feel perfectly calm. Look."

She held out her hand, palm downward.

"You see? Not a breath of wind. The water quite still. So black. No ripples."

"You're ill. I'm going to fetch someone."

Acland moved toward the steps, then stopped. It would be unwise, he knew, to leave her. He turned back, still hesitating. Constance remained staring in the direction of the lake, just visible still in the gathering dusk. Her face was white as chalk, her gaze wide-eyed and intent. The proximity of that lake made Acland afraid. No, he could not leave her.

As he stared out toward the water, there came a sudden sound, so startling after the silence that Acland flinched and then—with a reflex that remained, all those years after the war—lifted his arm to shield his face. He felt the sussuration of the air; saw, dimly, the passage, very close, of a black and indeterminate shape.

Even as he recognized it to be a swan, lifting into flight from the water, he thought: *Will I never be free of this?* And as he thought this, Constance screamed.

Her gull cry: one clear, high, piercing note. Acland swung around. Fear and confusion made time reverse. For a second, turning, he expected to see a child, white-faced, black-dressed, bending, straightening, screaming—and then freezing, fixing him with her accusatory eyes, black and unwavering in a small stone face.

No child, of course. Constance, in her gray coat, had also flinched. Her arm, too, was lifted before her face, as if to ward off a blow. As he looked at her she backed away from him, into the shadows, so her figure merged with them, so he could see only the pallor of her face.

She said—later he would think she said—"Don't. For the love of God. Don't."

She made a tiny sound, a whimpering sound, like a small and injured animal. Then, as Acland, recovering, made a gesture of concern, began hesitantly to move toward her, she dropped her arm and straightened up.

Acland stopped. Her face stopped him. Constance paused, seemed to consider, then walked forward a few steps. She lifted her head to look at him, dusk making her skin silvery, shadow dissolving, then re-forming the features of her face.

She said, in a clear precise voice: "Do you know what my father did once? He gave me my own blood to drink. In a very small glass. The tiniest glass. As small as a thimble. Or was it wine? No, I don't think it was wine. I couldn't be mistaken, could I? Wine tastes different from blood."

Before Acland could speak, she lifted her hand, then felt for his face.

"Poor Acland." Her expression changed, beneath that glassy overlay. Her hair merged into the dusk. "Poor Acland. I'm not ill. My mind never felt so clear. I understand now." She seemed to gather herself, or to summon some last vestige of her will. "I knew I would understand—in the end. All day today, I could feel it coming, closer and closer. You helped—I think you helped. The voice was always there, you see—I just had to listen to it. Did you hear it just now? I'm glad I listened. I should have listened before, but I was too afraid. I thought time would drown it out—but of course it couldn't. Not even twenty years, two whole decades, not the rest of my life, not the deepest water would silence that. After all, you can't drown a voice, can you? A person, yes—but not a voice."

She gave a small shake of the head. Acland felt her fingers trace his own features; then she let her hand fall.

"It's growing dark. I can't see you so very well. Let me look at you. Yes, I thought so. Such a small imagination. So quick, so clever—but you still don't understand, do you? Shall I show you? Shall I show you now? Yes, I think I shall. I owe you that."

She ran down the steps ahead of him. At the bottom of them she paused, looking back. She drew her gray coat close about her. She gazed at him for a moment, then turned and began to walk away up the path to the house.

The light was almost gone. Acland ran out after her. He heard the sound of her small feet, the crush of gravel underfoot, then the crack of a stick.

He peered into the dusk. Constance, clearly in sight a moment before, was now invisible.

Here I am. And here I am not. Acland felt alarm tighten in his chest, felt an acute sense of foreboding. He ran down the steps. He stared along the path. He could see the lights of the house in the distance, the pale thread of the gravel; shadows wavered; half-light witched his eyes.

He thought he saw, some way in the distance, her figure move. Constance, or a trick of the light? He hesitated, uncertain, afraid she might have turned away in the direction of the lake. He began to walk, then to run. A branch reached out and caught at his hair. A trunk twisted at him, startlingly white. His pace slowed. He stopped.

From the darkness ahead of him a voice called. He felt an

instinctual fear, a chill on the back of his neck. His mother's voice.

In the silence that followed he stood irresolute, telling himself that darkness distorted, that he imagined this. Then the voice came again, its accent and its tone unmistakable. A perfect piece of mimicry.

"Eddie," called his mother's voice. "Eddie. This way. I'm over here."

When Acland reached the house he paused in the hall. From the drawing room beyond he could hear the sounds of normality: the crackle of logs on the fire, the chink of teacups, the murmur of conversation. He listened: his wife's voice, Wexton's voice, an interjection from Steenie, some exchange of remarks between Freddie and Winnie; then, interspersed with the others, Constance's voice. He could catch only phrases, for Constance's voice was always low-pitched, but those phrases were enough to tell him: Constance had returned to the family circle. She was discussing, it seemed, varieties of honey. Her voice and manner of speech were not odd in any way. There was no indication of stress, or emotion, in her speech. Acland leaned against the wall. He closed, then opened his eyes. He thought: *I imagined this.*

Constance had always possessed this ability, to drag him through the looking glass, to make—of inversion—sense. He gazed at the staircase; he watched it branch. He was reluctant to leave the protection of this hall; he wanted to remain here, on the borderline, on the frontier. He did not want to look Constance in the face.

Standing there in the hall, Acland felt certain the events of the afternoon *had* taken place; he felt equally certain they had not. He found he could not remember precisely what Constance had said to him, or the order in which she had said it. His mind was full of scraps; he could assemble them in an infinite number of patterns. Their innate energy, their malevolent capacity for change, perturbed and confused him.

He was sure that, on the path, Constance had called back to him in his mother's voice. He thought he was sure of the words she had used. He understood that, if he had heard this, the voice that had called to him was the voice of patricide.

This, too, was possible, and impossible. He was not prepared to trust the accuracy of his own memory, or its implications. Constance, after all, was a liar, as well as a fantasist. Cross-examine. Decode. Acland tried to force his mind to work—he had prided himself, once upon a time, on the incisiveness of his reason.

If he had heard what he thought he had heard, then Constance was capable of murder, or was not sane, or, at the very least, had a seriously disturbed imagination. Guilt, as he knew, was a flexible, devious thing; it was possible to feel it for an action wished but never committed. Had she committed a crime, or merely *imagined* she had committed it? That was possible: He knew Constance's ability to believe her own fictions. Yes, he could talk this thing down, level by level, until it became something within the grasp of the rational. Yet he could not be certain. Flux, distortion, an almost infinite capacity for interpretation—nothing could be fixed. This crime—if it was a crime—was too old. There it lay, twenty years in the past, beyond the reach of reason, or forensics.

I shall know when I look at her, Acland told himself. So he crossed the hall and entered the drawing room. Constance's face told him nothing; her manner told him nothing. She was neither quieter nor more animated than usual. She took tea with his family. She sat there in a chair to the left of the fire, sipping tea, her small feet extended toward the warmth of the flames.

She had, it seemed, just presented her christening present, and Jane—disguising the dislike Acland knew she would have for such an object—rose to show it to him as he entered. An extravagant, costly, pagan-looking bracelet: a snake, with a jeweled head, designed to coil about the arm. Constance, negligent about this present, said she had not wanted to provide the usual predictable christening trinkets. This present was one Victoria could wear when she was older; it looked best on bare skin. Constance smiled. A pretty thing, she thought; she had bought it on impulse, the previous day, in Bond Street.

Nothing happened. Acland found this unnerving. His head began to ache. When he went to dress for dinner the pain worsened. He had suffered migraine attacks since the war (and was to continue to suffer them, throughout my Winterscombe childhood). Usually, the only cure for these attacks was silence and a darkened room—but that evening such cures were out of the question.

A special dinner had been planned in celebration of the christening—just a family dinner, but one he knew was important to his wife.

Acland took codeine to dull the edge of the pain. Looking toward light sources, he found them rimmed with black, a blackness that nauseated him, that probed some space behind the eyes, was an affliction to the retina.

At seven-thirty he went downstairs. All the household was assembled except Constance. Constance was to come down late; while the rest of the group drank glasses of sherry downstairs, Constance paced about her room. She turned back and forth before her mirror; she reassured herself of her own beauty. Glittery: as perfect as ice; her hair electric with purpose, her fingers like daggers.

Constance was planning her little scene. Should she say this first, or that? Should she just punish Acland for being ordinary—or should she punish them all, one after another? All of them, she decided.

She sent a mind-message to Montague, who was—she saw now—*not* ordinary; her husband, who would approve of what she was doing. *We are alike*, she said to him: *We know how to hate; if it came to it, we would both have the courage to leap into the chasm. Watch me pull the temple down, Montague*, she said—*watch. I know you will find it amusing.*

I shall wear your diamonds, for you, Constance said—and she strung them around her neck, a chain of water. She turned her throat, this way, then that; she watched lightning spring out from their facets.

Time to go. Her skin was white. Her dress was black. Her lips were red. *I can kill*, said her will; and then it said: *I can do anything.*

She turned out the lights, one by one. Even the darkness was not frightening. Then, taking the stairs slowly, admiring, as she went, the trimness of her tiny feet, the fit of her satin shoes, the buckles like prisms, she went down.

Hurt them, said Constance to herself. And, since she was a child in this respect as well as others, since she was never to understand that to punish others is a poor way to ensure the punishment of the self, her will gathered strength.

She entered the drawing room with confidence, as she always did when she was undivided in her purpose. She looked from face to face, and then—just as she had planned—she set about procuring her own banishment. Acland may have been the instrument for that exile, but I have no doubt that it was Constance who acted judge and jury. In ensuring that she became an outcast, she was passing sentence on herself.

Imagine it: it was an old-fashioned, a very formal dining room at Winterscombe. Reduced circumstances, yes, but the old rules still prevailing. A polished table, too large for seven people, and the numbers odd—a fact that was indisguisable. William, assisted by one of the elderly maids, was serving. He would have poured the claret (and it would have been a fine one) as he always did, with an air of reverence. The four men, in dinner jackets; the three women, in evening dress. Candlelight; a fire; heavy silver, well polished; over-ornate crested dinner service, four hundred individual pieces, once a source of pride to my grandfather Denton. A well-cooked plain meal—an English meal; the cook distrusts what she calls fancy dishes. No herbs here; not a whisper of garlic. The fillets of sole come curled up like small white fists; their only adornment, lemon. The roast is saddle of mutton—it is excellent, but will remain untasted. The puddings—a nod to Freddie here—are the kind Englishmen claim to prefer: nursery puddings; starchy, heavy, and reassuring. They would not be eaten either, for it was when the saddle of mutton had been brought out, and Acland—as was customary—had crossed to the sideboard to carve, that Constance began. It was Winnie, poor Winnie, who gave her her cue.

Winnie, loyal and devoted to Wexton, had been reading his latest collection of poems. It was dedicated to my parents—a fact Winnie mentioned in passing. Constance's mouth tightened.

Winnie explained, at some length, that she and Cootie (detained in London on regimental matters) liked to read these poems aloud to each other, often over cocoa at bedtime. One in particular was their favorite: a love sonnet. Winnie, oblivious to Wexton's embarrassment, went so far as to quote, from memory, certain lines.

She misinterpreted them, in a sense. Winnie was, and is, an innocent in many ways. To her, the poem was about love—it must therefore be about the kind of love Winnie understood, the kind of love she felt for her husband.

When she had finished her quotation, there was a small silence. Steenie, who had not yet had time to become properly drunk but who was heading that way fast, gave Wexton a surreptitious wink. Jane, who found the words moving, glanced toward Acland. Constance leaned forward.

"Of course," she said in a clear voice, "you do know, Winnie, that the poem was written to a man?"

Winnie, in the act of raising her wineglass to her lips, almost dropped it. She blinked. She stared at Wexton in consternation. Her neck, then her cheeks, blushed crimson.

"He is describing lovemaking, of course," Constance continued, into absolute silence, her voice thoughtful. "Lovemaking between two men. The kind Wexton prefers. The kind Steenie prefers too. Did you know, Winnie, that Steenie and Wexton used to be lovers?" She frowned. "I forget. Were you sixteen then, Steenie, or seventeen? Under-age, certainly."

There was a crash. The elderly maid, less imperturbable than
William, had dropped a large vegetable dish. Its silver lid clattered
across the floor. Roast potatoes spilled out, then slithered. The maid
knelt down, then attempted to pick them up.

"Homosexuals," Constance continued musingly. "I never use
the term *queers* myself. Nor *pansies*. I think those words stupid, and
rude—don't you, Winnie? People use them—"

Acland stopped carving. He laid down the knife. He gave a
small sign—and at that sign both servants departed. Over the sound
of their footsteps Constance continued.

"People use them—terms like that—because they find sexual
inversion frightening. Some people would say shameful—but I don't
believe that. No. Fear is involved, I feel sure. People like Steenie
and Wexton remind us that there are no rules—for love or for sex.
People will try to pretend that there are—which seems to me so very
tiresome! You, Winnie, for instance, how would you define normal
love? As heterosexual? And what about normal sex? As married? As
occurring once a week? As employing the missionary position? How I
wish your husband, Cootie, were here! Then he could tell us what
he thought. I mean, when it comes to fucking, are his views conservative or liberal? Could they be radical? Now, there's a thought!
When it comes to fucking, is the absent colonel a radical? And if
so . . ."

Winnie's chair scraped back. She was quivering from head to
foot. Her mouth opened, then closed.

Acland said, with some force, "Constance. Stop this."

Constance turned upon him a wide-eyed gaze.

"Acland, please—this is interesting. I make my case for the
deregulation of sex. And love—come to that. But the two do become
so inextricably entangled, don't you find? Which doesn't help for
clarity of viewpoint. People will get so hot under the collar! I cannot
think why. *Sodomy* now—let's consider that. We all know sodomy is
something homosexuals practice—"

"Biblical!" cried Steenie, rising dramatically to his feet. "Are
we going to be biblical, because if we are—"

"But after all," Constance went on, "sodomy is not a practice
confined to homosexuals. Heterosexuals, the most muscular Christians, they have been known to indulge in it too. So, is it a perversion? If so, why? Winnie, what would your attitude be? Would
Cootie consider it a perversion, do you think? Does he have a view
on—let me see—masturbation? On oral sex? On fornication? Personally, I've always taken the view that if it's pleasurable, it's permitted—

and if it isn't permitted, it's all the more fun. But then I never set myself up as a moralist. Oh dear." Constance gave a small sigh. "I feel sure that if Cootie were here, he could set me straight. Then I should understand at last—why one practice was more permissible than another. . . . Do you know, I think I have a *language* difficulty? Do you find that, Winnie? I cannot *quite* understand why we make lust a sin, and love a virtue, when love causes so much trouble in this troublesome world. But then, for that matter, I have *never* understood why laborious Latin terms are more acceptable than native ones. Would anyone truly prefer to say 'penis' when they could say—"

"*Never!*" said Winnie, finding her voice at last.

"—And then *fuck*. Quite apart from the fact that no other adequate verb exists, I find it a charming word—don't you, Wexton? It has poetic virtues. It is onomatopoeic, to begin with, and—"

"Never!" cried Winnie again, with gusty force. "Never in all my life—to hear a woman speak in this way—to hear *anyone* speak in this way. Is this woman deranged? Is she *drunk*?"

Winnie was wearing a shawl. As she spoke she gathered this shawl about her shoulders, straightened her back, and fixed Constance with a gimlet eye. Constance considered her wineglass.

"No, Winnie. I'm not drunk. I don't *think* I'm drunk. Actually, I never become drunk. I don't think I've ever been drunk in the whole of my life—"

"Then this display is all the sadder," replied Winnie with some venom. "I shall not listen to one more word of this—"

"Neither shall I," interjected Freddie. He rose. He looked around the table, his face dazed with blind distress. "Acland, can't you stop her? You know what she's like. Once she starts—"

"Constance—"

"Acland, don't be foolish. We are discussing language and morals. I am a woman. A rather small woman. What are you going to do, eject me?"

"*Leave*," replied Winnie smartly. "I for one intend to do just that. Freddie, if you would be so kind. I feel in need of a little fresh air."

Winnie swept toward the door. Freddie hesitated. He looked back at Constance, as if about to risk one last plea. Evidently the expression in Constance's eyes suggested this might be unwise; Freddie decided not to risk it. He headed for the door, offered Winnie his arm—a small gallantry that was later to be remembered, I think, in the years of Winnie's widowhood. Winnie's exit was regal; Freddie's, less so. The door shut.

Steenie said, "I feel sick." He slumped in his chair. He drank one glass of wine, then poured another. "Honestly, Connie—why do you do it?"

"Do what?" Constance looked from face to face, her expression innocent. "It was only a *discussion*."

"A pretty one-sided discussion." Wexton leaned forward. "In fact, I wouldn't have said it was a discussion at all. You set out to hurt Winnie."

"Well, perhaps I did." Constance gave a small smile. "Just a little. She *is* the tiniest bit stupid, don't you think? She made horrid faces at my hat, all morning. . . ."

"Jesus Christ," said Steenie.

"Besides, people like Winnie irritate me. You, too, Jane, if you will forgive my saying so. I hate moral codes that are self-limiting. Being blinkered is not moral—it's cowardly, and more than a little self-deluding. And Winnie really was terribly stupid about your poem, Wexton. Confess—she made your toes curl the second she started to recite."

"My toes curl when anyone recites my poems."

"Do they really? How high-minded. But then you are high-minded, Wexton. An Olympian teddy bear. May I ask you something?"

"Sure."

"I admire your poems, you know. Even I can see they are good. But I *never* understood how you could dedicate such good poems to a man like Steenie. Or fall in love with him, come to that. Now, Steenie, don't roll your eyes about and wave your hands—you know this is true. I love you dearly, and when you were younger and didn't drink so much, you were terribly pretty. But I would never have thought Wexton was the kind of man to fall for a pretty face—"

"*Don't*," said Steenie, both rolling his eyes and continuing to wave his hands. "Don't start on me, Connie, because if you do—"

"Well, be honest, Steenie. You *are* a dabbler. One exhibition of paintings—and then look what happened. You weren't faithful to Wexton for five seconds. The minute Boy shot himself, what did you do? You went running off to Conrad Vickers and leapt into bed. *And* you blamed Boy for your own unfaithfulness—which I must say I always thought a little cheap. But then *no one* told the truth about Boy's death, including Boy. All these years we all still pretend it was the war, shell shock. It was nothing to do with the war. Boy killed himself because he liked little girls—"

"What did you say?"

"He liked little girls, Acland—surely you guessed? If you doubt me, ask Freddie. Freddie saw the photographs Boy took of me when I was a child. I'm afraid they were rather pornographic. What Freddie *doesn't* know—none of you know—is that it wasn't just photographs." Constance paused. "May I use the word *fuck*, now Winnie's left us? Boy liked to fuck little girls. Me, for instance. And there's no point in looking at me like that, Acland—or you, Steenie. Facts are facts. If you think about it, Acland, you'll know I'm right. Don't you remember, that time you caught me coming out of Boy's room?"

"No, I don't remember. I don't believe this. I don't believe I'm hearing it. And I don't know what the hell you're talking about."

"Acland, I can quite see you may prefer to forget, but I remember the incident perfectly. I think I was twelve."

"It never damn well happened."

"None of it happened," Steenie interrupted, his voice rising in pitch. "Don't argue with her, Acland—there's no point. Constance bloody well tells lies. Her father was a nasty cheap little liar, and she's exactly the same—"

"Steenie, do be quiet." Constance gave him a dismissive glance. "Your mascara is running. You're about to burst into tears, as usual—"

"You're a bitch," said Steenie, whose powers of invective were never at their best when he was emotional. "You always were an absolute bitch. Boy's *dead*. He can't defend himself—"

"Steenie, it's really very silly, calling me names, when we both know you'll come running back to me, sweet as pie, three days from now. Also, you look awful. You always do when you lose your temper. You're beginning to look raddled, do you know that? Truly, Steenie, another few years and you'll be a pathetic old queen."

"Oh, really? *I* look raddled?" Steenie, sniffing, drew himself up. "Well, let me tell *you*, darling—I'm not the only one. Maud said you were ill-bred. She said it was beginning to show—and it is. Nasty little lines, all 'round your mouth, darling. By the time I'm a pathetic old queen, you'll look like a harpy. I should ring the plastic surgeon, dear—ring him quickly—"

"Steenie, do go away."

"My dear, I'm going." Steenie, even quivering, managed a certain dignity. "I shan't give you an audience. Not for a performance like this. I haven't seen so much ham in a theater in years. Way over the top, dear—even for you, and that's saying something. Wexton, are you coming?"

"No. You go. I'll stay." Wexton hunched himself in his chair. He fiddled with his knife and fork. "You're right. It is over the top. But it's kind of interesting. I want to see what she's planned for her finale."

"Well, when she gets there," said Steenie, on the move, flounc-
ing, "*do* ask her about the stevedore in New York. I gather that
should be *very* entertaining."

Steenie slammed the door. Wexton looked from Jane, who had
not spoken, to Acland, who had turned his back. He smiled. He
settled himself more comfortably in his chair. He poured himself
another glass of claret.

"You know," he began in an amiable way, "Steenie's wrong. I
don't want to know about the stevedore. I don't think it would be
entertaining. Now, you've gotten rid of all the people you wanted
out of the way—except me."

"Wexton! How unkind!"

"So why not come to the point? Jane's here. Acland's here.
You've fired your tracer bullets. I guess you can see your main target.
Go ahead."

"No, Wexton," Acland interrupted. "I've had enough of this.
This isn't a game. This is my family, my brothers. Steenie's right.
Boy isn't here to defend himself. I won't hear him spoken of in that
way."

"Heavens! What a cold voice! What are you going to do, Acland?
Manhandle me out of the room? I might like that."

"That won't be necessary. This is all just a little one-sided, it
seems to me. Before you go, Constance, why don't you tell us about
yourself? Why not tell us about this afternoon? After all, that's what
provoked all this, wasn't it?"

Constance gave a small sigh. "Do you know," she began slowly,
"I think it was. I realized something this afternoon, and I've just
seen it in action again. An English family, closing ranks. Perhaps all
families do that—perhaps it isn't purely an English quality. It shouldn't
surprise me, I suppose. I am the outsider here. I always was."

"That isn't true." Jane leaned forward, her voice indignant.
"Acland's family took you in. Even today—you asked to be a godmother. Acland agreed. I invited you here."

"Ah, but reluctantly, I think? Constance as a godmother. I know
you couldn't have wanted that."

"You're right. I did not want it."

"Well, well, I won't argue with that." Constance smiled. "A
very sensible attitude. I always did tend to bite the hand that feeds
me. A defect in my nature. Is it charity I resent? No. I don't like to
be patronized, I think."

"Is kindness patronage?"

"Jane, don't argue with her. It's pointless."

"Oh, Acland—don't stop your wife!" Constance glanced back at him with a radiant smile. "I love to listen to Jane's arguments. I find them edifying. Sometimes I think that if I listened to Jane long enough, I might reform. I could become just like her. Calm and good, unfailingly reasonable, invariably right. And then I think—no, I'd rather be dead. I like to . . . walk on the wild side, you see. I always did."

"Walk on the wild side. Jesus." Acland turned away. "That's what you call it? I never heard such crap."

"It's a term, a phrase. I can think of others. It's very odd . . ." Constance rose. She began to walk about the room. "Whenever I come to Winterscombe, I begin to feel . . . oh, very wicked. Like an anarchist. I look around me, at this splendid house and this splendid family—and sooner or later, I itch to blow it up. One bomb! A great conflagration! This whole edifice, hurtling up into the air. It's very strange. Five minutes in this house and I turn into the most ardent revolutionary."

"You're destructive, in other words," Acland replied shortly. "I suppose you always were."

"Is that destructive?" Constance seemed to consider the question seriously. "Perhaps it is. It doesn't feel like that—I see it as cleansing, all those flames licking up through the roof. No more good intentions. No more pretenses. No more secrets. You see, it always seems to me that Winterscombe is a very *flimsy* construct. So many cracks in the walls—and everyone busily papering them over. Now, when *I* see a crack, I always want to prise it open. I want to make it gape, wider and wider—and then I want to step through, into all the rubble and chaos. Where it's dangerous."

"Why?" Jane frowned. "Why do that?"

Constance gave a little shrug. "Just to see what's left, I think. To see if there's anything still standing. After all, who knows what I might find there?" She smiled. "I might find all the things people say are good. I might find love. Or truth. On the other hand, I might find nothing at all. Not one single thing. Don't you think that's brave of me? I do. None of you would risk following me. Well, Wexton might. But not you, Acland, or your wife. You'd rather stay here, where it's safe."

"Safe?" This word seemed to distress Jane. Color mounted in her cheeks. "That isn't true, Constance. If you'd seen the war at firsthand, you wouldn't say that. This house—this family—it isn't just a refuge. It's something I believe in, and Acland believes in. It's fragile, and vulnerable—we both know that. We have to struggle, every day, to make it work—"

"Your marriage, too—do you have to work at that?"

"Jane, don't argue with her. Can't you see that's what she wants?"

"I will." Jane's face had become fierce. "I won't sit here and let her dismiss everything I care about. She makes it sound so plausible, so attractive—and she's *wrong*. You're selfish, Constance. You tell lies, and you don't care who's hurt by them—"

"Lies? Have I told lies tonight? About Steenie? About Boy? Everything I said was true. Heavens!" Constance gave a small grimace of irritation. "It seems to me I've been very merciful. I never mentioned Freddie—and I could tell you some very amusing things about Freddie. As for Acland—"

"Leave Acland out of this—"

"Why should I? Acland is a perfect example of what I mean. I have a long memory. I remember how Acland used to be, before you set about taming him. And now look at him. The perfect husband. The perfect father—"

"Is that something to be ashamed of?"

"Not exactly." Constance paused. She picked up, and considered, her table knife. "He plays the role very well. I'm almost convinced. But not quite. Certain elements don't add up. After all, here we all are, gathered together for a christening. All this rejoicing for the birth of a little girl. A first child, at last. Except—she isn't a first child. Acland had a son once. By Jenna—whom he used to love. A little boy called Edgar, with eyes exactly like his father's."

"Stop this." Acland swung around. "Dear God, will you stop this—"

"No, Acland." Jane rose. She laid her hand on his arm. "Let her finish."

"Thank you, Jane. I was about to say, Edgar is dead. He's been conveniently dead for a long time—so I suppose it is easier to pretend he never existed, to continue to lie about him. After all, so long as we all go on assuming he was Jack Hennessy's child, we're safe—aren't we? We paper over that particular crack. But is that right—all that deception? Here we all are, downstairs—and who is upstairs minding the new baby? Jenna. And Jane is, apparently, devoted to Jenna. I find that astonishing. Is it the result of ignorance? I ask myself. Or is it true generosity of spirit? Is Jane stupid, or magnificent? Did you know, Jane? And if you knew, how did you manage? Are you never jealous?"

There was a silence. Acland turned away. He pressed his hand across his eyes. Jane and Constance continued to face each other.

Wexton—the bystander in all this, as he was later to say to me—continued to watch.

Jane did not reply for some while. She frowned a little, as if uncertain what to say. She clasped her hands together. The firelight flickered against her hair; her eyes rested on Constance's face.

"Constance," she said at last, "I *know* all this. You are not the only person to think of Edgar. I think of him too. I speak of him—to Acland and to Jenna. I thought of him this morning, in the church—and I am sure they did also. He is not forgotten, Constance." She hesitated. Faint color came to her cheeks.

"Acland and I have been married twelve years, Constance. Rather too long for secrets. Jenna once lost a child. I have lost two. We understand each other. Whatever happened in the past, it doesn't cause division. Can you understand that? It brings us closer together. Acland and I, and Jenna—we deal with this in our way."

There was a silence. Constance made an odd, faltering gesture. "Twelve years?" Her expression became confused. "Is it twelve years?"

"Constance, why do you do this?" Jane's voice was quiet. Moving forward, she laid her hand on Constance's arm. "To speak of a child in that way, to use a dead child as a weapon—why would you do such a thing, today of all days? Why ask to be a godmother, and then do this? I don't understand. Why go to such lengths to cause pain to others?"

"Leave me alone."

"Steenie's your friend—and you've hurt him." Jane paused. "Winnie may have misunderstood some aspects of Wexton's poem, but she understood the heart of it. Wouldn't it have been kinder to leave her with her illusions? Boy, Freddie, Acland—I know you care for them, Constance, so why behave as if you hate them?"

"I love them. They're my brothers."

"Then why hurt them, Constance? All it does is isolate you. Can't you see that you hurt yourself, far more than you could ever hurt us?"

The word *us* stung. It was gently said, but Constance flinched. She jerked her face away as if she had been slapped.

"Don't you pity me—don't you dare to pity me." She backed away until she was pressed up against the table. "You're stupid, you know that? The ex-nurse! I wouldn't come to you to bandage my finger. You know why Acland married you? For your money. Because *I* told him to."

Jane paused, then gave a small shrug of exasperation. "Very

well. And I have the opportunity to thank you at last. There isn't very much money left. Even so, you gave my husband good advice. For which we're both grateful."

As she said this, Jane glanced toward her husband. Perhaps it was the quality of that glance, affectionate and wry; perhaps the fact that Acland then moved to his wife; perhaps the fact that Wexton, the bystander, smiled. Whatever the reason, Constance's control snapped.

As always, her rage was sudden, and physical. Her hand smashed down on the table. She swung it in an arc. Knives, forks, plates, crashed to the floor. Wexton ducked, then rose to his feet. Constance began to hurl glasses. Crystal showered; wine dripped. Debris filled the air. There was a small violent whirlwind of energy in the room, a smashing, crashing concatenation. Then, eerily, silence.

"Shall I, Acland?" Constance said.

She stood in the midst of quick disorder, wrist outstretched. The stem of a wineglass, with one pointed shard still attached, was poised in her right hand.

The flurry of movement stopped; the group resolved itself. Wexton to one side of her, some few yards away; Jane and Acland to the other; the table behind her. Constance stood at bay, her face white, her eyes fixed and glittering, her black hair springing away from her small, set face.

"You think I won't? Don't come any nearer. You think people don't do that—they don't cut themselves up in other people's dining rooms? I will. Acland knows I will. I break all the rules—"

"Constance—"

"Get back. All of you. Come any nearer, and I'll do it."

Jane gave a gesture of alarm. Acland took a step forward, then stopped. Constance's face lit with triumph.

"Shall I, Acland? Which—wrist or throat? This glass is very sharp. Cut the right vein the right way, and it's very quick. One great fountain of blood. You can all watch."

"All right." Acland folded his arms. His voice became grim. "We'll watch. Go right ahead. Only make sure it's an artery and not a vein, if you want it to be quick."

"Acland, don't. She's ill." Jane took a step forward. "Constance. Put the glass down."

"Come any closer and I'll smash it in your stupid sanctimonious face—"

"Leave her alone. Stay where you are." Acland moved between Constance and his wife. Constance's eyes fixed themselves upon his face. She gave a small shiver. Her black eyes took on a dead look.

"Shall I, Acland? Shall I jump? Is it a very long way down?"

"Far enough." He hesitated. "It always was."

"You did understand—this afternoon?"

"Yes. I understood."

"How I hate this house! All the corners talk."

"Give me the glass, Constance."

"The dead walk up and down in this house. I can smell them."

"Give me the glass."

"Where's my father? Are you my father?"

"No, Constance."

"Isn't he here?" Her face dissolved in grief. "I thought he was here. I heard his voice."

"Constance. He isn't here. Now put the glass in my hand, quietly."

"Oh, very well." Constance sighed. The tension left her body. Her hand fell. "Maybe you're right. Live a little longer, then a little longer, inch by inch, day by day, step by step, night by night. Here you are, Acland. May I be alone? I want to be alone. I'll go to bed now. It's all right. Don't worry. I'll leave in the morning. What a horrid mess. I'm so sorry."

When she had left the room, there was a silence. Jane bent to pick up a plate, then left it. Wexton wandered up and down the room, then sat down in a chair. He said, "Jesus."

"I know." Acland turned away grimly. He looked at the smashed glass, the uneaten meal, the chaos of the table.

"I need a whisky," Wexton said.

"Good idea. Pour me one, would you?"

"Does she often go that far?"

"She's always liked to make scenes. This was one of the better ones. She controls it, up to a point. Then it goes wildly wrong—way out of control. As you just saw. Today, there were reasons."

"I guessed that."

"Acland." Jane had been staring into the fire. She turned. "Acland, you can't make her leave. She'll have to stay. She's ill. She needs help."

"No. She's leaving. And she's not coming back."

"You can't do that. We can't do that. There's something seriously wrong."

"I know that. And it's not my responsibility. I won't have her in this house. Not again. Not after tonight. You saw what happened, for God's sake—"

"You can't blame her, Acland. I see that now. She isn't responsible for her own actions."

"Then it's time she was. I'm not arguing about this. I don't want her anywhere near you, or Victoria."

"Acland, she's *ill*."

"I know her illnesses. She recovers from them very conveniently. You'll see—tomorrow morning she'll behave as if nothing happened. And expect everyone else to do the same. I told you: She's leaving, and she's not coming back. That's it. The whole goddam thing. It's over."

"You'll let her go back to New York—on her own? A long journey like that? Acland, you *can't*. It isn't safe."

"I can't? Just watch me."

"Her behavior tonight—all those things she said. The way she looked with that glass in her hand . . ." Jane hesitated. "Acland. She isn't altogether sane."

"She's not altogether mad, either, if that's what you mean. She might like you to think she was—but she isn't. I'm right, aren't I, Wexton?"

Wexton had been sitting, during this conversation, at one end of the table, his chin sunk in his hands, his whisky in front of him. Now he roused himself. He hunched himself up into his favorite position, that of a human question mark.

"Is Constance mad? That's the question? Well, I'd say—a bit like the play. You know: 'mad north-north-west; when the wind is southerly. . . .' "

He gave Jane one of his anxious, melancholy looks. "Acland's right, you know, Jane. She should leave. She wants to leave, anyway. No. Correction. She wants to be *made* to leave."

"Why should she want that?"

"Punishment, I guess." Wexton shrugged. "If other people won't oblige, she punishes herself. No, Acland—don't say anything. Whatever she told you, I don't want to know. This whole evening— that's what it was all about: Constance, making sure she got exiled. Okay, so she finally pulled it off. Let her go, Jane. She does have a husband."

Later that night, when Acland had explained to her the events of the afternoon, Jane did try cabling that husband. She sent a second cable the next day. Morning, and Constance was leaving.

Jane, in her bedroom above, could hear the muted sounds of her departure. She moved to the bay window.

Only Steenie was there to bid Constance goodbye. He seemed to have forgiven her, as Constance had predicted. He embraced her tightly, standing on the portico steps. He was not wearing a coat, although the morning was cold and the lawns white with frost. His scarf fluttered in the wind; Constance's little white hands linked behind his neck. She kissed him once, twice, three times.

When she released him, she turned and looked about her. A tiny, erect figure in a scarlet coat, the only vivid point of color in a bleached and monochrome landscape. Jane saw her face turn back toward the house, then jerk in the direction of the lake and the woods. She was wearing no hat; the wind lifted her black hair away from her face. She pulled on first one glove, then the other.

Constance's final farewell to Winterscombe. For once, it seemed, she had nothing to say. Having looked around her, she climbed into the back of the waiting car. The door was closed. It pulled away. Jane watched it, a large, black, somewhat funereal Daimler, as it disappeared down the drive and out of sight. She turned back to her husband, who had not wished to witness this departure. Acland sat by the fire, gazing into the coals. Across the room, his child slept.

"She's gone, Acland," Jane said gently.

"Has she? I hope so. I wish I felt sure of it."

Jane knelt and took his hand in hers. "She couldn't have done it, Acland," she said quietly. "You must know that. She may imagine she did—but kill her own father? It's not possible. It's unthinkable. She was a ten-year-old child."

"I know. I don't believe it either. But she does. I suppose that's what's wrong with her."

"Do you think Stern knows?"

"He knows most things. I don't think it would be easy to keep a secret from him. But in this case—no, I think not. If you'd seen her in the Stone House, you'd understand. First—she seemed so convinced it was me. Then she kept talking—you know how she talks. She talks the way people dream. She cried out—I remember that. She said something about listening to a voice. I can't remember exactly. Then she said she'd show me, and she ran out. It was as if the idea came to her then, for the first time. She looked . . . I can't describe how she looked—"

"She frightens me, Acland."

"I know. She frightens me too. You see now, why I won't have her here? It was my fault. My mistake. Nothing and no one is safe from her. She talks about my own brother, about Boy—and I feel I never knew him. She distorts everything, but she does it in such a way that I can't see anymore. I begin to think maybe she's right, maybe it was the way she says it was—I can't explain. All I know is, she hurts people. And I don't want her to hurt you. Or Victoria."

"Acland." Jane knelt back. She looked at him. "We must make sure Stern understands. Not everything, perhaps. But he should know she's ill. If nothing else, he must understand that."

"You see, she could have been different." With a sudden, restless gesture, Acland rose. He began to pace about the room. "She could. I still believe that. When she was younger. Even now—some of the things she says. She can be . . . extraordinary."

Jane looked down at the floor. She said:

"She's very beautiful."

"Yes. But I don't mean that. She *isn't* beautiful—not in any classical sense, not if you analyze her, feature by feature. But you can't analyze her. Not once you look at her. She's so very alive. She has so much energy—"

"Do you love her, Acland?"

Acland stopped pacing and turned around. He stared at his wife.

"Love her? No. I don't."

"But you did . . . once?" Jane raised her eyes to his face. "Tell me, Acland. I'd rather know."

"I can't answer that. I don't even *know* the answer. There was a time—before the war, at the beginning of the war. She—bewitched me a little, I think."

"Bewitched you?" Jane looked away. "Oh, Acland, that's not your kind of word. It's all right. I understand. She's very lovely and very strange. Any man might fall in love with her."

"And I gather a number do," Acland replied drily. He crossed and put his arm around his wife. "It didn't last—that's the point. I found you."

"Ah, the wife."

"Don't say it like that. I won't let you."

"Oh, but I will—and all women would." Jane gave a wry smile. She rose to her feet. "Even the most virtuous wives, you know, feel a little envy for the mistresses—for the mistress type."

A glint of amusement came into Acland's eyes. He said, "They do?"

"But of course. I'd make a very bad mistress, for instance—I know that. I'm aware of my own limitations. But I'm not nearly as strait-laced as Constance seems to think. I've considered, from time to time, how it would be—to be the other kind of woman. To be an object of desire. Beautiful. Careless. Capricious."

"Expendable."

"Perhaps. I'm not so sure about that. The perfect mistress—"

"Is there such a thing?"

"The perfect mistress is . . . unattainable. Like the perfect lover. She can be . . . achieved, but never possessed."

"And you think men imagine such a woman—want such a woman? You think I do that?"

Jane smiled. "I'm a wife. I told you. And sensible wives are discreet. I shall never ask you, Acland—and no, don't tell me either way, because I shan't listen."

"All I was going to say"—he kissed her—"is that you have a rather feminine view of the male imagination. Most men, I think, are rather more basic. Either they are like me—exemplary, devoted—or they want diversion. And the point about the diversions is that they're easily and immediately available. Easily disposed of, too. Darling—"

"Acland, I'm being serious."

"I know you are. It's delightful. It's also very funny."

"You think I'm wrong? Then how do you explain Constance's success?"

"With men?" Acland frowned. "Ah, I see the trap. She's certainly had her fair share of worshippers. Also victims. Perhaps you're right. Steenie calls her the *femme fatale* of Fifth. She seems to like that. I'm not sure I believe in *femmes fatales*, though—"

"I do." Jane turned away. "Especially when the woman concerned is also a *femme enfant.*"

"What did you say?"

"She has no children." Jane's face was pressed to the window. She did not look around. "She has never grown up. She is a woman *and* a child. I think there are men who like women like that." She paused. "Sometimes, I think *all* men like women like that."

Her voice sounded suddenly tired. Acland hesitated, but he did not answer her.

He thought of the Stone House, the previous day. The sharp scent of Constance's hair came back to him. He saw the curve of her white throat, the redness of her parted lips, the pleading and childish anxiety in her eyes. He put his arms around a child; his fingers brushed against a woman's breast. He thought: *I could have stayed when she asked me to. What would have happened if I had?*

Abruptly he turned away and crossed the room.

"I'll write to Stern," he said. "If he doesn't reply to the cables by tonight, I'll cable his office tomorrow."

Acland sent his letter, to which he received no reply. The cables, both those to Stern's house and to his offices, remained unanswered. Neither Jane nor Acland were to see or hear from him again.

"You can't do this," Constance said. "*Why* are you doing this?"

"If you would just sign there, Constance, and initial the first page. My secretaries can witness the signature later."

"I won't sign. You don't want me to sign. I love you. I came back to tell you I loved you. I took the very first boat. I ran into the apartment. It was cruel to do that. To take all your things. I looked for your clothes. All the hangers were empty. They clattered about—"

"At the bottom of the second page, Constance. I've kept the details brief."

"I will *not*!" Constance pressed her small hands flat on her husband's desk. "You don't understand. You won't listen when I explain. Acland is nothing to me! You know what I discovered? He is just as you said. A boring Englishman, with tweeds and a wife and a cradle in the bedroom. There *was* no other Acland, except in my mind. I invented him. I know I've been stupid. Oh, I ran away so fast! Montague—why is your office so big? I hate this office. You look so far away, and so cold, sitting there across your desk. I'm not a *client;* I'm your wife. You love me—I know you do. And you try to hide it, just as I did. All those foolish games, Montague—can't you see? They're over now. Oh, we shall be so happy. Please—look—if I lean across the desk, won't you kiss me?"

"Just *sign*, Constance, if you would be so good. I have another appointment."

"Go to hell, then. I won't sign. Stupid papers. Lawyers' language. I hate lawyers."

"Constance, if you don't sign the separation agreement, I shall divorce you. It's as simple as that."

"Divorce? You wouldn't do that."

"Yes, I would. And in view of the number of correspondents I could cite, the terms would be a great deal less favorable to you financially than these are. So I suggest you sign."

"You're punishing me—that's all this is. You're punishing me for going to England—"

"Constance, don't be childish. We once made an agreement. You did not keep to its terms. It is now null and void."

"You think I believe that? It's nonsense. You're tired of me, that's all. You want to run off to that little Ursula of yours, with her lovely singing voice. You think I don't know?"

"Constance, I told you. Pyrotechnics can become tedious. I find the lies tedious and your lovers tedious. The way you change your mind becomes tedious. This marriage becomes tedious. Please sign."

"Acland didn't kill my father, you know. He wanted to, but he didn't. *That* was why I went to England. To ask him that. No other reason. You see—you had no need to be jealous."

"That may have been one of the reasons you went to England. I doubt it was the only one. And what you tell me now is something I already knew."

Constance's head jerked up. Her eyes widened.

"What? You knew Acland was not involved? But you said—"

"You misinterpreted what I said. Would you sign, please, Constance?"

"You knew? How did you know?"

Constance rose to her feet. She stared at her husband. Stern, who had remained seated, looked at her calmly.

"I told you, Constance. I was there that night. I was a houseguest, if you remember."

"You were with Maud. After the party you were with Maud. You told me."

"I was with Maud for a while. I did not remain with her. Later—not a great deal later—I was playing billiards. The one diversion gave me a taste for the other, perhaps. I used to be like that."

"I don't believe you."

"You may believe it or not, as you wish. It is true. I played billiards from around one-thirty to past three in the morning. As did a number of other men. They included Acland, and Freddie—who was drunk. They included Boy. So, obviously, I found it odd when you told me that Boy spent the night upstairs in his room, talking to you. Presumably, you mistook the night."

"You knew." Constance's eyes filled with tears. "All these years, you knew."

"My dear." Stern's manner became more gentle. "I tried to tell you. In the end—perhaps I thought it was better to let it rest. All I can tell you is that it made no difference then, and it makes none now. It is not something which I would ever discuss."

"Montague, please." Constance leaned forward. "You must see. I need you. If you're not there—I'll die. I can't live with myself. Not alone. It makes me so afraid to be alone. Please."

"Constance, you won't die. You are one of nature's survivors. You have a great deal of natural resilience. Now, please dry your eyes. If you would just sign, then the matter will be settled. There need be no more painful scenes. You see—if you look at the first page—the house will be sold, but you will be well provided for. I have added one clause. Maud's paintings should be returned to her, I think. They were a gift—no doubt one of my vulgar gifts, but still—"

"Montague, I beg you. Don't do this. You'll suffer, too—I know you will. You're not as hard as you pretend—"

"And you'll see, on the second page—the capital sum is a large one. You will be able to buy an apartment, of course. I thought you might consider starting a business of your own. Instead of advising your friends on their houses for nothing, why not charge them? You have a great deal of energy, Constance. Instead of wasting it all on love affairs, why not put it to practical use? You might find you liked to work. Work has its consolations."

"Kiss me." Constance crossed to him. "I defy you to kiss me and then make me sign. You can't. You'd have to admit then—this is a lie, all of this, the paper, the way you speak, everything. I am your wife. You—almost—love me."

Stern had risen as Constance spoke. She stepped forward and linked her arms about his waist. She tilted her face up to his. Stern looked down at her gravely.

"Oh, Montague. You see me. You always did. Please tell me what you see."

"You look very lovely, Constance," Stern said. "To me, you always did. I thought once . . . I wish . . ."

He bent his head and kissed her. He kissed first her lips, then her closed eyes. He wiped the tears from her cheeks and then kissed her once more. Constance, with a cry, bent her head against his chest. Stern stroked her hair, then the nape of her neck. He let his hand rest against her delicate throat until he had recovered his composure; then, after some minutes, he drew back.

Constance lifted her face to look at him. She made a small sound, perhaps of distress. In an impulsive way she pressed her hand against his cheek and then drew back.

"Ah, I see. I see what I've done. I can read it in your face. How I hate myself. Such regret."

She reached across the desk and picked up the separation document.

"Self-preservation, Montague?"

Stern glanced away. "Something like that."

"It's all right. I understand. I'll sign then. I'll sign because I . . . care for you. I care very much. There! You see?" Picking up the pen, Constance signed her name. She gave her husband a sideways glance. "How noble I am! It is a far far better thing I do now than I have ever done." She smiled. "Initial here? There. It is done." She slid the paper away from her, recapped the pen.

"We are alike?" she said, head bent.

"Oh, very alike."

"Montague . . ."

"Yes, my dear?"

"If we are not to see each other again, as you said—if I promise you to leave this room the minute you reply, may I ask you a question?"

"You'll keep this promise?"

"Absolutely. I can, you know."

"Very well. Ask."

"Must I ask? You know what the question is."

"Do I?"

"Yes. There was only ever one."

"I suppose there was." Stern hesitated.

"Is it so hard? I said it to you."

"The habits of a lifetime . . ." He shrugged.

"Oh, Montague, break them. Just for once."

"Very well. I love you, Constance. I have always loved you, very much."

There was a silence. Constance looked down at the floor.

"Despite what I am? What you know me to be? Even so?"

"Even so." Stern paused. "As I'm sure you know—rational considerations have nothing to do with it."

"Oh, I wish I were different." Constance gave a small, helpless gesture. "I wish I could unmake myself and begin again. I wish I could erase the past. Not all of it. There were times . . . Ah, well, I gave you my promise. It's very hard to keep it, now—but I will. Look the other way, Montague. Face the window. You see—such a gray day. Do you see the rain falling?"

Stern looked toward the window. Clouds moved in a slow sky. He heard no footfall, no sound of a door, but when he looked back, Constance had gone.

She had gone back, I think, to the past, to those black notebooks of hers, and to her final entry. It is undated, but I think it was written later that day, very shortly afterward. Constance's last attempt to square the past.

I read it very late at night, alone by a still-silent telephone, the fire burning low and the room growing cold around me.

The handwriting was jagged, uneven with emotion. Constance's confession must have been written at speed. As I read I pitied her.

Look, look, look, it begins, the words jabbed down with such force that some have ripped the paper. *Look, look, look. Listen, Montague. Constance will tell you how it happened.*

How it happened.

It was the rabbit that made Constance decide. If the rabbit hadn't died like that, she would never have done it. But the snare was wound so tight. It was cutting into the fur and into the flesh, so it made the rabbit bleed while it choked him. That was a wicked thing to do: wicked, wicked, wicked.

She never saw her mother die, but when the rabbit died, it twitched. Its eyes went dull. It hurts to die, Constance thought—yes, it hurts, I know how it feels—and she picked up a big stick and she whirled all round the clearing.

When she saw the trap, she thought—there it is; it's waiting. She could see that it was hungry. Give me something to eat, said the trap, and it had a metal voice, like rust mixed with syrup. Such a big mouth. It gaped; it wanted filling.

Constance was bad then. She buried the rabbit first, and she loved the rabbit, but she was bad all the time she buried him, because she knew she wanted to look, and peep, and spy, and the trap said, do it.

So, when the rabbit was safe, she ran back to the house, so fast, so fast. No one saw. It made her pant, all that running. She wasn't allowed in that part of the house, but she went anyway. Up the stairs, open the door, into the dressing room. It was red in there—the curtains were red, and the curtains were closed. She could hear them in there, the other side of the curtains. She could hear what they were doing.

Not the first time she'd heard it. She heard it in London, with the nurse, while she lay next door in her bed. Groans and gruntings and pantings. She knew it was a secret. She knew it was dirty. Should she look? She'd never looked before—kissing, yes; she'd spied on the kissing, but then she'd run away. This time, she thought, I shall take a look, just a little look, round the corner of that dark red curtain.

Her father did it to Gwen. Gwen was all trussed up, like a lovely white bird. And Papa did it to her, all those special things he did to Constance, the things that made him say he loved her.

Just the same. There was his bone in his hand, and he touched it. He rubbed his hands on it, so it got bigger and bigger, so it stood up, jutted out, Papa's big stick, her stick, the one he used to love her and to chastise her.

Constance thought—maybe he won't put it in. Maybe he only did that with me, because I am special, special. But he did put it in. He turned his back, then he put it in. Gwen screamed, but that didn't stop him. In and out. In and out. Jab, jab, jab. Just the same. No difference at all. Constance's mind went scratch, scratch, scratch. The curtains started screaming.

Such a wicked thing to do. Constance felt dead—deader than the rabbit. She couldn't move her feet, or her hands or her tongue or her eyes. She watched Gwen cry. She felt sorry for Gwen. It never stopped him, crying. Then Papa told Gwen he loved her. He used the very same voice he used to Constance, and the very same words. He wanted to do it again with Gwen. That very night. In the woods. After the comet.

Constance ran away then. She hid in a closet. It was dark in there, and no one could find her, not even Steenie. Then she went down to tea, and when he saw her, Papa said that horrible thing, the thing he'd promised her and promised her he wouldn't say, ever again, not in front of other people. He said she was an albatross, a great dead lump round his neck, weighing him down, choking him, the way the snare choked the rabbit.

When he said that, Constance thought: I will kill him. Lots of time to plan—all a spring evening. All his fault, said the wardrobe and the bed. The door said, he had it coming.

How Constance crept about. Easy, easy, easy. Up and down, in and out, all the secret places in the secret house. She was very cunning. She fetched Gwen. She told Gwen that Steenie was ill. She knew Gwen wouldn't leave the house, not then. She'd stay, the way she did before, when Steenie was ill, because she loved him.

There is a little place just outside the conservatory door. A big bush, with a hollow place inside it. Constance hid there. She waited, very, very patiently. She wasn't cold; she had thought of everything. She had a coat and a scarf and a pair of boots. She crouched down. It was exciting, waiting.

He came out at twelve. Smoking a cigar. She could see the red end glowing. Acland saw him leave too. She could see Acland, but he couldn't see her. There he was, on the terrace, in the shadows, watching. Acland knew. She knew. No one else did.

She watched Acland for a bit. She counted to fifty. Then she followed her father. Through the bushes, down to the wood. The same path. Sneaking through the trees. The red cigar glowing. The comet had gone. It was dark in the wood. It was exciting, and frightening.

He sat down in the clearing. He leaned up against a tree. His foot was very near the rabbit grave. Constance crept up on him. He looked at his watch. Then he looked at the sky. Then he shut his eyes. Constance waited. Then she understood. He was sleeping.

She crept up very close then, so close she could have touched him. She thought he might wake up, because the branches snapped, and the trap talked, but he didn't seem to hear them. Constance watched him breathe. His chest lifted, then fell. His mouth was open. When she leaned over, his breath puffed in her face, sweet port smell, like wine and honey.

Constance thought—I don't have to do it. I don't. She thought—I could say I loved him. She was afraid to do that. His eyes might hate her. He might hit her. He might bring out the bone and make her stroke it. She hated the bone, and she loved the bone. It made her head ache, all that love and hate mixed up. Constance thought: fire and brimstone.

Such a long time to wait. She crept away again. She hid in the bushes, just the other side of the trap. The bushes were damp. The leaves washed her clean, so her soul shone through her skin. The trap talked. Louder and louder, on and on in that metal jammy voice: hungry, hungry, hungry. One big mouth, and her father liked mouths. Swallow me up, he said to Constance once, swallow me up.

He woke up finally. He looked at his watch. He muttered a bit. Constance thought: Papa is drunk. She could see now, when he walked, he wasn't very steady. Weaving about. Weaving about. He peed against the tree. He peed on the tree, and the grass, and the rabbit's grave. That was a mistake. The trap didn't like it.

Suppose she told him—about the rabbit? Constance knew what he would say, Flip, flip, flip—one of his jokes. His jokes were like razor blades. Stupid Constance, that's what he'd say. You should have brought it home—made a pie of it. Stupid Constance. Ugly Constance. Papa said she smelled nasty. He said she tasted sour. He said she was small, her fault she was bleeding. Stupid little bitch, he said, your hands are clumsy.

I'll show him how stupid I am, Constance said to herself, and she called to him.

Eddie, she called. Eddie, I'm over here. This way. The voice was as right as right. He liked that voice, much more than he ever liked hers, and he went to it. Slipping about in the bracken. He swore. My, but he was clumsy. She called one more time. Only one more time. Then the trap got him.

Swallow, swallow, swallow, Constance said. She danced about, the way she does when she is angry. Swallow, swallow, swallow, black, black, black. The trap snapped. Its teeth ground. All that bone and all that blood. The trap smacked its lips. It gurgled. It said he was juicy.

She ran away then. Fast, then faster still. All she could hear was the wind in her ears. Just the wind. No screaming.

No screaming then. The screams waited. They came at night. When her eyes closed, out they came. How Constance ached with those screams, but the albatross said: No, they are lovely things. They lift me up. Watch, Constance. He smothered all the pain with his soft white feathers, and then he soared on the pain, up and up, higher and higher, far beyond the reach of men, which was wise, for the albatross had so many enemies. On and on he flew, to the ends of the earth and back again; then one night, when he returned, he said to Constance: Be at peace. It wasn't you; it was Acland.

Look in his eyes, the albatross said. He knew you wanted it. And Constance did look. She saw it at once, all that clean black hate, as deep as the very deepest water, the very mirror of her own. She loved him at once. Acland loved her in return, instantly. You are my twin, Constance used to say to him. If you look very deep in my eyes, Acland, you can drown in them.

They went inside the glass then, and in its circle they were close. One day they would be closer still. Constance tried to tell him. She said: Look, we will lie down at the end of the world, Acland. Our mouths will match. There will be such symmetry. Don't you see, both of us, Acland and Constance, bloody from head to foot, the most perfect jointure of all—a man and a woman, you and I, lovers and murderers.

Acland said no; he said that place was a black place, he wouldn't go there. So Constance went on her own. She was afraid at first, going down into that black black place. She took a step, then another step. She went deeper and deeper. She became quite brave. She dug with her hands, faster and faster, all day yesterday, all day today. She thought— she believed—Constance believed—that if you went right down inside the sin, if you burrowed down as far as you could go, you came through. You reached the place on the far side of sin, and once you were there, the light washed you.

It said: You are here, Constance. Lay down your burdens. Look at the loveliness of the world. You see? The leaves are inevitable. The grass springs up. Night is followed by day. The planets keep to their appointed course. A man dies and a child is born. This is the world—can you see the providence in its patterns? That was what the light said, on the other side of the dark.

Don't write any more, it said. It anointed my head. It said: All alone.

You can rest now, Constance.

It was late when I finished reading this strange entry. The fire had burned down. The room was quiet. I closed the black cover and put the last of the notebooks away.

I thought that Constance could not have written this unless she had been mad. I thought that Constance could not have written this unless she had been sane. Her opposites touched me, love and hate, sanity and insanity, death and birth—I suppose even those childhood terms, words I had not heard pronounced for many years: sin and redemption. It was as if Constance took my hands, right and left, and placed them on two terminals; a current flowed through me.

It must have been, I think, about three or even four o'clock in the morning; the dawn was still hours away. I went to the windows, pulled back the curtains, and looked out.

There was a full moon and a hard frost. Winterscombe was monochrome. I could see the gunmetal lake and the copper cockerel on the stable roof; I could see the band of black that was the woods, and there, on a rise to one side of the gardens, beyond the hothouses and the orchards, the spire of the church where I was baptized— where Constance, too, was baptized, on the same day. I think she believed that, as I did.

I did not want to sleep, though I think I did, in the end, fall into some kind of sleep, wakeful, uncomfortable, propped up in a chair, half dreaming, half alert.

At six, when it grew light outside, I rose. I walked around the room and then, quietly, the sleeping house. I think I was saying my last goodbye to Winterscombe, to all the people I now saw there. It felt a next and necessary step. As I went from room to room I thought I knew why Constance had given me those journals. I thought that if they were full of death, they were also full of life, and love; Constance had tried to be evenhanded. I thought: *How odd; they have freed me.*

I went from place to place; it was like a pilgrimage. I stood in the conservatory, where Boy proposed, where the frames were now rotten and the glass falling in. I went up the stairs, to the nurseries, to the King's bedroom, to my parents' room with its bay window. I went back down to the ballroom, where Constance had selected her husband, and I had waltzed with Franz-Jacob. Just rooms, quiet, many of them empty—and yet, not just rooms. As I left each one, I closed the door behind me.

When I returned to the drawing room I stood at its far end, in the alcove where my mother's piano had been. That piano, on which she had played on the night of the comet party, was long gone, but I remembered its position exactly.

I stood where my mother would have sat that night, facing an invisible keyboard and the room beyond. I waited. I watched, as people on a film set watch while cameras are repositioned: time for the reverse shot. If I could see these past events with Constance's eyes, I could also see them with my mother's.

I was her child, too—I could see that now. Her identity rested upon me; it fused with that of my father. I resembled them, not just in the physical sense—that did not matter—but in the heart and in the mind. I stood very still; I could hear the music from that piano quite distinctly. Note after note; its resonance filled the house.

I felt a great and most powerful sense of love—love past and love present. Its force was in the air all around me. My parents' love for each other; Constance's love for Stern and his for her: love enduring, and love wayward. Opening the doors, I walked out into the morning.

So many places to visit one last time: I went to the gazebo, where my father once read a Scott novel upside down. I went to the birch grove, where Boy died; to the Stone House; to the church; to the stables.

I looked up at the loft window from which Jenna and my father watched a comet's light decline. I looked up at the nursery window, where a small child planned her father's murder while she spied. Constance and Edward Shawcross, fighting it out to the death. Constance might have killed her father, I thought, but he had killed her first. Both of them, parent and child, were murder victims.

Last of all, I turned back to the lake. I walked along the shore, by the reed beds. I watched the gray shape of a heron rise from the water. I thought: *I can do it now. I shall walk through the woods to the clearing.*

I took the path Shawcross must have taken that night, the path

Constance must have taken when she followed him. In summer it would have been impassable; even in autumn the track was faint. I walked on through the early morning. The woods were filled with the industry of animals. The woods were light, sun filtering through the tracery of the branches. I saw a hare break from a thicket. I could breathe in hope; I trod upon optimism.

Even in the clearing; even there. I found it in the end. Light slanted; the grass was cropped short by rabbits; the only sound was birdsong. If there had ever been, here, the shadow of past events, it was long gone; the place had been purified by the passing of the seasons. The air smelled of the morning, of damp leaves, of woodsmoke. Beneath the oak tree the ground was thick with fallen leaves. I bent, brushing them to one side, making a space here, a space there, but too much time had passed, of course. The little grave Constance once made was not visible.

There were no snares here now, no keepers, no game to protect. The woods might have been colonized once, but they had been reclaimed, long reclaimed, by nature. I bent a leaf between my fingers. I held it up to the light and traced its veins with my fingers. I straightened. I heard . . . well, let's say I heard my name being called, although the woods were silent.

I began to walk back. I walked slowly, sure there was no need to hurry. *Ein Zauber Ort.* I thought: *I shall walk down to the lake and along the shore and across the lawns, and when I reach the lawns I shall hear the telephone ringing. I shall begin to run then, although there is no need—it will continue to ring for as long as need be. I will run, though, up the slope to the house, across the terrace.* I looked at my watch. I calculated that particular distance. I thought: *I shall hear his voice, in twenty minutes.*

In this I was wrong. As I left the woods and came out into the open, as I looked out across the lake and the gardens, I saw Frank on the far side of the water. His face, too far away for me to make out his features, was turned in my direction. His hands were thrust deep into the pockets of his coat. He waited.

I can tell you what the distance was between us then: It was no distance, and a quarter of a mile. I can tell you the length of time it took us both, between us, to traverse it: five minutes, maybe six. When I reached his side it was seven-thirty on an autumn morning.

I touched his hand, and then his face. He was calmer—somewhat calmer—than I was. It was eight—I think it was eight—when we turned back to the house together.

"Why is it," Frank said, "that when you write me letters, I seem never to receive them? What did this note of yours say?"

"If you walk out on receptions in your honor, and go out the back way and climb in your car and drive miles in the dark and then walk about in the gardens here half the night . . . Did you really do that?"

"Yes. I was thinking."

"Then you don't receive my messages."

"Or I do. But indirectly. What did it say?"

"Nothing important. Nothing that matters now. Nothing that could ever matter again."

"You're sure?"

"Quite sure. It was very brief. A question of moves. A chess problem."

Frank stopped. He said, "I love your memory."

"Did you see me at the lecture, Frank?"

"No. But I knew you were there. In mind, I thought. I lost the sense, mid-sentence. Had I known you were actually there, I would have thrown my notes to the four winds—"

"You weren't speaking from notes. It was extempore."

"I would have rushed down from the platform. The professors would have parted before me like the waves of the Red Sea before Moses. And . . ."

"And?"

"I would have given that very distinguished audience something much better than a lecture. A demonstration. Of some more elemental forms of biochemistry."

"Frank," I said, after a pause and on a note of warning, "you do know Wexton is staying at the house?"

"No, but it doesn't matter. Wexton is a tactful man. He will remain invisible. It is a little cold, kissing in the open air, I think. We'll go inside, yes? Besides, there's something I want to show you."

"Something to show me?"

"Yes. A present, I think. Once meant for us both. I haven't opened it yet. It was delivered to my hotel last night. No message. Just a label, with my name. I recognized the writing."

I recognized the writing too. A small leather valise, an old-fashioned luggage label: DR. FRANK GERHARD. The strokes of the letters were bold; the ink, black.

I lifted the case, which was heavy. I looked at Franz. "Do you know what this is?"

"I think I do. Yes."

"So do I. Shall we open it?"

"Later, I think. Now—there is no urgency."

We finally opened it the next morning, sitting there in the drawing room at Winterscombe. We laid the case down on the carpet; we opened it up—and there they were, all our letters. As the lid was lifted, they spilled out upon the floor, all those old, now-faded envelopes, still sealed. My handwriting, round and unformed; Frank's handwriting, which was, and is, European. American stamps, English stamps, French stamps, German stamps. We counted them; they were all there. Not a single one was missing.

It was a gesture, as Frank was later to say, which had all Constance's hallmarks: surprise; reversal; a certain defiance. What I should also have seen was that it was a final gesture, Constance's last piece of stagecraft, her way of ringing down the curtain on a life in which she had never given less than a bravura performance.

Frank, I think, did see that aspect of this gift, though he said nothing at the time. I did not see; I was too happy—and besides, I knew by then I had nothing to fear from Constance.

Frank and I were married in London, with a rumpled Wexton as best man and a beaming Freddie, a triumphant Winnie, as witnesses. That wedding was in November—almost twenty years ago now as I write—but I remember it with the greatest clarity. For me (as Constance would have said) it is yesterday.

Constance waited. I still believe that, although Frank remains uncertain. She waited until the marriage had safely taken place, and then—when she could perhaps wait no longer—she acted.

The news of her death reached us some three weeks later. I heard of it first, not from a friend but from an unknown reporter, a Scottish stringer for a London newspaper, seeking confirmation for his story.

That would have pleased Constance, who so liked indirection. It would have pleased her, too, that the circumstances of her death should remain unexplained, and be attributed, finally, to accident. Constance succeeded in dying, as she had lived, amid speculation and puzzlement.

That, at least, is the public version of her death, the one accepted by newspapers, by her colleagues, friends, lovers, and rivals. It is not my version. I have always been quite sure what happened—but then, I had read her journals.

Constance chose to die—and I have no doubt that she chose to investigate that last best secret of hers—in the place where she had spent her honeymoon. That house, once my grandfather's, had been purchased by Stern. Stern had willed it to Constance, as you know. I think that until the occasion of her death, it was a place she had never revisited.

Shall we walk to the wilderness? Constance had been walking in that direction for some time; once the news reached me, I began to understand that. Her timing remains her secret—as, no doubt, she wished. Why *then?* I would ask myself—and there was no certain answer.

Sometimes I would think Constance began on that last journey of hers when Steenie died; at other times I would think, no, she embarked on it much earlier, perhaps even at the time of her husband's death. Sometimes I would feel she was guided by coincidence, by the symmetry of numbers: She was thirty-eight when she entered my life; I was thirty-eight when she departed it. On the whole, though, I think the likeliest explanation was the simplest one: Just as Constance, once upon a time, would announce at midnight that she would leave for Europe the next morning, so, perhaps, one day she woke up, snapped her fingers, and said, *Enough of this. Let's see what it's like—death.*

But if I cannot explain her timing, there are things I can tell you. I can tell you, for instance, about her route.

First stop: that cocktail-age apartment on Park Avenue, kept unchanged from the days Stern owned it, where she had left me her journals. After that, a trail of visitations, the details of which emerged in the weeks after her death. There are gaps—but there are also certainties. I know she went to two of the London houses she and Stern once rented. I know she went in search of Stern's childhood home, in Whitechapel. When I retraced her steps, I found the same house, the same Bengali family; they recognized her photograph.

Whether she was searching for Stern in those months before she took her train to Scotland, I'm not sure. I think, rather, that—like me—she circumnavigated a part of her past before she said farewell to it. She was certainly alone when she did so; no evidence was ever produced of any traveling companion. I thought of that last telephone call she had made to me, from a station. I thought I knew the identity of the man she had said grew impatient, was waiting.

Perhaps this is true; perhaps I invent, and read too much into a series of chances and coincidences. But walk to Stern's wilderness she did, in the end. She stayed in that red sandstone mock-baronial house for one week, alone except for an elderly housekeeper.

At the end of that week, on a clear fine day, not a breath of wind, the sun shining, the air icy, she walked from the house down the track to that black loch which she had always hated.

It was a sea-loch, and subject to tides; she had calculated those tides, it seemed, with some precision. She took one of the boats that were left pulled up above the waterline, and she must have rowed herself, or allowed herself to drift, some way out, for she was seen sitting in the boat in the distance, in the late morning, by a passing fisherman.

She was too far out for him to discern whether the figure in the boat was a man or a woman. A man, he assumed, and—thinking nothing of it—continued his walk back to his village. Later the same day, in the afternoon, he returned that way with his dog. He saw the boat still drifting; he saw it was empty. Some time, then, between eleven and three: a time when the tides were ebbing.

Frank and I flew to Scotland as soon as the news came. I went to a house I knew only at second hand, from Constance's journals. We talked to the housekeeper, to the fisherman, to the police, to the men from air-sea rescue. In the afternoon, when we were finally alone, Frank and I walked down the track to the loch.

I looked at the mountains on the farther side, whose peaks were reflected in the water's black and glassy surface. It was just as Constance had described it: a desolate yet beautiful place, not one to be alone in.

Bravado *and* bravery, don't you think? I certainly thought so then, and do so still. Frank and I stood for a long time in silence, looking at the surface of that water. Preternaturally still, it would sometimes shift, heave, and then subside, like the flank of a great animal. When it did so, the images of the mountains bent; they fractured before re-forming.

I thought: *Full fathom five thy father lies*—but of course the water was many fathoms deeper than that, and it was a sea-loch. They never found her body.

AFTER WORDS

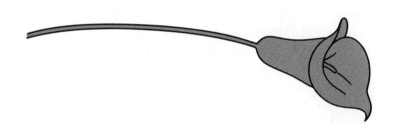

FOUR YEARS AGO, FOR THE FIRST TIME in almost twenty years, I went back to Winterscombe. It was January of 1986; our two children (they are almost grown up now) remained in America. Frank and I went to England. There were two reasons for our visit, which Frank categorized as the major one and the minor one. The minor one was professional: Frank was giving an address to the Royal Society, of which he had recently been made a fellow; the major, he insisted, concerned my uncle Freddie. Freddie had, that previous summer, reached his ninetieth year—a fact of which he was exceedingly proud. Belatedly, we were to celebrate his birthday. But how? Neither Freddie's nor Winnie's zest for life had diminished by one iota; it was difficult to plan a birthday treat that would be sufficiently splendid.

Such a great age! A trip to a restaurant or a theater seemed a little tame for a couple who had visited the Amazon at eighty. A party? Freddie, who had outlived almost all his contemporaries, now disliked parties.

The matter was still unresolved when we reached London. It remained unresolved until the night after Frank's speech, when we returned to our hotel room. I was looking through London listings in some desperation, wondering which musical (they all seemed to be musicals; they were all by the same composer) Freddie might enjoy. Frank was leafing through the glossy brochures for glossy hotels which came supplied with our room. Frank, who rarely stayed in such places if he could avoid them, was fascinated by them nonetheless. That evening, riffling through pages, he gave a sudden exclamation, then brandished the brochure in my face. I looked down, and there was Winterscombe.

I had finally sold Winterscombe, not long after our marriage, to some educational reformers, a husband and wife who had decided that Winterscombe was the perfect base from which to revolutionize British schooling. Their reforms had not caught on; they had later sold, I heard, to a pension fund. The pension fund, I believe, later sold to a computer millionaire, who used the house as his company headquarters. Winterscombe's capacity to adapt to time and changing circumstances was apparently endless. Now, it seemed, it had been transformed into a fashionable country-house hotel.

I looked at the photographs in disbelief. This was, and was not, Winterscombe. It had been redecorated, lavishly, by an American interior decorator I knew well. He had remade it into a grand Edwardian country house—or, rather, into everyone's *idea* of such a house—at the same time incorporating every modern luxury and convenience. The cellars had been converted into a swimming pool and gymnasium that might have diverted a Caesar. The ballroom was now the restaurant. My grandfather would have loved the restoration of the billiards room: much grander than it had ever been in his day, every wall was adorned with large, gory depictions of hunting. There was a helicopter landing pad, a jogging track around the lake for jaundiced executives. Not a bedroom was without a four-poster. It was clever, and preposterous. No, no, no, I said—don't even *suggest* it. We can't take Freddie and Winnie there—they would hate it.

I was wrong. The next day, in Little Venice, Freddie and Winnie took one look at the brochure, and I knew: They loved it. Silently, I despaired. I was by no means sure I wanted to revisit Winterscombe.

"What a jolly good idea," said Freddie.

"We'd be tickled pink," said Winnie.

Frank telephoned, there and then: bookings were made for the coming weekend. Winnie crossed to her neat desk; in her methodical way she entered this event in her calendar. As she did so, she showed signs of new excitement. Her cheeks became pink.

"Freddie!" she said. (She shouted, in fact; Uncle Freddie had become rather deaf.) Winnie brandished the calendar; Freddie twiddled with his hearing aid.

"Freddie—imagine this! We'll be able to watch it from Winterscombe. How *splendid*! That weekend. It's visible then. It was in *The Times*. I made *particular* note of it."

"What? What?" said Freddie. The hearing aid gave a piercing squeak.

"The *comet*!" Winnie replied, on a note of triumph. "Halley's comet. That weekend is one of the times it's visible. We'll be able to watch it. How exciting! I missed it last time. I was with my Papa. In Peking, I think."

"Fancy that," said Freddie, when this information sank in. He beamed. "Twice in one lifetime. And from the same spot too. I bet there's not many people who can say *that*."

So, the next weekend, we returned to Winterscombe. Freddie and Winnie had last been there for Steenie's funeral. Frank and I had last seen it more than seventeen years before, when we left to live in America.

The landscape had changed in Wiltshire, as it had in so many parts of England. The long lines of elm trees had gone; hedgerows had been plowed up; the nearest town, once thirty miles away, now encroached to within six miles of Winterscombe.

We drove through high gates, and for a moment—looking out over the lake and the bowl of the valley, seeing the house and the gardens in the soft light of a late winter afternoon—I thought little had changed. Then I saw this was an illusion. Winterscombe was *managed* now. The drive was freshly raked; all bumps and ruts had been removed; it smelled faintly of weedkiller. An attempt was being made, I think, to convey the impression that the hotel staff were old family retainers: At the house, our luggage was taken by a man wearing a garment I had not seen in forty years. He was young and zippy; he wore a green baize apron.

A man dressed in the manner of a butler greeted us distantly at reception. Reception consisted of an Edwardian partners' desk. To check in, you signed a leather visitors' book; the room keys bore names, not numbers. Presumably there were computers somewhere, and other technological aids, but if so they were well hidden. Rugs had been replaced upstairs by thick pile carpets. A man passed us carrying a fishing rod and complaining that the river was polluted. (It was out of season for fishing.) Another passed carrying a portable telephone. Freddie and Winnie seemed to be the only English guests; all the other accents we heard, like Frank's and mine, were foreign.

Once we were in our bedroom and the man in the green baize apron had departed, Frank and I looked at each other.

The room, a former guest room, was huge. It was dominated by one of the reproduction four-posters. The windows were double-glazed, the radiators red-hot, the room temperature about seventy-five degrees. There were carefully chosen homogenous antiques.

The pictures on the walls were safe and irreproachable. The covers on the chairs matched the quilt and the curtains. On one of the chests, arranged symmetrically, were two small bottles of complimentary sherry, a basket containing fruit under cling-wrap, some overarranged dried flowers, and a twenty-four-hour room service menu. Frank and I began to laugh.

"What would Maud say?" Frank asked. "Oh, what would Maud say?"

"I know exactly what Maud would say—and do. Maud could be the most terrific snob, but always about the oddest things. If she were here, if she came in now—you know the very first thing she'd do?"

"What?"

"This." I pulled back the quilt on the bed and laid my hand on the pillowcase. "She'd say: 'Oh, Victoria, this *won't* do. It's cotton, not linen.' "

We were a little delayed that evening, calling America—our son, Max, and our daughter, Hannah. When we went down to dinner that night, Freddie and Winnie were there in the hotel lounge (once the drawing room) awaiting us. They were sitting on a red velvet chesterfield, by a large log fire, attracting a number of curious stares.

Freddie was wearing a very ancient and slightly greenish dinner jacket, which had seen better days. Winnie was wearing a full-length dress that could never have been fashionable, but which had come closest to fashionability around 1940. Pinned to the front of her battleship bosom was a jet brooch the size of a coffee-cup saucer. She was wearing lipstick, which she did only on the most important occasions.

Both of them wore a look of happy and bemused expectation.

"My dear, you'll never guess where they've put us," said Winnie, in a lowered voice that could have been heard at the far end of the gardens. "The King's bedroom, Vicky! Imagine that!"

"That's not the best part." Freddie was rocking with delight. "In the bathroom—in the bathroom there's this absolutely incredible machine. You put the water in, then some of that bubble-bath stuff—"

"Which is there in the room. Free!" Winnie put in. "In sachets!"

"And then you press this switch, and *whoosh!* It turns into a kind of whirlpool."

"It's a Jacuzzi, Freddie," I said.

"Is it?" Freddie looked very interested at this. "They have that sort of thing now, do they, in hotels? Quite extraordinary. There's a carpet, too—in a bathroom! Well, well, well." He paused. "Can you buy them—those Jack things? I wouldn't mind having one at home. I said to Winnie, what a place for a murder! What would Inspector Coote make of that?"

Freddie was still talking about the Jacuzzi, to the considerable mirth of the other guests, when we went in to dinner. There, in the former ballroom, Freddie and Winnie encountered for the first time the delights of *nouvelle cuisine*. These impressed them rather less than the Jacuzzi.

"My goodness me," said Freddie when he was presented with a small artwork of three different-colored mousses in the middle of a large white plate. "Is this all you get? It looks a bit like baby food. What do you think, Winnie? I seem to have a rose on my plate. Can it be a rose? Good Lord, well I'm jiggered—it's a tomato."

The food, in fact, was excellent, and Freddie became more converted as course succeeded course, though he still lamented the absence of what he called "proper" food, such as steak-and-kidney pudding.

At half past nine, which was the time when he and Winnie always retired to bed, Uncle Freddie downed his regulation whisky. He patted his tummy—a firm and rounded one—with the air of a man greeting a familiar friend.

"Do you know," he said to Frank in a confiding way, "during the war—the Great War, that is—my mother took me to see a doctor, a most eminent man, and he said I had a weak heart. Something a bit iffy about the valves—I forget now. Well, I think, considering, that I haven't done too badly—ninety years old. What do you think, Frank?"

"I think," Frank replied, "that we will bring you and Winnie here again. But that time it will be for your one hundredth birthday, Freddie."

This made Freddie very pink in the face. He pressed Frank's hands, then, recovering himself, shook hands energetically.

"You have a very nice husband, Vicky," Winnie said as I followed them out to the foot of the stairs. "A very nice husband *indeed*. Freddie and I chose very well for you—didn't we, Freddie?"

They began to mount the stairs to their room, with the firm intention—Winnie said—of watching for the comet from their bedroom window. The fact that it was a cloudy night, with poor visibility, made no difference to Winnie, who remained a woman of undaunted spirit. She expected the comet, I think, to oblige her by passing directly outside her window at a slow, highly visible pace.

"Will there be sparks, Freddie?" she said when they were halfway up.

"I can't remember, Winnie. I don't *think* there are sparks."

"Oh, I do hope there will be." Winnie sounded wistful. "Lots of sparks, and a big tail. Do you know what I think, Freddie? I think it will look exactly like a flying bomb—yes, that's it! Like a doodle-bug, Freddie . . ."

"We won't see it, you know," Frank said in a regretful voice some while later. We had put on coats; we were on the terrace.

Frank looked up at the sky in a melancholy way.

"You can hardly see the moon. I can't see a single star. The only way anyone is going to see that comet tonight is with a radiotelescope."

"It doesn't matter. It's there. We know it's there, even if we can't see it."

"I suppose so." Frank, the scientist, did not seem convinced by this. "I'd like to have seen it once. Just once. After all—every seventy-six years. We shall never be able to see it again."

"Max and Hannah may—they can watch it for us."

"Do you believe that?"

"I half believe it. Yes. I feel as if, tonight, I'm watching for all the people who saw it here last time. For my mother and father, my grandparents. For Maud, Montague Stern and Constance, Steenie and Boy, Jenna. All of them." I looked around the empty terrace. "Yes. I do feel that."

"Let's walk." Frank took my hand. "Shall we? Shall we walk—oh, a long way? I'd like to do that. I don't want to go back in there."

"No, neither do I. Let's walk. I love to walk at night." So we left the terrace; we set off down the path toward the lake. At first we walked side by side; then—as often happened when we took walks together—Frank drew ahead. Neither of us minded this: Frank's strides were longer than mine. He still walked, as my uncle Steenie had once said, with a certain lack of moderation. He had a questing walk; he liked always to press on, to the next bend or the next vantage point. I liked to walk more slowly, sometimes looking back.

There were still swans on the lake—white ones now. We watched them stealing upon us out of the dark—silent, white, like beautiful ghosts, the cleft between the arch of their wings as black as ebony.

We walked on. I watched the clouds scud across the face of the moon. I watched the trees move. The air was damp against my skin. I thought, with affection, of the dead. I thought of those who had died most recently: Wexton, and (a few years before him) Jenna. Jenna, whom I had succeeded in tracing, some years after my marriage; Jenna, whom I had last seen in the center of her new family, with her husband, her stepchildren, her grandchildren. Jenna had found happiness in the end, and I was glad of that.

I thought of those I had lost before this, in the middle period of my life: of Steenie, and of Constance. I thought of those who had died even longer ago: my own parents, an uncle I never knew except at second hand, Frank's lost family. So many ghosts: there, and yet absent. I wished they had been more substantial; I would have liked to speak to them.

"Not through the woods," Frank called as we approached them.

"No, not through the woods. Shall we take that track?"

"Where does it lead?"

"We took it once, with Freddie's greyhounds. It goes on for miles. Out of the valley, up onto the plain. It goes as far as the circle, farther maybe. When we took it, we stopped up there, on the hill."

"The circle? The stone circle? I've never seen that. How far is it?"

"Four miles. Five, maybe."

"Shall we do it? I want to walk a long way tonight. On and on, without stopping."

And so we walked on. It was a wide cart-track, clearly defined. The moon gave just enough light to show the path winding ahead, out of the Winterscombe valley and up to that harsher landscape beyond.

As we walked, the wind strengthened; the sky began to clear. We saw, first, the polestar, then—as if they were being unveiled for our benefit—the brightness of the constellations. I thought: Cassiopeia, Orion, the twins Castor and Pollux. It was perhaps then that I decided to write down the story of my parents, and of Constance.

When thinking of this idea before, I had discussed it once or twice with Frank. I think he read my mind, and knew I was thinking of it then, as we walked. We crested one rise. We began to mount a second.

"If I did write it down, Frank—"

"Winterscombe?"

"Yes, Winterscombe. Where should I begin?"

"Oh, I know that. That's easy. You must begin with the fortuneteller."

"The fortuneteller? Why?"

"Well, you should begin with magic, I think."

"Why magic?"

"Because of all the other magic, of course. Wasn't there magic when Constance was ill and then recovered? When your father recovered, come to that? What happened to your mother in those caves? What was it I sensed, back there in that wood? All those things are magic. So begin with the magic. Begin with your fortuneteller."

"Do you believe in magic?"

"Certainly."

"Even though you are a scientist?"

"Perhaps *because* I am a scientist. And when you get to us"—he paused—"be sure to mention the arithmetic. . . ."

I smiled. Frank strode on ahead. He stopped at the summit of the hill. I watched the figure of my husband outlined against the sky. Whatever it was he could see from this vantage point seemed to please him, for he lifted his arms. One of his odd, impulsive gestures, half triumph, half jubilation. I watched him with love as he moved against the sky. I walked on, and as I reached the top he held out his hand to me.

"Look this way first."

I turned and looked back to Winterscombe. The moonlight was stronger now, the terrain clear. I could see the bowl of the valley, the dark thread of the river bellying out into the lake, the shelter of the belt of woodland, and the great mass of the house, its black roofs, its bays, its turrets, its ranked windows and their lights.

"Now this way."

He turned me to face the other way. I drew in my breath. There, at the base of the bare and treeless hills, was the monument. A huge and lonely circle of stones, a place prehistory: The stones were white as bones in the moonlight.

Beyond the pillars and their immense capitals, the clouds banked on the horizon, the night sky above them clear. As we looked I saw those clouds were edged with light: Their extremities, frayed, diffuse, constantly in motion, gathering, dissipating, were tinged with an unearthly and sulfurous luminosity. They were at once massed and striated.

This silenced us. We watched the clouds thicken, converge, disperse.

"Is it the comet, Frank? Is it?"

"I'm not sure."

"I never thought it would look like that. There, and not there."

"Neither did I."

We stood watching some time longer. The moon rose, and as its light grew stronger, the discoloration of the clouds grew less intense. What had been burnished faded to an opalescent silver, then to gray, and finally to black.

"Look at us. How small we are."

Frank looked at the sweep of the hills.

"Small—and large. Both at once. Do you feel that?"

"Yes. I do."

"I want to walk down there. All the way down." He pointed to the monument. "I want to stand there tonight, right in the center of that circle. With you."

He began to walk down the hill at a fast pace. The wind whipped his hair about his face. Frank, always indifferent to the elements, ignored this.

I looked one last time back, toward the lights of Winterscombe, the enclosure of its valley. Frank turned; he waited for me.

I ran down to join him. He took my hand once more, and hand in hand, the wind in our faces, we walked down toward the circle of stones.